"Writers are made, not born," Ayn Rand wrote in another context. "To be exact, writers are self-made." In this fascinating collection of Ayn Rand's earliest work—including a previously unpublished piece, "The Night King"—her own career proves her point. We see here not only the budding of the philosophy that would seal her reputation as a champion of the individual, but also the emergence of a great narrative stylist whose fiction would place her among the most towering figures in the history of American literature.

Dr. Leonard Peikoff worked with Ayn Rand for thirty years; he is her legal heir and the executor of her estate.

THE
EARLY AYN RAND

A Selection from Her Unpublished Fiction

REVISED AND EXPANDED EDITION

Edited and with an
Introduction and Notes by
LEONARD PEIKOFF

A SIGNET BOOK

SIGNET
Published by New American Library, a division of
Penguin Group (USA) Inc., 375 Hudson Street,
New York, New York 10014, USA
Penguin Group (Canada), 90 Eglinton Avenue East, Suite 700, Toronto,
Ontario M4P 2Y3, Canada (a division of Pearson Penguin Canada Inc.)
Penguin Books Ltd., 80 Strand, London WC2R 0RL, England
Penguin Ireland, 25 St. Stephen's Green, Dublin 2,
Ireland (a division of Penguin Books Ltd.)
Penguin Group (Australia), 250 Camberwell Road, Camberwell, Victoria 3124,
Australia (a division of Pearson Australia Group Pty. Ltd.)
Penguin Books India Pvt. Ltd., 11 Community Centre, Panchsheel Park,
New Delhi - 110 017, India
Penguin Group (NZ), 67 Apollo Drive, Rosedale, North Shore 0632,
New Zealand (a division of Pearson New Zealand Ltd.)
Penguin Books (South Africa) (Pty.) Ltd., 24 Sturdee Avenue,
Rosebank, Johannesburg 2196, South Africa

Penguin Books Ltd., Registered Offices:
80 Strand, London WC2R 0RL, England

Published by Signet, an imprint of New American Library, a division of Penguin Group (USA) Inc. This edition of *The Early Ayn Rand* contains a new preface and two new selections, "The Night King," which is being published for the first time in this volume, and the "The Simplest Thing in the World," which appeared in Ayn Rand's *The Romantic Manifesto*.

First Printing (Revised Edition), April 2005
10 9 8 7 6

Copyright © Leonard Peikoff, Paul Gitlin, Eugene Winick, Executors of the
Estate of Ayn Rand, 1983, 1984
Introduction and Editor's Note copyright © Leonard Peikoff, 1984
Copyright © The Estate of Ayn Rand, 2005
All rights reserved

 REGISTERED TRADEMARK—MARCA REGISTRADA

Contents

Preface to the Revised Edition

This revision adds two short stories to the collection, thereby placing all six short stories by Ayn Rand in one volume. The previously unpublished story, "The Night King," has been included, as well as the story "The Simplest Thing in the World," reprinted from *The Romantic Manifesto*. The first of these, most likely written in 1926, seems to be her first attempt at fiction in English. The second, written in 1940, demonstrates the command of the English language she achieved over this fourteen-year period.

Nearly a decade of organizing and cataloging her papers by the Ayn Rand Archives has allowed some refinement in dating the original manuscripts, which is reflected in this edition. References to the sales figures of her novels have been updated to the present day. Other than that, Leonard Peikoff's Introduction and prefaces are exactly duplicated from the previous editions of *The Early Ayn Rand*.

—Richard E. Ralston
Revision Editor
August 2004

Introduction

In 1926, Ayn Rand was a twenty-one-year-old Russian immigrant to America struggling with her first short story in English; she was barely able to speak the language, let alone handle complex ideas or project a convincing hero. In 1938, a mere twelve years later, she was writing *The Fountainhead*, in full command of her distinctive philosophy, aesthetic approach, and literary style. A progression such as this represents an astonishing intellectual and artistic growth.

The present book is an anthology of Ayn Rand's fiction from this early period, arranged chronologically. I have decided to publish this material because I believe that admirers of Miss Rand will be interested to learn by what steps she developed her literary abilities. They can now see the steps for themselves.

Only one of the pieces *(Think Twice)* can be considered finished, mature work. The others are offered not as finished ends-in-themselves, but primarily for the light they shed on Ayn Rand's development during her most critical formative decade as a writer. None of the pieces has been published before, nor did Miss Rand intend to publish them.

The novels of the mature Ayn Rand contain superlative values that are unique in our age. *The Fountainhead* and *Atlas Shrugged* offer profound and original philosophic themes, expressed in logical, dramatic plot structures. They portray an uplifted vision of man, in the form of protagonists characterized by strength, purposefulness, integrity—heroes who are not only idealists, but happy idealists, self-confident, serene, at home on earth. The books are written in a highly calculated literary style intent on achieving precision and luminous clarity, yet that style is at the same time brilliantly colorful, sensuously evocative, and passionate. Just as Ayn Rand's philosophy, Objectivism, rejects the mind-body dichotomy, so her art sweeps aside the false alternatives this dichotomy has spawned: her novels prove that one can unite philosophy and suspense thrillers, art and entertainment, morality and practicality, reason and emotion.

She could not do all of the above, however, at the beginning. She had to create her own abilities gradually, by a prodigious effort.

What kinds of themes concerned her as a young woman, before she could deal with the deeper issues of ethics or epistemology? What kinds of stories did she tell before she could invent complex plots involving an entire society or even the whole world? What kinds of characters did she write about before she was able to project Howard Roark or John Galt? *How* did she write in these years, when she was first learning the craft?

The eleven selections in this book answer such questions. They exhibit Ayn Rand's continuous growth in every area: depth of theme, ingenuity of plot structure, stature of hero. Most of all, they exhibit the maturation of her style, from the broken English of "The Husband I Bought" to the power and poetry of *The Fountainhead*.

Miss Rand's development seems to fall into three rough stages, reflected in the three parts of this anthology.

Part I covers the 1920s and includes her earliest fiction in English. The short stories from this period are a beginner's exercises written as literary practice, and never meant for any audience.

Part II covers the early 1930s and represents Miss Rand's first professional work. It includes a lengthy synopsis of a movie original *(Red Pawn);* two excerpts from the manuscript of *We the Living* that were cut before publication; and an early stage play *(Ideal)* which, though finished work, is not fully consonant with Miss Rand's later viewpoint.

Part III covers the late 1930s and represents Ayn Rand's first mature work. It includes an intriguing stage play, the philosophical murder mystery *Think Twice;* and two sets of excerpts from *The Fountainhead* manuscript that were cut before publication. One of these tells the story of Roark's first love affair, before he met Dominique.

An early short story has been omitted from this collection, along with several screenplays (adapting other authors' stories) from her days in Hollywood, some scenarios for the silent screen, and a version of *We the Living* written for the stage. Aside from these items, there is no more of Ayn Rand's fiction that remains unpublished. (There are no excerpts from the *Atlas Shrugged* manuscript long enough to warrant publication.)

By the nature of this anthology, most of the material is imperfect, unedited and/or undeveloped Ayn Rand. But it is still Ayn Rand—and that is the second reason for publishing it. Despite all the flaws, despite everything she has still to learn, her vision of man and of life, and even some of her power to convey that vision in words, are there at the beginning. They are real, they are able to break through, to be felt, to haunt us. For those who admire her work, as I do, this is reason enough to grasp at these early pieces.

I first met Ayn Rand in 1951 at her home in California. She was writing *Atlas Shrugged* at the time; I was a pre-medical student who loved *The Fountainhead* and was brimming over with philosophical questions to ask her about it. That meeting changed my life.

Ayn Rand was unlike anyone I had ever imagined. Her mind was utterly firsthanded. On intellectual issues, she said what no one else said or perhaps had ever even thought, but she said these things so logically—so simply, factually, persuasively—that they seemed to be self-evident. And she was passionate about ideas; she radiated the kind of intensity that one could imagine changing the course of history. Her brilliantly perceptive eyes looked straight at you and missed nothing; neither did her methodical, painstaking, virtually scientific replies to my questions miss anything. She convinced me that night that philosophy *is* a science, with objective, provable answers to its questions; it is the science that moves the world, she argued, whether men acknowledge the fact or not. It did not take me long to give up medicine and decide on philosophy as a career.

As the years passed, I came to work closely with Miss Rand, first as an informal student of hers, then as a writer and lecturer on her ideas. The two of us regularly talked ideas, not infrequently for twelve hours (or more) at a stretch. I learned more about philosophy listening to her than I did from ten years in graduate school getting a Ph.D. in the subject.

Not long after I met Miss Rand, she let me read the two plays in the present collection, *Ideal* and *Think Twice;* she was pleased with both and hoped to see them produced one day. (This, I think, is why she never tried to have them published.) I also came to read the short story "Good Copy" and to hear Miss Rand's analysis of it; she regarded this piece as a worthy, though flawed, attempt by a beginning writer. Of the rest of this collection, I read nothing at all during Miss Rand's lifetime (though I heard from her in passing about a few items, which she regarded as ancient history). I was astonished, after her death, to find so much fiction that was new to me in her "trunk."

Out of this new material, I have three personal favorites: "Vesta Dunning," for the quality of the writing; "Kira's Viking," for its fairy-tale romanticism; and "The Husband I Bought," because it is a rare window on Ayn Rand's soul at the beginning, before she knew much about philosophy, art, or English—a window that reveals eloquently her own intense dedication to values. Along with the material I already knew, these pieces are what convinced me, as her literary executor, to publish the total.

To those unfamiliar with Ayn Rand, however, I want to say that this book is not the place to begin. Read her novels first. If their ideas interest you, you might then turn to her nonfiction works, such as *The Virtue of Selfishness* (on ethics), or *Capitalism: The Unknown Ideal* (politics), or *The Romantic Manifesto* (aesthetics). Then, if you wish, pick up the present collection.

If any reader wants more information—about Miss

Rand's other published essays; about courses, schools, and publications that carry on her philosophy; or about further material of hers yet to be brought out (journals, letters, lectures)—I suggest that he write to Objectivism EA, P.O. Box 177, Murray Hill Station, New York, NY 10157. I regret that owing to the volume of mail, personal replies to such letters are not possible; but in due course inquirers will receive literature from several sources indicating the direction to pursue if they want to investigate Ayn Rand's ideas further, or to support them.

Ayn Rand has long been beloved by a broad public. Here then for all to read is her early fiction: the first of her stories, and also the last—the last, that is, for us to discover and to experience. I hope you enjoy them as much as I did.

—Leonard Peikoff
New York City

Part I

THE TWENTIES

The
Husband I Bought

c. 1926

Editor's Preface

Ayn Rand arrived in the United States from Russia in February 1926, at the age of twenty-one, and spent several months with relatives in Chicago before leaving for Hollywood. Although she had studied some English in Russia, she did not know the language well, and she devoted herself at first to writing scenarios for the silent screen. "The Husband I Bought" seems to be the only writing other than scenarios from these early months. It is the first story she wrote in English.

Miss Rand was aware that this story (like all her work in the 1920s) was a beginner's exercise, written in effect in a foreign language, and she never dreamed of publishing it. She did not even sign her name to it privately (although she had chosen the name "Ayn Rand" before she left Russia). She signed it with a pseudonym invented for this one case and never used again: Allen Raynor.

Many years later, Ayn Rand was asked to give a lecture defining the goal of her work. "The motive and purpose of my writing," she said, "is the projection of an ideal man. The portrayal of a moral ideal, as my ultimate literary goal, as an end in itself . . ." *(The Romantic Manifesto)*.

Prior to *The Fountainhead,* however, she did not consider herself ready for this task; she knew that she had too much still to learn, both as a philosopher and as a writer. What she did regard as possible to her in these early years was the depiction of a woman's *feeling* for the ideal man, a feeling which she later called "man-worship." She herself had experienced this feeling as a driving passion since childhood, primarily in response to the projections of heroes she discovered in Romantic literature.

Concepts such as "worship," "reverence," "exaltation," and the like are usually taken as naming emotions oriented to the supernatural, transcending this world. In Ayn Rand's view, however, this concedes to religion or mysticism what are actually

> the highest moral concepts of our language. . . . [S]uch concepts do name actual emotions, even though no supernatural dimension exists; and these emotions are experienced as uplifting or ennobling, without the self-abasement required by religious definitions. What, then, is their source or referent in reality? It is the entire emotional realm of man's dedication to a moral ideal. . . . It is this highest level of man's emotions that has to be redeemed from the murk of mysticism and redirected at its proper object: man.*

"Man-worship" means the enraptured dedication to values—and to man, man the individual, as their only achiever, beneficiary, and ultimate embodiment. This is basically a metaphysical-ethical feeling, open to either sex, a feeling uniting all those "who see man's highest potential and strive to actualize it"—those "dedicated to the *exaltation* of man's self-esteem and the *sacredness* of his happiness on earth."†

When a woman with this kind of character sees her deepest values actualized and embodied in a specific man, man-worship becomes (other things being equal) romantic love. Thus the special quality of the Ayn Rand romantic love: it is the union of the abstract and the

---

The Fountainhead, 25th Anniversary Edition, Introduction.

†Ibid.

concrete, of ideal and reality, of mind and body, of up-lifted spirituality and violent passion, of reverence and sexuality.

Throughout the early years, female protagonists predominate in Ayn Rand's fiction; and one of their essential traits is this kind of man-worship. The early heroes are merely suggested; they are not fully realized until Roark. But whatever the language and literary problems still unresolved, the motif of the woman's feeling for a hero *is* realized. Even in this first story, Ayn Rand can write eloquent scenes on this theme (especially the moving farewell scene). Even this early, she can make effective use of the dramatic, short-sentence style that became famous with *The Fountainhead*.

Henry, in the present story, is the earliest ancestor of Leo (in *We the Living*), of Roark, of Francisco or Rearden (in *Atlas Shrugged*). Those who know the later heroes can see the first faint glimmer of them here. The focus, however, lies in Irene's response to him, which may be symbolized by a single line: "When I am tired, I kneel before the table [on which Henry's picture stands] and I look at him."

On the surface, this story might appear to be quite conventional. I can imagine someone reading it as the tragic story of an unloved wife "selflessly" removing herself from her husband's path. But the actual meaning is the opposite. Irene is not a selfless wife, but a passionate valuer; her decision to leave Henry is not self-sacrifice, but self-preservation and the reaffirmation of *her* values. She cannot accept anyone less than Henry, or any relationship with him less than what she has had.

Nor does Irene draw a tragic conclusion from her suffering. The glory of her life, she feels, is that Henry exists, that she had him once, and that she will love him always. Even in the agony of unrequited love, her implicit focus is on values, not on pain. This is especially clear in her desire to protect her ideal from suffering, to protect him for her *own* sake, although she is leaving him, to keep her supreme value whole, radiant, godlike, not dimmed or diminished by loss and sorrow. "Henry, you must be happy, and strong, and glorious. Leave suffering to those that cannot help it. You must smile at life. . . . And never think about those that cannot. They are not worthwhile."

The story's events are conventional—but their meaning and motivation are vintage Ayn Rand, and utterly unconventional. What makes this possible is the profound *seriousness* of Irene's passion. This is what transforms and transfigures an otherwise ordinary tale.

There are, of course, major flaws in the story's execution. Important events are not dramatized, but merely narrated (and sometimes only sketchily explained). This is a practice opposite to that of the mature Ayn Rand. The moral code of the small town—the narrow respectability of sixty years ago—is thoroughly dated, and, in our age, virtually unbelievable. Above all, there is the problem of the language, which reflects a mind still unfamiliar with many essentials of English grammar, vocabulary, and idiom; as a result, the dialogue in particular is often stilted and unreal. I have edited out the most confusing lapses of English grammar and wording and the most obvious foreignisms, but have allowed the rest of the text to stand as written, so as to leave to posterity a record of where Ayn Rand began. Those who have read her novels can judge for themselves how far she was able to travel.

It may be wondered why Ayn Rand chose to present man-worship first of all in the form of a story of unrequited love. My conjecture—it is only that—is that this aspect of the story was autobiographical. Ayn Rand as a college student was in love with a young man in Russia who was the real-life source of the character of Leo. She remembered this young man, and her feeling for him, all her life. The relationship between them, however, was never fulfilled—whether for personal reasons or political ones (I believe he was exiled to Siberia) I do not know. But, either way, it is easy to imagine that alone in a new country, on the threshold of a new life, she should be drawn to focus as a kind of farewell on the man she loved and had now lost forever—or, more exactly, to focus on her own feeling for that man and loss.

—L. P.

The Husband I Bought

I should not have written this story. If I did it all—I did it only by keeping silent. I went through tortures, such as no other woman on earth, perhaps just to keep silent. And now—I speak. I must not have written my secret. But I have a hope. My one and only, and last hope. And I have no time before me. When life is dead and you have nothing left on your way—who can blame you for taking a last chance, a poor little chance . . . before the end? And so I write my story.

I loved Henry. I love him. It is the only thing I know and I can say about myself. It is the only thing, that was my life. There is no person on earth that has never been in love. But love can go beyond all limits and bounds. Love can go beyond all consciousness, beyond your very soul.

I never think of how I met him. It has no importance for me. I *had* to meet him and I did. I never think of how and when I began to love him or how I realized that he loved me. The only thing I know is that two words only were written on my life: "Henry Stafford."

He was tall and slim, and beautiful, too beautiful. He was intensely ambitious and never made a step to realize it. He had an immense, indefinite longing and did not trouble himself to think about it. He was the most perfectly refined and brilliant man, whom society admired and who laughed at society. A little lazy, very skeptical, indifferent to everything. Haughty and self-conceited for himself—gracious and ironical for everybody.

In our little town Henry Stafford was, of course, the aim and target of all the girls and "homemade" vamps. He flirted openly with everyone; that made them all furious.

His father had left him a big business. He managed it just enough to have the necessary money and the least trouble possible. He treated his business with the same smile of perfect politeness and perfect indifference with which he spoke to our society ladies or read a popular best-seller, from the middle.

Mr. Barnes, an old lawyer and a friend of mine, said once, with that thoughtful, indefinite look afar that was so characteristic to him: "That impossible man . . . I could envy the girl he shall love. I would pity the one he will marry."

For the moment, I could have been envied by Mr. Barnes, and not by Mr. Barnes only: Henry Stafford loved me. I was twenty-one then, just graduated from one of the best colleges. I had come to live in my little native town, in the beautiful estate that belonged to me after my parents' death. It was a big, luxurious house, with a wonderful old garden, the best in the town. I had a considerable fortune and no near relatives at all. I was accustomed to ruling my existence quietly and firmly myself.

I tell the whole truth here, so I must tell that I was beautiful. And I was clever, I knew it; you always know it when you are. I was considered a "brilliant girl," "a girl with a great future" by everybody in our society, though they did not like me too much, for I was a little too willful and resolute.

I loved Henry Stafford. It was the only thing I ever understood in my life. It was my life. I knew I would never have another one, never could have. And I never did. Perhaps you should not love a human being like this. I cannot tell and I will not listen, if someone tells me you should not. I cannot listen: it was my whole life.

Henry Stafford loved me. He loved me seriously. It was the first thing he did not smile at in his life.

"I did not know I would be so helpless before love," he said sometimes. "It was impossible, that you would not be mine, Irene. I must always have the things I wish, and it is the only thing I ever wished!" He kissed my arms, from the fingertips to the shoulder. . . . As for me, I looked at him and felt nothing else. His every movement, his manners, the sound of his voice made me tremble. When a passion like this gets hold of you, it never lets you go, never till your last breath. It burns all in you, and still flames, when there is nothing more to burn. . . . But then, how happy, oh! how happy I was!

I remember one day better than everything. It was summer and there was as much sun on the bushes in my garden as water in a flood. We were flying on a swing, he and I. Both all in white, we stood at each side of the long, narrow plank, holding strongly to the ropes with both hands, and making the swing fly madly from one side to the other. We went so fast that the ropes cracked piteously and I could hardly breathe. . . . Up and down! Up and down! My skirt flew high above my knees, like a light white flag.

"Faster, faster, Irene!" he cried.

"Higher, higher, Henry!" I answered.

With his white shirt open at the chest and the sleeves rolled above the elbows, he held the ropes with his arms, burned by the sun, and pushed the swing by easy, gracious movements of his strong, flexible body. His hair was flying in the wind. . . .

And in the breathtaking speed, in the glowing sun, I saw and felt nothing but the man with the flying hair that was before me.

Then, without saying anything to each other, with one thought, we jumped down from the highest position of our swing, in its fastest moment. We scratched our arms and legs badly in falling; but we did not mind it. I was in his arms. He kissed me with more madness than there had been in our flight. It was not for the first time, but I shall never forget it. To feel his arms around me made me dizzy, almost unconscious. I clutched his shoulders with my hands, so that my nails must have scratched him through his shirt, till blood. I kissed his lips. I kissed his neck, where the shirt was open.

The only words we said then were pronounced by him,

or rather whispered, so that he could hardly distinguish them himself: "Forever . . . Irene, Irene, say that it is forever. . . ."

I did not see him the next day. I waited anxiously till the evening. He did not come. Neither did he on the second day. A young fellow, a very self-confident and very clumsy "sheik," who tried hopelessly to win a little attention from me, called upon me that day and, talking endlessly and quickly about everything imaginable, like a radio, dropped finally: "By the way, Henry Stafford has got into some business trouble . . . serious, they say."

I learned the whole terrible news in the next days: Henry was ruined. It was a frightful ruin: not only had he lost everything, but he owed a whole fortune to many persons. It was not his fault, even though he had always been so careless with his business. It was circumstance. Everybody knew it; but it looked like his fault. And it was a terrible blow, a mortal blow to his name, his reputation, all his future.

Our little town was greatly excited. There were persons who sympathized with him, but most of them were maliciously, badly glad. They had always resented him, despite the admiration they surrounded him with, or just because of it, perhaps. "I would like to see what kind of face he'll make now," said one. "O-oh! That's great!" "Such a shame!" said others.

Many remarks turned upon me, also. They had always resented me for being Henry's choice. "Don't know what he'd find 'bout that Irene Wilmer," had said once Patsy Tillins, the town's prize vamp, summing up the general opinion. Now, Mrs. Hughes, one of our social leaders, a respectable lady, but who had three daughters to marry, said to me, with a charming smile: "I am sincerely happy that you escaped it in time, dear child. . . . Always thought that man was good for nothing"; to which Patsy Tillins added, in a white cloud, as she was quickly powdering her nose: "Who's it you'll pick up next, dearie?"

I did not pay any attention to it all and I was not hurt. I only tried to understand the position and wondered if it was really so serious for Henry or not. One sentence only, pronounced by a stern, serious businessman whom I always respected, explained all to me and cleared the terrible truth. "He is an honest man," he said to a friend, not knowing that I heard it, "but the only honorable thing left to him is to shoot himself, and the sooner the better." Then I understood. I did not think long. I threw a wrap on my shoulders and ran to his house.

I trembled when I saw him. I scarcely even recognized him. He was sitting at his desk, with a stone face and immobile eyes. One of his arms was hanging helplessly by his side and I saw that only his fingers were trembling, so lightly I could scarcely notice it. . . .

He did not hear me enter. I approached him and fell at his feet, burying my head in his knees. He shuddered. Then he took my arms strongly and forced me to rise. "Go home, Irene," he said with a stern, cold, expressionless voice, "and never come again."

"You . . . you don't love me, Henry?" I muttered.

There was suffering now in his voice, but anger also when he answered: "There can be nothing between us, now. . . . Can't you understand it?"

I understood. But I smiled, I just smiled from fun, because it was too impossible to be true. Money was now between us, money pretended to take him from me. Him! . . . I laughed, a frightful laugh. But would you not laugh if one would try to deprive you of your whole life, your one and only aim, your god . . . because that god has no money? . . .

He did not want to listen to me. But I made him listen . . . I could not tell how many long, horrible hours I spent begging and imploring him. He refused. He was tender at times, asking me to forget him; then he was cold and stern, and turned his back to me, not to hear my words, ordering me to leave him. But I saw the passionate love in his eyes, the despair that he tried in vain to hide. I remained. I fell on my knees; I kissed his hands. "Henry . . . Henry, I cannot live without you! . . . I just cannot!" I cried.

It took a long time to conquer him. But I was desperate and despair always finds a way. He surrendered himself at last and agreed . . . And when he held me in his arms, covering my face with kisses, flooded by tears, when he whispered: "Yes . . . Irene . . . yes," and his lips trembled, I knew that he loved me, that an immense love made his eyes so dark with emotion. . . .

The town exploded with surprise when they learned the news. No one was able to believe it, at first. When they did—the terror was general. Even Mrs. Hughes rushed to me and cried with a real sincerity and a sincere terror: "But . . . but you will not marry him, Irene! . . . It's foolish! Why, but it's . . . it's foolish!" She was unable to find another word. "The girl is crazy!" said her friend, Mrs. Brogan, who was not so particular about expressions.

Mr. Davis, an old friend of my parents, came to speak to me. He asked me to think it over again. He advised me not to marry Henry, to remember that if I gave my fortune to pay my husband's debt, it would take all I possess—and could I be sure of the future? All this only made me laugh. I was so happy!

The most farsighted of all was Mr. Barnes. He looked at me with his long, thoughtful glance. He had a sad, kind smile, which his experience with life and men had given him. He said: "I fear you will be very unhappy, Irene. . . . One is never happy with a passion like this."

Then he said to Henry, in a voice unusually stern for him: "Now, be careful with yourself, Stafford."

"I think it was superfluous to tell me this," answered Henry coldly.

We were married. Some persons say there is no perfect happiness on earth. There was. I was. I could not even call it happiness—the word is too small.

I was his wife. I was not Irene Wilmer any longer, I was Irene Stafford. I can hardly describe the first time of my married life. I do not remember anything. If one asks me what was then, I could answer one word only: "Henry!" He was there, and what could I have noticed besides this? We sold all I had, the debt was paid, and he was saved. We could live just for one another, with nothing to disturb us, in the maddest, the wildest of happiness two human beings had ever experienced.

The day came, however, when we were obliged to think of the future. We had paid all the money I possessed, sold my estate and my jewels. So we had to think of some work. Henry had been educated as an engineer. He found employment. It was not a very big position, but it was good enough for the beginning, considering the fact he had never worked in his specialty before.

I rented a little flat. And then we lived, and I took all my strength, all my soul to make his life as it should be. I helped him in his work. He had not enough character to do it always with the necessary energy. He would often, in the middle of an important work, lie down on the sofa, his feet on his desk, with some eccentric new book in hand and a current of smoke from his cigarette. I always found a way to make him work and be more and more successful.

I never allowed myself to become just his "pal," his good friend and servant-for-all-work. I was his mistress, as well as his wife, and he was my lover. I managed to put a certain indefinite aloofness about me, that made me always seem somewhat inaccessible. He never noticed who was doing all the housework for him. I was a queen in his house, a mysterious being, that he was never sure to possess wholly and unquestionably, that he could never call his property and habitual commodity. I can say, we did not notice our home life; we had no home life. We were lovers, with an immense passion between us. Only.

I made a romance out of his life. I made it seem different, strange, exciting every day, every moment. His house was not a place to rest, eat, and sleep in. It was an unusual, fascinating palace, where he had to fight, win, and conquer, in a silent, thrilling game.

"Who could have thought of creating a woman like you, Irene!" he said sometimes, and his kisses left burning red marks on my neck and shoulders. "If I live it is only because I have you!" I said nothing. I never showed him all my adoration. You must not show a man that he is your whole life. But he knew it; he felt it. . . .

The town's society, which had met our marriage with such disapproval, began to look more kindly at us, after a while. But through the first hard time of fight, work, and loneliness, I led him, I alone, and I am proud to say that he did not need anyone else, through all those years.

A frequent guest of ours and my best friend was Mr. Barnes. He watched our life attentively. He saw our impossible, unbelievable happiness. It made him glad, but thoughtful. He asked me once: "What would happen if he stopped loving you?"

I had to gather all my strength to make my voice speak: "Don't ever repeat it. There are things too horrible that one must not think about."

Time went, and instead of growing cold and tedious, our love became greater and greater. We could understand each other's every glance, every movement now. We liked to spend long evenings before a burning fireplace in his study. I sat on a pillow and he lay on the carpet, his head on my knees. I bent to press my lips to his, in the dancing red glow of the fire. "I wonder how two persons could have been made so much for one another, Irene," he said.

We lived like this four years. Four years of perfect, delirious happiness. Who can boast of such a thing in his life? After all, I wonder sometimes whether I have the right to consider myself unhappy now. I paid a terrible price to life, but I had known a terrible happiness. The price was not too high. It was just. For those days had been, they were, and they were mine.

Society had taken us back, even with more appreciation than before, perhaps. Henry became the most popular, the most eagerly expected guest everywhere. He had made a rapid career. He was not very rich yet, but his name began to be mentioned among those of the most brilliant engineers. When a man is so interesting, so fascinating as he was, lack of money will never mean much to society. . . .

Then it happened. . . . I have had the strength to live through it, I shall have the strength to write it down. . . .

A new woman came to our town and appeared in our society. Her name was Claire Van Dahlen. She was divorced and had come from New York after a trip to Europe to rest in our little town, where she had some distant relatives. I saw her on the first evening she appeared in our society, at a dancing party.

She had the body of an antique statuette. She had

golden skin and dark-red lips. Her black hair was parted in the middle, combed straight and brilliant, and she wore long, hanging perfume-earrings. She had slow, soft, fluent movements; it seemed that her body had no bones at all. Her arms undulated like velvet ribbons. She was dressed very simply, but it was the simplicity that costs thousands of dollars. . . . She was gorgeously, stunningly beautiful.

Our society was amazed with admiration; they had never seen a woman like this. . . . She was perfectly charming and gracious with everybody, but she had that haughty, disinterested smile of women accustomed to and tired of admiration.

Henry looked at her . . . he looked too long and too fixedly. The glance with which he followed her every movement was full of a strange admiration, too intense for him. He danced with her several times.

At the end of the party, a crowd of young men rushed to ask the favor of bringing Mrs. Van Dahlen home. "I will have to choose," she said, with a charming, indulgent smile.

"Choose from everyone present!" proposed one of her eager new admirers.

"From everyone?" she repeated, with her smile. She paused, then: "Well, it will be Mr. Stafford."

Henry had not asked for the favor; he was astonished. But it was impossible to refuse. Mr. Barnes brought me home.

When Henry came back and I asked his opinion of her, he said shortly and indifferently: "Yes, very interesting." I had seen that he was much more impressed than this, but I did not pay any attention to it.

The next time we had to go to a party, Henry had no desire to go out that evening. He was tired, he had work to do. "Why, Henry, they expect us," I said. "There will be many persons tonight: Mr. and Mrs. Harwings, Mr. and Mrs. Hughes, Mrs. Brooks, Mrs. Van Dahlen, Mr. Barnes . . ."

"Well, yes, I think we might go," he said suddenly.

He danced with Claire Van Dahlen that evening more than anyone else. Her dress had a very low neck in back, and I saw his fingers sometimes touch her soft silken skin. The look in her eyes, which were fixed straight into his, between her long, dark lashes, astonished me. . . . At the table, they were placed near one another: the hostess wanted to please Mrs. Van Dahlen.

After this Henry missed no party where she appeared. He took her for rides in his automobile. He called at her relatives', where she lived. He managed to be in theaters the evenings she was there. He had a strange look, eager and excited. At home, he was always busy, working with an unusual speed, then hurrying somewhere.

I saw it, I was astonished; that was all. I had no suspicion whatever. The thing I could have suspected was so horrible, so unbelievably atrocious, that it simply could not slip into my mind. I could not think of it.

Then, suddenly, he broke off every relation with her. He did not want to go out. He refused sternly every invitation. He was dark, and beneath his darkness I distinguished one thing—fear.

Then I understood. His courtship had meant nothing to me; his break told me everything. Oh, not immediately, of course. These things never happen immediately. First, a vague, uncertain thought, a supposition, that made my blood cold. Then a doubt. A desperate fight against this doubt, which only made it stronger. Then an attentive, frightful study. Then—certainty. Henry loved Claire Van Dahlen. . . . Yes, it is my own hand that writes this sentence.

There are things, there are moments in life, which you must not speak about. That was what I felt when I told this sentence to myself for the first time. I found some gray hair on my head that day.

Then came a madness. I could not believe it. It was there and it could not enter into my brain. Oh, that awful feeling of everything falling, falling down, everything around me and in me! . . . There were days when I was calm, hysterically calm, and I cried it was impossible. There were nights when I bit my hands till blood. . . . And then I resolved to fight.

There was a cold, heavy terror in my head now, and life had changed its whole appearance for me. But I gathered all my strength. I told myself that one must not give up one's husband so easily. He had been mine—he might be again.

I understood clearly what was going on in his soul. He had flirted with Claire at first, thinking he was just a little interested in her as in a new acquaintance. The supposition of something serious seemed as impossible to him as it seemed to me. He did not think of it. And it came. And when it came—he broke all off, resolved to crush it immediately.

So we both fought. I, for him; he, against himself. Oh, it was long and hard! We fought bravely. We lost—both.

He was never cold, stern, or irritable with me during those days of his struggle. He was tender as ever. I was gay, quiet as always, attractive as never before. But I could not win him back even for a moment: it was done, and finished.

"Henry," I said once, very calmly and very firmly, "we shall go to this party." We had been refusing all invitations for a long time. Now we went to the party.

He saw her and I watched him. We both knew what we wanted to know. There was no use fighting any longer.

I did not sleep that night. I made all my efforts to breathe. Something strangled me. "One of us has to go through this torture, for life," I thought, "he or I. . . . It shall be I. . . ." I breathed with effort. "He will tell me everything at last . . . and I shall give him a divorce. . . . And if he should be too sorry for me . . . I shall tell him that I do not love him as much as before . . . if I have the strength to do it. . . ." One thing only was clear and without doubt—he could never be happy with me again.

"Henry," I asked one evening, sitting at the fireplace with him and forcing my voice not to tremble, "what will you say . . . if I tell you I do not love you any more?"

He looked into my eyes, kindly and seriously. "I will not believe it," he answered.

Time passed and he did not say a word to me about the truth. I could not understand him. He pitied me, perhaps; but he must tell it sooner or later. He was calm, quiet, and tender; but I saw his pale face, the drooping corners of his mouth, his dark, desperate eyes. When a passion like this gets him—a man is helpless, and I could not blame him. He must have gone through a terrible torture. But he was silent.

In those heartbreaking days, there was one thing which made me furious, for it looked as though fate was playing a grim joke on me. This thing was Gerald Gray. He was a young English aristocrat who came to our town not long ago for a trip. He was thirty years old, elegant, flawlessly dressed, gracious and polite to the points of his nails, and flirting was his only occupation in life. Many women in our town had fallen in love with him. I do not know what made him become interested, too much interested in me. Gracious, polite, yet firm in his courtship, he called upon me, even after I almost plainly threw him out. And this during the time when I awoke every morning, thinking that it is the last day, that I shall hear the fatal words from Henry, at last!

But I waited and Henry said nothing. He refused any possibility of meeting Claire Van Dahlen. She did all she could to meet him. We were flooded with invitations. She sent an invitation to him herself, at last. He refused.

Then came the day when I understood everything. And that day decided my fate. I went to a party alone that evening. Henry stayed at home, as usual, and besides, he had work to do. I could not refuse this invitation without seriously offending the hostess. So I went, but it was a kind of torture for me. I waited with the greatest impatience for the time when it would be possible for me to leave.

I never regretted afterwards that I went to that party. As I was passing near a curtain, I heard two women speaking on the other side of it. It was Mrs. Hughes and Mrs. Brogan. They were speaking about Henry and Claire; they were speaking about me. "Well, she has given all her fortune," said Mrs. Hughes, "she paid enough for him. He cannot leave her now."

"I'll say so," said Mrs. Brogan. "She bought her husband. He might be miserable as a starving dog now—he could not show it!"

I stuffed my handkerchief into my mouth. I knew, now. . . .

I went home alone, on foot. . . . I bought my husband . . . I *bought* my husband! . . . So this was the mystery. He could not leave me. He will never tell me. He will be tortured and keep silent. He cannot be happy with me and his life will be ruined . . . because of my money! . . . Oh! if he will not speak, I must speak!

Perhaps I would not have done what I did, had it not been for that money. I would have fought more, perhaps, and might have gained him back. But now—I could not. I had no right. If he ever came back to me, how would I know whether it was love or thankfulness for my "sacrifice" and the resolution to sacrifice himself in his turn? How would I know that he was not ruining his happiness to recompense me for that money?

I must give him up now—voluntarily and myself. I must give him up—because he owed me too much. I had no right to my husband any more—because I had done too much for him. . . .

I must act now. But what to do? Offer him a divorce? He will not accept it. Tell him I do not love him? He will not believe.

I took off my hat; I could not keep it on. Little drops of rain fell on my forehead and the wind blew my hair—it was such a relief!

I saw a light in the window of Henry's study as I approached our house. I went in noiselessly, not to disturb him. And when I passed by the door of his study, I heard a sound that made my heart stop. I approached the door and looked through the opening, not believing my ears. Sitting at the desk with his arms on his plans and his head on his arms, Henry was sobbing. I saw his back, which shuddered, racked by deep, desperate sobs.

I made a step from the door. I looked before me with senseless eyes. . . . *Henry cried!* . . .

". . . He might be miserable as a starving dog now—he could not show it!"

I knew what I had to do. He will not believe that I do not love him? I must make him believe it! . . .

I went up to my room. I entered it mad, horrified, desperate. I came out in the morning, quiet and calm. What had gone on in me during that night—I will never speak about it with any living creature.

"What is the matter, Irene?" asked Henry, looking into my face, when I came downstairs in the morning.

"Nothing," I answered. "It was a bad dream; it's over now."

I was conscious of one thing only then: I must find a way, an opportunity to prove to Henry my unfaithfulness, so that there should remain no doubt. I found that opportunity. It came the same day.

I returned home after being out, and, entering the hall, I heard a voice in Henry's study. I knew that voice. It was Claire Van Dahlen. I was not astonished. I approached the study door calmly and listened, looking through the keyhole. She was there. I saw her long, bright-green silk shawl on a tan suit. She was perfectly beautiful.

I heard Henry's voice: "Once more, I ask you to leave my house, Mrs. Van Dahlen. I do not want to see you. Do you not understand this?"

"No, I don't, Mr. Stafford," she answered. She looked at him with half-closed eyes. "You are a coward," she said slowly.

He made a step towards her and I saw him. His face was white and, even from the distance where I was, I could see his lips tremble.

"Go away," he said in a strangled voice.

She opened her eyes wholly then. They had a strange look of passion, command, and immense tenderness, that she tried to hide. "Henry . . ." she said slowly, and her voice seemed velvet like her body.

"Mrs. Van Dahlen . . ." he muttered, stepping back.

She approached him more. "You cannot fight . . . I love you, Henry! . . . I want you!"

He was unable to speak. She continued, with a haughty, lightly mocking smile: "You love me and you know it, as well as I. Will you dare to deny it?"

There was torture in his eyes that I could not look upon; and, as though he felt it, he covered them with his hand. "Why did you come here!" he groaned.

She smiled. "Because I want you!" she answered. "Because I love you, Henry, I love you!" She slowly put her hands on his shoulders. "Tell me, Henry, do you love me?" she whispered.

He tore his hand from his eyes. "Yes! . . . Yes! . . . Yes! . . ." he cried. He seized her wildly in his arms and pressed his lips to hers with a desperate greediness.

I was not stricken. There was nothing new for me in all this. But to see him kiss her—it was hard. I closed my eyes. That was all.

"I expected it long ago," she said at last, with her arms embracing him more passionately than she wanted to show.

But he pushed her aside, suddenly and resolutely. "You will never see me again," he said sternly.

"I will see you tonight," she answered. "I will wait for you at nine o'clock at the Excelsior."

"I shall not come!"

"You shall!"

"Never! . . . Never!"

"I ask you a favor, Henry. . . . Till nine o'clock!" And she walked out of the study. I had just time to throw myself behind a curtain.

When I looked into his room again, Henry had fallen on a chair, his head in his hands. I saw all his despair in the fingers that clutched his hair convulsively.

I had found my opportunity. Now—I had to act.

I went to my room, took off my hat and overcoat. I moved towards the door, to go downstairs, to Henry . . . and begin. Then I stopped. "Do you realize," I muttered to myself, "do you understand whom and what you are going to lose?" I opened my mouth to take a breath.

There was a photograph of Henry on my table, the best he had ever taken. There was an inscription on it: "To my Irene—Henry—Forever." I approached it. I fell on my knees. I looked at it with a silent prayer. "Henry . . . Henry . . ." I whispered. I had no voice to say more. I asked him for the strength to do what I had to do.

Then I arose and walked downstairs.

"Henry," I said, entering his room, "I have received a letter from Mrs. Cowan. She is ill and I am going to visit her." Mrs. Cowan was an old acquaintance that lived in a little town four hours' ride from ours. I visited her very rarely.

"I would not like you to go," answered Henry, tenderly passing his hand on my forehead. "You look pale and tired; you must need a rest."

"I am perfectly well," I answered. "I shall be back tomorrow morning."

I had a telephone in my room, and Henry could not hear me talk. At seven o'clock I called Gerald Gray. "Mr. Gray," I said, "would you be at half past eight at the Excelsior?"

"W-what? . . . Oh! Mrs. Stafford!" he muttered in the telephone, losing his perfect countenance before this unexpected favor. I hung up the receiver.

My plan was simple. Henry shall come to the Excelsior for Claire Van Dahlen and he shall see me with Mr. Gray. I had told him that I was going away for the whole night. That's all.

I dressed myself slowly and carefully. I tried to be very attentive, very busy with my toilet, and to drown all thoughts in it. I put on my best gown, a silver gauze dress, all glimmering with rhinestones. I made up my face to look as pretty as possible: I had to use a lot of rouge for it.

Then, suddenly, a thought flashed through my mind, a thought that made me jump from my chair. What if Henry did not come to the Excelsior? He had cried "Never! Never!" so resolutely. . . . What if he had the strength to resist Claire?

The porcelain powder box which I held dropped from my hand and broke to pieces.

Oh, then, if he does not come, it means that he does not love her so much! Then, I will run home and fall at his feet and tell him everything! . . . I had not cried all day; now, tears rolled down my cheeks, so big that I was astonished. Once a person has lost hope, its return is more cruel than the most terrible tortures. I was calm when I began to dress. Now my hands trembled, so that I could hardly touch things.

When I was ready, I put on my traveling overcoat; it hid my evening dress completely. Then I went downstairs.

"Take care of yourself, Irene," said Henry, fastening tightly and carefully the collar of my overcoat. "Don't tire yourself. Don't take too much out of your strength."

"No, Henry, I won't. . . . Goodbye, Henry." I kissed him. For the last time, perhaps. . . .

I walked on foot through the dark streets. It was a cold night and the wind ran under my overcoat, on my naked arms and shoulders. I felt the soft cloud of silver gauze blown close to my legs. I walked firmly and steadily, with a high head.

The Excelsior was a big nightclub in our town. It had not a bad reputation, but somehow women came there with their husbands or did not come at all. I saw the gigantic electric letters "Excelsior," so white that it hurt the eyes to look upon, above the wide glass entrance. I went upstairs. I did not hear my own footsteps on the deep, soft carpets, and the waiters' metallic buttons gleamed like diamonds in the strong, unnatural light around me.

The sharp, piercing rumble of a jazz band struck my head like a blow when I entered the great hall. I saw big round white lanterns, white tables, black suits and naked shoulders. I saw glittering glasses, silk stockings, and diamonds.

Mr. Gray was waiting for me. He looked like the best pictures in the most exclusive men's style magazine. As a perfect gentleman, he did not show the slightest sign of astonishment or surprise at all this. He smiled as courteously and respectfully as it is possible for a man to smile. I chose a table behind a screen, from where I could see the entrance door. Then I sat looking at it, and, strangely, all seemed to be veiled by a cloud. I distinguished the room very vaguely, as in a mist, while I saw the door clearly, precisely, as though through a magnifying glass, with every little detail, to the slightest reflection of the glass, to the smallest curves of the knob.

I remember that Mr. Gray spoke about something and I spoke. He smiled and I smiled, probably, also. . . . There was a clock above the entrance door. It was eight-thirty when I arrived. The hands on the dial moved. I watched them. And if someone could look into my soul then—he would have seen there a round white dial with moving hands. Nothing more.

Just at nine, in the very second when the big hand reached the middle of the 12, the wide glass door opened. I knew it would be opened. . . . However, it was not Henry, no. But it was Claire Van Dahlen.

She was alone. She had a plain black velvet dress, just a piece of soft velvet wrapped around her body; but she had the most gorgeous diamond tiara on her head, with sparkling stones falling to her beautiful golden shoulders.

She stopped at the door and inspected the hall with a quick glance around. She saw at once that he was not there. Her lips had an imperceptible movement of anger and grief. She moved slowly across the hall and sat at a table. I could observe her through a hole in the screen.

Nine-fifteen. . . . The door opened every two minutes. Men in dress coats and women in silk wraps and furs entered and walked noiselessly into the brilliant crowd. I watched the endless torrent of patent-leather shoes and little silver slippers on the soft lavender carpet at the entrance. Oh, why, why were there so many visitors in this restaurant! Every time I heard the door open, with a sinister creaking sound, a cold shudder ran through my back and knees.

My eyes could not leave the door for a second. "Careful, Mrs. Stafford!" I heard Mr. Gray's voice, as in a dream. I noticed that I had been holding a glass of water and the water was spilling on my dress. I took a little piece of ice from the glass and swallowed it. Mr. Gray looked at me with astonishment.

Nine twenty-five. . . . My knees trembled convulsively. It seemed to me that I would never be able to walk. I looked at Claire through the screen's hole. She, too, was waiting. Her eyes were also fixed at the door. She was nervously breaking a flower's stem in her fingers.

Nine-thirty. . . . I could not have told whether the jazz band was rumbling or it was the heavy, striking, knocking noise in my temples. . . . I held my throat with my hand: there was so little air in this hall and a strange leaden humming strangled me.

At nine forty-five he came. The door opened and I saw Henry. For a second it seemed to me that he was standing in the air: there was nothing around. Then I saw the door, but did not see him, though he was standing there: I saw a black hole. Then I saw him again and he moved. And there was a strange dead silence around. No sounds in my ears.

Then I threw back my head and cried: "Let us be merry, Mr. Gray!" I flung my arms around his neck and, burying my face in his shoulder, I bit convulsively his coat: I understood plainly one thing only—I must not shout.

Mr. Gray was amazed; he had been sitting with his back to the door and had not seen Henry. But with his perfect, courteous self-possession, he remained calm and even passed his hand cautiously on my hair.

I raised my head and he could read nothing in my face now. But my eyes must have been horrible, for he looked into them and grew a little uneasy. I seized nervously at all the glasses that were on the table. "Where is the wine, Mr. Gray?" I cried. "Why is there no wine? I want wine!" Afraid to make any opposition, he called a waiter and whispered some words, and the waiter winked.

I looked through the screen's hole. Henry approached Claire. She had involuntarily jumped from her chair and smiled, with more happiness and passionate tenderness than she wanted to show, perhaps. She must have been very anxious, for she did not even say a word about his delay. He was pale and serious. This delay told me more than anything: he had struggled, oh! horribly struggled, and lost. . . . He sat at her table. I saw his eyes light with an unconquerable joy as he looked at her, and his lips smiled. . . . And he was so beautiful!

The waiter brought the wine, two bottles. Mr. Gray wanted to pour it. I seized the bottle from his hand and filled a glass, so that the wine ran over, on my dress. Then I lifted the glass as high as I could and let it fall to the floor, breaking with a sharp, ringing sound. I burst into a loud, piercing, provocative laugh.

Mr. Gray was amazed. "Laugh!" I whispered threateningly. "I want you to laugh! Laugh loudly!" He laughed. I looked through the hole. Many persons glanced in our direction, wondering who could be making that vulgar noise. That was what I wanted.

I seized my hair and brought it to a wild disorder, so that threads flew in all directions. Then I seized a bottle of wine and flung it to the floor, with a terrible noise. I laughed again and cried: "O-oh! Gerry!" Then I overturned my chair and jumping on Mr. Gray's knees, embracing him, I pressed my face to his, as though I was kissing him. He could not notice that I pushed the screen with my foot in the same moment. The screen fell and there I was, on "Gerry's" lap!

Many persons arose from their seats to look, and when I arose, pretending to be very vexed and ashamed—I stood face to face with Henry.

I shall never forget his eyes. . . . We were silent. . . . "Irene . . . Irene," he muttered.

I pretended to be stricken, afraid, terrified the first minutes. Then I raised my head and looking at him with the greatest insolence: "Well?" I asked.

He stepped back. He shuddered. He passed his hand over his eyes. Then he said slowly: "I will not disturb you." He turned and walked to Mrs. Van Dahlen. "Let us go to another restaurant . . . Claire," he said. They walked out. I followed them with my eyes, till they disappeared behind the door. That was all. . . .

I was completely, deeply calm now. I turned to Mr. Gray. He had put the screen around our table again. "Do not grieve yourself, Mrs. Stafford," he said. "It is for the best, perhaps."

"Yes, Mr. Gray, it is for the best," I answered.

We sat down and we finished our dinner, calmly and quietly. I had all my consciousness now. I spoke, and smiled, and flirted with him so gently, so graciously, that he was wholly charmed and forgot the wild scene. At half past ten I asked him to take me home. He was disappointed that our meeting was so short, but said nothing and courteously brought me to my house door, in an automobile. "Shall we meet again soon?" he asked, holding my hand in his.

"Yes, very soon . . . and very often," I answered. He went away, completely happy.

I entered our apartment. I stood motionless, I could not tell for how long. . . . It was done. . . .

I entered Henry's study. I saw some papers on the floor and, picking them up, replaced them on the desk. A chair was pushed into the middle of the room—I put it back. I adjusted the pillows on the sofa. I put in order the plans and drawings that covered all the desk. His rulers, compasses, and other objects were thrown all over the room. I put them on the desk. I made a fire in the fireplace. . . . It was for the last time that I could do a wife's duty for him.

When there was nothing more to arrange, I went to the fireplace and sat on the floor. Henry's armchair was standing by the fire, and there was a pillow near it, on which he put his feet. I did not dare to sit in the armchair. I lay on the floor and put my head on the pillow. . . . The wood was burning with a soft red glow in the darkness and a little crackling sound in the silence. I lay motionless, pressing the pillow to my lips. . . .

I arose quickly when I heard a key turn in the entrance door's lock. I went into the hall. Henry was pale, very pale. He did not look at me. He took off his hat and overcoat and hung them on the clothes peg. Then he walked to his study and, passing by me, looked at me with a long glance. He entered first; I followed him.

We were silent for a long time. Then he spoke, sternly and coldly: "Will you explain to me anything?"

"I have nothing to explain, Henry," I answered. "You have seen."

"Yes," he said, "I have seen."

He walked up and down the room, then stopped again. He smiled, a smile of disgust and hatred. "It was great!" he said. I did not answer. He trembled with fury. "You . . . you . . ." he cried, clasping his fists. "How could you?" I was silent. "And I called my wife during four years a woman like that!" He pressed his head. "You make me crazy! It is impossible! It is not you! You were not like this! You could not be like this!"

I said nothing. He seized me by the arms and flung me to the floor. "Speak, dirt! Answer! Why did you do it?"

I looked at him, I looked straight into his eyes and told a lie. It was the most atrocious lie that could be and the only one he could believe and understand. "I hid it from you because I did not want to make you unhappy. I struggled a long time against this love and could not stand it any longer," I said.

And he understood this. He left my arms and stepped back. Then laughed. "Well, I can make you happy, then!" he cried. "I don't love you at all and I am not unhappy at all! I love another woman! I am only happy now!"

"You are happy, Henry?"

"Yes, immensely! I see that you are disappointed!"

"No, Henry, I am not disappointed. It is all right."

"All right? . . . What are you doing lying on the floor? Get up! . . . All right? You have the insolence to say that?"

He walked up and down the room. "Don't look at me!" he cried. "You have no right any more even to look at me! I forbid it to you!"

"I will not look, Henry," I answered, bowing my head.

"No, you will! You will look at yourself!" he cried and, seizing me by the arm, flung me to the looking glass. "Look at your dress!" he cried. Dark wine spots covered the silver gauze of my dress.

"You loved him, you went with him, well. But wine! But kisses! But that conduct in a public place!" he cried. Oh, my plan had worked perfectly! I said nothing.

He was silent for some time, then he said, more calmly and coldly: "You understand that there will be nothing between us, now. I wish I could forget that there ever was. . . . And I want you to forget that I was your husband. I want you to give me back everything you have from me, any kind of remembrance."

"Well, Henry, I can give them now," I answered.

I went to my room and brought everything, all his pictures, his presents, some letters, all I had from him. He took them all and threw them into the fireplace. "May I . . . may I keep this one, Henry?" I asked, handing him the best picture, with the inscription. My fingers trembled. He took it, looked, and threw it back to me disdainfully. It fell on the floor. I picked it up.

"I will see to it that we are divorced as soon as possible," he said. He fell into an armchair. "Let me alone now," he added.

I walked to the door, then stopped. I looked at him. And I said, with a voice that was very firm and very calm: "Forgive me, Henry . . . if you can . . . and forget me. . . . And don't grieve with grim thoughts, think about Claire, and be happy . . . and don't think about me . . . it is not worthwhile."

He looked at me. "You were like this . . . before," he said slowly.

"I was . . . I am no longer. . . . Everything changes, Henry . . . everything has an end. But life is beautiful . . . life is great. . . . You must be happy, Henry."

"Irene," he said, in a very low voice, "tell me, why have you changed?"

I have gone through it all calmly. This simple sentence, my name, his low voice, made something rise in my throat. But for one second only. "I could not help it, Henry," I answered.

Then I went upstairs to my room.

I bit my lips, when I entered, so that I felt the heavy taste of blood in my mouth. "That's nothing," I muttered. "That's nothing, Irene. . . . That's nothing. . . ." I felt a strange necessity to speak; to say something; to drown with words something that has no name and that was there, waiting for me. "That's nothing . . . nothing. . . . It will be over . . . it will be over . . . just one minute, Irene, it will be over . . . one minute. . . ."

I knew I was not blind, but I did not see anything. I did not hear a sound. . . . When I began to hear again I noticed that I was repeating senselessly, ". . . one minute . . . one minute . . ."

Henry's picture, which I held, fell to the floor. I looked at it. Then, suddenly, I saw clearly, wholly, and exactly what had happened and what was going to happen. It lasted less than a second, as though in the glow of a sudden lightning, but it seized me at the throat, like pincers of red-hot iron. And I shouted. I uttered a cry. It was not even a cry, it was not a human sound. It was the wild howl of a wounded animal; the primitive, ferocious cry of life for help.

I heard running footsteps on the staircase. "What happened?" cried Henry, knocking at my door.

"Nothing," I answered. "I saw a mouse." I heard him go downstairs.

I wanted to move, to take some steps. But the floor was running under my feet, running down, down. And there was a black smoke in my room that turned, turned, turned in columns with a frightful speed. I fell. . . .

When I opened my eyes, I was lying on the floor. It was quite dark in the room, and cold. A window had been left open and the curtains moved slowly, blown by the wind. "I was unconscious," I said to myself.

I rose to my feet and tried to stand. My knees seemed broken. I let myself slowly down again. Then I saw his picture on the floor. A long shudder ran through all my body.

I took the picture and put it in an armchair. Then I whispered, and my voice was human now, weak and trembling: "Henry . . . Henry . . . my Henry . . . that is nothing. . . . It is not true, is it, Henry? It was a dream, perhaps, and we shall awaken soon. . . . And I will not cry. Don't look at my eyes, Henry, I am not crying . . . it will be over . . . in a minute. . . . Because, you see, it was hard . . . I think it was even very hard. . . . But that is nothing. You are with me, aren't you, Henry? . . . And you know everything. . . . You do. . . . I am foolish to grieve like this, am I not, Henry? Say that I am. . . . Smile, Henry, and laugh at me . . . and scold me for torturing myself like this, when there is nothing . . . nothing at all. . . . Nothing happened . . . and you know everything. . . . You see, I am smiling. . . . And you love me. . . . You are my Henry. . . . I am a little tired, you know, but I will take a rest . . . and it will be over. . . . No, I am not crying, Henry . . . I love you . . . Henry. . . ."

Tears ran down my cheeks, big, heavy, silent tears. I did not cry, there were no sobs, no sound. I spoke and I smiled. Only tears rolled down, without interruption, without sound, without end. . . .

I do not remember much about the months that followed. We had applied for a divorce, on the ground of wife's unfaithfulness. Waiting for it, I lived in Henry's house. But we did not meet often. When we met, we greeted one another politely.

I managed to live, somehow. I remember that I read books, lots of books. But I cannot remember a word of them now, their titles or how they looked; not one of them. I walked much too, in the little deserted streets of the poorest neighborhoods, where nobody could see me. I think I was calm then. Only I remember that I once heard a boy say, pointing at me: "Here's one that's goofy!"

I met Gerald Gray often, as often as I could, and I flirted with him, I had to. I do not remember one of our meetings. But I must have played my part perfectly well, for I remember, as though out of a deep fog, one sentence said by him: "You are the most bewitching, the most exquisite of women, Mrs. Stafford, and your husband is a fool . . . for which I am immensely happy." I do not know how I could have done it; I must have acted with the precision and unconsciousness of a lunatic.

One thing I remember well: I watched Henry. He spent all his time with Claire. His eyes were brilliant, and sparkling, and smiling, now. I, who knew him so well, who understood every line of his face, I saw that he was happy. He seemed to have come out of a heavy nightmare, which his existence for the last months had been, and to breathe life again, and as before to be young, strong, beautiful, oh! too beautiful!

I watched Claire, also. She loved Henry. It was not a mere flirt for her, or a victory that flattered her pride. It was a deep, great passion, the first in her life, perhaps. She was no "vamp." She was a clever, noble, refined woman, as clever as she was beautiful. . . . He will be happy.

I saw them together once. They were walking in the street. They were talking and smiling. She wore an elegant white suit. They looked perfectly happy.

The town was indignant at our divorce, indignant with me, of course. I was not admitted in any house any more. Many persons did not greet me in the street. I noticed disdainful, mocking smiles, despising grins on the faces of persons that had been my friends. I met Mrs. Brogan once. She stopped and told me plainly, for she always said what she thought: "You dirty creature! Do you think nobody understands that you sold yourself for Gray's money?" And Patsy Tillins approached me once in the street and said: "You've made a bad bargain, dearie: I wouldn't have changed Henry Stafford for no one, from heaven to hell!"

The day came when we got the divorce. . . . I was Irene Wilmer again; divorced for unfaithfulness to my husband. That was all.

When Henry spoke to me about money that I might need, I refused to take anything and said cynically: "Mr. Gray has more money than you!"

Gerald Gray was to leave for New York, just on the next day, to take a ship for Europe from there. I was to go with him.

That evening, Mr. Barnes called upon me. He had been out of town for the last months and, returning only today, heard about everything. He came to me immediately. "Now, Irene," he said very seriously, and his voice trembled in spite of him, "there is some terrible mistake in what I have heard. Would you tell me?"

"Why, Mr. Barnes," I answered calmly, "I don't think there could be any mistake: I am divorced, just today."

"But . . . but . . . but is it really your fault? Are you really guilty?"

"Well, if you call it guilty . . . I love Gerald Gray, that's all."

His face grew red, purple, then white. He could not speak for some long minutes. "You . . . *you* don't love your husband?" he muttered at last.

"Henry Stafford, you mean? He is not my husband any longer. . . . No, I don't love him."

"Irene . . ." He tried to speak calmly and there was a strange solemn strength in his voice. "Irene, it is not true. I will tell everybody that you could not have done it."

"I'm no saint."

He stepped back and his grayish old head shook piteously. "Irene," he said again, and there was almost a plea in his voice, "you could not have traded a man like your husband for that silly snob."

"I did."

"You, Irene, *you?* I cannot believe it!"

"Don't. Who cares?"

This was too much. He raised his head. "Then," he

said slowly, "I have nothing more to say. . . . Farewell, Irene."

"Bye-bye!" I answered with an indifferent insolence.

I looked through the window, when he was going away. His poor old figure seemed more bent and heavy than ever. "Farewell, Mr. Barnes," I whispered. "Farewell . . . and forgive me."

That night, the last night I spent in my home, I awoke very late. When all was silent in the house, I went noiselessly downstairs. I thought that I could not say farewell to Henry, tomorrow, and I wanted to say it. I cautiously opened the bedroom door: he was sleeping. I entered. I raised slightly the window curtain, to see him. I stood by his bed, that had been mine also. I looked at him. His face was calm and serene. The dark lashes of his closed eyes were immobile on his cheeks. His beautiful lips seemed carved of marble on his face, pale in the darkness. I did not dare to touch him. I put my hand slowly and cautiously on the pillow, near his head.

Then I knelt down, by the bed. I could not kiss his lips; it would have awakened him. I took his hand cautiously and pressed it to my lips. "Henry," I whispered, "you shall never know. And you must not know. Be happy, very happy. . . . And I shall go through life with one thing, one right only left to me: the right to say that I loved you, Henry . . . and the right to love you . . . till the end." I kissed his hand with a long, long kiss.

Then I arose, closed the curtain, and went out.

It was a cold, gray day, the next and the last. There was a little chilly rain sometimes, and a wind that carried gray smoky clouds in the sky.

The train was leaving our town at ten-fifteen P.M. Mr. Gray called me in the morning. He was radiant with joy. He wanted to come in the evening to bring me to the station. I refused. "Wait for me there," I said shortly. "I shall come myself."

It was already dark and I sat in my room waiting. Waiting with such a despair that it astonished me, for I thought that I was unable to feel anything now. I waited for Henry. He was not at home. He must have gone to Claire, to spend with her the first day of his freedom. I could not say farewell to him, no; but I wanted to take a last look at him, the last one before going forever. And he was not there. . . . I sat by the window. It was cold, but I opened it. I watched the street. The roofs and pavement were wet and glittering. There were few passersby that walked rarely, with a nervous hurry, lonely, hopeless shadows in glittering raincoats. . . .

It was nine-thirty. Henry had not come.

I closed the window and took a little bag. I had not much to pack. I put some linen in it and one dress—my wedding dress, with the veil; I put in Henry's photograph. It was all I took with me.

When I was closing the bag, I heard a key turn in the entrance door and footsteps, his footsteps. He had come!

I put on my hat and overcoat, took my bag. "I shall pass through the hall and open the door of his study a little. He will not notice and I shall take a look, just one look," I thought.

I went downstairs. I entered the hall and opened his door: the study was empty; he was not there. I took a deep breath and walked to the entrance door. I put my hand on the knob.

"Irene, are you not going to say farewell to me?" I turned. It was Henry. His voice was calm and sad.

I was so stricken that I almost lost all my self-possession in the first second. "Yes . . . yes . . ." I muttered incoherently.

We entered his study. There was a fire in the fireplace. He looked at me with his dark eyes, and they were very clear and very sad.

"We are parting forever, perhaps, Irene," he said, "and we had meant much to one another."

I nodded. My voice would have betrayed me, if I spoke.

"I cannot blame or judge you, Irene. . . . That evening, in the restaurant, it was a sudden madness, perhaps, that you did not realize yourself. . . . I do not think you are really the woman you were then."

"No, Henry . . . perhaps not." I could not help whispering.

"You are not. I shall always think of you as the

woman I loved." He paused. I had never seen him so quiet and hopeless.

"Life goes on," he continued. "I shall marry another woman and you—another man. . . . And everything is over." He took my hands in his and there was a sudden light in his eyes when he said: "But we were so happy, Irene!"

"Yes, Henry, we were," I answered firmly and calmly.

"Did you love me then, Irene?"

"I did, Henry."

"That time has gone. . . . But I could never forget you, Irene. I cannot. I shall think about you."

"Yes, Henry, think about me . . . sometimes."

"You will be happy, Irene, won't you? I want you to be happy."

"I will be, Henry."

"I will be also. . . . Maybe even as happy as I was with you. . . . But we cannot look behind now. One has to go on. . . . Will you think about me a little, Irene?"

"I will, Henry."

His eyes were dark and there was a deep sorrow in them. I raised my head. I put my hand on his shoulder. I spoke with a great calm, with a majesty, perhaps, to which I had the right now.

"Henry, you must be happy, and strong, and glorious. Leave suffering to those that cannot help it. You must smile at life. . . . And never think about those that cannot. They are not worthwhile."

"Yes . . . you are right. . . . Everything finished well. It could have broken the life of one of us. I am so happy it did not!"

"Yes, Henry, it did not. . . ."

We were silent. Then he said: "Farewell, Irene. . . . We shall never meet on this earth again. . . ."

"Life is not so long, Henry." I trembled when I said this, but happily he did not understand. "Who knows?" I added quickly. "We shall meet, perhaps . . . when we are sixty."

He smiled. "Yes, perhaps . . . and then we shall laugh at all this."

"Yes, Henry, we shall laugh. . . ."

He bent his head and kissed my hand. "Go now," he whispered, and added, in a very low voice: "You were the greatest thing in my life, Irene." He raised his head and looking into my eyes: "Will you not say something to me . . . for the last time?" he asked.

I looked straight into his eyes. All my soul was in my answer: *"I loved you, Henry."*

He kissed my hand again. His voice was a very faint whisper when he said: "I shall be happy. But there are moments when I wish I would never have met that woman. . . . There is nothing to do. . . . Life is hard, sometimes, Irene."

"Yes, Henry," I answered.

He took me in his arms and kissed me. His lips were on mine; my arms—around his neck. It was for the last time, but it was. And no one can deprive me of it now.

He went with me outside. I called a taxi and entered it. I looked through the window: he was standing on the steps. The wind blew his hair and he was immobile like a statue. It was the last time I ever saw him.

I closed my eyes and when I opened them—the taxi was stopped before the station. I paid the driver, took my bag, and went to the train.

Gerald Gray was waiting for me. He had a brilliant traveling costume, a radiant smile, and a gigantic bouquet of flowers, which he presented to me. We entered the car.

At ten-fifteen there was a crackling, metallic sound, the wheels turned, the car shook and moved. The pillars of the station slipped faster and faster beyond us, then some lanterns, on corners of the dark streets, some lights in the windows. And the town remained behind us. . . . The wheels were knocking quickly and regularly.

We were alone in our part of the car. Mr. Gray looked at me and smiled. Then he smiled again, as though to make me smile in answer. I sat motionless. "We are free and alone at last," he whispered and tried to put his arm around me. I moved from him.

"Wait, Mr. Gray," I said coldly. "We shall have time enough for that."

"What is the matter with you, Mrs. Stafford . . . Miss Wilmer, I mean?" he muttered. "You are so pale!"

"Nothing," I answered. "I am a little tired."

For two hours we sat, silent and motionless. There was nothing but the noise of the wheels around us.

After two hours' ride, there was the first station. I took my bag and rose. "Where are you going?" asked Mr. Gray, surprised. Without answer, I left the train. I approached the open window of the car where he sat looking at me anxiously, and I said slowly: "Listen, Mr. Gray: there is a millionaire in San Francisco waiting for me. You were only a means to get rid of my husband. I thank you. And don't ever say a word about this to anybody—they will laugh at you terribly."

He was stricken, furious and disappointed, oh, terribly disappointed. But as a perfect gentleman, he did not show it. "I am happy to have rendered you that service," he said courteously. The train moved at this moment. He took off his hat, with the most gracious politeness.

I remained alone on the little platform. There was an immense black sky around me, with slow, heavy clouds. There was an old fence and a wretched tree, with some last, wet leaves. . . . I saw a dim light in the little window of the ticket office.

I had not much money, only what was left in my pocketbook. I approached the lighted window. "Give me a ticket, please," I said, handing over all my money, with nickels and pennies, all.

"To which station?" asked the employee shortly.

"To . . . to . . . That is all the same," I answered.

He looked at me and even moved a little back. "Say . . ." he began.

"Give me to the end of the line," I said. He handed me a ticket and pushed back some of my money. I moved from the window, and he followed me with a strange look.

"I shall get out at some station or other," I thought. A train stopped at the platform and I went in. I sat down at a window. Then I moved no more.

I remember it was dark beyond the window, then light, then dark again. I must have traveled more than twenty-four hours. Perhaps. I don't know.

It was dark when I remembered that I must alight at some station. The train stopped and I got out. On the platform I saw that it was night. I wanted to return to the car. But the train moved and disappeared into the darkness. I remained.

There was nobody on the wet wooden platform. I saw only a sleepy employee, a dim lantern, and a dog rolled under a bench, to protect himself from the rain. I saw some little wooden houses beyond the station, and a narrow street. The rails glittered faintly and there was a poor little red lantern in the distance.

I looked at the clock: it was three A.M. I sat on the bench and waited for the morning.

All was finished. . . . I had done my work. . . . Life was over. . . .

I live in that town now. I am an employee in a department store and I work from nine to seven. I have a little flat—two rooms—in a poor, small house, and a separate staircase—nobody notices me when I go out or return home.

I have no acquaintances whatever. I work exactly and carefully. I never speak. My fellow workers hardly know my name. My landlady sees me once a month, when I pay my rent.

I never think when I work. When I come home—I eat and I sleep. That is all.

I never cry. When I look into a looking glass—I see a pale face, with eyes that are a little too big for it; and with the greatest calm, the greatest quietness, the deepest silence in the world.

I am always alone in my two rooms. Henry's picture stands on my table. He has a cheerful smile: a little haughty, a little mocking, very gay. There is an inscription: "To my Irene—Henry—Forever." When I am tired, I kneel before the table and I look at him.

People say that time rubs off everything. This law was not for me. Years have passed. I loved Henry Stafford. I love him. He is happy now—I gave him his happiness. That is all.

They were right, perhaps, those who said that I bought my husband. I bought his life. I bought his happiness. I paid with everything I had. I love him. . . . If I could live life again—I would live it just as I did. . . .

Women, girls, everyone that shall hear me, listen to this: don't love somebody beyond limits and consciousness. Try to have always some other aim or duty. Don't love beyond your very soul . . . if you can. I cannot.

One has to live as long as one is not dead. I live on. But I know that it will not be long now. I feel that the end is approaching. I am not ill. But I know that my strength is going and that life simply and softly is dying away in me. It has burned out. It is well.

I am not afraid and I am not sorry. There is only one thing more that I dare to ask from life: I want to see Henry once again. I want to have one look more, before the end, at him that has been my whole life. Just one look only. That is all I ask.

I cannot return to our town, for I will be seen and recognized at once. I wait and I hope. I hope hopelessly. There is not much time left. When I walk in the street— I look at every face around me, searching for him. When I come home—I say to his picture: "It is not today, Henry. . . . But it will be tomorrow, perhaps. . . ."

Shall I see him again? I tell myself that I shall. I know that I shall not. . . .

Now I have written my story. I gathered all my courage and I wrote it. If he reads it—he will not be unhappy. But he will understand all. . . .

And then, perhaps, after reading it, he will . . . oh, no! not come to see me, he will understand that he must not do it . . . he will just pass by me in the street, seeming not to notice me, so that I might see him once again, once more . . . and for the last time.

The Night King

c. 1926

Editor's Preface

This story represents the writing of the *very* early Ayn Rand. She wrote the story, probably in 1926, while living at the Hollywood Studio Club. She was still learning English—especially the use of American slang and how to re-create the same on the printed page.

"The Night King" clearly reflects her admiration of O. Henry. (See Leonard Peikoff's preface to "Escort.")

This story is being published here with minimal editing in order accurately to convey her literary and linguistic starting point, and thus her development as a writer both of fiction and of English in the ensuing years.

—R.E.R.

The Night King

That one was to be the best crime I ever pulled off, if I say so myself, it was to be a masterpiece. And a masterpiece it was, all right, but every time I think of it my blood boils with fury and I wonder if I'm not going to be a murderer instead of a mild, harmless hold-up man.

Some people may be so heartless as to feel a certain lack of respect for me, when they hear of this memorable affair. But I defy anyone to tell me that he would have acted differently, that he would have been *able* to act differently in this strange case.

I'm not an average crook and my mind is the best in the business. I sacrificed two years of my valuable life to that one job. Believe it or not, for two whole years I was as straight as a telegraph pole and earned my modest living by holding the honorable, respectable position of a valet. The cops back in Chicago would never believe that of me, Steve Hawkins, the great Steve Hawkins who used to pull stick-up jobs faster than the crime reporters could write down in short-hand. Me—to become a valet! Yet that's just what I had been doing—for two years. For, you see, I was after the most precious thing and against the most dangerous man in New York.

The thing was the Night King; the man—Winton Stokes.

Winton Stokes had a nasty smile, sixteen million dollars and no fear whatsoever.

He also had the Night King.

He was one of those wealthy loafers that spend their

lives looking for danger and never getting enough of it. Big-game hunting, aviation, jungle-exploring, mountain-peak climbing—there wasn't a thing that man hadn't had time to do in the thirty-four years of his life. And he always took a particular pleasure in doing the things that would shock people, that nobody could expect or think of. Some brain, too! The keenest, sharpest and, damn it!, queerest brain I ever came across. I often thought it was too bad he was born a millionaire, for he would have made a perfect crook—just the type for it.

His smile? I hated it. I hated almost everything about him: his slow, soft movements that looked as though his bones were of velvet, and with it his tanned skin that looked as though his body were of bronze; and then, his grey eyes, the eyes of a tamed tiger, that you weren't so sure whether it's tamed or not. But his smile was the worst of all. He always had it when he looked at people—just two little wrinkles in the corners of his mouth, which seemed to say you were terribly funny, but that he was too polite to laugh.

The Night King was a black diamond; one of those perfect gems that have a world-renown, and their owners—a world-envy. A marvelous stone, famous like a movie star, but different from one in that it never had a double.

Was it valuable? Well, you could buy a small city, inhabitants and all, for the price of that one little splinter of black fire. Winton Stokes was so proud of it that he wouldn't have traded it for all the rest of his possessions—and that was plenty.

There had been more loss of life from trying to get that stone than there is from traffic accidents in a big city. All of our big guys tried it. Then, it was given up as impossible. No one could get it; not with Winton Stokes as the owner.

But I told them that there was nothing impossible to Steve Hawkins, the master-criminal. I had made up my mind to succeed where all had failed. They laughed at me for giving up my brilliant hold-up career and slaving as Winton Stokes' valet. During the two years of my working at his New York residence, I never once got even a hint of where the Night King was hidden, no matter how hard I tried. I don't believe anybody on earth knew that secret, except Winton Stokes. But I waited and played the part of as honest a guy as they make 'em. I was a model valet and just as sweet and white as sugar. Then, finally, my big chance came—and oh! How it did come!

I wanted to show them all an unusual crime to knock them cockeyed with amazement. And they *were* amazed, though not quite in the way I had expected. But just try to mention the Night King case to the New York cops and see what happens!

It started like this: Winton Stokes was going on a trip to San Francisco. He was engaged to some charming little girl who lived there. I've seen her picture on his desk. A blonde little thing, with a smile like a glass of champagne and legs like a hosiery ad. Winton Stokes was to marry her there, in her home town. But I knew something else about this trip of his, something that no one knew, but me, and Stokes, and his girl.

I learned it in a very simple manner, but the news was as unexpected to me as a fresh orchid in a garbage can. You may be sure that for two years I've been opening secretly all of Winton Stokes' letters that I could lay my hands on. So I opened this particular one that he had ordered me to mail. I don't remember a word of it, except one sentence, and here is the sentence that took hold of my brains, memory and consciousness so as to knock out everything else I had on my mind:

"My dearest one, I'll bring with me, as my wedding gift, the thing that has been my most precious possession, but isn't any more—not since I looked into the blue diamonds of your eyes—I'll bring the Night King, that you asked me about once."

Oh boy!

The first thing I did when I read this was to take a deep breath. The second—to swear, energetically. The third—to laugh. The big fool! To give *that* stone away like this to a woman! Just like him, too.

Well, here was my chance.

In the day that followed I turned my brain upside

down and back again, trying to figure out a way to accompany him on this trip. But I didn't have to think much. He saved me the trouble.

I was called into his study on that beautiful spring morning. He was sitting in a deep, Oriental chair, his legs crossed, a long cigarette between his lips, looking at me with half-closed eyes.

"Williams," he said (this being the name I had adopted), "you might be interested to know that in three days you are leaving with me for San Francisco."

There must have been something funny in my face, for he added:

"What is it? Are you surprised?"

I muttered something about how grateful I was for the honor. Fact is, I was so grateful that I almost felt like sparing him and not touching his diamond at all!

"Your services have been most satisfactory during the time you have worked for me and I chose you to accompany me on this trip," he explained, adding, "I trust you more than my other men."

Now, I had to act and act quick. After some careful deliberation, a plan was ready in my mind, a brilliant plan that only a bright thinker like me could have devised.

That evening, I made my way to a certain part of New York, very far from the residential district and very different from it. I went directly to a certain pool-parlor, unofficially called "The Hanged Cat," which was a pool-parlor and many other things besides. Since the time I started on my valet job, I didn't mix with any rough work, as I've said before, but I knew where to find the boys if I needed them. "The Hanged Cat" was their favorite social club.

It didn't take me long to choose my men—three of them—and to get them into a dark corner, around an old, shaking table that had four legs all of different lengths.

"Boys," I said, "I have a job for us and if we pull it through we can all retire and start putting burglar-proof alarms on our safes!"

I explained the whole thing. I told them just what I wanted them to do and also just how much they'd get from me. Two of them, Pete Crump and "Snout" Timkins, agreed at once, and enthusiastically, too. But the third, and I might have expected it, started trouble. The third was Mickey Finnegan.

I had known Mickey back in my Chicago days and we had always been rivals in business. That sap had the nerve to think he was as good as me, and just as much of a master-crook! Every success of mine always made him green with jealousy and every one of his didn't make me pink, either.

Mickey was a big, husky fellow, with fists like watermelons, hair like a floor-mop, lips like beef-steaks, eyes like a fish and an atrocious odor of tobacco that he was always chewing, slowly and senselessly, like a cow. I had no respect whatever for that big brute's mentality, of which he had a nickel's worth. But I had to admit he was strong, and that's what I needed now—strength.

I had hesitated before choosing him for my accomplice, but his hairy fists looked so promising and besides, I thought our old misunderstandings were forgotten. I was mistaken.

"It's all right, Steve," he said in his slow, dragging voice, "it's fine—except one thing, which's this: I'm gonna get half of it, see? Fifty-fifty."

"What? You don't mean that . . . !"

"Yeh, I do. I wasn't never Steve Hawkins' under-dog yet and I don't crave to start now, neither. I'm just as good as you, and I'll get just as much, so I will."

"Well, for pity sakes, Mickey! Isn't it my job? Didn't I prepare it? Didn't I spend two years on it?"

"That," said Mickey, "don't make no difference to me."

I argued for some time, for a long time. But what was the use? Mickey had always been as stubborn as a bull-dog.

"Shut up," he said finally, "you're wastin' yer breath and my time, and one o'them is valuable. It's either I gets half of it or I don't and if I don't you don't see none of Mickey Finnegan with your gang, either."

"Mickey," I said solemnly, "you're a skunk."

"Am I?" roared Mickey, and then followed something which is hard to describe, and which was stopped only by the other boys stepping between Mickey and me and tearing us apart. And the result of it was that I had to spit from my mouth two teeth knocked out by Mickey's fist.

My two friends assured me that we could manage the job between the three of us and didn't need Mickey at all. So I told him just what I thought of him and went home.

But when I got there and glanced into a mirror, I was terrified to see what my face looked like. My jaw was swollen and as I open my mouth very wide when I talk, the empty black hole on the side was very much in evidence.

What would Winton Stokes think when he saw his model valet with a mug like that? He might change his mind about taking me along. And he might even suspect something. My brilliant plan might be ruined because of Mickey. I shuddered.

"What happened to your face?" asked Winton Stokes calmly, when he saw me on the next morning.

"I—I had a fall. . . ." I stammered, rather uncertainly. "I fell on the basement steps in the dark, last night."

He looked at me fixedly for some moments, as though thinking it over. "He suspects!" I trembled. But he said, rather indifferently:

"Well, see to it that you have a more decent appearance by the day of our departure, and have some false teeth put in—it doesn't look proper."

He sent me to a dentist, and forgot about this episode, and I felt an immense relief. But I made up my mind that someday I'd make Mickey Finnegan pay dearly for it.

In the days that preceded our departure I watched Winton Stokes like a police-dog that trails a crook. I watched his every movement. There wasn't a place where I didn't manage to follow him, and watch. I didn't sleep nights. I hoped to see him take the Night King out of its mysterious hiding-place and see where he was going to put it for the trip. I didn't see a thing. I didn't get the slightest clue. I didn't see him make one move that could be connected with the diamond, or that even looked suspicious.

And so, the day of our departure came and we started on our trip, just Winton Stokes, me, and a little suitcase of his. He didn't take any other baggage.

Now, I knew that he had the Night King with him somewhere. He would never disappoint a lady and he would take the stone to her in spite of all danger. Besides, it was just the kind of thing he would enjoy doing.

But what got me mad was his utter, perfect calm. He was just as serene as a summer morning; not the slightest shade of worry or preoccupation. And just as we were leaving the house, I remarked that he had left behind the automatic he always carried.

"I won't need it," he said, "not on this trip."

Not on this trip!

When we found ourselves in the luxurious express flying westward, Winton Stokes sat by a window, calm and indifferent, his head thrown back and his eyes half closed. And I, Steve Hawkins, fidgeted nervously in my corner, biting my dry lips and looking anxiously around.

My big moment was approaching. Two years of my life! I thought of the financial loss I had suffered by being out of business for such a long time. The Night King would make up for it all. I had a customer all ready and it takes my breath away when I think of the sum he had offered me for it.

I looked over the car and watched the passengers. I was afraid there might be some detective around, hired by Stokes for protection. But there didn't seem to be any. My heart was beating fast and I was as nervous as an author on his play's first night. Winton Stokes was immobile, like an inscrutable Oriental idol.

All of a sudden I jumped in my seat and stuck both my gloves into my mouth to stifle a cry. In a far corner I noticed a gentleman who seemed to be slumbering in his seat, his head hanging down on his breast and a fly walking across his red, moist forehead. That gentleman had a dirty shirt-collar, a brand new suit that didn't fit, fat legs squeezing out of patent-leather shoes, and all the appearance of one who isn't used to decent clothes. His mouth was chewing slowly and heavily. It was Mickey Finnegan.

What was he doing here? What was he going to do?

Would he betray me, or try to pull the job for himself? For the first time it occurred to me he knew the secret of the Night King's trip and might wish to try his own luck at it.

I felt cold in my spine. But there was nothing I could do, except watch Mickey carefully and hope that he wouldn't have time to act before I did. After a while I was a little reassured: I decided that a master-mind like me didn't have to fear the rivalry of that brainless boob. Besides, Mickey didn't seem to have any accomplices around and he looked dead tired and sleepy.

I could hardly wait for night to come. The hours just dragged forever. The speeding strokes of car-wheels on the rails sounded like a slow funeral march to me. But everything comes to him who waits.

It was near midnight. Winton Stokes was still sitting in the day coach. He always went to sleep very late and I had counted on it. The night was black as ink. The train stopped at a miserable little station that had only one dim, dirty light and two sleepy, dirty employees on its deserted platform.

I asked Stokes for permission to go out and buy some cigarettes. I went and, having made sure that everything was as I had prepared, returned into the car.

"I thought you might like to know, sir," I said, "that Mr. Harvey Clayton is traveling with this train, too, in the next car."

Harvey Clayton was a good friend of his and was, probably, by this time, sleeping peacefully in his New York apartment.

"Harvey Clayton? On this train?" asked Winton Stokes, surprised.

"Yes, sir. I just saw him in the next car, as I was going out."

Winton Stokes got up and walked towards the next car. I cast a quick glance at Mickey Finnegan in his corner. I drew a breath of relief. That fat fool was sound asleep.

Unseen behind the door, I watched what happened then on the car's little platform. As Winton Stokes stepped out he found himself between Pete Crump and

"Snout" Timkins and felt two guns pressed against his ribs.

"Now you follow and not a squeal outta you, or we'll pump you full o'holes like a lace curtain!" whispered Pete Crump.

There was no one around to witness the little scene. Pete and "Snout" put their arms under Stokes', one on each side, and stepped down from the train. Stokes followed calmly. They walked away across the dark station platform. They looked like three good friends. No one could notice the two guns that were pressed against Stokes' body, under his arms. The sleepy station employees couldn't see anything suspicious.

I rushed back to the place where Winton Stokes had been sitting and took his coat, hat and suitcase. Then I followed my boys.

They had taken Stokes to a car parked on a dark street-corner, behind the station. Before joining them I tied a handkerchief around my face and put on a big, long coat they had prepared for me, so that Stokes wouldn't recognize me by my clothes.

I jumped into the car and we drove away into the darkness.

The whole little town had about two streets, one grocery store and a dozen houses. In a moment we were out in the country, flying along a deserted, muddy road. We saw in the distance the train going away to San Francisco, without its most valuable passenger this time. The long line of lighted car windows rolled faster and faster under a rain of red sparks from the puffing engine. It whistled away into the night and disappeared with a moaning of trembling rails. We were alone in the dark country, going at full speed, with all lights turned off. Nothing but desolated plains, lonely bushes and an immense black sky around us.

We all were tense and silent. But Winton Stokes was perfectly calm and seemed to be curious about it all.

We came to a stop before a shabby little hot-dog stand on the road, a couple of miles from the town. I can't imagine what kind of a business it was doing in that God-forsaken spot, but it fitted our purpose perfectly. It was locked for the night. We forced the lock easily and took our prisoner in.

The old shack was full of dirty pans, onion-peels, bread crumbs, rusty cans and an odor of cheap grease. We lighted a kerosene lamp and awakened a cloud of flies and night-bugs that came buzzing around and beating against the dusty, smoked lamp-chimney.

"Mr. Stokes," I said gracefully, "you are a sensible man and so are we. You realize that you are entirely in our power, and you can save yourself a lot of trouble by giving to us peacefully and of a free will the Night King, which is as good as ours already."

"It never pays," answered Winton Stokes, "to jump to conclusions."

"Yeh?" I said, less gracefully. "If you don't obey, that stone'll be in my hand here within the next ten minutes!"

"That," answered Winton Stokes, "remains to be seen."

"All right!" I sneered. "Look!"

At a sign from me, the boys seized him and started the search, while I busted his suitcase open and looked it over myself. Winton Stokes seemed amused and he had the nasty light smile that I hated playing on his lips.

We searched carefully and thoroughly. During the first five minutes of it I was casting mocking glances at Winton Stokes and whistling a musical comedy tune. At the end of ten minutes I stopped the whistling. At the end of half an hour I began to think that my blood was getting unusually cold.

We looked over every inch of his clothes; we tore off the lining of his coat; we examined every grain of dust in his suitcase—to no avail.

"Hang it!" burst out Pete. "The stone ain't big, but it couldn't have gone into thin air, could it?"

"We'll find it, if we have to spend all night here!" I said.

"Take your time, boys, I'm not in a hurry," remarked Winton Stokes.

"Listen," I groaned to him in a hoarse whisper. "Get this into your head: I'll have that stone!"

"Well, what's stopping you?" he inquired.

At the end of three hours we sat down on the floor and looked helplessly at each other: we didn't know what more we could search. We had torn every seam in his clothes; we had broken his suitcase to pieces; we had busted the heels of his shoes; squeezed his hat into a pan-cake; crushed flat all his cigarettes; chopped to pieces his soap and towel; ragged his underwear into a mass of fringe; smashed every object he had in his suitcase. We had a pile of wreckage before us and no sign of anything like a diamond.

Pete was perspiring. "Snout" was shaking. I was breathing heavily. Winton Stokes looked indifferent and slightly bored. Believe it or not, he even yawned once.

"Damn you!" I roared, at last. "You'll tell me where it is or we'll make you tell, if we have to tear your whole damn body to bits, too!"

"I'll tell you."

"Yeah?!"

"I'll tell you that you're a fool: nothing on earth can tear a sound from me when I want to be silent—and you know it!"

I answered by a series of expressions that I can't write down.

"I have been thinking," he said suddenly, "that I know your voice."

And before I had time to jump back, he seized the handkerchief covering my face and pulled it off.

All his self-control was not enough to stop a gasp. He stepped back and looked at my face.

"Surprised, eh?" I sneered. He didn't answer.

"Listen, you," I yelled. "I'd give my life, hear me?— my life to get that stone! And I wouldn't mind taking yours, if it would help me to find it!"

At that—he laughed uproariously, a long, loud, inso-lent laugh . . .

When morning came and a cold grey light crawled into the shack through the dusty window, we were still there, hopeless, broken, beaten. We didn't even talk any more. There was nothing to be done. We couldn't stay here much longer: the owner would come soon to open his stand. And besides, what should we stay for?

Silently, without looking at each other, we went to our

car and rode away. Of course, we didn't take Winton Stokes with us. I remember I turned around and saw him standing at the door of the shack, following us with his eyes, his beautiful brown body trembling slightly in the morning cold under the torn rags of his clothes . . .

I was half insane when I got back to New York. I walked around in a daze. "The Night King!" was the only name on my brain. It haunted me. Everything black and round, even shoe-buttons and raisins in bread-loaves seemed to me black diamonds that were tempting, mocking, torturing me.

For hours I sat in a dark corner, in some joint, racking my brain hopelessly over that unexplainable mystery, gnawing over and over again at the same questions: What had happened? Where had that stone been hidden? Where was it now, while I was eating my soul away for it? I drank like a sponge.

So if you have any imagination, imagine, for I can't describe it, imagine my feelings when I saw the following headlines on newspaper extras:

THE NIGHT KING STOLEN
Winton Stokes Robbed on Trip West

Was I going goofy? I read the paper, hardly believing my eyes. It didn't say much. It said only that the well-known young millionaire, Winton Stokes, had been robbed of his famous black diamond, "The Night King," on his way to San Francisco. And that the police were looking for a certain notorious criminal who committed the robbery and whose name they were keeping a secret.

It was a long time before I gathered my senses and even then I couldn't understand a thing. It occurred to me that Winton Stokes might have faked that news himself, to protect his diamond from further attempts. But I soon realized that I was mistaken: for Stokes was back in New York and didn't start on another trip, and was reported seriously perturbed; besides, the police were in a big turmoil and really searching for some one.

And then the thought struck me: Mickey Finnegan! Yes, that must be it. How on earth had that big sap managed to do it when I had failed was more than I could understand. It was unbelievable. Yet, Mickey was the only human being that had been in on the secret.

I turned green with fury. Then, I thought it over. Then I almost felt happy.

The first thing I wanted to do was to learn something of Mickey's present whereabouts. That evening I went to "The Hanged Cat" to try and get some information.

And whom should I see there, right before my eyes, sitting alone at a table in a dark corner, but Mickey Finnegan himself! Well, he was just enough of a dumbbell to do that. He was sipping slowly some booze and his face had a senseless expression, if any.

I walked to his table and sat down.

"Hello!" I said, amiably.

"Hello," he answered, dark and surprised.

"Mickey, I have an offer for you: give me half of it."

"Half o'what?"

"You know very well—half of the Night King's price."

He looked at me with open mouth and didn't answer.

"I know you got it," I said impatiently, "I know you have it. And it's healthier for you to be partners with me, Mickey Finnegan, understand?"

"Whatcha talking about?"

"Aw, can that stuff! If you were so lucky as to get it, you owe it to me, for I gave you the tip. It's only fair that we split now. And if you don't—I'll go straight to police headquarters and tell them who's got the Night King and where to find him!"

"Listen, buddy, you're cracked. How could I have gotten it when you grabbed it first? Yeh, I was on the train, an' I figured to try it, but I was too damn tired an' I fell asleep, an' when I woke the Stokes guy was gone—so who pulled it?"

"I didn't know you were such a good actor, Mickey Finnegan! But it's no use, you can't fool me. Now, do I get half of it or do I not?"

"I know you've got it yerself, an' you're lying, but I'll be damned if I can understand why."

"Mickey," I said desperately, "Mickey! We've always been good friends. Give me that stone, Mickey! Show it to me! Let me see it!"

"You've been drinkin', buddy."

"For the last time, Mickey, are we partners?"

"Like fun we are!"

I got up. "All right," I growled, "all right. So long, Mickey Finnegan. You know where I'm going!"

"Go to hell!" was Mickey's answer.

There was but one feeling left in me and it was a blind fury against Mickey Finnegan. Forgetting everything else, I had but one thought now—revenge. I decided to go straight to headquarters. I hesitated for a moment, thinking that they were probably looking for me, too, after my attempted robbery. But I reassured myself with the thought that they wouldn't know me, for Stokes never had a picture of me, and besides, I would be forgiven and maybe even rewarded for helping to catch the real thief.

I remembered the fist fight and all that I had suffered from Mickey Finnegan and my mad fury choked me. I went to headquarters.

I walked right in, head high and with assured steps, like an honest, respectable citizen. I asked proudly and imperatively to see the Chief Inspector.

The cops were looking at me with the queerest looks I ever saw in human eyes. When I asked for the Chief Inspector, two or three of them rushed to his office much too hurriedly.

When I walked into the Chief's office, he looked at me with bulging eyes.

"Well, for goodness' sake!" he gasped.

"Inspector," I said solemnly, "I know who stole the Night King and I know the man you're looking for: it's Mickey Finnegan!"

He looked at me silently for a long time, with the funniest expression on his face.

"You're mistaken, Hawkins," he said slowly at last, "it isn't Finnegan we're looking for—it's you!"

"Me?! Me? W-why?"

"Because you've got the Night King."

"What?!!"

"You've got it and what's more, you're going to return it."

"Who the hell told you that?"

"Mr. Stokes did. And I'm going to get in touch with him at once and tell him that we've got you."

"Mr. Stokes?!" I roared. "Mr. Stokes? Why, the guy's gone bugs! Call him, call him at once! He knows it's a lie! He ought to know!"

When I confronted Winton Stokes, he looked at me with that darned mocking smile of his twisting his mouth.

"What the hell does that mean?" I yelled. "You know damn well I didn't get your sparkler! You know it as well as I do, don'tcha?"

"That's just it," he said, so very kindly, "that's just the trouble: I happen to know a little more than you do."

The cops around were grinning so that their mouths almost reached their ears.

"What's the joke?" I asked furiously.

"Oh boy!" roared one of them.

"We owe the gentleman an explanation," said Winton Stokes. "You fooled me, Hawkins, and it's a compliment I don't pay to people often. I believed you to be an honest, trustworthy servant and I chose you for a very important mission. You see, I had to carry the Night King with me and I had to hide it in a place where no one would think of looking for it. I knew it wasn't safe anywhere on my person. By chance, you yourself gave me the idea for its hiding-place. But even though I trusted you, I didn't want to take any chances and give you any temptations. So I made you serve my purpose without your knowing it. The only person I had to trust with the secret was a good old friend of mine who happens to be a dentist. Well, the whole thing turned out to be more unusual than I had expected. Open your mouth!"

In the next moment I uttered a yell, the yell of a mad beast, and if the cops hadn't seized me in time, I would have jumped at Winton Stokes and murdered him on the spot: for I opened my mouth wide, he unscrewed something in it and there, in my teeth, *in my own false teeth*, was the Night King!

Good Copy

c. 1927

Editor's Preface

This story was written a year or more after "The Husband I Bought," probably sometime in 1927, when Ayn Rand was living at the Hollywood Studio Club, had obtained a position as a junior screenwriter for Cecil B. DeMille, and was just beginning to date Frank O'Connor, her future husband. The spirit of the story matches these auspicious events.

Miss Rand's silent-screen synopses from the 1920s—about a dozen remain—are examples of pure, even extravagant Romanticism. Most are imaginative adventure stories, with daring heroes, a strong love interest, nonstop action, and virtually no explicit philosophy. "Good Copy" is one of the few works of this type that are not scenarios. As such, it represents a major change in mood from "The Husband I Bought."

"The Husband I Bought" portrays the dedication of the passionate valuer, who will bear the greatest suffering, if necessary, rather than settle for something less than the ideal. "Good Copy" reminds us of another crucial aspect of Ayn Rand's philosophy: her view that suffering is an exception, not the rule of life. The rule, she held, should not be pain or even heroic endurance, but gaiety and lighthearted joy in living. It is on this premise that "Good Copy" was written.

I first heard the story some twenty-five years ago,

when it was read aloud in a course on fiction-writing given by Ayn Rand to some young admirers. The class was told merely that this was a story by a beginning writer, and was asked to judge whether the writer had a future. Some students quickly grasped who the author was, but a number did not and were astonished, even indignant, when they found out. Their objection was not to the story's flaws but to its essential spirit. "It is so unserious," the criticism went. "It doesn't deal with big issues like your novels; it has no profound passions, no immortal struggles, no philosophic meaning."

Miss Rand replied, in effect: "It deals with only one 'big issue,' the biggest of all: can man live on earth or not?"

She went on to explain that malevolence—the feeling that man by nature is doomed to suffering and defeat—is all-pervasive in our era; that even those who claim to reject such a viewpoint tend to feel, today, that the pursuit of values must be a painful, teeth-clenched crusade, a holy but grim struggle against evil. This attitude, she said, ascribes far too much power to evil. Evil, she held, is essentially impotent (see *Atlas Shrugged*); the universe is not set against man, but is "benevolent." This means that man's values (if based on reason) *are* achievable here and in this life; and therefore happiness is not to be regarded as a freak accident, but, metaphysically, as the normal, the natural, the to-be-expected.

Philosophically, in short, the deepest essence of man's life is not grave, crisis-ridden solemnity, but lighthearted cheerfulness. A story reflecting this approach, she concluded, a story written specifically to project pure "benevolent universe," should be written as though all problems have already been answered and all big issues solved, and now there is nothing to focus on but man acting in the world and succeeding—nothing but unobstructed excitement, romance, adventure.

In *Atlas Shrugged,* Dagny hears Francisco laughing: "it was the gayest sound in the world. . . . The capacity for unclouded enjoyment, she thought, does not belong to irresponsible fools . . . to be able to laugh like that is the end result of the most profound, most solemn thinking." In these terms, we may say that if her more philosophic works represent Ayn Rand's profound thinking, then "Good Copy" is like the unclouded laugh of Francisco.

The story, of course, is still very early, and must be read in part for its intention, which is not consistently realized.

Laury, the young hero, is but a faint, even humorous suggestion of the heroes still to come. Reflecting the primacy of women in the early works, Jinx, the heroine, is the more mature character, and the one dominant in the action. She is ahead of Laury all the way. Yet, as one would expect from Ayn Rand, Jinx's feeling for Laury is one of the most convincing elements in the story—and she is the opposite of a feminist. "Women," she tells Laury warmly at one point, "are the bunk."

As a piece of writing, "Good Copy" represents a major advance over "The Husband I Bought." The author's command of English, though still imperfect, has increased substantially. The originality of certain descriptions and the sudden flashes of wit begin to foreshadow what is to come. The dialogue, especially the use of slang, is still not quite right; and the tone of the piece is unsteady, verging, I think, on being overly broad. But despite these flaws, the story as a whole does manage to convey a real exuberance of spirit.

Decades later, after she had completed *Atlas Shrugged,* Ayn Rand occasionally said that she wanted to write a pure adventure story without any deep philosophical theme. (At one point, she had even chosen the hero's name—Faustin Donnegal—and his description; like Laury McGee, he was to have dimples.) But she never did write it.

"Good Copy," therefore, though early and imperfect, is all we have from her in this genre. It reflects a side of Ayn Rand that her admirers will not find isolated in this pure form anywhere else.

A note on the text: In the 1950s, for the reading to her class, Miss Rand modernized some of the period expressions in the piece, substituting "sports car" for "roadster," "panties" for "step-ins," and the like. I have retained these changes in the following.

—L. P.

Good Copy

"I wish there was a murder! Somebody chopped to pieces and blood all over the pavements. . . . And I wish there was a fire, an immense fire, so that the gas tank would bust like a peanut and half the town'd be blown up! . . . And I'd like to see somebody stick up the bank and sweep it to the last nickel, clean like a bald head! . . . And I wish there was an earthquake!"

Laury McGee walked fast, fast, so that each step struck the pavement furiously, like a blow to an enemy. His shirt collar thrown open, the veins in his sunburnt neck trembled and tensed as he tried to draw his lips into a grim, straight line. This was very difficult, for Laury McGee's lips were young, delightfully curved, with tempting, mischievous dimples in the corners that always looked as though he was trying to hold back a sparkling smile. But he was very far from any desire to smile, now.

His steps rang like gunshots in the sweet peace of the summer afternoon—and the summer afternoon on Dicksville's Main Street was very sweetly peaceful. There were almost no passersby, and those that did pass moved with a speed implying human life to be five hundred years long. The store windows were hot and dusty, and the doors wide open, with no one inside. A few old, overheated tomatoes were transforming themselves into catsup on the sidewalk in front of the Grocery Market. In the middle of Dicksville's busiest traffic thoroughfare a dog was sleeping in the sun, cuddled in a little depression of the paving. Laury was looking at it all and clenching his fists.

It was Laury McGee's twenty-third summer on earth and his first on the *Dicksville Dawn*. He had just had a significant conversation with his City Editor. This conversation was not the first of its kind; but it was to be the last.

"You," said City Editor Jonathan Scraggs, "are a sap!"

Laury looked at the ceiling and tried to give his face an expression intended to show that his dignity was beyond anything the gentleman at the desk might choose to say.

"One more story like that from you and I'll send you to wash dishes in a cafeteria—if they'll take you in!"

Laury could not help following with his eyes the Editor's powerful five fingers as they closed over his beautiful, neatly typed pages, crunched them with the crisp, crackling sound of a man chewing celery, and flung them furiously into an overflowing wastebasket; the pages that he had hoped would double the *Dicksville Dawn*'s circulation with his name on the front page.

Laury was very sure of being perfectly self-possessed, but he bit his lips in a way that might have been called self-possession—in a bulldog.

"If you don't like it," he threw at the Editor, "it's your own fault, yours and your town's. No story is better than its material!"

"You aren't even a cub!" roared Jonathan Scraggs. "You're a pup, and a lousy one! Just because you were the star quarterback at college doesn't mean that you can be a reporter now! I still have to see you use your head for something besides as a show window to parade your good looks on!"

"It's not my fault!" Laury protested resolutely. "I've got nothing to write about! Nothing ever happens in this swamp of a town!"

"You're at it again, aren't you?"

"Since I've been here you've sent me on nothing but

funerals, and drunken quarrels, and traffic accidents! I can't show my talent on such measly news! Get somebody else for your fleas' bulletins! Let me have something big, *big*!—and you'll see what's in my head besides good looks, which I can't help, either!"

"How many times have I told you that you've got to write about *anything* that comes along? What do you expect to happen? Dicksville is no Chicago, you know. Still, I don't think we can complain—things are pretty lively and the *Dawn* is doing nicely, and I can't say that much of the *Dicksville Globe,* for which the Lord be praised! You should be proud, young man, to work for Dicksville's leading paper."

"Yeah! Or for Dicksville's leading paper's wastebasket! But you'll learn to appreciate me, Mr. Scraggs, when something happens worthy of my pen!"

"If you can't write up a funeral, I'd like to see you cover a murder! . . . Now you go home, young man, and try to get some ideas into your head, if it's possible, which I doubt!"

Somebody had said that Laury's gray eyes looked like a deep cloudy sky behind which one could feel the sun coming out. But there was no trace of sun in his eyes when they stared straight at City Editor Jonathan Scraggs, and if there was anything coming behind their dark gray it looked more like a thunderstorm, and a serious one.

"Mr. Scraggs," he said slowly, ominously, *"things are going to happen!"*

"Amen!" answered Mr. Scraggs, and turning comfortably in his chair lit a cigar, then dropped his head on his breast and closed his eyes to enjoy the peace of the Dicksville afternoon, with the hot summer air breathing in through the open windows that needed a washing.

Laury took his coat from an old rack in a corner and looked fiercely at the room; no one had paid any attention to the conversation. The city room was hot and stuffy, and smelled of print, dust, and chewing gum. One walked as though in a forest on a thick carpet of fallen leaves cracking under the feet—a carpet of old, yellow newspapers, cigarette wrappers, bills, ads, everything that has ever been made out of paper. The walls were an art museum of calendars, drawings, cartoons, comic strips, pasted on the bare bricks and alternated by philosophical inscriptions such as "Easy on the corkscrew!" and "Vic Perkins is a big bum!" The dusty bottle of spring water on a shaking stand was hopelessly and significantly empty; water, after all, was not the only drink that had been used in the room.

The energetic activity of Dicksville's leading paper made Laury grind his teeth. The chief copy man was very busy making a sailboat out of a paper drinking cup. The sports editor was carefully drawing a pair of French-heeled legs on the dust of a file bureau. Two reporters were playing an exciting game of rummy; and a third was thoroughly cleaning his fingernails with a pen and trying to catch a fly that kept annoying him. The copy boy was sound asleep on a pile of paper, his back turned disdainfully on the room, his face red like his hair and his hair red like a carrot, his decided snores shaking the mountain of future newspapers under him.

However, at one of the central desks, under an imposing sign of: "Don't park here. Busy" Vic Perkins, the *Dawn*'s star reporter, was profoundly absorbed in some serious work. Vic Perkins had a long, thin face and a little black mustache under his nose that looked like he needed a handkerchief, more than like anything else. He always wore his hat on the back of his head and never condescended to use a toothbrush. He was chewing zealously the end of a pencil and looking up at a green-shaded lamp, in deep meditation.

"Any news?" asked Laury, approaching him.

"There's always news for the man who's smart enough to write 'em!" replied Vic Perkins in a tone of disdainful superiority.

Laury glanced at the story he was writing. It was a gripping account of Dicksville's latest sensational crime—$550 cash and a silver pepper shaker stolen by Pug-Nose Thomson, the town's desperate outlaw.

Laury swung on his heels and walked out of the building, slamming the door ferociously, hoping one of the dusty glass panes would bust for a change; but it didn't.

Laury had graduated from college with a B.A. degree, high honors, and the football championship, this spring.

He had accepted the first opportunity to work on a newspaper, to start on the road of his buoyant ambition. He came to the *Dicksville Dawn* with an overflowing energy, a wild enthusiasm, an irresistible smile, and no experience whatsoever. And he was disappointed.

He had expected a glorious career full of action, danger, and thrills, the career of a glamorous being whose every word on the printed pages sends thousands of hearts beating fast, like a sonorous trumpet that rings through the country thrilling and terrifying men. And now he had found himself hustling after news that wouldn't disturb a mosquito. . . .

Laury walked fast, his hands in his pockets, a lock of unruly hair falling down to mix with his long, long eyelashes. The sky was blue, blue like a color postcard. An odor of frying grease floated from the open door of Ye Buttercup Tea Room. In a music shop a hoarse radio was singing "My Blue Heaven." Clampitt's Grocery Market was having a big event—a canned-goods sale.

Oh, if only something would happen here! Laury's heart throbbed. But what could happen—*here*?

A drowsy newsboy was muttering: "*Dicksville Dawn* poiper," as though he were selling sleeping tablets. Laury threw a quick glance at the front page, passing by. The headline announced the birth of the town Mayor's fifth child; there was a prominent news item about the Spinsters' Club annual convention; and an editorial by Victor Z. Perkins on the importance of animal pets.

Were these, then, the scorching, flamboyant headlines, roaring into people's eyes, that he had dreamed about? Oh, if only somebody would do something! Somebody, *anybody*. . . . It seemed hopeless in Dicksville. And yet . . . was it so hopeless? Wasn't it possible to . . . ?

Laury quickened his steps and clenched his fists in his pockets. His eyes narrowed and glistened. His heart beat faster. For City Editor Jonathan Scraggs' opinion to the contrary notwithstanding, Laury McGee *had* an idea.

It would be dangerous, he knew. He had had that idea for a long time. It would be a mad chance to take, a frightful risk. And yet . . . and yet . . .

"Sap!!"

He felt a strong knock across his body and when he

turned his head all he could see was a slim, swift, sparkling sports car, like a thrown torpedo, speeding away, and a wild mass of brown hair flying above it like a flag.

He realized that he had been crossing a street, too absorbed in his serious thoughts to notice anything, automobiles included. The result of which was a considerable pain and a greasy line on his tan trousers where the sports car's fender had struck him.

He looked again at the disappearing car and started as though hit by a sudden inspiration. He had recognized the driver. It was Miss Winford, the "dime-a-hair girl"; called so for being the sole heiress to her father's fortune, that could number a dime for each hair on her head; which may not seem much, but try to figure it out!

Christopher A. Winford was a big steel magnate from Pittsburgh who had the bad taste to spend his summers in Dicksville. He owned half the town and the white residence on a hill overlooking it, a royal building whose glass-and-marble turrets looked like glistening fountains thrown to the blue sky from a sea of green foliage.

Miss Winford was eighteen and the absolute leader of Dicksville's younger set, of her parents, and of her sports car. Laury had never met her, but he had seen her often in town. She looked like an antelope and acted like a mustang. She had big, slightly slanting, ominously glistening eyes that made people feel a little nervous wondering just what was going on behind their suspicious calm; she had thin, dancing eyebrows and a determined mouth. Her brown hair was thrown behind her ears in a long, disheveled cut. From the tips of her little feet to that stormy tangle of hair she was slim, straight, strong like a steel spring.

Her ambitious mother had christened her Juliana Xenia. But her friends of the younger set, to the horror of said mother, called her simply Jinx.

Laury stood staring at her car long after it had disappeared. He had a strange, fixed, enraptured expression on his face, the expression of a man who has just been struck by an idea for the invention of an interplanetary communication. That girl . . . was it a coincidence? His idea—this was just what he needed for his idea. He had the aim—here was the means. . . .

He walked home without noticing the streets around him, the sky above or the pavement under his feet. . . .

That night, in his apartment, Laury McGee sat on the desk, his feet on a chair, his elbows on his knees, his chin on his fists, his eyes unblinking—and thought. The result of these thoughts was the lively happenings which occurred in Dicksville in the days that followed.

———*II*———

Jinx Winford was speeding home at fifty miles an hour, as usual; and at midnight, as usual, too. She had been visiting a girl friend out of town and now was on her way back, not in the slightest measure disturbed by the fact that her little gray sports car was the only sign of life on the dark, deserted road. Under a heavy black sky the endless plain stretched like a frozen sea with immobile waves of hills. Far ahead, a pale glow rose to the sky like a faint luminous fog, and the lights of Dicksville twinkled mysteriously, in straight lines bordering streets and in lonely, disorderly sparks, as though a tangle of golden beads had been thrown into the dark plain and some strings had broken in the fall.

The gray sports car was flying down the road like a swift, humming bug with two long, shuddering feelers of light sweeping the ground and tiny wings beating in the wind—the silk scarf on Jinx's shoulders. Her two firm hands on the wheel, Jinx was whistling a song. And she remained perfectly calm when, turning a sharp curve, she saw an automobile standing straight across the road, barring the way. It was an old sports car with no one at the wheel. But its lights were turned on, two glaring white spots that made the darkness beyond it seem empty and impenetrable, like a bottomless black hole.

She stepped on the brakes just in time to make her car stop with a jerk and a sharp, alarmed creaking a few inches from the strange sports car.

"Hey, what's the idea?" she threw into the darkness where it seemed she could distinguish the shadow of a man.

In the darkness, behind the old sports car, Laury

McGee was ready. He had been waiting there for two hours. He had a black mask and a revolver. The lips under the mask were grim and determined; the fingers clutching the revolver trembled. Laury McGee was not hunting for news any more—he was making it.

The time had come. He looked, catching his breath, at the girl in the gray sports car, who sat clutching the wheel and peering into the darkness interrogatively, with raised eyebrows.

"How will she take it?" he shuddered. "I hope she doesn't scream too loud! Oh, I hope she doesn't faint!"

Then, resolutely, with broad steps, he walked towards her and stopped in full light, his threatening eyes behind the mask and the muzzle of his revolver looking straight at her. He waited silently for the effect that his appearance would produce. But there was no particular effect. Jinx raised one eyebrow higher and looked at him with decided curiosity, waiting.

"Don't scream for help!" he ordered in his most lugubrious voice. "No man can save you!"

"I haven't screamed yet," she observed. "Why suggest it?"

"Not a sound from you nor a movement! And step out of that car!"

"Well, I can't do that, you know," she answered sweetly.

Laury bit his lips. "I mean, get out of your car at once! Men like me are used to having their slightest order obeyed immediately!"

"Well, I haven't had the pleasure of meeting any men like you before, I'm sorry to say. As it happens, I'm not well acquainted with the profession."

"Then you better remember that my name is whispered with terror from coast to coast!"

"What's your name? Mine's Jinx Winford."

"You'll be sorry to learn my name! Everybody will tell you that my hand is of steel; that my heart is of granite; that I pass in the night like a death-bearing lightning, leaving terror and desolation behind!"

"Oh, really? I *am* sorry and you have all my sympathy: it must be awfully hard to live up to such a reputation!"

Laury looked at her strangely. Then he remembered

that great bandits are always courteous to women. So he spoke gallantly:

"However, you have nothing to fear: I crush all men, but I spare women!"

"That's nothing to be proud of: women are the bunk and you ought to know it!"

"I'm profoundly sorry that I have to do this," he continued, "but you'll be treated with the greatest respect and courtesy, so you don't have to be afraid."

"Afraid? What of?"

"Say, will you please step out of your car and get into mine?"

"Is that absolutely necessary?"

"Yes!"

"Will you please kindly tell me what the hell this is all about?" she asked very suavely.

"You are being kidnapped," he explained politely.

"Oh!"

He didn't like that "Oh!"—it was not what he had expected at all. There was no terror or indignation in it; it sounded rather simple, matter-of-fact, as a person would say: "Oh, I see!"

She jumped lightly to the ground, her short skirt whirling high above graceful legs in tight, glistening stockings. The wind blew her clothes tight around her body and for a moment she looked like a slim little dancer in a wet, clinging dress, on an immense black stage, torn out of the darkness by the bright circle of the car's spotlight. And behind her, as a background— a gray, sandy piece of hill with bushes of dry, thorny weeds sticking out like deer horns.

"Will you please kindly wait while I lock my car?" she asked. "I don't mind being kidnapped, but I don't want some other gentleman to get the notion of kidnapping my car."

Calmly, she turned off the headlights, locked the car, and slipped the key into her pocketbook. She approached his old sports car and looked it over critically.

"Your business doesn't pay, does it?" she asked. "That buggy of yours doesn't look as though you get three meals a day."

"Will you please step in!" he almost shouted, exasperated. "We have no time to waste!"

She stepped in and snuggled comfortably on the seat, stretching her pretty legs far out on the slanting floor-board, her pleated skirt hardly covering the knees. He jumped to the wheel beside her.

"Do you expect a lot of money out of this?" she asked.

He did not answer.

"Are you desperately in love with me, then?"

"I should say not!" he snapped.

With a sharp, hoarse growl and a convulsive jerk from top to tire, the sports car tore forward, snorted, shuddered and rolled, wavering, into the darkness, towards the lights of Dicksville.

The wind and the dark hills rushed to meet them and rolled past. They were both silent. She studied him furtively from the corner of her eye. All she could see was a black mask between a gray cap and gracefully curved lips. He did not look at her once. All he knew of her presence was a faint, expensive perfume and tangled locks of soft hair that the wind blew into his face occasionally.

The first houses of Dicksville rose by the side of the road. Laury drove into town cautiously, choosing the darkest, emptiest streets. There were few streetlamps and no passersby. He stepped on the gas involuntarily, when passing through the white squares of light streaming from lonely corner drugstores.

Laury lived in an old apartment house in a narrow little street winding up a hill, in a new, half-built neighborhood. The house had two floors, big windows, and little balconies with no doors to them. There was an empty, unfinished bungalow next to it and a vacant lot across the street. Only two apartments on the first floor were occupied. Laury was the sole tenant on the second floor.

As the car swung around the corner into his street, Laury turned off the headlights and drove up to the house as noiselessly as he could. He looked carefully around before stopping. There was no one in sight. The little street was as dark and empty as an abandoned stage setting.

"Now, not a sound! Don't make any noise!" he whispered, clutching the girl's arm and dashing with her to the front door.

"Sure, I won't," she answered. "I know how you feel!"

They tiptoed noiselessly up the carpeted steps to Laury's door. The first thing that met Jinx's eyes, as Laury politely let her enter first, was one of his dirty shirts in the middle of the little hall, that had rolled out of an open clothes closet. Laury blushed under his mask and kicked it back into the closet, slamming its door angrily.

The living room had two windows and a soft blue carpet. A desk stood between the windows, a tempestuous ocean of papers with a typewriter as an island in it. The blue davenport had a few cushions on it, also a newspaper, a safety razor, and one shoe. The only big, low armchair was occupied by a pile of victrola records with an alarm clock on top of them; and a portable victrola stood next to it on a soap box covered with an old striped sweater. A big box marked "Puffed Wheat Cereal" served as a bookcase. A graceful glass bowl on a tall stand, intended for goldfish, contained no water, but cigarette ashes and a telephone, instead. The rest of the room was occupied by old newspapers, magazines without covers, covers without magazines, a tennis racket, a bath towel, a bunch of dry, shriveled flowers, a big dictionary, and a ukulele.

Jinx looked the room over slowly, carefully. Laury threw his coat and cap on a chair, took off the mask, wiped his forehead with a sigh of relief, and ran his fingers through his hair. Jinx looked at him, looked again, then took out her compact, powdered her face quickly, and passed the lipstick over her lips with unusual care.

"What's your name?" she asked in a somewhat changed voice.

"It doesn't matter, for the present," he answered.

She settled herself comfortably on the edge of his desk. He looked at her now, in the light. She had a lovely figure, as her tight silk sweater showed in detail, he thought. She had inscrutable eyes, and he could not decide whether their glance, fixed on him, was openly mocking or sweetly innocent.

"Well, you showed good judgment in choosing me for kidnapping," she said. "I don't know who else would be as good a bet. If you had less discrimination you might have chosen Louise Chatterton, perhaps, but, you know, her old man is so tight he never gets off a trolley before the end of the line, to get all his money's worth!"

She glanced over the room.

"You're a beginner, aren't you?" she asked. "Your place doesn't look like the lair of a very sinister criminal."

He looked at the room and blushed. "I'm sorry the room looks like this," he muttered. "I'll straighten it out. I'll do my best to make you comfortable. I hope your stay here will be as pleasant as possible."

"There's no doubt about that, I'm beginning to think. But then, where's your sweetheart's picture? Haven't you got a 'moll'?"

"Are you hungry?" Laury asked briskly. "If you want something to eat, I can . . ."

"No, I do not. Have you got a gang? Or are you a lonely mastermind?"

"If there's anything you want . . ."

"No, thanks. Have you ever been in jail yet? And how does it feel?"

"It's getting late," Laury said abruptly. "Do you want to sleep?"

"Well, you don't expect me to stay up all night, do you?"

Laury arranged the davenport for her. For himself he had fixed something like a bed out of a few chairs and an old mattress, in the kitchen.

"Tomorrow," he said before leaving her, "I'll have to go out for a while. You'll find food in the icebox. Don't make any attempts to run away. Don't make any noise— no one will hear you. You will save yourself a lot of trouble if you will promise me not to try to escape."

"I promise," she said, and added with a strange look straight into his sunny gray eyes: "In fact, I'll do my best *not* to escape!" . . .

Laury's heart was beating louder than the alarm clock at his side when he stretched himself on his uncomfortable couch in the dark kitchen. The couch felt like a mountainous landscape under his body and there was an odor of canned chili floating from the sink above his head. But he felt an ecstasy of triumph beating rapturously, like victorious drums, over all his body, to his very fingertips. He had done it! There had been no one in that dump of a town bright enough to commit a good crime. He had committed it; a crime worthy of his pen; a crime that would make good copy. Tomorrow, when the *Dawn*'s headlines would thunder like wild beasts . . .

"Mr. Gunman!" a sweet voice called from the living room.

"What's the matter?" he cried.

"Is it an RCA victrola you have there in the corner?"

"Yes!"

"That's fine. . . . Goodnight."

"Goodnight."

----*III*----

The headlines on the *Dicksville Dawn* were three inches high and blazed on the front pages like huge, black mouths screaming to an astounded world:

SOCIETY GIRL KIDNAPPED

And an army of newsboys rolled over Dicksville like a tidal wave, with swift currents branching into every street and an alarming, tempestuous roar of hoarse voices: "Extray! Extra-a-ay!"

The eager citizens who snatched from each other the crisp, fresh sheets, with the black print still wet and smearing under their fingers, read, shivering, of how the charming young heiress, Miss Juliana X. Winford, had disappeared on her way home from a visit and of how her sports car had been examined by the police on a lonely road two miles out of town. The sports car had two bullet holes in its side and one in a rear tire; the windshield was broken, the upholstery ripped and torn.

Everything indicated a grim, desperate struggle. The sports car had been discovered, the *Dicksville Dawn* proudly announced, by "our own reporter, Mr. L. H. McGee."

There was a big photograph of Miss Winford, where all one could distinguish were bare legs, a tennis racket, and an intoxicating smile. The thrilling front-page story that related all these events was entitled: "Society Beauty Victim of Unknown Monster"—by Laurence H. McGee. It started with: "A profound sorrow clutched our hearts at the news that our fair city's peace and respect for law, of which we had always been so proud, was suddenly disturbed by a most atrocious, terrifying, revolting crime. . . ."

The old building of the *Dicksville Dawn* looked like an anthill that somebody had stepped on. The presses thundered; the typewriters cracked furiously like machine guns; a current of frenzied humanity streamed down the main stairs and another one rolled up. City Editor Jonathan Scraggs dashed around, sweat streaming down his red face, rubbing his hands with a grin of ecstatic satisfaction at the thought that the *Dawn* had received the great news two hours before its rival, the *Dicksville Globe.* Laury McGee sat on the Editor's desk, his legs crossed, calmly smoking a cigarette.

"Great stuff, that story of yours, Laury, my boy!" Mr. Scraggs repeated. "Never thought you had it in you!"

The telephones screamed continuously, calls from all over the town, anxious voices begging news and details.

Chief Police Inspector Rafferty himself dropped in to see the City Editor. He was short, square, and nervous. He had a big black mustache, like a shaving brush, and little restless, suspicious eyes always watching for someone to offend his dignity.

"Cats and rats!" he shouted. "What's all this? Now, I ask you, what the hell is all this?"

"It's quite an unexpected occurrence," agreed Jonathan Scraggs.

"Occurrence be blasted! That any scoundrel should have the nerve to pull that off in my town! Cats and rats! I'll be hashed into hamburger if I know who the lousy mongrel could be! It isn't Pug-Nose Thomson, 'cause he was seen stewed like a hog in some joint, last night!"

"The affair does seem rather mysterious and . . ."

"I've sent every man on the force to comb the town! I'll fire them all, each goddamn boob, if they don't pull the bum out by the gullet!"

That afternoon, Mr. Christopher A. Winford's gray automobile stopped before the *Dawn* building and the tall gentleman walked up to the city room, with a step that implied a long acquaintance with respectfully admiring eyes and news cameras. He was cool, poised, distinguished. He had gray eyes, and a mustache that matched his eyes, and a suit that matched his mustache.

"Yes, it's most annoying," he said slowly, his eyes half-closed as one used to conceal his superior thoughts. "I wish my daughter back, you understand."

There was a slight wonder in his voice, as though he was unable to see how his wish could be disobeyed.

"Certainly, certainly, Mr. Winford," Mr. Scraggs assured him. "You have all our sympathy. A father's heart in a misfortune like this must . . ."

"I came here personally to arrange for an announcement in your paper," Mr. Winford went on slowly, "that I will pay a reward to anyone who furnishes information leading to the discovery of my daughter's whereabouts. Name the sum yourself, whatever you find necessary. I will pay for everything."

He had the calm tone of a man who knows the surest means of attaining his desires and does not hesitate to use it.

"There's an extra for us!" Mr. Scraggs cried enthusiastically when Mr. Winford left. "Rush to your mill, Laury, old pal, and fix us a good one! 'Heartbroken father in *Dawn*'s office' . . . and all that, you know!"

"You seem to be in an unusually happy humor, today," Mr. Scraggs chuckled, watching Laury's sparkling eyes and swift fingers dancing on the typewriter keys. "So am I, boy, so am I!"

When Laury went home, late that evening, there was under every streetlamp an enthusiastic newsboy yelling himself hoarse with:

"Extree-e! Big ree-word for missin' goil! Here's yer cha-ance!"

And the headlines announced:

DESPERATE FATHER OFFERS $5,000 REWARD

That, in Mr. Scraggs' eyes, had been the most sensational sum he could name. . . .

Laury's heart missed a few beats when he walked up the steps to his apartment and turned the key in the door lock. Was everything all right?

As he entered, Jinx dashed gaily to meet him. He gasped. She was wearing his best violet silk pajamas! They were too big for her and she draped them gracefully in soft, clinging folds around her little body.

"Hello, darling!" she greeted him. "Why so late? I've missed you terribly!"

"Why . . . why did you put these on?"

"These? Pretty, aren't they? Well, you didn't leave me anything to change and I was tired of wearing the same dress for two days!"

She led the way into the living room, and he stopped short with another gasp. The living room had been thoroughly cleaned, and not a single object stood in its former place. The whole room had been rearranged to look like a very impressionistic stage setting. The window curtains were hanging over the davenport, forming a cozy, inviting tent. The sofa cushions were capriciously thrown all over the floor. Jinx's colored silk scarf hung on the wall over his desk, like an artistic banner. The fishbowl stood at the foot of the davenport, and some incense that she had unearthed in one of his desk drawers was burning in it, a long, thin column of blue smoke swaying gracefully like a light, misty scarf.

"What did you do that for?" he muttered, amazed.

"Don't you like it?" She smiled triumphantly. "Your room looked as though it needed a woman's influence badly. I thought that you ought to have a little beauty in your hard life, to relax after a day of danger and gun-shooting!"

Laury laughed. She looked at him calmly, with a sweet look that seemed too innocent to be trusted.

"By the way," she said casually, "you better disconnect that phone. You left it here and I might have called up the police, you know!"

Laury's face went crimson, then white; with one jump, he snatched the phone and tore the wires furiously out of the wall. Then he turned to her, puzzled.

"Well, why didn't you?" he asked.

She smiled, a smile that seemed at once indulgent, cunning, and perfectly naive.

"I wanted to," she answered innocently, "but I had no time, I was too busy." And she added imperatively: "Take off your coat. Dinner is ready."

"What?"

"Dinner! And hurry up, 'cause it's late and I'm darn hungry!"

"But . . . but . . ."

"Come on, now, help me pull that table out!"

In a few seconds he was seated at a neatly arranged table covered with one of his pillowcases, there being no tablecloth in the house. And Jinx was serving a delicious dinner, hot, steaming dishes whose tempting odor made him realize how very tired and hungry he really was after this exciting day.

"Now, don't look so dumbfounded!" she said, settling down to her plate. "I'm a good cook, I am. I got the first prize in high school. I don't care much about cooking, but I like first prizes, no matter what for!"

"I must thank you," Laury muttered, eating hungrily, "although I didn't expect you to . . ."

"I bet you haven't had a homemade dinner in ages," she remarked sympathetically. "I bet you're used to eating in dingy pool parlors and saloons, where you meet to divide the loot with your gangsters. See, I know all about it. They must have pretty tough food, though, don't they?"

"Why . . . y-yes . . . yes, they do," Laury agreed helplessly.

After dinner, she asked for a cigarette, crossed her legs in the violet silk trousers, like a little Oriental princess, and leaned comfortably back in her chair, sending slowly graceful snakes of smoke to float into space.

"Get me a drink!" she ordered.

"Oh, sure!" He jumped up, eager to serve her in turn. "What do you wish? Tea, coffee?"

She smiled and winked at him significantly.

"Well, what do you wish?" he repeated.

"Well, now, as though you didn't understand!" She frowned impatiently.

"No, I don't understand. Surely, you don't mean to say that . . . that you want . . . liquor?"

"Oh, any kind of booze you've got will do!"

Laury stared at her with open mouth.

"Well, what's the matter?" she asked.

"I never thought that you would . . . that you might . . . that you . . ."

"You don't mean to say that you haven't got any?"

"No, I haven't!"

"Well, I'll be hanged! A crook, a real crook, with nothing to drink in his house! What kind of a gangster are you, anyway?"

"But, Miss Winford, I never thought that you . . ."

"You've got a lot to learn, my child, you've got a lot to learn!"

Laury blushed; then remembered that he was the kidnapper and had to show some authority.

"Now, don't disturb me," he ordered, sitting down at his desk before the typewriter. "I've got something very important to write. . . . Here," he added, "you might be interested in this!" And he threw to her the day's newspapers.

"O-oh! Sure!" she cried. "The papers!"

She jumped on the sofa, the cushions bouncing under her, folded her legs criss-cross, and bent eagerly over the papers, her tousled hair hanging down over her face, almost touching the wide sheets.

He attacked the typewriter furiously, pounding the keys energetically in an attempt to write the important message he had in mind. But it was not so easy. The words did not seem to him impressive enough. He started one sheet after another, and tore them to pieces, and flung them into the wastebasket.

Jinx interrupted him every few seconds with a gasp of sincere delight: "Oh, look, *my* picture! . . . Oh, what a fuss for the old town! . . . Aren't they dumbfounded! . . .

Don't worry, they'll never find you out, not that bunch of saps! . . . Lizzie Chatterton's going to chew her nails to the bone from envy—she's never been kidnapped! . . . Say, what's this about my car? Who wrecked it and why?"

"Some reporter must have done it," Laury answered disdainfully. "It makes better copy."

"Oh, listen to this!" she laughed happily. " 'Every heart in our town is convulsed with anxiety at the thought of this helpless young beauty in the cruel claws of some pitiless beast. . . .' Oh boy! Who wrote that? Gee, what a sap that McGee fellow must be!"

Laury was working hard, very hard—writing the ransom letter. It was not easy, since it had to be good front-page stuff. And a blissful smile of satisfaction spread on his face when he finished it at last and turned to Jinx.

"Here," he said. "Listen—it concerns you."

And he read:

Dear Sir,
    This is not an offer or a request, this is a command and you will do well to obey it at once or hell itself will seem a sweet baby's dream compared to the fate I have in store for you. At an hour and place that I will communicate to you later, you will deliver into my hands ten thousand dollars cash, as the price of your daughter's freedom. Be careful not to oppose me, for you are dealing with the most dangerous enemy that any mortal has ever encountered. You are warned.

                                            Damned Dan

Jinx sprang to her feet, her eyes blazing, her body shaking with indignation.

"How dare you?" she cried. "You cheap scoundrel! How dare you ask my father for *ten* thousand dollars?"

She snatched the letter from him and tore it to pieces furiously.

"Now sit down!" she commanded, pointing proudly at the typewriter. "Sit down and write another one—and ask for *one hundred thousand dollars!*"

And as Laury did not move, she added:

"Ten thousand dollars! It's an insult to be sold for ten

thousand! I won't stand for my price being that low! Why, it's only the price of a car, and of not such a very good one, at that!"

It was a long time before Laury had recovered enough to sit at the typewriter and obey her order. . . .

"But that is not all, Miss Winford," he said severely, when he had finished the new ransom message. "You, too, are going to write a letter to your father."

"Oh, with pleasure!" she answered willingly.

He gave her a pen and a sheet of paper. She wrote quickly: "Dear Pop."

"What do you mean?" he shouted. "Dear Pop! Do you realize that your letter will be published in all the papers? You write what I dictate!"

"All right," she agreed sweetly and took another sheet.

"Dear Father," he dictated solemnly. "If there is in your heart a single drop of pity for your unfortunate daughter, you will . . ."

"I never write like that," she observed.

"Never mind, write now! '. . . you will come to my rescue at once.' Exclamation point! 'I can't tell you all the suffering I am going through.' Have you got that? 'Please, oh! please save me.' Exclamation point! 'If you could only see what your poor daughter is doing now . . .' "

"Say, don't you think that if he could see that, he'd be rather surprised, and not in the way you want?"

"Go on, write what I say! '. . . is doing now, your heart would break!' "

"Most probably!"

"Go on! 'I can't write very well, because my eyes are dimmed with tears . . .' "

"Aren't you laying it on too thick?"

" '. . . with tears! I implore you to spare no effort to save me!' Now sign it! 'Your desperate daughter . . .' No! Gosh! Not Jinx! 'Juliana Xenia Winford.' "

"Here you are," she said, handing him the letter.

He read it and frowned slightly.

"Let's make it a little stronger," he said. "Write a postscript to it: 'P.S. I'm miserable, miserable.' Exclamation point—two of them! Have you finished? Here, fold it and put it into this envelope. Fine! Thank you, Miss Winford!"

He put the envelope with the two letters into his pocket. He smiled triumphantly. It had turned out better than he had expected. Of course, he did not intend to take any ransom money from Mr. Winford; he did not even intend to fix an hour and place for it; and he was certain that, anyway, Mr. Winford would never agree to pay ten thousand dollars, much less a hundred thousand.

He stretched himself with a sigh of relaxation.

"Well, I'm going to bed. I've got to get up early tomorrow."

"Are you going out tomorrow?" Jinx asked.

"Yes. Why?"

"I've got a little errand for you. There are a few things that you'll have to buy for me tomorrow."

"A few things? What things?"

"Why, if you intend to keep me here for quite a while, you can't expect me to wear the same clothes all the time, can you? A woman needs a few little things, you know. Here's the list I've written for you."

He took the list. It occupied four pages. It included everything from dresses and slippers to underwear and nightgowns to nail polish and French perfume at forty dollars an ounce.

He blushed. He thought with a shudder of what would be left of his bank account, if anything. But he was too much of a gentleman to refuse.

"All right," he said humbly. "You'll get it tomorrow."

"Now, don't forget, I want the chiffon dress flame-red and the silk one electric-blue. And I want the panties real short, see, like the ones I have."

And she held out the dainty little cloud of lace that she had thrown into one of his desk drawers. She didn't blush; but he did.

"All right," he said, "I'll remember. . . . Goodnight, Miss Winford."

"Goodnight—Mr. Damned Dan!"

——IV——

"I can't figure it out!" Vic Perkins was saying acidly, on the next morning. "Spray me with insect powder if I can figure it out! For one thing, I don't see anything so brilliant in these stories of his. And for two things, all this news he's getting first, well, it's just a fool's luck. And why all this fuss the Editor's raising over that McGee bum what never got two words in print before is more than my intellect can digest!"

Vic Perkins was not quite satisfied with the turn of events. The *Dawn*'s morning number had come out with blazing stories, each bearing a line in big black print: "by Laurence H. McGee." Practically the whole front page was by Laurence H. McGee. There was even a picture of him. And Victor Z. Perkins, the *Dawn*'s star, had to be satisfied with two measly columns on the third page, where he expressed his opinions on the great crime, and they sounded like a mouse's squeal, compared to the roar of Laury's flaming stories.

It had been reported, to City Editor Jonathan Scraggs' extreme satisfaction, that the *Dicksville Globe* was seriously perturbed by his brilliant new reporter's activity. There could be no one to compete with Laurence H. McGee. He was getting all the news hours ahead of everybody else. He seemed to know just where to go to get it. He interviewed Miss Winford's parents, her servants, her friends. He wrote heartbreaking stories on the vanished girl. He wrote terrifying warnings to parents to watch their children. He seemed to burst with inspiration, and Dicksville's citizens were beginning to gulp eagerly every issue of the *Dawn* for its gripping, thrilling articles.

"My congratulations, Mr. McGee," said the Managing Editor himself, when Mr. Scraggs announced Laury's raise in salary. "I have a presentiment of a brilliant future for you!"

"Great, Laury, kid, great!" Mr. Scraggs chuckled rapturously. "You have a positive genius for that kind of stuff! Oh boy, ain't we cleaning up, though! Extras go like pancakes!"

Laury sat in Mr. Scraggs' comfortable armchair, his

feet on the editorial desk, and looked bored. Some of the *Dawn* staff's elite had found a few minutes to gather around him and congratulate the new star. Laury was smoking one of Mr. Scraggs' cigars, and it made him sick, but he looked superior.

"Your stories are . . . are gorgeous! Just simply . . . simply wonderful!" muttered an enthusiastic and anemic little cub.

"How d'you do it?" asked Vic Perkins gruffly.

"It's all in the day's work," answered Laury modestly.

"Oh, Mr. McGee!" cackled Aurelia D. Buttersmith, the flower of the *Dawn*'s womanhood, who wore glasses and had never been kissed. "I'm doing a story on Miss Winford's personality. Do you think it will be appropriate to call her 'a sweet little lily-of-the-valley that the slightest wind could break'? Will it suit her?"

"Perfectly, Miss Buttersmith," Laury answered. "Oh, perfectly!"

"That whole affair is a godsend!" Mr. Scraggs enthused. "By gum, I almost feel I could thank the guy who pulled it!"

Early that afternoon, Mr. Scraggs had another thrill that sent him jumping in his chair like a rubber ball. Laury rushed into the city room, his shirt collar flung open, his hair like a storm, his eyes like lightning.

"An extra!" he cried. "Quick! I've got the letters Winford received from the kidnapper!"

"O-oo-ooh!" was all Mr. Scraggs could answer.

It was lucky for Laury that no one noticed the fact that the *Dicksville Dawn* received the copy of the two letters half an hour before the postman delivered the originals to Mr. Winford. . . .

While the fresh extras were flowing from the press, Laury went out again, "to look for news," he said. But this time, he went "to look for news" in Harkdonner's big department store.

Laury thought that if he deserved a punishment for his crime, he got it, and plenty, in the hours that he spent at Harkdonner's department store. He went from counter to counter, Jinx's list in hand, perspiration gluing his shirt to his back and his hair to his forehead, and his face red as a tomato. He thought he had acquired a habit of stuttering for life before he got through with the lingerie counter. He did not dare to look at the courteous saleslady, for fears she would be blushing, too.

"It's . . . it's for my wife . . . for my wife," he repeated helplessly, hoping desperately that no one would see him in the store.

And as it always happens in such cases, two stenographers from the *Dawn* passed by, saw him at the ladies' lingerie counter, waved to him, giggled, and winked significantly.

And he almost murdered the salesman who, with an understanding grin, offered him a weekend suitcase.

Finally, with four huge boxes, two in each hand, Laury emerged from the store, put the boxes in his faithful old sports car, and left the car in a garage where no one could see it until evening. Then he walked back to the *Dawn* building.

His good humor returned to him on the way. Damned Dan's name was all over Dicksville. It blazed on headlines of extras everywhere. It echoed in the terrified whispers of little groups of people gathered all along Main Street. It ran like the swift fire of a dynamite cord, spreading over the whole town to explode in a frenzy of general panic. Laury felt a personal pride.

Besides, he noticed that many passersby looked at him, pointed him out to each other, whispered, and turned around. "The one that writes those marvelous stories in the *Dawn*," he heard.

And two charming young ladies even had the courage to stop him.

"Oh, Mr. McGee!" sang one of them in a lovely voice from lovely lips. "Excuse our boldness, but we recognized you and couldn't help stopping you to ask about that terrible crime. Do you really think that man is as horrible as he seems?"

"Do you really think all of us girls are in danger?" breathed the other one, very becomingly frightened. "Your stories are so fascinating! I thought, 'Here's a man to protect us all!' "

And it was hard to decide whether their smiles sparkled with admiration for the stories or for the big gray eyes and tempting lips of the young man before them.

So Laury entered the *Dawn* offices, head high, whistling nonchalantly, with the proud air of a conqueror tired of victories.

"Hey, where on earth have you been?" shouted the copy boy, meeting him on the stairs. "The Editor's hollering for you!"

Laury strolled into the city room, a superior smile on his lips.

"You nearsighted, blind boob!" Mr. Scraggs greeted him. "You brainless, straw-stuffed sap!"

"W-why, Mr. Scraggs!" Laury suffocated.

"Why the hell," Mr. Scraggs roared, "why the hell when you brought us Miss Winford's letter did you leave out the best part of it?"

"What?"

"Why did you omit the second postscript?"

"The *second* postscript?!"

"Look here!" And Mr. Scraggs threw to him an extra of the *Dicksville Globe* that had just come out, an hour after the *Dawn,* with the two sensational letters that Mr. Winford had received. Laury found Jinx's letter and read:

Dear Father,

If there is in your heart a single drop of pity for your unfortunate daughter, you will come to my rescue at once! I can't tell you all the suffering I am going through. Please, oh! please save me! If you could only see what your poor daughter is doing now your heart would break. I can't write very well because my eyes are dimmed with tears. I implore you to spare no effort to save me.

Your desperate daughter,
Juliana Xenia Winford.

P.S. I'm miserable, miserable!!
P.S.II Like fun I am!

"When interviewed on the subject," the *Globe* added, "Mrs. Winford remarked: 'Unfortunately, only the second postscript sounds like my daughter's style of self-expression!'"

Laury entered his apartment that evening with a scowl

on his face, darker than printing ink. He threw the four boxes in the middle of the room, without answering Jinx's greeting, and slumped down on the sofa, turning his back to her.

"O-oh! Isn't that sweet of you!" Jinx cried, throwing herself eagerly on the packages.

In a second the living-room floor looked like a combination salad made out of a woman's boudoir after an earthquake. And Jinx sat on the carpet in the middle of the waves of lace and silk, enthusiastically examining her new possessions.

"My goodness! What's this?" she cried suddenly.

And she pulled out the nightgown that Laury had chosen for her. As his excuse it must be said that he had no way of knowing what girls wear at night and so he had chosen the most decent-looking gown in the store, which was an immense thing of heavy flannel with long sleeves, high collar, and little pockets, a dignified garment to which his grandmother could have found no objection.

"What do you think this is, an Eskimo raincoat?" Jinx asked indignantly, waving the gown before Laury's eyes.

"Well, but . . ." he muttered, embarrassed.

"Have you ever seen a woman in a nightgown like that?" she thundered.

"No, I haven't!" he answered sharply.

His face was dark and indifferent. And it did not change when, after carrying her new things away, Jinx emerged suddenly from the kitchen, wearing one of her new dresses.

It was the flame-red chiffon. The light red mist clung to her slim waist tightly like a bathing suit and then flowed down to her knees in wide waves that floated around her like trembling tongues of fire. She stood immobile, her head thrown back. Her hair looked tornado-blown. Her lips were parted, glistening like wet petals; and her eyes sparkled strangely with a joyous, intense, and eager glitter.

"Do you like it?" she asked softly.

"Yes!" he threw indifferently, without looking at her.

She laughed. She turned on the victrola, a thundering jazz record.

"Let's dance!" she invited.

Laury turned to her abruptly.

"What did you write that second postscript for?" he asked.

"Oh! Wasn't that clever?" she laughed, dancing all over the room, her body shaking with the gracefully convulsive jerks of a fox-trot. "You're not angry, are you—Danny?"

"Please stop that dancing, Miss Winford! Do you want the neighbors to hear you?"

"Don't call me Miss Winford!"

"What shall I call you? And leave that ukulele alone! You'll wake up the whole house, Miss Winford!"

"My name's Jinx!"

"No wonder!"

She laughed again. With one graceful leap she landed on her knees at his feet and her strong little hands turned his head towards her.

"Now, Danny," she whispered tenderly, her hair brushing his chin, her laughing eyes fixed straight on his, "can't you smile, just once?"

He did not want to, but he could not help it and he smiled. When Laury smiled he had little dimples playing on his cheeks, gay like flickers of light, and in his eyes—dancing sparks, mischievous like dimples. And the strange, eager, almost hungry look glittered again in Jinx's eyes.

She pulled him up to his feet and threw his arms around her and pushed him into the gay rhythm of a fox-trot. He laughed wholeheartedly and obeyed. They glided, swaying, over the room. The victrola screamed joyously and in the buoyant roar of the jazz orchestra some instrument knocked dryly, rhythmically, like a cracking whip spurring the sounds to dance. Laury's hands clasped her slim little body, the tremulous red cloud with the faint, sweet perfume. And Jinx pressed herself to him, closer, closer.

They danced until their feet could move no longer and then they both fell on the sofa, in the cozy tent of the window curtains that Jinx had arranged. She looked at him with smiling, encouraging, impatient eyes.

"You're a wonderful dancer, Miss Winford," he said.

"Thanks! So are you," she answered indifferently.

"Are you tired?"

"No!" she threw coldly.

They were silent for several minutes.

"Have you ever kidnapped a girl before?" she asked suddenly.

"Now, just why do you want to know that?" he inquired.

"Oh, I just wonder . . . I just wonder if you ever kiss the girls who are your prisoners."

"You don't have to be afraid of that!" he answered, with a sincere indignation.

And he could not quite make out what the look that she gave him meant. . . .

They danced again; then, he played the ukulele and sang to her the songs he knew; and she sang the ones he didn't know; and they sang together; and she taught him a new dance; and she thought that Lizzie Chatterton had certainly missed something having never been kidnapped.

When he finally stretched himself on his mountainous bed in the kitchen and turned off the light, Laury somehow did not feel like sleeping and the sweet perfume lingered with him, as though breathing from the other room, and he looked at the closed door.

"Oh! . . . Danny!!" a frightened voice screamed in the living room.

He jumped up and rushed to her. She threw her arms around him and clung to him, trembling, making him fall on his knees by the side of her bed.

"Oh! . . . I heard a noise . . . as though somebody was moving in the hall!" she whispered with a terror that looked almost perfectly genuine.

Her blanket was half thrown off and she clung to him, trembling, frightened, helpless. His hands clasped her nightgown, and the body under the nightgown, and he felt her heart beating under his fingers.

"There's no one there. . . . What are you afraid of . . . Jinx?" he whispered.

"Oh!" she breathed. "Oh, I'm afraid the police might come!"

Laury was surprised to see that he was trembling when

he returned to his kitchen and that it had cost him a hard effort to return there.

"I wish," he thought, closing his eyes, "I wish the police would never come here . . . and for more reasons than one!"

———V———

"Extray! . . . Extray-ay!"

The sun was shining so gaily in the sky and in Laury's eyes, on this following morning, that he did not pay any particular attention to the ominous roar bursting suddenly in the street under the city room windows. The sky was blue and Laury's desk at the window looked like a square of gold. He had won back Mr. Scraggs' favor by his brilliant story on the mysterious personality of Damned Dan, in the morning number. He was writing another article now, and the cubs around him looked respectfully at the great journalist at work.

So when the unexpected roar of yelling voices thundered in the street, proclaiming some eventful news, Laury was not disturbed and only wondered dimly what the *Globe* could have an extra for.

But he did not have much time for meditation. He was summoned hurriedly to Mr. Scraggs' desk. His heart fell when he saw the Editor's face. He knew at once that something had happened, something frightful.

"What excuse have you got to offer?" Mr. Scraggs asked with sinister calm.

"Excuse . . . for what?" Laury muttered, steadying his voice.

"I had an impression that you were supposed to cover the Winford case, young man?"

"Well . . ."

"Then how do you account for the fact," Mr. Scraggs roared, "that a punk, lousy, measly paper like the *Globe* gets such news ahead of us?" And he waved a *Globe* extra into Laury's face.

"News, Mr. Scraggs? News on the Winford case?"

"And how! . . . Or perhaps you wouldn't call it news that Winford received a second letter from the kidnapper?"

"What?!"

"You heard me! And the letter orders him to deliver the money tonight!"

Laury saw stars swimming between him and Mr. Scraggs. He seized the extra, almost tearing it in half; and he read the great news. Mr. Winford had received this morning a second message from Damned Dan, fixing the time and place for the ransom money to be delivered. Mr. Winford had decided to obey, for, he had declared: "I would rather search for my money than for my daughter." Therefore, he had refused to make public all of the letter and the place appointed for the meeting. The *Globe's* reporter was only able to state that the kidnapper's letter was written with a pencil on a piece of brown wrapping paper; and that it started with:

Deer Ser enuff monkay biznes. Come across with the dough and make it pretti darn snappi or I'l get sor and wat'l hapen to yur gal then will be plenti. . . .

It was signed:

Veri trooli yur's
Dammd Dan

Laury swayed on his feet, and Mr. Scraggs wondered at the color of his face.

"It's . . . it's impossible!" he muttered hoarsely. "It's impossible!"

"What's impossible? The *Globe* getting it first and you asleep on your job?"

"But . . . but it can't be, Mr. Scraggs! Oh, God! It can't be!"

"Just why can't it be?"

Laury straightened himself slowly, straight and tense like a piano string.

"There's something happening somewhere, Mr. Scraggs!" he said, white as a sheet. "Something horrible!"

"There sure is," answered Mr. Scraggs, "and it's right here, in my city room, from which you're going to be kicked out, head first, if you ever miss a piece of news like this again!"

Eight hours passed after this conversation; eight desperate hours that Laury spent ransacking the town in search of some clue to that inexplicable development. He was too astounded to be quite conscious of what he was doing. He wondered if he was not going insane—the thing seemed so ridiculously incredible. He was searching frantically for something that would give him the faintest suspicion of an explanation.

He interviewed Mr. Winford and saw the first half of the letter on brown wrapping paper; he interviewed the police; he went around town actually hunting for news on the Winford case, looking for—Damned Dan! The idea made him laugh—with a gnashing of teeth.

And when he dragged himself back towards the *Dawn* building at six-thirty P.M., he had discovered nothing. The sun was setting far at the end of Main Street and red fires blazed on the windshields of cars rolling west. The peaceful traffic streamed by as usual and the shop awnings were being pulled up over darkened windows, locked for the night, as usual; but it seemed to Laury that somewhere behind these quiet houses, somewhere in this peaceful town, an invisible, frightful doom was silently awaiting him. . . .

"No," said Mr. Scraggs, when Laury reached the city room, "you can't go home tonight. You'll be needed here. Grave developments are coming, I feel. Take an hour off for dinner and then be back on the job. Hang around Winford, be the first to learn the results of the ransom meeting this evening. And be sure to get here before the deadline!"

Laury walked home, his hands deep in his pockets and his thoughts deep in misery. What was he to do now? He could not let Mr. Winford be robbed of that huge sum, robbed and cheated, for he knew that the second "Dammd Dan" could not deliver Jinx to her father. He must warn him. But how? He did not dare to act, now that he felt himself watched and had not the slightest idea of the enemy he was dealing with.

Just the same, he jerked his head up proudly and muttered behind a firmly set mouth:

"But if that lousy bum, whoever he is, thinks he can scare me, he has a surprise coming that he'll long remember! I'll learn what his game is and damn soon!"

"Congratulations, buddy!" said a thick voice above his ear.

He stopped short and wheeled around. A tall, huge shadow towered above him in the coming darkness. That shadow had a crumpled little cap, too small for its big head, and greasy clothes that smelled of whiskey. It had a flat face, heavy eyes, and a broken, prizefighter's nose. Laury recognized it at once: it was Pug-Nose Thomson.

"Sir?" Laury asked indignantly, backing away from the man's strange, significant grin.

"Yeah, buddy, yeah, I says it was a slick one!" answered the man with a slow chuckle.

"What are you talking about? I don't know you! Whom do you think you're talking to?" Laury threw sharply.

"I'm talkin' to Damned Dan hisself!" the man answered happily.

Laury wanted to make a reply and couldn't.

"I says, yuh pulled the best job any guy ever tried in this burg," the man went on. "For an amatcher it was pretty slick, I'll say!"

"I don't know what you're talking about!" Laury pronounced with a tremendous effort, wondering himself at the calm of his voice. "Leave me alone! You've been drinking!"

"So I have. Which don't make no difference," answered Pug-Nose Thomson quietly. "An' yuh better don't pull that line on me, kiddo, 'cause I know what I know, an' yuh know it, too. . . . But I don't mean no offense to yuh, on the conterry, I mean to pay my compliments. If that's yer begginin', yuh'll go far, young fella, yuh'll go far!"

"I don't understand you!" Laury insisted. "You're taking me for somebody else!"

"No, I ain't! Now, lissen here, I've got a offer fer yuh: Let's be partners on this job!"

"You crazy fool! If you think . . ."

"Aw, cut that out, I'm talkin' bizness! I know pretty damn well that yuh're the guy what writes all them stories in the poipers an' what's got the Winford dame locked up in his own joint! Which's pretty darn smart, I agrees!"

"But . . ."

"An' if yuh wanna know how I knows it, it's right simple: I read the poipers an' I noticed as how yuh was gettin' all them news on this bizness first. 'That's funny,' I thought to myself, 'nobody never heard of this guy before.' An' then I watched yuh, an' I saw yuh buy all them Jane's duds an' yuh ain't never got a sweetie, so there! An' I watched yer joint from acrost the street an' sure thing, there was the Winford gal at yer winder!

"Now keep yer mouth shut!" he went on, without giving Laury time to reply. "No use tryin' to fool me! Here's the main thing: I wrote that second letter to the Winford gent an' he's bringin' the dough over tonight, in an hour. Yuh bring the gal an' we go fifty-fifty on it!

"That's still plenty fer yuh," he added, as Laury remained silent and immobile. "No one ever got fifty grand fer his first job!"

Laury looked calmly, steadily into the man's eyes.

"All right, then, if you are so well informed," he said coldly, narrowing his eyes. "Now, suppose I refuse your offer?"

"Yuh won't," Pug-Nose declared with conviction, " 'cause then I go an' tell the bulls what I know on this case. An' I get the five grand of reward. So yuh better accept my offer!"

"Well," said Laury, "I accept it!"

"Great, buddy! Now . . ."

"I accept it on one condition: you give me twenty-four hours. We'll meet Winford at the same time tomorrow!"

"Why should I?" Pug-Nose protested. "I don't wanna wait!"

"Then go to the police at once, and denounce me, and get your five thousand, instead of the fifty you'll get tomorrow! I won't bring the girl tonight, and that's final!"

"Well, okay," said Pug-Nose slowly, after some deliberation. "We'll make it tomorrow. Yuh meet me here, same time, with the gal."

"Yes!" said Laury. "Goodnight, partner!"

"Goodnight!"

The darkness was gathering and Pug-Nose Thomson disappeared behind a corner so swiftly that Laury hardly heard his footsteps. There was no one around that could have witnessed their meeting. Lonely streetlamps flared up feebly in the deserted street with two rows of silent, drooping houses, in the brown shadows of a rusty sunset. A woman was gathering the wash from a clothesline in a backyard, and a car rattled through the silence, somewhere in the distance.

Cold sweat was rolling down Laury's face. He hurried home. But his mind was made up when he entered his apartment.

"Take your things and come on," he said to Jinx sternly.

"Where?" she asked.

"I've decided to take you back to your parents tonight!"

"That's too bad," she said sweetly, with a smile of compassion for him. "I won't go!"

He stepped back and stared at her, wide-eyed.

"What did you say?" he asked.

"Just that I won't go," she repeated calmly, "that's all!"

"How . . . how am I to understand that?"

"Oh, any way you please! Just any way!"

"You mean, you don't want to be free?"

"No! . . . I enjoy being a prisoner . . . your prisoner!"

There was only one shaded little lamp lighted in the room. She was wearing her electric-blue silk dress, tight, luminous, glittering faintly, and in the half-darkness she looked like a phosphorescent little firefly.

"Danny," she said softly, "you aren't going to send me away like that, are you?"

He did not answer. He was surprised to feel his heart beating furiously somewhere in his throat. She smiled scornfully:

"Why, there's no fun in being kidnapped if that's all there is to it!"

"But, Miss Winford . . ."

"Do you realize that I'm your prisoner and you can do with me anything you want?"

He was silent.

"Oh, Damned Dan!" she threw at him. "Aren't you going to take advantage of a girl who is in your power?"

He turned to her sharply and looked at her with half-closed eyes, curious, a little mocking, unexpectedly masterful, a dangerous look. And she felt that look like a hand squeezing her heart with delightful pain.

She stood straight, immobile, from the tips of her feet to her wide, sparkling eyes—waiting. "You have no right! You have no right! What are you thinking about?" he cried soundlessly to himself.

He turned away. "Come on, you're going home!" he ordered sharply.

"I'm not!" she answered.

"You're not, eh?" He turned to her fiercely. "You terrible little thing! You're the worst little creature I ever saw! I'm glad to get rid of you! You'll go now, do you hear me?"

He seized her wrist with a bruising grip. She whirled around and threw her body close against his.

"Oh, Danny! I don't want to go away!" She breathed so softly and she was so close that he heard it with his lips rather than his ears.

And then he closed his eyes, and crushed his lips against hers, and thought, when his arms clasped her, that he was going to break her in two. . . .

"Jinx . . . darling . . . darling!"

"Danny, you wonderful thing! You most adorable of all."

They seemed to be cut away from the whole world by the little tent over the sofa, and not by the little tent only. His arms closed around her, like the gates of a kingdom that no more than two can ever enter. Their eyes were laughing soundlessly at each other. And he was saying to her the most eloquent things which a man's lips can say and for which no words are needed.

And Laury forgot all about having ever been a reporter. . . .

It was ten minutes to nine when he remembered.

"Oh, my goodness!" he cried, jumping up. "The deadline!"

"The dead who?"

"The deadline! I must run now! Dearest, I'll be back soon!"

"Oh! Do you have to go? Well, hurry back then—you know how I'll miss you, darling!"

Laury threw his old sports car as fast as it could go, flying towards the *Dawn* building. He was too happy to think much about anything else. His soul was dancing, and so was his sports car. The old machine went zigzagging to right and left, jumping buoyantly and senselessly, like a young calf turned loose for the first time in a green, sunny meadow. The drivers around him swore frantically; Laury laughed joyously, his head thrown back.

Then he remembered that he had no story for Mr. Scraggs. He seized his notebook and jotted words down hurriedly. It was a miracle that he reached the *Dawn* building without an accident, driving as he was with his one hand on the wheel, his other on the notebook, and his mind on a pair of slanting, sparkling eyes and soft, laughing lips, back home.

"Ah, so here you are!" Mr. Scraggs exclaimed ominously, when Laury whirled into the city room.

Laury was too far away in his overflowing happiness to notice the storm on Mr. Scraggs' face.

"Yes! I'm on time, am I not?" he cried gaily.

"You are? And what about the news?"

"The news? Oh, sure, the news! . . . I got it! Most sensational news, Mr. Scraggs! Winford came to the meeting place and—Damned Dan was not there to meet him!"

Such a dead silence fell over the city room that Laury looked around, surprised.

"I'd like to know," Mr. Scraggs said slowly with the tense, shivering calm of a fury hard to restrain, "I'd like to know where the hell you are getting your news from!"

"Why . . . why, what's the matter?"

"What's the matter? You blockheaded, half-witted, confounded idiot! Nothing's the matter, except that the *Globe* came out half an hour ago with the news and . . ."

"Oh, well . . ."

". . . and Damned Dan *did* come to the meeting, you skunk of a reporter!"

"He . . . *came*?"

"Where have you been all that time, you lazy cub? Sure, he came, but he didn't bring the girl, so he got one grand in advance and promised to bring her later!"

Laury had no strength to make a comment or an answer; he stood, his eyes closed, his arms drooping helplessly.

"In fact," Mr. Scraggs added, "he promised to bring her in an hour!"

"What?" Laury jumped forward as though he was going to choke Mr. Scraggs.

"I'd like to know," Mr. Scraggs cried in furious amazement, "what the hell is the meaning of your strange . . . Where are you going?! Hcy! Stop! Come here at once! Where are you going?"

But Laury did not hear him. He was flying madly down the stairs, out into the street, into his sports car. . . .

His apartment was empty when he got there. Jinx's perfume was still lingering in the air. A pair of adorable little slippers was thrown into a chair. The sofa cushions were still crumpled where they had been sitting together. . . .

He found a note on his desk.

Deer partner I changed my mind. Wy shood I wait fer a haff toomoro wenn I can hav oll of it too-nyt? I'l giv yu a litle of it later fer a consolashun. So good lukk and happi dreems. Dont skueel coz then I'l skueel too.

Pug Noz Thomson

——*VI*——

"You gentlemen of the press," said Mr. Winford to Laury, "are most decidedly aggravating, I must say. You should realize that I am not exactly in the mood to give you interviews and information on this painful subject. . . . No, I repeat, the individual who calls himself Damned Dan did not come to this second meeting, as he promised, an hour after the first. I waited for him to no avail and I just returned home. That is all I know. . . . But I do wish that you gentlemen would not be so insistent in paying me visits that are becoming rather too frequent."

Laury stared at him hopelessly.

"And, young man," Mr. Winford added severely, "I would give a little more consideration to my personal appearance before calling at people's houses, if I were you."

Laury glanced indifferently into a big, full-size mirror in the white marble hall of the Winford residence, and the mirror showed to him a haggard, disheveled young man, with his hair hanging down on his wet forehead, his cap backwards on his head, his shirt torn open and his necktie on his shoulder.

The sight did not affect him at all; he had had too many shocks this day to retain any faculty of reaction. The last shock had been the worst of all; from his apartment he had rushed straight to the Winford residence, hoping to find Jinx there; he had found only Mr. Winford just returned from his second appointment with Pug-Nose Thomson and Pug-Nose had *not* come to this meeting! Why? Jinx was in his power now. What had happened?

Laury bowed to Mr. Winford wearily.

"I'm sorry, Mr. Winford," he said in a dull voice. "I'm rather upset over a very serious matter. . . . Thank you for the information. . . . Goodnight!"

He turned and left the wide, empty hall dimly lighted by crystal chandeliers reflected in the dark mirrors and polished marble floor, Mr. Winford's lonely figure motionless among tall, white columns and the faint sound of Mrs. Winford's sobs, somewhere in a distant room.

He drove his rattling sports car on the graveled road of the Winford gardens, rolling downhill, with a fountain tinkling somewhere in the darkness like breaking glass and the lights of Dicksville glittering far down under his feet between the branches of tall, black cypresses.

With each turn of the wheels his face was becoming grimmer and grimmer. He was calm now, and implacable. There was only one thing to do—and he had decided to do it.

He was going straight to Police Headquarters to throw

them on Pug-Nose Thomson's trail. He knew that once Pug-Nose was caught, it would be the end of him, too, for the bum certainly would not keep silent. For the first time he felt a cold shudder at the thought of jail. So that was the fate awaiting him! Such was to be the end of his glorious journalistic career that had just been starting so brilliantly! A kidnapper, a criminal, a convict. . . . Oh, well, it had to be done!

He did not hesitate for a moment, for there was only one reason, expressed in one word, that pushed him to action: Jinx! His whole being was one immense anxiety for her. Where was she now and what was happening to her? He closed his eyes not to see Pug-Nose Thomson's picture that rose in his mind. . . .

It was a proud, determined Laury that entered Chief Police Inspector Rafferty's office; a Laury cold, imperative, and impersonal, like a general ready for a dangerous battle, calm with the calm of a great moment.

"Get your men, Inspector," he ordered, "to arrest Miss Winford's kidnapper!"

"Cats and rats!!" cried Chief Police Inspector Rafferty.

Pug-Nose Thomson's hangouts were pretty well known to the police. It would not take long to make their round, and Inspector Rafferty decided to go himself in his excitement over the biggest case of his whole career. He called two husky policemen to accompany him.

Laury, true to his duty to the last, rushed to a telephone.

"Mr. Scraggs?" he cried, when he got the *Dawn*'s editorial desk. "It's McGee speaking! Send your best man over to Police Headquarters right away! There's going to be a knockout of a story! . . . No, I won't be able to cover it! . . . You'll learn why, very soon! . . . Goodbye! Hurry!"

Such was the interest aroused by the Winford case that when Inspector Rafferty, Laury, and the two policemen were leaving Headquarters, Mr. Jonathan Scraggs in person bounced out of a speeding taxi before it had quite stopped, and joined them. He was accompanied by Vic Perkins.

"So Pug-Nose Thomson is Damned Dan?" asked Mr. Scraggs, a note of disappointment in his voice, as the police car dashed into the dark streets, its siren screaming piercingly.

"Well, not quite. But you're going to find Damned Dan, too," answered Laury with resignation. . . .

They found Pug-Nose Thomson in the dirty back room of an old, miserable tenement. The room had one tiny window with dusty pieces of broken glass sticking out and a wretched little gas lamp that hardly gave enough light to distinguish Pug-Nose Thomson's huge bulk huddled over an old, unpainted table, drinking desperately. He was alone.

"Where's Miss Winford?" cried Laury.

Pug-Nose looked with hazy eyes at the group of men in his doorway, and the gleaming brass buttons were the first thing he understood.

"So yuh squealed, yuh goddamn louse, yuh did?" he yelled, jumping at Laury, but the two policemen seized him, one by each arm, and handcuffed his big, hairy fists.

"Where's the girl?" asked Inspector Rafferty in a threatening voice.

"The girl? The girl, she's gone, damn her, she escaped from me!"

"How could she escape?"

"How *could* she? Oh boy! The only thing I wonder 'bout is how that boob managed to keep her fer three days!" And he shook his fist at Laury.

"What do you mean?" cried Mr. Scraggs.

"Haw-haw! So yuh don't know, do yuh? Damned Dan—there he is, in his own person! Shake hands an' make yerself acquainted!" And he bellowed his ferocious laugh into Laury's face.

"The man's insane!" Mr. Scraggs exclaimed.

"Who's insane, yuh old fool? Sure, I stole the girl, but I stole her from him! He's the one that pulled the whole thing! Yuh thought maybe I wouldn't squeal on yuh, yuh dirty double-crosser?"

Five pairs of bulging eyes turned to Laury. He looked at them, cold, silent, immobile. He did not want to deny it; he knew that his guilt could be proved too easily.

"Why . . . Laury! . . . Why . . ." choked Mr. Scraggs.

Silently, Laury stretched his hand out to Inspector Rafferty for the handcuffs.

"My stars in heaven!" was all Mr. Scraggs could utter.

"Hot diggity dog!" added Vic Perkins. . . .

Laury was silent in the car all the way down to the jail, and the five men did not dare to look at him. Pug-Nose snored by his side.

The big door of the damp, gray jail building opened like a gaping mouth, eager to swallow Laury, and the heavy iron gratings clicked like hungry teeth. Inspector Rafferty had to kick the jailer on the back to get him out of the trance he had fallen into, on learning who his new prisoner was and why.

When the rusty grate of his cell closed after him, Laury turned suddenly and handed a piece of paper to the jailer with a few words written in the form of a headline. The words were:

RENEGADE IN OUR MIDST: OUR OWN REPORTER— ATROCIOUS KIDNAPPER!

"Give that to Mr. Scraggs," said Laury sadly. "That, too, will make good copy!"

"I suppose," said Inspector Rafferty, entering his office with Mr. Scraggs, Vic Perkins, and the two policemen, "I suppose Miss Winford is safe at home by this time. I shall inquire."

He called up the Winford residence and asked if Miss Winford had returned home.

"No! Oh, my God, no!" answered Mrs. Winford's hysterical voice.

The five men looked at each other, dumbfounded.

"Well, I'll be damned!" cried Inspector Rafferty, falling into a chair. "What a case! What's happened now?"

Laury's apartment being the only place they could think of searching, all five of them rushed back to the car and hurried there at full speed. They were not only anxious by this time, they were panic-stricken.

When they entered Laury's apartment, Jinx herself met them. She had one of Laury's shirts draped gracefully instead of an apron, with the two sleeves tied around her waist, and she was in the kitchen, cooking dinner.

"To what do I owe the honor of this visit?" she asked with the charming smile of a gracious hostess.

"Miss . . . Miss Winford!" gulped Inspector Rafferty. He was the only one that had retained the use of his voice.

Jinx stood facing them, perfectly poised, smiling, unperturbed, a slight interrogative frown raising her eyebrows, as though waiting politely for an explanation.

"I . . . I'm glad to see you safe, Miss Winford," muttered Inspector Rafferty, not at all sure whether he quite understood just what the situation was. "I'm glad we managed to rescue you at last!"

"Oh, you did?"

"Yes, Miss Winford! You have nothing to fear from him any more!"

"Fear from whom?"

"The young man that kidnapped you, Laurence McGee!"

"Laurence McGee?" Jinx shouted. *"Laurence McGee?"*

And such a thunder of laughter exploded like a bomb with splinters ringing all over the room, that Inspector Rafferty and his companions started, terrified.

"Oh . . . oh, how adorable!" Jinx laughed, understanding the real meaning and reason of the whole case.

"You are glad that we arrested him, is that it?" asked Inspector Rafferty timidly, very much surprised.

"Arrested? *Him?* Oh, my God! . . . Inspector, you must release him immediately!"

Vic Perkins, who had been taking notes, dropped his pad and pencil.

"It's all a big misunderstanding, Inspector!" Jinx said quickly, still anxious, but regaining her calm.

"A misunderstanding, Miss Winford?"

"You see, I've never been kidnapped," she explained, so sweetly, so sincerely that it would have been hard to doubt the straight look of her bold, mocking eyes. "I feel that you ought to know the truth, and I must confess everything. Mr. McGee did not kidnap me. We have known each other for a long time, and we were in love, and we eloped to get married; because, you see, my parents would have objected to it. So we made it look like a kidnapping to throw them off the track. It was all my idea!"

The five faces before her were frozen with the queerest expressions she had ever seen.

"Of course, I escaped from that broken-nosed bum, who tried to butt in, and then I came right back here. So there wasn't any particular need to rescue me."

"I . . . I don't . . . I've never in my life . . . I . . ." Inspector Rafferty felt that his power of speech had been knocked out together with the rest of his reasoning abilities.

"Oh, dear Inspector!" Jinx gave him her sweetest smile and her most innocent look. "Surely you won't break my heart and be too severe with my poor fiancé?"

"Of . . . of course . . . I see that it . . . it changes the situation," stuttered Inspector Rafferty.

"Where is he now?"

"In jail, Miss Win—"

"In jail? How dare you! Come, at once, set him free!"

And she rushed out, flying like a bullet down the stairs, the five men hardly able to follow her.

She jumped at the wheel of the police car, pushing the chauffeur aside.

"Never mind, I'm a better driver than any of you!" she cried in reply to Inspector Rafferty's protest. "Jump in! Hurry!"

And the big car tore forward like a rocket, with a deafening whistle of the siren, in the hands of the little bluc driver with wild, flying hair. . . .

"Don't try to write it, Vic, old boy!" Mr. Scraggs cried, striving to be heard above the roar of the speeding machine. "No words will ever cover *that* story!"

Jinx had to wait in the jail reception room, while Inspector Rafferty and the jailer went to bring Laury.

They found him lying on his cot, his face in his hands. But he jumped up when they entered the cell and faced them calmly, the brave gray eyes steady and unfaltering.

"I must apologize, Mr. McGee," said Inspector Rafferty, "though, of course, you shouldn't have kept silent. But I'm glad to say that you are free to go now."

"I'm . . . free?"

"Yes, we know the whole truth. Miss Winford confessed everything."

"She did?"

Laury was stupefied, but he had learned by this time that it was better not to protest against anything Jinx said.

He walked to the reception room. Jinx rushed to him, threw her arms around his neck, and kissed him, before the eyes of all the witnesses.

"Oh, *Laury* darling, I'm so sorry you had to suffer like that for me!" she cried.

"It was very noble of you to keep silent, but, really, you should have told them the truth," she went on, as though without noticing the amazed look in his eyes. "I told them everything, how we eloped to get married and how I made up the kidnapping story to deceive my parents. You can tell them it's true now, darling!"

"Oh! Yes! . . . Yes, it's true!" confirmed Laury enthusiastically, for he would not have denied it, even if he could.

"Oh, Laury!" cried Mr. Scraggs with admiration. "And to think that he works on our paper!"

"The headlines, Mr. Scraggs," said Jinx to the Editor, "the headlines will be: 'Society Beauty Elopes with Our Own Reporter!' "

"Don't thank me, you helpless, unimaginative sap of a criminal!" Jinx whispered to Laury, squeezing his hand, as they walked down the steps and his arm encircled her in the darkness of the narrow jail stair way. "So you wanted to give them sensational news, didn't you? Now think of the sensation *my* news is going to give them!"

Escort

c. 1929

Editor's Preface

This brief story seems to have been written in 1929, the year Ayn Rand married Frank O'Connor. One of his earliest gifts to her was a pair of small, stuffed lion cubs, christened Oscar and Oswald, who soon became to the young couple a private symbol of the "benevolent universe." Every Christmas the cubs were brought out, dressed in colorful hats, to preside over the gaiety of the season.

I mention this because "Escort," in manuscript, is signed by one "O. O. Lyons." This means, I take it, that the story is intended as humor, the kind of fine, twinkling humor that Ayn Rand associated with her husband, and with Oscar and Oswald.

Ayn Rand by this time had read a great deal of O. Henry. She admired his cheerful lightheartedness and virtuoso plot ingenuity. "Escort" (and "The Night King") may be read as her own private salute to O. Henry, her own attempt at his kind of twist ending.

—L. P.

Escort

Before he left the house, Sue asked:

"You won't be back until morning, dear?"

He nodded dejectedly, for he had heard the question often and he wished his wife would not ask it. She never complained, and her blue eyes looked at him quietly and patiently, but he always felt a sadness in her voice, and a reproach. Yet tonight, the question and the voice seemed different somehow. Sue did not seem to mind. She even repeated:

"You won't be back until the small hours?"

"God knows, darling," he protested. "I don't like it any better than you do. But a job's a job."

He had explained it so many times so very carefully: shipping clerks in warehouses could not choose their hours; and since he could not choose jobs, he had to work nights, even though he knew how wistfully she looked at the women whose husbands came home each evening, after the day's work, to a bright dinner table under a bright lamp. And Sue had done such a grand job of their little house with less than nothing to go on. He had not noticed how the dreary shack they had rented had turned into a bright, warm little miracle, with rows of red-and-white-checkered dishes gleaming in the kitchen, and Sue among them in a wide, starched dress of red and white checks, slim and blond and gay as a child among toys. It was the third year of their marriage, and such a far cry from the first, when he had come, fresh from college, to these same rooms, then full of dust and cracked paint and desolation, when he had brought his young bride here, with nothing to offer her save the menacing monster of rent to be paid, which stared at them each month and which they could not pay. When he thought of those days, his lips tightened grimly and he said:

"I've got to hang on to this job, sweetheart, much as you hate it. I hate it too, but I won't let you go through what we've been through ever again."

"Yes," said Sue, "of course." But she seemed to be looking past him, without hearing his voice.

He kissed her and hurried to the door, but Sue stopped him.

"Larry," she reminded him sweetly, "it's Saturday."

So it was. He had forgotten. He groped for his billfold and slipped her weekly allowance into her hand. Her hand seemed much too eager as it closed over the bills.

Then she smiled at him, her gay, impish smile, her eyes sparkling and open and innocent. And he left.

He raised the collar of his neat, modest gray overcoat against the thin drizzle of the street. He looked back once, with regret, at the light over their door, over the number 745, his number, his home, 745 Grant Street. Then he hurried to the subway.

When he alighted upon the milling platforms of Grand Central, Larry Dean did not walk to an exit. He hurried to a locker room instead, opened a locker, took from it a neat suitcase, and then walked to the men's room. Fifteen minutes later, he emerged from it, and the fat black attendant looked with respectful admiration at his tall, slender figure in full dress clothes, trim and resplendent from the tips of his shining pumps to his shining top hat set at the right careless angle of a dazzling man of the world bent upon a gay evening. He put the suitcase with his modest working clothes back in the locker, snapped his fingers lightly, and walked to an exit, carelessly, without hurry.

The gold-braided doorman at a magnificent entrance on Park Avenue greeted Larry with a respectful bow denoting a long acquaintance. Larry entered the elevator with just the right touch of nonchalant swagger. But he stopped and his gay smile vanished before an imposing door marked: CLAIRE VAN NUYS ESCORT BUREAU.

Larry hated the place and he hated his job. Each evening, night after night, he had to accompany fat dowagers, rich spinsters, and foolish, giggling out-of-town matrons on an endless round of dinners, suppers, dances, nightclubs. He had to bow gracefully, and smile enchantingly, and laugh, and dance, and throw tips to waiters as if he were a millionaire. He had to keep going an endless stream of charming, entertaining drivel, and listen to more drivel in answer, and try to know what he was talking about, while his thoughts ran miserably miles away, to a quiet little room and Sue's lonely shadow under the lamp.

At least, Sue did not know of this and she would never know. He would rather die than let her guess the kind of job he really had. It was respectable enough, oh yes, most respectable! Miss Van Nuys saw to that. But it was no job for a man, Larry felt. Still, he had to be grateful, for it was a job and it kept the little house at 745 Grant Street going.

Sue must never know of his sacrifice, the shy, quiet Sue who would be horrified at the thought of a nightclub and who had never seen one. At first, she had asked him timidly to take her out some night, but his anger had made her drop the subject, and she never asked it again. He could not let her enter one of those vile, noisy places where he was so well known, and his job as well. Besides, he was sick of the glitter, of the jazz, of the waiters.

He sighed, squared his shoulders for the night's ordeal, and walked into Miss Van Nuys' office. . . .

When Larry had left his house, Sue stood for a long time looking at the closed door, the money clutched in her hand. Then she took out the little tin box hidden deep in a kitchen drawer, and added the last dollar to her secret fund. It was a hundred dollars now, an even hundred, and this was the night she had been waiting for.

She had saved the money out of the household allowance, so carefully, with such painstaking little economies, for such a long time. Now she was ready. She went to a closet and took out her evening gown, her lovely blue, shimmering evening gown, which she had had no chance to wear for two years. She laid it out cautiously on the bed, and stood looking at it happily. For one night, for just one night, she would wear it, and dance, and laugh, and see one of those brilliant nightclubs she had heard so much about ever since she came to New York. She was deceiving Larry, she thought, but it was such a harmless deception! Just a few hours of dancing and some innocent fun, which Larry would not understand, the earnest, hardworking Larry who never thought of such things. She loved him so much, she was so happy in their little home, but the lonely evenings were so long, and she was still young, and she looked so pretty in her blue evening gown. Just one night . . . there was no harm in that, and Larry need never know.

It would be different if she allowed some man to take her out. But she wasn't going to. She was going to pay for it herself, and do it right, one hundred dollars for one grand, reckless smash. She had heard how it could be arranged safely and respectably. Her heart beating, she went to the phone.

In the office on Park Avenue, a trimly permanented, efficient secretary looked up at Larry Dean standing before her desk.

"Your assignment for tonight, Mr. Dean," she said, "will be dinner, dancing, best place in town, full dress clothes. You are to call in an hour for Mrs. Dean—no relation, I presume?—at 745 Grant Street."

Her Second Career

c. 1929

Editor's Preface

"Her Second Career" seems to date from 1929. It was probably written soon after Ayn Rand had begun working in the office of the RKO wardrobe department (a job she hated, but had to hold for three years, until she began to earn money by writing).

The subject matter of "Her Second Career" remains, in a broad sense, that of the early stories: the importance of values in human life. But here the focus is on the negative, on those who do not live life but merely posture at it, those who do something *other* than pursue values.

By 1929, Ayn Rand had a fund of observations on this subject: she had been working in and around Hollywood for three years. She respected the potential of the film medium, and she loved certain movies (her favorites were the great German Romantic silent films, with stars such as Conrad Veidt and Hans Albers, and directors such as Ernst Lubitsch and Fritz Lang). But she rejected out of hand the syrupy, platitudinous stories enshrining mediocrity, offering odes to "the boy next door" or "the sweet maiden next door." She despised what she saw as Hollywood's trite values, its undiscriminating taste, its "incommunicable vulgarity of spirit," as she put it in *The Romantic Manifesto*.

Unlike most critics, however, Ayn Rand did not ascribe the movies' low estate to "commercialism" or "box-office chasing." She singled out as the basic cause an inner mental practice or default, described by the hero in this story as follows:

> There's no one in this business with an honest idea of what's good and what's bad. And there's no one who's not scared green of having such an idea for himself. They're all sitting around waiting for someone to tell them. Begging someone to tell them. Anyone, just so they won't have to take the awful responsibility of judging and valuing on their own. So merit doesn't exist here.

The Fountainhead would not appear in print for fourteen years; but here is its author's first recognition in writing of the psychology of Peter Keating, the second-hander, the man who abdicates his inner sovereignty, then lives without real thought or values, as a parasite on the souls of others. Claire Nash in this story—again, a woman in the central role—is Peter Keating's earliest ancestor; she is the antonym of Irene in "The Husband I Bought"; she is the woman who does not even know that values exist.

"Her Second Career" is not, however, a psychological study or a serious analysis of secondhandedness. It is a satire and, like "Good Copy," an essentially jovial, lighthearted piece. (This story, too, is signed by "O. O. Lyons.") Claire, despite her character, is a mixed case, with enough virtue to be attracted to the hero. Moreover, events reveal that there is, after all, a place for merit, even in Hollywood, and this functions as a redeeming note, making the satire a relatively gentle element in the context of a romantic story, rather than a biting denunciation or a bitter commentary.

This story, I believe, is the last of the preliminary pieces composed by Miss Rand before she turned to her first major literary undertaking, her novel *We the Living*. Several signs of her increasing maturity are apparent. Winston Ayers and Heddy Leland are more recognizably Ayn Rand types of hero and heroine than any of the figures in earlier stories. Though there is still a certain foreign awkwardness and, as in "Good Copy," an overly broad tone at times, the writing as a whole is more assured. Parts of the story, especially on the set during the filming, are genuinely funny. Above all, "Her Second Career" presents, for the first time in the early pieces, an element essential to the mature Ayn Rand: an intriguing plot situation, integrated with the broader theme. On the whole, the logic of the events has been carefully worked out (although I have some doubt about Claire's motivation in accepting Ayers' wager, and about an element of chance that occurs near the end).

With developments such as these, the period of private writing exercises draws to a close. Ayn Rand is now ready for professional work.

A note on the text: three pages of the original manuscript are missing. To preserve the continuity, I have inserted in their place several paragraphs—about one-third the length of the missing pages—from an earlier version of the story which happens to have been preserved. The inserted material runs from the sentence "She reached the little hotel she was living in" through the sentence ". . . I am sure that I could not have found a better interpreter for my story."

—L. P.

Her Second Career

"*Heart's Desire* narrowly misses being the worst picture
of the year. The story is mossgrown and the direction
something we had better keep charitably silent about.
BUT . . . but Claire Nash is the star. And when this is
said, everything has been said. Her exquisite personality
illuminates the picture and makes you forget everything
but her own matchless magic. Her portrayal of the innocent country maiden will make a lump rise in the most
sophisticated throat. Hers is the genius that makes
Screen History. . . ."

The newspaper hanging lightly, rustling between two
pink-nailed fingertips, Claire Nash handed it to Winston
Ayers. Her mouth, bright, pink, and round as a straw-
berry, smiled lightly her subtlest smile of indulgent pity.
But her eyes, soft violets hidden among pine needles of
mascara, watched closely the great Winston Ayers
reading.

He read and handed the paper back to her without
a word.

"Well?" she asked.

"Perhaps I shouldn't have said what I said, Miss
Nash," he answered in his low, clear voice, and she could
not tell whether it was perfectly polite or perfectly mocking. "But you asked for my candid opinion, and when
I'm asked I usually give it."

"You still hold to that opinion?"

"Yes. Perhaps I should add I'm sorry."

She gave a little unnatural laugh which tried to be gay and friendly, but failed. "You realize that it's a rather . . . well, unusual opinion, Mr. Ayers, to put it gently?"

"Quite," he answered with a charming smile, "and I'm certain that it means nothing whatever."

"Quite," she was tempted to reply, but didn't. Of course, his opinion should mean nothing to Claire Nash, because she was Claire Nash. She had a palace in Beverly Hills and two Rolls-Royces, and she had immortalized the ideal of sweet maidenhood on the screen. For her, five gentlemen had committed suicide—one of them fatally—and she had had a breakfast cereal named in her honor. She was a goddess, and her shrines were scattered all over the world, little shrines of glass with a tiny window in front, through which an endless stream of coins poured night and day; and the sun never set on that golden stream. Why should she feel such anger at the insult of any single man?

But Winston Ayers had come to Hollywood, and Winston Ayers had been expected and invited and begged to come to Hollywood for more than three years. Winston Ayers was England's gift to the theaters of the world, or perhaps the theaters of the world had been a gift thrown into Winston Ayers' nonchalant, expert hands; and these hands had created without effort or notice such miracles of drama and laughter that Ayers' opening nights became riots, and from the theatrical pages of the world press there looked upon his worshiping public the face of a new playwright, a young playwright who looked bored. Winston Ayers had been offered one hundred thousand dollars for one screen story. And Winston Ayers had refused.

Claire Nash tightened the soft, luminous folds of her sky-blue negligee around her shoulders, pink as clouds of dawn over the satin sky. She bent her head wistfully to one shoulder, her head with the golden tangle of hair as a sun rising from the clouds, and she smiled the sweet smile of a helpless child which had made her famous. It had cost more sleepless nights and diplomacy than she cared to imagine for Mr. Bamburger, president of Wonder-

Pictures, to arrange this interview between his great star and the man he wished to become his great scenarist. Mr. Bamburger had hoped that Claire Nash would succeed where all had failed, as she usually did, and induce the Box-Office Name to sign. "Don't stop at the price," Mr. Bamburger had instructed her, and she hadn't known whether he had meant himself or her.

But the interview did not seem to succeed. For the Box-Office Name had said a thing . . . a thing . . . well, she would not care to repeat it to Mr. Bamburger nor to anyone else.

The soft twilight of her dressing room hid the angry little flash of red on Claire's cheeks. She looked at the man who sat before her. He was tall, young, inexplicable. He had very clear, very cold eyes, and when he spoke, he narrowed his eyelids with a strange, slow movement that seemed to insult whatever he was looking at; she hated the movement, yet found herself watching eagerly to see it. "Much too handsome for a writer," she decided in her mind.

"So you think," she began bravely, "that screen actresses . . ." She could not force herself to finish the sentence.

". . . are not worth writing for," he finished it for her courteously, just as courteously as he had said it before, in the same even, natural voice that seemed utterly unconscious of the bombshell his words set off in her mind.

"Of course . . ." She fumbled desperately for something brilliant and shattering to say. "Of course, I . . ." She failed and ended up in a furious hurry of stumbling words. "Of course I wouldn't hold myself as an example of a great screen actress, far from it, but there are others who . . ."

"On the contrary," he said charmingly, "on the contrary. You are the perfect example of a great screen actress, Miss Nash." And she didn't know whether she should smile gratefully or throw him out.

The pink telephone on a crystal stand by her side rang sharply. She took the receiver.

"Hello? . . . Yes. . . ." She listened attentively. She wasn't yawning, but her voice sounded suddenly as if she were. "My dear, how many times do I have to say it? It was final. . . . No. . . . A definite no! . . . To the Henry Jinx Films as well. . . . I'm sorry."

She let the receiver drop from her hand and leaned back on the pillows of her chaise longue, little sparks glittering through the mascara needles. "My manager," she explained lazily. "My contract here expires after this picture, and all the studios are hounding the poor man to death. I wish he wouldn't bother me about it."

This was what she said; what she wanted to say was: "You see?"

The telephone rang again before she had a chance to observe the effect.

"Hello? . . . Who? . . . About Heddy Leland?" Claire's face changed suddenly. Her round cheeks drew up with a jerk and swallowed her eyes, so that there were no violets left, but only two slits of black needles across her face, sticking out like iron lances lowered for battle; and no fan would have recognized the sweet, world-famous voice in the shrill barks showered suddenly upon the pink receiver which seemed to blush under the flow: "You dare ask me again? . . . No! I said, no! . . . I won't allow it! I never want to see that girl on my set again! . . . I don't give a damn about her excuses! . . . You heard me? I'm not accustomed to repeating twice! . . . And I hope, my dear Mr. Casting Director, that you won't bother me again for any five-dollar extra!"

She slammed the receiver down so hard that the crystal stand rang under it with a thin, musical whine. Then she noticed an expression, an actual expression in the eyes of Winston Ayers, the first she had seen in them: it was an expression of mocking astonishment. The look on her face did not quite suit the ideal of sweet maidenhood; she realized that.

She shrugged her beautiful shoulders impatiently. "An insolent extra," she tried to explain calmly. "Imagine, today, on the set, I was doing my best scene—oh, what a scene! I had had such a hard time getting into the mood of it—and I'm so sensitive to things like that—and just as I got it, right in the midst of it, that creature tumbled from the sidelines straight into me! Almost knocked me down! Of course, the scene was ruined. We had to retake it and I couldn't do it again! Because of an extra!"

"She did it on purpose, of course?" he asked lightly, and the tone of his voice answered his own question.

"I don't care! She said someone pushed her. It makes no difference. I told them I won't have her on my set again!" She took a cigarette, then broke it and flung the pieces away. "Let us return to our interesting subject, Mr. Ayers. You were saying . . ."

"I'll enter anyway!" a young, ringing voice exploded suddenly behind the door. The door flew open. Something wild, tall, disheveled burst in, slammed the door behind, and stood suddenly still.

The girl wore a tight little suit that ended abruptly above the knees of two strong, thin, exquisite legs. The legs seemed grown fast to the floor, straight and taut; the light from the pink lamp cut a thin, glittering line on each stocking, and they looked like two jets from a fountain, flung up and frozen. She seemed to be standing on tiptoe, but it was only her small, high-heeled pumps that made her seem so, the pumps and the tenseness of her slim body stopped abruptly in flight. Her short hair was thrown back in disorder, as it had been left after she had torn off her screen costume, and a thin line of greasepaint still showed at the edge of her forehead. Her face had odd, irregular lines, impish and solemn and somber all at once. Her eyes, immense, glittering, incredible, were dark and still.

Claire Nash jumped to her feet and stood looking at the intruder, her little mouth hanging open in amazement.

"Excuse me for entering like this, Miss Nash," said the girl. Her voice was unexpectedly steady, as if she had had time to pull some reins within her and to bring it under control.

"Why . . . Heddy Leland!" Claire stammered, incredulous and suffocated.

"Your secretary wouldn't let me enter," the girl said evenly, "but I had to enter. It was my last opportunity to see you. If they send me away tonight, I won't be able to get on the lot again."

"Miss Leland, I . . . I really fail to understand how . . ." Claire began grandly, and ended much more naturally, exploding, "Of all the brazen nerve . . . !"

"Please excuse me and listen to me, Miss Nash," the girl said quietly and firmly. "It was not my fault. I am very sorry. I ask your forgiveness. I promise you that it will never happen again."

Claire seated herself slowly on the chaise longue and draped the blue folds of the negligee carelessly and majestically about her. She was beginning to enjoy it. She said leisurely:

"No, it will never happen again. Haven't you understood that I do not want you back on my set?"

"Yes. I have. That's why I came. I thought that perhaps you hadn't understood what my work here meant to me. I was promised two weeks. Please, allow me to remain. I . . ." She hesitated for the first time. "I . . . need it very much."

"Really?" said Claire. "Were you under the impression that a studio is a charitable institution?"

The girl's lean, tanned cheeks blushed very slightly, so slightly that Winston Ayers was alone to notice it. She made an effort, as if forcing herself on against an overwhelming desire to say something quite different from what she actually said in her level, steady voice:

"Forgive me. You are quite right. It was in very bad taste on my part to mention that. That doesn't matter. But, you see, I'm just starting in Hollywood. It's difficult to get an opening, even for extra work, to be seen. My whole career may depend on what I do in this picture."

"Your whole career?" said Claire sweetly. "But, my dear girl, what makes you think that you have a career before you?"

The girl hadn't expected it. She looked at Claire closely. Two soft, mocking dimples creased Claire's cheeks. She continued, shrugging, "There are thousands and thousands of girls like you in Hollywood and every one of them thinks she has a career waiting for her."

"But . . ."

"Let me give you some advice, Miss Leland. Friendly advice—really, I don't hold that little incident against you. Think of the thing you can do best—then go and do it. Forget the movies. I am more experienced than you are and I know the business: the screen is not for you."

"Miss Nash . . ."

"Oh, don't say it's heartbreaking and all that! Let me tell you the truth. You are not particularly pretty. Thousands of better-looking girls are starving here. You haven't a chance. It really doesn't matter whether you work here or not. You won't get far anyway. Go back home and try to marry some nice, respectable fellow. That would be the best thing for you."

Heddy Leland looked at her; looked at the man who sat silently watching them.

"Please excuse my intrusion, Miss Nash," she said as if she were reciting disjointed words without meaning, for her voice had no expression at all. She turned and walked out and closed the door evenly behind her. The soft curtains of peach velvet rustled and billowed slightly and fell back to immobility.

Claire lit a cigarette with magnificent disdain.

"Why did you give that advice to the girl?" Winston Ayers asked.

"Oh!" Wrinkles gathered on Claire's pretty little nose. "Oh, it makes me sick! When I see one of those girls who gets five bucks a day and wants to be a star! Everybody wants to be a star. They think that to be a star means nothing at all!"

"Precisely, Miss Nash. It means *nothing at all.*"

Claire spilled ashes on her blue satin without noticing it. "You're saying that to me?" she breathed.

"I was under the impression," he answered, "that I had said it before. You were kind enough to inquire why I refuse to write for Hollywood. Perhaps I can make myself clear now. You see, I believe that screen actresses are not great artists, rare talents, exceptions. They are not one in a thousand, they are just one out of the thousand, chosen by . . ."

"By?"

". . . *chance.*"

Claire said nothing. No proper words would come to her.

"Look about you," he continued. "Thousands and

thousands of girls struggle for a place in the movies. Some are as beautiful as you are, and some are more beautiful. All can act as you act. Have they a right to fame and stardom? Just as much or just as little as you have."

"Do you realize," said Claire, and her voice made funny little gurgling sounds in her throat, but she was past caring about her voice or what it said, "do you realize, Mr. Ayers, that you are speaking to a woman who is considered one of the world's geniuses?"

"The world," said Winston Ayers, "would never have seen that genius, if someone hadn't told it so—by chance."

"Really," Claire stammered, "I don't mean to be begging for compliments, Mr. Ayers, but . . ."

"Neither do I mean to be insulting, Miss Nash. But look at it objectively. There's no one in this business with an honest idea of what's good and what's bad. And there's no one who's not scared green of having such an idea for himself. They're all sitting around waiting for someone to tell them. Begging someone to tell them. Anyone, just so they won't have to take the awful responsibility of judging and valuing on their own. So merit doesn't exist here. What does exist is someone's ballyhoo which all the others are only too glad to follow. And the ballyhoo starts with less discrimination and from less respectable sources than the betting at a racetrack. Only this is more of a gamble, because at a track all the horses are at least given a chance to run."

Claire rose. "Most unusual, Mr. Ayers," she said, smiling icily. "I do wish we could continue this stimulating discussion. But I am so sorry, I do have an early call on the set tomorrow and . . ."

"Keep this, Miss Nash," he said, rising, "as a little memento of me. You have made your career. I do not ask how you made it. You are famous, great, admired. You are considered one of the world's geniuses. But you could not make a *second career*."

Claire stopped; looked at him; walked back to him.

"A second career? What do you mean?"

"Just that. If you were to start at the beginning now, you would see how easy it is to get your talent recognized. You'd see how many people would notice it. How many people would be eager to notice. How pleasant they would make it for you. How many of them would give a damn!"

"Sit down," she ordered. He obeyed. "What are you driving at?"

He looked at her, and his eyelids narrowed. And he explained exactly what he was driving at. Claire Nash sat before him, her mouth open, her eyes swimming in fascinated terror.

"Well?" he asked.

She hesitated. But there was one thing to Claire Nash: she believed in her own greatness, deeply, passionately, devotedly. Her belief was the warm glow that greeted her when she awakened each morning; that filled her days with radiance; that rose over the set, brighter than the arc lights, and drove her to her best scenes; that shone, as a halo, over her head when she passed other women in the street, those women who were not like her. It was true that she had married a producer's nephew many years ago, at the beginning of her career, and divorced him since; but that had been only a short-cut and it proved nothing. Her genius alone could open the gates of Hollywood again and as many times as she wished. Besides, there was the tall man with the narrowed eyelids before her. She liked him—she hated to admit it—yes, she liked him definitely. Most definitely. She knew suddenly that she wanted to see him again. What triumph there would be in making him retract all those words, in seeing him bow, him, like all those countless others!

"Well?" he repeated.

She raised her head and laughed suddenly.

"Of course," she said. "I'll do it."

He looked at her and bowed graciously.

"Miss Nash," he said, "I admire you—for the first time."

She was angry at herself for the senseless pleasure these words gave her.

"Well, then, remember," he continued. "You are starting all over again, at the very beginning. You are taking your real name—Jane Roberts, isn't it? You allow yourself no more money than an average extra girl can have. You know no one in Hollywood. No one has ever heard of you. I wish you luck."

"I shan't need it," said Claire gaily.

"Then, when you have seen what you shall see, you can return to your stardom and bring Claire Nash back. I hope she will enjoy her fame in a somewhat different manner then."

"We'll see."

"And to prove to you the other side of my theory, Miss Nash," he said, "while you try to break into the movies, I'll make a star out of an extra, any extra, the first one we choose—say, out of that little Heddy Leland who was here."

A burst of ringing laughter was the answer.

Claire Nash was leaving for Europe. She had finished her last picture and was going to take, as the newspapers had explained, a much needed vacation.

When the hour came for her to enter the luxurious car of the Chief, a mob of fans was there to see her departure. She appeared, slow, regal, radiant as a sunrise. She crossed the platform through the waves of flowers and worshipers. Newsmen snapped pictures of her, one thin pump poised gracefully on the car step, a huge bouquet hiding the rest of her, all but the blond head bent wistfully to one shoulder, a trim little French hat pulled low over one eye, the lips smiling sadly and gently. Three reporters asked questions she could not hear through the roar, and wrote down answers they never heard. A sob sister rammed her spectacles into Claire's ear, and screamed demands to know Claire's opinion on the European war situation, which Claire gave solemnly and which the woman wrote down in mad haste not to lose a single precious word. The fans fought for a rose that had fallen from Claire's bouquet. A woman fainted. It rained. Policemen worked hard to maintain order. Six citizens were hurt.

The train moved. Standing on the observation platform, Claire Nash bowed graciously to right and left, smiled sweetly and waved a tiny lace handkerchief. . . .

No passenger paid any attention when, at the first

stop, a slender little woman in gray slipped quietly from the train. When the train moved again, no one knew that behind the forbidding locked door of Claire Nash's compartment, there was no star left, but only a prim, slightly bewildered secretary going on alone for a much needed vacation.

The slender woman in a plain gray coat took the first train back to Los Angeles. Claire Nash was gone, was far away on her journey to Europe. Jane Roberts was coming to Hollywood to break into the movies.

"The story will be ready in two weeks, Mr. Bamburger."

"Oh, Mr. Ayers!"

"One hundred thousand dollars?"

"Yes, Mr. Ayers."

"We sign?"

"Yes, indeed, yes, Mr. Ayers."

Mr. Bamburger pushed the papers forward, thrust a fountain pen toward the hand of the man before him, as if fearing that the hand might change its mind, missed, dropped the pen to the floor, and saw a gurgling spot of blue spread on the rug. Mr. Bamburger plunged down for it, jammed the pen into the man's hand, and mopped his forehead, adding streaks of blue to the shining glow of perspiration. Mr. Bamburger prided himself on his self-control, but here, in his office, at his desk, sat the great Winston Ayers in person, and the great Winston Ayers had surrendered!

"I supervise the production of the story?"

"Certainly, Mr. Ayers."

"I choose the director?"

"Yes, Mr. Ayers."

"And remember, Mr. Bamburger: I choose the cast."

"Yes, Mr. Ayers."

"Can't promise anything. But we might be using crowds later. Drop in next week."

Heddy Leland repeated to herself the words of the casting director in his short, indifferent voice. "Next week . . . for the sixth time," she added in her own voice, soft and tired.

She was walking home from the studio, from the seventh studio she had visited that day. The answers in the others had been the same. No, not quite the same. She had waited for two hours in one of them, only to be told that the casting director would see no one else today. In another, an assistant, a skinny boy with a dripping nose, had said: "Nothing today, sister," and when she had tried to remind him of his boss' promise, he had snapped: "Who's running this place? Get going, sister."

Six weeks without work. Forty-two days of getting up in the morning, dressing herself like a Parisian doll—while being careful that no one should notice the tears in her silk stockings, hidden by her pumps, the tears in her lace blouse, hidden by her trim jacket—walking into a casting office, asking the same question with the same smile and the same sinking of the heart; and hearing the same answer, always, each day, for all eternity.

She reached the little hotel she was living in. "Did the Henry Jinx Films call me, Mrs. Johns?" she asked at the desk, her voice trembling a little.

"Miss Leland? . . . Let's see . . . the Henry Jinx Films—yes. They called. A message: they are sorry, but they have nothing right now. They hope that next week . . ."

Heddy was sitting on the bed, in her room, her elbows in the pillow and her chin in her hands, in a dark meditation, when the telephone rang, with a dry, sharp noise.

"Hello."

"Miss Leland?"

"Yes."

"This is Wonder Pictures. Mr. Bamburger wants to see you at once."

"Mr. Bamb—"

"Mr. Bamburger, yes. At once."

"Miss Leland—Mr. Ayers." Mr. Bamburger introduced them. Winston Ayers looked at her with his slow, cold, curious look. She looked at him with her calm, dark, resolute eyes. He opened his eyelids slightly wider. Hers remained motionless.

"I am very glad to meet you, Miss Leland," he said in his slow, charming voice, a smiling voice from serious lips, "and I am sure that I could not have found a better interpreter for my story."

"I am very grateful for your choice, Mr. Ayers," she answered evenly, "and I shall try to live up to it."

Winston Ayers looked at her again. He knew that only a few minutes ago, Mr. Bamburger had told this girl that the great author himself had chosen her for the part which Hollywood's biggest stars dreamed of playing. She seemed too calm, much too calm. He shrugged his shoulders and turned away, his eyes narrowing indifferently, as Mr. Bamburger resumed his nervous, hurried speech; but he found himself looking again at the strange, thin profile, the long lashes, the hard, set mouth. It isn't indifference in her, he thought, it's something else. He wished suddenly to know the something else, even if he had to break the arrogant little creature to learn it.

The tips of her fingers pressed to the edge of Mr. Bamburger's desk, the only thing to keep her from swaying and falling before them, Heddy Leland had the strength to stand still, to listen, to hear Mr. Bamburger saying: ". . . for this one picture only . . . three hundred dollars a week . . . as a beginning . . . the future depends on your work. . . ." Then Winston Ayers' slow voice: "You'll have the script at once, Miss Leland, and you can get acquainted with the part of Queen Lani."

Her round cheeks rouged delicately, her blond curls fluttering in the wind, under the brim of her cheapest little hat (she was being honest about it, for the hat had cost a mere thirty dollars and it was most becoming!), a huge round collar of blinding white lace billowing under her chin, Claire Nash was the very picture of sweet girlhood on its way to see the casting director of the Henry Jinx Film Company.

She had a hard time trying not to smile and she lowered her eyes modestly, to keep from looking at the passersby and from betraying in one laughing glance her whole mad adventure. She had been bored in Hollywood for so many months, and she did not remember such a thrilling morning for a long, long time.

She saw the Henry Jinx Studio rise before her, white, majestic, and royally welcoming, as she turned a corner.

With her brisk, assured, graceful little step, she walked up the broad, polished steps to the glittering entrance. A sign stopped her. It was a dirty little cardboard sign with crooked letters drawn by hand: CASTING OFFICE AROUND THE CORNER. It hung there as a silent insult. She made a little grimace, shrugged gaily, and walked obediently around the corner.

The thing whose narrow door carried the faded sign CASTING OFFICE was not a building, was not even a shack. It was a dump heap of old boards, upon which no one had wanted to waste the precaution of beams or the courtesy of paint. It seemed to announce silently for whose entrance it had been designed and what the studio thought of those who entered here. Claire had not turned that corner for many years. She stopped, because she thought unreasonably that someone had just slapped her in the face. Then she shrugged, not quite so gaily, and entered.

The room before her had a floor, a ceiling, four walls, and two wooden benches. All these must have been clean sometime, Claire thought, but she doubted it. Without looking left or right, she walked straight to the little window in the wall across the room.

A blond, round-faced, short-nosed youth looked at her and yawned.

"I want to see the casting director," said Claire; she had meant to say it; she commanded, instead.

"Gotta wait your turn," the youth answered indifferently.

She sat down on the corner of a bench. She was not alone. There were others, all waiting for the casting director. A tall, red-haired girl in a tight black dress with flowing sleeves of blue chiffon, tomato-red lips, no stockings, and a slave-bracelet on the left ankle. A tall, athletic young gentleman with dark, languorous eyes, a very neat haircut, and a not so neat shirt collar. A stout woman with a red face, a man's overcoat, and a drooping ostrich plume on her hat. An assortment of short, plump little things who remained determinedly "flappers," with fat legs squeezing out of shoes many sizes too small. A sloppy woman with an overdressed child.

Claire pulled her skirt closer to her and tried to look

at nothing but the window. She did not know how long she sat there. But she knew that time was passing, for she noticed the flappers producing their compacts and remaking their faces several times. She would permit herself no such vulgarity in public. She sat still. Her right leg went to sleep, from the knee down. She waited.

A door banged against a wall like an explosion. She saw the flash of a man's heavy stomach and above it the face of an angry bulldog, which, she realized in a few seconds, was the man's face after all. "Who's first?" he barked.

Claire rose hastily. Something streaked past her toward the door, hurling her aside roughly in its progress; the door was slammed before she realized that it had been one of the flappers and heard consciously the angry words left in its wake: "Wait your turn, sneak!"

Claire sat down again. She felt damp beads on her upper lip. She took out her compact and remade her face.

Her turn came an hour later. She walked into the next room slowly, conscious of the precise grace of each moving muscle, timing her entrance as carefully as if she were advancing toward a grinding camera.

"Well?" snapped the bulldog behind the desk, without raising his eyes from the papers before him.

Well, thought Claire, what did one say here? She was suddenly, utterly blank. She smiled helplessly, waiting desperately for him to raise his head; no words would be necessary then. He raised his head and looked at her blankly. "Well?" he repeated impatiently.

"I . . . I want to work in pictures," she stammered foolishly. It was foolish, she thought, and it was not her fault; couldn't he tell at a glance what he had before him and what he should do about it?

It seemed as if he couldn't. He wasn't even looking at her, but was pulling some paper forward.

"Ever done extra work before?"

"*Extra* work?"

"That's what I asked."

"*Extra work?*"

"Yes, madam!"

She wanted to argue, to explain, but something choked

her, and what did come out of her throat was not what she had intended to say at all:

"No, I'm just beginning my career."

The man pushed the paper aside.

"I see. . . . Well, we don't use extras who've had no previous experience."

"Extras?"

"Say, what's the matter with you? Did you mean to ask for a bit straight off the bat?"

"A . . . a bit?"

"Lady, we have no time to waste here." He pushed the door open with his foot. "Who's next?"

There was no reason, Claire Nash was telling herself as she walked out into the street, there was no reason to take the whole farce so seriously. No reason at all, she was saying, while she twisted the handle of her bag till she wrenched it off and went on, the bag dangling violently on a broken strap.

But she went on. She went to the Epic Pictures Studio, and three hours later saw its casting director.

"Ever been in pictures before?" the lean, weary, skeptical gentleman asked as if her answer were the last thing in the world he cared to hear.

"No!" she answered flatly, as a challenge.

"No experience?"

"But . . . no. No experience."

"Whatchur name?"

"Clai—Jane Roberts."

"Well, Miss Roberts," he yawned, "we do not make a practice of it, but we could . . ." he yawned, ". . . use you someday, let you try, when . . ." he yawned, ". . . oh, dear me! . . . when we have a very big crowd of extras. Leave your name and phone number with my secretary. Can't promise anything. Come and remind us—next week. . . ."

When a month had passed, Claire Nash had heard "Next week" four times each from six studios; from three others she heard nothing—their casting directors did not interview beginners; from the last one there was nothing to hear—its casting director was away on a trip to Europe to scout for new screen talent.

*   *   *

His eyes fixed, thoughtful, more troubled than he cared to show, Winston Ayers watched the shooting of the first scenes. Work on *Child of Danger,* his story, had begun. He was watching—with an emotion which made him angry and which he could not control—the camera and that which stood before the camera. For before the camera stood an old fortress wall, a mighty giant of huge, rough stones; and on the wall was Queen Lani.

Queen Lani was the heroine of his story, a wild, sparkling, fantastic creature, queen of a barbarous people in the age of legends; a cruel, lawless, laughing little tyrant who crushed nations under her bare feet. He had seen her vaguely, uncertainly in his dreams. And now she was here, before him, more alive, more strange, more tempting than he had ever imagined her, more "Queen Lani" than the Queen Lani of his script. He looked at her, stricken, motionless.

Her hair flying in the wind, her slim body wrapped only in a bright, shimmering shawl, her naked legs, arms, and shoulders hard as bronze, her huge eyes glittering with menace and laughter, Heddy Leland sat on the rocks of the wall, under the eyes of the cameras, a reckless, wild, incredible, dazzling queen looking down at her limitless dominions.

There was a dead silence on the set. Werner von Halz, the scornful, aristocratic imported director, bit his megaphone in a frenzy of admiration.

"Dat," pronounced Mr. von Halz, pointing a fat finger at the girl, "dat iss de virst real actress I efer vork vit!"

Mr. Bamburger nodded, mopped his forehead, dropped his handkerchief, forgot to pick it up, nodded again, and whispered to the silent man beside him:

"Some find, eh, Mr. Ayers?"

"I . . . I didn't know . . . I didn't expect . . ." Winston Ayers stammered, without tearing his eyes from the girl.

When the scene was over, he approached her as she stepped off the wall.

"It was splendid," he said, tensely, harshly, as if grudgingly, his eyes dark between half-closed, insulting eyelids.

"Thank you, Mr. Ayers," she answered; her voice was polite and meaningless; she turned abruptly and walked away.

"I want," Mr. Bamburger was shouting, "I want articles in all the fan magazines! I want interviews and I want them syndicated! I want photos—where's that fool Miller, has he been sleeping?—photos in bathing suits and without bathing suits! Wonder-Pictures' new discovery! Discovery, hell! Wonder-Pictures' new gold mine!"

Claire Nash struggled, wept, wrote letters, wasted nickels in phone booths, fought for and obtained an interview at Central Casting.

She sat—trembling and stammering, unable to control her part any longer and the part running away with her—before the desk of a thin, gentle, pitiless woman who looked like a missionary. Central Casting ruled the destinies of thousands of extras; it flung opportunities and ten-dollar-a-day calls by the hundreds each single day. Wasn't there, Claire begged with an indignation merging into tears, wasn't there room for one more?

The woman behind the desk shook her head.

"I am sorry, Miss Roberts," she said precisely and efficiently, "but we do not register beginners. We have thousands of experienced people who have spent years in the business and who are starving. We cannot find enough work for them. We are trying to cut our lists in every way possible, not augment them with novices."

"But I . . . I . . ." stammered Claire, "I *want* to be an actress! I may have a great talent . . . I . . . God! I *know* I have a great talent!"

"Very possible," said the woman sweetly and shatteringly. "But so say ten thousand others. It is very ill advised, Miss Roberts, for a lovely, inexperienced young girl like you to be thinking of this hard, heartbreaking business. Very ill advised. . . . Of course," she added, as Claire rose brusquely, "of course, if your situation is . . . well, difficult, we can suggest an organization which undertakes to provide the fare back home for worthy girls who . . ."

Claire forgot her part for the moment; she did a thing

which no beginner would have dared to do: she rushed out and slammed the door behind her.

They are fools, Claire thought, sitting in her hotel room, all of them just blind, lazy fools. It was their job to find talent, yet they did not see it, because . . . because it seemed that they didn't give a damn. Who had said that to her before, so long ago? Then she remembered who had said it, and the cold, mocking eyes of the speaker, and she jumped to her feet with a new determination; a new determination and a brand-new feeling of loneliness.

If they had no eyes to see for themselves, she decided, she would show them. If it's acting experience they want, she would throw the experience in their faces. She started on a round of the little theaters that flourished like mushrooms on Hollywood's darkest corners. She learned that one did not get paid for acting in the wretched little barns, because the "chance to be *seen*" was considered payment enough for the weeks of rehearsals. She was willing to accept this, even though she did wonder dimly how she would have been able to accept it were she a real beginner left alone to struggle on her own earnings. But her willingness brought no results. In four of the theaters, she was told that they employed no one without previous stage experience. In three others, her name and phone number were taken with the promise of a call "if anything came up," a promise made in such a tone of voice that she knew this would be the end of it, and it was.

But in the eighth theater, the fat, oily manager took one look at the thirty-dollar hat and bowed her eagerly into his office.

"But of course, Miss Roberts," he gushed enthusiastically, "of course! You are born for the screen. You have the makings of a star, a first-class star! Trust me, I'm an old horse in this business and I know. But talent's gotta be seen. That's the secret in Hollywood. You gotta be *seen*. Now I have just the play for you and a part—boy, what a part! One part like this and you're made. Only, unfortunately, our production has been delayed because of financial difficulties, most unfortunate. Now, two hundred dollars, for instance, wouldn't be too much for you to invest in a future that would bring you millio— Well," said the manager to his secretary, blinking at the slammed door, "what do you suppose is the matter with her?"

The agents, Claire thought, the agents; they made their money on discovering new talent and they would be honest about seeking it. Why hadn't she thought of them before?

She was careful to call only on those agents who had never met Claire Nash in person. She found that the precaution was unnecessary: she was never admitted any farther than the exquisite, soft-carpeted waiting rooms, modernistic riots of glass, copper, and chromium, where trim secretaries sighed regretfully, apologizing because Mr. Smith or Jones or Brown was so busy in conference; but if Miss Roberts would leave her telephone number, Mr. Smith would be sure and call her. Miss Roberts left the number. The call never came.

The agents who had no waiting rooms and no chromium, but only a hole facing a brick wall, and a mid-Victorian armchair shedding dirty cotton upon a spotted rug, were delighted to meet Miss Roberts and to place her name upon the lists of their distinguished clients; which was as much as they were able to accomplish for Miss Roberts.

One of them, tall and unshaved, seemed more delighted to meet her than all the others. "You have come to the right man, kid," he assured her, "the right man. You know Joe Billings down at Epic Pictures? The assistant director? Well, Joe's a partic'lar friend of mine and he's got a lotta pull at Epic. All I gotta do is slip a coupla words to Joe and bingo! you get a screen test. A real, genuine screen test. How about dinner tonight down at my place, kiddo?" She fled.

Her face . . . her face that had been called "one of the screen's treasures" so often . . . her face seemed to make no impression on anyone. With a single exception. One of the agents, whom she had never seen before, did look at her closely for a long moment, and then he exclaimed:

"By God but you're a dead ringer for Claire Nash, sister!"

Then he looked again, shook his head, and changed his mind.

"Nope," he said, "not exactly. Claire's eyes are lighter, and her mouth smaller, and she's got it over you as far as the figure's concerned. Great friend of mine, Claire. . . . Tell you what we'll do: you leave your phone number and I'll get you a swell job as Claire's stand-in. You look like her—or near enough for that. Only we'll have to wait—she's away in Europe right now."

Jane Roberts' opportunity came; not exactly in the way she had expected it to come, but it came anyhow.

One evening, as she sat on the bed in her stuffy hotel room, her slippers flung into a corner and her feet aching miserably, a neighbor came in to ask if she hadn't two nickels for a dime. The neighbor was a tall, cadaverous girl with a long nose and seven years of movie-extra experience.

"No luck around the studios, eh?" she asked sympathetically, seeing Claire's eyes. "It's tough, kid, that's what it is, tough. I know." Then she brightened suddenly. "Say, want a bit of work for tomorrow?"

Claire jumped to her feet as if her life depended on it.

"You see," the girl was explaining, "they got a big crowd tomorrow morning and my friend, the propman, got me in and I'm sure he can fix it up for you too."

"Oh, yes!" Claire gasped. "Oh, yes, please!"

"The call's for eight in the morning—ready and made-up on the set. We'll have to be at the studio at six-thirty. I'll go phone the boy friend, but I'm sure it'll be okay."

She was turning to leave the room, when Claire asked:

"What studio is it and what picture?"

"The Wonder-Pictures Studio," the girl answered. "*Child of Danger,* you know, their big special with that new star of theirs—Heddy Leland."

Claire Nash sat, shivering with cold, in the corner of a bus. Snorting and groaning, the bus rambled on its way to the studio through the dark, empty, desolate streets of early morning. The bus shook like a cocktail shaker on wheels, jumbling its passengers against one another, throwing them up at each rut, to fall and bounce upon the sticky leather seats. All the passengers had the same destination—with their tired faces and old, greasy makeup boxes.

Claire felt cold and broken. Her eyelids felt like cotton and closed themselves against her will. She thought dully, dimly, through the crazy unreality around her, that a director, a real director, would know genius when he saw it.

She was still thinking it as she trudged wearily through the gates of the Wonder-Pictures Studio. Claire Nash had worked for seven years on the Wonder-Pictures lot. But it was for the first time in her life that she entered it through the shabby side-gate of the "Extra Talent Entrance." She kept her head bowed cautiously and her scarf under her nose, not to be recognized. She soon found that she had nothing to fear: no one could pick her out in the dismal stampede of gray shadows streaming past the casting office window; no one could and no one showed any inclination to try. The boy in the window handed her her work ticket without raising his head or looking at her. "Hurry up!" her companion prodded her impatiently, and Claire started running with the others in the mad rush to the wardrobe.

Three stern-faced, gloomy-eyed, frozen individuals in shirtsleeves stood behind a wooden counter, distributing the extras' costumes. They fished the first rags they could reach out of three hampers filled with filthy junk and pushed them across the counter into uncomplaining hands. When Claire's turn came, the lordly individual threw at her something heavy, huge, discolored, with dirty pieces of faded gold ribbon, with a smell of stale makeup and perspiration. "Your ticket?" he ordered briefly, extending his hand for it.

"I don't like this costume," Claire declared, horrified.

The man looked at her incredulously.

"Well, isn't that just too bad!" he observed, seized her ticket, punched it, and turned, with an armful of rags, to the next woman in line.

The extras' dressing room was cold as a cellar, colder than the frozen air outside. With stiff fingers, Claire undressed and struggled into her costume. She looked into a mirror and closed her eyes. Then, with an effort, she looked again: the huge garment could have contained easily three persons of her size; the thick folds gathered clumsily into a lump on her stomach; she tried to adjust them, but they slipped right back to her stomach again; she was awkward, obese, disfigured.

Suffocating, she sat down on a wooden bench before a little crooked mirror on a filthy, unpainted wooden counter—to make up her face. But she knew little about screen makeup and had long since forgotten what she had known. For the last seven years she had had her own expert makeup man who knew how to correct the little defects of her face. Now she realized suddenly that her eyes were a little too narrow; that her cheeks were a little too broad; that she had a slight double chin. She sat twisting the greasy tube helplessly in her fingers, trying to remember and do the best she could.

Around her, the big barrack was full of busy, noisy, hurrying and gossiping females. She saw half-naked, shivering bodies and flabby muscles, vapor fluttering from mouths with every word, barbarian tunics and underwear—not very clean underwear.

She was about to rise when a strong hand pushed her down again.

"What's the hurry, dearie? Put on yar wig, willya?"

A short, plump girl in a blue smock stood before her, with hairpins in her mouth and in her hand something that looked like the fur of a very unsanitary poodle.

"*That* . . . for me?" Claire gasped. "But . . . but I'm blond! I . . . I can't wear a black wig!"

"D'ya suppose we got time to monkey around with every one of ya?" the girl asked, swishing the hairpins in her mouth. "Ya can't have bobbed hair in this picture. It's the ancient times, this is. Take what ya get. We ain't gonna bother about the color of two hundred heads!"

"But it will look awful!"

"Well, who do ya think ya are? It will ruin the picture, I suppose, will it?"

The wig was too small. The hairdresser rammed it down till it squeezed Claire's temples like a vise. She wound a huge turban over it to keep it in place, and stuck a dozen hairpins inside with such violence that she skinned Claire's skull.

"Now ya're okay. Hurry up, ya got five minutes left to get on the set."

Claire threw a last glance in the mirror. The black poodle fur hung in rags over her face; the huge turban slid down to her eyes; she looked like a mushroom with a lump in the middle. She was safe; no one would recognize her; she couldn't recognize herself.

"Ef-fry-body on de set!" Werner von Halz roared through his megaphone.

Obedient as a herd, the huge crowd filled the stone-paved yard of Queen Lani's castle. Four hundred pairs of eyes rose expectantly to the high platform where Mr. von Halz's majestic figure stood among seven cameras.

In the solemn silence, Mr. von Halz's voice rang imperiously:

"Vat you haff to do iss diss. Der iss a var going on and your country she hass just von a great fictory. Your queen announces it to you from her castle vall. You greet de news mitt vild joy."

The mighty castle rose proudly to the clear, blue sky, a giant of impregnable granite and plaster in a forest of wooden scaffoldings and steel wires. An army of overalls moved swiftly through the castle, placing metal sheets and mirrors in, under, above the ramparts. The hot rays of the sun focused on the crowd. Hasty, nervous assistant directors rushed through the mob, placing extras all over the set.

Claire followed every assistant with an eager, hopeful glance. No one noticed her. She was not chosen for the best, prominent spots. And when, once, an assistant pointed her out to another, that other shook his head: "No, not that one!"

The cameramen were bent over their cameras, tense, motionless, studying the scene. Werner von Halz watched critically through a dark lens.

"A shadow in de right corner!" he was ordering. "Kill dat light on your left! . . . I vant sefen more people on dose steps. . . . Break dat line! You're not soldiers on a parade! . . . Dun't bunch up like sardines on vun spot! Spread all ofer de yard! . . . All right!" he ordered at last. "Let's try it!"

Heddy Leland's slim, quick figure appeared on the castle wall. She spoke. The crowd roared without moving, only hundreds of arms shot vigorously in every direction, as though practicing their daily dozen.

"Stop! Hold it!!" Werner von Halz roared. "Iss dat de vay people iss glad? Iss dat de vay you vould meet your queen speaking of fictory? Now try to tink she iss saying dat you are going to haff lunch at vunce! Let's see how you vill meet dat!"

Queen Lani spoke again. Her subjects greeted her words enthusiastically. Mr. von Halz nodded.

"Diss vill be picture!" he announced.

Frantic assistants rushed through the crowd, throwing their last orders: "Hey, you there! Take off your spectacles, you fool! . . . Don't chew gum! . . . Hide that white petticoat, you, over there! . . . No chewing gum! They didn't chew gum in that century!"

"Ready?" boomed Werner von Halz. The huge set froze in silence, a reverent silence.

"Cam'ra-a-a!!"

Seven hands fell as levers. Seven small, glistening eyes of glass were suddenly alive, ominous, commanding the scene as seven cannons fixed upon it. Four hundred human beings in a panic of enthusiasm stormed like a boiling kettle of rags at the foot of the castle. On the wall, two thin, strong arms rose to the sky and a young voice rang exultantly through the roar of the crowd.

And Claire Nash felt herself torn off her feet, pushed, knocked, tumbled over, thrown to left and right by human bodies gone mad. She tried to act and register joy. Pressed between two huge, enthusiastic fellows, she could not tell on which side stood the cameras and on which the castle; all she could see was a piece of blue sky over red, sweating necks. She tried to fight her way out. She was thrown back by someone's elbow in her ribs and someone's knee in her stomach. A woman screaming frantically: "Long live our Queen!" was spitting into her face. A gentleman with the figure of a prizefighter stepped on her bare foot, taking the skin off three toes. She smiled pitifully and muttered: "Long live our Queen," waving a limp hand over her head. Even the hand could not be seen by the cameras. . . .

When, at last, the piercing siren blew and assistants shouted "Hold it," when the cameras stopped, when Claire drew a deep breath and pulled the wig's hair out of her mouth, Mr. von Halz wiped his forehead with satisfaction and said:

"Dat's good. . . . Vunce more, pleaz!"

Claire had been standing on her feet for three hours when the cameras were moved at last, and she was able to hobble towards a nurse, to get Mercurochrome smeared over the scratches on her arms and legs, to breathe, to powder her face and to look around.

She saw the tall, slender figure of a man in the simplest gray suit, insolently elegant in its simplicity. Her heart did a somersault. She recognized the clear, contemptuous eyes, the scornful, irresistible smile. He was bending over Heddy Leland, talking to her intently, as if they were alone on the set. Heddy Leland was sitting in a low, comfortable canvas chair, a dark silk robe drawn tightly over her costume, her thin, brown hands motionless on the chair's arms. She was looking up at Winston Ayers, listening quietly, her face inscrutable; but she was looking at him as if he were the only man on the set.

Claire felt suddenly as if something had struck her through the ribs. She did not mind the set, nor the crowd, nor her place in it, nor Heddy Leland's place. It was the man in gray and the look with which he spoke to the girl in the chair. Claire was surprised to learn how much she minded that. She walked away hastily, with one last, bitter glance at the chair with the black inscription on its canvas back: "Keep off. Miss Heddy Leland."

She fell down wearily on the first chair she could find. " 'scuse me, please!" snapped a prop boy and, without waiting for her to rise, snatched the chair from under her and carried it away. She saw that it was marked: "Keep off. Mrs. McWiggins, Wardrobe." She stumbled away and sat down on the steps of a ladder. " 'scuse me, please!" snapped an electrician and carried the ladder away. She dragged herself into a shady corner and fell miserably down on an empty box.

"Ef-fry-body on de set!" roared Werner von Halz.

She stumbled heavily back to the set, swaying slightly, the white glare of the sun on the metal reflectors blinding her. A swift shadow fell across her face as someone passed by. She opened her eyes and found herself looking straight upon Winston Ayers. He stopped short and looked at her closely. One of his eyebrows rose slowly; he opened his mouth and quickly closed it again. Then he bowed, calmly, precisely, graciously, without a word, turned and walked on. But Claire had seen that his lips were trembling in a tremendous effort to stop the laughter that choked him. She grew crimson as a beet, even through the thick layers of brown makeup.

When the new scene was being rehearsed, Claire pushed her way, resolute and desperate, to the edge of the crowd, in front of the cameras. "They'll notice me!" she whispered grimly. They did.

"Who's dat girl in brown?" asked Werner von Halz after the first rehearsal, pointing his thumb at Claire Nash, who was struggling fiercely with the lump gathering on her stomach and the turban sliding off her head. "Take her out of dere! Put somebody dat can act in front!"

At the end of the day, every bone in her body aching and her feet burning like hot irons, with dust in her eyes and dust creaking on her teeth, Claire Nash stood in line at the cashier's window, curious and anxious, watching girls walk away with seven-fifty and ten-dollar checks. When she asked for her payment, the little slip of paper she received bore the words: "Pay to the order of Jane Roberts—the sum of five dollars."

Claire Nash was an indomitable woman. Besides, the thought of Winston Ayers' trembling lips kept her awake all night. On the following day at the studio, she got a bit.

She remembered the beginning of her first career. She smiled and winked at an assistant director; she spoke to him—not too sternly. And as a result, when Mr. von Halz asked for a girl to do a bit, she was pushed forward.

Mr. von Halz looked her over critically, bending his head to one side. "Vell, try it," he said at last, indifferently. "Dat man"—he pointed to a tall, lean, pitiful extra—"iss a covard, he iss afraid of var. You"—he pointed to Claire—"are angry und laugh at him. You are . . . vat dey call it? . . . vun rough-und-ready woman."

"I?" gasped Claire. "I—a rough-and-ready woman? But it's not my type!"

"Vat?" said Mr. von Halz, astounded. "You dun't vant to do it maybe?"

"Oh, yes!" said Claire hastily. "Oh, yes, I do!"

The cameras clicked. The coward trembled, covering his face with his hands. Claire laughed demoniacally, her fists on her hips, and slapped him on the back, trying to forget as much of the ideal of sweet maidenhood as she could forget. . . .

On the following evening, Claire saw the rushes of her scene in the projection room. No extra could be admitted lawfully into the sacred mystery of a projection room; but she smiled wistfully upon the susceptible assistant director and he surrendered and smuggled her in through the narrow door, when the lights were off and all the great ones had settled down comfortably in deep leather armchairs: Mr. Bamburger, Mr. von Halz, Mr. Ayers, Miss Leland. Claire stood in a dark corner by the door and looked anxiously at the screen.

She had to confess to herself that she did not photograph as well as she used to; and she remembered that for seven years she had had her own cameraman who knew the secret of the lights which made her face what the fans thought it to be. Besides, rough-and-ready women were definitely not her forte.

Mr. von Halz's opinion was more detailed. "Hm," she heard him say, "dat girl hass not got vun nickel's vorth of personality. And she duss not photograph. And she iss no actress. Cut dat out!"

She did not remember what happened after that. She remembered standing in a dark studio alley, with her head raised to the wind, a cold wind that would not cool her flaming, throbbing forehead; while the assistant director was pleading foolishly, mumbling something about dinner and about something she had promised. She got rid of him at last and fled blindly.

At the studio gate, she saw a long, low roadster sparkling faintly in the moonlight. A slim young girl stood with one foot on the running board, wrapped tightly in a short coat with a huge fur collar; a tall man in gray held the door open for her. They were speaking softly, in low voices Claire could not hear.

Two girls passed by and looked at them. "That's Winston Ayers and his discovery," Claire heard the girls whisper. They heard it too. They looked at each other, looked straight into each other's eyes. They smiled. His smile was warm and soft. Her smile was hard and bitter. She swung behind the wheel, and slammed the door, and was gone. He stood motionless and watched the car disappearing down the long dark road.

"You can think what you wish!" said Claire Nash to Winston Ayers, who had met her in an obscure restaurant at her request. "I'm through with it! I don't think anything and I'm tired of thinking. It's all too silly. I'm putting an end to the stupid comedy."

"Certainly, Miss Nash," he answered imperturbably. "It can be done easily. I am sorry if this little adventure has given you cause for annoyance." It was all he said. He asked no questions. He never mentioned the *Child of Danger* set, as if he had never seen her there.

She tried to forget it all, and she smiled at him warmly, invitingly, hopefully. The cold, hard face before her remained unmoved. She had known on their first meeting that there was little hope for the wish this man awakened in her. She knew now that there was no hope at all. Something had changed him. She thought she could know also what that was, if she but put her certainty into words; but she did not want to know.

She walked alone back to her hotel room, feeling very tired and very empty.

This was on a Monday. On Wednesday, the screen columns of the Hollywood papers announced that Claire Nash had sailed from Europe, outwitting the reporters who had tried to learn the name of the boat she was taking; she was, the papers further stated, to fly back to Hollywood immediately upon landing in New York.

Claire bought all the papers. She sat in her room looking at them. It seemed to her that she was coming out of a nightmare.

Then she sent a long, detailed wire to her secretary in New York. The secretary was to take a Deluxe Transcontinental Flyer for Hollywood in five days; she was to register herself aboard as Claire Nash; she, Claire, would meet the plane at the last stop before Los Angeles and they would exchange places; then a proper welcome would greet her in Hollywood.

She dispatched the wire, entered the first bar she saw, and ordered a drink. She had spent too many nights alone in her room, afraid to venture into the gay night spots where her old friends would see and recognize her. She could stand it no longer. She could not wait another week. She didn't care. But nothing happened at the bar. No one saw her.

The banquet was coming to an end. The long white table, precise and formal, was like a river frozen under a mantle of snow, dotted with crystal, like chunks of ice, with flashes of silver like sparkling water in the cracks of the snow, with flowers floating like islands in midstream. The cash value of the names borne by those who filled the great hall would have stretched in a line of figures from one end of the table to the other. Hollywood's great and costly were gathered to celebrate the signing of a five-year starring contract between Miss Heddy Leland and Wonder-Pictures, Inc.

In the place of honor, a thin little figure modeled in white rose from the billowing waves of an immense skirt, a cloud of white chiffon with rhinestones sparkling as lost raindrops in the mist. She sat, straight, poised, calm, as correct as the occasion demanded, all but her hair, brushed back off her forehead, wild, untamed, ready to fly off and to carry the white cloud away with it, away from the frightening place where she had to smile, and bow, and hide her eyes and her wish to scream. On her left sat Mr. Bamburger's huge, beaming smile and Mr. Bamburger's huge, beaming diamond shirt studs. On her right sat Winston Ayers.

He sat motionless, silent, grim; he seemed to have lost his impeccable manners and forgotten to compose his face into the proper smile of enthusiasm; he showed no enthusiasm whatever; in fact, he seemed not to know or care where he was. Heddy knew suddenly that this day, this day for which she had waited and struggled through such hell, meant nothing to her compared to the thoughts which she could not guess in the mind of the man beside her. He made no effort to speak to her. So she did not turn to him, but smiled dutifully at Mr. Bamburger, at the flowers, at the endless, ringing sentences of the speakers:

"Miss Leland, whose incomparable talent . . . Miss Leland, whose brilliant youth has achieved . . . Hollywood is proud to welcome . . . Fame never smiled so brightly upon a greater future . . . We, who are ever on the lookout for the great and the gifted . . ."

"Miss Leland . . ." Winston Ayers overtook her in a dark gallery of the building, where she had fled to be alone, to leave the great banquet unnoticed and escape. She stopped short. At least, someone had missed her; he had, he who had not seemed to know that she was there.

She stood still, white as a statue in the darkness. A cold wind blew from the Hollywood hills, flaring her skirt out like a sail. He approached. He stood looking down at her. The look in his eyes did not seem to fit the words she heard in his slow, mocking voice:

"I have neglected my duties on this great day, Miss Leland," he said. "Consider yourself congratulated."

She answered without moving:

"Thank you, Mr. Ayers. And thank you—for everything."

"Unnecessary," he shrugged. "From now on, you need no further help from me." She knew he said it as an insult; but it sounded like regret.

"I'm glad of it!" she said suddenly, before she knew she was saying it, her voice alive for the first time, alive and trembling. "I still owe it all to you, but I wish I didn't. Not to you. To anyone but you. Gratitude is such a hard thing to bear. Because it can . . . it can . . ." She could not say it. "Because it can take the place of everything else, be considered to cover, to explain everything else, to . . . I don't want to be grateful to you! Not grateful! I wish I could die for you, but not because of gratitude! Because I . . ."

She stopped in time. She didn't know what she was saying; surely, she thought, he couldn't know it either. But he stood very close to her now. She looked up at him. She knew what his eyes were saying, she knew it so clearly all of a sudden, that she hardly heard his words and paid no attention to them, his words that were still struggling against that to which his eyes had surrendered.

"You owe nothing to me," he was saying coldly. "I've wanted to tell you this for a long time. I knew I'd have to. I didn't select you because I had faith in you or because I saw anything in you. I'm just as much of a fool as the others. I selected you as a trick, a gag—to prove something unimportant to someone even less important. I'll tell you the whole story someday. I can't claim your gratitude. I can claim nothing from you. I didn't think it would ever make any difference to me, but it does. It does." He finished in a grim, low voice, still hard, still cold, but something in its coldness had broken: "Because I love you."

It was not the mocking, skeptical writer who took in his arms the trembling little white figure and whose lips met hers hungrily. . . .

"Oh, my dear, my dear," said Winston Ayers when he led Heddy Ayers into his apartment, three days later, "more than movie careers depends on chance!"

More than movie careers depends on chance. . . .

"Extry! Extry!" the newsboys were yelling on street corners. "Horrible catastrophe! Airliner crashes with twelve passengers!"

Eager citizens tore the papers out of the boys' hands, with the hungry joy of a big sensation. And the sensation grew when the next editions appeared with huge black headlines:

CLAIRE NASH DEAD

In smaller type it was explained that the star had been registered among the passengers of the ill-fated liner which crashed on its way to the last stop before Los

Angeles; that no one aboard had survived; that the bodies were mangled beyond recognition.

Then the flood broke loose. From coast to coast, tragic articles sobbed over the terrible loss in miles of close-printed black columns. It was said that the screen had been deprived of its brightest luminary; that her name was written in the book of Immortality; that the whole world would feel her absence; that there never would be another Claire Nash; that Wonder-Pictures, Inc., had signed Lula Del Mio, the famous ingenue, for the starring part in *Heart and Soul,* which the unforgettable Claire Nash was to have made.

In her little hotel room, having come back from the city where her plane never landed, Claire Nash sat among an ocean of newspapers. No obituary notices had ever had such a happy reader. That, thought Claire joyously as she read, was that. This was what she meant to the world. They knew her true value, after all. What publicity and what buildup! What sensation to come, when the world would learn suddenly that its brightest luminary was still shining! She delayed her resurrection for a few days. The bright crop of glowing words that fell into her hands with each new paper was like wine to her battered, thirsty soul.

She frowned for the first time, though, when the producer's nephew, whom she had thoroughly forgotten, appeared in print with an article about their years-old divorce; a sad, gentle article which, however, brought out some intimate details of the matter that had better been kept hidden. No doubt, he had been well paid for it and a mangled corpse could not bring suit, but still, there were the Women's Clubs, and that sort of thing did not help a star's reputation.

She stopped smiling entirely when a featured player of smoldering Latin charm, long since unemployed, whose name she had trouble in recalling, published a lengthy confession of his love life with Miss Nash, the details of which she recalled only too well. And the Sunday supplements carried such stories, with snapshots and facsimiles of letters, that she decided the time had definitely come to stop it. What the country was beginning to whisper about Claire Nash was neither as sad nor as beautiful as the obituary notices.

"I really cannot understand, madam, how you can persist in that queer statement," said Mr. Bamburger to Claire Nash, a haggard, green-faced, wild-eyed Claire Nash who sat in his office after her long, desperate struggle to gain admittance.

"But, Jake . . ." she stammered. "But you . . . I . . . for God's sake, Jake, you can't make me think I'm crazy! You know me. You recognize me!"

"Really, madam, I have never seen you before in my life."

Mr. Bamburger's secretary left the room. Mr. Bamburger rose hastily and closed the door.

"Listen, Claire . . ."

She jumped to her feet, a radiant smile drying her gathering tears.

"Jake, you fool! What's the gag?"

"Listen, Claire. Of course, I recognize you. But I won't recognize you in public. Now, don't stare at me like that. I won't—for your own good."

She sat down again, for she was going to fall.

"I . . . I don't understand," she muttered.

"You understand," said Mr. Bamburger, "only too damn well. You've read those articles, haven't you? What producer do you think will want to touch you now with a ten-foot pole?"

"But I can . . ."

"No, you can't. You can't sue those fellows, because they'll prove it all. You know it and I know it. And we know also that the Women's Clubs and all the Moral Uplifters would boycott a studio off the face of the earth, if any of us were fool enough to star you again."

"But . . ."

"Where were you all this time, you nitwitted idiot? Why did you let all those obituaries go on? If that alone weren't enough! Do you think the public would love you for that kind of a publicity stunt? Capitalizing on a catastrophe! It would ruin all confidence in the picture business, if they knew! The day is past for cheap, fantastic press-agent tricks like these!"

"But I've explained it to you! I did it only because . . ."

"Oh, so you think you're going to confess the real story? Tell the world that you weren't on that plane because you were pulling a silly, lousy trick on the studios? And do you expect us producers to back you up in that and make ourselves look like a bunch of jackasses?"

"But . . . but . . . but I'm popular . . . I'm a great star . . . I'm a box-offi—"

"You were. You were also slipping. Oh, definitely slipping, my girl. Take a look at the reports on your last two pictures. The public's getting sick of ingenues. Besides, we have signed Lula Del Mio to take your place. We don't need two of a kind. . . .

"Take my advice, Claire," Mr. Bamburger was saying half an hour later to the white ghost of a woman who was leaving his office. "Stay dead officially, leave Hollywood, and give up the movies. Better for your reputation and your peace of mind. Of course, you can prove your identity easily. But the public won't take you. You'll only make yourself ridiculous. And no producer will take you. Ask them. They'll tell you the same things. You've made quite a fortune in pictures. You don't have to work. Rest and enjoy it. Try to marry some nice, respectable millionaire. Forget the movies. I am more experienced than you are and I know the business: the screen is not for you any more."

Mr. Bamburger objected violently. Werner von Halz objected with a string of invectives in five European languages. But Winston Ayers and Heddy Leland Ayers, his wife, insisted quietly and irrevocably. So Jane Roberts was signed for the second feminine lead in *Child of Danger*. The character appeared only in the second half of the picture and the part had not yet been filled.

Mr. Bamburger surrendered on condition that Jane Roberts remain strictly Jane Roberts, change the color of her hair and the shape of her eyebrows, keep to herself socially, and let no breath reach the press about any connection between her and Claire Nash.

"Still," sighed Mr. Bamburger, "still the public will know."

"I hope," said Winston Ayers earnestly, "I hope from the bottom of my heart that they do. But I have my own doubts."

Jane Roberts' part was that of a sweet, innocent country maiden in Queen Lani's kingdom. It was not a big part, but it was worth ten starring roles. It gave her an opportunity for all the dramatic emotions she cared to display. It fitted her to perfection. It was a brilliant condensation of all the great parts she had played.

Claire Nash gathered all her strength. She remembered all her famous roles and took the best from each. She brought to her part the sweet, helpless glances, the tremulous lips, the famous smile of innocence, all the movements, manners, and graces that had been admired so much by fans and critics. She did everything she had ever done and more. Never had she acted so well in her life.

Six months later came the reviews:

"*Child of Danger* is the picture of the century. Words are inadequate before the magnificence of this miracle of the screen. One must see it in order to comprehend the enchantment of this cinematic triumph. The story is as great as its author—Winston Ayers. And when this is said, everything has been said. Werner von Halz gains his right to immortality by his brilliant direction of this one masterpiece. Heddy Leland, the new star, is a discovery that surpasses anything ever seen on the screen before. Her acting bears the flaming seal of that genius which makes Screen History. . . .

"If we may be permitted to carp on minor flaws in such a stupendous achievement, we would like to remark in passing on a small annoyance in a perfect evening. We are speaking of the second feminine lead. It's one of those innocent, insipid little things with nothing but a sweet smile and a pretty face. She reminds us of some star or other, but her weak, colorless portrayal of the country maiden shows the disadvantages of a good part in the hands of an inexperienced amateur. The part is played by one Jane Roberts."

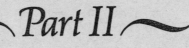

Part II

THE EARLY THIRTIES

Red Pawn

c. 1931–32

Editor's Preface

In 1930, while still working in the RKO wardrobe department, Ayn Rand began to outline *We the Living*. But she interrupted the novel late in 1931 to write a movie original, hoping to earn enough money to enable her to write full-time. Ayn Rand regarded *Red Pawn* as her first professional work. Happily, it was also her first sale: she sold it to Universal Pictures in 1932 for $1,500, and was thus finally able to escape RKO. The payment of $1,500 was for a synopsis of the story as well as the screenplay.

Universal later traded the story to Paramount (for a property that had cost Paramount $20,000). All rights are now owned by Paramount Pictures, which has never produced the story, but which has granted permission to reprint the synopsis here.

Red Pawn presents Ayn Rand's first serious, philosophical theme: the evil of dictatorship—specifically, of Soviet Russia. Miss Rand's full objection to dictatorship involves her whole system of philosophy, including her view of the nature of reality and of the requirements of the human mind (see *Capitalism: The Unknown Ideal*). But in *Red Pawn* the argument is reduced to its essence. Communism demands that the individual renounce his independence and his happiness, in order to become a cipher selflessly serving the group. Communism, therefore, is the destroyer of the individual and of human joy. Or, as we may put it in terms of the themes of "The Husband I Bought" and "Good Copy," the philosophic issue is: Communism vs. man-worship and Communism vs. the "benevolent universe," i.e., Communism vs. *values*. This is the link between the political theme of the story and Ayn Rand's lifelong ethical concerns.

The answer to Communism, Ayn Rand held, is the recognition of man's right to exist—to exist by his own mind and for his own sake, sacrificing neither himself to others nor others to himself. The goal and badge of such a man is the kind of happiness symbolized in this story by the "Song of Dancing Lights." This song is, in effect, Ayn Rand's refutation of Communism; the song's laughing spirit—the fact that such joy is possible to man—is the answer to the apostles of selfless toil. To demand the renunciation of such joy, Ayn Rand held, is evil, no matter what benefit any recipient claims to gain from the sacrifice.

Red Pawn has a subtheme: the philosophic identity of Communism and religion. Both subordinate the individual to something allegedly higher (whether God or the state), and both equate virtue with selfless service. From her early teens, Ayn Rand saw clearly that Communism, contrary to its propaganda, is not the alternative to religion, but only a secularized version of it, with the state assuming the prerogatives once reserved to the supernatural. (The alternative is a philosophy of reason and rational self-interest.)

The plot situation in *Red Pawn,* like the theme, is very similar to that of *We the Living.* Both works involve a triangle: a passionate woman (who dominates the action), her anti-Communist lover (or husband), and a dedicated Communist who holds power over him, and whom she must court in order to save the lover's life. In the conventional triangle of this kind, the heroine despises the second man, and sleeps with him only for practical reasons. In the Ayn Rand version, however, the Communist is not a villain, but a misguided idealist whom the heroine grows to love; this gives the heroine a much more painful situation to resolve, and the story an incomparably greater suspense.

As in most Ayn Rand fiction, the story leaves one with a special, uplifted sense of human stature, and even grandeur, because the essential conflict is not between good and evil, but between good and good (the two men). In accordance with her view that evil is impotent, the villains in Ayn Rand's fiction rarely rise to the role of dominant, plot-determining figures. For the most part, like Fedossitch in this story, they are peripheral creatures doomed by their own irrationality to failure and defeat. The focus of the story, therefore, is not on man the sordid, but on man the heroic. (In *The Fountainhead,* the main conflict is not Roark against Toohey or Keating, but Roark against Dominique and Wynand. In *Atlas Shrugged,* the main conflict is Dagny and Rearden against Galt and the other strikers.)

In *Red Pawn,* as befits a story for the screen, the central situation is presented in simplified terms. The husband (Michael) is a prisoner on a desolate island, the Communist (Kareyev) is the Commandant, and the goal of the wife (Joan) is to help the husband escape. The details and the pace are thus very different from what they are in *We the Living*—and so is the ending, which is in itself a brilliant touch; the suspense is resolved by four unexpected but logical, even inevitable, words uttered by Joan to the soldiers. The title seems to be a play on words: Joan is a pawn made available to Kareyev by the red state, but Kareyev is a red who is a pawn of Joan's own plan.

By its nature, a movie synopsis focuses on dramatic action open to the camera to record. This synopsis offers a Romantic director an abundance of such drama. One can almost see the close-up of Michael's face as he waits table on his wife and rival, torn by jealousy but unable to speak; or the spotlight stabbing an urgent message into the void, accompanied by the pealing of the bells; or, at the end, the two sleighs moving slowly apart, in opposite directions across the trackless snow, with Joan's eyes intent on a head that is held proudly high as its owner rides to his death.

The most brilliant visualization of the theme occurs in the prison library. Kareyev is standing between a Communist poster and a painting left on the island by ancient monks. The poster depicts ant-sized men sweating beneath a slogan demanding sacrifice for the collective; the painting depicts a saint ecstatically burning at the stake. And across from both there is Joan with "her head thrown back, her body on the dark altar steps, tense, listening to the song [of Dancing Lights] . . . seem[ing to be] a sacrificial offering to the Deity she was serving." Here is the reverence of man-worship contrasted with its two destroyers—and all of it captured in one *visual* scene. *That* is "writing for the movies."

It is astonishing how much of purely literary worth this mere synopsis contains. There is Ayn Rand's eloquent economy of means, enabling one or two words in the right context to speak volumes. (For example, when Kareyev asks Joan why she came to the island, she tells him she heard that he was the loneliest man in the republic. "I see," he says. "Pity?" "No. Envy.") There are the dramatic antitheses in the style of Victor Hugo, whose novels Ayn Rand admired above all others. ("The civil war had given him a scar on his shoulder and a contempt of death. Peace gave him Strastnoy Island and a contempt of life.") There are the sensuous descriptions with their evocative images (for instance, the description of the monastery at twilight, or of the waves at night).

After *Red Pawn* and *We the Living,* Ayn Rand rarely wrote again about Soviet Russia. She had had her say about the slave state in which she had grown up. Thereafter, her interest moved from politics to the fundamental branches of philosophy, and from slavery to the achievements (and problems) of life in a human country.

A note on the text: Ayn Rand wrote an original draft of this synopsis, then edited about twenty pages, to the point where Michael first sees Joan on the island. Presumably, these pages were sufficient as a submission to the studios and further editing proved unnecessary. This is why the early pages are somewhat tighter and smoother than the rest.

In her editing, Miss Rand changed the names and backgrounds of some of the characters. Joan was originally Tania, a Russian princess; Michael was Victor, a Russian prince; and the prisoners generally were drawn from the Russian nobility. I have had to make many small changes to render the manuscript consistent with the new opening. I have not, however, written new sentences; I have merely changed the necessary names and deleted references to backgrounds that were altered.

—L. P.

Red Pawn

——I——

"No woman," said the young convict, "could accept such a thing."

"As you can observe," said the old convict, shrugging, "there's one who has."

They leaned over the tower parapet to look far out at the sea. From the frost-glazed stone under their elbows, the tower was a straight drop of three hundred feet to the ground below; far out at sea, where the white clouds rolled softly like a first promise of snowdrifts to come, a boat plowed its way toward the island.

Down on the shore guards were ready, waiting under the wall, on a landing of old, rotted boards; on the wall, guards stopped in their rounds; they leaned on their bayonets and looked at the boat. It was a serious breach of discipline.

"I've always thought," said the young convict, "that there was a limit to a woman's voluntary degradation."

"That," said the old convict, pointing at the boat, "proves there isn't any."

He shook his hair, for it got tangled in his monocle; there was a strong wind and he needed a haircut.

A faded gilt cupola rose high over them, like the countless peaks that raised gold crosses into the heavy sky over Russia; but its cross had been broken off; a flag floated over it, a bright, twisted, flickering tongue of red,

154

like a streak of flame dancing through the clouds. When the wind unfurled it into a straight, shivering line, a white sickle and hammer flashed for a second on the red cloth—the crossed sickle and hammer of the Soviet Republic.

In the days of the Czar the island had been a monastery. Fanatical monks had chosen this bit of land in the Arctic waters off the Siberian coast; they had welcomed the snow and the winds, and bowed in voluntary sacrifice to a frozen world no man could endure for many years. The revolution had dispersed the monks and brought new men to the island, men who did not come voluntarily. No letter ever left the place; no letter ever reached it. Many prisoners had landed there; none had returned. When a man was sentenced to Strastnoy Island, those he left behind whispered the prayers for the dead.

"I haven't seen a woman for three years," said the young convict. There was no regret in his voice; only a wistful, astonished wonder.

"I haven't seen a woman for ten years," said the old convict. "But this one won't be worth looking at."

"Maybe she's beautiful."

"Don't be a fool. Beautiful women don't have to do things like this."

"Maybe she'll tell us what's happening . . . outside."

"I'd advise you not to speak to her."

"Why?"

"You don't want to give up the last thing you've got."

"What?"

"Your self-respect."

"But maybe she . . ."

He stopped. No one had told him to stop and he had heard nothing behind them, no steps or sound. But he knew that a man stood behind them, and he knew who it was, and he turned slowly, without being asked to turn, wishing he could leap off the tower rather than turn to face that man.

Commandant Kareyev stood there, at the head of the stairs. People always knew when Commandant Kareyev entered a room, perhaps because he was never conscious of them, of the room, or of his entering it. He stood without moving, looking at the two convicts. He was tall, straight, thin. He seemed to be made of bones, skin, and anesthetized nerves. His glance held no menace, no anger. It held no meaning at all. His eyes never held any human meaning. The convicts had seen him reward some guard for distinguished service or order a prisoner to be flogged to death—with the same expression. They could not say who feared him more—the guards or the prisoners. His eyes never seemed to see people; they saw, not men, but a thought; a single thought many centuries ahead; and so when people looked at him, they felt cold and lonely, as if they were walking into an endless distance on an open plain at night.

He said nothing. The two convicts moved past him, to the stairs; and went down, hastily, not too steadily; he heard one of them stumbling, if he heard or noticed them at all. He had not ordered them to go.

Commandant Kareyev stood alone on the tower platform, his hair flying in the wind. He leaned over the parapet and looked at the boat. The sky above him was gray as the steel of the gun at his belt.

Commandant Kareyev had worn a gun at his belt for five years. For five years he had been Commandant of Strastnoy Island, the only one of the garrison who had been able to stand it that long. Years before, he had carried a bayonet and fought in the civil war, against some of the men whose prison he was now guarding, and against the parents of others. The civil war had given him a scar on his shoulder and a contempt of death. Peace gave him Strastnoy Island and a contempt of life.

Commandant Kareyev still served the revolution as he had served it in the civil war. He had accepted the island as he had accepted night attacks in the trenches; only this was harder.

He walked sharply, lightly, as if each step were a quick electric shock throwing him forward; a few white streaks shone in his hair, as his first decoration of the North; his lips were motionless when he was pleased, and smiled when he wasn't; he never repeated an order. At night, he sat at his window and looked somewhere, without movement, without thought. They called him "Comrade

Commandant" when they met him; behind his back, they called him "the Beast."

The boat was approaching. Commandant Kareyev could distinguish figures on deck. He bent over the parapet; there was no eagerness in his glance, and no curiosity. He could not find the figure he expected. He turned and went down the stairs.

The guard on the first landing straightened quickly at his approach; the guard had been looking at the boat.

At the foot of the stairs, two convicts leaned over a windowsill overlooking the sea.

". . . he told them he was lonely," he heard one of them say.

"I wouldn't want what he's getting," said the other.

He walked down a deserted corridor. In one of the cells he saw three men standing on a table pushed against a small barred window. They were looking at the sea.

In the hall he was stopped by Comrade Fedossitch, his assistant. Comrade Fedossitch coughed. When he coughed his shoulders shook, drooping forward, and his long neck dipped like the beak of a starving bird. Comrade Fedossitch's eyes had lost their color; they stared, reflecting, like a frozen mirror, the gray of the monastery walls. They stared timidly and arrogantly at once, as if fearing and inviting an insult. He wore a leather whip at his belt.

Comrade Fedossitch had been told that Strastnoy Island was not good for his cough. But it was the only job he knew where he could wear a whip. Comrade Fedossitch had stayed.

He saluted the Commandant, and bowed, and said with a little grin, a servile grin spread like lacquer over the sharp edges of his words:

"If you please, Comrade Commandant. Of course, the Comrade Commandant knows what's best, but I was just thinking: a female citizen coming here against all regulations and . . ."

"What do you want?"

"Well, for instance, our rooms are good enough for us, but do you think the comrade woman will like hers? Do you want me to fix it up a little and . . ."

"Never mind. It's good enough for her."

In the yard, convicts were busy chopping logs. A wide archway opened upon the sea, and a guard stood in the archway, his back to the convicts, watching the boat that rocked softly, growing, approaching in the pale green fog of waves and sky.

A few axes struck the logs indifferently, once in a while; the convicts, too, were looking at the sea. A stately gentleman, erect in his ragged prison garb, whispered to his companions:

"Really, it's the best story I've ever heard. You see, Commandant Kareyev had sent in his resignation. I presume five years of Strastnoy Island was too much, even for his red nerves. But how would they ever run the place without the Beast? They asked him to stay."

"Where would they find another fool who'd freeze his blood away for the sake of his duty to the revolution?"

"And this was his condition to the authorities on the mainland: 'I'll stay, if you send me a woman; any woman.' "

"Just that: any woman."

"Well, gentlemen, that's only natural: a good red citizen lets his superiors select his mates. Leaves it to their judgment. All in the line of duty."

"You can imagine how far a woman must fall to accept such an invitation."

"And a man to make it."

Michael Volkontzev stood aside from the others. He did not look at the sea. The ax flashed over his head in a wide silver circle, as he chopped the logs vigorously, rhythmically, without stopping. A lock of black hair rose and fell over his right eye. One of his sleeves was torn, and the muscles of his arm stood out, young and strong. He did not take part in the conversation. But when he was not busy he usually spoke to his fellow convicts, spoke often and long; only the more he spoke, the less they could learn about him. They knew one thing for certain, however: when he spoke, he laughed; he laughed gaily, easily, with an air of mocking, boyish defiance; it was sufficient to know that about him; to know that he was the kind of man who could still laugh like that after two years on Strastnoy Island. He was the only one who could.

The prisoners liked to talk about their past. Their memories were the only future they had. And there were many memories to exchange: memories of the universities where some of them had taught, of the hospitals where others had attended the sick, of the buildings they had designed, of the bridges they had built. There were men of many professions. All of them had been useful and had worked hard in the past. All of them had one thing in common: that the Red State had chosen to discard them and to throw them into jail, for some reason or another, often without reason; perhaps because of some careless word they had uttered somewhere; perhaps simply because they had been too able and had worked too hard.

Michael Volkontzev was the only one among them who would not speak about his past. He would speak about anything under the sun, and often on a subject and at a time when it would have been far safer to remain quiet; he would risk his life drawing caricatures of Commandant Kareyev on the walls of his cell; but he would not speak about his past. No one knew where he had come from or why. They suspected that he had been an engineer at some time in his life, because he was always assigned to any work that required an engineer's skill, such as repairing the dynamo that operated the wireless high in a room on top of the tower. They could discover nothing else about him.

The boat's siren roared hoarsely outside. A convict waved his arm in the direction of the sea and announced:

"Gentlemen, salute the first woman on Strastnoy Island!"

Michael raised his head.

"Why all this excitement," he asked indifferently, "about some cheap tramp?"

Commandant Kareyev had stopped at the entrance to the yard. He walked slowly toward Michael. He stood, watching him silently. Michael did not seem to notice it, but raised his ax and split another log in two. Kareyev said:

"I'm warning you, Volkontzev. I know how little you're afraid of and how much you like to show it. But you're not to show it on the subject of that woman. You're to leave her alone."

Michael threw his head back and looked at Kareyev innocently.

"Certainly, Commandant," he said with a charming smile. "She'll be left alone. Trust my good taste."

He gathered an armful of logs and walked away, down the steps of the cellar.

The boat's siren roared again. Commandant Kareyev went to meet it at the landing.

The boat came to the island four times a year. It brought food and new prisoners. There were two convicts aboard, this time. One of them was mumbling prayers and the other one was trying to hold his head high, but it was not convincing, because his lips trembled as he looked at the island.

The woman stood on deck and looked at the island, too. She wore a plain, black coat. It did not look expensive, but it was too plain, and fitted too well, and showed a slim, young body, not the kind that Commandant Kareyev had seen tramping wearily the dark streets of Russian cities. Her hand held her fur collar tightly under her chin. Her hand had long, slender fingers. There was a quiet curiosity in her large, wide eyes, and such an indifferent calm that Commandant Kareyev would not believe she was looking at the island. No one had ever looked at it like that. But she did.

He watched her walking down the gangplank. The fact that her steps were steady, light, assured was astonishing; the fact that she looked like a woman who belonged in exquisite drawing rooms was startling; but the fact that she was beautiful was incredible. There had been some mistake: she was not the woman sent to him.

He bowed curtly. He asked:

"What are you doing here, citizen?"

"Commandant Kareyev?" she inquired. Her voice had a strange, slow, indifferent calm—and a strange foreign accent.

"Yes."

"I thought you were expecting me."

"Oh."

Her cool eyes looked at him as they had looked at his island. She had nothing of the smiling, inviting, professional charm he had expected. She was not smiling. She did not seem to notice his astonishment. She did not seem to find the occasion unusual at all. She said:

"My name is Joan Harding."

"English?"

"American."

"What are you doing in Russia?"

She took a letter from her pocket and handed it to him. She said:

"Here is my letter of introduction from the GPU at Nijni Kolimsk."

He took the letter, but did not open it. He said curtly:

"All right. Come this way, Comrade Harding."

He walked up the hill, to the monastery, stiff, silent, without offering a hand to help her up the old stone steps, without looking back at her, followed by the eyes of all the men on the landing and by the unusual, long-forgotten sound of French heels.

The room he had prepared for her was a small cube of gray stone. There was a narrow iron cot, a table, a candle on the table, a chair, a small barred window, a stove of red bricks built in the wall. There was nothing to greet her, nothing to show that a human being had been expected to enter that room, only a thin red line of fire trembling in the crack of the stove's iron door.

"Not very comfortable," said Commandant Kareyev. "This place wasn't built for women. It was a monastery—before the revolution. The monks had a law that a woman's foot could not touch this ground. Woman was sin."

"You have a better opinion of women, haven't you, Comrade Kareyev?"

"I'm not afraid of being a sinner."

She looked at him. She spoke slowly, and he knew she was answering something he had not said:

"The only sin is to miss the things you want most in life. If they're taken from you, you have to reclaim them—at any price."

"If this is the price you're paying for whatever it is you want, it's pretty high, you know. Sure it's worth it?"

She shrugged lightly:

"I've been accustomed to rather high-priced things."

"So I notice, Comrade Harding."

"Call me Joan."

"It's a funny name."

"You'll get used to it."

"What are you doing in Russia?"

"In the coming months—anything you wish me to do."

It was not a promise nor an invitation; it was said as an efficient secretary might have said it, and more coldly, more impersonally than that; as one of the guards might have said it, awaiting orders; as if the sound of her voice added that the words meant nothing—to him or to her.

He asked:

"How do you happen to be in Russia at all?"

She shrugged lazily. She said:

"Questions are so boring. I've answered so many of them at the GPU before they sent me here. The GPU officials were satisfied. I'm sure you never disagree with them, do you?"

He watched her as she took her hat off, and threw it down on the table, and shook her hair. Her hair was short, blond, and stood like a halo over her face. She walked to the table and touched it with her finger. She took out a small lace handkerchief and wiped the dust off the table. She dropped the handkerchief to the floor. He looked at it. He did not pick it up.

He watched her thoughtfully. He turned to go. At the door he stopped and faced her suddenly.

"Do you," he asked, "whoever you are, understand what you're here for?"

She looked straight into his eyes, a long, quiet, disconcerting look, and her eyes were mysterious because they were too calm and too open.

"Yes," she said slowly, "I understand."

The letter from the GPU said:

Comrade Kareyev,
As per your request, we are sending to you the bearer of

this, Comrade Joan Harding. We vouch for her political trustworthiness. Her past reputation will guarantee that she will satisfy the purpose of your request and lighten the burden of your difficult duty on the far outpost of our great proletarian Republic.

> With Communistic greetings,
> Ivan Veriohoff,
> Political Commissar

Commandant Kareyev's bed had a coarse gray blanket, like those on the prisoners' cots. His cell of damp gray stone looked emptier than theirs; there was a bed, a table, two chairs. A tall glass door, long and narrow like a cathedral window, led to an open gallery outside. The room looked as if a human being had been flung there in a hurry for a short moment: there were rows of old nails on the bare stone walls bearing clothes and arms, wrinkled shirts hanging by one sleeve, old leather jackets, rifles, trousers turned inside out, cartridge belts; there were cigarette butts and ashes on the bare stone floor. The human being had lived there for five years.

There was not a single picture, not a book, not an ashtray. There was a bed because the human being had to sleep; and clothes, because he had to dress; he needed nothing else.

But there was one single object which he did not need, his single answer to any questions people could ask looking at his room, although no one had ever asked them: in a niche where ikons had been now hung, on a rusty nail, Commandant Kareyev's old Red Army cap.

The unpainted wooden table had been pulled to the center of the room. On the table stood heavy tin dishes and tin cups without saucers; a candle in an old bottle; and no tablecloth.

Commandant Kareyev and Joan Harding were finishing their first dinner together.

She raised a tin jug of cold tea, with a smile that should have accompanied a glass of champagne, and said:

"Your health, Comrade Kareyev."

He answered brusquely:

"If it's a hint—you're wasting your time. No drinks here. Not allowed. And no exceptions."

"No exceptions and no hints, Comrade Kareyev. But still—your health."

"Cut the nonsense. You don't have to drink my health. You don't have to smile. And you don't have to lie. You'll hate me—and you know it. And I know it. But you may not know that I don't care—so you're warned in advance."

"I didn't know I'll hate you."

"You know it now, don't you?"

"Less than ever."

"Listen, forget the pretty speeches. That's not part of your job. If you expect any compliments—you might as well be disappointed right now."

"I wasn't expecting any compliments when I took the boat for Strastnoy Island."

"And I hope you weren't expecting any sentiment. This is a business deal. That's all."

"That's all, Comrade Kareyev."

"Did you expect a companion like me?"

"I've heard about you."

"Have you heard what I'm called?"

"The Beast."

"You may find I deserve the name."

"You may find I like it."

"No use telling me about it—if you do. I don't care what you think of me."

"Then why warn me about it?"

"Because the boat's still here. It goes back at dawn. There's no other for three months."

She had lighted a cigarette. She held it in two straight fingers, looking at him.

"Were you in the civil war, Comrade Kareyev?"

"Yes. Why?"

"Did you acquire the habit of retreating?"

"No."

"Neither have I."

He leaned toward her, his crossed elbows on the table, watching her in the trembling glow of the candle, his eyes narrow, mocking. He said:

"I've seen some soldiers overestimate their strength."

She smiled, and reached over and flicked the ashes off her cigarette into his empty plate.

"Good ones," she answered, "take chances."

"Listen," he said impatiently, "you don't like questions, so I won't bother you, because I don't like to talk either. But there's just one thing I'm going to ask you. That letter from the GPU said you were all right politically, but you don't look as . . . as you should look at all."

She blew at the smoke and did not answer. Then she looked at him and shrugged lightly.

"The letter told you about my present. The past is dead. If I'm not thinking of it, why should you?"

"No reason," he agreed. "Makes no difference."

A convict, waiting on the Commandant's table, had removed the dishes, sliding silently out of the room. Joan rose.

"Show me the island," she said. "I want to get acquainted. I'm staying here for a long time—I hope."

"I hope you'll repeat that," he answered, rising, "three months from today."

When they walked out, the sky was red behind the monastery towers, a shivering red, as if the light were dying in gasps. The monastery looked silently upon them, with small barred windows like reluctant eyes opened upon a sinful world, guarded by menacing saints of gray stone; cold evening shadows settled in the wrinkles of the saints' faces cut by reverent hands, stormy winds, and centuries. A thick stone wall encircled the shore, and sentinels walked slowly on the wall, with measured steps, with bayonets red in the sunset, with heads bowed in resignation, watchful and weary like the saints by the windows.

"The prisoners aren't locked up in their cells here," Commandant Kareyev explained to her. "They have the freedom to move around. There's not much space to move in. It's safe."

"They get tired of the island, don't they?"

"They go mad. Not that it matters. It's the last place they'll see on earth."

"And when they die?"

"Well, no room for a cemetery here. But a strong current."

"Has anyone ever tried to escape?"

"They forget the word when they land here."

"And yourself?"

He looked at her, without understanding. "Myself?"

"Have you ever tried to escape?"

"From whom?"

"From Commandant Kareyev."

"Come on. What are you driving at?"

"Are you happy here?"

"No one's forcing me to stay."

"I said: are you happy?"

"Who cares about being happy? There's so much work to be done in the world."

"Why should it be done?"

"Because it's one's duty."

"To whom?"

"When it's duty, you don't ask why and to whom. You don't ask any questions. When you come up against a thing about which you can't ask any questions—then you know you're facing your duty."

She pointed far out at the darkening sea and asked:

"Do you ever think of what lies there, beyond the coast? Of the places where I came from?"

He answered, shrugging contemptuously:

"The best of that world beyond the coast is right here."

"And that is?"

"My work."

He turned and walked back to the monastery. She followed obediently.

They walked down a long corridor where barred windows threw dark crosses on the floor, over the red squares of dying light, and figures of saints writhed on ancient murals. From behind every door furtive eyes watched the stranger. The eyes were eager and contemptuous at once. Commandant Kareyev did not notice them; Joan was braver—she did, and walked on, not caring.

They had reached the foot of the stairs where, at tall

windows, a group of prisoners loitered, as if by chance, aimlessly studying the sunset.

Her foot was on the first step when a cry stopped her, the kind of cry she would have heard if the martyrs of the murals had suddenly found voice.

"Frances!"

Michael Volkontzev stood grasping the banister, barring her way. Many people were looking at his face, but his face looked like a thing that should not be seen.

"Frances! What are you doing here?"

The men around them could not understand the question, because of the way his voice sounded—and because he spoke it in English.

Her face was cool and blank and a little astonished—politely, indifferently astonished. She looked straight at him, her eyes calm and open.

"I beg your pardon," she said, in Russian. "I don't believe I know you."

Kareyev stepped between them and seized Michael's shoulder, asking:

"Do you know her?"

Michael looked at her, at the stairway, at the men around them.

"No," he muttered. "I was mistaken."

"I warned you," said Kareyev angrily, and threw him out of the way, against the wall. Joan turned and walked up the steps. Kareyev followed.

The prisoners watched Michael pressed to the wall, as he had fallen, not moving, not straightening himself, only his eyes watching her go up and his head nodding slowly as if counting each step.

There was no door to connect Joan's cell with Commandant Kareyev's. For five years Commandant Kareyev had not spoken to a woman, but almost forty years had gone before he had ever spoken to a woman like this guest of his. She was his prize, his reward, the pawn from the red republic for the hours and years of his life, for his blood, for his gray hair. She was his as his salary, as the rations of bread citizens got on their provision cards. But she had helpless white fingers and cool eyes that did not invite and did not forbid and looked at him with an open, wondering calm beyond his understanding. He had waited for five years; he could wait one night longer.

He had closed his door and listened. He could hear the moaning of waves outside; and the steps of sentinels on the wall; and the rustle of her long dress against the stone floor, in the next cell.

It was long after midnight, and the monastery towers had dissolved into the black sky, and only the smoking lanterns of the guards floated over the darkness, when a hand knocked on Joan's door. She had not been sleeping. She was standing at a bare stone wall, under the faint square of a barred window, and the lighted candle tore out of the darkness the white spots of her hands and bowed face. The wax of the candle had frozen in long rivulets across the table. She hesitated for only a second. She tightened the folds of her long, black robe and opened the door.

It was not Commandant Kareyev; it was Michael.

He put his hand on the door so that she could not close it. His lips were determined, but his eyes were desperate, tortured, pleading.

"Keep quiet," he whispered. "I've got to see you alone."

"Get out of here," she ordered, in a whisper. "At once."

"Frances," he begged, "this . . . all this isn't possible. I can't understand . . . I've got to hear a word, a . . ."

"I don't know who you are. I don't know what you want. Let me close this door."

"Frances, I have to . . . I can't . . . I must know the reason you . . ."

"If you don't go, I'll call Commandant Kareyev."

"Oh, you will?" He raised his head defiantly. "Well, let me see you do it."

She opened her door wider and called:

"Comrade Kareyev!"

She did not have to call twice. He threw his door open and faced them, hand on the gun at his belt.

"I didn't come here to be annoyed by your prisoners, Comrade Kareyev," she said evenly.

Commandant Kareyev did not say a word. He blew

his whistle. Down the long corridor, the echoes of their heavy boots pounding against the vaults, two guards ran to his summons.

"Into the pit," he ordered, pointing at Michael.

Michael's eyes were not desperate any longer. A contemptuous smile pulled down the corners of his mouth. His hand went to his forehead in a military salute to Joan.

She stood, motionless, until the guards' footsteps died in the darkness beyond the stairs, leading Michael away. Then, Kareyev entered her room and closed the door. He looked at her throat, white against the black robe.

"After all," said Commandant Kareyev, "he had the right idea."

He did not know whether the soft warmth under his hands was the velvet or the body under the velvet. For one short second, it seemed to him that her eyes had lost their hard calm, that they were helpless and frightened and childish, like the fluffy blond hair that fell over his arm. But he did not care, for then her lips parted in a smile and his closed them again.

——*II*——

Joan was unpacking her trunks. She was hanging her clothes on a row of nails. Just enough light crawled in through the barred window to make the satins and laces glimmer, shivering and surprised, in the stone niche built for monks' robes.

The light seemed to rise out of the sea and the sky hung over it, a dead gray reflecting feebly a borrowed glow. The leaden waves moved restlessly; they did not run towards the shore; they seemed to boil and knock against each other, furious whitecaps flashing up and disappearing instantly, as if the sea, a huge tank, had been shaken and its waters stirred, swaying against unseen walls.

From her window, Joan could watch the statue of St. George on a cornice. His huge, awkward face looked straight at the far horizon, without bending towards the dragon under his horse's hoofs. The dragon's head hung over the sea, limp under centuries of threat from a heavy stone spear, as if the last drops of blood had been drained through its gaping mouth into the waves far below.

Joan was hanging a shawl to cover the niche, a square piece of old linen heavy with crosses of embroidery. Commandant Kareyev entered when she struck her finger with the hammer, trying to drive a nail into the hard wooden frame around the niche.

"It's your fault," she said, a little smile softening her lips in a wordless greeting. "You promised to help me."

He took her hand without hesitation, possessively, and looked, worried, at the little red spot.

"I'm sorry. Here, I'll nail it for you."

"You've left me alone three times this morning," she complained.

"Sorry. I had to go. A disturbance down there. One of the fools chopped his toe off."

"Accident?"

"No. Madness. Thought he'd be sent to the mainland to a hospital."

"Didn't you send him?"

"No. Had the doctor tend to him. The doctor's a useful prisoner to have; been a surgeon at the Medical Academy in St. Petersburg. He's cauterizing the idiot's foot now—with red iron. . . . What's all this here?"

"My clothes."

"Why do you have so many?"

"Why do you carry that gun?"

"That's my profession."

"That"—she pointed to the niche—"is mine."

"Oh." He looked at the clothes, at her, frowned. "Yes, and a paying one. . . . And if it paid so well, why did you come here?"

"I was tired. I heard about you—and liked it."

"What did you hear?"

"I heard that you were the loneliest man in this republic."

"I see. Pity?"

"No. Envy."

She bent and took out of the trunk a dress of soft, dark satin.

"Hold it," she ordered, taking out a wrap, shaking its fluffy fur collar, stroking it gently, hanging it carefully in the niche. He held the dress cautiously, his fingers moving slowly in the smooth, lustrous folds, soft and bewildering as some unknown beast's skin. He said:

"You won't need such things here."

"I thought you might like them."

"I don't notice rags."

"Give me that dress. Don't hold it up by the hem like that."

"What's the use of such a thing?"

"It's beautiful."

"It's useless."

"But it's beautiful. Isn't that reason enough to bring it along, Comrade Kareyev?"

"One of us," said Commandant Kareyev, "has a lot to learn."

"One of us," she answered slowly, "has."

She bent into the trunk and took out a long satin nightgown. She displayed the luxury of her exquisite possessions in a natural, indifferent manner, as if they were to be expected, as if she did not notice Kareyev's surprised eyes; as if she did not know that this elegance of a fashionable boudoir transplanted into a monk's cell was a challenge to the frozen walls, to the grim Communist, to the very duty she had accepted. Under the dusty bottle that held a candle on the table, she put down a huge white powder puff.

He asked gruffly:

"Where do you think you are?"

"I think," she answered with her lightest smile, "that you may wish to think of places where you haven't been—someday."

"I don't have many wishes," he answered sternly, "except those that come on official blanks with a Party seal. If they tell me to stay here—I'll stay."

He looked at the row of dresses in the niche. He kicked an open trunk impatiently.

"Are you through with that?" he asked. "I haven't much time to waste here helping you."

"You haven't given me much time," she complained. "They have been calling you away all morning."

"They'll call me again. I have more important things to do than to hang up that junk of yours."

She brought out a satin slipper. She studied its buckle thoughtfully, attentively.

"That man who came to my room last night," she asked, "where did you put him?"

"Into the pit."

"The pit?"

"Fifty feet under the ground. Could swim down there if all the water on the walls wasn't frozen. But it's frozen. And I gave him the limit."

"The limit of what?"

"Of light. When we give the limit, we close the big shutter over the hole above. Until we open it to throw him food, he might as well be blind for all the good his eyes will do him."

"How long is his sentence?"

"Ten days."

She bent for the second slipper. She put them down carefully under the folds of a long robe. She asked with a light smile:

"Do men think that kind of punishment satisfies a woman?"

"What would a woman do?"

"I would make him apologize."

"You wouldn't want me to have him shot, would you? For disobedience? He'll never apologize."

"Suspend his sentence if he does."

"He's a hard one. I've broken many a hard one here, but he's steel—so far. Strastnoy Island hasn't put its rust on him, yet."

"Well? Are you only after those you know are easily broken?"

Commandant Kareyev walked to the door, opened it, and blew his whistle.

"Comrade Fedossitch," he ordered his assistant when shuffling feet stopped at the door, "bring Citizen Volkontzev here."

Comrade Fedossitch looked, surprised, at Kareyev. He looked into the room at Joan, a veiled glance of resentful hatred. He bowed and shuffled away.

They heard his steps again mingled with the resonant

stride of Volkontzev. Comrade Fedossitch pushed the door open with his boot and, stepping aside, drawing his head into his shoulders in the obsequious bow of a headwaiter, his elbows pressed tightly to his body, let Michael enter, approached Kareyev and remarked, smiling softly, his smile timidly apologetic and arrogantly remonstrative at once:

"It's against the law, Comrade Commandant. The sentence was ten days."

"Has Comrade Fedossitch forgotten," Kareyev asked, "that *my* order brought Citizen Volkontzev here?"

And he slammed the door, leaving his assistant outside.

Commandant Kareyev looked at Michael, pale, erect in his old jacket that fitted so well; then, he looked at Joan, who faced the prisoner, studying with an indifferent curiosity the patches on that jacket and the blue, frozen hands in its sleeves.

"You are here, Volkontzev," said Commandant Kareyev, "to apologize."

"To whom?" Michael asked calmly.

"To Comrade Harding."

Michael made a step toward her and bowed graciously.

"I'm sorry, madam," he smiled, "that you made the worthy Commandant break a law—for the first time in his life. But I warn you, Comrade Commandant, laws are easily broken by . . . er . . . Comrade Harding."

"Citizen Volkontzev is not a fair judge of women," Joan answered, her voice expressionless.

"I should hate to judge all women, Comrade Harding, by some I have known."

"You're here to apologize," reminded Kareyev. "If you do, your sentence will be suspended."

"And if I don't?"

"I've been here five years and all the prisoners until now have obeyed me. If I stay here longer, *all* of them will learn to obey me. And I'm not leaving—yet."

"Well, then, you can feed me to the rats in the pit; or you can have me flogged till I stop bleeding; but you won't hear me apologize to this woman."

Commandant Kareyev did not answer, for the door

flew open and Comrade Fedossitch saluted, out of breath.

"Comrade Commandant! There's a disturbance in the kitchen!"

"What's the matter?"

"The convicts on vegetable duty refuse to peel the potatoes. They say the potatoes are frozen and rotten and not fit to cook."

"Well, they'll eat them raw."

He hurried out, and Comrade Fedossitch followed.

In one swift movement, Joan was at the closed door. She listened, her ear and her hands pressed to the panel. She waited till the last step echoed against the vaults far downstairs.

Then, she turned. She said one word, her voice alive, tremulous, ringing like the first blow to a bursting dam, pleading and triumphant and anguished:

"Michael!"

The word slapped him in the face. He did not move. He did not soften, did not smile. Only his lips quivered when he asked almost without sound:

"Why are you here?"

She smiled softly, her smile pleading, radiant. Her hands rose, hungrily, imperiously, to his shoulders. He seized her wrists; it was an effort that shook every muscle of his body, but he threw her hands aside.

"Why are you here?" he repeated.

She whispered, a faint trace of reproach in her voice:

"I thought you had enough faith in me to understand. I couldn't recognize you yesterday—I was afraid of being watched. I'm here to save you."

He asked grimly:

"How did you get here?"

"I have a friend in Nijni Kolimsk," she whispered hurriedly, breathlessly. "A big English merchant, Ellers. His place is right across the street from the GPU. He knows men there, influential men he can *order*, you understand? We heard about that . . . that invitation of Kareyev's. Ellers arranged it—and I was sent here."

She stopped, looking at his white face. She asked:

"Why so . . . stern, dearest? Won't you smile to reward me?"

"Smile at what? My wife in the arms of a foul Communist?"

"Michael!"

"Did you really think that you'd find me willing to be saved—at such a price?"

She smiled calmly. "Don't you know how much a woman can promise—and how little fulfill?"

"My wife can't pretend to play a part like that."

"We can't choose our weapons, Michael."

"But there is an honor that . . ."

She spoke proudly, solemnly, her head high, her voice tense, ringing, throwing each word straight into his face:

"I have a shield that my honor will carry high through any battle: I love you. . . . Look at these walls. There's frozen water in the stone. A few more years—your eyes, your skin, your mind will freeze like that, crushed by this stone, by the days and hours that do not move. Do you want me to go away, to wander through the world with but one thought, one desire, and leave you to wither in this frozen hell?"

He looked at her. He took a step toward her. She did not move. She made no sound, but her bones crackled when his arms tore her off the ground, his lips sinking into her body, hungry with the dreams, the despair, the sleepless nights of two long years.

"Frances! . . . Frances . . ."

She was the first one to tear herself away from him. She listened at the door and threw a long gold thread of hair off her temple with the back of her hand, her fingers drooping limply, a quick, sharp movement.

He whispered breathlessly:

"Do it again."

"What?"

"Your hair . . . the way you threw it back. . . . I've been dreaming—for two years—of how you did that . . . and the way you walked, and the way you turned your head with that hair over one eye. . . . I've tried to see it—as if you were here—so many times. And now you're here . . . here . . . Frances . . . but I want you to go back."

"It's too late to go back, Michael."

"Listen." His face was grim. "You can't stay here. I thank you. I appreciate what you've tried to do. But I can't let you stay. It's insane. There's nothing you can do."

"I can. I have a plan. I can't tell you now. And there's no other way for me to save you. I've tried everything. I've spent all the money I had. There's no way out of Strastnoy Island. No way but one. You have to help me."

"Not while you're here."

She walked away from him, turned calmly, stood, her arms crossed, her hands grasping her elbows, the golden thread of hair falling over one eye, looking at him calmly, the faintest wrinkle of a mocking smile in the corners of her long, thin mouth.

"Well?" she asked. "I'm here. What can you do about it?"

"If you don't go, I can tell one thing to Kareyev. Just one name. Yours."

"Can you? Think of it, Michael. Don't you know what he'd do to me if he learned the truth?"

"But . . ."

"It will be worse for me than for you, if you betray me. You could try to kill him. You'd never succeed, but you'd be executed and you'd leave me alone—in his power."

"But . . ."

"Or you could kill yourself—if you prefer. It would still leave me—alone."

She knew that she had won. She whirled toward him suddenly, her voice vibrant, passionate, commanding:

"Michael, don't you understand? I love you. I ask you to believe in me. There has never been a time when you could prove your faith, as you can do now. I'm asking the hardest of sacrifices. Don't you know that it's much harder sometimes to stand by and remain silent than to act? I'm doing my part. It's not easy. But yours is worse. Aren't you strong enough for it?"

His face set, his eyes on hers, a new fire in his eyes, he answered slowly:

"Yes."

She whispered, her lips close to his:

"It's not for your sake only, Michael. It's our life. It's the years awaiting us, and all that is still left to us, still possible—if we fight for it. One last struggle and then . . . then . . . Michael, I love you."

"I'll do my part, Frances."

"Keep away from me. Pretend you've never seen me before. Remember, your silence is your only way to protect me."

The vaults downstairs rang faintly as if from quick electric shocks. Kareyev's steps hurried up the stairs.

"He's coming, Michael," she whispered. "Here's your beginning. Apologize to me. It will be your first step to help me."

When Commandant Kareyev entered, Joan was standing by the table, examining indifferently a pair of stockings. Michael stood by the door. His head was bowed.

"Well, Volkontzev," the Commandant inquired, "have you had time to think it over? Have you changed your mind?"

Michael raised his head. Joan looked at him. Not a line moved in her calm face, not even the muscles around her eyes. But her eyes looked into his with a silent, desperate plea he alone could understand.

Michael made a step forward and bowed slightly.

"I have been mistaken about you, Comrade Harding," he said steadily, distinctly. "I'm sorry."

* * *

Editor's Note

In one summary of Red Pawn, *Ayn Rand wrote the following about the background of Joan and Michael. Presumably, this information would belong somewhere in the preceding sequence.*

"Three years ago, as an engineer in charge of a Soviet factory, Michael had been sent on a mission to America. He had met Joan and married her there. But he was forced to return to Russia, because his mother was held as a hostage for his return. Joan had come to Russia with him. Then, during one of the usual political purges, Michael was arrested; the authorities had been suspicious of him for some time, because he showed too much ability, and men of ability are considered dangerous in Russia; besides, he hud been abroad and was married to an

American who, it was felt, must have taught him many
dangerous ideas of freedom. Michael was sent to Strast-
noy Island—for life. It had taken Joan two years to find
out where he was."

——*III*——

The Strastnoy Island library was in the former chapel.
Here, prisoners and guards off duty were allowed to
spend their long days, to try and forget that their days
had twenty-four hours—all of them alike.

The sacred emblems and ikons which could be removed had been taken down. But the old paintings on
the walls could not be removed. Many centuries ago, the
unknown hand of a great artist had spent a lifetime of
dreary days immortalizing his soul on the chapel's walls.
None could tell what dark secret, what sorrow had
thrown him out of the world into its last, forgotten outpost. But all the power and passion, all the fire and re-
bellious agony of his tortured spirit had been poured
into the somber colors on the walls, into majestic figures
of a magnificent life, the life his eyes had seen and renounced. And the bodies of tortured saints silently cried
of his ecstasy, his doubt, his hunger.

Through three narrow slits of windows, a cold haze of
light streamed into the library, like a gray fog rolling in
from the sea. It left the shadows of centuries to doze in
the dark, vaulted corners. It threw white blotches on the
rough, unpainted boards of bookshelves that cut into the
angels' snowy wings, into the foreheads of saintly patri-
archs; on the procession following the cross-bearing Jesus
to the Golgotha; and above it—on the red letters on a
strip of white cotton: PROLETARIANS OF THE WORLD UNITE!

Tall candles in silver stands at the altar had to be
lighted in the daytime. Their little red flames stood immobile, each candle transformed into a chandelier by the
myriads of tiny reflections in the gilded halos of carved
saints; they burned without motion, without noise, a silent, resigned service in memory of the past—around a
picture of Lenin.

Above, on the vaulted ceiling, the unknown artist had

placed his last work. A figure of Jesus floated in the clouds, His robe whiter than snow. He looked down with a sad, wise smile, His arms outstretched in silent invitation and blessing.

The library was the creation of Comrade Fedossitch, who liked to talk of "our duty to the new culture." The murals did not harmonize with his new culture and Comrade Fedossitch had tried to improve them. He had painted a red flag into the raised hand of Saint Vladimir as that first Christian ruler converted his people to the new faith; he had painted a sickle and hammer on Moses' tablets. But the ancient glazing that protected the murals, its secret lost with the monks, did not take fresh paint well. The red flag ran down the wall and peeled off in pieces. So Comrade Fedossitch had given up the idea of artistic alterations. He had compromised by tacking over Saint Vladimir's stomach a bright-red poster bearing a soldier and an airplane, and the inscription: COMRADES! DONATE TO THE RED AIR-FLEET!

On the shelves were *The Constitution of the U.S.S.R., The ABC of Communism,* the first volume of a novel, a book of verse without a cover, a *Ladies' Guide to Fine Needlework,* a manual of arithmetical problems for the first grade, and others.

Joan had brought a radio. She walked into the library carrying it under her arm, a square box with an awkward loudspeaker.

The men in the room rose, bowing to her, smiling a timid welcome. It was different from her first entrance into the library a week ago. Then they had ignored her, as if the door had opened to admit her and no one had entered the room; they had stepped out of her way, cautiously and speedily, as if she were a poisonous plant they did not care to touch. She had won them and none of them could say that she had tried. It was her fluffy, childish hair, and her wise, mysterious smile, and her eyes so defiantly open that they concealed her thoughts by exposing them, and her slow, leisurely steps that carried her down the monastery halls like a vision from these men's pasts, like the women they had left far behind in the years that had gone, in the halls of mansions that had crumbled.

An old surgeon and a former Senator did not greet her, however. They were playing chess on a corner of the long library table, where a chessboard had been traced on the unpainted wooden boards with cheap purple ink. The chess figures had been modeled out of stale bread. The Senator had a long black beard; he never shaved; he talked little and had trouble in shifting his eyes: they always looked straight into one spot for hours. He did not raise his head when Joan entered; neither did the surgeon.

An old general who wore a patched jacket and St. George's ribbon did not greet her, either. He was sitting alone, by a window, bending, his eyes squinting painfully in the dim light, busily carving wooden toys.

And still another man did not move when she entered: Michael sat alone under a tall candle reading a book for the third time. He turned a page and bent lower when the door opened to admit her.

"Good morning, Miss Harding," a prisoner who had been a Count greeted her. "How lovely you are today! May I help you? What is this?"

"Good morning," said Joan. "It's a radio."

"A radio!"

They surrounded her, stunned, eager, curious, looking at that box from somewhere where history, which had stopped for them, was still marching forward.

"A radio!" said the Count, adjusting his monocle. "So I'm not going to die without seeing one, after all."

"What's a radio, anyway?" asked an old professor.

Comrade Fedossitch, who had been painting a poster while sitting alone at a table in a corner, put his brush down and looked up, resentfully, frowning.

Joan put the radio down on the altar, under Lenin's picture. She said:

"This will cheer us all a little."

"A charming thought." The Count clicked his heels gallantly. "And what a charming gown! We of the old world said that woman was the flower of creation—and clothes the petals."

"Nothing can extinguish the torch of human progress," the gray-haired professor said solemnly. His hair was white as the angels' wings on the walls, and his eyes sad and innocent as theirs.

A tall young convict, his blond hair disheveled over a face still pale from fifty lashes he had received, said softly, his hesitant fingers touching the radio timidly:

"I haven't heard any music . . . for three years."

"The first concert," Joan announced, "on Strastnoy Island."

The radio coughed, hissed, as if clearing its throat. Then—the first notes of music dropped into the chapel like pebbles cutting into a deep, stagnant pool, tearing in sweet agony the virginal air that had never been disturbed by the sound of life.

"The hand of fate draws an eternal trace,
I see your face again so close to mine . . ."

It was a woman's voice singing a song of memories, with a poignant joy as a shadow softening its sorrow, slow and resigned, like an autumn day, still breathing of a past sunshine, but giving it up without thunder, without a storm, with just one teardrop of a first, cold rain.

It rolled into the tortured murals, into the bookshelves and posters and candles from the world outside where life breathed and sent them one faint draught. And they stood, their mouths and their hearts open, gasping for the draught, reverent as at a sacred mass, hearing the music more with a strange, contracted spot in their breasts than with their ears.

They did not speak until the voice of the radio announcer had told them that it was a station in Leningrad. Then, the blond youth broke the silence:

"That was beautiful, Miss Harding. Almost . . ." A violent cough interrupted him, shaking his thin shoulders. "Almost as beautiful as you are. . . . Thank you. . . ."

He grasped her hand and pressed it to his lips, and held it there longer than mere gratitude dictated.

"Leningrad," the Count remarked, adjusting his monocle, an effort bringing back to his lips his old nonchalant smile. "It was St. Petersburg in my day. Funny how time flies. . . . The quays of the Neva were all white. The snow squealed under the sleighs. We had music, too, at the Aquarium. Champagne that sparkled like music, and girls that sparkled like champagne. . . ."

"I'm from Moscow," said the professor. "I gave lectures . . . at the University. 'The History of Aesthetics'—that was my last course. . . ."

"I'm from the Volga," said the blond youth. "We were building a bridge across the Volga. It gleamed in the sun—like a steel knife that was to slash across the river's body."

"When Mademoiselle Collette danced at the Aquarium," said the Count, "we threw gold coins on the table."

"Young students listened to me," the professor whispered. "Rosy cheeks . . . bright eyes. . . . Young Russia. . . ."

"It was to be the longest bridge in the world. . . . Perhaps, someday . . . I might go back and . . ." He did not finish; he coughed.

"I have faith in Russia." The professor spoke solemnly, like a prophet. "Our Saint Russia has known dark years before and has risen triumphant. What if we have to fall on the way as dry leaves swept by a torrent? Russia will live."

"It seems to me, citizen"—Comrade Fedossitch rose slowly, frowning, approaching Joan—"that it must be against the law to play this here radio of yours."

"Is it, Comrade Fedossitch?"

"Well, if you ask me, it is. But then, I don't have the say. It may be all right for Comrade Kareyev. It was against the law to let a female citizen in here. But then, how could they refuse anything to such a worthy comrade as Commandant Kareyev?"

He walked out, slamming the door. Five years ago, in Nijni Kolimsk, Comrade Fedossitch had been a candidate for the post of Commandant of Strastnoy Island. But the GPU had chosen Comrade Kareyev.

"I gather," said the Count, following Fedossitch with his eyes, "that the male citizen does not care for the fine art of music. And I observe that he is not alone. How about you, Volkontzev? Not interested?"

"I've heard music before," Michael answered abruptly, turning a page.

"I think that men who let some pet prejudice of theirs stand against the most wonderful woman in the world," said the young engineer, "ought to be thrown into the pit."

"Leave him alone," said the Count. "I'm sure Miss Harding will excuse his unreasonable antipathy."

"But will she forgive mine?" a hoarse voice asked.

They all turned to the sound.

The old general got up, looking straight at Joan, a timid, awkward apology in his old, stubborn face. He made a step forward, came back, picked up his wooden toy; then walked to her, clutching his precious work in his big, stubby fingers.

"I'm sorry, Miss Harding"—he clicked his heels in bast shoes, as if hoping to hear the old sound of military spurs—"if I've been rather . . . Can you forget?"

"Certainly, General." Joan smiled, her smile warm as a caress, and extended her hand.

The general quickly transferred the toy to his left hand and shook hers in a tight grasp.

"That . . ." He indicated the box from which the soft tune of a folk song floated into the room. "Is that played in St. Petersburg?"

"Yes."

"I'm from St. Petersburg. Eleven years. I've left my wife there. And Iura, my grandson. He's the grandest little fellow. He was two years old when I left. He had blue eyes, just like . . . like my son."

He stopped suddenly. Joan noticed the awkward silence that none of the men seemed willing to break.

The Count proved to be the bravest.

"What are you making now, General? A new one?" he asked, pointing at the toy. "You know, Miss Harding, our general is a proud old man. We have a little workshop here where we're allowed to make things: boots, baskets, and such. When the boat comes, they collect it all and take it away, to the cities. They bring us cigarettes, woolen scarfs, socks—in exchange. The boots are the most profitable to make. But the general won't make boots."

"No one shall say," the general interrupted proudly, "that a general of the Army of his Imperial Majesty stooped to making boots."

"He makes wooden toys, instead," the Count explained. "He invents them himself."

"This is a new one." The general smiled eagerly. "I'll show you."

He raised the toy and pulled a little stick; a wooden peasant and bear armed with hammers struck an anvil in turn, jerking awkwardly. As the tiny hammers knocked rhythmically through the music, the Count whispered into Joan's ear:

"Don't ever mention his son. He was a captain in the old army. The reds hanged him—before his father's eyes."

"You see," the general was explaining, "I'm always thinking that my toys go out into the world and children play with them, little chubby, rosy fellows, like Iura. . . . And sometimes, I think, wouldn't it be funny if one of the toys fell into his hands, and . . . But then, how stupid of me! . . . Eleven years . . . he's a full-grown young man, by now. . . ."

"Checkmate, Doctor," the Senator's raucous voice boomed suddenly. "Were you paying any attention to the game? Or am I going to lose the last man I can speak to?"

He shot a dark, significant glance at the general, and left the room, slamming the door.

"Poor fellow," sighed the general. "You mustn't be angry at him, Miss Harding. He won't speak to anyone that speaks to you. He's not quite sane."

"He can't forgive you," explained the Count, "for what he presumes to be your . . . shall we say ethical differences? . . . with his code. . . . You see, he shot his own daughter—and also the Bolshevik who had attacked her."

Comrade Fedossitch found Commandant Kareyev inspecting the guard posts on the wall.

"I'm taking the liberty to report to the Comrade Commandant"—he saluted—"that there are unlawful doings going on in the library."

"What's the trouble?"

"It's the comrade woman. She's playing music."

"On what?"

"On a radio."

"Well, isn't that great? I haven't heard one for five years."

When Commandant Kareyev entered, there was a strange, tense silence in the library. The men were surrounding Joan. She knelt by the radio, turning the dial slowly, listening intently, frowning in concentration. He felt the suspense and stopped at the door.

"I think I have it," Joan's triumphant voice greeted a faint rumble from the loudspeaker.

A blast of jazz music exploded into the room, like a skyrocket bursting out of the loudspeaker, rising and breaking into flaming colors under the dark vaults.

"Abroad," said one of the men, breathlessly, reverently, as if he were saying: "Heaven."

The music was the end of a dance. It finished abruptly in a burst of applause. It was an unusual sound to enter the library. The men grinned and applauded, too.

A nasal Oriental voice spoke an announcement in French. Joan translated:

"This is the Café Electric, Tokyo, Japan. We are now going to hear the lightest, gayest, maddest tune that ever conquered the capitals of Europe: the 'Song of Dancing Lights.' "

It was a challenge, it was an insulting burst of laughter right into the grim face of Strastnoy Island. It was like a ray of light split by a mirror, its sparkling bits sent flying, dancing over the dark, painted walls. It was the halting, drifting, irregular raving of a music drunk on its own gaiety. It was the voice of streetlights on a blazing boulevard under a dark sky, of electric signs, of automobile headlights, of diamond buckles on dancing feet.

Still kneeling by the radio, like a solemn priestess to that hymn of living, Joan spoke. She spoke to the men, but her eyes were on Commandant Kareyev. He stood at the door. At one side of him was a painting of a saint burning at the stake, his face distorted into a smile of insane ecstasy, renouncing the pleasures and the tortures of the flesh for the glory of his heaven; at the other side—a poster of a huge machine with little ant-sized men, sweating at its gigantic levers, and the inscription: "Our duty is our sacrifice to the red collective of the Communistic State!"

Joan was speaking:

"Somewhere, they are dancing to this music. It's not very far. It's on this same earth. Over there, the man is holding the woman in his arms. They, too, have a duty. It's a duty to look into each other's eyes and smile at life an answer beyond all doubts, all questions, all sorrows."

Her head thrown back, her body on the dark altar steps, tense, listening to the song with its every muscle, seemed a sacrificial offering to the Deity she was serving. The candlelight drowned in her hair, golden as the saints' halos.

She did not feel Michael's hungry eyes. She was smiling at Commandant Kareyev.

Commandant Kareyev did not say a word. He walked to the altar. He turned the radio dial without looking at it, his eyes on her. He turned until he found a voice speaking in stern, familiar, Party accents:

". . . and in closing this meeting of the workers of the first Moscow Textile factory, let me remind you, comrades, that but one devotion has a place in our lives: our devotion to the great aim of the world revolution."

The radio coughed applause. Another voice announced:

"Comrades! We shall close this meeting by singing our great anthem—the 'Internationale.' "

The slow, majestic notes of the red hymn marched solemnly into the air.

"All men—stand up!" ordered Commandant Kareyev.

It seemed that red banners unrolled under the vaults, under Jesus' white robes. It seemed that drums beat through the singing chorus, drums and footsteps of men marching gladly, steadily into battle, their lives a ready sacrifice to the call of the song.

Commandant Kareyev did not say a word. He looked at Joan, a little wrinkle of a smile in the corners of his mouth, the song giving her his answer.

Joan stood up. She leaned over the radio. She looked

at him, calm, undefeated. Her lips parted in a slow, mysterious, indulgent smile.

——*IV*——

Snow was falling beyond the library windows. It gathered on the sills outside, rising slowly, closing the barred squares one by one. White flakes crashed silently into the glass panes and stayed there like fluffy, broken stars. It made the library darker. New candles burned at the altar.

Commandant Kareyev's hand had long, sinewy fingers. They grasped things tightly, precisely, as if closing over the trigger of an aimed gun. Commandant Kareyev was turning the radio dial impatiently.

"I can't get it, dear," he said. "No one seems to be playing our 'Song of Dancing Lights' today."

Joan's hand covered his and led it, turning the dial slowly, together. She bent over the radio, her cheek pressed to his forehead, her blond hair brushing his temple, blinding him, getting tangled in his dark eyelashes.

They caught the familiar tune in the middle of a laughing sentence. It came like the unseen hand of the outside world, drawing a curtain of tumbling notes over the snow-laden windows, making Commandant Kareyev's lips smile gaily, eagerly, a young happiness relaxing his stern wrinkles.

The library was deserted. He sat on the altar steps, drawing Joan close to him.

"Here it is," he said, "the anthem of our duty."

Her finger was wandering over his forehead, following the veins on his temple. She said:

"They play it well tonight. It's night in Japan now."

"And there are lights . . . dancing lights . . ."

"Not candles, like here."

"If we were there tonight, I'd take you to this place where they are playing our song. And if there's snow on the ground, like here, I'd carry you out of the car in my arms so that the snow wouldn't touch your little slippers."

"They have no snow there. They have cherry trees in blossom—all white."

"Like your shoulders under the lights. There are men sitting at tables there, the kind of men who wear black suits and diamond studs. They'll look at you. I want them to look at you. At your shoulders. I want them to know you're mine."

"Cherry blossoms and music . . . no footsteps on the wall outside; no groans from the pit."

"But you came to all this—and to me. And you've stayed with me."

"I came because I was desperate. I stayed because I found something I didn't expect."

Her hand moved slowly from his forehead down to his chin, studying tenderly every line.

"It's strange, Joan . . . I've tracked a cross over Russia, through forests and swamps, with a gun and a red flag. I thought I was marching toward the dawn of the world revolution. It has always been there, ahead of me. And now, when I look ahead, the golden dawn is nothing but," he finished with a laughing tenderness, drawing her closer, "a lock of your hair loose in the wind because you forgot to comb it."

He sat on the altar steps. She knelt by his side, erect, her hands on his shoulders. Behind them tall candles burned before golden saints; above them was the picture of Lenin; the radio played the "Song of Dancing Lights."

Through the windows where the rising snow was growing whiter against a darkening sky came the shrill whistle of a boat. He did not seem to notice it, but Joan started.

"The boat," she said. "The last boat before the sea freezes."

He did not turn to look at the window. He smiled slyly, happily.

"I have a little surprise for you, Joan. And will you do something for me? Will you wear tonight, for dinner, the blue dress I like?"

She walked to the window and peered through the frosted pattern. The boat had stopped at the old landing. Most of the prisoners had been ordered to unload the cargo; there was more freight than usual.

The general was the first to appear, bent under a huge

crated object. Joan heard his heavy steps in the corridor. She opened the library door and watched him pass on his way upstairs.

"I think it's an armchair," the general grinned at her, passing by. "It feels like one. Although I've never yet felt an armchair from the underside."

The next one to come was Comrade Fedossitch. He shuffled to the library door and stopped, saluting, out of breath.

"It's here, Comrade Commandant. It's arrived," he reported, servility fighting indignation in his voice. "The boat's arrived. Don't you want to come down and watch the men—under the unusual circumstances?"

Commandant Kareyev waved his hand, annoyed.

"I thought I told you to watch them. You can do it. I'm busy."

More packages came, carried through the corridor, up the stairs to Kareyev's room. The prisoners' boots left tracks of dirty, melting snow as they passed.

The professor and the Senator came with a long, heavy roll of carpet. The professor smiled at Joan. The Senator, his beard longer, his cheeks whiter than before, turned his head away.

The young engineer carried a box in which something rattled with a metallic sound. His cheeks were beginning to acquire an unnatural bright rosiness. His eyes sparkled with a feverish vivacity.

"I think it's for Miss Harding," he said aloud as if to himself, passing by the library door, rattling the box, watching Joan from the corner of his eye. "I admire the Commandant—for the first time."

The Count carried a carefully crated box stuffed with straw. He held it with the reverence due a priceless load. The load made the sound of clinking glass.

"Congratulations, Miss Harding," he smiled triumphantly, winking at the box. "*That* is what I call a real victory!"

Commandant Kareyev watched Joan's wide, questioning eyes as they followed the procession up the stairs. He did not explain.

Michael stopped at the open door. His tall shoulders were beginning to droop; so did the corners of his mouth. His eyes were darker than usual; and that darkness, like a wave of unbearable pain, seemed to have overflown his eyes and frozen in blue puddles of circles under them. The sparkling defiance of Michael Volkontzev was gone; a brooding bitterness had taken its place.

He carried on his shoulders a large bundle sewn in heavy burlap. It seemed soft and light. He looked at Joan and Kareyev in the doorway, her head resting on his shoulder.

"These are pillows, I believe," said Michael. "Do they go to your room or her room—or does it make any difference?"

Joan did not raise her head.

"To my room," said Kareyev.

Joan wore her blue dress for dinner. The dark velvet clung to her body tightly, almost too tightly; but a severe military collar clasped her neck high under her chin.

One candle burned on the table in the middle of Commandant Kareyev's room. It made a little island of light in the darkness, and a bright flame in the black panes of the window. She saw the shadows of long dark drapes; she felt a soft carpet under her feet. Two big armchairs stood at the table. A white stain in the darkness by the wall was a heavy lace spread on the bed with faint glimmers of candlelight in the new satin pillows.

"It's all for your room," Kareyev hurried to explain, smiling happily, almost bashfully, before she could say a word. "It's here . . . just for a surprise."

Across the swaying candle flame, Joan smiled at him. His eyes did not leave her. He watched for her to notice the snow-white tablecloth, the delicate china dishes, the little red sparks dancing in the silverware and the tall cut-glass goblets.

Joan's eyes had melted into a soft, dreamy warmth. When she looked at Kareyev they sparkled with more than the candlelight's reflection. They stopped one second longer than a glance required, lingering in a caress for the two of them alone to understand.

They were not alone. A waiter stood by the wall. It was Michael's turn to wait on the Commandant's table.

He stood, hunching his shoulders, thrusting his head

forward, watching solicitously Commandant Kareyev's every movement, stiff and smiling discreetly, an exaggerated picture of a correct waiter. He had thrown a white napkin over his arm—which had never been required. The maître d'hôtel of one of the fashionable restaurants which Michael Volkontzev used to visit would not have approved, however, of the look in that perfect waiter's eyes.

"This is our anniversary, Joan," said Kareyev, when they sat down. "Don't you remember? You came here three months ago."

She smiled, indicating the table:

"And such is the end of Commandant Kareyev."

"No. The beginning."

He leaned closer to her, speaking eagerly.

"I'll bring everything you want here. I'll make this island for you—what you make it for me."

"What I've made it—for us."

She did not notice Michael's eyes that seemed to gather her every syllable, tearing them, in silent, ferocious agony, off her lips.

Kareyev shook his head slowly. "I don't like that word. I've served it for such a long time. For *us*. We— the people, the collective, the millions. I've fought on barricades—for us. I've fought in the trenches. I've shot at men and men have shot at me. For us, for them, for those countless others somewhere around me, those for whom I've given a lifetime, my every moment, my every thought, my blood. For us. I don't want to hear the word. Because now—it's for *me*. You came here—for *me*. You're mine. I won't share that with anyone on earth. *Mine*. What a word that is—when you begin to understand it!"

She smiled, mocking, a little reproachful.

"Why, *Comrade* Kareyev!"

He smiled timidly, apologetically.

"Yes, Comrade Kareyev—tomorrow. And after tomorrow. And for many days to come. But not tonight. I can have one night for my own, can't I? Look." He pointed at the table proudly. "I ordered all this for you—by wireless. I have money in the bank at Nijni Kolimsk. My salary. Had nothing to do with it for five years. . . . I guess it wasn't money alone that I've been missing for five years—for more than thirty-five years."

"It's never too late while one lives—if one still wants to live."

"It's strange, Joan. I've never really known what it was to want to live. I've never thought of tomorrow. I didn't care what bullet ended me—or when. But now, for the first time, I want to be spared. Am I a traitor, Joan?"

"One cannot be a traitor to anything," said Joan, "except to oneself."

"Loyalty," said Michael, "is like rubber: one can stretch it so far, and then—it snaps."

Kareyev looked at him surprised, as if noticing him for the first time.

"Where did you get these perfect waiter's manners, Volkontzev?" he asked.

"Oh, I've had a lot of experience, sir," Michael answered calmly, "from a slightly different angle, though. We had banquets in my day, too. I remember one. We had many flowers and guests. We had a wedding such as those of the old days. She held a bouquet more gracefully than any woman I've ever seen. She wore a long white veil—then."

Commandant Kareyev looked at him, looked at a convict with a shadow of sympathy—for the first time.

"Do you miss her?" he asked.

"No," said Michael. "I wish I did."

"And she?"

"She's the kind that doesn't stay lonely for a long time."

"I wouldn't say that about a woman I had loved."

"You and I, Commandant, did not love the same woman."

"After dinner," Joan said slowly, looking at Michael, "will you bring some wood to my room? I've burned the last logs. It's very cold at night."

Michael bowed silently.

Commandant Kareyev pointed to a dark bottle that stood on the table. Michael poured, filling their glasses.

The wine was dark red, and when he poured it, little

ruby sparks tumbled into the glasses, as a draft waved the candle flame.

Commandant Kareyev rose holding his glass, looking at Joan. She rose, too.

"To love," he said calmly, solemnly.

He had pronounced the word for the first time.

Joan held her glass out to his. They met over the candle. It threw a trembling red glow over their faces through the dark liquid, and the shadows swayed over their cheeks, as the flame in the draft.

Her hand jerked suddenly, when she sat down. She spilled a red drop on the white tablecloth. Michael hurried to refill her glass.

"To love, madame," he said, "that *is*—and that *was*."

She drank.

Joan was alone in her room when Michael entered carrying the wood.

She watched him silently, standing at the window, her arms crossed, without moving. He dropped the logs by the stove. He asked, without looking at her:

"Is that all?"

"Start the fire," she ordered.

He obeyed, kneeling by the stove. He struck a match and the crisp bark crackled, curling, twisting, bursting into little white flames. She approached him and whispered:

"Michael, please listen. I . . ."

"How many logs, madame?" he asked coldly.

"Michael, what were you trying to do? Do you want to ruin my plan?"

"I didn't know there was any plan left to ruin."

"Your faith doesn't last long, does it?"

"My faith? What about his? I've seen what you've done to that."

"Isn't that what I set out to do?"

"Yes, but I can see the way you look at him. I can see the way you talk to him. What am I to believe?"

"My love."

"I believe in that. Yes. Your love. But for whom?"

"Don't you know?"

"He trusts you, too. Which one of us are you deceiving?"

She looked at him, her eyes narrowing with the indifferent, even, enigmatic glance that no one could answer. She said slowly, with the innocence of a perfect calm:

"Maybe both."

He stepped toward her, his voice tense, his eyes pleading:

"Frances, I trust you. I wouldn't last here one day if I didn't trust you. But I can't stand it. We've tried. There's nothing we can do. You must see that now. It's hopeless. The boat leaves at dawn. It's the last one before the sea freezes. You'll go back. You'll take that boat tomorrow."

She spoke slowly, without changing her voice, her words lazy, indifferent:

"I won't take that boat, Michael. Someone else is taking it."

"Who's taking it?"

"You."

He stared at her, speechless.

"Keep working on that fire," she ordered.

He obeyed. She bent over him, whispering quickly, eagerly:

"Listen carefully. You'll get on board. You'll hide in the hold. The Commandant won't make his inspection rounds tonight, I'll see to that."

"But . . ."

"Here are the keys to the outside door and the gate. There's only one guard on the wall who can see the landing. Watch him. At midnight he'll be removed."

"How?"

"Leave that to me. When you see him go—hurry to the boat."

"And you?"

"I'm staying here."

He stared at her. She added:

"I'm staying here just a little longer. To keep him from discovering your escape. Don't worry. There's no danger. He'll never know who helped you."

He took her hand. "Frances . . ."

"Dearest, not a word. Please! I've lived three long

months for just this night. We can't weaken now. We can't retreat. It's our last battle. You understand?"

He nodded slowly. She whispered:

"I'll join you in a free country where we'll take these last two years of our lives, and seal them, and never open them again."

"But I'd like to read again about what you've done."

"There's only one thing I want you to read and remember, only one thing that I'll write over these years: I love you."

They heard Kareyev's steps outside. Michael went out as he entered. Joan stood at the open door of the stove where a bright flame whistled merrily. She said to Michael, aloud:

"Thank you, this will warm the room. I'll feel much better—tonight."

—— *V* ——

The island was blue under the moon, blue-white, sparkling like hard clean sugar. Dark shadows cut black holes in the snow, with sharp gaping edges. The sky, a black precipice above, twinkled with a white foam of stars floating over its smooth surface, as the foam that crashed furiously against the island, leaping in silver sprays high over the top of the walls. On the black precipice of the sea below floated the white shadows of the first ice.

The lights were out in the monastery. The entrance door had been locked for the night. The gray flag fought the wind on the tower.

Michael sat on his cot in the darkness and watched the wall outside. A guard walked there slowly, back and forth. His lantern seemed a little red eye winking at Michael. His muffler flapped in the wind.

Michael's roommate, the old professor, had gone to bed. But he could not sleep. He sighed in the darkness, and made the sign of the cross.

"Aren't you going to bed, Michael?"

"Not yet."

"Why do you keep your coat on?"

"I'm cold."

"That's funny. I feel stuffy in here. . . . Well, goodnight."

"Goodnight."

The professor turned to the wall. Then he sighed. Then he turned to Michael again.

"Do you hear the sea? It has been beating there for centuries. It's been moaning before we came here. It will be moaning long after we're gone."

He made the sign of the cross. Michael was watching the guard's lantern.

"We wander in the darkness," said the professor. "Man has lost sight of beauty. There is a great beauty on this earth of ours. A beauty one's spirit can approach only bare-headed. But how many of us ever get a glimpse of it?"

Commandant Kareyev's window was a long, thin, blue cut in the darkness of his room. The moonlight made a long, thin band across the floor, checkered into panes, pointed as the door of an ancient cathedral. In the darkness by the window, Joan's head was leaning against the back of an armchair, her face a pale white with soft blue shadows under her cheekbones, with a glowing blue patch in the triangle under her chin thrown back, her mouth dark and soft and tender, glistening with a few lost sparks of moonlight. The darkness swallowed her body and only her hands were white on her knees, and in her hands lay the face of Commandant Kareyev at her feet. He did not move. The light of a single candle on the table did not reach them. He whispered, his dark hair brushing her white wrists:

". . . and then, someday, you may want to leave me. . . ."

She shook her head slowly.

"You may be lonely here in winter. The sea freezes. The nights are so long."

"Nights like this?"

He looked at the window, smiling.

"Lovely, isn't it? I've never noticed that before. As if . . . as if it were a night for just the two of us."

Somewhere, far downstairs, an old clock slowly chimed twelve. She repeated softly at the last stroke:

"Yes . . . for just the two . . . of us. Let's step outside. It's lovely."

Commandant Kareyev wrapped her winter cloak around her shoulders. The huge collar of fluffy gray fox swallowed her head, rising over the tips of her blond curls.

On the gallery outside, a soft silver glow streamed from the heavy, sparkling fringe of icicles on the cornices above their heads. A guard with a lantern passed slowly on the wall before them. Beyond the wall rose the black funnel of the boat.

Commandant Kareyev looked at her. It had been his first wine in five years. It had been his first celebration. He drew her closer. His hand slipped under the fluffy fox collar. She jerked herself away.

"What's the matter?" he whispered.

"Not here."

"Why?"

Calmly, she pointed to the guard on the wall, a few steps away. Commandant Kareyev smiled. He blew his whistle. The guard turned abruptly, raised his head, saluted.

"Report to post number four at once," Kareyev shouted over the roar of the waves. "Patrol it until further orders."

The guard saluted, climbed down, hurried away across the white yard, snow crunching under his boots.

Commandant Kareyev's lips sank into Joan's. His arms crushed her body against his.

"Did you ever feel a moment when you knew why you had been living, my dearest . . . dearest . . ." he whispered. "I'm happy . . . Joan."

Her head was thrown far back, so far that he could see the reflection of the stars in her eyes; so far that she could see the yard below. Her body fell backwards recklessly, limp against his arm. She was smiling triumphantly, deliriously.

"Why do you look so strange, Joan? Why do you smile like that?"

"I'm happy—tonight," she whispered at the stars.

Michael opened the entrance door noiselessly. He tried with his foot the frozen, slippery steps outside. He felt the gun in his pocket. He stepped out. It took him three minutes to pull the door closed again, slowly, gradually, without a sound. He locked it behind him.

The blue snow glared at him. But there was a narrow line of shadow under the wall of the building. He could follow it to the landing gate. He glided silently into the deep snow, pressing himself against the wall. The snow rose higher than his boots. He could feel it sliding inside. It felt hot as a burn against the holes in his old woolen socks. He moved slowly, his eyes on the empty wall where the guard had been, drawn by it as by a magnet.

He stopped across from the landing gate. He could see the boat's funnel beyond it. There was no sound on the island but the beating of waves against the wall. He could see two little red dots of lanterns far away. He had to cross to the gate in the open, in the snow. But the guards were too far. The lights were out in the building.

He threw himself down in the snow and crawled as fast as he could toward the gate. He felt the snow biting his wrists between his gloves and sleeves. Halfway across, he raised his head to look back at the building. He stopped.

High on an open gallery, he saw two figures. They were immobile in a passionate embrace. The man's back was to the yard below.

Michael rose to his feet. He stood in the open, in the glaring snow, and looked at them. One glove slid from his hand, but he didn't notice it. There was no sound as the glove fell; no sound of his breathing, not even of his heart. Then he ran through the snow, in the moonlight, back to the monastery door.

Commandant Kareyev and Joan turned when the door of his room was flung open. Joan screamed. Michael stood on the threshold, snow dripping from his clothes.

"You might need these," he said and threw the keys into Kareyev's face. "I've tried to escape. I don't care what you do to me. And I don't care what you do to her."

"Michael!" Joan screamed. "Get out of here! Keep quiet!"

"She's afraid," said Michael, "that I'll tell you that she's my wife!

"Oh, that's all right," he continued, as no answer came. "You can have her, with my compliments and permission. Only I don't think you needed the permission."

Commandant Kareyev looked at Joan. She stood straight, looking at him. The cloak with the fluffy collar had fallen to her feet.

Commandant Kareyev bent down and picked up the keys. Then he blew his whistle three times. A little drop of blood rolled from his lips where the keys had struck him.

Comrade Fedossitch and two guards appeared at the door. Comrade Fedossitch was hastily pulling his nightshirt into his trousers.

"Put Citizen Volkontzev in the tower detention cell," Commandant Kareyev ordered.

"Why don't you throw me into the pit?" asked Michael. "You'll be rid of me quicker. Then you can enjoy my wife without any trouble."

"Did you say—your *wife,* Citizen Volkontzev?" gasped Comrade Fedossitch.

"Put Citizen Volkontzev in the tower detention cell," repeated Commandant Kareyev.

The guards grasped Michael's arms. He walked out, head high, laughing. Comrade Fedossitch followed.

The long flame of a candle on the table hissed in the silence, smoking, reaching the end of the little wax butt. Commandant Kareyev looked at Joan. She stood leaning against the table, her head bent, looking at her toe buried in the fur collar on the floor.

Commandant Kareyev walked to a shelf, took a new candle, lighted it, replaced the old one. He stood waiting. She did not look at him, did not speak. He asked:

"What are you going to say?"

"Nothing."

"Is it true?"

"My name is Frances Volkontzeva."

"You love him?"

She looked at him slowly, fixedly, from under her eyelids, without raising her head.

"I didn't say that," she answered.

He waited. She was silent.

"Is that all you have to say to me?" he asked.

"No . . . but that's all I'm going to say."

"Why?"

"I won't explain. You won't believe me."

"That's for me to decide."

His words were an order; but his eyes were a plea.

She studied him again from under her eyelids. Then she raised her head. She looked straight at him. Her eyes were clear and haughty, as they always were when she was proud of the truth in her words or prouder of the lie.

"Well, yes, I'm his wife. Yes, I came here only to save my husband. I came here hating all Communists. But I stayed because I loved one."

He did not move. But she noticed that he made an effort not to move and she knew that she could go on.

"At first it was just a game, like my name Joan. But, you see, Joan killed Frances, and now it's Joan who lives . . . and loves."

"She did not forget Frances' plans, however."

"Oh, don't you understand? I wanted him out of the way. How could I remain here with that threat, that reminder always before me? I wanted his freedom to feel that I had earned mine. But you don't have to believe me."

Her eyes were defiant; but her lips trembled, soft and childish, and her body leaned against the table, suddenly frail, helpless, calling for his protection.

"I was young when I married Michael. I thought I loved him. I didn't learn what love could be until it was too late."

In his arms was all the strength of his despair, of his faith grateful to be forced to believe again.

"It's never too late," he whispered, "while one lives— if one still wants to live."

She was laughing through his kisses, laughing happily.

"Let him escape," she whispered. "You can't leave him here. And you can't kill him. He'll always stand between us."

"Don't talk about him, now, dear. Let's just keep silent, and let me hold you like this . . . close."

"Let him go. I'll stay here with you . . . forever."

"You don't know what you're asking. If I let him go, there will be an investigation. They'll learn your real name and arrest you. We'll be separated. Forever."

"I can't stay here if he does."

"And as long as I'm Commandant here, I can't betray my Party's confidence."

"Well, then, do you have to be Commandant here?"

He let her out of his arms, stepped back, and looked at her. He was not indignant, just surprised.

"Oh, don't you see?" Her voice fell to a passionate, breathless whisper. "I've betrayed my whole past when I said I loved you. Do the same. Let's kill the years behind us with one blow—and start life again from the same grave."

"What do you mean, Joan?"

"Let's escape all together—the three of us. I know that you can't leave without permission, but we'll take the emergency motorboat. We'll go to Nijni Kolimsk. I have a friend there—an English merchant. He has connections in the GPU—it's right across the street."

"And . . . then?"

"He'll arrange our passage on an English ship to foreign lands, far, far away. To America. There Michael will give me my freedom. It's a fair exchange. And then . . ."

"Joan, I've belonged to a Party for twenty-two years. A Party that fought for the revolution."

"That fought for *them*? The people, the collective? Look at them, your millions. They sleep, they eat, they marry, they die. Is there one among them who will shed one tear in honor of a man that gave up his desire of desires for their sake?"

"They're my brothers, Joan. You don't understand our duty, our great struggle. They're hungry. They have to be fed."

"But your own heart will die of starvation."

"They've toiled hopelessly for centuries."

"But you'll give up your own last hope."

"They've suffered so much."

"But you're going to learn what suffering means."

"There is a great duty . . ."

"Yes, we all have a great duty. A sacred inviolable duty, and we spend our lives trying to violate it. Our duty to ourselves. We fight it, we stifle it, we compromise. But there comes a day when it gives us an order, its last, highest order—and then we can't disobey any longer. You want to go. With me. You *want* it. That's the highest of all reasons. You can't question it. When you can't ask any questions—then you know you're facing your duty."

He moaned helplessly:

"Oh, Joan, Joan!"

She stood before him, solemn as a priestess looking into the future, but her words were soft, dreamy, as if her voice were smiling between her stern lips, and it seemed to him that it was not her voice, not her words, but the soft, faint movements of her mouth that drew him, tempting, irresistible, into a future it knew, but he had never known.

"Over there, far away, electric fires will blaze on dark boulevards . . . and they'll play the 'Song of Dancing Lights' . . ."

He whispered obediently:

". . . and I'll carry you out of the car . . ."

". . . and I'll teach you to dance . . ."

". . . and I'll laugh, laugh, and will never feel guilty . . ."

"Are we going?"

He seemed to awaken suddenly. He stepped aside. He closed his eyes. When he opened them again she saw the look she had forgotten on the Beast's face.

"The boat is to leave at dawn," he said slowly. "I'll order it to wait till noon. You can pack your clothes. At noon, you'll go—alone."

"Is that your choice?"

"I know what I'm missing. But there are some things I can't do. I want you to go—before it is too late for me."

"Repeat it again." Her voice was calm, like his, and indifferent.

"Tomorrow—at noon—you will go—alone."

"All right, Commandant. I'll go to sleep, since I have

to travel tomorrow. . . . Goodnight. . . . When you think of me, remember only that I . . . loved you."

———*VI*———

The big trunk stood open in the middle of Joan's room. She folded her dresses slowly and put them in, one by one. She wrapped her slippers in paper. She gathered her stockings, that made a film thin as smoke over her fingers; her white powder puffs, her crystal bottles of perfume. She moved through the room quietly, without hurry. She was as calmly indifferent as on the day when she had unpacked that trunk.

She could hear, above the roar of the sea, the low droning of bells that moaned when the wind was very strong. The sea, a dirty white, turbid like dishwater, swayed furiously, ready to be slung out of the pail. The spurting sprays of foam soiled the sky to a muddy gray.

Twice, Joan had stepped out into the hall and looked at the room next to hers. Its door was open. It was empty. Its new carpet was a deep blue in the daylight. The lace spread and pillows on the bed had not been disturbed. One pillow had been flung against the wall in a far corner.

The monastery was silent. The wind whistled in the old abandoned cells high on top of the towers. Below, in the long, dim halls, whispers crawled eagerly, stealthily, as hushed gusts of wind.

". . . and all the time she was his wife."

"I don't envy him."

"I do. I wish I had a woman who loved me like that."

In a huddled group on a stair landing, the old professor whispered, sighing:

"How lonely this place will be without her!"

"I'm glad she's going," a weary voice answered, "for her sake."

At a window, the general leaned on the Count's shoulder. They were watching the sea.

"Well, the Beast has made people suffer," the general whispered. "It's his turn."

"He's getting the loan back," the Count remarked, "with *plenty* of interest."

Comrade Fedossitch leaned heavily, crouching, against a windowsill. He was not looking at the sea. He was looking, his shrewd, narrow pupils fixed tensely, up at the tower platform under the bells. The tall figure of a man stood there, at the parapet. Comrade Fedossitch had a good idea of what the Commandant was thinking.

Commandant Kareyev stood on the tower, the wind tearing his hair. He was looking far out to where the clouds, as a heavy gray curtain, had descended over the coast and all that lay beyond the coast. Commandant Kareyev had faced long city streets where barricades rose red with human flags and human blood, where, behind every corner, from every rooftop, machine guns coughed a death rattle deadlier than that of a consumptive. He had faced long trenches where behind rusted barbed wire thin, bluish blades of steel waited, silent, sure, pitiless. But his face had never looked as it did now.

Steps grated on the stairs behind him. He turned. The young engineer was coming up, carrying a stepladder and a new red flag. The old flag was gray, shivering desolately in its last convulsions, high over the cupola white with snow.

The engineer looked at him. In his young, blue eyes was a sorrow he knew they were sharing. He said slowly:

"It's a bad morning, Commandant. Gray. No sun."

"There will be no sun for a long time," said Kareyev.

"I'm cold. I'm so cold. And . . ." He looked straight into Kareyev's eyes. "I'm not the only one, Commandant."

"No," said Commandant Kareyev, "you're not the only one."

The engineer put his stepladder against the tower wall. Then he turned again. He said, as if each word were to pierce the grim, fathomless pupils of the man he had hated until that moment:

"If I found that the climate here wasn't good for my lifeblood, I'd flee to the end of the world—*if I were free.*"

Kareyev looked at him. Then he looked slowly up, at

the old flag fighting the wind between the clouds and the snow. He said thoughtfully, irrelevantly, pointing up:

"Look at that red flag. Red against the white snow. Doesn't look well together."

"The flag has faded," the engineer said slowly. "The snow has taken its color away."

"It was of cheap material. Good stuff keeps its color—in all weather."

"It's due for a change, Commandant. It has served its time."

He climbed up the ladder. He turned again to look down at the man before him. He spoke suddenly, with an impetuous fire, with the solemn gravity of a prophet, his voice clear, vibrant in the wind:

"A thousand years from now, Commandant, whether the world is red as this flag or white as the snow, who will care that a certain Communist on a speck of an island gave up the very blood of his heart—for the glory of the world revolution?"

Joan's door was left open. Commandant Kareyev passed by. He hesitated. She saw him and called:

"Good morning."

"Good morning," he answered.

"Won't you come in? We're not parting like enemies, are we?"

"Of course not."

"Maybe you'll help me to pack? Here, can you fold this blue velvet dress for me?"

She handed him the dress she had worn the night before, his favorite one. He folded it; he handed it back to her; he said brusquely:

"I'm sorry. I can't help you much. I'm busy."

He walked away. In the corridor, Comrade Fedossitch stopped him. Comrade Fedossitch bowed. Comrade Fedossitch said gently:

"The boat is waiting for Frances Volkontzeva, Comrade Commandant."

"Well?"

"Do I understand it correctly that she is going away free, that she is not to be arrested for her counterrevolutionary, treacherous plan?"

"She is going away free."

"I should think our duty is to send her to the GPU in Nijni Kolimsk. I should think hers is a serious offense against the State, punishable by . . ."

"Someday, Comrade Fedossitch, you may be Commandant of this island. Someday. Not yet."

Commandant Kareyev saw Joan again in the library. She was saying goodbye to the convicts. She was leaving the radio to them to remember her by, she said. She noticed him at the door, but did not turn.

A strange thing happened. The pale, bearded Senator, who had never looked at her, got up. He walked straight to her, took her hand, and raised it to his lips in the most courtly manner.

"I want to tell you, Citizen Volkontzeva," he said in his hoarse, dead voice, "that you are a great woman."

"Thank you, Senator," she answered. "Only, when I go away, I shall not be Citizen Volkontzeva any more. I'm going as Joan Harding."

Commandant Kareyev hurried away. Outside, on the wharf, the pockmarked, one-eyed captain was leaning on the rail of the boat, smoking his pipe. He looked at the sky and called:

"Almost noon, Comrade Commandant. The woman ready?"

"Not yet," Kareyev answered.

Soundlessly, as a shadow, Comrade Fedossitch suddenly stood at his elbow. Comrade Fedossitch saluted and said sweetly:

"Of course, Comrade Commandant, there's no question of our loyalty to you. All this will never be known. But I was just thinking that if one of us Party members here decided to go and tell the GPU about the aristocrat who got away . . ."

"The emergency motorboat is at the service of the first one who wants to go," said Kareyev. "Ask me for the key when you need it."

A guard came running down the hill, saluting, reporting breathlessly:

"Citizen Volkontzeva wants to see you, Comrade Commandant!"

Kareyev ran up to the monastery, through the snow,

leaping two steps at once. The guard looked after him, surprised. Comrade Fedossitch nodded slowly.

Joan's trunk was closed.

"I think it's time," she said calmly when Kareyev entered. "Will you have the men take my trunk down?"

"You'll have to wait a little," he answered desperately. "The boat isn't ready."

Then he went to his room and slammed the door. She listened at the wall of her cell, but could not hear a sound.

Then she heard his steps again. She opened her door.

He fell at her feet, as if all strength had gone out of his body and spirit.

"You won't go alone . . . you won't go alone . . ." was all he could whisper.

She stroked his head, smiling, kissing his hair. She whispered:

"Dear . . . we'll be so happy . . . so happy . . ."

He buried his face in the folds of her dress. He did not speak. His hands clasped her legs, holding her, in a desperate panic of fear that she would vanish from his fingers, disappear forever. She whispered:

"It will be easy. . . . Tonight. We'll take the motorboat. The three of us."

"You won't leave me . . . you'll never leave me."

"No, dear, never. . . . Tell the captain to go."

"And they'll play the 'Song of Dancing Lights' . . . just for the two of us. . . ."

"Get the motorboat ready."

"I'll buy you little satin slippers. Lined with soft pink feathers. I'll slip them myself on your bare feet. . . ."

"Destroy the wireless, so they can't give an alarm."

The wind had chased the clouds. A red, shivering line panted soundlessly over the sea where the sun had drowned. Red stains died slowly in the snow of the cupolas.

The convicts had finished their supper. Commandant Kareyev could hear the clinking of dishes in the kitchen. But there was no sound of voices. He knew what they were all thinking. When he walked through the corridors, he saw all eyes turn away from him with a forced indifference; and he felt these eyes staring at him behind his back.

Passing by the guard room, he heard Comrade Fedossitch. Comrade Fedossitch was speaking to his friend, the head of the guards. He noticed Kareyev and did not lower his voice.

". . . silver, carpets, wine . . . that's what bourgeois luxuries lead to. I never approved of the idea of bringing the bitch here. I knew she was a White."

Commandant Kareyev passed, without entering.

Comrade Fedossitch followed him.

"The Comrade Commandant inspected the motorboat today," he remarked. "Anything wrong with it?"

"No. But it's going to be used."

"Ah . . . when?"

"Tomorrow. Citizen Volkontzeva is under arrest. She'll be sent to the GPU in the morning."

"Alone?"

"No. With a trusted escort. Maybe—you."

He turned to go.

"If Citizen Volkontzeva is under arrest"—Comrade Fedossitch hunched his shoulders more ingratiatingly than ever—"will you want me to put a guard at her door?"

"If I were you, I'd be careful, Comrade Fedossitch. Someone else here might find himself with a guard at his door."

When it had grown dark, Commandant Kareyev approached the steps of the tower that guarded the wireless. There were no candles on the stairway. There was no glass in the windows. Snow gathered on the steps, blown in by the wind. He could distinguish the windows by the twinkling stars; the walls of the tower were black as the sky.

He went up slowly, carefully, trying to muffle the sound of snow creaking under his feet.

On the first landing he saw a shadow against the stars. The shadow coughed hoarsely, heaving its shallow chest.

"Good evening, Comrade Fedossitch," said the Commandant. "What are you doing here?"

"Just taking a stroll, Comrade Commandant. Like yourself."

"Have a cigarette?"

Kareyev struck a match. Their eyes met for a second over the quivering little flame. The wind blew it out. The two red lighted dots remained in the darkness.

"There's a strong wind tonight," said Comrade Fedossitch, "and the sea is rough. Dangerous for sailing."

"The cold isn't good for your lungs, Comrade Fedossitch. You should be careful of things that aren't good for you."

"I never mind it in the line of my duty. Good Communists don't let anything stand in the way of their duty. Good Communists like you and me."

"It's a pretty late hour for any duty you may have to perform."

"True, Comrade Commandant. I don't have as many responsibilities as you have. And, speaking of responsibilities, did it ever occur to you that it's a bit careless the way we leave our wireless in a lonely tower where anyone can reach it?"

Commandant Kareyev made a step forward and ordered slowly:

"Go back to your room. And stay there."

Comrade Fedossitch barred the stairs with his body, his outstretched arms touching the walls.

"You won't go up!" he hissed.

"Get out of my way!" Commandant Kareyev whispered.

"You won't get that wireless, you traitor!"

Commandant Kareyev's hand seized the long sinewy throat; his other hand pulled the gun out of Comrade Fedossitch's belt. He kicked him, and the comrade tumbled down several steps. When he straightened himself he felt Commandant Kareyev's gun in his back.

"Go down, rat. If you open your mouth—I shoot."

Comrade Fedossitch did not make a sound. Commandant Kareyev led him down to the yard. He blew his whistle.

"Citizen Fedossitch is under arrest," he said to the guards calmly, "for insubordination. Take him into the pit."

Comrade Fedossitch did not say a word. He choked, coughing, his shoulders heaving convulsively. The guards led him away, and Commandant Kareyev followed.

In a dark, clammy, low-vaulted room, the guards opened a heavy stone trapdoor with an old brass ring. They tied a rope around Comrade Fedossitch's waist. In the light of a smoked lantern, its flame swaying in a draft, his face was the color of a shell with damp, greenish pearls on his forehead. The guards unrolled the rope, lowering him into the pit. They heard his cough growing fainter as he went down. Commandant Kareyev stood watching.

The wireless room was high up in the tower. No one could hear, in the yard below, when the wireless set cracked, breaking in Commandant Kareyev's strong hands. He made sure the parts were crushed beyond repair. He had to hold them up to the starlight to see. He did not strike a match. The wind blew the hair from his wet forehead.

Commandant Kareyev opened Joan's door soundlessly, without knocking.

"Come on," he whispered. "All's ready."

She had been waiting, wrapped in a warm coat, a fur collar tight under her chin, a fur cap over her blond curls.

"Don't make any noise," he ordered. "We'll go down and get Volkontzev."

She raised her smiling lips for a kiss. He kissed them calmly, tenderly. There was no hesitation in his movements, no doubt in his eyes. He was the Communist Kareyev who had fought in the civil war.

Michael was sitting on his cot when the door of his cell was thrown open. He jumped up. Joan entered first. Commandant Kareyev followed. Michael stood, his dark eyes a silent question. Kareyev threw to him a fur-lined leather jacket.

"Put this on," he ordered. "And don't make any noise. And follow."

"Where?" Michael asked.

"You're escaping. And so am I. The three of us."

Michael's wide eyes did not leave Joan.

"I suppose you understand the bargain," said Commandant Kareyev. "It's your life in exchange for your woman."

"Supposing," Michael asked, "I don't accept the bargain?"

Joan stood facing him, her back to Kareyev. Her voice was calm, indifferent; but her eyes were trying silently, desperately to make Michael understand.

"There are things you don't understand, Michael. And some that you forget."

"The three of us," said Kareyev, "have an account to settle, Volkontzev. And we can settle it better on free ground. Are you afraid to go?"

Michael shrugged and put on the jacket slowly.

"But aren't you afraid of the settlement, Commandant?" he asked.

"Come on," said Joan. "We have no time to talk."

"You'd better take this," said Kareyev, slipping a gun into Michael's hand. "We may need it."

Michael looked at him for a second, in silent appreciation of his trust; then he took the gun.

The head of the guards was having a night inspection of his staff in the yard back of the monastery, according to Commandant Kareyev's orders. There were no red lanterns moving on the walls.

Through the thunder of the waves, no one could hear the roar of the motorboat as it shot out into the darkness.

The waves rose high as swelling breasts heaving convulsively. The moon dropped long blotches of a cold, silver fire into the water and the sea tore it into glimmering rags. The stars drowned in the water, and knocking furiously against each other, the waves tried to throw them back in white, gleaming sprays.

The waves rose slowly and hung over the boat, motionless as walls of black, polished glass. Then a white foam burst on their crest, as if a cork had popped, and roared down the black side, throwing the boat up, out of the water, to land on the boiling crest of another mountain.

Commandant Kareyev bent over the wheel. His eyebrows made one straight line across his face and his eyes held one straight line ahead, into the darkness. He could feel every muscle of his body tensed to the will of his fingers that clutched the wheel like claws. The loops of his bent arms worked as the wings, as the nerves of the boat. He had lost his cap. His hair rose straight in the wind like a pennant.

"Volkontzev! Hold Joan!" he yelled once.

Joan looked back at the island. She saw it for the last time as a lonely black shadow, with a faint silver glow in its cupolas, that speeded away, disappearing behind the peaks of the waves.

At midnight, they saw red sparks gleaming faintly ahead. Kareyev swerved to the right, speeding away from the twinkling village. The boat crushed into the soft bottom and stopped. Kareyev carried Joan ashore.

A deserted beach ran into a forest of tall pines, silent, asleep, their branches heavy with snow. A mile to their left was the village; to their right, many miles down the white beach, the searchlight of a coast guard station revolved slowly, groping the sea.

A little lane wound itself on the outskirt of the forest. Snow had covered all tracks. Only two deep ruts left by peasants' wheels still remained like rails cut into the frozen ground.

Commandant Kareyev walked first; Joan followed. Michael came last, his hand on his gun.

They walked in silence. The wind had died. The moon beyond the forest threw long, black shadows of pine trees over the lane and far out across the beach. Farther, by the water, the snow gleamed, throwing up a hard, blue light.

A low branch bent under its white load, shuddered, powdering them with frozen dust. A white rabbit stuck its long ears from behind a shrub and darted into the forest, a leaping, soundless snowball.

They selected a lonely house on the outskirts of the village. Commandant Kareyev knocked at the door. A dog barked somewhere, choking in a long alarming howl.

A sleepy peasant opened the door fearfully, a sheepskin coat trembling on his shoulders, his eyes blinking over a candle.

"Who goes there?"

"Official business, comrade," said Kareyev. "We need two good horses and a sleigh."

"So help me God, Comrade Chief," the peasant whined, bowing, making the sign of the cross with a freckled hand, "we have no horses, so help me God. We're poor people, Comrade Chief."

One of Commandant Kareyev's hands crumpled significantly a wad of paper money; the other one closed over the butt of his gun.

"I said we needed two good horses and a sleigh," he repeated slowly. "And we need them quickly."

"Yes, Comrade Chief, yes, sir, as you wish."

Bowing, chewing nervously his long, reddish beard, the peasant led them to the stables behind his house, the candle dripping wax on his trembling hand.

Commandant Kareyev selected the horses. Michael gathered straw from the stable floor and filled the bottom of the sleigh around Joan's feet, wrapping them in an old fur blanket. Commandant Kareyev jumped to the driver's seat. He threw the wad of bills into the red beard. He warned:

"This is confidential official business, comrade. If you breathe a word about it—it's the Revolutionary Tribunal for you. Understand?"

"Yes, sir, Comrade Chief, the Lord bless you, yes, sir . . ." the peasant muttered, bowing.

He was still bowing when the sleigh flashed out of his yard in a cloud of snow.

——*VII*——

At midnight, the head of the guards sneaked noiselessly to the door of the pit. He listened cautiously; he heard no sound in the monastery. He pulled the trapdoor open and called down, raising his lantern over the pit:

"Are you there, Grisha?"

"Is it . . ." came from far below, in a gust of coughing, ". . . you, Makar?"

"It is. Wanted to know how you were getting along, pal."

At the bottom of a deep well with icicles sparkling in the crevices of its stone walls, Comrade Fedossitch huddled in the straw, his thin fingers at his throat, his eyes like two black puddles in his livid face. He hissed, a growl that ended in a moan:

"It took you long enough to get curious."

"His orders. Said not to come near you."

"Seen him around in the last few hours?"

"No."

"Let me out!"

"Are you in your right mind, Grisha? Against his orders?"

"You blind fool! See if you can find him. Or the woman. Or the motorboat."

"Lord help us, Grisha! Do you think . . ."

"Hurry! Go and see! Then let me out!"

Comrade Fedossitch laughed when Makar came running back, blubbering crazily, incredulously:

"He's gone! He's gone! They're gone! The boat's gone!"

"I'm the head of this island, now," said Comrade Fedossitch, his teeth chattering, when the rope jerked him out of the pit. "And it's my boot into the teeth of the first one who doesn't obey orders!"

"Bring Citizen Volkontzev here!" was the first order.

Makar departed obediently and returned wide-eyed, reporting that Citizen Volkontzev had gone, too.

"Well," laughed Comrade Fedossitch, "the Comrade Commandant was a bigger fool than I thought."

Up the old tower stairs to the wireless room Comrade Fedossitch ran, stumbling, stopping to cough, shadows dancing crazily around the shaking lantern in his hand. Makar followed, bewildered. Comrade Fedossitch's boot kicked the door open. The light of the lantern shuddered in a red circle over the crushed remains of the wireless set.

"I'll get him," Comrade Fedossitch choked. "I'll get him! That great red hero! That arrogant Beast!"

Then he raised his lantern, and waved it triumphantly, and yelled, pointing to a dark object in a corner:

"The spotlight, Makar! The spotlight! We'll signal the coast! We'll get him! Connect it and bring it up! To the bell tower!"

Comrade Fedossitch's woolen scarf slapped him furiously in the face when he emerged upon the platform of the bell tower. He threw himself forward against the wind, as if pushing aside an unseen, gigantic hand that tried to hurl him back down the stairs; his long shadow leaped dizzily over the parapet and into space.

He put his lantern down and seized the rope of the bells. It burned his bare hand. He tore the scarf off his neck and wound it around his fingers. Then he pulled the rope.

In clear weather the bells could be heard on the mainland. The sky was clear. The wind was blowing towards the coast.

The bells gave a long, moaning cry. Frozen snow showered Comrade Fedossitch's shoulders. A shudder ran through the old monastery, from the tower down to the pit.

The bells roared in agony, the brass ringing in long, clamorous sobs. Furious blows hammered like a huge metal whip, and the droning thunder rose heavily, floating slowly away, high over the sea.

Comrade Fedossitch swung the rope ferociously. He dropped his scarf. He did not feel his bare hands freezing to the rope. He laughed deliriously, coughing. He ran across the platform and swung back, his legs and arms twisted around the rope, flying, swaying over the tower like a monstrous pendulum.

Makar came up the stairs with the spotlight, dragging, like a snake rustling against the steps, a long wire that connected it with a dynamo in the room below. He stood still, terrified. Comrade Fedossitch yelled, swinging, twisting the rope:

"They've got to hear! They've got to hear!"

Across the sea, at the coast guard station, the moving searchlight stopped suddenly.

"Do you hear?" asked a soldier who wore a peaked khaki cap with a red star.

"Funny," said his assistant. "Sounds like a bell."

"Can't be coming from anywhere but hell, perhaps."

"It's from Strastnoy Island."

And as they stood, listening, peering into the darkness, a bright tongue of light flashed far out on the horizon, like a lance slashing the black sky, and the wound quickly closed again.

"Trouble," said the soldier in the peaked cap. . . .

Comrade Fedossitch was signaling his message to the mainland. He crouched by the spotlight, on his knees, pressing it feverishly to his chest, as a precious child which he had to shield from the wind, which he could not let go, clasping it with fingers stiff as pliers. He clawed his chest, trying to warm his fingers, tearing his shirt, without feeling the wind on his naked throat. He laughed. His laughter rolled a long howl of moans and coughs and triumph into the wind, following the streaks of light that flashed as darts shooting straight into the breast of an unseen enemy far away in the darkness.

Makar stood, paralyzed, but for one hand that made quickly, fearfully, the sign of the cross.

The soldiers at the coast guard station knew the code. The white streaks beyond the sea panted slowly, letter by letter:

"C-O-M-M-A-N-D-A-N-T C-O-N-V-I-C-T W-I-F-E E-S-C-A-P-E."

From under eight hoofs eight spurts of snow dust flew up like coils of steam; out of the horses' nostrils steam flew up like spurts of snow dust. The whip in Commandant Kareyev's hand whirled over their heads and sank into the horses' heaving ribs.

Under them the white earth rolled backwards as if streaming like a waterfall down into a precipice under the sleigh. By their side snow and tree stumps melted into a long white belt. Above them huge pines slowly swam past, carried immobile on a speeding ground.

The horses bent into arcs; their fore and hind legs met under their bodies; then they sprang into straight lines, flying over the ground, their legs stretched out, immobile.

Joan's eyes were fixed on the whip that whistled as if in the hand of the executioner on Strastnoy Island; as if beating the darkness ahead. She could feel the speed with her lips, the wind pounding against her teeth. Michael's arm held her tightly, his fingers sinking into her coat.

Through miles of forest, where the pines seemed to close, meeting across the road ahead, and the road, like a white knife cut them apart in its flight; through clearings and plains where the black sky swallowed the white snow into one ball of darkness and the road seemed a gray cloud carrying them over an abyss; over ruts, and snow heaps, and fallen logs they flew through the night, every mile and every hour a victory.

"Are you cold, *Joan*?"

"Button your collar, *Frances*. It's open."

When the lights of a village sparkled ahead through the fog of snow dust, Commandant Kareyev turned abruptly and sent the sleigh bumping through narrow side roads. As they flew past they could see, at a distance, the gleaming cross of the church over the low roofs, and the dark flag—red in the daytime—over the house of the village Soviet. Commandant Kareyev did not look at the flag; only his whip bit ferociously into the horses' ribs.

Down the dark village streets, dots of lanterns were hurrying, gathering in twinkling groups, rushing away. A bell was ringing, as a long, tremulous, alarming call.

"Hold on to Joan, Volkontzev! Sharp turn!"

The moon had set and clouds, like a black fog, swam slowly up, swallowing the stars. A light down of snow fluttered lazily.

"Look at that snow, Frances," said Michael. "We won't see any for a long, long time. This is our farewell to Russia."

"This is a farewell," said Kareyev, "for two of us."

"Yes," said Michael, "for two of us."

Ahead of them, a faint white thread, whiter than the snow, cut the sky from the darkness of the earth.

"Tomorrow, at dawn, we'll be far away at sea," said Kareyev, "and the boat will be flying towards a *new* country for Joan."

". . . where she can forget all about Strastnoy Island."

". . . and all that brought her to it."

"No matter what the future," said Joan, "I'll never forget some of the past. One of us will need this. I want him to remember it."

"One of us," said Kareyev, "will not need it. The other one may not want it."

Joan's head dropped back. The snow down caught on her eyelashes.

She started with a cry; she jumped up, but the speed of the sleigh threw her down again.

"There . . . there . . . look!"

They turned. The snow plain stretched like a gray fog behind them. Through the fog, far down the road they had passed, a black spot rolled toward them. It looked like a beetle with two long legs clawing the snow. But it moved too fast for a beetle.

Commandant Kareyev's whip rose straight up in the air, and the sleigh jerked as it fell.

"That's nothing," he said. "Some peasant going to town."

"He's going pretty fast for a peasant," said Michael.

Kareyev's eyes met his over Joan's head, and Michael understood.

"Nothing to worry about," said Kareyev.

The horses were exhausted. But the reins tensed like wires in Kareyev's hands. They flew faster.

As they flew, two things grew slowly, ominously, running a silent race: the white line ahead and the black spot behind them.

"Don't look at it, Joan!" The whip swished down in Kareyev's hand. "You're making yourself nervous." The whip swished down. "It's nothing. We're faster than they are." The whip swished down. "They can't . . ."

A shot rang through the silence where hoofbeats drummed like a heart.

Michael seized Joan and threw her brutally down on her knees in the straw on the bottom of the sleigh, bending over her, covering her with his body, holding her down.

"Michael! Let me get up! Let me get up!"

She struggled frantically. He pressed her down roughly.

"That's it!" shouted Commandant Kareyev. "Keep her down, Volkontzev! Keep her down!"

Commandant Kareyev had jumped to his feet. His tall body swayed, bent forward, his arm one with the tense reins. His whip flashed like a circle. Red streaks tore the horses' ribs.

"Stop!" came the distant cry. "Stop in the name of the law!"

Michael drew his gun.

"Don't, Volkontzev!" cried Kareyev. "Save your bullets! They're too far away! We'll escape!"

Two more shots ripped the darkness behind them. Joan heaved up convulsively against her living armor. Standing, Kareyev pressed one knee into her back to keep her down.

The road shot straight into a growth of pines and made a sharp turn. They whirled around the corner, Kareyev's body swaying perilously and straightening again. They lost the white thread in the forest; and the black spot lost them.

A winding side lane branched off the road, disappearing into the wilderness of pines; not even a lane, but a forgotten clearing barely wide enough for a sleigh, leading nowhere. With a quick movement of his whole body, Kareyev pulled the reins and sent the sleigh straight into the side lane, swiftly, as if his body, more than the worn-out horses, had thrown it forward.

They raced blindly through the snow and the pines. They soon lost all trace of a lane. They wound their way between tall, red trunks, tearing through bushes, knocking against trees, their slides cutting into the bark; diving into hollows, crashing and whirling off tree stumps. Low branches flogged them. Joan's fur cap was torn off. A branch hit Kareyev across the eyes; he shook the snow and pine needles out of his hair, red drops rolling down his temple.

The horses snorted; their ribs heaved; their nostrils quivered in terror. The whip, tearing their flesh, forced them forward; the whip was in the merciless hand of the Beast from Strastnoy Island.

One horse stumbled and fell. For a moment, they heard the silence of the forest, a silence of deep snow and trackless wilderness.

Commandant Kareyev jumped into the snow. His feet were not steady on the ground. He staggered to the horse. He brushed the hair out of his eyes. He looked at the red on his hand, felt his temple; he took a handful of snow and washed the temple; he flung the pink snow away.

Michael waded to him. They pulled the horse to its feet. The whip whistled again.

"Don't be afraid, Joan. They won't get us." Commandant Kareyev's voice rang clear, vibrant. "One night, many years ago, I was carrying priceless documents for the Red Army. Three horses were shot under me. I delivered the documents. My charge is more precious—tonight."

——VIII——

When they stumbled out into a clearing, the horses could barely move. Commandant Kareyev's whip was broken. A bare, wide plain stretched to the black line of another forest. Beyond, the clouds were torn off a broad band of glowing pink.

An old, crumbling shack leaned against the last pines of the forest, its unpainted boards black from age and weather, its roof caved in, one window staring like an empty socket—without glass.

Commandant Kareyev knocked at the door. No answer came. He kicked the door. It was not locked. He went in, then called:

"It's all right. Come in."

Michael followed, carrying Joan in his arms.

There was an empty stone hearth, and an old wooden table, and snow under the broken roof, and pine needles on the floor.

"We're safe here—for a while," said Kareyev.

The two men looked at each other. Commandant Kareyev's leather jacket hung in strips. He had lost his muffler. His shirt was torn at the throat. Michael's head was a tangle of black hair and pine needles. He smiled, flashing sparkling teeth, young and vibrant, a trim, healthy animal in the joy of his first real battle.

"Great work, Commandant," said Michael.

"Well, we've done it," said Kareyev, "—together."

It was only a second, but their eyes held each other in the silent understanding of their common danger, with the first, faint, hidden spark of admiration in their understanding. Then they looked at the woman who stood leaning against the open door, her blond hair hanging over one eye, the soft blond hair golden as ripe wheat in the sun, against the white desolation of snow and black pines raw in the frost. They did not look at each other again.

Commandant Kareyev closed the door and pulled an old wooden latch, locking it. He said:

"We'll let the horses rest. Then we'll go. The town isn't far. Just a few more hours."

Michael spread the fur blanket on the floor. They sat silently. Joan's head leaned on Kareyev's shoulder. He ran his fingers through her hair, tenderly, removing pine needles from her tangled curls. She noticed anxiously Michael's dark eyes that were watching Kareyev fixedly. Michael removed her boots, rubbed her feet in woolen socks damp with snow. She watched Kareyev's eyes following Michael's movements silently, his eyebrows drawn tightly in a dark frown.

"Let's go now," she said suddenly.

"We can't, Joan. We have plenty of time."

"I hate it here."

"You've gone through many things you've hated, Frances," said Michael. "You've been brave. It's the end, now. Think of what's awaiting us."

"What's awaiting us," said Kareyev slowly, "is for two—only."

"Yes," said Michael. "Only. And I hope the third one steps aside as bravely as he has been behaving."

"I hope he does," said Kareyev.

"It's too cold here," Joan complained.

"I'll make a fire, Frances."

"Don't. They may notice the smoke."

"Let me hold you close, Joan. You'll be warmer."

Commandant Kareyev drew her into his arms.

"Take your hands off her," said Michael slowly.

"What?"

"I said, take your hands off her."

Commandant Kareyev did. He put Joan aside gently and rose to his feet. So did Michael.

Joan stood between them, her eyes dark, scornful.

"Keep quiet!" she ordered. "Both of you seem to forget where we are—and when."

"We may as well settle this now, once and for all," said Kareyev. "He forgets that he has no more rights to you."

"And you, Commandant," said Michael, "forget that you never had any."

"I bought her from you in exchange for the next fifty years of your life."

"She wasn't for sale."

"I wouldn't stand in a woman's way after she had asked me to get out."

"I wish you would remember that."

Commandant Kareyev turned to Joan. He said very gently:

"It's been a game, Joan, and a bad one. I know the truth, but you must tell it to him. You've been too cruel with him."

"Oh, please! please . . ." she begged, backing away from him. "Don't. Not now. Not here."

"Right here, Frances," said Michael. "Now."

She stood straight, facing them. She raised her head high. Her eyes and her voice were clear. It was not her apology. It was the proud, defiant verdict of her sublime right.

"I love—one of you. No matter what I've done, don't you understand that there is a love beyond all justice?"

"Which one?" asked Michael.

"We want a proof, Joan," said Kareyev. "One beyond doubt."

A hand knocked at the door.

"In the name of the law . . . open this door!"

Michael leaped to the window. His gun flashed. He fired. Shots answered from outside, the bark of several rifles.

Michael dropped his gun. His hand grasped the edge of the window. He pulled himself up to his full height, shuddered, and fell backwards, his arms swinging in a wide circle over his head.

Joan's cry did not sound like a woman's voice. She threw herself over his body, tearing his jacket, fumbling for his heart, blood running over her fingers.

"Come here!" she screamed to Kareyev. "Help him!"

Kareyev was pressed to the door, trying to hold it

against furious blows, his gun in a crack of the wall, shooting blindly at those outside.

"Come here!" she cried. "Help him! Come here!"

He obeyed. Michael's head fell limply over his arm. He tore the jacket, felt a faint beating under his fingers, looked at the little hole in the chest that spurted a dark stream with each beat.

"He's all right, Joan. Just fainted. The wound isn't serious."

She looked at the sticky red that thickened into a web between her fingers. She pulled her collar open, tore a piece of her dress, pressed it to the wound.

She did not hear the door crash into splinters under the butts of rifles. She did not see the two soldiers who jumped in through the window, nor the two others who stood at the door.

"Hands up!" said the soldier who entered first. "You're under arrest."

Commandant Kareyev rose slowly and raised his arms. Joan looked up indifferently.

The soldiers wore shaggy sheepskin coats that smelled of sweat; the long fur of their big caps stuck to their wet foreheads; their boots left tracks of snow on the floor.

"And that, citizens," said their leader, "is how all counterrevolutionaries get their white necks twisted."

His stomach bulged over his cartridge belt. He spread his heavy, square boots wide apart. He pushed his fur cap at the back of his head, scratched his neck, and laughed. He had a wide grin and short teeth.

"Pretty smart, aren't you, citizens?" The cartridge belt shook under his stomach. "But the hand of the proletarian republic is long, and has good sharp claws."

"What are the orders from those who sent you?" Commandant Kareyev asked slowly.

"Not so fast, citizen. Why the hurry? You'll have plenty of time to find out."

"Let's go," said Joan, rising. "This man here is wounded. Take him to a doctor."

"He won't need one."

"Their horses are here, behind the house," a soldier reported, entering.

"Bring them out. . . . Such is the end, citizens, of all who dare to raise a hand against the great will of the proletariat."

"What are your orders?" repeated Commandant Kareyev.

"The orders are to save your valuable chests for better bullets than ours. The convict, the woman's husband, is to be taken right back to Strastnoy Island, to be executed. The woman and the traitor Commandant are to be taken for trial to Nijni Kolimsk, to the GPU. Nice place, your ladyship, right across the street from a rich English merchant."

Joan's eyes met Kareyev's. In the house across the street from the rich English merchant, doors could be left unlocked, guards could be absent, prisoners could disappear without trace: for execution—or for freedom.

There were three of them. Two were saved—if they reached that house. One was doomed.

"And, by the way," asked the soldier, "which one is your husband?"

Joan stood by the table. She leaned far back against it, her tense arms propped against the edge, her head in her shoulders. Her hands grasping the table seemed to hold her body from falling backwards. But her eyes looked straight at the soldier; there was no fear in them, there was the last, desperate resolution of a cornered animal.

"This is my husband," she answered and pointed at Kareyev.

Commandant Kareyev looked at her. His eyes were calm and grew calmer as they studied hers. Hers were not pleading; they were proud with a defiant hopelessness.

He had asked for a proof of the truth; one beyond doubt. He had it.

Commandant Kareyev looked at the sky where dawn, like a child, smiled its first hope to the beginning of life. Then, he turned to the soldier.

"Yes," he said calmly, "I am her husband."

Joan's body slid from the edge of the table. Her arms pulled it up again. Her eyes widened looking at that for which she had not dared to hope.

"Let's go," said the soldier. "You must be crazy, Citizen Convict. I don't see anything to be smiling about."

The soldiers bent over Michael. He stirred faintly.

"The traitor's all right," said the leader. "He can make the journey to Nijni Kolimsk. Put him into our sleigh, and the woman, too, and take them to town. I'll take the convict back to the coast. Send an order to have a boat for Strastnoy waiting there."

Joan did not look at the men lifting Michael and carrying him out to the sleigh. She did not notice the figures passing before her. Her eyes were frozen, staring at Kareyev.

There was a great calm in Commandant Kareyev's face; a calm that seemed to erase softly the wrinkles of many years on the Beast's face. He was not looking at Joan. He was staring, wondering, at something he seemed to understand for the first time. He was not smiling; but his face looked as if it were.

"Well, come on," said the soldier. "What's the matter, citizen woman? Stop staring at him like that."

"May I," asked Kareyev, "say goodbye . . . to my wife?"

"Go ahead. But make it quick."

Commandant Kareyev turned and met her eyes. Then, he smiled softly and took her hands.

"Goodbye, Joan."

She did not answer. She was staring at him.

"There is a love beyond all justice, Joan. I understand."

She did not seem to hear. He added:

"And also there is a love beyond all sorrow. So don't worry about me."

"I can't let you go," her lips said almost without sound.

"You have been mine. You gave me life. You have a right to take it."

"I'd rather . . ."

"You'd rather keep quiet. . . . You have a duty to me, now. You must be happy—for my sake."

"I'll be . . . happy," she whispered.

"You're not crying, are you, Joan? It's not as bad as all that. I don't want to be a ghost who will ruin the life awaiting you. Are you strong enough to promise that you will always smile when you think of me?"

"I'm . . . smiling . . . dear. . . ."

"Remember me only when—in the countries where you'll be sent by . . . the house across the street from the English merchant—you see the lights . . . dancing."

She raised her head. She stood straight as a soldier at attention. She said slowly, each word steady and solemn as a step to the scaffold:

"I can't thank you. I only want you to know that of all the things I've done, the one I'm doing now is the hardest."

He took her in his arms and kissed her. It was a long kiss. He wanted to sum up his life in it.

They walked out together, her hand in his. The sun greeted them, rising over the forest. It rose slowly, and its rays were like arms outstretched in a solemn blessing. Far away in the forest, snow glistened on the branches like tears that had dropped from the flaming sunrise and rolled, overfilling the forest, over the wide plain. But the tall, old trees raised their dark heads straight into the sky, above the snow, triumphant, greeting life that was starting again for the first time. And over the white plain little sparks burned in the snow, little twinkling, dancing lights of all colors, like a rainbow.

"To the glory of the world revolution!" said the soldier and wiped his nose with the back of his hand.

Two sleighs were waiting, their horses turned in opposite directions. Two soldiers sat in one sleigh, waiting for their prisoner. In the other, Michael was propped against the seat. He moaned feebly, still unconscious. A soldier sat next to him, holding the reins.

Joan stopped. She had no strength to go on. Commandant Kareyev smiled calmly. He noticed that her fur collar was open and fastened it. The soldiers' leader pulled her towards the sleigh.

She stopped and turned, facing Kareyev. She stood straight, leaning against the sunrise, her golden hair in the wind. She smiled proudly, gallantly, in sublime sanction of life.

Kareyev walked to the other sleigh, without an order,

stepped in calmly, and sat down between the two soldiers.

A rough hand pulled Joan into the sleigh. She put her arm around Michael and held him, his head on her shoulder.

The soldier clicked his whip. The horses jerked forward, into the sunrise. Their harness creaked. Snow spurted up.

Joan turned to look at the other sleigh. Commandant Kareyev did not turn back when the horses tore forward. She saw his hair waving in the wind and above it the white line of his forehead: Commandant Kareyev's head was held high.

We the Living
(unpublished excerpts)

1931

Editor's Preface

Ayn Rand returned to *We the Living* in 1932, but interrupted it again the next year to write her first stage play, *Night of January 16th,* produced in Hollywood in 1934, then on Broadway in 1935. (This play has been separately published by New American Library.) The novel was completed in March 1934, but could find no publisher until 1936. After issuing a first edition of 3,000 copies, the publisher, despite indications of rising sales, destroyed the type, and the book was not to reach its audience for a quarter of a century. In 1959, it was reissued by Random House, and in 1960 in paperback by New American Library. Since that time, more than three million copies of *We the Living* have been sold.

Ayn Rand's view of the theme and current relevance of *We the Living,* and of its place in her work, can be found in her foreword to the reissued edition.

In looking through the manuscript of the novel, I found several passages or "outtakes" that had been cut from the final version. Ayn Rand was a champion of literary economy; she was ruthless in cutting passages she considered inessential. There should not, she held, be an unnecessary scene or word in a piece of writing; in judging any element, the standard is not its interest on its own terms, but its contribution to the total.

Several of the cut passages, however, are of some interest. They can be enjoyed as separate pieces, even while one agrees with Miss Rand that they are not parts of the novel, and must not be viewed as such. I have selected for this anthology two such pieces from the early part of *We the Living,* both probably written in 1931. Neither has received Ayn Rand's customary editing and polishing. The titles are my own invention.

"No" is an eloquent montage of life in Soviet Russia after the Revolution. It offers a glimpse of the kind of daily existence Ayn Rand herself had to endure before she could leave for America. Some elements of this montage were retained in the novel, in the form of brief paragraphs integrated with the development of the story. Evidently, Miss Rand judged that a separate extended treatment would be too static. Perhaps she thought also that it would repeat what was already clear elsewhere in the book.

The "month to wait" mentioned in the opening lines is the month Kira, the heroine, must wait between meetings with Leo, the man she loves and is not to see again until October 28.

In the novel, there is one paragraph describing a story about a Viking that the young Kira had read; the Viking became her private symbol of man the hero. I had always loved this brief reference and was delighted to find that the story had originally been given a fuller treatment.

"Kira's Viking" may be read as a lushly Romantic fairy tale for adults, as well as for children. The language is simple, evocative, Biblical in its cadence and power. Miss Rand's admirers will recognize the similarity in this regard to her later novelette *Anthem*—and also to the legends about John Galt in *Atlas Shrugged.* Ayn Rand was expert in creating the mood and reality of this kind of haunting, timeless legend, and I could not let this small example of her talent stay buried. (Besides, it is the only fairy tale I know with a viewpoint on the relationship between statism and religion.)

The story was cut, presumably, because it was not necessary for the purpose of the novel at this point—that is, to establish Kira's character.

The last paragraph of "Kira's Viking," which I have

placed after a sequence break, originally appeared much later, near the end of the book, in Kira's death scene; it was cut when the story was cut.

"No" is the world Ayn Rand escaped from. "Kira's Viking" is why she escaped—what she wanted to find in the world instead.

—L. P.

"No"

A month to wait is a fortnight in Paris, a week in New York, a year in Soviet Russia.

"No," said the saleslady in the bookstore, "we have no foreign magazines, citizen. Foreign magazines? You must be new in Petrograd. We have no more publications from *abroad* than from Mars, citizen. Unsuitable ideology, you know. What can one expect of bourgeois countries? . . . Here's a nice selection, citizen: *The Young Communist, Red Weekdays, Red Harvest*. . . . No? . . . We have splendid novels, citizen. *Naked Year*—all about the civil war. *Sickle and Hammer*—it's the class awakening of the village—futuristic, you know—but very profound."

The shelves were bright with white covers and red letters, white letters and red covers—on cheap, brownish paper and with laughing, defiant broken lines and circles cutting triangles, and triangles splitting squares, the new art coming through some crack in the impenetrable barrier, from the new world beyond the borders, whose words could not reach the little store where a picture of Lenin winked slyly at Kira, from above a sign: "State Publishing House."

"No," said Galina Petrovna, "we have no money to waste on theater tickets. You ought to be glad we have enough for tramway tickets."

In the streets, there were big posters with little blue letters announcing the opening season of the "State Academic Theaters"—the three theatrical giants of Petrograd that were called "the Imperial Theaters" five years ago: the Alexandrinsky, with a chariot high on its roof, stone horses' hoofs suspended over the city, with five balconies of red and gold inside, watching Russia's best dramas; the Marinsky—blue and silver, solemn and majestic, a temple to operas and the fluttering skirts of ballet; the Michailovsky—orange and silver, friendly and impudent, winking at its two serious brothers with the newest daring plays and the gayest light operas.

"No," said the cashier, "no tickets under three hundred and fifty rubles. Then we have profunion nights—free tickets from your union. . . . If you're not a union member, citizen, who cares if you don't get to see a show?"

"No," said Irina Dunaeva, "I get no new dresses this winter either. So you don't have to worry, Kira. We'll look alike. . . . Yes, I have powder. Soviet powder. Doesn't stay on very well. But do you know Vava Miloslavsky, Victor's girl—for the time being? Her father's a doctor—a Free Profession, they call it—you see, he doesn't 'exploit labor' so they leave him alone—and he makes money—and Vava—now don't talk about it—she has a box of Coty's powder . . . yes, French. Yes, real. From *abroad*. Smuggled. Ten thousand rubles a box. . . . I think Vava uses lipstick. You know, I think it's going to be a fashion. Daring, isn't it? But they say they use it—*abroad*. . . . Vava, she has a pair of silk stockings. Don't say I told you. She likes to show them off—and I don't want to give her the satisfaction."

"No!" said the red letters on a poster. "The Proletarian Consciousness is not Contaminated by Paltry Bourgeois Ideology. Comrades! Tighten our Class Welding!"
The poster showed a milling crowd of workers, the size of ants, in the shadow of a huge wheel.

"No," said the student in the red bandanna, "you gotta stand in line for the bread, same as us all, citizen. Sure, it might take two hours. And it might take three hours. What's the hurry, citizen? You ain't got anything better to do with your time. Expecting privileges, perhaps? Too good to stand in line with us proletarians? Don't wiggle your feet, citizen. Certainly, I'm cold, too. . . . Sure, you'll miss the lecture. And I'll miss a meeting of the Cell. But this is Bread Day."

Every student had a provision card. The floor of the University shop was covered with sawdust. The clerk at the counter briskly shoved hunks of dried bread at the line moving slowly past him, and dipped his hand into a barrel to fish out the pickles, and wiped his hand on the bread. The bread and pickles disappeared, unwrapped, into briefcases filled with books.

"No," said the article in *Pravda,* "the New Economic Policy is not a surrender of our revolutionary ideology. It is a temporary compromise with a historical necessity. The fight isn't over. Come on, comrades, let's show the fat-bellied foreign imperialists, our new, united ranks on the front of economic recovery! This is the day of the factory and the tractor instead of the bayonet! This is the day to demonstrate our red discipline in the slow, monotonous routine of proletarian State Construction! This is the time of heroic Red weekdays!"

"No," said Galina Petrovna, "I didn't break the kerosene stove. There's no kerosene. If you mix the coarse flour with cold water, it'll taste like gruel."

"No," said the militia man, "you can't cross the street, citizen. What's the hurry? Don'tcha see there's a demonstration of the toilers?"

A string of women waddled down Nevsky, spreading to fill its broad expanse, stopping the trucks and tramways, mud flying in little spurts from under heavy shoes. The red banner at the head of the demonstration said:

"The Women of the First Factory of the Red Food-trust Protest Against the Imperialistic Greed of England and Lord Chamberlain!"

The women hid their hands in their armpits, to warm them, and sang:

> "We are the young red guard
> and our aim is set.

We're told: don't hang your guns
and bravely march ahead . . ."

*   *   *

"No," said the drunken sailor in the darkness under
the window, on the street far below, "I ain't gonna stop.
I'm a free citizen. To hell with your sleep."

And he pulled the harmonica as if he were going to
tear it apart, and it squealed in terror, and he sang, leaning against a lamp post, throwing his raucous words at
the moon over the dark roofs above:

"Vanka 'nd Mashka fell in love
and he swore by stars above
'I will treat you good
and I'll buy you wood
and the wood is pure birch-tree
lots of heat for you and me' . . .
Lamtsa-dritsa-tsa-tsa!"

*   *   *

"No," said the Upravdom, "you can't be no exception,
citizen. Even if you are a student. Social duty comes
above all. Every tenant gotta attend the meeting."

So Kira sat in the long, bare room, the largest in the
house, in the apartment of a tramway conductor. Behind
her sat Galina Petrovna in her oldest dress, and Alexander Dimitrievitch stretching out his run-down boots, and
Lydia shivering in a torn shawl. Every tenant in the
house was present. The apartment had electrical connections and one bulb burned in the center of the ceiling.
The tenants chewed sunflower seeds.

"Seeing as how I'm the Upravdom," said the Upravdom, "I declare this meeting of the tenants of the
house . . . on Moika open. On the order of the day is
the question as regards the chimneys. Now, comrades
citizens, seeing as how we are all responsible citizens
and conscious of the proper class consciousness, we gotta
understand that this ain't the old days when we had
landlords and didn't care what happened to the house
we lived in. Now this is different, comrades. Owing to
the new regime and the dictatorship of the proletariat,

and seeing as how the chimneys are clogged we gotta do something about it, seeing as how we're the owners of the house. Now if the chimneys are clogged, the stoves won't burn, and if the stoves won't burn we'll have the house full of smoke, and if we have the house full of smoke— it's sloppy, and if we're sloppy—that's not true proletarian discipline. And so, comrades citizens . . ."

The smell of food burning came from the hall and a housewife fidgeted nervously, glancing anxiously at the clock. A fat man in a red shirt was twiddling his thumbs. A young man, with a pale mouth hanging open, was scratching his head, occasionally producing something which he rolled in his fingers and dropped on the floor.

". . . and the special assessment will be divided in proportion as to the . . . Is that you, Comrade Argounova, trying to sneak out? Well, you better don't. You know what we think of people what sabotage their social duties. You better teach your young one the proper consciousness, Citizen Argounova. . . . And the special assessment will be divided in proportion as to the social standing of the tenants. The workers pay three percent, and the free professions, ten, and the private traders the rest. . . . Who's for—raise your hands. . . . Comrade Secretary, count the citizens' hands. . . . Who's against— raise your hands. . . . Comrade Michliuk, you can't raise your hand for and against on the one and same proposition. . . ."

In the mornings—there was millet and the smell of kerosene when there was no wood, and smoke when there was no kerosene.

In the evenings—there was millet, and Lydia rocking back and forth on a rickety chair, moaning:

"The pagans! The sacrilegious apostates! They're taking the ikons, and the gold crosses from the churches. To feed their damn famine somewhere. No respect for anything sacred. What're we coming to?"

And Galina Petrovna wailed:

"What's Europe waiting for? How far do we have to go?"

And Alexander Dimitrievitch asked timidly:

"May I, Galina? Just a spoonful more?"

And Maria Petrovna came to visit, trembling by the stove, coughing as if her chest were torn into shreds, fighting with words and coughs:

". . . and Vassia had another fight with Victor . . . over politics . . . and Irina got nothing but dried fish at the University . . . this week . . . no bread . . . and I made a nightgown out of the old blanket . . . old . . . rips if you breathe on it . . . and Acia needs galoshes . . . and Vassia won't take a Soviet job, won't hear of it. . . . Yes, I take cough medicine. . . . Did you hear about Boris Koulikov? In a hurry, tried to jump on a crowded tramway—at full speed—both legs cut off. . . . Acia's learning to spell at school and what words do they teach it with? Marxism and Proletariat and Electrification. . . ."

On the floor crumbled sheets of *Pravda* rustled underfoot:

"Comrades! True Proletarians have no will but that of the collective. The iron will of the Proletariat, the victorious class, will lead humanity into . . ."

And Kira stood by a window, her hand on the dark, cold glass, and her body felt young, cold and hard as the glass, and she thought that one could stand a lot, and forget a lot, if one kept clear and firm one final aim and cause. She did not know what the aim was; but she did not ask herself the question, for the aim was beyond questions and doubts; she knew only that she was awaiting it. Perhaps, it was the twenty-eighth of October.

Kira's Viking

There was only one book Kira remembered. She was
ten years old when she read it. It was the story of a
Viking. It was written in English. Her governess gave it
to her. She heard later that the author had died very
young. She had not remembered his name; in later years,
she had never been able to find it.

She did not remember the books she read before it;
she did not want to remember the ones she read after.

The Viking had a body against which the winds broke
like a caress. The Viking's step was like the beating of
waves upon the rocks: steady and irrevocable. The Viking's eyes never looked farther than the point of his
sword; but there was no boundary for the point of his
sword.

The Viking's ship had patched sails and blade-scarred
flanks; and a banner that had never been lowered. There
was on the ship a crew of men whose hearts froze at a
home-fire; whose heads never bowed but to the Viking's
voice. Among the northern rocks of his homeland, the
ship lay hidden in a harbor no one dared to enter.

The ship had to be hidden, for high in the mountains
was a city surrounded by gray walls, where, at night, a
smoked lantern burned by the locked gates and a lonely
cat walked down the old stone wall. In the city there
was a King, and when he passed in the street, the people
bowed so low that wrinkled foreheads left marks in the
soft dust. The King hated the Viking.

The King hated him, for when peaceful lights twinkled

in his subjects' homes and smoke rose over houses where mothers cooked the evening meal, the Viking watched the city from a high cliff, and the wind carried the smoke high into the mountains, but not high enough to reach the Viking's feet. The King hated him, for walls fell at a motion of the Viking's hand, and when he walked in their ruins, the sun made a crown over his head, but he walked, light and straight, without noticing its weight.

So the King had promised a reward for the Viking's head. And in the narrow streets, on the doorsteps slippery with onion peelings, the people waited and hoped for the reward, so that they could have a big supper.

Far down in a deep valley was a temple that the sun-rays reached but one hour each day; and where the rays struck the temple was a tall window of dark painted glass. When the sun pierced the window, the huge shadow of a tortured saint spread over the backs of those who knelt in prayer, and the gold of the sun turned red as the blood of suffering. The Priest of the temple hated the Viking.

The Priest hated him, for the Viking laughed under the cold, black vaults and his laugh sounded as if the painted window had been broken. The Priest hated him, for the Viking looked at heaven only when he bent for a drink over a mountain brook, and there, overshadowing the sky, he saw his own picture.

So the Priest had promised forgiveness of all sins for the Viking's head. And skinning their knees on the temple steps, the people waited and hoped for the forgiveness, so that they could sleep safely with their neighbor's wife.

Far away in the polar seas, where the bridges of northern lights connected the waves and the clouds, and no ship dared to break the connection, stood the sacred city. From a long distance, sailors had seen its white walls rising to the snows of the mountains. But they did not look at the city in spring, for when the spring sun struck the white walls, their blaze sent many a sailor home—blind.

At dawn, from a long distance, sailors could see the queen-priestess rise to the tall white tower. Her white robe and golden hair fell to the ground, but her slender body swaying back in a tense effort, her arms were raised, high and straight, to a pale, young sky. And in the still mirror of the sea, from the bottom of a tall white tower, a slender, white figure stretched her arms down into the depth.

It was spring when the Viking said he was leaving to conquer the sacred city.

People ran into their houses and closed the shutters over their windows. But the King smiled, and offered him forgiveness and the royal banner for his enterprise.

"For your King," he said.

The Priest smiled, and offered him forgiveness, and the banner of the temple.

"For your Faith," he said.

But the Viking took neither. When his ship cut the waves towards the blazing white spot, on the tall mast, lashing the wind, was his own banner, that had never been lowered.

There were many days and many storms. When the waves rose high, fighting the wind for his dark cape and light hair, the Viking stood on the prow and looked ahead.

It was night when the Viking's ship approached the sacred city, and its walls were blue under the stars.

When the stars had gone and the sky glowed, transparent with the coming light, white stones crumbled to meet the waves where the walls had been; over the gates flung wide open to the sea the Viking's banner was nailed.

Alone over the city, his clothes torn, the Viking stood on top of the tall white tower. There was a wound across his breast and red drops rolled slowly down to his feet.

From the ravaged streets below, conquerors and conquered alike looked up at him. There was much wonder in their eyes, but little hatred. They raised their heads, but did not rise from their knees.

On the tower stairs the slender queen-priestess of the sacred city lay at the Viking's feet. Her head bent so low that her golden hair swept the steps and he could see her breasts as, breathing tremulously, they touched the ground. Her hands lay still and helpless on the steps, the palms turned up, hungry in silent entreaty. But it was not mercy they were begging of him.

The sun had not risen. A pale sky looked into a pale, still sea, both misty green and transparent, touched by the first faint promise of color. Behind the city, a red glow mounted in the sky, rising slowly, ominously, like a victorious banner unrolling into the sky from the heart of the earth. The Viking's body stood alone, cutting the fire.

Faint waves beat at the foot of the ruins. The waves had seen unknown shores and lost, faraway cities; beyond the line where they melt into the sky, was a great earth alive with a promise of so much that was possible. And the earth lay still, tense in reverent waiting, as if its very heart and meaning were rising to the morning sky; and the morning was like a slow, triumphant overture for the song to come.

The Viking smiled as men smile when they look up, at heaven; but he was looking down. His right arm was one straight line with his lowered sword; his left arm, straight as the sword, raised a goblet of wine to the sky. The first rays of a coming sun, still unseen to the earth, struck the crystal goblet. It sparkled like a white torch. Its rays lighted the faces of those below.

"To a life," said the Viking, "which is a reason unto itself."

A Viking had lived, who had laughed at Kings, who had laughed at Priests, who had laughed at Men, who had held, sacred and inviolable, high over all temples, over all to which men knew how to kneel, his one banner—the sanctity of life. He had known and she knew. He had fought and she was fighting. He had shown her the way. To the banner of life, all could be given, even life itself.

Ideal

1934

Editor's Preface

Ideal was written in 1934, at a time when Ayn Rand had
cause to be unhappy with the world. *We the Living* was
being rejected by a succession of publishers for being
"too intellectual" and too opposed to Soviet Russia (this
was the time of America's Red Decade); *Night of January
16th* had not yet found a producer; and Miss Rand's
meager savings were running out. The story was written
originally as a novelette and then, probably within a year
or two, was extensively revised and turned into a stage
play. It has never been produced.

After the political themes of her first professional
work, Ayn Rand now returns to the subject matter of
her early stories: the role of values in men's lives. The
focus in this case, as in "Her Second Career," is negative, but this time the treatment is not jovial; dominantly,
it is sober and heartfelt. The issue now is men's lack of
integrity, their failure to act according to the ideals they
espouse. The theme is the evil of divorcing ideals from
life.

An acquaintance of Miss Rand's, a conventional
middle-aged woman, told her once that she worshiped a
certain famous actress and would give her life to meet
her. Miss Rand was dubious about the authenticity of
the woman's emotion, and this suggested a dramatic
idea: a story in which a famous actress, so beautiful that

she comes to represent to men the embodiment of their deepest ideals, actually enters the lives of her admirers. She comes in a context suggesting that she is in grave danger. Until this point, her worshipers have professed their reverence for her—in words, which cost them nothing. Now, however, she is no longer a distant dream, but a reality demanding action on their part, or betrayal.

"What do you dream of?" Kay Gonda, the actress, asks one of the characters, in the play's thematic statement.

"Nothing," he answers. "Of what account are dreams?"

"Of what account is life?"

"None. But who made it so?"

"Those who cannot dream."

"No. Those who can *only* dream."

In a journal entry written at the time (dated April 9, 1934), Miss Rand elaborates this viewpoint:

I believe—and I want to gather all the facts to illustrate this—that the worst curse on mankind is the ability to consider ideals as something quite abstract and detached from one's everyday life. The ability of *living* and *thinking* quite differently, in other words eliminating thinking from your actual life. This applied not to deliberate and conscious hypocrites, but to those more dangerous and hopeless ones who, alone with themselves and to themselves, tolerate a complete break between their convictions and their lives, and still believe that they have convictions. To them—either their ideals or their lives are worthless—and usually both.

Such "dangerous and hopeless ones" may betray their ideal in the name of "social respectability" (the small businessman in this story) or in the name of the welfare of the masses (the Communist) or the will of God (the evangelist) or the pleasure of the moment (the playboy Count)—or they may do it for the license of claiming that the good is impossible and therefore the struggle for it unnecessary (the painter). *Ideal* captures eloquently the essence of each of these diverse types and demonstrates their common denominator. In this regard, it is an intellectual tour de force. It is a philosophical guide to hypocrisy, a dramatized inventory of the kinds of ideas and attitudes that lead to the impotence of ideals—that is, to their detachment from life.

(The inventory, however, is not offered in the form of a developed plot structure. In the body of the play, there is no progression of events, no necessary connection between one encounter and the next. It is a series of evocative vignettes, often illuminating and ingenious, but as theater, I think, unavoidably somewhat static.)

Dwight Langley, the painter, is the pure exponent of the evil the play is attacking; he is, in effect, the spokesman for Platonism, who explicitly preaches that beauty is unreachable in this world and perfection unattainable. Since he insists that ideals are impossible on earth, he cannot, logically enough, believe in the reality of any ideal, even when it actually confronts him. Thus, although he knows every facet of Kay Gonda's face, he (alone among the characters) does not recognize her when she appears in his life. This philosophically induced blindness, which motivates his betrayal of her, is a particularly brilliant concretization of the play's theme, and makes a dramatic Act I curtain.

In her journal of the period, Miss Rand singles out religion as the main cause of men's lack of integrity. The worst of the characters, accordingly, the one who evokes her greatest indignation, is Hix, the evangelist, who preaches earthly suffering as a means to heavenly happiness. In an excellently worked-out scene, we see that it is not his vices, but his religion, including his definition of virtue, that brings him to demand the betrayal of Kay Gonda, her deliberate sacrifice to the lowest of creatures. By gaining a stranglehold on ethics, then preaching sacrifice as an ideal, religion, no matter what its intentions, systematically inculcates hypocrisy: it teaches men that achieving values is low ("selfish"), but that giving them up is noble. "Giving them up," in practice, means betraying them.

"None of us," one of the characters complains, "ever chooses the bleak, hopeless life he is forced to lead." Yet, as the play demonstrates, all these men do choose the lives they lead. When confronted by the ideal they profess to desire, they do not want it. Their vaunted "idealism" is largely a form of self-deception, enabling them to pretend to themselves and others that they aspire to something higher. In fact and in reality, however, they don't.

Kay Gonda, by contrast, is a passionate valuer; like Irene in "The Husband I Bought," she cannot accept anything less than the ideal. Her exalted sense of life cannot accept the ugliness, the pain, the "dismal little pleasures" that she sees all around her, and she feels a desperate need to know that she is not alone in this regard. There is no doubt that Ayn Rand herself shared Kay Gonda's sense of life, and often her loneliness, too—and that Kay's cry in the play is her own:

> I want to see, real, living, and in the hours of my own days, that glory I create as an illusion! I want it real! I want to know that there is someone, somewhere, who wants it, too! Or else what is the use of seeing it, and working, and burning oneself for an impossible vision? A spirit, too, needs fuel. It can run dry.

Emotionally, *Ideal* is unique among Ayn Rand's works. It is the polar opposite of "Good Copy." "Good Copy" was based on the premise of the impotence and insignificance of evil. But *Ideal* focuses almost exclusively on evil or mediocrity (in a way that even *We the Living* does not); it is pervaded by Kay Gonda's feeling of alienation from mankind, the feeling, tinged by bitterness, that the true idealist is in a minuscule minority amid an earthful of value-betrayers with whom no communication is possible. In accordance with this perspective, the hero, Johnnie Dawes, is not a characteristic Ayn Rand figure, but a misfit utterly estranged from the world, a man whose virtue is that he does not know how to live today (and has often wanted to die). If Leo feels this in Soviet Russia, the explanation is political, not metaphysical. But Johnnie feels it in the United States.

In her other works, Ayn Rand herself gave the answer to such a "malevolent universe" viewpoint, as she called it. Dominique Francon in *The Fountainhead,* for instance, strikingly, resembles Kay and Johnnie in her idealistic alienation from the world; yet she eventually discovers how to reconcile evil with the "benevolent universe" approach. "You must learn," Roark tells her, "not to be afraid of the world. Not to be held by it as you are now. Never to be hurt by it as you were in that courtroom." Dominique does learn it; but Kay and Johnnie do not, or at least not fully. The effect is untypical Ayn Rand: a story written *approvingly* from Dominique's initial viewpoint.

Undoubtedly, the intensity of Miss Rand's personal struggle at the time—her intellectual and professional struggle against a seemingly deaf, even hostile culture—helps to account for the play's approach. Dominique, Miss Rand has said, is "myself in a bad mood." The same may be said of this aspect of *Ideal*.

Despite its somber essence, however, *Ideal* is not entirely a malevolent story. The play does have its lighter, even humorous side, such as its witty satire of Chuck Fink, the "selfless" radical, and of the Elmer Gantry-like Sister Essie Twomey, with her Service Station of the Spirit. The ending, moreover, however unhappy, is certainly not intended as tragedy or defeat. Johnnie's final action is *action*—that is the whole point—action to protect the ideal, as against empty words or dreams. *His* idealism, therefore, is genuine, and Kay Gonda's search ends on a positive note. In this respect, even *Ideal* may be regarded as an affirmation (albeit in an unusual form) of the benevolent universe.

—L. P.

Ideal

CHARACTERS

BILL McNITT, screen director
CLAIRE PEEMOLLER, scenario writer
SOL SALZER, associate producer
ANTHONY FARROW, president of the Farrow Film Studios
FREDERICA SAYERS
MICK WATTS, press agent
MISS TERRENCE, Kay Gonda's secretary
GEORGE S. PERKINS, assistant manager of the Daffodil Canning Co.
MRS. PERKINS, his wife
MRS. SHLY, her mother
KAY GONDA
CHUCK FINK, sociologist
JIMMY, Chuck's friend
FANNY FINK, Chuck's wife
DWIGHT LANGLEY, artist
EUNICE HAMMOND
CLAUDE IGNATIUS HIX, evangelist
SISTER ESSIE TWOMEY, evangelist
EZRY
COUNT DIETRICH VON ESTERHAZY
LALO JANS
MRS. MONAGHAN
JOHNNIE DAWES

SECRETARIES, LANGLEY'S GUESTS, POLICEMEN

Place   Los Angeles, California

Time   Present; from afternoon to early evening of the following day

Synopsis of scenes

Prologue

Late afternoon. Office of ANTHONY FARROW *in the Farrow Film Studios. A spacious, luxurious room in an overdone modernistic style, which looks like the dream of a second-rate interior decorator with no limits set to the bill.*

Entrance door is set diagonally in the upstage Right corner. Small private door downstage in wall Right. Window in wall Left. A poster of KAY GONDA, *on wall Center; she stands erect, full figure, her arms at her sides, palms up, a strange woman, tall, very slender, very pale; her whole body is stretched up in such a line of reverent, desperate aspiration that the poster gives a strange air to the room, an air that does not belong in it. The words "KAY GONDA IN* FORBIDDEN ECSTASY" *stand out on the poster.*

The curtain rises to disclose CLAIRE PEEMOLLER, SOL SALZER, *and* BILL McNITT. SALZER, *forty, short, stocky, stands with his back to the room, looking hopelessly out of the window, his fingers beating nervously, monotonously, against the glass pane.* CLAIRE PEEMOLLER, *in her early forties, tall, slender, with a sleek masculine haircut and an exotically tailored outfit, reclines in her chair, smoking a cigarette in a lengthy holder.* McNITT, *who looks like a brute of a man and acts it, lies rather than sits in a deep armchair, his legs stretched out, picking his teeth with a match. No one moves. No one speaks. No one looks at the others. The silence is tense, anxious, broken only by the sound of* SALZER's *fingers on the glass.*

McNITT: [*Exploding suddenly*] Stop it, for Christ's sake!

[SALZER *turns slowly to look at him and turns away again, but stops the beating. Silence*]

CLAIRE: [*Shrugging*] Well? [*No one answers*] Hasn't anyone here a suggestion to offer?

SALZER: [*Wearily*] Aw, shut up!

CLAIRE: I see absolutely no sense in behaving like this. We can talk about something *else,* can't we?

McNITT: Well, talk about something else.

CLAIRE: [*With unconvincing lightness*] I saw the rushes of *Love Nest* yesterday. It's a smash, *but* a smash! You should see Eric in that scene where he kills the old man and . . . [*A sudden jerk from the others. She stops short*] Oh, I see. I beg your pardon. [*Silence. She resumes uneasily*] Well, I'll tell you about my new car. The gorgeous thing is so chic! It's simply dripping, *but* dripping with chromium! I was doing eighty yesterday and not a bump! They say this new Sayers Gas is . . . [*There is a stunned, involuntary gasp from the others. She looks at two tense faces*] Well, what on earth is the matter?

SALZER: Listen, Peemoller, for God's sake, Peemoller, don't mention it!

CLAIRE: What?

McNITT: The name!

CLAIRE: What name?

SALZER: *Sayers,* for God's sake!

CLAIRE: Oh! [*Shrugs with resignation*] I'm sorry.

[*Silence.* McNITT *breaks the match in his teeth, spits it out, produces a match folder, tears off another match, and continues with his dental work. A man's voice is heard in the next room. They all whirl toward the entrance door*]

SALZER: [*Eagerly*] There's Tony! He'll tell us! He must know something!

[ANTHONY FARROW *opens the door, but turns to speak to someone offstage before entering. He is tall, stately, middle-aged, handsomely tailored and offensively distinguished*]

FARROW: [*Speaking into the next room*] Try Santa Barbara again. Don't hang up until you get her personally. [*Enters, closing the door. The three look at him anxiously, expectantly*] My friends, has any of you seen Kay Gonda today? [*A great sigh, a moan of disappointment, rises from the others*]

SALZER: Well, that's that. You, too. And I thought you knew something!

FARROW: Discipline, my friends. Let us keep our heads. The Farrow Studios expect each man to do his duty.

SALZER: Skip it, Tony! What's the latest?

CLAIRE: It's preposterous! *But* preposterous!

McNITT: I've always expected something like this from Gonda!

FARROW: No panic, please. There is no occasion for panic. I have called you here in order to formulate our policy in this emergency, coolly and calmly and . . . [*The interoffice communicator on his desk buzzes sharply. He leaps forward, his great calm forgotten, clicks the switch, speaks anxiously*] Yes? . . . You did? Santa Barbara? . . . Give it to me! . . . *What?!* Miss Sayers won't speak to *me*?! . . . She *can't* be out, it's an evasion! Did you tell them it was Anthony Farrow? Of the Farrow Films? . . . Are you sure you made it clear? *President* of the Farrow Films? . . . [*His voice falling dejectedly*] I see. . . . When did Miss Sayers leave? . . . It's an evasion. Try again in half-an-hour. . . . And try again to get the chief of police.

SALZER: [*Desperately*] That I could have told you! The Sayers dame won't talk. If the papers could get nothing out of her—we can't!

FARROW: Let us be systematic. We cannot face a crisis without a system. Let us have discipline, calm. Am I

understood? . . . [*Breaks in two a pencil he has been
playing with nervously*] . . . *Calm!*

SALZER: Calm he wants at a time like this!

FARROW: Let us . . . [*The intercom buzzes. He leaps to
it*] Yes? . . . Fine! Put him on! . . . [*Very jovially*] Hello, Chief! How are you? I . . . [*Sharply*] What do you
mean you have nothing to say? This is *Anthony Farrow* speaking! . . . Well, it usually *does* make a difference. Hel . . . I mean, Chief, there's only one question
I have to ask you, and I think I'm entitled to an answer. Have there or have there not been any charges
filed in Santa Barbara? [*Through his teeth*] Very
well. . . . Thank you. [*Switches off, trying to control
himself*]

SALZER: [*Anxiously*] Well?

FARROW: [*Hopelessly*] He won't talk. No one will talk.
[*Turns to the intercom again*] Miss Drake? . . . Have
you tried Miss Gonda's home once more? . . . Have
you tried all her friends? . . . I know she hasn't any,
but try them anyway! [*Is about to switch off, then
adds*] And get Mick Watts, if you can find the bast—
if you can find him. If anyone knows, *he* knows!

McNITT: That one won't talk either.

FARROW: And that is precisely the thing for us to do.
Silence. Am I understood? *Silence.* Do not answer any
questions on the lot or outside. Avoid all references
to this morning's papers.

SALZER: *Us* the papers should avoid!

FARROW: They haven't said much so far. It's only rumors. Idle gossip.

CLAIRE: But it's all over town! Hints, whispers, questions. If I could see any point in it, I'd say someone
was spreading it intentionally.

FARROW: Personally, I do not believe the story for a
minute. However, I want all the information you can
give me. I take it that none of you has seen Miss
Gonda since yesterday?

[*The others shrug hopelessly, shaking their heads*]

SALZER: If the papers couldn't find her—we can't.

FARROW: Had she mentioned to any of you that she was going to have dinner with Granton Sayers last night?

CLAIRE: When has she ever told anyone anything?

FARROW: Did you notice anything suspicious in her behavior when you saw her last?

CLAIRE: I . . .

McNITT: I should say I did! I thought at the time it was damn funny. Yesterday morning, it was. I drove up to her beach home and there she was, out at sea, tearing through the rocks in a motorboat till I thought I'd have heart failure watching it.

SALZER: My God! That's against our contracts!

McNITT: What? My having heart failure?

SALZER: To hell with you! Gonda driving her motorboat!

McNITT: Try and stop her! So she climbs up to the road, finally, wet all over. "You'll get killed someday," I say to her, and she looks straight at me and she says, "That won't make any difference to me," she says, "nor to anyone else anywhere."

FARROW: She said that?

McNITT: She did. "Listen," I said, "I don't give a damn if you break your neck, but you'll get pneumonia in the middle of my next picture!" She looks at me in that damnable way of hers and she says, "Maybe there won't be any next picture." And she walks straight back to the house and her damn flunkey wouldn't let me in!

FARROW: She actually said that? Yesterday?

McNITT: She did—damn the slut! I never wanted to direct her anyway. I . . .

[*Intercom buzzes*]

FARROW: [*Clicking the switch*] Yes? . . . *Who?* Who is Goldstein and Goldstein? . . . [*Exploding*] Tell them to go to hell! . . . Wait! Tell them Miss Gonda does *not* need any attorneys! Tell them you don't know what on earth made them think she did! [*Switches off furiously*]

SALZER: God! I wish we'd never signed her! A headache we should have ever since she came on the lot!

FARROW: Sol! You're forgetting yourself! After all! Our greatest star!

SALZER: Where did we find her? In the gutter we found her! In the gutter in Vienna! What do we get for our pains? Gratitude we get?

CLAIRE: Down-to-earthiness, that's what she lacks. You know. No finer feelings. *But* none! No sense of human brotherhood. Honestly, I don't understand what they all see in her, anyway!

SALZER: Five million bucks net per each picture—that's what *I* see!

CLAIRE: I don't know why she draws them like that. She's completely heartless. I went down to her house yesterday afternoon—to discuss her next script. And what's the use? She wouldn't let me put in a baby or a dog, as I wanted to. Dogs have such human appeal. You know, we're all brothers under the skin, and . . .

SALZER: Peemoller's right. She's got something there.

CLAIRE: And furthermore . . . [*Stops suddenly*] Wait! That's funny! I haven't thought of this before. She did mention the dinner.

FARROW: [*Eagerly*] What did she say?

CLAIRE: She got up and left me flat, saying she had to dress. "I'm going to Santa Barbara tonight," she said. Then she added, "I do not like missions of charity."

SALZER: My God, what did she mean by that?

CLAIRE: What does she mean by anything? So then I just couldn't resist it, *but* couldn't! I said, "Miss Gonda, do you really think you're so much better than everybody else?" And what did she have the nerve to answer? "Yes," she said, "I do. I wish I didn't have to."

FARROW: Why didn't you tell me this sooner?

CLAIRE: I had forgotten. I really didn't know there was anything between Gonda and Granton Sayers.

McNITT: An old story. I thought she was through with him long ago.

CLAIRE: What did *he* want with her?

FARROW: Well, Granton Sayers—you know Granton Sayers. A reckless fool. Fifty million dollars, three years ago. Today—who knows? Perhaps, fifty thousand. Perhaps, fifty cents. But cut-crystal swimming pools and Greek temples in his garden, and . . .

CLAIRE: . . . And Kay Gonda.

FARROW: Ah, yes, and Kay Gonda. An expensive little

plaything or art work, depending on how you want to look at it. Kay Gonda, that is, two years ago. Not today. I know that she had not seen Sayers for over a year, previous to that dinner in Santa Barbara last night.

CLAIRE: Had there been any quarrel between them?

FARROW: None. Never. That fool had proposed to her three times, to my knowledge. She could have had him, Greek temples and oil wells and all, anytime she winked an eyelash.

CLAIRE: Has she had any trouble of any kind lately?

FARROW: None. None whatever. In fact, you know, she was to sign her new contract with us today. She promised me faithfully to be here at five, and . . .

SALZER: [*Clutching his head suddenly*] Tony! It's the contract!

FARROW: What about the contract?

SALZER: Maybe she's changed her mind again, and quit for good.

CLAIRE: A pose, Mr. Salzer, just a pose. She's said that after every picture.

SALZER: Yeah? You should laugh if you had to crawl after her on your knees like we've done for two months. "I'm through," she says. "Does it really mean anything?" Five million net per each picture—does it mean anything! "Is it really worth doing?" Ha! Twenty thousand a week we offer her and she asks is it worth doing!

FARROW: Now, now, Sol. Control your subconscious. You know, I have an idea that she will come here at five. It would be just like her. She is so utterly unpredictable. We cannot judge her actions by the usual standards. With her—anything is possible.

SALZER: Say, Tony, how about the contract? Did she insist again . . . is there anything in it again about Mick Watts?

FARROW: [*Sighing*] There is, unfortunately. We had to write it in again. So long as she is with us, Mick Watts will be her personal press agent. Most unfortunate.

CLAIRE: That's the kind of trash she gathers around her. But the rest of us aren't good enough for her! Well, if she's got herself into a mess now—I'm glad. Yes,

glad! I don't see why we should all worry ourselves
sick over it.

McNITT: I don't give a damn myself! I'd much rather direct Joan Tudor anyway.

CLAIRE: And I'd just as soon write for Sally Sweeney.
She's such a sweet kid. And . . .

[*The entrance door flies open.* MISS DRAKE *rushes in,
slamming it behind her, as if holding the door against
someone*]

MISS DRAKE: She's here!

FARROW: [*Leaping to his feet*] Who? Gonda?!

MISS DRAKE: No! Miss Sayers! Miss Frederica Sayers!

[*They all gasp*]

FARROW: What?! Here?!

MISS DRAKE: [*Pointing at the door foolishly*] In there!
Right in there!

FARROW: Good Lord!

MISS DRAKE: She wants to see you, Mr. Farrow. She *demands* to see you!

FARROW: Well, let her in! Let her right in, for God's
sake! [*As* MISS DRAKE *is about to rush out*] Wait! [*To
the others*] You'd better get out of here! It may be
confidential. [*Rushes them to private door Right*]

SALZER: [*On his way out*] Make her talk, Tony! For
God's sake, make her talk!

FARROW: Don't worry!

[SALZER, CLAIRE, *and* McNITT *exit Right.* FARROW *whirls
on* MISS DRAKE]

FARROW: Don't stand there shaking! Bring her right in!

[MISS DRAKE *exits hurriedly.* FARROW *flops down behind his desk and attempts a nonchalant attitude. The
entrance door is thrown open as* FREDERICA SAYERS
*enters. She is a tall, sparse, stern lady of middle age,
gray-haired, erect in her black clothes of mourning.*

MISS DRAKE *hovers anxiously behind her.* FARROW *jumps to his feet*]

MISS DRAKE: Miss Frederica Sayers, Mr. Far—

MISS SAYERS: [*Brushing her aside*] Abominable discipline in your studio, Farrow! That's no way to run the place. [MISS DRAKE *slips out, closing the door*] Five reporters pounced on me at the gate and trailed me to your office. I suppose it will all appear in the evening papers, the color of my underwear included.

FARROW: My *dear* Miss Sayers! How do you do? So kind of you to come here! Rest assured that I . . .

MISS SAYERS: Where's Kay Gonda? I must see her. At once.

FARROW: [*Looks at her, startled. Then:*] Do sit down, Miss Sayers. Please allow me to express my deepest sympathy for your grief at the untimely loss of your brother, who . . .

MISS SAYERS: My brother was a fool. [*Sits down*] I've always known he'd end up like this.

FARROW: [*Cautiously*] I must admit I have not been able to learn all the unfortunate details. How *did* Mr. Sayers meet his death?

MISS SAYERS: [*Glancing at him sharply*] Mr. Farrow, your time is valuable. So is mine. I did not come here to answer questions. In fact, I did not come here to speak to you at all. I came to find Miss Gonda. It is most urgent.

FARROW: Miss Sayers, let us get this clear. I have been trying to get in touch with you since early this morning. You must know who started these rumors. And you must realize how utterly preposterous it is. Miss Gonda happens to have dinner with your brother last night. He is found dead, this morning, with a bullet through him. . . . Most unfortunate and I do sympathize, believe me, but is this ground enough for a suspicion of murder against a lady of Miss Gonda's standing? Merely the fact that she happened to be the last one seen with him?

MISS SAYERS: And the fact that nobody has seen her since.

FARROW: Did she . . . did she really do it?

MISS SAYERS: I have nothing to say about that.

FARROW: Was there anyone else at your house last night?

MISS SAYERS: I have nothing to say about that.

FARROW: But good God! [*Controlling himself*] Look here, Miss Sayers, I can well understand that you may not wish to give it out to the press, but you can tell me, in strict confidence, can't you? What were the exact circumstances of your brother's death?

MISS SAYERS: I have given my statement to the police.

FARROW: The police refuse to disclose anything!

MISS SAYERS: They must have their reasons.

FARROW: Miss Sayers! Please try to understand the position I'm in! I'm entitled to know. What actually happened at that dinner?

MISS SAYERS: I have never spied on Granton and his mistresses.

FARROW: But . . .

MISS SAYERS: Have you asked Miss Gonda? What did she say?

FARROW: Look here, if you don't talk—I don't talk, either.

MISS SAYERS: I have not asked you to talk. In fact, I haven't the slightest interest in anything you may say. I want to see Miss Gonda. It is to her own advantage. To yours also, I suppose.

FARROW: May I give her the message?

MISS SAYERS: Your technique is childish, my good man.

FARROW: But in heaven's name, what is it all about? If you've accused her of murder, you have no right to come here demanding to see her! If she's hiding, wouldn't she be hiding from you above all people?

MISS SAYERS: Most unfortunate, if she is. Highly ill advised. Highly.

FARROW: Look here, I'll offer you a bargain. You tell me everything and I'll take you to Miss Gonda. Not otherwise.

MISS SAYERS: [*Rising*] I have always been told that picture people had abominable manners. Most regrettable. Please tell Miss Gonda that I have tried. I shall not be responsible for the consequences now.

FARROW: [*Rushing after her*] Wait! Miss Sayers! Wait a moment! [*She turns to him*] I'm so sorry! Please forgive me! I'm . . . I'm quite upset, as you can well understand. I beg of you, Miss Sayers, consider what it means! The greatest star of the screen! The dream woman of the world! They worship her, millions of them. It's practically a cult.

MISS SAYERS: I have never approved of motion pictures. Never saw one. The pastime of morons.

FARROW: You wouldn't say that if you read her fan mail. Do you think it comes from shopgirls and school kids, like the usual kind of trash? No. Not Kay Gonda's mail. From college professors and authors and judges and ministers! Everybody! Dirt farmers and international names! It's extraordinary! I've never seen anything like it in my whole career.

MISS SAYERS: Indeed?

FARROW: I don't know what she does to them all—but she does something. She's not a movie star to them—she's a goddess. [*Correcting himself hastily*] Oh, forgive me. I understand how you must feel about her. Of course, you and I know that Miss Gonda is not exactly above reproach. She is, in fact, a very objectionable person who . . .

MISS SAYERS: I thought she was a rather charming young woman. A bit anemic. A vitamin deficiency in her diet, no doubt. [*Turning to him suddenly*] Was she happy?

FARROW: [*Looking at her*] Why do you ask that?

MISS SAYERS: I don't think she was.

FARROW: That, Miss Sayers, is a question I've been asking myself for years. She's a strange woman.

MISS SAYERS: She is.

FARROW: But surely you can't hate her so much as to want to ruin her!

MISS SAYERS: I do not hate her at all.

FARROW: Then for heaven's sake, help me to save her name! Tell me what happened. One way or the other, only let's stop these rumors! Let's stop these rumors!

MISS SAYERS: This is getting tiresome, my good man. For the last time, will you let me see Miss Gonda or won't you?

FARROW: I'm so sorry, but it is impossible, and . . .

MISS SAYERS: Either you are a fool or you don't know where she is yourself. Regrettable, in either case. I wish you a good day.

[*She is at the entrance door when the private door Right is thrown open violently.* SALZER *and* McNITT *enter, dragging and pushing* MICK WATTS *between them.* MICK WATTS *is tall, about thirty-five, with disheveled platinum-blond hair, the ferocious face of a thug, and the blue eyes of a baby. He is obviously, unquestionably drunk*]

McNITT: There's your precious Mick Watts for you!

SALZER: Where do you think we found him? He was . . . [*Stops short seeing* MISS SAYERS] Oh, I beg your pardon! We thought Miss Sayers had left!

MICK WATTS: [*Tearing himself loose from them*] Miss *Sayers*?! [*Reels ferociously toward her*] What did you tell them?

MISS SAYERS: [*Looking at him coolly*] And who are you, young man?

MICK WATTS: *What did you tell them?*

MISS SAYERS: [*Haughtily*] I have told them nothing.

MICK WATTS: Well, keep your mouth shut! Keep your mouth shut!

MISS SAYERS: That, young man, is precisely what I am doing. [*Exits*]

McNITT: [*Lurching furiously at* MICK WATTS] Why, you drunken fool!

FARROW: [*Interfering*] Wait a moment! What happened? Where did you find him?

SALZER: Down in the publicity department! Just think of that! He walked right in and there's a mob of reporters pounced on him and started filling him up with liquor and—

FARROW: Oh, my Lord!

SALZER:—and here's what he was handing out for a press release! [*Straightens out a slip of paper he has crumpled in his hand, reads:*] "Kay Gonda does not cook her own meals or knit her own underwear. She does not play golf, adopt babies, or endow hospitals for homeless horses. She is not kind to her dear old mother—she *has* no dear old mother. She is not just like you and me. She never was like you and me. She's like nothing you bastards ever dreamed of!"

FARROW: [*Clutching his head*] Did they get it?

SALZER: A fool you should think I am? We dragged him out of there just in time!

FARROW: [*Approaching* MICK WATTS, *ingratiatingly*] Sit down, Mick, do sit down. There's a good boy.

[MICK WATTS *flops down on a chair and sits motionless, staring into space*]

McNITT: If you let me punch the bastard just once, he'll talk all right.

[SALZER *nudges him frantically to keep quiet.* FARROW *hurries to a cabinet, produces a glass and a decanter, pours*]

FARROW: [*Bending over* MICK WATTS, *solicitously, offering him the glass*] A drink, Mick? [MICK WATTS *does not move or answer*] Nice weather we're having, Mick. Nice, but hot. Awfully hot. Supposing you and I have a drink together?

MICK WATTS: [*In a dull monotone*] I don't know a thing. Save your liquor. Go to hell.

FARROW: What *are* you talking about?

MICK WATTS: I'm talking about nothing—and that goes for everything.

FARROW: You could stand a drink once in a while, couldn't you? You look thirsty to me.

MICK WATTS: I don't know a thing about Kay Gonda. Never heard of her. . . . Kay Gonda. It's a funny name, isn't it? I went to confession once, long ago—and they talked about the redemption of all sins. It's useless to yell "Kay Gonda" and to think that all your sins are washed away. Just pay two bits in the balcony—and come out pure as snow.

[*The others exchange glances and shrug hopelessly*]

FARROW: On second thought, Mick, I won't offer you another drink. You'd better have something to eat.

MICK WATTS: I'm not hungry. I stopped being hungry many years ago. But she is.

FARROW: Who?

MICK WATTS: Kay Gonda.

FARROW: [*Eagerly*] Any idea where she's having her next meal?

MICK WATTS: In heaven. [FARROW *shakes his head help-lessly*] In a blue heaven with white lilies. Very white lilies. Only she'll never find it.

FARROW: I don't understand you, Mick.

MICK WATTS: [*Looking at him slowly for the first time*] You don't understand? She doesn't either. Only it's no use. It's no use trying to unravel, because if you try, you end up with more dirt on your hands than you care to wipe off. There are not enough towels in the world to wipe it off. Not enough towels. That's the trouble.

SALZER: [*Impatiently*] Look here, Watts, you must know something. You'd better play ball with us. Remember, you've been fired from every newspaper on both coasts—

MICK WATTS:—and from many others in between.

SALZER:—so that if anything should happen to Gonda, you won't have a job here unless you help us now and . . .

MICK WATTS: [*His voice emotionless*] Do you think I'd want to stay with the lousy bunch of you if it weren't for her?

McNITT: Jesus, it beats me what they all see in that bitch!

[MICK WATTS *turns and looks at* McNITT *fixedly, ominously*]

SALZER: [*Placatingly*] Now, now, Mick, he doesn't mean it, he's kidding, he's—

[MICK WATTS *rises slowly, deliberately, walks up to* McNITT *without hurry, then strikes him flat on the face, a blow that sends him sprawling on the floor.* FARROW *rushes to help the stunned* McNITT. MICK WATTS *stands motionless, with perfect indifference, his arms limp*]

McNITT: [*Raising his head slowly*] The damn . . .

FARROW: [*Restraining him*] Discipline, Bill, discipline, control your . . .

[*The door is flung open as* CLAIRE PEEMOLLER *rushes in breathlessly*]

CLAIRE: She's coming! She's coming!

FARROW: Who?!

CLAIRE: Kay Gonda! I just saw her car turning the corner!

SALZER: [*Looking at his wristwatch*] By God! It's five o'clock! Can you beat that!

FARROW: I knew she would! I knew it! [*Rushes to intercom, shouts:*] Miss Drake! Bring in the contract!

CLAIRE: [*Tugging at* FARROW's *sleeve*] Tony, you won't tell her what I said, will you, Tony? I've always been her best friend! I'll do anything to please her! I've always . . .

SALZER: [*Grabbing a telephone*] Get the publicity department! Quick!

McNITT: [*Rushing to* MICK WATTS] I was only kidding, Mick! You know I was only kidding. No hard feelings, eh, pal?

[MICK WATTS *does not move or look at him.* WATTS *is the only one motionless amid the frantic activity*]

SALZER: [*Shouting into the phone*] Hello, Meagley? . . . Call all the papers! Reserve the front pages! Tell you later! [*Hangs up*]

[MISS DRAKE *enters, carrying a batch of legal documents*]

FARROW: [*At his desk*] Put it right here, Miss Drake! Thank you! [*Steps are heard approaching*] Smile, all of you! Smile! Don't let her think that we thought for a minute that she . . .

[*Everyone obeys, save* MICK WATTS, *all eyes turned to the door. The door opens.* MISS TERRENCE *enters and steps on the threshold. She is a prim, ugly little shrimp of a woman*]

MISS TERRENCE: Is Miss Gonda here?

[*A moan rises from the others*]

SALZER: Oh, God!

MISS TERRENCE: [*Looking at the stunned group*] Well, what is the matter?

CLAIRE: [*Choking*] Did you . . . did *you* drive up in Miss Gonda's car?

MISS TERRENCE: [*With hurt dignity*] Why, certainly. Miss Gonda had an appointment here at five o'clock, and

I thought it a secretary's duty to come and tell Mr. Farrow that it looks as if Miss Gonda will not be able to keep it.

FARROW: [*Dully*] So it does.

MISS TERRENCE: There is also something rather peculiar I wanted to check on. Has anyone from the studio been at Miss Gonda's home last night?

FARROW: [*Perking up*] No. Why, Miss Terrence?

MISS TERRENCE: This is *most* peculiar.

SALZER: *What* is?

MISS TERRENCE: I'm sure I can't understand it. I've questioned the servants, but they have not taken them.

FARROW: Taken what?

MISS TERRENCE: If no one else took them, then Miss Gonda must have been back at home late last night.

FARROW: [*Eagerly*] Why, Miss Terrence?

MISS TERRENCE: Because I saw them on her desk yesterday after she left for Santa Barbara. And when I entered her room this morning, they were gone.

FARROW: What was gone?

MISS TERRENCE: Six letters from among Miss Gonda's fan mail.

[*A great sigh of disappointment rises from all*]

SALZER: Aw, nuts!

McNITT: And I thought it was something!

[MICK WATTS *bursts out laughing suddenly, for no apparent reason*]

FARROW: [*Angrily*] What are you laughing at?

MICK WATTS: [*Quietly*] Kay Gonda.

McNITT: Oh, throw the drunken fool out!

MICK WATTS: [*Without looking at anyone*] A great quest. The quest of the hopeless. Why do we hope? Why do we seek it, when we'd be luckier if we didn't think that it could exist? Why does she? Why does she have to be hurt? [*Whirls suddenly upon the others with ferocious hatred*] God damn you all! [*Rushes out, slamming the door*]

CURTAIN

Act I

When the curtain rises, a motion-picture screen is disclosed and a letter is flashed on the screen, unrolling slowly. It is written in a neat, precise, respectable handwriting:

Dear Miss Gonda,

I am not a regular movie fan, but I have never missed a picture of yours. There is something about you which I can't give a name to, something I had and lost, but I feel as if you're keeping it for me, for all of us. I had it long ago, when I was very young. You know how it is: when you're very young, there's something ahead of you, so big that you're afraid of it, but you wait for it and you're so happy waiting. Then the years pass and it never comes. And then you find, one day, that you're not waiting any longer. It seems foolish, because you didn't even know what it was you were waiting for. I look at myself and I don't know. But when I look at you—I do.

And if ever, by some miracle, you were to enter my life, I'd drop everything, and follow you, and gladly lay down my life for you, because, you see, I'm still a human being.

Very truly yours,

George S. Perkins
. . . S. Hoover Street
Los Angeles, California

When the letter ends, all lights go out, and when they come on again, the screen has disappeared and the stage reveals the living room of GEORGE S. PERKINS.

It is a room such as thousands of other rooms in thousands of other homes whose owners have a respectable little income and a respectable little character.

Center back, a wide glass door opening on the street. Door into the rest of the house in wall Left.

When the curtain rises, it is evening. The street outside is dark. MRS. PERKINS *stands in the middle of the room, tense, erect, indignant, watching with smoldering emotion the entrance door where* GEORGE S. PERKINS *is seen outside turning the key in the lock.* MRS. PERKINS *looks like a dried-out bird of prey that has never been young.* GEORGE S. PERKINS *is short, blond, heavy, helpless, and over forty. He is whistling a gay tune as he enters. He is in a very cheerful mood.*

MRS. PERKINS: [*Without moving, ominously*] You're late.

PERKINS: [*Cheerfully*] Well, dovey, I have a good excuse for being late.

MRS. PERKINS: [*Speaking very fast*] I have no doubt about that. But listen to me, George Perkins, you'll have to do something about Junior. That boy of yours got D again in arithmetic. If a father don't take the proper interest in his children, what can you expect from a boy who . . .

PERKINS: Aw, honeybunch, we'll excuse the kid for once—just to celebrate.

MRS. PERKINS: Celebrate what?

PERKINS: How would you like to be Mrs. Assistant Manager of the Daffodil Canning Company?

MRS. PERKINS: I would like it very much. Not that I have any hopes of ever being.

PERKINS: Well, dovey, you are. As of today.

MRS. PERKINS: [*Noncommittally*] Oh. [*Calls into house*] Mama! Come here!

[MRS. SHLY *waddles in from door Left. She is fat and looks chronically dissatisfied with the whole world.* MRS. PERKINS *speaks, half-boasting, half-bitter*]

Mama, Georgie's got a promotion.

MRS. SHLY: [*Dryly*] Well, we've waited for it long enough.

PERKINS: But you don't understand. I've been made *Assistant Manager*—[*Looks for the effect on her face, finds none, adds lamely*]—of the Daffodil Canning Company.

MRS. SHLY: Well?

PERKINS: [*Spreading his hands helplessly*] Well . . .

MRS. SHLY: All I gotta say is it's a fine way to start off on your promotion, coming home at such an hour, keeping us waiting with dinner and . . .

PERKINS: Oh, I . . .

MRS. SHLY: Oh, we ate all right, don't you worry! Never seen a man that cared two hoops about his family, not two hoops!

PERKINS: I'm sorry. I had dinner with the boss. I should've phoned, only I couldn't keep him waiting, you know, the boss asking me to dinner, in person.

MRS. PERKINS: And here I was waiting for you, I had something to tell you, a nice surprise for you, and . . .

MRS. SHLY: Don't you tell him, Rosie. Don't you tell him now. Serves him right.

PERKINS: But I figured you'd understand. I figured you'd be happy—[*Corrects his presumption hastily*]—well, *glad* that I've been made—

MRS. PERKINS:—Assistant Manager! Lord, do we have to hear it for the rest of our lives?

PERKINS: [*Softly*] Rosie, it's twenty years I've waited for it.

MRS. SHLY: That, my boy, is nothing to brag about!

PERKINS: It's a long time, twenty years. One gets sort of tired. But now we can take it easy . . . light . . . [*With sudden eagerness*] . . . you know, *light* . . . [*Coming down to earth, apologetically*] . . . easy, I mean.

MRS. SHLY: Listen to him! How much you got, Mr. Rockafeller?

PERKINS: [*With quiet pride*] One hundred and sixty-five dollars.

MRS. PERKINS: A *week*?

PERKINS: Yes, dovey, a week. Every single week.

MRS. SHLY: [*Impressed*] Well! [*Gruffly*] Well, what're you standing there for? Sit down. You must be all tired out.

PERKINS: [*Removing his coat*] Mind if I slip my coat off? Sort of stuffy tonight.

MRS. PERKINS: I'll fetch your bathrobe. Don't you go catching a cold. [*Exits Left*]

MRS. SHLY: We gotta think it over careful. There's lots a man can do with one-sixty-five a week. Not that there ain't some men what get around two hundred. Still, one-sixty-five ain't to be sneezed at.

PERKINS: I've been thinking . . .

MRS. PERKINS: [*Returning with a flashy striped flannel*

bathrobe] Now put it on like a good boy, nice and comfy.

PERKINS: [*Obeying*] Thanks. . . . Dovey, I was sort of planning . . . I've been thinking of it for a long time, nights, you know . . . making plans . . .

MRS. PERKINS: Plans? But your wife's not let in on it?

PERKINS: Oh, it was only sort of like dreaming . . . I wanted to . . .

[*There is a thunderous crash upstairs, the violent scuffle of a battle and a child's shrill scream*]

BOY'S VOICE: [*Offstage*] No, ya don't! No, ya don't! Ya dirty snot!

GIRL'S VOICE: Ma-a-a!

BOY'S VOICE: I'll learn ya! I'll . . .

GIRL'S VOICE: Ma-a! He bit me on the pratt!

MRS. PERKINS: [*Throws the door Left open, yells upstairs*] Keep quiet up there and march straight to bed, or I'll beat the living Jesus out of the both of you! [*Slams the door. The noise upstairs subsides to thin whimpers*] For the life of me, I don't see why of all the children in the world I had to get these!

PERKINS: Please, dovey, not tonight. I'm tired. I wanted to talk about . . . the plans.

MRS. PERKINS: What plans?

PERKINS: I was thinking . . . if we're very careful, we could take a vacation maybe . . . in a year or two . . . and go to Europe, you know, like Switzerland or Italy . . . [*Looks at her hopefully, sees no reaction, adds*] . . . It's where they have mountains, you know.

MRS. PERKINS: Well?

PERKINS: Well, and lakes. And snow high up on the peaks. And sunsets.

MRS. PERKINS: And what would we do?

PERKINS: Oh . . . well . . . just rest, I guess. And look around, sort of. You know, at the swans and the sailboats. Just the two of us.

MRS. SHLY: Uh-huh. Just the *two* of you.

MRS. PERKINS: Yes, you were always a great one for making up ways of wasting good money, George Perkins. And me slaving and skimping and saving every little penny. Swans, indeed! Well, before you go thinking of any swans, you'd better get us a new Frigidaire, that's all I've got to say.

MRS. SHLY: And a mayonnaise mixer. And a 'lectric washing machine. And it's about time to be thinking of a new car, too. The old one's a sight. And . . .

PERKINS: Look, you don't understand. I don't want anything that we need.

MRS. PERKINS: What?

PERKINS: I want something I don't need at all.

MRS. PERKINS: George Perkins! Have you been drinking?

PERKINS: Rosie, I . . .

MRS. SHLY: [*Resolutely*] Now I've had just about enough of this nonsense! Now you come down to earth, George Perkins. There's something bigger to think about. Rosie has a surprise for you. A pretty surprise. Tell him, Rosie.

MRS. PERKINS: I just found it out today, Georgie. You'll be glad to hear it.

MRS. SHLY: He'll be tickled pink. Go on.

MRS. PERKINS: Well, I . . . I've been to the doctor's this morning. We have a baby coming.

[*Silence. The two women look, with bright smiles, at* PERKINS' *face, a face that distorts slowly before their eyes into an expression of stunned horror*]

PERKINS: [*In a choked voice*] Another one?

MRS. PERKINS: [*Brightly*] Uh-huh. A brand-new little baby. [*He stares at her silently*] Well? [*He stares without moving*] Well, what's the matter with you? [*He does not move*] Aren't you glad?

PERKINS: [*In a slow, heavy voice*] You're not going to have it.

MRS. PERKINS: Mama! What's he saying?

PERKINS: [*In a dull, persistent monotone*] You know what I'm saying. You can't have it. You won't.

MRS. SHLY: Have you gone plumb outta your mind? Are you thinking of . . . of . . .

PERKINS: [*Dully*] Yes.

MRS. PERKINS: Mama!!

MRS. SHLY: [*Ferociously*] D'you know who you're talking to? It's my daughter you're talking to, not a street woman! To come right out with a thing like that . . . to his own wife . . . to his own . . .

MRS. PERKINS: What's happened to you?

PERKINS: Rosie, I didn't mean to insult you. It's not even dangerous nowadays and . . .

MRS. PERKINS: Make him stop, Mama!

MRS. SHLY: Where did you pick that up? Decent people don't even know about such things! You hear about it maybe with gangsters and actresses. But in a respectable married home!

MRS. PERKINS: What's happened to you today?

PERKINS: It's not today, Rosie. It's for a long, long time back. . . . But I'm set with the firm now. I can take good care of you and the children. But the rest—Rosie, I can't throw it away for good.

MRS. PERKINS: What are you talking about? What better use can you find for your extra money than to take care of a baby?

PERKINS: That's just it. Take care of it. The hospital and the doctors. The strained vegetables—at two bits the can. The school and the measles. All over again. And nothing else.

MRS. PERKINS: So that's how you feel about your duties! There's nothing holier than to raise a family. There's no better blessing. Haven't I spent my life making a home for you? Don't you have everything every decent man struggles for? What else do you want?

PERKINS: Rosie, it's not that I don't like what I've got. I like it fine. Only . . . Well, it's like this bathrobe of mine. I'm glad I have it, it's warm and comfortable, and I like it, just the same as I like the rest of it. Just like that. And no more. There should be more.

MRS. PERKINS: Well, I like that! The swell bathrobe I picked out for your birthday! Well, if you didn't like it, why didn't you exchange it?

PERKINS: Oh, Rosie, it's not that! It's only that a man can't live his whole life for a bathrobe. Or for things that he feels the same way about. Things that do nothing to him—inside, I mean. There should be some-

thing that he's afraid of—afraid and happy. Like going
to church—only not in a church. Something he can
look up to. Something—high, Rosie . . . that's it, *high*.

MRS. PERKINS: Well, if it's culture you want, didn't I sub-
scribe to the Book-of-the-Month Club?

PERKINS: Oh, I know I can't explain it! All I ask is, don't
let's have that baby, Rosie. That would be the end of
it all for me. I'll be an old man, if I give those things
up. I don't want to be old. Not yet. God, not yet! Just
leave me a few years, Rosie!

MRS. PERKINS: [*Breaking down into tears*] Never, never,
never did I think I'd live to hear this!

MRS. SHLY: [*Rushing to her*] Rosie, sweetheart! Don't cry
like that, baby! [*Whirling upon* PERKINS] See what
you've done? Now don't let me hear another word
out of that filthy mouth of yours! Do you want to kill
your wife? Take the Chinese, for instance. They go in
for abortions, that's why all the Chinks have rickets.

PERKINS: Now, Mother, who ever told you that?

MRS. SHLY: Well, I suppose I don't know what I'm talking
about? I suppose the big businessman is the only one
to tell us what's what?

PERKINS: I didn't mean . . . I only meant that . . .

MRS. PERKINS: [*Through her sobs*] You leave Mama
alone, George.

PERKINS: [*Desperately*] But I didn't . . .

MRS. SHLY: I understand. I understand perfectly, George
Perkins. An old mother, these days, is no good for
anything but to shut up and wait for the graveyard!

PERKINS: [*Resolutely*] Mother, I wish you'd stop trying
to . . . [*Bravely*] . . . to make trouble.

MRS. SHLY: So? So that's it? So I'm making trouble? So
I'm a burden to you, am I? Well, I'm glad you came
out with it, Mr. Perkins! And here I've been, poor
fool that I am, slaving in this house like if it was my
own! That's the gratitude I get. Well, I won't stand
for it another minute. Not one minute. [*Rushes out
Left, slamming the door*]

MRS. PERKINS: [*With consternation*] George! . . . George,
if you don't apologize, Mama will leave us!

PERKINS: [*With sudden, desperate courage*] Well, let her
go.

MRS. PERKINS: [*Stares at him incredulously, then:*] So it's come to that? So that's what it does to you, your big promotion? Coming home, picking a fight with everybody, throwing his wife's old mother out into the gutter! If you think I'm going to stand for . . .

PERKINS: Listen, I've stood about as much of her as I'm going to stand. She'd better go. It was coming to this, sooner or later.

MRS. PERKINS: You just listen to me, George Perkins! If you don't apologize to Mama, if you don't apologize to her before tomorrow morning, I'll never speak to you again as long as I live!

PERKINS: [*Wearily*] How many times have I heard that before?

[MRS. PERKINS *runs to door Left and exits, slamming the door.* PERKINS *sits wearily, without moving. An old-fashioned clock strikes nine. He rises slowly, turns out the lights, pulls the shade down over the glass entrance door. The room is dim but for one lamp burning by the fireplace. He leans against the mantelpiece, his head on his arm, slumped wearily. The doorbell rings. It is a quick, nervous, somehow furtive sound.* PERKINS *starts, looks at the entrance door, surprised, hesitates, then crosses to door and opens it. Before we can see the visitor, his voice a stunned explosion:*] Oh, my God!! [PERKINS *steps aside.* KAY GONDA *stands on the threshold. She wears an exquisitely plain black suit, very modern, austerely severe; a black hat, black shoes, stockings, bag, and gloves. The sole and startling contrast to her clothes is the pale, luminous gold of her hair and the whiteness of her face. It is a strange face with eyes that make one uncomfortable. She is tall and very slender. Her movements are slow, her steps light, soundless. There is a feeling of unreality about her, the feeling of a being that does not belong on this earth. She looks more like a ghost than a woman*]

KAY GONDA: Please keep quiet. And let me in.

PERKINS: [*Stuttering foolishly*] You . . . you are . . .

KAY GONDA: Kay Gonda. [*She enters and closes the door behind her*]

PERKINS: W-why . . .

KAY GONDA: Are you George Perkins?

PERKINS: [*Foolishly*] Yes, ma'am. George Perkins. George S. Perkins. . . . Only how . . .

KAY GONDA: I am in trouble. Have you heard about it?

PERKINS: Y-yes . . . oh my God! . . . Yes. . . .

KAY GONDA: I have to hide. For the night. It is dangerous. Can you let me stay here?

PERKINS: *Here?*

KAY GONDA: Yes. For one night.

PERKINS: But how . . . that is . . . why did you . . .

KAY GONDA: [*Opens her bag and shows him the letter*] I read your letter. And I thought that no one would look for me here. And I thought you would want to help me.

PERKINS: I . . . Miss Gonda, you'll excuse me, please, you know it's enough to make a fellow . . . I mean, if I don't seem to make sense or . . . I mean, if you need help, you can stay here the rest of your life, Miss Gonda.

KAY GONDA: [*Calmly*] Thank you. [*She throws her bag on a table, takes off her hat and gloves, indifferently, as if she were quite at home. He keeps staring at her*]

PERKINS: You mean . . . they're really after you?

KAY GONDA: The police. [*Adds*] For murder.

PERKINS: I won't let them get you. If there's anything I can . . . [*He stops short. Steps are heard approaching, behind the door Left*]

MRS. PERKINS' VOICE: [*Offstage*] George!

PERKINS: Yes . . . dovey?

MRS. PERKINS' VOICE: Who was that who rang the bell?

PERKINS: No . . . no one, dovey. Somebody had the wrong address. [*He listens to the steps moving away, then whispers*:] That was my wife. We'd better keep quiet. She's all right. Only . . . she wouldn't understand.

KAY GONDA: It will be dangerous for you, if they find me here.

PERKINS: I don't care. [*She smiles slowly. He points to the room helplessly*] Just make yourself at home. You can sleep right here, on the davenport, and I'll stay outside and watch to see that no one . . .

KAY GONDA: No. I don't want to sleep. Stay here. You and I, we have so much to talk about.

PERKINS: Oh, yes. Sure . . . that is . . . about what, Miss Gonda?

[*She sits down without answering. He sits down on the edge of a chair, gathering his bathrobe, miserably uncomfortable. She looks at him expectantly, a silent question in her eyes. He blinks, clears his throat, says resolutely:*]

Pretty cold night, this is.

KAY GONDA: Yes.

PERKINS: That's California for you . . . the Golden West . . . Sunshine all day, but cold as the . . . but very cold at night.

KAY GONDA: Give me a cigarette.

[*He leaps to his feet, produces a package of cigarettes, strikes three matches before he can light one. She leans back, the lighted cigarette between her fingers*]

PERKINS: [*He mutters helplessly*] I . . . I smoke this kind. Easier on your throat, they are. [*He looks at her miserably. He has so much to tell her. He fumbles for words. He ends with:*] Now Joe Tucker—that's a friend of mine—Joe Tucker, he smokes cigars. But I never took to them, never did.

KAY GONDA: You have many friends?

PERKINS: Yes, sure. Sure I have. Can't complain.

KAY GONDA: You like them?

PERKINS: Yes, I like them fine.

KAY GONDA: And they like you? They approve of you, and they bow to you on the street?

PERKINS: Why . . . I guess so.

KAY GONDA: How old are you, George Perkins?

PERKINS: I'll be forty-three this coming June.

KAY GONDA: It will be hard to lose your job and to find yourself in the street. In a dark, lonely street, where you'll see your friends passing by and looking past you, as if you did not exist. Where you will want to scream and tell them of the great things you know, but no one will hear and no one will answer. It will be hard, won't it?

PERKINS: [*Bewildered*] Why . . . When should that happen?

KAY GONDA: [*Calmly*] When they find me here.

PERKINS: [*Resolutely*] Don't worry about that. No one will find you here. Not that I'm afraid for myself. Suppose they learn I helped you? Who wouldn't? Who'd hold that against me? Why should they?

KAY GONDA: Because they hate me. And they hate all those who take my side.

PERKINS: Why should they hate you?

KAY GONDA: [*Calmly*] I am a murderess, George Perkins.

PERKINS: Well, if you ask me, I don't believe it. I don't even want to ask you whether you've done it. I just don't believe it.

KAY GONDA: If you mean Granton Sayers . . . no, I do not want to speak about Granton Sayers. Forget that. But I am still a murderess. You see, I came here and, perhaps, I will destroy your life—everything that has been your life for forty-three years.

PERKINS: [*In a low voice*] That's not much, Miss Gonda.

KAY GONDA: Do you always go to see my pictures?

PERKINS: Always.

KAY GONDA: Are you happy when you come out of the theater?

PERKINS: Yes. Sure. . . . No, I guess I'm not. That's funny, I never thought of it that way. . . . Miss Gonda, you won't laugh at me if I tell you something?

KAY GONDA: Of course not.

PERKINS: Miss Gonda, I . . . I cry when I come home after seeing a picture of yours. I just lock myself in the bathroom and I cry, every time. I don't know why.

KAY GONDA: I knew that.

PERKINS: How?

KAY GONDA: I told you I am a murderess. I kill so many things in people. I kill the things they live by. But they come to see me because I am the only one who makes them realize that they want those things to be killed. Or they think they do. And it's their whole pride, that they think and say they do.

PERKINS: I'm afraid I don't follow you, Miss Gonda.

AYN RAND INFORMATION

If you find the ideas in this book engaging and would like to learn more about Ayn Rand and her philosophy, mail in this card to receive free information about:

- The Ayn Rand Institute: the authoritative source for information about Ayn Rand and her ideas

- Books, recorded lectures and courses, CDs, and DVDs by Ayn Rand and others on her philosophy

- Conferences, seminars and other Ayn Rand-related events

- University clubs, programs and activities

Information on all these is yours FREE, with no obligation. Just fill out this card and drop it in the mail today or go to www.aynrandinfo.com.

NAME

STREET ADDRESS   APT.

CITY   STATE   ZIP

E-MAIL (OPTIONAL)

BUSINESS REPLY MAIL

FIRST-CLASS MAIL   PERMIT NO 14564   IRVINE CA

POSTAGE WILL BE PAID BY ADDRESSEE

AYN RAND INFO
PO BOX 51808
IRVINE CA 92619-9930

KAY GONDA: You'll understand someday.

PERKINS: Did you really do it?

KAY GONDA: What?

PERKINS: Did you kill Granton Sayers? [*She looks at him, smiles slowly, shrugs*] I was only wondering why you could have done it.

KAY GONDA: Because I could not stand it any longer. There are times when one can't stand it any longer.

PERKINS: Yes. There are.

KAY GONDA: [*Looking straight at him*] Why do you want to help me?

PERKINS: I don't know . . . only that . . .

KAY GONDA: Your letter, it said . . .

PERKINS: Oh! I never thought you'd read the silly thing.

KAY GONDA: It was not silly.

PERKINS: I bet you have plenty of them, fans, I mean, and letters.

KAY GONDA: I like to think that I mean something to people.

PERKINS: You must forgive me if I said anything fresh, you know, or personal.

KAY GONDA: You said you were not happy.

PERKINS: I . . . I didn't mean to complain, Miss Gonda, only . . . I guess I've missed something along the way. I don't know what it is, but I know I've missed it. Only I don't know why.

KAY GONDA: Perhaps it is because you wanted to miss it.

PERKINS: No. [*His voice is suddenly firm*] No. [*He rises and stands looking straight at her*] You see, I'm not unhappy at all. In fact, I'm a very happy man—as happiness goes. Only there's something in me that knows of a life I've never lived, the kind of life no one has ever lived, but should.

KAY GONDA: You know it? Why don't you live it?

PERKINS: Who does? Who can? Who ever gets a chance at the . . . the very best possible to him? We all bargain. We take the second best. That's all there is to be had. But the . . . the God in us, it knows the other . . . the very best . . . which never comes.

KAY GONDA: And . . . if it came?

PERKINS: We'd grab it—because there *is* a God in us.

KAY GONDA: And . . . the God in you, you really want it?

PERKINS: [*Fiercely*] Look, I know this: let them come, the cops, let them come now and try to get you. Let them tear this house down. I built it—took me fifteen years to pay for it. Let them tear it down, before I let them take you. Let them come, whoever it is that's after you . . . [*The door Left is flung open.* MRS. PERKINS *stands on the threshold; she wears a faded corduroy bathrobe and a long nightgown of grayish-pink cotton*]

MRS. PERKINS: [*Gasping*] George! . . .

[KAY GONDA *rises and stands looking at them*]

PERKINS: Dovey, keep quiet! For God's sake, keep quiet . . . come in . . . close the door!

MRS. PERKINS: I thought I heard voices . . . I . . . [*She chokes, unable to continue*]

PERKINS: Dovey . . . this . . . Miss Gonda, may I present— my wife? Dovey, this is Miss Gonda, Miss Kay Gonda! [KAY GONDA *inclines her head, but* MRS. PERKINS *remains motionless, staring at her.* PERKINS *says desperately:*] Don't you understand? Miss Gonda's in trouble, you know, you've heard about it, the papers said . . . [*He stops.* MRS. PERKINS *shows no reaction. Silence. Then:*]

MRS. PERKINS: [*To* KAY GONDA, *her voice unnaturally emotionless*] Why did you come here?

KAY GONDA: [*Calmly*] Mr. Perkins will have to explain that.

PERKINS: Rosie, I . . . [*Stops*]

MRS. PERKINS: Well?

PERKINS: Rosie, there's nothing to get excited about, only that Miss Gonda is wanted by the police and—

MRS. PERKINS: Oh.

PERKINS:—and it's for murder and—

MRS. PERKINS: Oh!

PERKINS:—and she just has to stay here overnight. That's all.

MRS. PERKINS: [*Slowly*] Listen to me, George Perkins: either she goes out of the house this minute, or else I go.

PERKINS: But let me explain . . .

MRS. PERKINS: I don't need any explanations. I'll pack my things, and I'll take the children, too. And I'll pray to God we never see you again. [*She waits. He does not answer*] Tell her to get out.

PERKINS: Rosie . . . I can't.

MRS. PERKINS: We've struggled together pretty hard, haven't we, George? Together. For fifteen years.

PERKINS: Rosie, it's just one night. . . . If you knew . . .

MRS. PERKINS: I don't want to know. I don't want to know why my husband should bring such a thing upon me. A fancy woman or a murderess, or both. I've been a faithful wife to you, George. I've given you the best years of my life. I've borne your children.

PERKINS: Yes, Rosie . . .

MRS. PERKINS: It's not just for me. Think of what will happen to you. Shielding a murderess. Think of the children. [*He doesn't answer*] And your job, too. You just got that promotion. We were going to get new drapes for the living room. The green ones. You always wanted them.

PERKINS: Yes . . .

MRS. PERKINS: And that golf club you wanted to join. They have the best of members, solid, respectable members, not men with their fingerprints in the police files.

PERKINS: [*His voice barely audible*] No . . .

MRS. PERKINS: Have you thought of what will happen when people learn about this?

PERKINS: [*Looks desperately for a word, a glance from* KAY GONDA. *He wants her to decide. But* KAY GONDA *stands motionless, as if the scene did not concern her at all. Only her eyes are watching him. He speaks to her, his voice a desperate plea*] What will happen when people learn about this?

[KAY GONDA *does not answer*]

MRS. PERKINS: I'll tell you what will happen. No decent person will ever want to speak to you again. They'll fire you, down at the Daffodil Company, they'll throw you right out in the street!

PERKINS: [*Repeats softly, dazedly, as if from far away*] . . . in a dark, lonely street where your friends will be passing by and looking straight past you . . . and you'll want to scream . . . [*He stares at* KAY GONDA, *his eyes wide. She does not move*]

MRS. PERKINS: That will be the end of everything you've ever held dear. And in exchange for what? Back roads and dark alleys, fleeing by night, hunted and cornered, and forsaken by the whole wide world! . . . [*He does not answer or turn to her. He is staring at* KAY GONDA *with a new kind of understanding*] Think of the children, George. . . . [*He does not move*] We've been pretty happy together, haven't we, George? Fifteen years. . . .

[*Her voice trails off. There is a long silence. Then* PERKINS *turns slowly away from* KAY GONDA *to look at his wife. His shoulders droop, he is suddenly old*]

PERKINS: [*Looking at his wife*] I'm sorry, Miss Gonda, but under the circumstances . . .
KAY GONDA: [*Calmly*] I understand.

[*She puts on her hat, picks up her bag and gloves. Her movements are light, unhurried. She walks to the door Center. When she passes* MRS. PERKINS, *she stops to say calmly*:]

I'm sorry. I had the wrong address.

[*She walks out.* PERKINS *and his wife stand at the open door and watch her go*]

PERKINS: [*Putting his arm around his wife's waist*] Is mother asleep?
MRS. PERKINS: I don't know. Why?
PERKINS: I thought I'd go in and talk to her. Make up, sort of. She knows all about raising babies.

CURTAIN

SCENE 2
When the curtain rises, another letter is projected on the screen. This one is written in a small uneven, temperamental handwriting:

Dear Miss Gonda,
    The determinism of duty has conditioned me to pur-

sue the relief of my fellow men's suffering. I see daily before me the wrecks and victims of an outrageous social system. But I gain courage for my cause when I look at you on the screen and realize of what greatness the human race is capable. Your art is a symbol of the hidden potentiality which I see in my derelict brothers. None of them chose to be what he is. None of us ever chooses the bleak, hopeless life he is forced to lead. But in our ability to recognize you and bow to you lies the hope of mankind.

Sincerely yours,

Chuck Fink
. . . Spring Street
Los Angeles, California

Lights go out, screen disappears, and stage reveals living room in the home of CHUCK FINK. *It is a miserable room in a run-down furnished bungalow. Entrance door upstage in wall Right; large open window next to it, downstage; door to bedroom in wall Center. Late evening. Although there are electric fixtures in the room, it is lighted by a single kerosene lamp smoking in a corner. The tenants are moving out; two battered trunks and a number of grocery cartons stand in the middle of the room; closets and chests gape open, half emptied; clothes, books, dishes, every conceivable piece of household junk are piled indiscriminately into great heaps on the floor.*

At curtain rise, CHUCK FINK *is leaning anxiously out of the window; he is a young man of about thirty, slight, anemic, with a rich mane of dark hair, a cadaverous face, and a neat little mustache. He is watching the people seen hurrying past the window in great agitation; there is a dim confusion of voices outside. He sees someone outside and calls:*

FINK: Hey, Jimmy!
JIMMY'S VOICE: [*Offstage*] Yeah?
FINK: Come here a minute!

[JIMMY *appears at the window outside; he is a haggard-looking youth, his clothes torn, his eyes swollen, blood running down the side of his face from a gash on his forehead*]

JIMMY: Oh, that you, Chuck? Thought it was a cop. What d'you want?

FINK: Have you seen Fanny down there?

JIMMY: Huh! Fanny!

FINK: Have you seen her?

JIMMY: Not since it started.

FINK: Is she hurt?

JIMMY: Might be. I seen her when it started. She threw a brick plumb through their window.

FINK: What's happened out there?

JIMMY: Tear gas. They've arrested a bunch of the pickets. So we beat it.

FINK: But hasn't anyone seen Fanny?

JIMMY: Oh, to hell with your Fanny! There's people battered all over the place. Jesus, that was one swell free-for-all!

[JIMMY *disappears down the street.* FINK *leaves the window. Paces nervously, glancing at his watch. The noise subsides in the street.* FINK *tries to continue his packing, throws a few things into cartons halfheartedly. The entrance door flies open.* FANNY FINK *enters. She is a tall, gaunt, angular girl in her late twenties, with a sloppy masculine haircut, flat shoes, a man's coat thrown over her shoulders. Her hair is disheveled, her face white. She leans against the doorjamb for support*]

FINK: Fanny! [*She does not move*] Are you all right? What happened? Where have you been?

FANNY: [*In a flat, husky voice*] Got any Mercurochrome?

FINK: What?

FANNY: Mercurochrome. [*Throws her coat off. Her clothes are torn, her bare arms bruised; there is a bleeding cut on one forearm*]

FINK: Jesus!

FANNY: Oh, don't stand there like an idiot! [*Walks resolutely to a cabinet, rummages through the shelves, produces a tiny bottle*] Stop staring at me! Nothing to get hysterical over!

FINK: Here, let me help.

FANNY: Never mind. I'm all right. [*Dabs her arm with Mercurochrome*]

FINK: Where have you been so late?

FANNY: In jail.

FINK: Huh?!

FANNY: All of us. Pinky Thomlinson, Bud Miller, Mary Phelps, and all the rest. Twelve of us.

FINK: What happened?

FANNY: We tried to stop the night shift from going in.

FINK: And?

FANNY: Bud Miller started it by cracking a scab's skull. But the damn Cossacks were prepared. Biff just sprung us out on bail. Got a cigarette? [*She finds one and lights it; she smokes nervously, continuously throughout the scene*] Trial next week. They don't think the scab will recover. It looks like a long vacation in the cooler for yours truly. [*Bitterly*] You don't mind, do you, sweetheart? It will be a nice, quiet rest for you here without me.

FINK: But it's outrageous! I won't allow it! We have some rights . . .

FANNY: Sure. Rights. C.O.D. rights. Not worth a damn without cash. And where will you get that?

FINK: [*Sinking wearily into a chair*] But it's unthinkable!

FANNY: Well, don't think of it, then. . . . [*Looks around*] You don't seem to have done much packing, have you? How are we going to finish with all this damn junk tonight?

FINK: What's the hurry? I'm too upset.

FANNY: What's the hurry! If we're not out of here by morning, they'll dump it all, right out on the sidewalk.

FINK: If that wasn't enough! And now this trial! Now you had to get into this! What are we going to do?

FANNY: I'm going to pack. [*Starts gathering things, hardly looking at them, and flinging them into the cartons with ferocious hatred*] Shall we move to the Ambassador or the Beverly-Sunset, darling? [*He does not answer. She flings a book into the carton*] The Beverly-Sunset would be nice, I think. . . . We shall need a suite of seven rooms—do you think we could manage in seven rooms? [*He does not move. She flings a pile of under-*

wear into the carton] Oh, yes, and a private swimming pool. [*Flings a coffee pot into carton viciously*] And a two-car garage! For the Rolls-Royce! [*Flings a vase down; it misses the carton and shatters against a chair leg. She screams suddenly hysterically*] Goddamn them! Why do some people have all of that!

FINK: [*Languidly, without moving*] Childish escapism, my dear.

FANNY: The heroics is all very well, but I'm so damn sick of standing up to make speeches about global problems and worrying all the time whether the comrades can see the runs in my stockings!

FINK: Why don't you mend them?

FANNY: Save it, sweetheart! Save the brilliant sarcasm for the magazine editors—maybe it will sell an article for you someday.

FINK: That was uncalled for, Fanny.

FANNY: Well, it's no use fooling yourself. There's a name for people like us. At least, for one of us, I'm sure. Know it? Does your brilliant vocabulary include it? Failure's the word.

FINK: A relative conception, my love.

FANNY: Sure. What's rent money compared to infinity? [*Flings a pile of clothing into a carton*] Do you know it's number five, by the way?

FINK: Number five what?

FANNY: Eviction number five for us, Socrates! I've counted them. Five times in three years. All we've ever done is paid the first month and waited for the sheriff.

FINK: That's the way most people live in Hollywood.

FANNY: You might *pretend* to be worried—just out of decency.

FINK: My dear, why waste one's emotional reserves in blaming oneself for what is the irrevocable result of an inadequate social system?

FANNY: You could at least refrain from plagiarism.

FINK: Plagiarism?

FANNY: You lifted that out of *my* article.

FINK: Oh, yes. *The* article. I beg your pardon.

FANNY: Well, at least it was published.

FINK: So it was. Six years ago.

FANNY: [*Carrying an armful of old shoes*] Got any accep-
tance checks to show since then? [*Dumps her load
into a carton*] Now what? Where in hell are we going
to go tomorrow?

FINK: With thousands homeless and jobless—why worry
about an individual case?

FANNY: [*Is about to answer angrily, then shrugs, and turning away stumbles over some boxes in the semidarkness*] Goddamn it! It's enough that they're throwing
us out. They didn't have to turn off the electricity!

FINK: [*Shrugging*] Private ownership of utilities.

FANNY: I wish there was a kerosene that didn't stink.

FINK: Kerosene is the commodity of the poor. But I understand they've invented a new, odorless kind in
Russia.

FANNY: Sure. Nothing stinks in Russia. [*Takes from a
shelf a box full of large brown envelopes*] What do you
want to do with these?

FINK: What's in there?

FANNY: [*Reading from the envelopes*] Your files as
trustee of the Clark Institute of Social Research . . .
Correspondence as Consultant to the Vocational
School for Subnormal Children . . . Secretary to the
Free Night Classes of Dialectic Materialism . . . Ad-
viser to the Workers' Theater . . .

FINK: Throw the Workers' Theater out. I'm through with
them. They wouldn't put my name on their letter-
heads.

FANNY: [*Flings one envelope aside*] What do you want
me to do with the rest? Pack it or will you carry it
yourself?

FINK: Certainly I'll carry it myself. It might get lost. Wrap
them up for me, will you?

FANNY: [*Picks up some newspapers, starts wrapping the
files, stops, attracted by an item in a paper, glances at it*]
You know, it's funny, this business about Kay Gonda.

FINK: What business?

FANNY: In this morning's paper. About the murder.

FINK: Oh, that? Rubbish. She had nothing to do with it.
Yellow press gossip.

FANNY: [*Wrapping up the files*] That Sayers guy sure had
the dough.

FINK: Used to have. Not anymore. I know from that time when I helped to picket Sayers Oil last year that the big shot was going by the board even then.

FANNY: It says here that Sayers Oil was beginning to pick up.

FINK: Oh, well, one plutocrat less. So much the better for the heirs.

FANNY: [*Picks up a pile of books*] Twenty-five copies of *Oppress the Oppressors*—[*Adds with a bow*]—by Chuck Fink! . . . What the hell are we going to do with them?

FINK: [*Sharply*] What do you *think* we're going to do with them?

FANNY: God! Lugging all that extra weight around! Do you think there are twenty-five people in the United States who bought one copy each of your great masterpiece?

FINK: The number of sales is no proof of a book's merit.

FANNY: No, but it sure does help!

FINK: Would you like to see me pandering to the middle-class rabble, like the scribbling lackeys of capitalism? You're weakening, Fanny. You're turning petty bourgeois.

FANNY: [*Furiously*] Who's turning petty bourgeois? I've done more than you'll ever hope to do! I don't go running with manuscripts to third-rate publishers. I've had an article printed in *The Nation*! Yes, in *The Nation*! If I didn't bury myself with you in this mudhole of a . . .

FINK: It's in the mudholes of the slums that the vanguard trenches of social reform are dug, Fanny.

FANNY: Oh, Lord, Chuck, what's the use? Look at the others. Look at Miranda Lumkin. A column in the *Courier* and a villa at Palm Springs! And she couldn't hold a candle to me in college! Everybody always said I was an advanced thinker. [*Points at the room*] *This* is what one gets for being an advanced thinker.

FINK: [*Softly*] I know, dear. You're tired. You're frightened. I can't blame you. But, you see, in our work one must give up everything. All thought of personal gain or comfort. I've done it. I have no private ego left. All I want is that millions of men hear the name of Chuck Fink and come to regard it as that of their leader!

FANNY: [*Softening*] I know. You mean it all right. You're real, Chuck. There aren't many unselfish men in the world.

FINK: [*Dreamily*] Perhaps, five hundred years from now, someone will write my biography and call it *Chuck Fink the Selfless.*

FANNY: And it will seem so silly, then, that here we were worried about some piddling California landlord!

FINK: Precisely. One must know how to take a long view on things. And . . .

FANNY: [*Listening to some sound outside, suddenly*] Sh-sh! I think there's someone at the door.

FINK: Who? No one'll come here. They've deserted us. They've left us to . . . [*There is a knock at the door. They look at each other.* FINK *walks to the door*] Who's there? [*There is no answer. The knock is repeated. He throws the door open angrily*] What do you . . . [*He stops short as* KAY GONDA *enters; she is dressed as in the preceding scene. He gasps*] Oh! . . . [*He stares at her, half frightened, half incredulous.* FANNY *makes a step forward and stops. They can't make a sound*]

KAY GONDA: Mr. Fink?

FINK: [*Nodding frantically*] Yes. Chuck Fink. In person. . . . But you . . . you're *Kay Gonda,* aren't you?

KAY GONDA: Yes. I am hiding. From the police. I have no place to go. Will you let me stay here for the night?

FINK: Well, I'll be damned! . . . Oh, excuse me!

FANNY: You want us to hide you here?

KAY GONDA: Yes. If you are not afraid of it.

FANNY: But why on earth did you pick . . .

KAY GONDA: Because no one would find me here. And because I read Mr. Fink's letter.

FINK: [*Quite recovering himself*] But of course! My letter. I knew you'd notice it among the thousands. Pretty good, wasn't it?

FANNY: I helped him with it.

FINK: [*Laughing*] What a glorious coincidence! I had no idea when I wrote it, that . . . But how wonderfully things work out!

KAY GONDA: [*Looking at him*] I am wanted for murder.

FINK: Oh, don't worry about that. We don't mind. We're broadminded.

FANNY: [*Hastily pulling down the window shade*] You'll be perfectly safe here. You'll excuse the . . . informal appearance of things, won't you? We were considering moving out of here.

FINK: Please sit down, Miss Gonda.

KAY GONDA: [*Sitting down, removing her hat*] Thank you.

FINK: I've dreamed of a chance to talk to you like this. There are so many things I've always wanted to ask you.

KAY GONDA: There are many things I've always wanted to be asked.

FINK: Is it true, what they say about Granton Sayers? You ought to know. They say he was a regular pervert and what he didn't do to women . . .

FANNY: Chuck! That's entirely irrelevant and . . .

KAY GONDA: [*With a faint smile at her*] No. It isn't true.

FINK: Of course, I'm not one to censure anything. I despise morality. Then there's another thing I wanted to ask you: I've always been interested, as a sociologist, in the influence of the economic factor on the individual. How much does a movie star actually get?

KAY GONDA: Fifteen or twenty thousand a week on my new contract—I don't remember.

[FANNY *and* FINK *exchange startled glances*]

FINK: What an opportunity for social good! I've always believed that you were a great humanitarian.

KAY GONDA: Am I? Well, perhaps I am. I hate humanity.

FINK: You don't mean that, Miss Gonda!

KAY GONDA: There are some men with a purpose in life. Not many, but there are. And there are also some with a purpose—and with integrity. These are very rare. I like them.

FINK: But one must be tolerant! One must consider the

pressure of the economic factor. Now, for instance, take the question of a star's salary . . .

KAY GONDA: [*Sharply*] I do not want to talk about it. [*With a note that sounds almost like pleading in her voice*] Have you nothing to ask me about my work?

FINK: Oh, God, so much! . . . [*Suddenly earnest*] No. Nothing. [KAY GONDA *looks at him closely, with a faint smile. He adds, suddenly simple, sincere for the first time:*] Your work . . . one shouldn't talk about it. I can't. [*Adds*] I've never looked upon you as a movie star. No one does. It's not like looking at Joan Tudor or Sally Sweeney, or the rest of them. And it's not the trashy stories you make—you'll excuse me, but they are trash. It's something else.

KAY GONDA: [*Looking at him*] What?

FINK: The way you move, and the sound of your voice, and your eyes. Your eyes.

FANNY: [*Suddenly eager*] It's as if you were not a human being at all, not the kind we see around us.

FINK: We all dream of the perfect being that man could be. But no one has ever seen it. You have. And you're showing it to us. As if you knew a great secret, lost by the world, a great secret and a great hope. Man washed clean. Man at his highest possibility.

FANNY: When I look at you on the screen, it makes me feel guilty, but it also makes me feel young, new and proud. Somehow, I want to raise my arms like this. . . . [*Raises her arms over her head in a triumphant, ecstatic gesture; then, embarrassed:*] You must forgive us. We're being perfectly childish.

FINK: Perhaps we are. But in our drab lives, we have to grasp at any ray of light, anywhere, even in the movies. Why not in the movies, the great narcotic of mankind? You've done more for the damned than any philanthropist ever could. How do you do it?

KAY GONDA: [*Without looking at him*] One can do it just so long. One can keep going on one's own power, and wring dry every drop of hope—but then one has to find help. One has to find an answering voice, an answering hymn, an echo. I am very grateful to you. [*There is a knock at the door. They look at one another.* FINK *walks to the door resolutely*]

FINK: Who's there?

WOMAN'S VOICE: [*Offstage*] Say, Chuck, could I borrow a bit of cream?

FINK: [*Angrily*] Go to hell! We haven't any cream. You got your nerve disturbing people at this hour! [*A muffled oath and retreating steps are heard offstage. He returns to the others*] God, I thought it was the police!

FANNY: We mustn't let anyone in tonight. Any of those starving bums around here would be only too glad to turn you in for a—[*Her voice changes suddenly, strangely, as if the last word had dropped out accidentally*]—a reward.

KAY GONDA: Do you realize what chance you are taking if they find me here?

FINK: They'll get you out of here over my dead body.

KAY GONDA: You don't know what danger . . .

FINK: We don't have to know. We know what your work means to us. Don't we, Fanny?

FANNY: [*She has been standing aside, lost in thought*] What?

FINK: We know what Miss Gonda's work means to us, don't we?

FANNY: [*In a flat voice*] Oh, yes . . . yes . . .

KAY GONDA: [*Looking at* FINK *intently*] And that which means to you . . . you will not betray it?

FINK: One doesn't betray the best in one's soul.

KAY GONDA: No. One doesn't.

FINK: [*Noticing* FANNY'S *abstraction*] Fanny!

FANNY: [*With a jerk*] Yes? What?

FINK: Will you tell Miss Gonda how we've always . . .

FANNY: Miss Gonda must be tired. We should really allow her to go to bed.

KAY GONDA: Yes. I am very tired.

FANNY: [*With brisk energy*] You can have our bedroom. . . . Oh, yes, please don't protest. We'll be very comfortable here, on the couch. We'll stay here on guard, so that no one will try to enter.

KAY GONDA: [*Rising*] It is very kind of you.

FANNY: [*Taking the lamp*] Please excuse this inconvenience. We're having a little trouble with our electricity. [*Leading the way to the bedroom*] This way, please. You'll be comfortable and safe.

FINK: Good night, Miss Gonda. Don't worry. We'll stand by you.

KAY GONDA: Thank you. Good night. [*She exits with* FANNY *into the bedroom.* FINK *lifts the window shade. A broad band of moonlight falls across the room. He starts clearing the couch of its load of junk.* FANNY *returns into the room, closing the door behind her*]

FANNY: [*In a low voice*] Well, what do you think of that? [*He stretches his arms wide, shrugging*] And they say miracles don't happen!

FINK: We'd better keep quiet. She may hear us. . . . [*The band of light goes out in the crack of the bedroom door*] How about the packing?

FANNY: Never mind the packing now. [*He fishes for sheets and blankets in the cartons, throwing their contents out again.* FANNY *stands aside, by the window, watching him silently. Then, in a low voice:*] Chuck . . .

FINK: Yes?

FANNY: In a few days, I'm going on trial. Me and eleven of the kids.

FINK: [*Looking at her, surprised*] Yeah.

FANNY: It's no use fooling ourselves. They'll send us all up.

FINK: I know they will.

FANNY: Unless we can get money to fight it.

FINK: Yeah. But we can't. No use thinking about it. [*A short silence. He continues with his work*]

FANNY: [*In a whisper*] Chuck . . . do you think she can hear us?

FINK: [*Looking at the bedroom door*] No.

FANNY: It's a murder that she's committed.

FINK: Yeah.

FANNY: It's a millionaire that she's killed.

FINK: Right.

FANNY: I suppose his family would like to know where she is.

FINK: [*Raising his head, looking at her*] What are you talking about?

FANNY: I was thinking that if his family were told where she's hiding, they'd be glad to pay a reward.

FINK: [*Stepping menacingly toward her*] You lousy . . . what are you trying to . . .

FANNY: [*Without moving*] Five thousand dollars, probably.

FINK: [*Stopping*] Huh?

FANNY: Five thousand dollars, probably.

FINK: You lousy bitch! Shut up before I kill you! [*Silence. He starts to undress. Then:*] Fanny . . .

FANNY: Yes?

FINK: Think they'd—hand over five thousand?

FANNY: Sure they would. People pay more than that for ordinary kidnappers.

FINK: Oh, shut up! [*Silence. He continues to undress*]

FANNY: It's jail for me, Chuck. Months, maybe years in jail.

FINK: Yeah . . .

FANNY: And for the others, too. Bud, and Pinky, and Mary, and the rest. Your friends. Your comrades. [*He stops his undressing*] You need them. The cause needs them. Twelve of our vanguard.

FINK: Yes . . .

FANNY: With five thousand, we'd get the best lawyer from New York. He'd beat the case. . . . And we wouldn't have to move out of here. We wouldn't have to worry. You could continue your great work . . . [*He does not answer*] Think of all the poor and helpless who need you. . . . [*He does not answer*] Think of twelve human beings you're sending to jail . . . twelve to one, Chuck. . . . [*He does not answer*] Think of your duty to millions of your brothers. Millions to one. [*Silence*]

FINK: Fanny . . .

FANNY: Yes?

FINK: How would we go about it?

FANNY: Easy. We get out while she's asleep. We run to the police station. Come back with the cops. Easy.

FINK: What if she hears?

FANNY: She won't hear. But we got to hurry. [*She moves to the door. He stops her*]

FINK: [*In a whisper*] She'll hear the door opening. [*Points to the open window*] This way. . . .

[*They slip out through the window. The room is empty for a brief moment. Then the bedroom door opens.*]

KAY GONDA *stands on the threshold. She stands still for a moment, then walks across the room to the entrance door and goes out, leaving the door open*]

CURTAIN

SCENE 3

The screen unrolls a letter written in a bold, aggressive handwriting:

Dear Miss Gonda,

   I am an unknown artist. But I know to what heights I shall rise, for I carry a sacred banner which cannot fail—and which is you. I have painted nothing that was not you. You stand as a goddess on every canvas I've done. I have never seen you in person. I do not need to. I can draw your face with my eyes closed. For my spirit is but a mirror of yours.

   Someday you shall hear men speak of me. Until then, this is only a first tribute from your devoted priest—

                                        Dwight Langley

                              . . . Normandie Avenue
                              Los Angeles, California

Lights go out, screen disappears, and stage reveals studio of DWIGHT LANGLEY. *It is a large room, flashy, dramatic, and disreputable. Center back, large window showing the dark sky and the shadows of treetops; entrance door center Left; door into next room upstage Right. A profusion of paintings and sketches on the walls, on the easels, on the floor; all are of* KAY GONDA; *heads, full figures, in modern clothes, in flowering drapes, naked.*

   A mongrel assortment of strange types fills the room: men and women in all kinds of outfits, from tails and evening gowns to beach pajamas and slacks, none too prosperous-looking, all having one attribute in common— a glass in hand—and all showing signs of its effect.

   DWIGHT LANGLEY *lies stretched in the middle of a couch; he is young, with a tense, handsome, sunburnt face, dark, disheveled hair, and a haughty, irresistible* smile. EUNICE HAMMOND *keeps apart from the guests, her eyes returning constantly, anxiously, to* LANGLEY; *she is a beautiful young girl, quiet, reticent, dressed in a smart, simple dark dress obviously more expensive than any garment in the room.*

As the curtain rises, the guests are lifting their glasses in a grand toast to LANGLEY, *their voices piercing the raucous music coming over the radio.*

MAN IN DRESS SUIT: Here's to Lanny!

MAN IN SWEATER: To Dwight Langley of California!

WOMAN IN EVENING GOWN: To the winner and the best of us—from the cheerful losers!

TRAGIC GENTLEMAN: To the greatest artist ever lived!

LANGLEY: [*Rising, waving his hand curtly*] Thanks.

[ALL *drink. Someone drops a glass, breaking it resonantly. As* LANGLEY *steps aside from the others,* EUNICE *approaches him*]

EUNICE: [*Extending her glass to his, whispers softly*] To the day we've dreamed of for such a long time, dear.

LANGLEY: [*Turning to her indifferently*] Oh . . . oh, yes . . . [*Clinks glass to hers automatically, without looking at her*]

WOMAN IN SLACKS: [*Calling to her*] No monopoly on him, Eunice. Not anymore. From now on—Dwight Langley belongs to the world!

WOMAN IN EVENING GOWN: Well, not that I mean to minimize Lanny's triumph, but I must say that for the greatest exhibition of the decade, it was rather a fizz, wasn't it? Two or three canvases with some idea of something, but the rest of the trash people have the nerve to exhibit these days . . .

EFFEMINATE YOUNG MAN: Dear me! It is positively preposterous!

MAN IN DRESS SUIT: But Lanny beat them all! First prize of the decade!

LANGLEY: [*With no trace of modesty*] Did it surprise you?

TRAGIC GENTLEMAN: Because Lanny's a geniush!

EFFEMINATE YOUNG MAN: Oh, my yes! Positively a genius!

[LANGLEY *walks over to a sideboard to refill his glass.*
EUNICE, *standing beside him, slips her hand over his*]

EUNICE: [*In a low voice, tenderly*] Dwight, I haven't had
a moment with you to congratulate you. And I do
want to say it tonight. I'm too happy, too proud of
you to know how to say it, but I want you to
understand . . . my dearest . . . how much it means
to me.

LANGLEY: [*Jerking his hand away, indifferently*] Thanks.

EUNICE: I can't help thinking of the years past. Remember, how discouraged you were at times, and I talked
to you about your future, and . . .

LANGLEY: You don't have to bring that up now, do you?

EUNICE: [*Trying to laugh*] I shouldn't. I know. Utterly
bad form. [*Breaking down involuntarily*] But I can't
help it. I love you.

LANGLEY: I know it. [*Walks away from her*]

BLOND GIRL: [*Sitting on the couch, next to the woman in
slacks*] Come here, Lanny! Hasn't anyone got a chance
with a real genius?

LANGLEY: [*Flopping down on the couch, between the two
girls*] Hello.

WOMAN IN SLACKS: [*Throwing her arms around his shoulders*] Langley, I can't get over that canvas of yours. I
still see it as it hung there tonight. The damn thing
haunts me.

LANGLEY: [*Patronizingly*] Like it?

WOMAN IN SLACKS: Love it. You do get the damnedest
titles, though. What was it called? Hope, faith, or charity? No. Wait a moment. Liberty, equality, or . . .

LANGLEY: *Integrity.*

WOMAN IN SLACKS: That's it. "Integrity." Just what did
you really mean by it, darling?

LANGLEY: Don't try to understand.

MAN IN DRESS SUIT: But the woman! The woman in your
painting, Langley! Ah, that, my friend, is a masterpiece!

WOMAN IN SLACKS: That white face. And those eyes.
Those eyes that look straight through you!

WOMAN IN EVENING GOWN: You know, of course, who
she is?

MAN IN DRESS SUIT: Kay Gonda, as usual.

MAN IN SWEATSHIRT: Say, Lanny, will you ever paint any other female? Why do you always have to stick to that one?

LANGLEY: An artist *tells*. He does not *explain*.

WOMAN IN SLACKS: You know, there's something damn funny about Gonda and that Sayers affair.

MAN IN DRESS SUIT: I bet she did it all right. Wouldn't put it past her.

EFFEMINATE YOUNG MAN: Imagine Kay Gonda being hanged! The blond hair and the black hood and the noose. My, it would be *perfectly* thrilling!

WOMAN IN EVENING GOWN: There's a new theme for you, Lanny. "Kay Gonda on the Gallows."

LANGLEY: [*Furiously*] Shut up, all of you! She didn't do it! I won't have you discussing her in my house!

[*The guests subside for a brief moment*]

MAN IN DRESS SUIT: Wonder how much Sayers actually left.

WOMAN IN SLACKS: The papers said he was just coming into a swell setup. A deal with United California Oil or some such big-time stuff. But I guess it's off now.

MAN IN SWEATER: No, the evening papers said his sister is rushing the deal through.

WOMAN IN EVENING GOWN: But what're the police doing? Have they issued any warrants?

MAN IN DRESS SUIT: Nobody knows.

WOMAN IN EVENING GOWN: Damn funny. . . .

MAN IN SWEATER: Say, Eunice, any more drinks left in this house? No use asking Lanny. He never knows where anything is.

MAN IN DRESS SUIT: [*Throwing his arm around* EUNICE] The greatest little mother-sister-and-all-the-rest combination an artist ever had!

[EUNICE *disengages herself, not too brusquely, but obviously displeased*]

·

EFFEMINATE YOUNG MAN: Do you know that Eunice darns his socks? Oh, my, yes! I've seen a pair. Positively the cutest things!

MAN IN SWEATER: The woman behind the throne! The woman who guided his footsteps, washed his shirts, and kept up his courage in his dark years of struggle.

WOMAN IN EVENING GOWN: [*To the* WOMAN IN SLACKS, *in a low voice*] Kept up his courage—and his bank account.

WOMAN IN SLACKS: No. Really?

WOMAN IN EVENING GOWN: My dear, it's no secret. Where do you suppose the money came from for the "dark years of struggle"? The Hammond millions. Not that old man Hammond didn't kick her out of the house. He did. But she had some money of her own.

EFFEMINATE YOUNG MAN: Oh, my yes. The Social Register dropped her, too. But she didn't care one bit, not one bit.

MAN IN SWEATER: [*To* EUNICE] How about it, Eunice? Where are the drinks?

EUNICE: [*Hesitating*] I'm afraid . . .

LANGLEY: [*Rising*] She's afraid she doesn't approve. But we're going to drink whether she approves of it or not. [*Searches through the cupboards frantically*]

WOMAN IN SLACKS: Really, folks, it's getting late and . . .

MAN IN DRESS SUIT: Oh, just one more drink, and we'll all toddle home.

LANGLEY: Hey, Eunice, where's the gin?

EUNICE: [*Opening a cabinet and producing two bottles, quietly*] Here.

MAN IN SWEATER: Hurrah! Wait for baby!

[*There is a general rush to the bottles*]

MAN IN DRESS SUIT: Just one last drink and we'll scram. Hey everybody! Another toast. To Dwight Langley and Eunice Hammond!

EUNICE: To Dwight Langley and his future!

[*All roar approval and drink*]

EVERYONE: [*Roaring at once*] Speech, Lanny! . . . Yes! . . . Come on, Lanny! . . . Speech! . . . Come on!

LANGLEY: [*Climbs up on a chair, stands a little unsteadily, speaks with a kind of tortured sincerity*] The bitterest moment of an artist's life is the moment of his triumph. The artist is but a bugle calling to a battle no one wants to fight. The world does not see and does not want to see. The artist begs men to throw the doors of their lives open to grandeur and beauty, but those doors will remain closed forever . . . forever . . . [*Is about to add something, but drops his hand in a gesture of hopelessness and ends in a tone of quiet sadness*] . . . forever. . . . [*Applause. The general noise is cut short by a knock at the door.* LANGLEY *jumps off his chair*] Come in!

[*The door opens, disclosing an irate* LANDLADY *in a soiled Chinese kimono*]

LANDLADY: [*In a shrill whine*] Mr. Langley, this noise will have to stop! Don't you know what time it is?

LANGLEY: Get out of here!

LANDLADY: The lady in 315 says she'll call the police! The gentleman in . . .

LANGLEY: You heard me! Get out! Think I have to stay in a lousy dump like this?

EUNICE: Dwight! [*To* LANDLADY] We'll keep quiet, Mrs. Johnson.

LANDLADY: Well, you'd better! [*She exits angrily*]

EUNICE: Really, Dwight, we shouldn't . . .

LANGLEY: Oh, leave me alone! No one's going to tell *me* what to do from now on!

EUNICE: But I only . . .

LANGLEY: You're turning into a damnable, nagging, middle-class female!

[EUNICE *stares at him, frozen*]

WOMAN IN SLACKS: Going a bit too far, Langley!

LANGLEY: I'm sick and tired of people who can't outgrow their possessiveness! You know the hypocritical trick—the chains of *gratitude*!

EUNICE: Dwight! You don't think that I . . .

LANGLEY: I know damn well what *you* think! Think you've bought me, don't you? Think you own me for the rest of my life in exchange for some grocery bills?

EUNICE: What did you say? [*Screaming suddenly*] I didn't hear you right!

MAN IN SWEATER: Look here, Langley, take it easy, you don't know what you're saying, you're . . .

LANGLEY: [*Pushing him aside*] Go to hell! You can all go to hell if you don't like it! [*To* EUNICE] And as for you . . .

EUNICE: Dwight . . . please . . . not now . . .

LANGLEY: Yes! Right here and now! I want them all to hear! [*To the guests*] So you think I can't get along without her? I'll show you! I'm through! [*To* EUNICE] Do you hear that? I'm through! [EUNICE *stands motionless*] I'm free! I'm going to rise in the world! I'm going places none of you ever dreamed of! I'm ready to meet the only woman I've ever wanted—Kay Gonda! I've waited all these years for the day when I would meet her! That's all I've lived for! And no one's going to stand in my way!

EUNICE: [*She walks to door Left, picks up her hat and coat from a pile of clothing in a corner, turns to him again, quietly*] Goodbye, Dwight . . . [*Exits*]

[*There is a second of strained silence in the room: the* WOMAN IN SLACKS *is the first one to move; she goes to pick up her coat, then turns to* LANGLEY]

WOMAN IN SLACKS: I thought you had just done a painting called "Integrity."

LANGLEY: If that was intended for a dirty crack . . . [*The* WOMAN IN SLACKS *exits, slamming the door*] Well, go to hell! [*To the others*] Get out of here! All of you! Get out!

[*There is a general shuffle for hats and coats*]

WOMAN IN EVENING GOWN: Well, if we're being kicked out . . .

MAN IN DRESS SUIT: That's all right. Lanny's a bit upset.

LANGLEY: [*Somewhat gentler*] I'm sorry. I thank you all. But I want to be alone. [*The guests are leaving, waving halfhearted goodbyes*]

BLOND GIRL: [*She is one of the last to leave. She hesitates, whispering tentatively:*] Lanny . . .

LANGLEY: Out! All of you! [*She exits. The stage is empty*

but for LANGLEY *surveying dazedly the havoc of his studio. There is a knock at the door*] Out, I said! Don't want any of you! [*The knock is repeated. He walks to the door, throws it open.* KAY GONDA *enters. She stands looking at him without a word. He asks impatiently:*] Well? [*She does not answer*] What do you want?

KAY GONDA: Are you Dwight Langley?

LANGLEY: Yes.

KAY GONDA: I need your help.

LANGLEY: What's the matter?

KAY GONDA: Don't you know?

LANGLEY: How should I know? Just who are you?

KAY GONDA: [*After a pause*] Kay Gonda.

LANGLEY: [*Looks at her and bursts out laughing*] So? Not Helen of Troy? Nor Madame Du Barry? [*She looks at him silently*] Come on, out with it. What's the gag?

KAY GONDA: Don't you know me?

LANGLEY: [*Looks her over contemptuously, his hands in his pockets, grinning*] Well, you do look like Kay Gonda. So does her stand-in. So do dozens of extra girls in Hollywood. What is it you're after? I can't get you into pictures, my girl. I'm not even the kind to promise you a screen test. Drop the racket. Who are you?

KAY GONDA: Don't you understand? I am in danger. I have to hide. Please let me stay here for the night.

LANGLEY: What do you think this is? A flop house?

KAY GONDA: I have no place to go.

LANGLEY: That's an old one in Hollywood.

KAY GONDA: They will not look for me here.

LANGLEY: Who?

KAY GONDA: The police.

LANGLEY: Really? And why would Kay Gonda pick my house to hide in of all places? [*She starts to open her handbag, but closes it again and says nothing*] How do I know you're Kay Gonda? Have you any proof?

KAY GONDA: None, but the honesty of your vision.

LANGLEY: Oh, cut the tripe! What are you after? Taking me for a . . . [*There is a loud knock at the door*] What's this? A frame-up? [*Walks to door and throws it open.*

A uniformed POLICEMAN *enters.* KAY GONDA *turns away quickly, her back to the others*]

POLICEMAN: [*Good-naturedly*] 'Evening. [*Looking about him, helplessly*] Where's the drunken party we got a complaint about?

LANGLEY: Of all the nerve! There's no party, officer. I had a few friends here, but they left long ago.

POLICEMAN: [*Looking at* KAY GONDA *with some curiosity*] Between you and me, it's a lotta cranks that call up complaining about noise. As I see it, there's no harm in young people having a little fun.

LANGLEY: [*Watching curiously the* POLICEMAN's *reaction to* KAY GONDA] We really weren't disturbing anyone. I'm sure there's nothing you want here, *is there*, officer?

POLICEMAN: No, sir. Sorry to have bothered you.

LANGLEY: We are really alone here—[*Points to* KAY GONDA]—*this lady* and I. But you're welcome to *look around*.

POLICEMAN: Why, no, sir. No need to. Good night. [*Exits*]

LANGLEY: [*Waits to hear his steps descending the stairs. Then turns to* KAY GONDA *and bursts out laughing*] That gave the show away, didn't it, my girl?

KAY GONDA: What?

LANGLEY: The cop. If you were Kay Gonda and if the police were looking for you, wouldn't he have grabbed you?

KAY GONDA: He did not see my face.

LANGLEY: He would have looked. Come on, what kind of racket are you really working?

KAY GONDA: [*Stepping up to him, in full light*] Dwight Langley! Look at me! Look at all these pictures of me that you've painted! Don't you know me? You've lived with me in your hours of work, your best hours. Were you lying in those hours?

LANGLEY: Kindly leave my art out of it. My art has nothing to do with your life or mine.

KAY GONDA: Of what account is an art that preaches things it does not want to exist?

LANGLEY: [*Solemnly*] Listen. Kay Gonda is the symbol of all the beauty I bring to the world, a beauty we can never reach. We can only sing of her, who is the unattainable. That is the mission of the artist. We can only strive, but never succeed. Attempt, but never achieve. That is our tragedy, but our hopelessness is our glory. Get out of here!

KAY GONDA: I need your help.

LANGLEY: Get out!!

[*Her arms fall limply. She turns and walks out.* DWIGHT LANGLEY *slams the door*]

CURTAIN

Act II

The letter projected on the screen is written in an ornate, old-fashioned handwriting:

Dear Miss Gonda,

Some may call this letter a sacrilege. But as I write it, I do not feel like a sinner. For when I look at you on the screen, it seems to me that we are working for the same cause, you and I. This may surprise you, for I am only a humble Evangelist. But when I speak to men about the sacred meaning of life, I feel that you hold the same Truth which my words struggle in vain to disclose. We are traveling different roads, Miss Gonda, but we are bound to the same destination.

Respectfully yours,

Claude Ignatius Hix
. . . Slosson Blvd.
Los Angeles, California

Lights go out, screen disappears. When the curtain rises on the temple of CLAUDE IGNATIUS HIX, *the stage is almost completely black. Nothing can be seen of the room save the dim outline of a door, downstage Right, open upon a dark street. A small cross of electric lights burns high on wall Center. It throws just enough light to show the face and shoulders of* CLAUDE IGNATIUS HIX *high above the ground (he is standing in the pulpit, but this cannot be distinguished in the darkness). He is tall, gaunt, clothed in black; his hair is receding off a high forehead. His hands rise eloquently as he speaks into the darkness.*

HIX: . . . but even in the blackest one of us, there is a spark of the sublime, a single drop in the desert of every barren soul. And all the suffering of men, all the twisted agonies of their lives, come from their treason to that hidden flame. All commit the treason, and none can escape the payment. None can . . . [*Someone sneezes loudly in the darkness, by the door Right.* HIX *stops short, calls in a startled voice:*] Who's there?

[*He presses a switch that lights two tall electric tapers by the sides of his pulpit. We can now see the temple. It is a long, narrow barn with bare rafters and un-painted walls. There are no windows and only a single door. Rows of old wooden benches fill the room, facing the pulpit*]

[SISTER ESSIE TWOMEY *stands downstage Right, by the door. She is a short, plump woman nearing forty, with bleached blond hair falling in curls on her shoulders, from under the brim of a large pink picture hat trimmed with lilies-of-the-valley. Her stocky little figure is draped in the long folds of a sky blue cape*]

ESSIE TWOMEY: [*She raises her right arm solemnly*] Praise the Lord! Good evening, Brother Hix. Keep going. Don't let me interrupt you.

HIX: [*Startled and angry*] *You?* What are *you* doing here?

ESSIE TWOMEY: I heard you way from the street—it's a blessed voice you have, though you don't control your belly tones properly—and I didn't want to intrude. I just slipped in.

HIX: [*Icily*] And of what service may I be to *you*?

ESSIE TWOMEY: Go ahead with the rehearsal. It's an in-spiring sermon you have there, a peach of a sermon. Though a bit on the old-fashioned side. Not modern enough, Brother Hix. That's not the way I do it.

HIX: I do not recall having solicited advice, Sister Two-mey, and I should like to inquire for the reason of this sudden visitation.

ESSIE TWOMEY: Praise the Lord! I'm a harbinger of good news. Yes, indeed. I got a corker for you.

HIX: I shall point out that we have never had any matters of common interest.

ESSIE TWOMEY: Verily, Brother Hix. You smacked the nail right on the head. That's why you'll be overjoyed at the proposition. [*Settling herself comfortably down on a bench*] It's like this, brother: there's no room in this neighborhood for you and me both.

HIX: Sister Twomey, these are the first words of truth I have ever heard emerging from your mouth.

ESSIE TWOMEY: The poor dear souls in these parts are

heavily laden, indeed. They cannot support two temples. Why, the mangy bums haven't got enough to feed the fleas on a dog!

HIX: Dare I believe, sister, that your conscience has spoken at last, and you are prepared to leave this neighborhood?

ESSIE TWOMEY: Who? *Me* leave this neighborhood? [*Solemnly*] Why, Brother Hix, you have no idea of the blessed work my temple is doing. The lost souls milling at its portals—praise the Lord! . . . [*Sharply*] No, brother, keep your shirt on. I'm going to buy you out.

HIX: What?!

ESSIE TWOMEY: Not that I really have to. You're no competition. But I thought I might as well clear it up once and for all. I want this territory.

HIX: [*Beside himself*] You had the infernal presumption to suppose that the Temple of Eternal Truth was for sale?

ESSIE TWOMEY: Now, now, Brother Hix, let's be modern. That's no way to talk business. Just look at the facts. You're washed up here, brother.

HIX: I will have you understand . . .

ESSIE TWOMEY: What kind of a draw do you get? Thirty or fifty heads on a big night. Look at me. Two thousand souls every evening, seeking the glory of God! *Two thousand* noses, actual count! I'm putting on a Midnight Service tonight—"The Night Life of the Angels"—and I'm expecting three thousand.

HIX: [*Drawing himself up*] There come moments in a man's life when he is sorely pressed to remember the lesson of charity to all. I have no wish to insult you. But I have always considered you a tool of the Devil. My temple has stood in this neighborhood for . . .

ESSIE TWOMEY: I know. For twenty years. But times change, brother. You haven't got what it takes anymore. You're still in the horse-and-buggy age—praise the Lord!

HIX: The faith of my fathers is good enough for me.

ESSIE TWOMEY: Maybe so, brother, maybe so. But not for the customers. Now, for instance, take the name of your place: "Temple of Eternal Truth." Folks don't go for that nowadays. What have I got? "The Little

Church of the Cheery Corner." That draws 'em, brother. Like flies.

HIX: I do not wish to discuss it.

ESSIE TWOMEY: Look at what you were just rehearsing here. That'll put 'em to sleep. Verily. You can't hand out that line anymore. Now take my last sermon— "The Service Station of the Spirit." There's a lesson for you, brother! I had a whole service station built— [*Rises, walks to pulpit*]—right there, behind my pulpit. Tall pumps, glass and gold, labeled "Purity," "Prayer," "Prayer with Faith Super-Mixture." And young boys in white uniforms—good-lookers, every one of 'em!—with gold wings, and caps inscribed "Creed Oil, Inc." Clever, eh?

HIX: It's a sacrilege!

ESSIE TWOMEY: [*Stepping up on the pulpit*] And the pulpit here was—[*Looks at her fingers*]—hm, dust, Brother Hix. Bad business! . . . And the pulpit was made up like a gold automobile. [*Greatly inspired*] Then I preached to my flock that when you travel the hard road of life, you must be sure that your tank is filled with the best gas of Faith, that your tires are inflated with the air of Charity, that your radiator is cooled with the sweet water of Temperance, that your battery is charged with the power of Righteousness, and that you beware of treacherous Detours which lead to perdition! [*In her normal voice*] Boy, did that wow 'em! Praise the Lord! It brought the house down! And we had no trouble at all when we passed the collection box made up in the shape of a gasoline can!

HIX: [*With controlled fury*] Sister Twomey, you will please step down from my pulpit!

ESSIE TWOMEY: [*Coming down*] Well, brother, to make a long story short, I'll give you five hundred bucks and you can move your junk out.

HIX: *Five hundred dollars for the Temple of Eternal Truth?*

ESSIE TWOMEY: Well, what's the matter with five hundred dollars? It's a lot of money. You can buy a good secondhand car for five hundred dollars.

HIX: Never, in twenty years, have I shown the door to

anyone in this temple. But I am doing it now. [*He points to the door*]

ESSIE TWOMEY: [*Shrugging*] Well, have it your own way, brother. They have eyes, but they see not! . . . I should worry, by Jesus! [*Raising her arm*] Praise the Lord! [*Exits*]

[*The minute she is out,* EZRY's *head comes peering cautiously from behind the door.* EZRY *is a lanky, gangling youth, far from bright*]

EZRY: [*Calls in a whisper*] Oh, Brother Hix!

HIX: [*Startled*] Ezry! What are you doing there? Come in.

EZRY: [*Enters, awed*] Gee, it was better'n a movie show!

HIX: Have you been listening?

EZRY: Gee! Was that Sister Essie Twomey?

HIX: Yes, Ezry, it was Sister Essie Twomey. Now you mustn't tell anyone about what you heard here.

EZRY: No, sir. Cross my heart, Brother Hix. [*Looking at the door with admiration*] My, but Sister Twomey talks pretty!

HIX: You mustn't say that. Sister Twomey is an evil woman.

EZRY: Yes, sir. . . . Gee, but she's got such pretty curls!

HIX: Ezry, do you believe in me? Do you like to come here for the services?

EZRY: Yes, sir. . . . The Crump twins, they said Sister Twomey had a airyplane in her temple, honest to goodness!

HIX: [*Desperately*] My boy, listen to me, for the sake of your immortal soul . . . [*He stops short.* KAY GONDA *enters*]

KAY GONDA: Mr. Hix?

HIX: [*Without taking his eyes from her, in a choked voice*] Ezry. Run along.

EZRY: [*Frightened*] Yes, sir. [*Exits hurriedly*]

HIX: You're not . . .

KAY GONDA: Yes. I am.

HIX: To what do I owe the great honor of . . .

KAY GONDA: To a murder.

HIX: Do you mean that those rumors are true?

KAY GONDA: You can throw me out, if you wish. You can call the police, if you prefer. Only do so now.

HIX: You are seeking shelter?

KAY GONDA: For one night.

HIX: [*Walks to the open door, closes it, and locks it*] This door has not been closed for twenty years. It shall be closed tonight. [*He returns to her and silently hands her the key*]

KAY GONDA: [*Astonished*] Why are you giving it to me?

HIX: The door will not be opened, until you wish to open it.

KAY GONDA: [*She smiles, takes the key and slips it into her bag. Then:*] Thank you.

HIX: [*Sternly*] No. Do not thank me. I do not want you to stay here.

KAY GONDA: [*Without understanding*] You—don't?

HIX: But you are safe—if this is the safety you want. I have turned the place over to you. You may stay here as long as you like. The decision will be yours.

KAY GONDA: You do not want me to hide here?

HIX: I do not want you to hide.

KAY GONDA: [*She looks at him thoughtfully, then walks to a bench and sits down, watching him. She asks slowly:*] What would you have me do?

HIX: [*He stands before her, austerely erect and solemn*] You have taken a heavy burden upon your shoulders.

KAY GONDA: Yes. A heavy burden. And I wonder how much longer I will be able to carry it.

HIX: You may hide from the men who threaten you. But of what importance is that?

KAY GONDA: Then you do not want to save me?

HIX: Oh, yes. I want to save you. But not from the police.

KAY GONDA: From whom?

HIX: From yourself. [*She looks at him for a long moment, a fixed, steady glance, and does not answer*] You have committed a mortal sin. You have killed a human being. [*Points to the room*] Can this place—or any place—give you protection from that?

KAY GONDA: No.

HIX: You cannot escape from your crime. Then do not try to run from it. Give up. Surrender. Confess.

KAY GONDA: [*Slowly*] If I confess, they will take my life.

HIX: If you don't, you will lose your life—the eternal life of your soul.

KAY GONDA: Is it a choice, then? Must it be one or the other?

HIX: It has always been a choice. For all of us.

KAY GONDA: Why?

HIX: Because the joys of this earth are paid for by damnation in the Kingdom of Heaven. But if we choose to suffer, we are rewarded with eternal happiness.

KAY GONDA: Then we are on earth only in order to suffer?

HIX: And the greater the suffering, the greater our virtue. [*Her head drops slowly*] You have a sublime chance before you. Accept, of your own will, the worst that can be done to you. The infamy, the degradation, the prison cell, the scaffold. Then your punishment will become your glory.

KAY GONDA: How?

HIX: It will let you enter the Kingdom of Heaven.

KAY GONDA: Why should I want to enter it?

HIX: If you know that a life of supreme beauty is possible—how can you help but want to enter it?

KAY GONDA: How can I help but want it here, on earth?

HIX: Ours is a dark, imperfect world.

KAY GONDA: Why is it not perfect? Because it cannot be? Or because we do not want it to be?

HIX: This world is of no consequence. Whatever beauty it offers us is here only that we may sacrifice it—for the greater beauty beyond. [*She is not looking at him. He stands watching her for a moment; then, his voice low with emotion:*] You don't know how lovely you are at this moment. [*She raises her head*] You don't know the hours I've spent watching you across the infinite distance of a screen. I would give my life to keep you here in safety. I would let myself be torn to shreds, rather than see you hurt. Yet I am asking you to open this door and walk out to martyrdom. That is my chance of sacrifice. I am giving up the greatest thing that ever came to me.

KAY GONDA: [*Her voice soft and low*] And after you and I have made our sacrifice, what will be left on this earth?

HIX: Our example. It will light the way for all the miserable souls who flounder in helpless depravity. They, too, will learn to renounce. Your fame is great. The story of your conversion will be heard the world over. You will redeem the scrubby wretches who come to this temple and all the wretches in all the slums.

KAY GONDA: Such as that boy who was here?

HIX: Such as that boy. Let him be the symbol, not a nobler figure. That, too, is part of the sacrifice.

KAY GONDA: [*Slowly*] What do you want me to do?

HIX: Confess your crime. Confess it publicly, to a crowd, to the hearing of all!

KAY GONDA: Tonight?

HIX: Tonight!

KAY GONDA: But there is no crowd anywhere at this hour.

HIX: At this hour . . . [*With sudden inspiration*] Listen. At this hour, a large crowd is gathered in a temple of error, six blocks away. It is a dreadful place, run by the most contemptible woman I've ever known. I'll take you there. I'll let you offer that woman the greatest gift—the kind of sensation she's never dared to imagine for her audience. You will confess to her crowd. Let her take the credit and the praise for your conversion. Let her take the fame. She is the one least worthy of it.

KAY GONDA: That, too, is part of the sacrifice?

HIX: Yes.

[KAY GONDA *rises. She walks to the door, unlocks it, and flings it open. Then she turns to* HIX *and throws the key in his face. It strikes him as she goes out. He stands motionless, only his head dropping and his shoulders sagging*]

CURTAIN

SCENE 2

The letter projected on the screen is written in a sharp, precise, cultured handwriting:

Dear Miss Gonda,

I have had everything men ask of life. I have seen it
all, and I feel as if I were leaving a third-rate show on
a disreputable side street. If I do not bother to die, it
is only because my life has all the emptiness of the
grave and my death would have no change to offer me.
It may happen, any day now, and nobody—not even
the one writing these lines—will know the difference.

But before it happens, I want to raise what is left of
my soul in a last salute to you, you who are that which
the world should have been. Morituri te salutamus.

Dietrich von Esterhazy

Beverly-Sunset Hotel
Beverly Hills, California

*Lights go out, screen disappears, and stage reveals
drawing room in the hotel suite of* DIETRICH VON ESTER-
HAZY. *It is a large, luxurious room, modern, exquisitely
simple. Wide entrance door in center wall Left. Smaller
door to bedroom in wall Right, upstage. Large window
in wall Left, showing the dark view of a park far below.
Downstage Right a fireplace. One single lamp burning.*

As the curtain rises the entrance door opens to admit
DIETRICH VON ESTERHAZY *and* LALO JANS. DIETRICH VON
ESTERHAZY *is a tall, slender man in his early forties,
whose air of patrician distinction seems created for the
trim elegance of his full dress suit.* LALO JANS *is an exquisite female, hidden in the soft folds of an ermine wrap
over a magnificent evening gown. She walks in first and
falls, exhausted, on a sofa downstage, stretching out her
legs with a gesture of charming lassitude.* DIETRICH VON
ESTERHAZY *follows her silently. She makes a little gesture,
expecting him to take her wrap. But he does not approach
her or look at her, and she shrugs, throwing her wrap
back, letting it slide halfway down her bare arms.*

LALO: [*Looking at a clock on the table beside her, lazily*]
Only two o'clock. . . . Really, we didn't have to leave
so early, darling. . . . [ESTERHAZY *does not answer. He
does not seem to hear. There is no hostility in his attitude, but a profound indifference and a strange tension.*

He walks to the window and stands looking out thoughtfully, unconscious of LALO'*s presence. She yawns, lighting a cigarette*] I think I'll go home. . . . [*No answer*] I said, I think I'll go home. . . . [*Coquettishly*] Unless, of course, you insist. . . . [*No answer. She shrugs and settles down more comfortably. She speaks lazily, watching the smoke of her cigarette*] You know, Rikki, we'll just have to go to Agua Caliente. And this time I'll put it all on Black Rajah. It's a cinch. . . . [*No answer*] By the way, Rikki, my chauffeur's wages were due yesterday. . . . [*Turns to him. Slightly impatient:*] Rikki?

ESTERHAZY: [*Startled, turning to her abruptly, polite and completely indifferent*] What were you saying, my dear?

LALO: [*Impatiently*] I said my chauffeur's wages were due yesterday.

ESTERHAZY: [*His thoughts miles away*] Yes, of course. I shall take care of it.

LALO: What's the matter, Rikki? Just because I lost that money?

ESTERHAZY: Not at all, my dear. Glad you enjoyed the evening.

LALO: But then you know I've always had the damnedest luck at roulette. And if we hadn't left so early, I'm sure I'd have won it back.

ESTERHAZY: I'm sorry. I was a little tired.

LALO: And anyway, what's one thousand and seventy something?

ESTERHAZY: [*Stands looking at her silently. Then, with a faint smile of something like sudden decision, he reaches into his pocket and calmly hands her a checkbook*] I think you might as well see it.

LALO: [*Taking the book indifferently*] What's that? Some bank book?

ESTERHAZY: See what's left . . . at some bank.

LALO: [*Reading*] Three hundred and sixteen dollars. . . . [*Looks quickly through the check stubs*] Rikki! You wrote that thousand-dollar check on this bank! [*He nods silently, with the same smile*] You'll have to transfer the money from another bank, first thing in the morning.

ESTERHAZY: [*Slowly*] I have no other bank.

LALO: Huh?

ESTERHAZY: I have no other money. You're holding there all that's left.

LALO: [*Her lazy nonchalance gone*] Rikki! You're kidding me!

ESTERHAZY: Far be it from me, my dear.

LALO: But . . . but you're crazy! Things like that don't happen like . . . like that! One sees . . . in advance . . . one knows.

ESTERHAZY: [*Calmly*] I've known it. For the last two years. But a fortune does not vanish without a few last convulsions. There has always been something to sell, to pawn, to borrow on. Always someone to borrow from. But not this time. This time, it's done.

LALO: [*Aghast*] But . . . but where did it go?

ESTERHAZY: [*Shrugging*] How do I know? Where did all the rest of it go, those other things, inside, that you start life with? Fifteen years is a long time. When they threw me out of Austria, I had millions in my pocket, but the rest—the rest, I think, was gone already.

LALO: That's all very beautiful, but what are you going to do?

ESTERHAZY: Nothing.

LALO: But tomorrow . . .

ESTERHAZY: Tomorrow, Count Dietrich von Esterhazy will be called upon to explain the matter of a bad check. *May* be called upon.

LALO: Stop grinning like that! Do you think it's funny?

ESTERHAZY: I think it's curious. . . . The first Count Dietrich von Esterhazy died fighting under the walls of Jerusalem. The second died on the ramparts of his castle, defying a nation. The last one wrote a bad check in a gambling casino with chromium and poor ventilation. . . . It's curious.

LALO: What are you talking about?

ESTERHAZY: About what a peculiar thing it is—a leaking soul. You go through your days and it slips away from you, drop by drop. With each step. Like a hole in your pocket and coins dropping out, bright little coins, bright and shining, never to be found again.

LALO: To hell with that! What's to become of me?

ESTERHAZY: I've done all I could, Lalo. I've warned you before the others.

LALO: You're not going to stand there like a damn fool and let things . . .

ESTERHAZY: [*Softly*] You know, I think I'm glad it happened like this. A few hours ago I had problems, a thick web of problems I was much too weary to untangle. Now I'm free. Free at one useless stroke I did not intend striking.

LALO: Don't you care at all?

ESTERHAZY: I would not be frightened if I still cared.

LALO: Then you are frightened?

ESTERHAZY: I should like to be.

LALO: Why don't you do something? Call your friends!

ESTERHAZY: Their reaction, my dear, would be precisely the same as yours.

LALO: You're blaming *me*, now!

ESTERHAZY: Not at all. I appreciate you. You make my prospect so simple—and so easy.

LALO: But good God! What about the payments on my new Cadillac? And those pearls I charged to you? And . . .

ESTERHAZY: And my hotel bill. And my florist's bill. And that last party I gave. And the mink coat for Colette Dorsay.

LALO: [*Jumping up*] What?!

ESTERHAZY: My dear, you really didn't think you were . . . the only one?

LALO: [*Looks at him, her eyes blazing. Is on the point of screaming something. Laughs suddenly instead, a dry insulting laughter*] Do you think I care—*now*? Do you think I'm going to cry over a worthless . . .

ESTERHAZY: [*Quietly*] Don't you think you'd better go home now?

LALO: [*Tightens her wrap furiously, rushes to the door, turns abruptly*] Call me up when you come to your senses. I'll answer—if I feel like it tomorrow.

ESTERHAZY: And if I'm here to call—*tomorrow*.

LALO: Huh?

ESTERHAZY: I said, if I'm here to call—tomorrow.

LALO: Just what do you mean? Do you intend to run away or . . .

ESTERHAZY: [*With quiet affirmation*] Or.

LALO: Oh, don't be a melodramatic fool! [*Exits, slamming the door*]

[ESTERHAZY *stands motionless, lost in thought. Then he shudders slightly, as if recovering himself. Shrugs. Walks into bedroom Right, leaving the door open. The telephone rings. He returns, his evening coat replaced by a trim lounging jacket*]

ESTERHAZY: [*Picking up receiver*] Hello? . . . [*Astonished*] At this hour? What's her name? . . . She won't? . . . All right, have her come up. [*Hangs up. Lights a cigarette. There is a knock at the door. He smiles*] Come in!

[KAY GONDA *enters. His smile vanishes. He does not move. He stands looking at her for a moment, two motionless fingers holding the cigarette at his mouth. Then he flings the cigarette aside with a violent jerk of his wrist—his only reaction—and bows calmly, formally*]

Good evening, *Miss Gonda.*

KAY GONDA: Good evening.

ESTERHAZY: A veil or black glasses?

KAY GONDA: What?

ESTERHAZY: I hope you didn't let the clerk downstairs recognize you.

KAY GONDA: [*Smiles suddenly, pulling her glasses out of her pocket*] Black glasses.

ESTERHAZY: It was a brilliant idea.

KAY GONDA: What?

ESTERHAZY: Your coming here to hide.

KAY GONDA: How did you know that?

ESTERHAZY: Because it could have occurred only to you. Because you're the only one capable of the exquisite sensitiveness to recognize the only sincere letter I've ever written in my life.

KAY GONDA: [*Looking at him*] Was it?

ESTERHAZY: [*Studying her openly, speaking casually, matter-of-factly*] You look taller than you do on the screen—and less real. Your hair is blonder than I thought. Your voice about a tone higher. It is a pity that the camera does not photograph the shade of your lipstick. [*In a different voice, warm and natural*] And now that I've done my duty as a fan reacting, sit down and let's forget the unusual circumstances.

KAY GONDA: Do you really want me to stay here?

ESTERHAZY: [*Looking at the room*] The place is not too uncomfortable. There's a slight draft from the window at times, and the people upstairs become noisy occasionally, but not often. [*Looking at her*] No, I won't tell you how glad I am to see you here. I never speak of the things that mean much to me. The occasions have been too rare. I've lost the habit.

KAY GONDA: [*Sitting down*] Thank you.

ESTERHAZY: For what?

KAY GONDA: For what you didn't say.

ESTERHAZY: Do you know that it is really I who must thank you? Not only for coming, but for coming tonight of all nights.

KAY GONDA: Why?

ESTERHAZY: Perhaps you have taken a life in order to save another. [*Pause*] A long time ago—no, isn't that strange?—it was only a few minutes ago—I was ready to kill myself. Don't look at me like that. It isn't frightening. But what did become frightening was that feeling of utter indifference, even to death, even to my own indifference. And then you came. . . . I think I could hate you for coming.

KAY GONDA: I think you will.

ESTERHAZY: [*With sudden fire, the first, unexpected emotion*] I don't want to be proud of myself again. I had given it up. Yet now I am. Just because I see you here. Just because a thing has happened which is like nothing I thought possible on earth.

KAY GONDA: You said you would not tell me how glad you were to see me. Don't tell me. I do not want to hear it. I have heard it too often. I have never believed it. And I do not think I shall come to believe it *tonight*.

ESTERHAZY: Which means that you have always believed it. It's an incurable disease, you know—to have faith in the better spirit of man. I'd like to tell you to renounce it. To destroy in yourself all hunger for anything above the dry rot that others live by. But I can't. Because you will never be able to do it. It's your curse. And mine.

KAY GONDA: [*Angry and imploring at once*] I do not want to hear it!

ESTERHAZY: [*Sitting down on the arm of a chair, speaking softly, lightly*] You know, when I was a boy—a very young boy—I thought my life would be a thing immense and shining. I wanted to kneel to my own future. . . . [*Shrugs*] One gets over that.

KAY GONDA: Does one?

ESTERHAZY: Always. But never completely.

KAY GONDA: [*Breaking down, suddenly eager and trusting*] I saw a man once, when I was very young. He stood on a rock, high in the mountains. His arms were spread out and his body bent backward, and I could see him as an arc against the sky. He stood still and tense, like a string trembling to a note of ecstasy no man had ever heard. . . . I have never known who he was. I knew only that this was what life should be. . . . [*Her voice trails off*]

ESTERHAZY: [*Eagerly*] And?

KAY GONDA: [*In a changed voice*] And I came home, and my mother was serving supper, and she was happy because the roast had a thick gravy. And she gave a prayer of thanks to God for it. . . . [*Jumps up, whirls to him suddenly, angrily*] Don't listen to me! Don't look at me like that! . . . I've tried to renounce it. I thought I must close my eyes and bear anything and learn to live like the others. To make me as they were. To make me forget. I bore it. All of it. But I can't forget the man on the rock. I can't!

ESTERHAZY: We never can.

KAY GONDA: [*Eagerly*] You understand? I'm not alone? . . . Oh, God! I can't be alone! [*Suddenly quiet*] Why did you give it up?

ESTERHAZY: [*Shrugging*] Why does anyone give it up? Because it never comes. What did I get instead? Racing boats, and horses, and cards, and women—all those blind alleys—the pleasures of the moment. All the things I never wanted.

KAY GONDA: [*Softly*] Are you certain?

ESTERHAZY: There was nothing else to take. But if it came, if one had a chance, a last chance . . .

KAY GONDA: Are you certain?

ESTERHAZY: [*Looks at her, then walks resolutely to the telephone and picks up the receiver*] Gladstone 2-1018. . . . Hello, Carl? . . . Those two staterooms on the *Empress of Panama* that you told me about—do you still want to get rid of them? Yes . . . yes, I do . . . At seven thirty a.m.? . . . I'll meet you there. . . . I understand. . . . Thank you. [*Hangs up.* KAY GONDA *looks at him questioningly. He turns to her, his manner calm, matter-of-fact*] The *Empress of Panama* leaves San Pedro at seven thirty in the morning. For Brazil. No extradition laws there.

KAY GONDA: What are you attempting?

ESTERHAZY: We're escaping together. We're outside the law—both of us. I have something worth fighting for now. My ancestors would envy me if they could see me. For my Holy Grail is of this earth, it is real, alive, possible. Only they would not understand. It is our secret. Yours and mine.

KAY GONDA: You have not asked me whether I want to go.

ESTERHAZY: I don't have to. If I did—I would have no right to go with you.

KAY GONDA: [*Smiles softly; then:*] I want to tell you.

ESTERHAZY: [*Stops, faces her, earnestly*] Tell me.

KAY GONDA: [*Looking straight at him, her eyes trusting, her voice a whisper*] Yes, I want to go.

ESTERHAZY: [*Holds her glance for an instant; then, as if deliberately refusing to underscore the earnestness of the moment, glances at his wristwatch and speaks casually again*] We have just a few hours to wait. I'll make a fire. We'll be more comfortable. [*He speaks gaily as he proceeds to light the fire*] I'll pack a few things. . . . You can get what you need aboard ship. . . . I haven't much money, but I'll raise a few thousands before morning. . . . I don't know where, as yet, but I'll raise it. . . . [*She sits down in an armchair by the fire. He sits down on the floor at her feet, facing her*] The sun is terrible down in Brazil. I hope your face doesn't get sunburnt.

KAY GONDA: [*Happily, almost girlishly*] It always does.

ESTERHAZY: We'll build a house somewhere in the jungle. It will be curious to start chopping trees down—that's another experience I've missed. I'll learn it. And you'll have to learn to cook.

KAY GONDA: I will. I'll learn everything we'll need. We'll start from scratch, from the beginning of the world—our world.

ESTERHAZY: You're not afraid?

KAY GONDA: [*Smiling softly*] I'm terribly afraid. I have never been happy before.

ESTERHAZY: The work will ruin your hands . . . your lovely hands. . . . [*He takes her hand, then drops it hurriedly. Speaks with a little effort, suddenly serious:*] I'll be only your architect, your valet, and your watchdog. And nothing else—until I deserve it.

KAY GONDA: [*Looking at him*] What were you thinking?

ESTERHAZY: [*Absently*] I was thinking about tomorrow and all the days thereafter. . . . They seem such a long way off. . . .

KAY GONDA: [*Gaily*] I'll want a house by the seashore. Or by a great river.

ESTERHAZY: With a balcony off your room, over the water, facing the sunrise. . . . [*Involuntarily*] And the moonlight streaming in at night. . . .

KAY GONDA: We'll have no neighbors . . . nowhere . . . not for miles around. . . . No one will look at me . . . no one will pay to look at me. . . .

ESTERHAZY: [*His voice low*] I shall allow no one to look at you. . . . In the morning, you will swim in the sea . . . alone . . . in the green water . . . with the first sun rays on your body. . . . [*He rises, bends over her, whispers*] And then I'll carry you up to the house . . . up the rocks . . . in my arms . . . [*He seizes her and kisses her violently. She responds. He raises his head and chuckles with a sound of cynical intimacy*] That's all we're really after, you and I, aren't we? Why pretend?

KAY GONDA: [*Not understanding*] What?

ESTERHAZY: Why pretend that we're important? We're no better than the others. [*Tries to kiss her again*]

KAY GONDA: Let me go! [*She tears herself away*]

ESTERHAZY: [*Laughing harshly*] Where? You have no

place to go! [*She stares at him, wide-eyed, incredulous*] After all, what difference does it make, whether it's now or later? Why should we take it so seriously? [*She whirls toward the door. He seizes her. She screams, a muffled scream, stopped by his hand on her mouth*] Keep still! You can't call for help! . . . It's a death sentence—or this. . . . [*She starts laughing hysterically*] Keep still! . . . Why should I care what you'll think of me afterwards? . . . Why should I care about tomorrow?

[*She tears herself away, runs to the door, and escapes. He stands still. He hears her laughter, loud, reckless, moving away*]

CURTAIN

SCENE 3
The letter projected on the screen is written in a sharp, uneven handwriting:

Dear Miss Gonda,
This letter is addressed to you, but I am writing it to myself.
I am writing and thinking that I am speaking to a woman who is the only justification for the existence of this earth, and who has the courage to want to be. A woman who does not assume a glory of greatness for a few hours, then return to the children-dinner-friends-football-and-God reality. A woman who seeks that glory in her every minute and her every step. A woman in whom life is not a curse, nor a bargain, but a hymn.
I want nothing except to know that such a woman exists. So I have written this, even though you may not bother to read it, or reading it, may not understand. I do not know what you are. I am writing to what you could have been.

Johnnie Dawes

. . . Main Street
Los Angeles, California

Lights go out, screen disappears, and stage reveals gar-

ret of JOHNNIE DAWES. *It is a squalid, miserable room with a low, slanting ceiling, with dark walls showing beams under cracked plaster. The room is so bare that it gives the impression of being uninhabited, a strange, intangible impression of unreality. A narrow iron cot, at wall Right; a broken table, a few boxes for chairs. A narrow door opens diagonally in the Left upstage corner. The entire wall Center is a long window check-ered into small panes. It opens high over the skyline of Los Angeles. Behind the black shadows of skyscrapers, there is a first hint of pink in the dark sky. When the curtain rises, the stage is empty, dark. One barely distin-guishes the room and sees only the faintly luminous pan-orama of the window. It dominates the stage, so that one forgets the room, and it seems as if the setting is only the city and the sky. (Throughout the scene, the sky lightens slowly, the pink band of dawn grows, rising.)*

Steps are heard coming up the stairs. A quivering light shows in the cracks of the door. The door opens to admit KAY GONDA. *Behind her,* MRS. MONAGHAN, *an old landlady, shuffles in, with a lighted candle in hand. She puts the candle down on the table, and stands pant-ing as after a long climb, studying* KAY GONDA *with a suspicious curiosity.*

MRS. MONAGHAN: Here ye are. This is it.

KAY GONDA: [*Looking slowly over the room*] Thank you.

MRS. MONAGHAN: And ye're a relative of him, ye are?

KAY GONDA: No.

MRS. MONAGHAN: [*Maliciously*] Sure, and I was thinking that.

KAY GONDA: I have never seen him before.

MRS. MONAGHAN: Well, I'm after tellin' ye he's no good, that's what he is, no good. It's a born bum he is. No rent never. He can't keep a job more'n two weeks.

KAY GONDA: When will he be back?

MRS. MONAGHAN: Any minute at all—or never, for all I know. He runs around all night, the good Lord only knows where. Just walks the streets like the bum he is, just walks. Comes back drunk like, only he's not drunk, 'cause I know he don't drink.

KAY GONDA: I will wait for him.

MRS. MONAGHAN: Suit yerself. [*Looks at her shrewdly*] Maybe ye got a job for him?

KAY GONDA: No. I have no job for him.

MRS. MONAGHAN: He's got himself kicked out again, three days ago it was. He had a swell job bellhoppin'. Did it last? It did not. Same as the soda counter. Same as the waitin' at Hamburger Looey's. He's no good, I'm tellin' ye. I know him. Better'n ye do.

KAY GONDA: I do not know him at all.

MRS. MONAGHAN: And I can't say I blame his bosses, either. He's a strange one. Never a laugh, never a joke out of him. [*Confidentially*] Ye know what Hamburger Looey said to me? He said, "Stuck up little snot," said Hamburger Looey, "makes a regular guy feel creepy."

KAY GONDA: So Hamburger Looey said that?

MRS. MONAGHAN: Faith and he did. [*Confidentially*] And d'ye know? He's been to college, that boy. Ye'd never believe it from the kind of jobs he can't keep, but he has. What he learned there the good Lord only knows. It's no good it done him. And . . . [*Stops, listening. Steps are heard rising up the stairs*] That's him now! Nobody else'd be shameless enough to come home at this hour of the night. [*At the door*] Ye think it over. Maybe ye could do somethin' for him. [*Exits*]

[JOHNNIE DAWES *enters. He is a tall, slender boy in his late twenties; a gaunt face, prominent cheekbones, a hard mouth, clear, steady eyes. He sees* KAY GONDA *and stands still. They look at each other for a long moment*]

JOHNNIE: [*Slowly, calmly, no astonishment and no question in his voice*] Good evening, Miss Gonda.

KAY GONDA: [*She cannot take her eyes from him, and it is her voice that sounds astonished*] Good evening.

JOHNNIE: Please sit down.

KAY GONDA: You do not want me to stay here.

JOHNNIE: You're staying.

KAY GONDA: You have not asked me why I came.

JOHNNIE: You're here. [*He sits down*]

KAY GONDA: [*She approaches him suddenly, takes his face in her hands and raises it*] What's the matter, Johnnie?

JOHNNIE: Nothing—now.

KAY GONDA: You must not be so glad to see me.

JOHNNIE: I knew you'd come.

KAY GONDA: [*She walks away from him, falls wearily down on the cot. She looks at him and smiles; a smile that is not gay, not friendly*] People say I am a great star, Johnnie.

JOHNNIE: Yes.

KAY GONDA: They say I have everything one can wish for.

JOHNNIE: Have you?

KAY GONDA: No. But how do you know it?

JOHNNIE: How do you know that I know it?

KAY GONDA: You are never afraid when you speak to people, are you, Johnnie?

JOHNNIE: Yes. I am very much afraid. Always. I don't know what to say to them. But I'm not afraid—now.

KAY GONDA: I am a very bad woman, Johnnie. Everything you've heard about me is true. Everything—and more. I came to tell you that you must not think of me what you said in your letter.

JOHNNIE: You came to tell me that everything I said in my letter was true. Everything—and more.

KAY GONDA: [*With a harsh little laugh*] You're a fool! I'm not afraid of you. . . . Do you know that I get twenty thousand dollars a week?

JOHNNIE: Yes.

KAY GONDA: Do you know that I have fifty pairs of shoes and three butlers?

JOHNNIE: I suppose so.

KAY GONDA: Do you know that my pictures are shown in every town on earth?

JOHNNIE: Yes.

KAY GONDA: [*Furiously*] Stop looking at me like that! . . . Do you know that people pay millions to see me? I don't need your approval! I have plenty of worshipers! I mean a great deal to them!

JOHNNIE: You mean nothing at all to them. You know it.

KAY GONDA: [*Looking at him almost with hatred*] I thought I knew it—an hour ago. [*Whirling upon him*] Oh, why don't you ask me for something?

JOHNNIE: What do you want me to ask you?

KAY GONDA: Why don't you ask me to get you a job in the movies, for instance?

JOHNNIE: The only thing I could ask you, you have given to me already.

KAY GONDA: [*She looks at him, laughs harshly, speaks in a new voice, strange to her, an unnaturally common voice*] Look, Johnnie, let's stop kidding each other. I'll tell you something. I've killed a man. It's dangerous, hiding a murderess. Why don't you throw me out? [*He sits looking at her silently*] No? That one won't work? Well, then, look at me. I'm the most beautiful woman you've ever seen. Don't you want to sleep with me? Why don't you? Right now. I won't struggle. [*He does not move*] Not that? But listen: do you know that there's a reward on my head? Why don't you call the police and turn me over to them? You'd be set for life.

JOHNNIE: [*Softly*] Are you as unhappy as that?

KAY GONDA: [*Walks to him, then falls on her knees at his feet*] Help me, Johnnie!

JOHNNIE: [*Bends down to her, his hands on her shoulders, asks softly:*] Why did you come here?

KAY GONDA: [*Raising her head*] Johnnie. If all of you who look at me on the screen hear the things I say and worship me for them—where do I hear them? Where can I hear them, so that I might go on? I want to see, real, living, and in the hours of my own days, that glory I create as an illusion! I want it real! I want to know that there is someone, somewhere, who wants it, too! Or else what is the use of seeing it, and working, and burning oneself for an impossible vision? A spirit, too, needs fuel. It can run dry.

JOHNNIE: [*He rises, leads her to the cot, makes her sit down, stands before her*] I want to tell you only this: there are a few on earth who see you and understand. These few give life its meaning. The rest—well, the rest are what you see they are. You have a duty. To live. Just to remain on earth. To let them know you do and can exist. To fight, even a fight without hope. We can't give up the earth to all those others.

KAY GONDA: [*Looking at him, softly*] Who are you, Johnnie?

JOHNNIE: [*Astonished*] I? . . . I'm—nothing.

KAY GONDA: Where do you come from?

JOHNNIE: I've had a home and parents somewhere. I don't remember much about them . . . I don't remember much about anything that's ever happened to me. There's not a day worth remembering.

KAY GONDA: You have no friends?

JOHNNIE: No.

KAY GONDA: You have no work?

JOHNNIE: Yes . . . no, I was fired three days ago. I forgot.

KAY GONDA: Where have you lived before?

JOHNNIE: Many places. I've lost count.

KAY GONDA: Do you hate people, Johnnie?

JOHNNIE: No. I never notice them.

KAY GONDA: What do you dream of?

JOHNNIE: Nothing. Of what account are dreams?

KAY GONDA: Of what account is life?

JOHNNIE: None. But who made it so?

KAY GONDA: Those who cannot dream.

JOHNNIE: No. Those who can *only* dream.

KAY GONDA: Are you very unhappy?

JOHNNIE: No. . . . I don't think you should ask me these questions. You won't get a decent answer from me to anything.

KAY GONDA: There was a great man once who said: "I love those that know not how to live today."

JOHNNIE: [*Quietly*] I think I am a person who should never have been born. This is not a complaint. I am not afraid and I am not sorry. But I have often wanted to die. I have no desire to change the world—nor to take any part in it, as it is. I've never had the weapons which you have. I've never even found the desire to find weapons. I'd like to go, calmly and willingly.

KAY GONDA: I don't want to hear you say that.

JOHNNIE: There has always been something holding me here. Something that had to come to me before I went. I want to know one living moment of that which is mine, not theirs. Not their dismal little pleasures. One moment of ecstasy, utter and absolute, a moment that must not be survived. . . . They've never given me a life. I've always hoped I would choose my death.

KAY GONDA: Don't say that. I need you. I'm here. I'll never let you go.

JOHNNIE: [*After a pause, looking at her in a strange new way, his voice dry, flat*] You? You're a murderess who'll get caught someday and die on the gallows.

[*She looks at him, astonished. He walks to the window, stands looking out. Beyond the window it is now full daylight. The sun is about to rise. Rays of light spread like halos from behind the dark silhouettes of skyscrapers. He asks suddenly, without turning to her:*]

You killed him?

KAY GONDA: We don't have to talk about that, do we?

JOHNNIE: [*Without turning*] I knew Granton Sayers. I worked for him once, as a caddy, at a golf club in Santa Barbara. A hard kind of man.

KAY GONDA: He was a very unhappy man, Johnnie.

JOHNNIE: [*Turning to her*] Was anyone present?

KAY GONDA: Where?

JOHNNIE: When you killed him?

KAY GONDA: Do we have to discuss that?

JOHNNIE: It's something I must know. Did anyone see you kill him?

KAY GONDA: No.

JOHNNIE: Have the police got anything on you?

KAY GONDA: No. Except what I could tell them. But I will not tell it to them. Nor to you. Not now. Don't question me.

JOHNNIE: How much is the reward on your head?

KAY GONDA: [*After a pause, in a strange kind of voice*] What did you say, Johnnie?

JOHNNIE: [*Evenly*] I said, how much is the reward on your head? [*She stares at him*] Never mind. [*He walks to the door, throws it open, calls:*] Mrs. Monaghan! Come here!

KAY GONDA: What are you doing? [*He does not answer or look at her.* MRS. MONAGHAN *shuffles up the stairs and appears at the door*]

MRS. MONAGHAN: [*Angrily*] What d'ye want?

JOHNNIE: Mrs. Monaghan, listen carefully. Go downstairs to your phone. Call the police. Tell them to come here at once. Tell them that *Kay Gonda* is here. You understand? Kay Gonda. Now hurry.

MRS. MONAGHAN: [*Aghast*] Yes, sir. . . . [*Exits hurriedly*]

[JOHNNIE *closes the door, turns to* KAY GONDA. *She tries to dash for the door. The table is between them. He opens a drawer, pulls out a gun, points it at her*]

JOHNNIE: Stand still. [*She does not move. He backs to the door and locks it. She sags suddenly, still standing up*]

KAY GONDA: [*Without looking at him, in a flat, lifeless voice*] Put it away. I will not try to escape. [*He slips the gun into his pocket and stands leaning against the door. She sits down, her back turned to him*]

JOHNNIE: [*Quietly*] We have about three minutes left. I am thinking now that nothing has happened to us and nothing will happen. The world stopped a minute ago and in three minutes it will go on again. But this— this pause is ours. You're here. I look at you. I've seen your eyes—and all the truth that man has ever sought. [*Her head falls down on her arms*] There are no other men on earth right now. Just you and I. There's nothing but a world in which you live. To breathe for once that air, to move in it, to hear my own voice on waves that touch no ugliness, no pain . . . I've never known gratitude. But now, of all the words I'd like to say to you, I'll say just three: I thank you. When you leave, remember I have thanked you. Remember—no matter what may happen in this room. . . . [*She buries her head in her arms. He stands silently, his head thrown back, his eyes closed*]

[*Hurried steps are heard rising up the stairs.* JOHNNIE *and* KAY GONDA *do not move. There is a violent knock at the door.* JOHNNIE *turns, unlocks the door, and opens it. A police* CAPTAIN *enters, followed by two* POLICE-MEN. KAY GONDA *rises, facing them*]

CAPTAIN: Jesus Christ! [*They stare at her, aghast*]

POLICEMAN: And I thought it was another crank calling!

CAPTAIN: Miss Gonda, I'm sure glad to see you. We've been driven crazy with . . .

KAY GONDA: Take me away from here. Anywhere you wish.

CAPTAIN: [*Making a step toward her*] Well, we have no . . .

JOHNNIE: [*In a quiet voice which is such an implacable command that all turn to him*] Stay away from her. [*The* CAPTAIN *stops.* JOHNNIE *motions to a* POLICEMAN *and points to the table*] Sit down. Take a pencil and paper. [*The* POLICEMAN *looks at the* CAPTAIN, *who nods, baffled. The* POLICEMAN *obeys*] Now write this: [*Dictates slowly, his voice precise, emotionless*] I, John Dawes, confess that on the night of May fifth, willfully and with premeditation, I killed Granton Sayers of Santa Barbara, California. [KAY GONDA *takes a deep breath, which is almost a gasp*] I have been absent from my home for the last three nights, as my landlady, Mrs. Sheila Monaghan, can testify. She can further testify that I was dismissed from my job at the Alhambra Hotel on May third. [KAY GONDA *starts laughing suddenly. It is the lightest, happiest laughter in the world*] I had worked for Granton Sayers a year ago, at the Greendale Golf Club of Santa Barbara. Being jobless and broke, I went to Granton Sayers on the evening of May fifth, determined to extort money from him through blackmail, under threat of divulging certain information I possessed. He refused my demands even at the point of a gun. I shot him. I disposed of the gun by throwing it into the ocean on my way back from Santa Barbara. I was alone in committing this crime. No other person was or is to be implicated. [*Adds*] Have you got it all? Give it to me. [*The* POLICEMAN *hands the confession to him.* JOHNNIE *signs it*]

CAPTAIN: [*He cannot quite collect his wits*] Miss Gonda, what have you got to say about this?

KAY GONDA: [*Hysterically*] Don't ask me! Not now! Don't speak to me!

JOHNNIE: [*Hands the confession to the* CAPTAIN] You will please let Miss Gonda depart now.

CAPTAIN: Wait a minute, my boy. Not so fast. There's a lot of explaining you have to do yet. How did you get into the Sayers house? How did you leave it?

JOHNNIE: I have told you all I'm going to tell.

CAPTAIN: What time was it when you did the shooting? And what is Miss Gonda doing here?

JOHNNIE: You know all you have to know. You know enough not to implicate Miss Gonda. You have my confession.

CAPTAIN: Sure. But you'll have to prove it.

JOHNNIE: It will stand—even if I do not choose to prove it. Particularly if I am not here to prove it.

CAPTAIN: Gonna be tough, eh? Well, you'll talk at headquarters all right. Come on, boys.

KAY GONDA: [*Stepping forward*] Wait! You must listen to me now. I have a statement to make. I . . .

JOHNNIE: [*Steps back, pulls the gun out of his pocket, covering the group*] Stand still, all of you. [*To* KAY GONDA] Don't move. Don't say a word.

KAY GONDA: Johnnie! You don't know what you're doing! Wait, my dearest! Put that gun down.

JOHNNIE: [*Without lowering the gun, smiles at her*] I heard it. Thank you.

KAY GONDA: I'll tell you everything! You don't know! I'm safe!

JOHNNIE: I know you're safe. You will be. Step back. Don't be afraid. I won't hurt anyone. [*She obeys*] I want you all to look at me. Years from now you can tell your grandchildren about it. You are looking at something you will never see again and they will never see—a man who is perfectly happy! [*Points the gun at himself, fires, falls*]

CURTAIN

SCENE 4

Entrance hall in the residence of KAY GONDA. *It is high, bare, modern in its austere simplicity. There is no furniture, no ornaments of any kind. The upper part of the hall is a long raised platform, dividing the room horizontally, and three broad continuous steps lead down from it to the foreground. Tall, square columns rise at the upper edge of the steps. Door into the rest of the house downstage in wall Left. The entire back wall is of wide glass panes, with an entrance door in the center.*

Beyond the house, there is a narrow path among jagged rocks, a thin strip of the high coast with a broad view of the ocean beyond and of a flaming sunset sky. The hall is dim. There is no light, save the glow of the sunset.

At curtain rise, MICK WATTS *is sitting on the top step, leaning down toward a dignified* BUTLER *who sits on the floor below, stiff, upright, and uncomfortable holding a tray with a full highball glass on it.* MICK WATTS' *shirt collar is torn open, his tie hanging loose, his hair disheveled. He is clutching a newspaper ferociously. He is sober.*

MICK WATTS: [*Continuing a discourse that has obviously been going on for some time, speaking in an even, expressionless monotone, his manner earnest, confidential*] . . . and so the king called them all before his throne and he said: "I'm weary and sick of it. I am tired of my kingdom where not a single man is worth ruling. I am tired of my lusterless crown, for it does not reflect a single flame of glory anywhere in my land." . . . You see, he was a very foolish king. Some scream it, like he did, and squash their damn brains out against a wall. Others stagger on, like a dog chasing a shadow, knowing damn well that there is no shadow to chase, but still going on, their hearts empty and their paws bleeding. . . . So the king said to them on his deathbed—oh, this was another time, he was on his deathbed this time—he said: "It is the end, but I am still hoping. There is no end. Ever shall I go on hoping . . . ever . . . ever." [*Looks suddenly at the* BUTLER, *as if noticing him for the first time, and asks in an entirely different voice, pointing at him:*] What the hell are you doing here?

BUTLER: [*Rising*] May I observe, sir, that you have been speaking for an hour and a quarter?

MICK WATTS: Have I?

BUTLER: You have, sir. So, if I may be forgiven, I took the liberty of sitting down.

MICK WATTS: [*Surprised*] Fancy, you were here all the time!

BUTLER: Yes, sir.

MICK WATTS: Well, what did you want here in the first place?

BUTLER: [*Extending the tray*] Your whiskey, sir.

MICK WATTS: Oh! [*Reaches for the glass, but stops, jerks the crumpled newspaper at the* BUTLER, *asks:*] Have you read this?

BUTLER: Yes, sir.

MICK WATTS: [*Knocking the tray aside; it falls, breaking the glass*] Go to hell! I don't want any whiskey!

BUTLER: But you ordered it, sir.

MICK WATTS: Go to hell just the same! [*As the* BUTLER *bends to pick up the tray*] Get out of here! Never mind! Get out! I don't want to see any human snoot tonight!

BUTLER: Yes, sir. [*Exits Left*]

[MICK WATTS *straightens the paper out, looks at it, crumples it viciously again. Hears steps approaching outside and whirls about.* FREDERICA SAYERS *is seen outside, walking hurriedly toward the door; she has a newspaper in her hand.* MICK WATTS *walks to door and opens it, before she has time to ring*]

MISS SAYERS: Good evening.

[*He does not answer, lets her enter, closes the door and stands silently, looking at her. She looks around, then at him, somewhat disconcerted*]

MICK WATTS: [*Without moving*] Well?

MISS SAYERS: Is this the residence of Miss Kay Gonda?

MICK WATTS: It is.

MISS SAYERS: May I see Miss Gonda?

MICK WATTS: No.

MISS SAYERS: I am Miss Sayers. Miss Frederica Sayers.

MICK WATTS: I don't care.

MISS SAYERS: Will you please tell Miss Gonda that I am here? If she is at home.

MICK WATTS: She is not.

MISS SAYERS: When do you expect her back?

MICK WATTS: I don't expect her.

MISS SAYERS: My good man, this is getting to be preposterous!

MICK WATTS: It is. You'd better get out of here.

MISS SAYERS: Sir?!

MICK WATTS: She'll be back any minute. I know she will. And there's nothing to talk about now.

MISS SAYERS: My good man, do you realize . . .

MICK WATTS: I realize everything that you realize, and then some. And I'm telling you there's nothing to be done. Don't bother her now.

MISS SAYERS: May I ask who you are and what you're talking about?

MICK WATTS: Who I am doesn't matter. I'm talking about—[*Extends the newspaper*]—this.

MISS SAYERS: Yes, I've read it, and I must say it is utterly bewildering and . . .

MICK WATTS: Bewildering? Hell, it's monstrous! You don't know the half of it! . . . [*Catching himself, adds flatly*] I don't, either.

MISS SAYERS: Look here, I must get to the bottom of this thing. It will go too far and . . .

MICK WATTS: It has gone too far.

MISS SAYERS: Then I must . . .

[KAY GONDA *enters from the outside. She is dressed as in all the preceding scenes. She is calm, but very tired*]

MICK WATTS: So here you are! I knew you'd be back now!

KAY GONDA: [*In a quiet, even voice*] Good evening, Miss Sayers.

MISS SAYERS: Miss Gonda, this is the first sigh of relief I've breathed in two days! I never thought the time should come when I'd be so glad to see you! But you must understand . . .

KAY GONDA: [*Indifferently*] I know.

MISS SAYERS: You must understand that I could not foresee the astounding turn of events. It was most kind of you to go into hiding, but, really, you did not have to hide from me.

KAY GONDA: I was not hiding from anyone.

MISS SAYERS: But where were you?

KAY GONDA: Away. It had nothing to do with Mr. Sayers' death.

MISS SAYERS: But when you heard those preposterous rumors accusing you of his murder, you should have come to me at once! When I asked you, at the house that night, not to disclose to anyone the manner of my brother's death, I had no way of knowing what suspicions would arise. I tried my best to get in touch with you. Please believe me that I did not start those rumors.

KAY GONDA: I never thought you did.

MISS SAYERS: I wonder who started them.

KAY GONDA: I wonder.

MISS SAYERS: I do owe you an apology. I'm sure you felt it was my duty to disclose the truth at once, but you know why I had to keep silent. However, the deal is closed, and I thought it best to come to you first and tell you that I'm free to speak now.

KAY GONDA: [*Indifferently*] It was very kind of you.

MISS SAYERS: [*Turning to* MICK WATTS] Young man, you can tell that ridiculous studio of yours that Miss Gonda did not murder my brother. Tell them they can read his suicide letter in tomorrow's papers. He wrote that he had no desire to struggle any longer, since his business was ruined and since the only woman he'd ever loved had, that night, refused to marry him.

KAY GONDA: I'm sorry, Miss Sayers.

MISS SAYERS: This is not a reproach, Miss Gonda. [*To* MICK WATTS] The Santa Barbara police knew everything, but promised me silence. I had to keep my brother's suicide secret for a while, because I was negotiating a merger with . . .

MICK WATTS: . . . with United California Oil, and you didn't want them to know the desperate state of the Sayers Company. Very smart. Now you've closed the deal and gypped United California. My congratulations.

MISS SAYERS: [*Aghast, to* KAY GONDA] This peculiar gentleman knew it all?

MICK WATTS: So it seems, doesn't it?

MISS SAYERS: Then, in heaven's name, why did you allow everybody to suspect Miss Gonda?

KAY GONDA: Don't you think it best, Miss Sayers, not to discuss this any further? It's done. It's past. Let's leave it at that.

MISS SAYERS: As you wish. There is just one question I would like to ask you. It baffles me completely. I thought perhaps you may know something about it. [*Points at the newspaper*] This. That incredible story . . . that boy I've never heard of, killing himself . . . that insane confession. . . . What does it mean?

KAY GONDA: [*Evenly*] I don't know.

MICK WATTS: Huh?

KAY GONDA: I have never heard of him before.

MISS SAYERS: Then I can explain it only as the act of a crank, an abnormal mind . . .

KAY GONDA: Yes, Miss Sayers. A mind that was not normal.

MISS SAYERS: [*After a pause*] Well if you'll excuse me, Miss Gonda, I shall wish you good night. I shall give my statement to the papers immediately and clear your name completely.

KAY GONDA: Thank you, Miss Sayers. Good night.

MISS SAYERS: [*Turning at the door*] I wish you luck with whatever it is you're doing. You have been most courteous in this unfortunate matter. Allow me to thank you.

[KAY GONDA *bows.* MISS SAYERS *exits*]

MICK WATTS: [*Ferociously*] Well?

KAY GONDA: Would you mind going home, Mick? I am very tired.

MICK WATTS: I hope you've . . .

KAY GONDA: Telephone the studio on your way. Tell them that I will sign the contract tomorrow.

MICK WATTS: I hope you've had a good time! I hope you've enjoyed it! But I'm through!

KAY GONDA: I'll see you at the studio tomorrow at nine.

MICK WATTS: I'm through! God, I wish I could quit!

KAY GONDA: You know that you will never quit, Mick.

MICK WATTS: That's the hell of it! That you know it, too! Why do I serve you like a dog and will go on serving you like a dog for the rest of my days? Why can't I resist any crazy whim of yours? Why did I have to go and spread rumors about a murder you never committed? Just because you wanted to find out something? Well, have you found it out?

KAY GONDA: Yes.

MICK WATTS: What have you found out?

KAY GONDA: How many people saw my last picture? Do you remember those figures?

MICK WATTS: Seventy-five million, six hundred thousand, three hundred and twelve.

KAY GONDA: Well, Mick, seventy-five million, six hundred thousand people hate me. They hate me in their hearts for the things they see in me, the things they have betrayed. I mean nothing to them, except a reproach. . . . But there are three hundred and twelve others—perhaps only the twelve. There are a few who want the highest possible and will take nothing less and will not live on any other terms. . . . It is with them that I am signing a contract tomorrow. We can't give up the earth to all those others.

MICK WATTS: [*Holding out the newspaper*] And what about this?

KAY GONDA: I've answered you.

MICK WATTS: But you are a murderess, Kay Gonda! You killed that boy!

KAY GONDA: No, Mick, not I alone.

MICK WATTS: But the poor fool thought that he had to save your life!

KAY GONDA: He has.

MICK WATTS: What?!

KAY GONDA: He wanted to die that I may live. He did just that.

MICK WATTS: But don't you realize what you've done?

KAY GONDA: [*Slowly, looking past him*] That, Mick, was the kindest thing I have ever done.

CURTAIN

Part III

THE LATE THIRTIES

Think Twice

1939

Editor's Preface

The Depression years in New York City (to which she moved in 1934) were a difficult financial struggle for Ayn Rand: she lived on the earnings from *Night of January 16th* and from a series of jobs she held as reader for various movie companies. She wrote when she could find the time. Nevertheless, the work moved ahead. In 1935, she began making notes for *The Fountainhead* and planning the architectural research that it would require. Realizing that the novel would be a long-term project, she interrupted it several times to do shorter pieces. In 1937, she wrote the novelette *Anthem* (published separately by New American Library). In 1939, she wrote a stage adaptation of *We the Living*, produced on Broadway under the title of *The Unconquered* (it was not successful). In the same year, she wrote her third and last original stage play, the philosophical murder mystery *Think Twice*. It has never been produced.

Think Twice, written five years later than *Ideal*, is finished, mature work, in all major respects characteristic of the author of *The Fountainhead*. It is the only such piece in the present collection. (*Red Pawn* is an unedited scenario, and *Ideal* is not fully representative.) The theme is the distinctive Ayn Rand approach to ethics: the evil of altruism, and the need of man to live an independent, egoistic existence. The hero, who now has primacy over the heroine, is a completely recognizable Ayn Rand type. The plot, fast-moving and logical, has an ingenious twist; the story presents an altruist who, acting on his ideas, specializes in seeking power over others; thereby giving them compelling reasons to want to kill him. (The Russian character was originally a German Nazi; in the 1950s, Miss Rand updated the play, turning him into a Communist.) The style is smoothly assured; the mechanics of alibis, motives, and clues are deftly handled; and the writing displays Ayn Rand's clarity, her sense of drama, her intellectual wit. There is even the first sign of the science-fiction element which, years later, would become John Galt's motor in *Atlas Shrugged*.

One of Ayn Rand's most impressive literary skills, brilliantly demonstrated in her novels, is her ability to integrate theme and plot. That ability is evidenced in *Think Twice*—in the union of philosophy and murder mystery. This is not a routine murder story, with some abstract talk thrown in for effect. Nor is it a drawing-room discussion interrupted now and again by some unrelated events. The play is a union of thought and action: the philosophic ideas of the characters actually motivate and explain their actions, which in turn concretize and demonstrate the philosophic point, and acquire significance because of it. The result is a seamless blend of depth and excitement, at once art and entertainment.

A decade later, in her journal of August 28, 1949, Ayn Rand wrote the following:

The idea that "art" and "entertainment" are opposites, that art is serious and dull, while entertainment is empty and stupid, but enjoyable—is the result of the nonhuman, altruistic morality. That which is *good* [in this view] must be unpleasant. That which is enjoyable is sinful. Pleasure is an indulgence of a low order, to be apologized for. The serious is the performance of a duty, unpleasant and, therefore, uplifting. If a work of art examines life seriously, it must necessarily be unpleasant and unexciting, because such is the nature of life for man. An entertaining, enjoyable play cannot possibly be true to the deeper essence of life, it must be superficial, since life is not to be enjoyed.

It is unlikely that Miss Rand had her early work in mind when she wrote these words, but the present piece does illustrate her point. *Think Twice* is an entertaining, enjoyable play that is true to the deeper essence of life.

I first read the play in the 1950s, with Miss Rand present, asking me now and then who I thought the murderer was. I guessed just about every possibility, except the right one. Each time, Miss Rand beamed and said: "Think twice." When I finished, she told me that anyone who knew her and her philosophy should have been able to guess right away. She could not, she went on, ever write a series of mysteries, because everyone would know who the murderers were. "How?" I asked.

Now see if you can guess the murderer. After the play, I will quote her answer.

—L. P.

Think Twice

CHARACTERS

WALTER BRECKENRIDGE
CURTISS
SERGE SOOKIN
HARVEY FLEMING
TONY GODDARD
STEVE INGALLS
BILLY BRECKENRIDGE
FLASH KOZINSKY
ADRIENNE KNOWLAND
HELEN BRECKENRIDGE
GREGORY HASTINGS
DIXON

Place   Living room of a home in Connecticut

Time   Act I, Scene 1—Afternoon of July 3rd
                 Act I, Scene 2—That evening
                 Act II, Scene 1—Half an hour later
                 Act II, Scene 2—Next morning

Act I

Afternoon of July 3rd. The living room of a home in Connecticut. A large room, not offensively wealthy, but evidencing both money and an unsuccessful attempt at good taste. The room is stately and Colonial—too deliberately so. Everything is brand-new, resplendently unused; one expects to see price tags on the furniture.

Large French windows, Center, opening upon a lovely view of the grounds with a lake in the distance, a view marred only by a dismal, gray sky. Stairway, Stage Right, leading to a door, and another door downstage, leading to the rest of the ground floor. Entrance door upstage Left. Downstage Left an unused fireplace, with logs stacked neatly, and above the fireplace—a large portrait of WALTER BRECKENRIDGE.

At curtain rise, WALTER BRECKENRIDGE *stands alone in front of the fireplace. He is a stately, gray-haired man of fifty, who looks like a saint; a very "human" saint, however: benevolent, dignified, humorous, and a little portly. He stands, looking up at the portrait, deeply absorbed, a gun in his hand.*

After a while, CURTISS, *the butler, enters from door Right, carrying two empty flower vases.* CURTISS *is elderly, and severely well-mannered. He deposits the vases on a table and a cabinet.* BRECKENRIDGE *does not turn and* CURTISS *does not see the gun.*

CURTISS: Anything else, sir? [BRECKENRIDGE *does not move*] Mr. Breckenridge . . . [*No answer*] Is anything the matter, sir?

BRECKENRIDGE: [*Absently*] Oh . . . no . . . no . . . I was just wondering . . . [*Points at the portrait*] Do you think that in the centuries to come people will say he was a great man? [*Turns to face* CURTISS] Is it a good likeness of me, Curtiss? [CURTISS *sees the gun and steps back with a little gasp*] What's the matter?

CURTISS: Mr. Breckenridge!

BRECKENRIDGE: What's the matter with you?

CURTISS: Don't do it, sir! Whatever it is, don't do it!

BRECKENRIDGE: [*Looks at him in amazement, then notices the gun in his own hand and bursts out laughing*]

341

Oh, that? . . . I'm sorry, Curtiss. I'd quite forgotten I held it.

CURTISS: But, sir . . .

BRECKENRIDGE: Oh, I just sent the car down to meet Mrs. Breckenridge at the station, and I didn't want her to find this in the car, so I brought it in. We mustn't tell her about . . . you know, about why I have to carry this. It would only worry her.

CURTISS: Yes, of course, sir. I'm so sorry. It just gave me a jolt.

BRECKENRIDGE: I don't blame you. You know, I hate the damn thing myself. [*Walks to a cabinet and slips the gun into a drawer*] Funny, isn't it? I'm actually afraid of it. And when I think of all the deadly stuff I've handled in the laboratory. Radioactive elements. Cosmic rays. Things that could wipe out the whole population of the state of Connecticut. Never been afraid of them. In fact, never felt anything at all. But this . . . [*Points to the drawer*] Do you suppose it's my old age and I'm being sensitive about any . . . reminder?

CURTISS: [*Reproachfully*] Your old age, sir!

BRECKENRIDGE: Well, time passes, Curtiss, time passes. Why do they celebrate birthdays? It's just one year closer to the grave. And there's so much to be done. [*Looks at the portrait*] That's what I was thinking when you came in. Have I done enough in my life? Have I done enough?

[SERGE SOOKIN *enters through the French doors.* SERGE *is about thirty-two, pale, blond, with the face and the manner of a fervent idealist. His clothes are neat, but very poor. His arms are loaded with an enormous bunch of freshly cut flowers*]

Ah, Serge . . . thank you. . . . So kind of you to help us.

SERGE: I hope this flowers Mrs. Breckenridge will like.

BRECKENRIDGE: She loves flowers. We must have lots of flowers. . . . Over here, Serge. . . . [*Indicating the vases as* SERGE *arranges the flowers*] We'll put them here—and over there, on the cabinet—and on the fireplace, just one or two sprays on the fireplace.

SERGE: [*Wistfully*] By us in Moscow, we had the more beautiful flowers.

BRECKENRIDGE: Try not to think of all that, Serge. There are things it's best to forget. [*To* CURTISS] Have you taken care of the cigarettes, Curtiss?

[CURTISS *busies himself filling cigarette boxes*]

SERGE: [*Grimly*] There are the things never one can forget. But I am so sorry. That we should not discuss about. Not today, no? This is a great day.

BRECKENRIDGE: Yes, Serge. This is a great day for me. [*Indicating an armchair*] I don't think that chair is right, over there. Curtiss, would you move it please this way, to the table? [*As* CURTISS *obeys*] That's better, thank you. We must have everything right, Curtiss. For our guests. They are very important guests.

CURTISS: Yes, sir.

[*From offstage, there comes the sound of Tchaikovsky's "Autumn Song" expertly played on the piano.* BRECKENRIDGE *looks in the direction of the sound, a little annoyed, then shrugs and turns to* SERGE]

BRECKENRIDGE: You will meet some very interesting people today, Serge. I want you to meet them. Perhaps it will give you a better idea of me. You know, one can judge a man best by his friends.

SERGE: [*Looking up the stairs, a little grimly*] Not always, I hope.

BRECKENRIDGE: [*Looking up*] Oh, Steve? You mustn't mind Steve. You mustn't let him upset you.

SERGE: [*Coldly*] Mr. Ingalls he is not kind.

BRECKENRIDGE: No. Steve's never been kind. But then, you know, strictly speaking, Steve is not a friend. He's my business partner—just a junior partner, as we call it, but darn useful. One of the best physicists in the country.

SERGE: You are so modest, Mr. Breckenridge. You are in the country the greatest physicist. That everybody knows.

BRECKENRIDGE: Perhaps everybody but me.

SERGE: You are to mankind the benefactor. But Mr. Ingalls he is not a friend to the world. In his heart for the world there is no place. Today the world needs friends.

BRECKENRIDGE: That's true. But—

[*Doorbell rings.* CURTISS *opens the door.* HARVEY FLEMING *stands on the threshold. He is a man in his late forties, tall, gaunt, disreputably unkempt. He looks like anything but an "important" guest: he needs a shave, his clothes need pressing; he is not drunk, but not quite sober. He carries a small, battered overnight bag. He stands for a moment, studying the room glumly*]

CURTISS: [*Bowing*] Good afternoon, sir. Come right in, sir.

FLEMING: [*Enters, without removing his hat. Snaps glumly:*] Billy arrived yet?

CURTISS: Yes, sir.

BRECKENRIDGE: [*Advancing toward* FLEMING *with a broad smile*] Well, Harvey! Greetings and welcome. Harvey, I want you to meet—

FLEMING: [*Nods curtly in the general direction of* BRECKENRIDGE *and* SERGE] Hello. [*To* CURTISS] Where's Billy's room?

CURTISS: This way, sir.

[FLEMING *exits with him through door Right, without a glance at the others*]

SERGE: [*A little indignant*] But what is the matter?

BRECKENRIDGE: You mustn't mind him, Serge. He is a very unhappy man. [*Looks impatiently in the direction of the music*] I do wish Tony would stop playing.

SERGE: It is so sad, this piece. It is not appropriate today.

BRECKENRIDGE: Ask him to stop, will you?

[SERGE *exits Right while* BRECKENRIDGE *continues rearranging the room. The music stops.* SERGE *returns, followed by* TONY GODDARD. TONY *is young, tall, slender, modestly dressed, and a little high-strung, which he does his best to conceal.* BRECKENRIDGE *speaks gaily:*]

Did you notice that there's a phonograph right by the piano, Tony? Why didn't you put on a record by Egon Richter? He plays that piece ever so much better.

TONY: It *was* the record.

BRECKENRIDGE: Well, well! That's one on me.

TONY: I know you don't like to hear me playing.

BRECKENRIDGE: I? Why shouldn't I, Tony?

TONY: I'm sorry. . . . [*Indifferently, but not at all offensively*] Have I wished you a happy birthday, Mr. Breckenridge?

BRECKENRIDGE: Yes, of course you have. When you arrived. Why, Tony! How unflattering!

TONY: Guess I shouldn't have asked. Makes it worse. I always do things like that.

BRECKENRIDGE: Anything wrong, Tony?

TONY: No. No. [*Listlessly*] Where are our host and hostess?

BRECKENRIDGE: [*With a broad smile*] They haven't arrived.

TONY: Not yet?

BRECKENRIDGE: No.

TONY: Isn't that rather peculiar?

BRECKENRIDGE: Why, no. Mrs. Dawson asked me to take care of everything—it was very kind of her, she wanted so much to please me.

SERGE: It is unusual, no?—your preparing the party for your own birthday in the house of somebody else?

BRECKENRIDGE: Oh, the Dawsons are old friends of mine—and they insisted that they wanted to give the party and give it here.

TONY: Well, the house isn't old. It doesn't look as if they'd ever lived in it.

BRECKENRIDGE: It was built very recently.

STEVE INGALLS: [*From the top of the stairway*] And in very bad taste.

[INGALLS *is a man of about forty, tall and lean, with a hard, inscrutable face. He looks like a man who should have great energy—and his appearance is a contrast to his manner and movements: slow, lazy, casual, indifferent. He wears simple sports clothes. He comes lazily down the stairs, while* BRECKENRIDGE *speaks sharply, looking up at him:*]

BRECKENRIDGE: Was that necessary, Steve?

INGALLS: Not at all. They could have chosen a better architect.

BRECKENRIDGE: That's not what I meant.

INGALLS: Don't be obvious, Walter. Was there ever a time when I didn't know what you meant? [*To* TONY] Hello, Tony. You here, too? As was to be expected. Sacrificial offerings—needed at one's birthday party.

SERGE: [*Stiffly*] It is *Mr. Breckenridge's* birthday party.

INGALLS: So it is.

SERGE: If you think you—

BRECKENRIDGE: Please, Serge. Really, Steve, do let's drop the personal remarks just for today, shall we? Particularly about the house and particularly when the Dawsons arrive.

INGALLS: When or if?

BRECKENRIDGE: What do you mean?

INGALLS: And another thing, Walter, is that you always know what I mean.

BRECKENRIDGE: [*Does not answer. Then looks impatiently at door Right*] I wish they'd bring Billy out. What is he doing there with Harvey? [*Goes to ring bell*]

TONY: Who else is coming?

BRECKENRIDGE: We're almost all here, except Adrienne. I've sent the car to meet Helen.

SERGE: Adrienne? It is not perhaps Miss Adrienne Knowland?

BRECKENRIDGE: Yes.

[CURTISS *enters Right*]

CURTISS: Yes, sir?

BRECKENRIDGE: Please tell Mr. Kozinsky to bring Billy out here.

CURTISS: Yes, sir. [*Exits Right*]

SERGE: It is not the great Adrienne Knowland?

INGALLS: There's only one Adrienne Knowland, Serge. But the adjective is optional.

SERGE: Oh, I am so happy that I should meet her in the person! I have seen her in that so beautiful play— *Little Women.* I have wondered so often what she is like in the real life. I have thought she must be sweet and lovely—like Mademoiselle Shirley Temple in the cinema, when I was a little boy in Moscow.

INGALLS: Yeah?

BRECKENRIDGE: Please, Steve. We know you don't like Adrienne, but couldn't you control it for just a few hours?

[HARVEY FLEMING *enters Right and holds the door open for* FLASH KOZINSKY, *who comes in pushing* BILLY BRECKENRIDGE *in a wheelchair.* BILLY *is a boy of fifteen, pale, thin, strangely quiet and a little too well-mannered.* FLASH *does not carry a college pennant, but "football hero" is written all over him as plainly as if he did. He is young, husky, pleasant-looking, and not too bright. As he wheels the chair in, he bumps it against the doorjamb*]

FLEMING: Careful, you clumsy fool!

BILLY: It's all right . . . Mr. Fleming.

BRECKENRIDGE: Well, Billy! Feel rested after the trip?

BILLY: Yes, Father.

INGALLS: Hello, Bill.

BILLY: Hello, Steve.

FLASH: [*Turns to* FLEMING. *It has taken all this time to penetrate*] Say, you can't talk to me like that!

FLEMING: Huh?

FLASH: Who are you to talk to me like that?

FLEMING: Skip it.

BRECKENRIDGE: [*Indicating* SERGE] Billy, you remember Mr. Sookin?

BILLY: How do you do, Mr. Sookin.

SERGE: Good afternoon, Billy. Feeling better, no? You look wonderful.

FLEMING: He looks like hell.

BILLY: I'm all right.

SERGE: You are not comfortable maybe? This pillow it is not right. [*Adjusts the pillow behind* BILLY'*s head*] So! It is better?

BILLY: Thank you.

SERGE: I think the footrest it should be higher. [*Adjusts the footrest*] So?

BILLY: Thank you.

SERGE: I think perhaps it is a little chilly. You want I should bring the warm shawl?

BILLY: [*Very quietly*] Leave me alone, will you please?

BRECKENRIDGE: There, there! Billy's just a little nervous. The trip was too much for him—in his condition.

[FLEMING *walks brusquely to the sideboard and starts pouring himself a glass of whiskey*]

BILLY: [*His eyes following* FLEMING *anxiously, his voice low and almost pleading*] Don't do that, Mr. Fleming.

FLEMING: [*Looks at him, then puts the bottle down. Quietly:*] Okay, kid.

SERGE: [*To* BRECKENRIDGE, *in what he intends to be a whisper*] Your poor son, how long he has this paralysis?

BRECKENRIDGE: Sh-sh.

BILLY: Six years and four months, Mr. Sookin.

[*There is a moment of embarrassed silence.* FLASH *looks from one face to another, then bursts out suddenly and loudly:*]

FLASH: Well, I don't know what the rest of you think, but I think Mr. Sookin shouldn't've asked that.

FLEMING: Keep still.

FLASH: Well, *I* think—

[*There is a frightening screech of brakes offstage and the sound of a car being stopped violently. A car door is slammed with a bang and a lovely, husky feminine voice yells: "Goddamn it!"*]

INGALLS: [*With a courtly gesture of introduction in the direction of the sound*] There's Mademoiselle Shirley Temple . . . !

[*The entrance door flies open as* ADRIENNE KNOWLAND *enters without ringing. She is as great a contrast to the conception of a Shirley Temple or of* Little Women *as can be imagined. She is a woman of about twenty-eight, beautiful and completely unconcerned about her beauty, with sharp, angular movements and a tense,*

*restless energy. Her clothes are simple and tailored,
such as a woman would wear for a walk in the country,
not the kind one would expect from a glamorous actress. She carries a small suitcase. She enters like a gust
of wind and whirls upon* BRECKENRIDGE]

ADRIENNE: Walter! Why in hell do they have a horse
running loose out there?

BRECKENRIDGE: Adrienne, my dear! How do you—

TONY: [*At the same time*] A *horse*?

ADRIENNE: A horse. Hello, Tony. Why do they have a
horse cavorting in the middle of the driveway? I almost killed the damn beast and I think I should have.

BRECKENRIDGE: I'm so sorry, my dear. Somebody's care-
lessness. I shall give orders to—

ADRIENNE: [*Forgetting him entirely, to* FLEMING] Hello,
Harvey. Where have you been hiding yourself lately?
Hello, Bill, old pal. I really came here just to see you
again. Hello, Flash.

BRECKENRIDGE: Adrienne, my dear, may I present Serge
Sookin, a new and very dear friend of mine?

ADRIENNE: How do you do, Mr. Sookin.

SERGE: [*Clicking his heels and bowing*] I am honored,
Miss Knowland.

ADRIENNE: [*Looking at the room*] Well, I think this place
is—[*Her glance stops on* INGALLS, *who is standing
aside. She throws at him curtly, as an afterthought:*]
Hello, Steve. [*She turns away from him before he has
had time to complete his bow*] I think this place is—
what one would expect it to be.

BRECKENRIDGE: Would you like to see your room, my
dear?

ADRIENNE: No hurry. [*Tears her hat off and tosses it halfway across the room. To* FLASH, *indicating her suitcase:*] Flash, be an angel and take my stuff out of the
way, will you? [FLASH *exits up the stairs with the suitcase.* ADRIENNE *walks to sideboard and pours herself a
drink*] Incidentally, where's the host?

BRECKENRIDGE: Mr. and Mrs. Dawson are not here yet.

ADRIENNE: Not here? That's a new one in etiquette. Oh,
and yes, of course, happy birthday.

BRECKENRIDGE: Thank you, my dear.

ADRIENNE: How's the infernal machine?

BRECKENRIDGE: The what?

ADRIENNE: The gadget with cosmic rays that the papers have been yelping about.

BRECKENRIDGE: The papers might do some real yelping about it soon. Very soon.

TONY: I heard it's really a colossal invention, Adrienne.

ADRIENNE: Another one? I think it's outrageous—the amount of space that the Breckenridge Laboratories have always managed to hog in the newspapers. But then, Walter has a genius for not remaining unnoticed. Like a stripteaser.

INGALLS: Or an actress.

ADRIENNE: [*Whirls to him, then away, and repeats calmly, her voice a little hard*] Or an actress.

SERGE: [*Breaks the uncomfortable little silence, speaking hotly and with a defiant sort of respect*] The stage—it is a great art. It helps such as suffer and are poor, all the misery and the sadness it makes forget for the few hours. The theater—it is the noble work of the humanitarianism.

ADRIENNE: [*Looks at him very coldly, then turns to* BRECKENRIDGE *and says dryly:*] Congratulations, Walter.

BRECKENRIDGE: What?

ADRIENNE: Your very dear friend is a real find, isn't he? Out of what gutter did you pick him up?

SERGE: [*Stiffly*] Miss Knowland . . .!

ADRIENNE: But, sweetheart, there's no need to look so Russian about it. I meant it in the nicest way. Besides, it goes for me, too, and for all of us here. We were all picked up by Walter out of one gutter or another. That's why he's a great man.

SERGE: I do not understand.

ADRIENNE: You didn't know? But it's no secret. I was singing in a dive, just one step better than a cat house—not a very long step—when Walter discovered me, and he built the Breckenridge Theater. Tony here is studying medicine—on a Breckenridge scholarship. Harvey has nothing but Breckenridge cash between him and the Bowery Mission—only nobody would let him into the Mission, just as nobody will give him a job, because he drinks. That's all right, Harvey—I do, too, at times. Billy here—

TONY: For God's sake, Adrienne!

ADRIENNE: But we're among friends. We're all in the same boat, aren't we? Except Steve, of course. Steve is a special case and the less you know about him, the better.

BRECKENRIDGE: Adrienne, my dear, we know you have a wonderful sense of humor, but why overdo it?

ADRIENNE: Oh, I just thought I'd initiate your Volga Boatman here. He's joining the brotherhood, isn't he? He's got all the earmarks.

SERGE: It is very strange, all this, Miss Knowland, but I think it is beautiful.

ADRIENNE: [*Dryly*] It is very beautiful.

[FLASH *comes back down the stairs*]

SERGE: And it is the noble thing—the Breckenridge Theater in the so very vile Fourteenth Street, for the poor people to see the drama. The art brought to the masses, as it should. I have often wondered how Mr. Breckenridge can do it, with the such low prices of the tickets.

INGALLS: He can't. The noble thing costs him a hundred thousand dollars a season, out of his own pocket.

SERGE: Miss Knowland?

INGALLS: No, Serge. Not Miss Knowland. The theater. That would have been much more sensible. But Walter never asks anything in return. He discovered her, he built the theater for her, he made her the star of Fourteenth Street, he made her famous—in fact, he made her in every sense but the proper one. Which is outrageous, when you look at Adrienne.

BRECKENRIDGE: Really, Steve!

SERGE: [*To* INGALLS] You are not able to understand the unselfish action?

INGALLS: No.

SERGE: You do not have the feeling that it is beautiful?

INGALLS: I've never had any beautiful feelings, Serge.

SERGE: [*To* ADRIENNE] I shall beg your forgiveness, Miss Knowland, since the person who should do so will not.

BRECKENRIDGE: Don't take Steve too seriously, Serge. He's not really as rotten as he sounds at times.

SERGE: By us in Moscow, a gentleman does not insult an artist.

BRECKENRIDGE: Oh, no matter what Steve says, he's always attended her every opening night.

ADRIENNE: [*It is almost a scream*] He . . . *what*?

BRECKENRIDGE: Didn't you know it? Steve's always been there, at every opening of yours—though I never caught him applauding, but the others made up for it; you've never lacked applause, have you, my dear?

ADRIENNE: [*She has been looking at* INGALLS *all through* BRECKENRIDGE's *speech. She asks, still looking at* IN-GALLS:] Walter . . . with whom?

BRECKENRIDGE: I beg your pardon?

ADRIENNE: With whom did he come to my openings?

BRECKENRIDGE: How can one ever ask "with whom" about Steve? Alone, of course.

ADRIENNE: [*To* INGALLS, *her voice trembling with anger*] You didn't see me in *Little Women*, did you?

INGALLS: Oh, yes, my dear, I did. You were very sweet and very coy. Particularly the way you let your hands flutter about. Like butterflies.

ADRIENNE: Steve, you didn't—

INGALLS: Yes, I did. I saw you in *Peter Pan*. You have beautiful legs. I saw you in *Daughter of the Slums*— very touching when you died of unemployment. I saw you in *The Yellow Ticket*.

ADRIENNE: Goddamn you, you didn't see *that*!

INGALLS: I did.

TONY: But, Adrienne, why are you so upset about it? Your greatest hits.

ADRIENNE: [*She has not even heard* TONY] Why did you go to my openings?

INGALLS: Well, my dear, there could be two explanations: either I'm a masochist or I wanted material for a conversation such as this.

[*He turns away from her, the conversation ended, as*

far as he's concerned. There is a silence. Then FLASH *says loudly:*]

FLASH: Well, I don't know about you all, but I don't think it was a nice conversation.

TONY: [*As* FLEMING *is about to snap at* FLASH] Never mind, Harvey. I'll kill him for you one of these days.

FLEMING: Why in hell should Billy have a moron for a tutor?

BRECKENRIDGE: And why, may I ask, should you exhibit public concern about Billy's tutors, Harvey?

[FLEMING *looks at him, then steps back, somehow defeated*]

FLASH: [*Belligerently*] Whom you calling a moron, huh? Whom?

FLEMING: You.

FLASH: [*Taken aback*] Oh. . . .

BILLY: Father, could I please be taken back to my room?

BRECKENRIDGE: Why, I didn't think you'd want to miss the party, Billy. However, if you prefer—

BILLY: [*Indifferently*] No. It's all right. I'll stay here.

[*Doorbell rings*]

TONY: The Dawsons?

BRECKENRIDGE: [*Mysteriously*] Yes, I think it's time for the Dawsons.

[CURTISS *enters Right and crosses to open the door.* HELEN BRECKENRIDGE *enters. She is a woman of about thirty-six, tall, blond, exquisitely groomed. She is the perfect lady in the best sense of the word and she looks like the picture of a perfect wife who has always been perfectly cared for. She carries a small gift package*]

HELEN: [*Astonished*] Why, Curtiss! What are *you* doing here?

CURTISS: [*Bowing*] Good afternoon, madam.

BRECKENRIDGE: Helen, my dear! [*Kisses her on the cheek*] What a pleasant surprise to see you enter! As a matter of fact, it's always a surprise to me. I can't get used to it—not after sixteen years of married life.

HELEN: [*Smiling*] Too nice, Walter, much too nice. [*To the others*] Shall I say "hello" collectively? I'm afraid I'm late and last, as usual.

[*The others answer ad-lib greetings.* CURTISS *whispers something to* BRECKENRIDGE, *who nods.* CURTISS *exits Right*]

HELEN: [*To* BILLY] How do you feel, dear? Was the trip too hard?

BILLY: It was all right.

HELEN: I really don't quite see why I wasn't allowed to come down with you.

BRECKENRIDGE: [*Smiling*] There was a reason, my dear.

HELEN: I had a perfectly beastly time getting away from the city. I envy you, Steve—living right here in Connecticut. You have no idea of the traffic on a holiday eve. Besides, I had to stop at a bookstore—and why is it that they never seem to have any clerks in bookstores? [*To* BRECKENRIDGE, *indicating her package*] I bought *How Deep the Shadows* for Mrs. Dawson. Mrs. Dawson has such a regrettable taste in books. But it was so nice of her—giving this party.

INGALLS: Too nice, Helen, much too nice.

HELEN: Not if it got you out of that laboratory of yours. How long since you last attended a party, Steve?

INGALLS: I'm not sure. Maybe a year.

HELEN: Maybe two?

INGALLS: Possible.

HELEN: But I'm being terribly rude. Shouldn't I say hello to our hostess? Where is our hostess?

[*Nobody answers. Then* BRECKENRIDGE *steps forward*]

BRECKENRIDGE: [*His voice gay and solemn at once*] Helen, my dear, *that is* my surprise. *You* are the hostess. [*She looks at him without understanding*] You have always wanted a house in the country. This is it. It's yours. I had it built for you. [*She stares at him, frozen*] Why, my dear, what's the matter?

HELEN: [*A smile coming very slowly—and not too naturally—to her face*] I . . . I'm just . . . speechless . . . Walter. [*The smile improving*] You can't expect me not to be a little—overwhelmed, can you? . . . And I haven't even thanked you yet. I'm late again. I'm always too late. . . . [*She looks about, a little helplessly, notices the package in her hand*] Well . . . well, I guess I'll have to read *How Deep the Shadows* myself. It serves me right.

BRECKENRIDGE: I am fifty years old today, Helen. Fifty. It's a long time. Half a century. And I was just . . . just vain and human enough to want to mark the occasion. Not for myself—but for others. How can we ever leave a mark—except upon others? This is my gift—to you.

HELEN: Walter . . . when did you start building it . . . this house?

BRECKENRIDGE: Oh, almost a year ago. Think of what I've spared you: all the bother and trouble and arguments with architects and contractors, and shopping for furniture and kitchen ranges and bathroom fixtures. Let me tell you, it's a headache and a heartache.

HELEN: Yes, Walter. You have never let me be exposed to a headache or a heartache. You have been very kind. . . . Well . . . well, I hardly know where to begin . . . if I'm to be hostess—

BRECKENRIDGE: Everything's taken care of, my dear. Curtiss is here, and Mrs. Pudget is in the kitchen, the dinner is ordered, the drinks are ready, even the soap is in the bathrooms. I wanted you to come and find the party complete—from guests to ashtrays. I planned it that way. I don't want you to exert yourself at all.

HELEN: Well, I suppose that's that. . . .

BRECKENRIDGE: [*Turning to* BILLY] And, Billy, I wouldn't forget *you* today. Did you see—from the window of your room—that horse out on the lawn?

BILLY: Yes, Father.

BRECKENRIDGE: Well, it's yours. That's *your* present.

[*There's a little gasp—from* ADRIENNE]

HELEN: [*With shocked reproach*] *Really,* Walter!

BRECKENRIDGE: But why are you all looking at me like that? Don't you understand? If Billy concentrates on how much he would like to be able to ride that horse—it will help him to get well. It will give him a concrete objective for a healthy mental attitude.

BILLY: Yes, Father. Thank you very much, Father.

FLEMING: [*Screams suddenly, to* BRECKENRIDGE] Goddamn you! You dirty bastard! You lousy, rotten sadist! You—

INGALLS: [*Seizing him as he swings out at* BRECKENRIDGE] Easy, Harvey. Take it easy.

BRECKENRIDGE: [*After a pause, very gently*] Harvey . . . [*The kindness of his tone makes* FLEMING *cringe, almost visibly*] I'm sorry, Harvey, that I should be the cause of your feeling as ashamed as you will feel later.

FLEMING: [*After a pause, dully*] I apologize, Walter. . . . [*He turns abruptly, walks to sideboard, pours himself a drink, swallows it, refills the glass. No one is looking at him, except* BILLY]

BRECKENRIDGE: It's all right. I understand. I'm your friend, Harvey. I've always been your friend.

[*Silence*]

FLASH: Well, *I* think Mr. Fleming is drunk.

[CURTISS *enters with a tray bearing filled cocktail glasses*]

BRECKENRIDGE: [*Brightly*] I think Mr. Fleming has the right idea—for the moment. It's time we all had a drink.

[CURTISS *passes the cocktails to the guests. When he comes to* ADRIENNE *he stands waiting politely. She is lost in thought and does not notice him*]

Adrienne, my dear . . .

ADRIENNE: [*With a little jerk of returning to reality*] What? [*Sees* CURTISS] Oh . . . [*Takes a glass absently*]

BRECKENRIDGE: [*Taking the last glass, stands solemnly facing the others*] My friends! Not I, but *you* are to be honored today. Not what I have been, but those whom I have served. You—all of you—are the justification of my existence—for help to one's fellow men is the only justification of anyone's existence. That is why I

chose you as my guests today. That is why we shall
drink a toast—not to me, but—[*Raising his glass*]—to
you, my friends! [*Drinks. The others stand silently*]

SERGE: I would so very much like to give the toast
also, please?

BRECKENRIDGE: If you wish, Serge.

SERGE: [*Fervently*] To the man who has his life devoted
so that the other men's lives should be better. To the
man the genius of whom to the world gave the machine for the Vitamin X separating, which little babies
makes so healthier. To the man who the new violet-
ray diffuser gave us, so cheaper that the poor people
in the slums the sunlight could have. To the man who
the electric saw for the surgery invented, which so
many lives has saved. To the friend of the mankind—
Walter Breckenridge!

INGALLS: Sure. Walter's invented everything but a bust
developer for social workers.

FLASH: *I* think that's in bad taste.

ADRIENNE: [*Rising*] And now that we've done our duty,
may I go up to my room, Walter?

BRECKENRIDGE: Wait, Adrienne, do you mind? There's
something I want you all to hear. [*To the others*] My
friends, I have an announcement to make. It is important. I want you to be the first to hear it.

INGALLS: More gifts?

BRECKENRIDGE: Yes, Steve. One more gift. My greatest—
and my last. [*To the others*] My friends! You have
heard of the invention on which I have worked for
the last ten years—the one Adrienne referred to so
charmingly as a "gadget." There has been quite a
great deal of mystery about it—unavoidably, as you
shall see. It is a device to capture the energy of cosmic
rays. You may have heard that cosmic rays possess a
tremendous potential of energy, which scientists have
struggled to harness for years and years. I was fortu-
nate enough to find the secret of it—with Steve's able
assistance, of course. I have been asked so often
whether the device is completed. I have refused to
answer. But I can say it now: it is completed. It is
tried, tested, and proved beyond doubt. Its possibilities
are tremendous. [*Pauses. Continues, very simply, al-*

most wearily:] Tremendous. And its financial promises are unlimited. [*Stops*]

INGALLS: Well?

BRECKENRIDGE: Well . . . My friends, a man controlling such an invention and keeping its secret could be rich. *Rich.* But I am not going to keep it. [*Pauses, looks at them, then says slowly:*] Tomorrow, at twelve o'clock noon, I shall give this invention to mankind. *Give,* not sell it. For all and any to use. Without charge. To all mankind. [TONY *emits a long whistle.* FLASH *stands with his mouth hanging open, and utters only one awed:* "*Gee!*"] Think what that will do. Free power—drawn out of space. It will light the poorest slum and the shack of the sharecropper. It will throw the greedy utility companies out of business. It will be mankind's greatest blessing. And no one will hold private control over it.

ADRIENNE: Beautiful showmanship, Walter. You've always been a master of the theater.

TONY: But I suppose it *is* sort of grand—

ADRIENNE:—opera.

HELEN: What exactly is to happen tomorrow at noon, Walter?

BRECKENRIDGE: I have invited the press to be at the laboratory tomorrow at noon. I shall give them the blueprints—the formulas—everything—to spread in every tabloid.

ADRIENNE: Don't forget the Sunday magazine sections.

BRECKENRIDGE: Adrienne, my dear, surely you don't disapprove?

ADRIENNE: What's it to me?

SERGE: Ah, but it is so beautiful! It is an example for the whole world to follow. To me Mr. Breckenridge has spoken about this gift many weeks ago and I said: "Mr. Breckenridge, if you do this, I will be proud a human being to be!"

BRECKENRIDGE: [*Turning to* INGALLS] Steve?

INGALLS: What?

BRECKENRIDGE: What do you say?

INGALLS: I? Nothing.

BRECKENRIDGE: Of course, Steve doesn't quite approve. Steve is rather . . . old-fashioned. He would have preferred to keep the whole thing secret in our own hands, and to make a tremendous fortune. Wouldn't you, Steve?

INGALLS: [*Lazily*] Oh, yes. I like to make money. I think money is a wonderful thing. I don't see what's wrong with making a fortune—if you deserve it and people are willing to pay for what you offer them. Besides, I've never liked things that are given away. When you get something for nothing—you always find a string attached somewhere. Like the fish when it swallows the worm. But then, I've never had any noble feelings.

SERGE: Mr. Ingalls, that is contemptible!

INGALLS: Cut it, Serge. You bore me.

BRECKENRIDGE: But, Steve, I want you to understand why—

INGALLS: Don't waste your time, Walter. I've never understood the noble, the selfless, or any of those things. Besides, it's not my fortune you're giving away. It's yours. I'm only a junior partner. All I lose is two bits to your dollar. So I'm not going to argue about it.

BRECKENRIDGE: I'm glad, Steve. I made this decision after a great deal of time and meditation.

INGALLS: You did? [*Rises*] You know, Walter, I think decisions are made quickly. And the more important the step—the quicker. [*Walks to stairs*]

SERGE: [*With a little touch of triumph*] I begged Mr. Breckenridge to do this.

INGALLS: [*Stops on the stairs on his way up, looks at him. Then:*] I know you did. [*Exits up the stairs*]

HELEN: [*Rising*] It seems so foolish to ask this—when I'm hostess—but what time is dinner ordered for, Walter?

BRECKENRIDGE: Seven o'clock.

HELEN: Would you mind if I took a look at what my house is like?

BRECKENRIDGE: But of course! How thoughtless of me! Holding you here—when you must be dying of curiosity.

HELEN: [*To the others*] Shall we make an inspection tour together? The hostess needs someone to guide her.

TONY: I'll show you. I've been all through the house. The laundry in the basement is wonderful.

HELEN: Shall we start with Billy's room?

BILLY: Yes, please, Mother. I want to go back to my room.

[*As* FLEMING *and* FLASH *are wheeling* BILLY *out, Right,* BRECKENRIDGE *is about to follow*]

ADRIENNE: Walter. I'd like to speak to you. [BRECKENRIDGE *stops, frowning*] For just a few minutes.
BRECKENRIDGE: Yes, of course, my dear.

[HELEN *and* TONY *exit after* BILLY, FLEMING, *and* FLASH. SERGE *remains*]

ADRIENNE: Serge, when you hear someone say to someone else: "I'd like to speak to you"—it usually means *"alone."*
SERGE: Ah, but of course! I am so sorry, Miss Knowland! [*Bows and exits Right*]
BRECKENRIDGE: [*Sitting down and indicating a chair*] Yes, my dear?
ADRIENNE: [*She remains standing, looking at him. After a moment, she says in a flat, hard, expressionless voice:*] Walter, I want you to release me from my contract.
BRECKENRIDGE: [*Leans back. Then:*] You're not serious, my dear.
ADRIENNE: Walter, please. Please don't make me say too much. I can't tell you how serious I am.
BRECKENRIDGE: But I thought it was understood, a year ago, that we would not discuss that subject again.
ADRIENNE: And I've stuck it out, haven't I? For another whole year. I've tried. Walter. I can't go on.
BRECKENRIDGE: You are not happy?
ADRIENNE: Don't make me say anything else.
BRECKENRIDGE: But I don't understand. I—
ADRIENNE: Walter. I'm trying so hard not to have another scene like last year. Don't ask me any questions. Just say that you will release me.
BRECKENRIDGE: [*After a pause*] If I released you, what would you do?
ADRIENNE: That play I showed you last year.
BRECKENRIDGE: For a commercial producer?

ADRIENNE: Yes.

BRECKENRIDGE: For a cheap, vulgar, commercial Broadway producer?

ADRIENNE: For the cheapest and most vulgar one I could find.

BRECKENRIDGE: Let's see. If I remember correctly, your part would be that of a very objectionable young woman who wants to get rich, who drinks and swears and—

ADRIENNE: [*Coming to life*] And how she swears! And she sleeps with men! And she's ambitious! And she's selfish! And she laughs! And she's not sweet— Oh, Walter! She's not sweet at all!

BRECKENRIDGE: You're overestimating yourself, my dear. You can't play a part like that.

ADRIENNE: Maybe not. I'll try.

BRECKENRIDGE: You want a disastrous flop?

ADRIENNE: Perhaps. I'll take the chance.

BRECKENRIDGE: You want to be panned?

ADRIENNE: Perhaps. If I have to be.

BRECKENRIDGE: And your audience? What about your audience? [*She doesn't answer*] What about the people who love you and respect you for what you represent to them?

ADRIENNE: [*Her voice flat and dead again*] Walter, skip that. *Skip that.*

BRECKENRIDGE: But you seem to have forgotten. The Breckenridge Theater is not a mere place of amusement. It was not created just to satisfy your exhibitionism or my vanity. It has a social mission. It brings cheer to those who need it most. It gives them what they like. They need you. They get a great deal from you. You have a duty and a standing above those of a mere actress. Isn't that precious to you?

ADRIENNE: Oh, Goddamn you! [*He stares at her*] All right! You asked for it! I hate it! Do you hear me? I hate it! All of it! Your noble theater and your noble plays and all the cheap, trite, trashy, simpering bromides that are so sweet! So sweet! God, so sweet I can hear them grating on my teeth every evening! I'm going to scream in the middle of one of those noble speeches, some night, and bring the curtain down! I can't go on with it, Goddamn you and your audience! I can't! Do you understand me? I can't!

BRECKENRIDGE: Adrienne, my child, I cannot let you ruin yourself.

ADRIENNE: Listen, Walter, please listen. . . . I'll try to explain it. I'm not ungrateful. I want the audience to like me. But that's not enough. Just to do what they want me to do, just because they like it—it's not enough. I've got to like it, too. I've got to believe in what I'm doing. I've got to be proud of it. You can't do any kind of work without that. That comes first. Then you take a chance—and hope that others will like it.

BRECKENRIDGE: Isn't that rather selfish?

ADRIENNE: [*Simply*] I guess it is. I guess I'm selfish. It's selfish to breathe, also—isn't it? You don't breathe for anyone but yourself. . . . All I want is a chance—for myself—to do something strong, living, intelligent, difficult—just once.

BRECKENRIDGE: [*Sadly*] I believed in you, Adrienne. I did my best for you.

ADRIENNE: I know. And I hate to hurt you. That's why I've stood it for such a long time. But, Walter, the contract—it's for five more years. I couldn't take five years. I couldn't even take it for five days this coming season. I've reached my last minute—it's very terrible, when a person is driven to his last minute, and very ugly. You must let me go.

BRECKENRIDGE: Who's been talking to you? Steve's influence?

ADRIENNE: Steve? You know what I think of Steve. When would I talk to him? When do I ever see him?

BRECKENRIDGE: [*Shrugging*] It just sounds like him.

ADRIENNE: Do you know what made me speak to you today? That stupendous thing you announced. I thought . . . you're doing so much for humanity, and yet . . . why is it that the people who worry most about mankind have the least concern for any actual human being?

BRECKENRIDGE: My dear, try to understand. I'm acting for your own good. I can't let you ruin your career.

ADRIENNE: Let me go, Walter. Give me my freedom.

BRECKENRIDGE: Freedom—for what? Freedom to hurt yourself.

ADRIENNE: Yes!—if necessary. To make mistakes. To fail. To be alone. To be rotten. To be selfish. But to be free.

BRECKENRIDGE: [*Rising*] No, Adrienne.

ADRIENNE: [*In a dead, flat voice*] Walter . . . do you remember . . . last summer . . . when I ran my car into a tree? . . . Walter, it was not an accident. . . .

BRECKENRIDGE: [*Severely*] I refuse to understand what you mean. You're being indecent.

ADRIENNE: [*Screams*] Goddamn you! Goddamn you, you rotten, holy, saintly bastard!

INGALLS: [*Appearing at the top of the stairs*] You'll ruin your voice, Adrienne—and you won't be able to do *Little Women* again.

[ADRIENNE *whirls around and stops short*]

BRECKENRIDGE: [*As* INGALLS *comes down the stairs*] I believe this is the kind of performance you'll enjoy, Steve. So I'll leave Adrienne to you. You'll find you have a great deal in common. [*Exits Right*]

INGALLS: The acoustics in this room are great, Adrienne. Does wonders for your diaphragm—and your vocabulary.

ADRIENNE: [*Stands looking at him with hatred*] Listen, you. I have something to tell you. Now. I don't care. If you want to make wisecracks, I'll give you something real to wisecrack about.

INGALLS: Go ahead.

ADRIENNE: I know what you think of me—and you're right. I'm just a lousy ham who's done nothing but trash all her life. I'm no better than a slut—not because I haven't any talent, but worse: because I have and sold it. Not even for money, but for someone's stupid, drooling kindness—and I'm more contemptible than an honest whore!

INGALLS: That's a pretty accurate description.

ADRIENNE: Well, that's what I am. I know also what you are. You're a hard, cold, ruthless egoist. You're just a laboratory machine—all chromium and stainless steel. You're as efficient and bright and vicious as a car going ninety miles an hour. Only the car would bump if it ran over someone's body. You wouldn't. You wouldn't even know it. You're going ninety miles every one of the twenty-four hours—through a desert island, as far as you're concerned. A desert island full of charts, blueprints, coils, tubes, and batteries. You've never known a human emotion. You're worse than any of us. I think you're the rottenest person I've ever met. I'm inexcusably, contemptibly, completely in love with you and have been for years. [*She stops. He stands motionless, looking at her silently. She snaps:*] Well? [*He does not move*] You're not going to pass up a chance like this for one of your brilliant wisecracks? [*He does not move*] Shouldn't you answer—something?

INGALLS: [*His voice is very soft and very earnest. It is the first sound of simple sincerity to be heard from him:*] Adrienne . . . [*She looks at him, astonished*] I am thinking that I haven't heard it. I can't answer. Had you said it to me yesterday—or the day after tomorrow—I'd answer. Today, I can't.

ADRIENNE: Why?

INGALLS: You know, sound vibrations never die in space. Let's think that what you said hasn't reached me yet. It will reach me day after tomorrow. Then—if I'm still able to hear it and if you still want me to hear it—I'll give you my answer.

ADRIENNE: Steve . . . what's the matter?

INGALLS: Day after tomorrow, Adrienne. Perhaps sooner. But if not then—then never.

ADRIENNE: Steve, I don't understa—

INGALLS: [*Picking up a magazine from the table, in his normal, conversational tone*] Have you seen this week's *World*? There's a very interesting article on the progressive income tax. It demonstrates how the tax works for the protection of mediocrity. . . . The problem of taxation, of course, is extremely complex.

ADRIENNE: [*She is turned away from him, her shoulders sagging a little, but she does her best to follow his lead and speaks obediently, in as good an imitation of a conversational tone as she can manage—but her voice sounds very tired*] Yes. I've never been able to figure out an income tax blank or an insurance policy.

[HELEN, BRECKENRIDGE, SERGE, *and* TONY *enter, coming down the stairs*]

INGALLS: Well? What do you think of the house, Helen?

HELEN: [*Without enthusiasm*] It's lovely.

BRECKENRIDGE: [*Proudly*] She couldn't think of one thing that I hadn't thought of already.

INGALLS: As usual.

BRECKENRIDGE: Oh say, I mustn't forget. I'll tell you all while Billy isn't here; it's a little surprise for him. Tonight, at ten o'clock, when it gets dark, I shall give you a demonstration of my invention. Its first public demonstration. We'll start celebrating the Fourth of July tonight, a little in advance. We'll have fireworks—I've had them lined up—[*Points*]—over there, on the other side of the lake. I'll set them off—from the garden—without touching them, without wires, by remote control—by mere electrical impulses through the air.

TONY: Could I see the machine?

BRECKENRIDGE: No, Tony. Nobody can see the machine till tomorrow. Don't try to find it. You won't. But you will all be the first witnesses of its action. [*Shrugs gaily*] Think of it! If someday they make a movie of my life, you will all be impersonated in that scene.

SERGE: They always make the lives of the great men in the cinema.

INGALLS: All that Walter needs now to be a great man is to get assassinated.

HELEN: Steve!

INGALLS: Well, he came pretty close to it once—so I guess that'll have to do.

HELEN: He . . . did what?

INGALLS: Didn't you know that Walter almost got bumped off—about a month ago?

HELEN: [*Aghast*] No! . . .

INGALLS: Oh, yes. Someone's tried to get him. Under very mysterious circumstances, too.

BRECKENRIDGE: Just an accident, probably. Why talk about it?

HELEN: Please tell me, Steve.

INGALLS: There isn't really much to tell. Walter and Serge drove down to Stamford, one evening, and stopped at the

laboratory, and dragged me down here to see the house—
the "Dawsons'" house—it was just being finished then.
Well, the three of us got separated, looking around, and
then I heard a shot—and I saw Walter picking up his hat,
with a hole through it. It was a new hat, too.

HELEN: Oh! . . .

INGALLS: Well, we called the police, and all the building
workers were searched, but we never found the man
who did it or the gun.

HELEN: But it's fantastic! Walter doesn't have an enemy
in the world!

INGALLS: I guess you never can tell.

[FLEMING *enters, Right, goes to sideboard, pours himself a drink, and stands drinking, ignoring the others*]

HELEN: And then?

INGALLS: That's all. . . . Oh, yes, there was another funny
thing. I had a bag in the car—just a small bag with
some old junk in it. When we got back to the car, we
found the lock of that bag broken open. There was
nothing inside that anyone would want, and whoever
did it hadn't even looked inside, because the things
were just as I'd left them, but the lock was broken.
We never figured that out, either.

HELEN: Walter! . . . Why didn't you tell me about this?

BRECKENRIDGE: That is precisely why, dear—so that you
wouldn't be upset, as you are now. Besides, it was
nothing. An accident or a crank. I told Curtiss about
it—told him not to admit any strangers to the house—
but nobody came and nothing happened.

INGALLS: I told Walter that he should carry a gun—just
in case—but he wouldn't do it.

HELEN: But you should, Walter!

BRECKENRIDGE: I do. I got one.

INGALLS: I don't believe it. You know, Walter is afraid
of guns.

BRECKENRIDGE: Nonsense.

INGALLS: You said so yourself.

BRECKENRIDGE: [*Indicating cabinet*] Look in that drawer.

[INGALLS *opens the drawer and takes out the gun*]

INGALLS: You're right—for once. [*Examining the gun*] Nice little job. That will take care of any—emergency.

HELEN: Oh, put it away! I don't like them myself.

[INGALLS *replaces the gun in the drawer and closes it*]

TONY: It doesn't make sense. A man like Mr. Breckenridge—why would anyone—

BRECKENRIDGE: Of course it doesn't make sense. And I don't see why Steve had to bring that up—today of all days. . . . Well, shall we go on to look at the grounds? Wait till you see the grounds, Helen!

HELEN: [*Rising*] Yes, of course.

[FLEMING *swallows another drink and exits Right*]

BRECKENRIDGE: Adrienne, my dear—coming?

ADRIENNE: [*In a flat voice*] Yes.

BRECKENRIDGE: No hard feelings, of course?

ADRIENNE: No.

BRECKENRIDGE: I knew you'd be all right. I wasn't angry. An actress' temper is like a summer storm.

ADRIENNE: Yes.

[*She walks out through the French doors, followed by* BRECKENRIDGE, SERGE, *and* TONY]

HELEN: [*Stops at the French doors, turns*] Coming, Steve?

[*He does not answer and stands looking at her. Then:*]

INGALLS: Helen . . .

HELEN: Yes?

INGALLS: You are not happy, are you?

HELEN: [*With amused reproach*] Steve! That's one of those questions that should never be answered—one way or the other.

INGALLS: I'm asking it only . . . in self-defense.

HELEN: In . . . your *own* defense?

INGALLS: Yes.

HELEN: [*Decisively*] Don't you think we'd better join the others?

INGALLS: No. [*She does not move. She stands looking at him. After a moment, he adds:*] You know what I'm going to say.

HELEN: No. I don't know . . . I don't know. . . . [*Involuntarily*] I don't want to know . . .!

INGALLS: I love you, Helen.

HELEN: [*Trying to be amused*] Really, Steve, we're about ten years too late, aren't we? I'm sure I am. I thought things like that weren't being said anymore. At least . . . not to me. . . .

BRECKENRIDGE'S VOICE: [*Calling from garden*] Helen! . . .

INGALLS: I have wanted to say it for more than ten years.

HELEN: It's too . . . foolish . . . and conventional, isn't it? My husband's partner . . . and . . . and I'm the perfect wife who's always had everything . . .

INGALLS: Have you?

HELEN: . . . and you've never seemed to notice that I existed. . . .

INGALLS: Even if I know it's hopeless—

HELEN: Of course it's hopeless. . . . It . . . it *should* be hopeless. . . . [*There is the sound of voices approaching from the garden.* INGALLS *moves suddenly to take her in his arms*] Steve! . . . Steve, they're coming back! They're—

[*The voices are closer. He stops her words with a violent kiss. Her first movement is to struggle against him, then her body relaxes in surrender, her arms rise to embrace him—very eagerly—just as* ADRIENNE, BRECKENRIDGE, SERGE, *and* TONY *enter from the garden.* HELEN *and* INGALLS *step apart, she shocked, he perfectly calm.* INGALLS *is first to break the silence*]

INGALLS: I've always wanted to know what one really did at such a moment.

SERGE: [*Choking with indignation*] This . . . this . . . it is monstrous! . . . It is unspeakable! . . . It is—

BRECKENRIDGE: [*With great poise*] Now, Serge. No hysterics please. From anyone. Let us act grown-up. [*To* HELEN, *gently*] I'm sorry, Helen. I know this is harder for you than for any of us. I shall try to make it easier, if I can. [*Notices* ADRIENNE, *who looks more stunned and crushed than all the others*] What's the matter, Adrienne?

ADRIENNE: [*Barely able to answer*] Nothing . . . nothing. . . .

BRECKENRIDGE: Steve, I should like to speak to you alone.

INGALLS: I have wanted to speak to you alone, Walter, for a long time.

CURTAIN

SCENE 2

That evening. The room is in semidarkness, with just one lamp burning on a table.

At curtain rise, BRECKENRIDGE *is sitting in an armchair, a little slumped, looking tired and dejected.* SERGE *sits on a low hassock—at a little distance, but almost as if he were sitting at* BRECKENRIDGE'S *feet.*

SERGE: It is terrible. It is too terrible and I am sick. I cannot help that it should make me sick.

BRECKENRIDGE: You're young, Serge. . . .

SERGE: Is it only the young who have the feeling of decency?

BRECKENRIDGE: It is only the young who condemn. . . .

SERGE: At the dinner . . . you were . . . as if nothing had happened. . . . You were magnificent.

BRECKENRIDGE: There's Billy to think about.

SERGE: And now? What is to happen now?

BRECKENRIDGE: Nothing.

SERGE: Nothing?

BRECKENRIDGE: Serge, my position does not allow me to make this public. People believe in me. I cannot have scandal attached to my name. Besides, think what it would do to Helen. Do you suppose I'd do that to her?

SERGE: Mrs. Breckenridge she did not think of you.

BRECKENRIDGE: [*Slowly*] There's something about it that I can't understand. It's unlike Helen. But it's much more unlike Steve.

SERGE: Mr. Ingalls? Of him I expect anything.

BRECKENRIDGE: That's not what I mean, Serge. It

wouldn't surprise me that Steve should be unscrupulous. But that he should be stupid!

SERGE: Stupid?

BRECKENRIDGE: If Steve had wanted to carry on a secret love affair with Helen, he could have done so for years and years, and none of us would ever guess—if he didn't want us to guess. He's clever. He's too terribly clever. But to start . . . to start an embrace in broad daylight—when he knew we'd be back for her any moment—a fool wouldn't do that. *That's* what I can't understand.

SERGE: What did he say when you spoke to him?

BRECKENRIDGE: [*Evasively*] We spoke of . . . many things.

SERGE: I cannot understand that this to *you* should happen! The gratitude it does not exist in the world.

BRECKENRIDGE: Ah, Serge. We must never think of gratitude. We must do what we think is good for our fellow men—and let kindness be its own reward. [FLASH *enters Right, wheeling* BILLY *in, followed by* FLEMING *and* HELEN. BRECKENRIDGE *rises*]

BILLY: You wanted me here, Father?

BRECKENRIDGE: Yes, Billy. Not too tired?

BILLY: No.

BRECKENRIDGE: [*To* HELEN, *indicating his chair*] Sit down, my dear. This is the most comfortable chair in the room. [HELEN *obeys silently.* INGALLS *enters from the garden and remains standing at the French doors*] But why are we sitting in the dark like this? [*Turns more lights on*] Your dress is so light, Helen. It's rather chilly tonight for this time of the year. Are you sure you're not too cold?

HELEN: No.

BRECKENRIDGE: [*Offering her a cigarette box*] Cigarette, my dear?

HELEN: No, thank you.

INGALLS: [*Without moving*] You're exceptionally rotten tonight, Walter. Worse than usual.

BRECKENRIDGE: I beg your pardon? [ADRIENNE *enters, coming down the stairs, but stops and stands watching those below*]

INGALLS: You know what I'd do if I were you? I'd yell

at Helen at the slightest provocation or without any. I'd swear at her. I think I'd slap her.

BRECKENRIDGE: *You* would.

INGALLS: And do you know what the result would be? It would make things easier for her.

HELEN: Please, Steve.

INGALLS: I'm sorry, Helen . . . I'm terribly sorry.

[*Silence.* ADRIENNE *comes down the stairs. At the bottom, she stops: she sees* INGALLS *looking at her. For a moment they stand face to face, holding the glance. Then she turns sharply and goes to sit down alone in a corner of the room*]

FLASH: [*Looking helplessly at everybody*] What the hell is going on in this house?

BRECKENRIDGE: Flash. You are not to swear in Billy's presence.

FLASH: Gee, I beg your pardon. But I feel something. You may not know it, but I'm sensitive.

SERGE: By us in Moscow, things like this would not happen.

INGALLS: [*Casually*] Say, Serge, I heard something interesting today about some compatriots of yours. About the Soviet Culture and Friendship Society.

SERGE: [*Looks at him for a distinct moment, then:*] So? What did you hear?

INGALLS: That the FBI has caught up with them. Seems they're just a front for Soviet espionage in this country. One of the biggest fronts. Heard the FBI has cracked down on them and seized their files.

SERGE: When? That is not true!

INGALLS: Today.

SERGE: I do not believe it!

INGALLS: It ought to be in the papers—by now. I got a tip from my old friend Joe Cheeseman of the New York *Courier*—the *Courier* was first to get the story—he said it would be on their front page this afternoon.

BRECKENRIDGE: Never knew you had friends among the press.

SERGE: Do you have the today's *Courier*?

INGALLS: No.

SERGE: [*To the others*] Has anybody the—

INGALLS: Why are you so interested, Serge? What do you know about the Soviet Culture and Friendship Society?

SERGE: What do I know! A great deal I know! I know for long time they are the Soviet spies. I knew Makarov, their president, in Moscow. He was one of the worst. When I escaped during the World War Number Two . . . That is why I escaped—because the men like him they betrayed the people. They had the noble ideals, but the so cruel methods! They did not believe in God. They lost the spirit of our Holy Mother Russia. They lost our beautiful dream of the brotherhood and the equal sharing and the—

BRECKENRIDGE: Don't talk about it, Serge.

SERGE: All the time I am in this country, I wanted to tell the police what I know about Makarov and the Soviet Culture and Friendship Society. But I could not speak. If I open my mouth . . . [*Shudders*] You see, my family—they are still in Russia. My mother . . . and my sister.

FLASH: Gee, Mr. Sookin! That's awful.

SERGE: But if the Soviet Culture and Friendship it got caught now—I'm glad. I'm so glad! . . . Has anyone the today's *Courier* here? [*All the others answer "No" or shake their heads*] But I must see it! Where can I get the New York newspapers?

BRECKENRIDGE: Nowhere around here—at this hour.

INGALLS: In Stamford, Serge.

SERGE: Ah, yes? Then I will go to Stamford.

BRECKENRIDGE: Oh, but Serge! It's a long drive—three quarters of an hour at the least, there and back.

SERGE: But I so much want to read it tonight.

BRECKENRIDGE: You will miss the . . . the surprise.

SERGE: But you will excuse me, Mr. Breckenridge, no? I will try most quick as I can to be back. Would you permit that I take the car?

BRECKENRIDGE: Certainly, if you insist.

SERGE: [*To* INGALLS] Where do I find the nearest place with the newspapers?

INGALLS: Just follow the road straight to Stamford. The first drugstore you come to—a little place called Lawton's, on the corner, near the Breckenridge Laboratories. They have all the papers. Let's see . . . [*Looks at his watch*] They get the last city editions at ten o'clock. In fifteen minutes. They'll have them by the time you get there. Joe Cheeseman said it would be in today's last edition.

SERGE: Thank you so much. [*To* BRECKENRIDGE] You will please excuse me?

BRECKENRIDGE: Sure. [SERGE *exits Left*]

FLASH: [*As no one seems inclined to talk*] And another thing that bothers me is why nobody ate any dinner tonight. The lobster was wonderful. [*There is the distant sound of a small explosion, and far away, beyond the lake, a rocket rises, bursts in the air and vanishes*]

BRECKENRIDGE: Our neighbors across the lake are celebrating early.

BILLY: I want to see it.

BRECKENRIDGE: You'll see something much bigger than this—in a little while.

[FLASH *turns the wheelchair toward the French doors. Another rocket goes off in the distance.* TONY *enters, Left*]

TONY: Say, where's Serge going in such a hurry? Just saw him driving off.

BRECKENRIDGE: To Stamford. To get a newspaper.

INGALLS: You haven't got today's *Courier* by any chance, have you, Tony?

TONY: The *Courier*? No. [*Hesitates, then:*] Mr. Breckenridge, could I speak to you? For just a moment. I've tried all day—

BRECKENRIDGE: Well, what is it, Tony? What is it?

TONY: It's . . . about Billy. I didn't want to—[*Looks at* BILLY]

FLEMING: About Billy? What?

BRECKENRIDGE: Surely it can't be a secret. Go ahead.

TONY: If you wish. I saw Professor Doyle this morning.

BRECKENRIDGE: Oh, *that*? You're not going to begin again to—

FLEMING: Doyle? That's the doctor who's taking care of Billy?

TONY: Yes. He's my teacher at college.

FLEMING: What did he say?

BRECKENRIDGE: Really, Tony, I thought we had settled—

FLEMING: What did he say?

TONY: [*To* BRECKENRIDGE] He said that I must speak to you and beg you on my knees if I have to. He said that if you don't send Billy to Montreal this summer and let Dr. Harlan perform that operation—Billy will never walk again. [FLEMING *makes a step forward slowly, ominously*]

BRECKENRIDGE: Just a minute, Harvey.

FLEMING: [*In a strange, hoarse voice*] Why didn't you tell me about this?

BRECKENRIDGE: Because I didn't have to.

TONY: Mr. Fleming, it's Billy's last chance. He's almost fifteen now. If we wait longer, the muscles will become atrophied and it will be too late. Professor Doyle said—

BRECKENRIDGE: Did Professor Doyle say also that we'd risk Billy's life in that operation?

TONY: Yes.

BRECKENRIDGE: That's my answer.

HELEN: Walter, please. Please let's reconsider. Professor Doyle said the risk wasn't too great. It's a small chance against . . . against the certainty of being a cripple for life!

BRECKENRIDGE: A small chance is too much—where Billy is concerned. I would rather have Billy as he is than take the risk of losing him.

FLEMING: [*Screams ferociously*] That's going too far, you lousy bastard! You won't get away with this! Goddamn you, not with this! I demand, do you hear me?— I *demand* that you let them do the operation!

BRECKENRIDGE: You demand? By what right? [FLEMING *stands looking at him, helplessness coming almost visibly to his gaunt, slumping figure*]

INGALLS: [*His voice hard*] Do you mind if I don't witness this? [*Turns and exits through the French doors*]

BRECKENRIDGE: I must warn you, Harvey. If we have any more . . . incidents such as this, I shall be forced to forbid you to visit Billy.

HELEN: Oh, no, Walter!

FLEMING: You . . . wouldn't do that, Walter? You . . . you *can't.*

BRECKENRIDGE: You know very well that I can.

BILLY: [*It is the first time that his voice is alive—and desperate*] Father! You won't do *that!* [*As* BRECKENRIDGE *turns to him*] Please, Father. I don't mind anything else. I don't have to have the operation. Only you won't . . . Mr. Fleming, it's all right about the operation. I don't mind.

BRECKENRIDGE: Of course, Billy. And I'm sorry that Harvey upsets you so much. You understand. Anything I do is only for your own good. I wouldn't take a chance on your life with some unproved new method. [*As* HELEN *is about to speak*] And so, Helen, we shall consider the matter closed.

[FLEMING *turns abruptly. On his way to the stairs, he seizes a bottle from the sideboard and exits up the stairs*]

FLASH: Well, I think this is one hell of a birthday party!

BRECKENRIDGE: We mustn't mind poor Harvey. He is an unfortunate case. [*Looks at his watch*] And now we'll turn to a much more cheerful subject. [*Rises*] Billy, my dear, just watch the lake. You'll see some-thing interesting in a few minutes. [*To the others*] Now, please, I don't want anyone to follow me. I don't want anyone to see how it's done. Not till tomor-row. You'll get the best view from here. [*Turns at the French doors*] Who knows? Perhaps what you arc about to see will be of great importance to all mankind. [*Exits through French doors and walks off Right into the garden*]

HELEN: [*Rises suddenly as if with a decision taken, starts toward the stairs, then stops and says to the others, vaguely, as an afterthought:*] You will excuse me, please? . . . [*Exits up the stairs*]

TONY: I'm sorry, Bill. I've tried.

BILLY: It's all right. . . .When you'll be a doctor on your own, Tony, I'll still be . . . like this. And then I'd like you to be my doctor.

TONY: [*With an oddly stressed bitterness*] When I'll be . . . a doctor. . . .

BILLY: Everybody says you'll be a good one. Father says very nice things about you. About your hands, too. He says you have the hands of a great surgeon.

TONY: [*Looks at his hands*] Yes . . . he does . . . doesn't he? [*Turns abruptly to go*]

FLASH: Say, don't you want to see the fireworks?

TONY: Oh, take your fireworks and shove—[*Exits Right*]

FLASH: [*Looking after him with open mouth*] Well, *I* think he meant . . .

ADRIENNE: Yes, Flash. He meant exactly what you think.

[*From offstage Right there comes the sound of Rachmaninoff's Prelude in G Minor played on the piano*]

BILLY: Don't go, Miss Knowland. Everybody's going.

ADRIENNE: I'll stay, Bill. Let's open the doors and turn out the light, we'll see better. [*She turns the light off, while* FLASH *throws the French doors open*]

BILLY: Why does Tony always play such sad things?

ADRIENNE: Because he's very unhappy, Bill.

FLASH: You know, I can't figure it out. Nobody's happy in this house.

BILLY: Father is happy. [*A magnificent rocket rises over the lake, much closer than the ones we've seen, and bursts into showers of stars*]

FLASH: There it goes!

BILLY: Oh! . . . [*The rockets continue at slow intervals*]

FLASH: [*Excitedly, between the sounds of the explosions*] You see, Billy . . . you see . . . that's your father's new invention! . . . It works! . . . Those rockets are set off without any wires . . . without touching them . . . just like that, through space. . . . Imagine? Just some sort of tiny little rays blasting those things to pieces!

ADRIENNE: Lovely precision . . . right on target. . . . What if one chose a larger . . . [*Then, suddenly, she gasps; it is almost a stifled scream*]

FLASH: What's the matter?

ADRIENNE: [*In a strange voice*] I . . . just thought of something. . . . [*She is suddenly panicky, as she makes a movement to rush out, stops helplessly before the vast darkness of the garden, whirls around to ask:*] Where's Walter? Where did he go?

FLASH: I don't know. We're not supposed to follow him.

ADRIENNE: Where's Steve?

FLASH: Don't know. I think he went out.

ADRIENNE: [*Screaming into the garden*] Steve! . . . Steve! . . .

FLASH: He won't hear you. This place is so big, there's miles and miles to the grounds, you can't find anybody out there at night.

ADRIENNE: I've got to—

BILLY: Look, Miss Knowland! *Look!*

[*The fireworks are now forming letters, high over the lake, taking shape gradually, one tiny dot of light after another. The letters spell out:* "GOD BLESS . . ."]

ADRIENNE: I've got to find Walter!

FLASH: Miss Knowland! Don't! Mr. Breckenridge will be angry!

[ADRIENNE *rushes out and disappears Left into the garden. The fireworks continue to spell:* "GOD BLESS AMER . . ." *Then, suddenly, the last dot of light flashes on with a jerk, spreads out, the letters tremble, smear, and vanish altogether. There is nothing but darkness and silence*]

Well! . . . what's the matter? . . . What happened? . . . [*They wait. Nothing happens*] Well, I guess maybe the invention's not right yet. Something's gone screwy there. Maybe the great discovery's not so perfect. . . .

BILLY: It will start again in a minute.

FLASH: Maybe the old-fashioned way is best. [*They wait. Nothing happens*] Say, Bill. What's the matter with everybody in this house?

BILLY: Nothing.

FLASH: I can't figure it out. You're the nicest people I ever lived with. But there's something wrong. Very wrong.

BILLY: Skip it, Flash.

FLASH: Now take you, for instance. That operation. You wanted it pretty badly?

BILLY: I guess maybe I did. . . . I don't know . . . I don't know how it really feels to want things. I've been trying to learn not to.

FLASH: Bill, what do you want most in the world?

BILLY: I? . . . [*Thinks for a moment, then:*] I guess . . . I guess to get a glass of water.

FLASH: *What?* Want me to get you a drink?

BILLY: No. You don't understand. To get a glass of water—*myself.* [FLASH *stares at him*] You see what I mean? To get thirsty and not to have to tell anybody about it, but to walk down to the kitchen, and turn the faucet, and fill a glass, and drink it. Not to need anybody, not to thank anybody, not to ask for it. To *get* it. Flash. You don't know how important it is— not to need anybody.

FLASH: But people *want* to help you.

BILLY: Flash, when it's—everything, all the time, everything I do . . . I can't be thirsty—alone, without telling somebody. I can't be hungry—alone. I'm not a person. I'm only something being helped. . . . If I could stand up just once—stand up on my own feet and tell them all to go to hell! Oh, Flash, I wouldn't tell them to! But just to know that I could! Just once!

FLASH: Well, what for, if you wouldn't? You don't make sense. People are very kind to you and—[*There is the sound of a distant explosion in the garden*] There! There it goes again! [*Looks out. There is nothing but darkness*] No. Guess it was a dud.

BILLY: They're kind to me. It's such a horrible thing— that sort of kindness. Sometimes I want to be nasty just to have somebody snap at me. But they won't. They don't respect me enough to get angry. I'm not important enough to resent. I'm only something to be kind to.

FLASH: *Listen,* how about that glass of water? Do you want me to get it or don't you?

BILLY: [*His head dropping, his voice dull*] Yes. Get me a glass of water.

FLASH: Look, water's not good for you. How about my fixing you some nice hot chocolate and a little toast?

BILLY: Yes.

FLASH: That's what I said: nobody ate anything tonight. All that grand dinner going to waste. It's a crazy house. [*Turns at the door*] Want the light on?

BILLY: No. [FLASH *exits Right.* BILLY *sits alone for a moment, without moving, his head down.* INGALLS *enters from the garden*]

INGALLS: Hello, Bill. What are you doing here alone in the dark? [*Switches the light on*] The fireworks over?

BILLY: Something went wrong. They stopped.

INGALLS: Oh? Where's Walter?

BILLY: Fixing it, I guess. He hasn't come back. [*As* IN-GALLS *turns to the stairs*] Steve.

INGALLS: Yes?

BILLY: Steve, do you know why I like you? . . . Because you've never been kind to me.

INGALLS: But I want to be kind to you, kid.

BILLY: That's not what I mean. You couldn't be what . . . what I'm talking about. I mean, people who use kindness like some sort of weapon. . . . Steve! It's a horrible weapon. I think it's worse than poison gas. It gets in deeper, it hurts more, and there's no gas mask to wear against it. Because people would say you're wicked to want such a mask.

INGALLS: Bill. Listen to me. It doesn't matter. Even your legs and the wheelchair—it doesn't matter, so long as you don't let anyone into your mind. Keep your mind, Bill—keep it free and keep it your own. Don't let anyone help you—inside. Don't let anyone tell you what you must think. Don't let anyone tell you what you must feel. Don't ever let them put your soul in a wheelchair. Then you'll be all right, no matter what they do.

BILLY: You understand. Steve, you're the only one who understands. [FLASH *enters Right*]

FLASH: Come on, Bill. The grub's ready. Do you want it here?

BILLY: I'm not hungry. Take me to my room, please. I'm tired.

FLASH: Aw, hell! After I went to all the bother—

BILLY: Please, Flash. [FLASH *starts wheeling the chair out*] Good night, Steve.

INGALLS: Good night, kid. [FLASH *and* BILLY *exit, and we hear* TONY's *voice in the next room*]
TONY'S VOICE: Going, Billy? Good night.
BILLY'S VOICE: Good night. [TONY *enters Right*]
TONY: What about the great fireworks? All over?
INGALLS: I guess so. Billy said something went wrong.
TONY: You didn't watch them?
INGALLS: No.
TONY: I didn't either.

[HELEN *appears at the top of the stairs. She has her hat and coat on, and carries a small suitcase. She stops short, seeing the two men below, then comes resolutely down the stairs*]

INGALLS: Helen? Where are you going?
HELEN: Back to town.
TONY: *Now?*
HELEN: Yes.
INGALLS: But, Helen—
HELEN: Please don't ask me any questions. I didn't know that someone would still be here. I wanted to . . . I wanted not to have to talk to anyone.
INGALLS: But what's happened?
HELEN: Later, Steve. Later. I'll talk to you afterward. Tomorrow, in town, if you wish. I'll explain. Please don't—

[*From a distance in the garden there comes* ADRIENNE's *scream—a horrified scream. They whirl to the French doors*]

INGALLS: Where's Adrienne?
HELEN: I don't know. She—

[INGALLS *rushes out into the garden.* TONY *follows him.* FLASH *comes running in, Right*]

FLASH: What was that?
HELEN: I . . . don't . . . know. . . .
FLASH: Miss Knowland! It's Miss Knowland! [CURTISS *enters Right*]

CURTISS: Madam! What happened!

[INGALLS, TONY, *and* ADRIENNE *enter from the garden.* INGALLS *is supporting* ADRIENNE. *She is trembling and out of breath*]

INGALLS: All right. Take it easy. Now what is it?

ADRIENNE: It's Walter . . . out there . . . in the garden. . . . He's dead. [*Silence, as they all look at her*] It was dark . . I couldn't see. . . . He was lying on his face. . . . And then I ran. . . . I think he's shot. . . . [HELEN *gasps and sinks into a chair*]

INGALLS: Did you touch anything?

ADRIENNE: No . . . no. . . .

INGALLS: Curtiss.

CURTISS: Yes, sir?

INGALLS: Go down there. Stand by. Don't touch anything. And don't let anyone near.

CURTISS: Yes, sir.

ADRIENNE: [*Pointing*] There . . . to the left . . . down the path. . . . [CURTISS *exits into the garden*]

INGALLS: Tony, take Helen to her room. Flash, go to Billy. Don't tell him. Put him to bed.

FLASH: Y-yes, sir.

[*Exits Right.* TONY *helps* HELEN *up the stairs and they exit, while* INGALLS *reaches for the telephone*]

ADRIENNE: Steve! What are you doing?

INGALLS: [*Into phone*] Operator? . . .

ADRIENNE: Steve! Wait!

INGALLS: [*Into phone*] Give me District Attorney Hastings.

ADRIENNE: No! . . . Wait! . . . Steve, I—

INGALLS: [*Into phone*] Hello, Greg? Steve Ingalls speaking. From the house of Walter Breckenridge. Mr. Breckenridge has been—[ADRIENNE *seizes his arm. He pushes her aside, not violently, but firmly*]— murdered. . . . Yes. . . . Yes, I shall. . . . Yes, the new house. . . . [*Hangs up*]

ADRIENNE: Steve . . . you wouldn't let me tell you . . .

INGALLS: Well? What is it?

ADRIENNE: [*Pulls a man's handkerchief from her pocket and hands it to him*] This. [*He looks at the initials on the handkerchief*] It's yours.

INGALLS: Yes.

ADRIENNE: It was caught on a branch—there—near the . . . body.

INGALLS: [*Looks at the handkerchief, then at her*] It's good evidence, Adrienne. [*Slips the handkerchief calmly into his pocket*] It's evidence that you still love me—in spite of everything—in spite of what happened this afternoon.

ADRIENNE: [*Stiffening*] Merely circumstantial evidence.

INGALLS: Oh, yes. But one can do a lot with circumstantial evidence.

CURTAIN

Act II

SCENE 1

Half an hour later. Before the curtain rises we hear the sound of Chopin's "Butterfly Etude" played on the piano. It is played violently, exultantly—the gay notes dancing in laughter and release. The music continues as the curtain rises.

STEVE INGALLS *is alone on stage. He is pacing the room impatiently; he glances at his wristwatch. Then there is the sound of a car driving up. He looks out. He walks to the entrance door Left and throws it open suddenly, at the right moment, before the bell is rung.* SERGE *stands outside.*

SERGE: [*As he enters, angrily*] How thoughtful of you. [*Pulls the* Courier *out of his pocket and throws it to him*] There is nothing in the *Courier* about the Soviet Culture and Friendship Society. Or the FBI.

INGALLS: No?

SERGE: No! I make all the long trip for nothing.

INGALLS: [*Glancing through the paper*] Guess Joe Cheeseman gave me the wrong dope.

SERGE: And where is everybody? [INGALLS *slips the paper into his pocket and doesn't answer*] Why is it in the house all the windows dark? [INGALLS *stands watching him silently*] What is the matter?

INGALLS: Serge.

SERGE: Yes?

INGALLS: Mr. Breckenridge has been murdered.

SERGE: [*Stands stock-still for a long moment, then emits one short, sick gasp—like a moan. Then snaps hoarsely and crudely:*] You are crazy! . . .

INGALLS: [*Without moving*] Mr. Breckenridge is lying dead in the garden.

SERGE: [*Sinks down into a chair, his head in his hands, and moans*] Boje moy! . . . Boje moy! . . .

INGALLS: Save it for the others, Serge. Save it for an audience.

SERGE: [*Jerks his head up, his voice harsh and deadly*] Who did it?

INGALLS: You. Or I. Or any of us.

SERGE: [*Jumping up, ferociously*] I?!

INGALLS: Pipe down, Serge. You see, it's the one question that none of us must ask—under the circumstances. Leave that to Greg Hastings.

SERGE: Who?

INGALLS: Greg Hastings. The district attorney. He will be here any moment. I'm sure he'll answer your question. He always does.

SERGE: I hope he's good, I hope—

INGALLS: He's very good. Not one unsolved murder in his whole career. You see, he doesn't believe that there can be such a thing as a perfect crime.

SERGE: I hope he should find the monster, the fiend, the unspeakable—

INGALLS: Let me give you a tip, Serge. Cut down on that kind of stuff around Greg Hastings. I know him quite well. He won't fall for the obvious. He'll always look further than that. He's clever. Too clever.

SERGE: [*His voice rising angrily*] But why do you say this to me? Why do you look at me? You do not think that I . . .

INGALLS: I haven't even begun to think, Serge. [TONY *enters Right*]

TONY: [*Gaily*] The cops arrived? [*Sees* SERGE] Oh, it's you, Serge, old boy, old pal.

SERGE: [*Startled*] I beg your pardon?

TONY: You look wonderful. The ride's done you good. It's wonderful to drive fast at night, against the wind, with nothing to stop you! To drive fast, so fast—and free!

SERGE: [*Aghast*] But what is this? [*Whirls on* INGALLS] Oh, I see! It was the joke. It was the horrible joke from *you*. . . . [*To* TONY] Mr. Breckenridge he is not dead?

TONY: [*Lightly*] Oh yes, Mr. Breckenridge is dead. Dead as a doornail. Dead as a tombstone. Good and dead.

SERGE: [*To* INGALLS] He has lost his mind!

INGALLS: Or just found it. [HELEN *enters, coming down the stairs*]

HELEN: Tony, why did you—

SERGE: Oh, Mrs. Breckenridge! Permit me to express the deepest sympathy at this terrible—

HELEN: Thank you, Serge. [*Her manner is now simple, young, more natural than it has ever been*] Why did you stop playing, Tony? It was so lovely. I've never heard you play like this before.

TONY: But you will hear me again. You will—for years—and years—and years—[INGALLS *exits up the stairs*]

SERGE: Mrs. Breckenridge—

HELEN: I will give you a piano, Tony. Now. Tomorrow.

[*There is the distant sound of a police siren approaching.* SERGE *looks up nervously. The others pay no attention*]

TONY: You won't give me a piano! Nobody's going to give me anything ever again! I think I can get a job at Gimbel's, and I will, and I'll save three dollars a week, and in a year I'll have a piano—a good, second-hand piano of my own! . . . But I like you, Helen.

HELEN: Yes. Forgive me.

SERGE: Mrs. Breckenridge! . . . What has happened?

HELEN: We don't know, Serge.

TONY: What's the difference?

SERGE: But who did it?

TONY: Who cares?

[*Doorbell rings.* TONY *opens the door.* GREGORY HASTINGS *enters. He is a man in his early forties, tall, suave, distinguished, and self-possessed. He enters calmly, he speaks quietly, as naturally and undramatically as possible—without overdoing it. He enters, stops, looks at* HELEN]

HASTINGS: Mrs. Breckenridge?

HELEN: Yes.

HASTINGS: [*Bowing*] Gregory Hastings.

HELEN: How do you do, Mr. Hastings.

HASTINGS: I am truly sorry, Mrs. Breckenridge, that I should have to be here tonight.

HELEN: We'll be glad to help you in any way we can, Mr. Hastings. If you wish to question us—

HASTINGS: A little later. First, I shall have to see the scene of—

HELEN: [*Pointing*] In the garden. . . . Tony, will you show—

HASTINGS: It won't be necessary. I'll keep my men out of your way as much as possible. [*Exits Left*]

TONY: This is going to be interesting.

SERGE: But . . . you are inhuman!

TONY: Probably. [INGALLS *enters, coming down the stairs*]

INGALLS: Was that Greg Hastings?

TONY: Yes. The police.

INGALLS: Where are they?

TONY: [*Pointing to garden*] Sniffing at footprints, I guess.

SERGE: There will not be any footprints. There will not be anything. It is going to be terrible.

INGALLS: How do you know there won't be anything, Serge?

SERGE: There never is in a case like this.

INGALLS: You never can tell. [*Pulls the* Courier *out of his pocket*] Anyone here want the evening paper that Serge was nice enough to bring us?

TONY: [*Taking the paper*] Does the *Courier* have any comic strips? I love comic strips. [*Turns the paper to the funny page*] They don't have "Little Orphan Annie," though. That's my favorite—"Little Orphan Annie."

HELEN: [*Looking over his shoulder*] I like "Popeye the Sailor."

TONY: Oh, no! Annie's better. But Popeye has his points—particularly when they bring in Mr. Wimpy. Mr. Wimpy is good.

HELEN: Lord Plushbottom is good, too.

TONY: Lord Plushbottom is from another strip.

SERGE: *That's* what I drive the three-quarters of an hour for!

HELEN: Oh, yes, Serge, wasn't there some story you wanted to read?

SERGE: There was! But there isn't! Not a word in the damn paper about the Soviet Culture and Friendship Society!

TONY: And not even "Little Orphan Annie" or "Popeye the Sailor."

[FLEMING *comes down the stairs. He is sober and walks*

calmly, steadily. There is an air about him as if he were holding his head up for the first time in his life. His clothes are still disreputable, but he is shaved and his tie is straight]

FLEMING: Steve, you won't—by any chance—need a janitor down at the laboratory?

INGALLS: No. But we will need an engineer.

FLEMING: A has-been engineer?

INGALLS: No. A shall-be engineer.

FLEMING: [*Looks at him, then in a low voice:*] Steve, you're—

INGALLS: a cold-blooded egoist. I've never been called anything else. I wouldn't know what to do if I were. Let it go at that.

FLEMING: [*Nods slowly, solemnly. Then sits down and picks up part of the newspaper*] The police are out there in the garden. Guess they'll want us all here.

INGALLS: Yes, it won't be long now.

SERGE: [*Walks to sideboard, pours himself a drink*] Do you want a drink, Mr. Fleming?

FLEMING: [*With slow emphasis*] No, thank you.

SERGE: [*Swallows a stiff drink in one gulp. Then:*] The laboratory—who will run it now?

INGALLS: I will.

SERGE: And . . . what is to happen to the invention?

INGALLS: Ah, yes, the invention. Well, Serge, only two men knew the secret of that invention—Walter and I. Walter is dead.

SERGE: He wanted to give it to mankind.

INGALLS: He did. Now I'm going to sit and loaf and collect a fortune. It's too bad about mankind.

SERGE: You have no respect for the wishes of a—

INGALLS: I have no respect for anything, Serge.

SERGE: [*Cautiously*] But if you should now carry out the wish of Mr. Breckenridge—then perhaps the police will not think that *you* had a reason to kill him.

INGALLS: Oh, but Serge! You wouldn't suggest that I try to deceive the police, would you? [HASTINGS *enters from the garden. His face looks earnest*]

HASTINGS: Mrs. Breckenridge . . . [*Sees* INGALLS] Oh, hello, Steve.

INGALLS: Hello, Greg.

HASTINGS: I'm glad you're here. It will make things easier for me.

INGALLS: Or harder—if I did it.

HASTINGS: Or hopeless, if you did it. But I know one or two things already which seem to let you out. [*To* HELEN] Mrs. Breckenridge, I'm sorry, but certain facts make it necessary for everyone here to be fingerprinted.

HELEN: Of course. I'm sure none of us will object.

HASTINGS: If you will please ask everybody to step into the library—my assistant is there with the necessary equipment. After that I should like to have everybody here.

HELEN: Very well.

HASTINGS: Steve, will you please go down there—[*Points to the garden*]—and take a look at that electrical apparatus that Breckenridge was operating? I have the butler's statement about the invention and the fireworks display that was interrupted. I want to know what interrupted it. I want you to tell me whether that machine is out of order in any way.

INGALLS: Will you take my word for it?

HASTINGS: I'll have to. You're the only one who can tell us. Besides, my men are there and they'll be watching you. But first, come to the library and get fingerprinted.

INGALLS: All right.

[*They all exit, Right.* HELEN *is the last to go. She turns out the lights, then follows the others. The stage is dark and empty for a few moments. Then a man's figure enters Right. We cannot see who it is. The man gathers quickly all the sheets of the newspaper, twists them into one roll, and kneels by the fireplace. He strikes a match and sets fire to the paper. We see his two hands, but nothing else. He lets the paper burn halfway, then blows out the fire. Then he rises and exits Right*]

[*After a moment,* HELEN *and* HASTINGS *come back, Right.* HELEN *turns on the light. We can see part of the rolled newspaper among the logs in the fireplace*]

HASTINGS: May I apologize in advance, Mrs. Brecken-ridge, for anything that I might have to say or do? I'm afraid this is going to be a difficult case.

HELEN: Will you forgive me if I say that I *hope* it will be a difficult case?

HASTINGS: You do not wish me to find the murderer?

HELEN: I suppose I should, but . . . No. I don't.

HASTINGS: It might mean that you know who it is. Or—it could mean something much worse.

HELEN: I don't know who it is. As to the "much worse"—well, we'll all deny that, so I don't think my denial would be worth more than any of the others. [CURTISS *enters Right*]

CURTISS: Mr. Hastings, could you ask the coroner please to attend to Mrs. Pudget?

HELEN: Good God, Curtiss! You don't mean that Mrs. Pudget has been—

CURTISS: Oh no, madam. But Mrs. Pudget has a bad case of hysterics. [FLEMING *and* SERGE *enter Right*]

HASTINGS: What's the matter with her?

CURTISS: She says that she positively refuses to work for people who get murdered.

HASTINGS: All right, ask the coroner to give her a pill. Then come back here.

CURTISS: Yes, sir. [*Exits Right*]

HASTINGS: [*To* HELEN] I understand that your son wit-nessed the fireworks from this room?

HELEN: Yes, I believe so.

HASTINGS: Then I'm afraid I shall have to ask you to have him brought here.

FLEMING: And get him out of bed? At this hour? [HAS-TINGS *looks at him with curiosity*]

HELEN: But of course, Harvey. It can't be avoided. It's quite all right. I'll ask Flash to bring him down.

FLEMING: *I* will. [*Exits Right, as* TONY *enters*]

HASTINGS: [*To* HELEN] Do you know why I think this case is going to be difficult? Because motive is always the most important thing. Motive is the key to any case. And I'm afraid I'll have a hard time finding one single motive among all the people here. I can't imag-ine any reason for killing a man of Mr. Brecken-ridge's character.

HELEN: Neither could Walter. And I hope whoever did it told him the reason before he died. [*He looks at her, astonished*] Yes, I'm really as cruel as that—though I didn't know it before. [ADRIENNE *enters Right. She is pale, tense and barely able to control herself*]

TONY: I didn't know fingerprinting was as simple as that, did you, Adrienne? Wasn't it fun?

ADRIENNE: [*Curtly*] No.

TONY: [*Taken aback*] Oh . . . I'm sorry, Adrienne. . . . But I thought . . . you'd be the one to feel better than any of us.

ADRIENNE: [*Bitterly*] Oh, you did?

HELEN: Adrienne, may I get you a drink?

ADRIENNE: [*Looks at her with hatred. Then, to* HASTINGS:] Get this over with, will you, so I can get out of here?

HASTINGS: I shall try, Miss Knowland. [INGALLS *enters from the garden*] What about the machine, Steve?

INGALLS: In perfect order.

HASTINGS: Nothing the matter with it?

INGALLS: Nothing.

HASTINGS: Doesn't look as if anybody had tried to monkey with it?

INGALLS: No. [CURTISS *enters Right*]

HASTINGS: Now, I should like to ask you all to sit down and be as comfortable as we can be under the circumstances. I won't have a stenographer taking down anybody's words or gestures. I shan't need that. Let's just relax and talk sensibly. [*To* HELEN] Is everybody here now?

HELEN: Yes, except Billy and his tutor and Mr. Fleming.

HASTINGS: Now as to the servants—there are the butler, the cook and her husband, the chauffeur. Is that all?

HELEN: Yes.

HASTINGS: And—who are the nearest neighbors?

HELEN: I . . . don't know.

INGALLS: The nearest house is two miles away.

HASTINGS: I see. All right. Now we can begin. As you see, I don't believe in conducting an investigation behind closed doors and trying to play people against one another. I prefer to keep everything in the open. I know that none of you will want to talk. But my job requires that I make you talk. So I shall start by giving you all an example. I don't believe it's necessary—though it's usually done—to keep from you the facts in my possession. What for? The murderer knows them—and the others should want to help me. Therefore, I shall tell you what I know so far. [*Pauses. Then:*] Mr. Breckenridge was shot—in the back. The shot was fired at some distance—there are no powder burns around the wound. The body was lying quite a few steps away from the electrical machine which Mr. Breckenridge was using for the fireworks display. The watch on Mr. Breckenridge's wrist was broken and stopped at four minutes past ten. There was nothing but grass and soft earth where the body had fallen, so the watch crystal could not have been smashed like that by the fall. It looks as if someone stepped on the watch. The gun was lying on the ground, near the machine. Curtiss has identified it as Mr. Breckenridge's own gun. Only one shot had been fired. The gun shows an excellent set of fingerprints. We shall soon know whether they are the prints of anyone here. That's all—so far. Now I should like to—[FLEMING *and* FLASH *enter Right wheeling* BILLY *in.* BILLY *wears a bathrobe over his pajamas*]

HELEN: This is Billy, Mr. Hastings.

HASTINGS: How do you do, Billy. I'm sorry I had to get you out of bed.

HELEN: [*Looks questioningly at* FLEMING, *who shakes his head. She turns to* BILLY, *says gently:*] Billy, dear, you must try to be calm and grown-up about what I'm going to tell you. It's about Father. You see, dear, there was an accident and . . . and . . .

BILLY: You mean he's dead?

HELEN: Yes, dear.

BILLY: You mean he's been murdered?

HELEN: You mustn't say that. We don't know. We're trying to find out what happened.

BILLY: [*Very simply*] I'm glad. [*Silence as they all look at him. Then:*]

HASTINGS: [*Softly*] Why did you say that, Billy?

BILLY: [*Very simply*] Because he wanted to keep me a cripple.

HASTINGS: [*This is too much even for him*] Billy . . . how can you think such a thing?

BILLY: That's all he wanted me for in the first place.

HASTINGS: What do you mean?

BILLY: [*In a flat monotone*] He wanted a cripple because a cripple has to depend on him. If you spend your time helping people, you've got to have people to help. If everybody were independent, what would happen to the people who've got to help everybody?

FLEMING: [*To* HASTINGS, *angrily*] Will you stop this? Ask him whatever you have to ask and let him go.

HASTINGS: [*Looks at him, then:*] What's your name?

FLEMING: Harvey Fleming.

HASTINGS: [*Turns to* BILLY] Billy, what made you think that about Mr. Breckenridge?

BILLY: [*Looks at him, almost contemptuously, as if the answer were too enormous and too obvious. Then says wearily:*] Today, for instance.

HASTINGS: What happened today?

BILLY: They asked him to let me have an operation— the last thing they could do for me or I'd never walk at all. He wouldn't. He wouldn't, even when—[*Looks at* FLEMING. *Stops short*]

HASTINGS: [*Softly*] Even when—what, Billy?

BILLY: That's all.

FLEMING: Say it, kid. It's all right. Even when I cursed him and threatened him.

HASTINGS: You did? [*Looks at him, then:*] Mr. Fleming, why are you so concerned about Billy?

FLEMING: [*Astonished by the question, as if his answer were a well-known fact*] Why? Because I'm his father. [HASTINGS *turns to look at* HELEN] *No*, not what your dirty mind is thinking. I thought you knew. They all know. Billy's my own legitimate son—and my wife's. My wife is dead. Walter adopted him five years ago. [HASTINGS *looks at him, startled.* FLEMING *takes it for reproach and continues angrily:*] Don't tell me I was a Goddamn fool to agree to it. I know I was. But I didn't know it then. How was I to know? [*Points at the others*] How were any of them to know what would happen to them? I was out of work. My wife had just died. Billy'd had infantile paralysis for a year. I'd have given anything to cure him. I gave all I had to give—

I gave *him* up, when Walter asked to adopt him. Walter was rich. Walter could afford the best doctors. Walter had been so kind to us. When I saw what it really was—it took me two years to begin to guess—there was nothing I could do . . . nothing. . . . Walter owned him.

HASTINGS: [*Slowly*] I see.

FLEMING: No, you don't. Do you know that we came from the same small town, Walter and I? That we had no money, neither one of us? That I was the brilliant student in school and Walter hated me for it? That people said I'd be a great engineer, and I'd made a good beginning, only I didn't have Walter's gift for using people? That he wanted to see me down, as far down as a man can go? That he helped me when I was out of work—because he knew it would keep me out of work, because he knew I was drinking—when my wife died—and I didn't care—and it seemed so easy. . . . He knew I'd never work again, when he took the last thing I had away from me—when he took Billy to make it easier for me—to make it easier! If you want to finish a man, just take all burdens—and all goals—away from him! . . . He gave me money—all these years—and I took it. I took it! [*Stops. Then says, in a low, dead voice:*] Listen. I didn't kill Walter Breckenridge. But I would have slept prouder—all the rest of my life—if it was I who'd killed him.

HASTINGS: [*Turns slowly to* HELEN] Mrs. Breckenridge . . .

HELEN: [*Her voice flat, expressionless*] It's true. All of it. You see, we couldn't have any children, Walter and I. I had always wanted a child. I remember I told him once—I was watching children playing in a park—I told him that I wanted a child, a child's running feet in the house. . . . Then he adopted Billy. . . . [*Silence*]

BILLY: [*To* FLEMING] I didn't want to say anything . . . Dad. . . . [*To* HELEN, *a little frightened*] It's all right, now?

HELEN: [*Her voice barely audible*] Yes, dear. . . . You know it wasn't I who demanded that you . . . [*She doesn't finish*]

BILLY: [*To* FLEMING] I'm sorry, Dad. . . .

FLEMING: [*Puts his hand on* BILLY'S *shoulder, and* BILLY *buries his face against* FLEMING'S *arm*] It's all right, Bill. Everything will be all right now. . . . [*Silence*]

HASTINGS: I'm sorry, Mr. Fleming. I almost wish you hadn't told me. Because, you see, you did have a good motive.

FLEMING: [*Simply, indifferently*] I thought everybody knew I had.

TONY: What of it? He wasn't the only one.

HASTINGS: No? And what is your name?

TONY: Tony Goddard.

HASTINGS: Now, Mr. Goddard, when you make a state-ment of that kind, you're usually asked to—

TONY:—finish it? What do you suppose I started for? You won't have to question me. I'll tell you. It's very simple. I'm not sure you'll understand, but I don't care. [*Stretches his hands out*] Look at my hands. Mr. Breckenridge told me that they were the hands of a great surgeon. He told me how much good I could do, how many suffering people I could help—and he gave me a scholarship in a medical college. A very gener-ous scholarship.

HASTINGS: Well?

TONY: That's all. Except that I hate medicine more than anything else in the world. And what I wanted to be was a pianist. [HASTINGS *looks at him.* TONY *continues, calmly, bitterly:*] All right, say I was a weakling. Who wouldn't be? I was poor—and very lonely. Nobody had ever taken an interest in me before. Nobody seemed to care whether I lived or died. I had a long struggle ahead of me—and I wasn't even sure that I had any musical talent. How can you ever be sure at the beginning? And the road looks so long and so hopeless—and you're hurt so often. And he told me it was a selfish choice, and that I'd be so much more useful to men as a doctor, and he was so kind to me, and he made it sound so right.

HASTINGS: But why wouldn't he help you through a music school, instead?

TONY: [*Looks at him, almost pityingly, like an older man at a child, says wearily, without bitterness:*] Why? [*Shrugs in resignation*] Mr. Hastings, if you want to have men dependent on you, don't allow them to be happy. Happy men are free men.

HASTINGS: But if you were unhappy, why didn't you leave it all? What held you?

TONY: [*In the same wise, tired voice*] Mr. Hastings, you don't know what a ghastly weapon kindness can be. When you're up against an enemy, you can fight him. But when you're up against a friend, a gentle, kindly, smiling friend—you turn against yourself. You think that you're low and ungrateful. It's the best in you that destroys you. That's what's horrible about it. . . . And it takes you a long time to understand. I think I understood it only today.

HASTINGS: Why?

TONY: I don't know. Everything. The house, the horse, the gift to mankind . . . [*Turns to the others*] One of us here is the murderer. I don't know who it is. I hope I never learn—for his sake. But I want him to know that I'm grateful . . . so terribly grateful. . . . [*Silence*]

HASTINGS: [*Turns to* INGALLS] Steve?

INGALLS: Yes?

HASTINGS: What did *you* think of Walter Breckenridge?

INGALLS: [*In a calm, perfectly natural voice*] I loathed him in every way and for every reason possible. You can make any motive you wish out of that. [HASTINGS *looks at him*]

ADRIENNE: Stop staring at him like that. People usually prefer to look at me. Besides, I'm not accustomed to playing a supporting part.

HASTINGS: You, Miss Knowland? But *you* didn't hate Mr. Breckenridge.

ADRIENNE: *No?*

HASTINGS: But—why?

ADRIENNE: Because he kept me doing a noble, useful work which I couldn't stand. Because he had a genius for finding people of talent and for the best way of destroying them. Because he held me all right—with a five-year contract. Today, I begged him to let me go. He refused. We had a violent quarrel. Ask Steve. He heard me screaming.

HELEN: Adrienne, I'm so sorry. I didn't know about this.

ADRIENNE: [*Looks at her, doesn't answer, turns to* HAS-

TINGS] How soon will you allow us to leave? It was bad enough staying here when it was Walter's house. I won't stand it for very long—when it's hers.

HASTINGS: *Why,* Miss Knowland?

TONY: Adrienne, we don't have to—

ADRIENNE: Oh, what's the difference? He'll hear about it sooner or later, so he might as well have it now. [*To* HASTINGS] This afternoon, Walter and I and the others came in from the garden just in time to interrupt a love scene, a very beautiful love scene, between Helen and Steve. I've never been able to get any leading man of mine to kiss me like that. [*To* HELEN] Was Steve as good at it as he looked, my dear? [HELEN *stands staring at her, frozen.* ADRIENNE *whirls to* HASTINGS] You didn't know that?

HASTINGS: No. I didn't know either of these two very interesting facts.

ADRIENNE: Two?

HASTINGS: First—the love scene. Second—that it should have impressed you in this particular manner.

ADRIENNE: Well, you know it now.

INGALLS: Adrienne, you'd better stop it.

ADRIENNE: Stop what?

INGALLS: What you're doing.

ADRIENNE: You don't know what I'm doing.

INGALLS: Oh, yes, I think I do.

HASTINGS: Well, I don't know if any of you noticed it, but I've made one mistake about this case already. I thought nobody would want to talk.

INGALLS: I noticed it.

HASTINGS: You would. [*Turns to* BILLY] Now, Billy, I'll try not to hold you here too long. But you were here in this room all evening, weren't you?

BILLY: Yes.

HASTINGS: Now I want you to tell me everything you remember, who left this room and when.

BILLY: Well, I think . . . I think Steve left first. When we were talking about the operation. He walked out.

HASTINGS: Where did he go?

BILLY: In the garden.

HASTINGS: Who went next?

BILLY: It was Dad. He went upstairs.

FLASH: And he took a bottle from the sideboard with him.

HASTINGS: You're Billy's tutor, aren't you?

FLASH: Yes. Flash Kozinsky—Stanislaw Kozinsky.

HASTINGS: And you stayed here with Billy all evening?

FLASH: Yes.

HASTINGS: Now who went next?

BILLY: Mr. Breckenridge. He went into the garden. And he said that he didn't want anybody to follow him.

HASTINGS: What time was that?

FLASH: About ten o'clock.

HASTINGS: And then?

FLASH: Then Mrs. Breckenridge got up and said "Excuse me" and went upstairs. And then Tony told me to . . . to do something with the fireworks which I couldn't possibly do—and went into the library.

BILLY: And then we heard Tony playing the piano in the library.

FLASH: Then the fireworks started—and nobody was there to see it but us two and Miss Knowland. They were very beautiful fireworks, though. And Miss Knowland said that it was lovely, good target shooting, or something like that—and suddenly she kind of screamed and said she had thought of something and wanted to find Mr. Breckenridge right away.

[INGALLS *makes a step forward*]

HASTINGS: Ah. . . . What did you think of, Miss Knowland?

ADRIENNE: I thought . . . [*Looks at* INGALLS. *He is watching her*]

INGALLS: [*Slowly*] What did you think of, Adrienne?

ADRIENNE: I thought . . . I thought that Steve would take advantage of Walter's absence and . . . and that Steve would be upstairs with Helen, and I wanted to tell Walter about it.

HASTINGS: I see. And what did you do?

ADRIENNE: I went out into the garden—to find Walter.

HASTINGS: And then?

BILLY: Then the fireworks stopped.

HASTINGS: How soon after Miss Knowland left did the fireworks stop?

FLASH: Almost immediately. Almost before she could've been a step away.

HASTINGS: And then?

FLASH: Then we waited, but nothing happened. We just talked and—[*Stops. Gasps:*] Jesus Christ!

HASTINGS: What is it?

FLASH: Jesus Christ, I think we heard it when Mr. Breckenridge was murdered!

HASTINGS: *When?*

FLASH: Bill, do you remember the dud? Remember there was a kind of crack outside and I thought the fireworks were starting again, but nothing happened and I said it was a dud?

BILLY: Yes.

CURTISS: I heard it too, Mr. Hastings. But there had been so many rockets outside that I thought nothing of it at the time.

HASTINGS: Now that's interesting. You heard it *after* the fireworks had stopped?

FLASH: Yes. Quite a bit after. Five minutes or more.

HASTINGS: What happened after that?

BILLY: Nothing. Then Steve came back from the garden, and we talked, and then Flash took me to my room.

HASTINGS: You didn't see Mrs. Breckenridge or Mr. Fleming come back down these stairs while you were here?

BILLY: No.

HASTINGS: Now, Curtiss, you were in the pantry all that time?

CURTISS: Yes, sir. I was polishing the silver.

HASTINGS: Could you see the back stairway from the second floor all the time you were there?

CURTISS: Yes, sir. The pantry door was open.

HASTINGS: Did you see anyone coming down the stairs?

CURTISS: No, sir.

HASTINGS: [*To* FLEMING] Well, I guess that lets *you* out.

FLEMING: [*Shrugging*] Not necessarily. There's a window in my room.

HASTINGS: What were you doing in your room? Getting drunk?

FLEMING: *Staying* drunk.

HASTINGS: And you, Mrs. Breckenridge, were you in your room?

HELEN: Yes.

HASTINGS: Since I can't see you climbing out of a window, I presume at least that it lets you out.

HELEN: Not necessarily. There's a balcony outside my room with a perfectly functional stairway leading to the garden.

HASTINGS: Oh. . . . What were you doing in your room?

HELEN: Packing.

HASTINGS: *What?*

HELEN: My suitcase. I wanted to go back to New York.

HASTINGS: *Tonight?*

HELEN: Yes.

HASTINGS: Why?

HELEN: Because I felt that I couldn't stay in this house. [HASTINGS *looks at her. She continues quietly:*] Don't you see? I had always wanted a house of my own. I wanted a small, very modern house, simple and healthy, with huge windows and glass brick and clean walls. I wanted to hunt for the latest refrigerators and colored washstands and plastic floor tiles and . . . I wanted to work on it for months, to plan every bit of it. . . . But I was never allowed to plan anything in my life. . . . [*Controls herself. Continues in a matter-of-fact voice:*] I was ready to leave. I came downstairs. Steve and Tony were here. I was about to go when we heard Adrienne scream . . . and . . . [*Finishes with a gesture of her hand, as if to say: "And that was that"*]

HASTINGS: I see. . . . Now, Miss Knowland. What were you doing in the garden?

ADRIENNE: I was looking for Walter. But I went in the wrong direction. I went toward the lake. I got lost in the dark. Then I came back and—I found him. Dead. [*Looks at* HASTINGS, *adds:*] Of course, I could have been doing anything.

HASTINGS: Is that what you want me to think?

ADRIENNE: I don't care what you think.

HASTINGS: You know, I *would* think it—if it weren't for one fact. The fireworks stopped too soon after you left. You wouldn't have had the time to get from here to the spot where Mr. Breckenridge was found. And I think it was the murderer who stopped those fireworks—or interrupted Mr. Breckenridge and caused him to stop. Because there's nothing wrong with the machine it-self. I think the murderer got there when the fire-works stopped. Perhaps earlier. But not later. [*Turns to* INGALLS] Now, Steve. What were you doing in the garden?

INGALLS: I have no alibi at all, Greg.

HASTINGS: None?

INGALLS: None. I just went for a walk through the grounds. I saw no one and no one saw me.

HASTINGS: Hm. . . . Now, Mr. Goddard. You were playing the piano in the library?

TONY: Yes.

HASTINGS: [*To* BILLY *and* FLASH] How long did you hear him playing? Till after the fireworks stopped?

BILLY: Yes, till quite a bit after.

FLASH: Yes.

HASTINGS: [*To* TONY] Well, that lets *you* out.

TONY: Not necessarily. If you look through the phonograph records, you will see that there is one of Rachmaninoff's Prelude in G Minor.

HASTINGS: [*Leans back in his chair, disgusted*] Is there anyone here who does *not* want to be the murderer?

FLASH: Oh, *I* don't.

SERGE: I think it is horrible! It is horrible that these people should act like this after the death of their benefactor!

HASTINGS: [*Turns to look at him with curiosity. Then, to* HELEN:] Who is this gentleman?

HELEN: Mr. Serge Sookin. A friend of my husband's.

HASTINGS: Mr. Sookin, we seem to have forgotten you. Where were you all that time?

SERGE: *I* was not here at all.

HASTINGS: You weren't?

BILLY: That's right. I forgot him. Mr. Sookin left long before everybody else. He went to Stamford.

HASTINGS: [*Interested, to* SERGE:] You drove to Stamford?

SERGE: Yes. To get the evening newspaper.

HASTINGS: What newspaper?

SERGE: The *Courier.*

HASTINGS: What time did you leave?

SERGE: I am not certain, I think it was—

INGALLS: A quarter to ten. I looked at my watch. Remember?

SERGE: That is right. You did.

HASTINGS: When did you get back?

SERGE: Just a few minutes before you arrived here.

HASTINGS: Which was at ten-thirty. Well, you made pretty good time. You couldn't have gotten to Stamford and back any faster than that. I presume you didn't stop anywhere on your way?

SERGE: No.

HASTINGS: Did anyone see you buying that newspaper?

SERGE: No. It was the drugstore, you know, with the newspapers on the box outside the door, and I just took the newspaper and left the five cents.

HASTINGS: What drugstore was it?

SERGE: It was . . . yes, it was called Lawton's.

HASTINGS: You didn't speak to anybody at Lawton's?

SERGE: No. [*Begins to understand, looks startled for a second, then laughs suddenly*] Oh, but it is funny!

HASTINGS: What is?

SERGE: [*Very pleased*] You see, there is no place between here and the Lawton's drugstore where I could buy a newspaper.

HASTINGS: No, there isn't.

SERGE: And Mr. Ingalls he said that the Lawton's drugstore they do not get the last edition of the *Courier* until ten o'clock, so I could not have had it with me earlier. And I left here at one quarter to ten. And I came back with the last edition of the *Courier.* And I could not have waited somewhere till four minutes past ten and killed Mr. Breckenridge, because then I could have only twenty-six minutes to get to Stamford and back, and you say that this would not be possible. And it is funny, because it was Mr. Ingalls who gave me the real alibi like that.

INGALLS: I sincerely regret it.

HASTINGS: Where is the paper you brought, Mr. Sookin?

SERGE: Why, right here . . . right . . . [*Looks around. Others look also*] But that is strange. It was right here. They were reading it.

TONY: That's true. I saw the paper. I read the comic strips.

HASTINGS: It was the *Courier*?

TONY: Yes.

HASTINGS: Who else saw it here?

INGALLS: I did.

HELEN: I did.

FLEMING: I did, too.

HASTINGS: Did any of you notice whether it was the last edition?

INGALLS: No, I didn't. [*The others shake their heads*]

HASTINGS: And Mr. Sookin did not seem to mind your reading that paper he brought? He did not seem in a hurry to take it away from you?

HELEN: Why, no.

[INGALLS, TONY, *and* FLEMING *shake their heads*]

HASTINGS: No. What I'm thinking wouldn't be like Mr. Sookin at all.

SERGE: [*Still looking for it*] But where is it? It was right here.

HASTINGS: Did anyone take that paper?

[*They all answer "No" or shake their heads*]

SERGE: But this is ridicable!

HASTINGS: Oh, I guess we'll find it. Sit down, Mr. Sookin. So you have a perfect alibi . . . unless, of course, you telephoned to some accomplice to get that paper for you.

SERGE: *What?!*

HASTINGS: Did anyone see Mr. Sookin using the telephone? [*They ad-lib denials*] And, of course, there's no other place to phone from, closer than Lawton's. No, I don't really think you phoned, Mr. Sookin. I just mentioned it. . . . How long have you been in this country, Mr. Sookin?

SERGE: I escaped from Russia during the World War Number Two.

HASTINGS: How long have you known Mr. Breckenridge?

SERGE: About three months.

HASTINGS: What do you do for a living?

SERGE: In my country I was a physicist. That is why Mr. Breckenridge he took an interest in me. Now I am unemployed.

HASTINGS: What do you live on?

SERGE: I get from the Refugees' Committee the fifteen dollars each week. It is quite sufficient for me.

HASTINGS: And Mr. Breckenridge didn't help you?

SERGE: Ah, Mr. Breckenridge he offered many times to help me. But money I would not take from him. I wanted to get work. And Mr. Breckenridge wanted to give me the job in his laboratories. But Mr. Ingalls refused.

HASTINGS: Oh? [*To* INGALLS] Is that right, Steve?

INGALLS: That's right.

HASTINGS: Why did you refuse?

INGALLS: Well, I'll tell you: I don't like people who talk too much about their love for humanity.

HASTINGS: But how could you override Mr. Breckenridge's wish?

INGALLS: That was a condition of our partnership. Walter received seventy-five percent of the profits and he had sole authority over the disposition to be made of our products. But I had sole authority over the work in the laboratory.

HASTINGS: I see. . . . Now tell me, Steve, how many hours a day did you usually spend in the laboratory?

INGALLS: I don't know. About twelve, I guess, on the average.

HASTINGS: Perhaps nearer to sixteen—on the average?

INGALLS: Yes, I guess so.

HASTINGS: And how many hours a day did Mr. Breckenridge spend in the laboratory?

INGALLS: He didn't come to the laboratory every day.

HASTINGS: Well, average it for the year. What would it make per day?

INGALLS: About an hour and a half.

HASTINGS: I see. . . . [*Leans back*] Well, it's very interesting. Any of you could have committed the murder. Most of you have halfway alibis, the kind that make it possible, but not probable. You're worse off than the rest, Steve. You have no alibi at all. At the other end—there's Mr. Sookin. He has a perfect alibi. [*Pauses, then:*] Here's what makes it interesting: someone deliberately smashed Mr. Breckenridge's watch. Someone was anxious that there should be no doubt about the time of the murder. Yet the only person who has a good alibi for that particular time is Mr. Sookin—who was, at four minutes past ten, just about driving into Stamford.

SERGE: Well?

HASTINGS: I'm just thinking aloud, Mr. Sookin.

[DIXON *enters Right, carrying some papers in his hand. He is an energetic, efficient young man who does not waste much time. He walks to* HASTINGS, *and puts one paper on the table before him*]

DIXON: The statements of the cook and the chauffeur, Chief.

HASTINGS: [*With a brief glance at the paper*] What do they say?

DIXON: They went to bed at nine o'clock. Saw nothing. Heard nothing—except Curtiss in the pantry.

HASTINGS: Okay.

DIXON: [*Handing him the other papers. His voice a little less casual:*] And here are the fingerprints off the gun—and another set.

HASTINGS: [*Looks carefully at two cards of fingerprints. Then puts them on the table, facedown. Then raises his head and looks slowly at all the people in the room, from face to face. Then says slowly*:] Yes. The fingerprints on that gun are those of someone in this room. [*Silence. He turns to* DIXON] Dixon.

DIXON: Yes, Chief?

HASTINGS: Have the boys examine the shrubbery and the ground under Mr. Fleming's window. Have them examine the balcony and the stairs leading down from it. Look through the phonograph records and see if you find one of Rachmaninoff's Prelude in G Minor.

Search the house and bring me all the newspapers you find. Look particularly for a copy of today's *Courier.*

DIXON: Okay, Chief. [*Exits Right*]

SERGE: [*Jumping up suddenly*] Mr. Hastings! I know who did it! [*They all look at him*] I know! And I will tell you! You are wasting the time when it is so clear! I know who did it! It was Mr. Ingalls!

INGALLS: By us in America, Serge, when you say a thing like that—you're expected to prove it.

HASTINGS: Now, Mr. Sookin, why do you think that Mr. Ingalls did it?

SERGE: Mr. Ingalls hated Mr. Breckenridge, because Mr. Breckenridge was fine and noble, and Mr. Ingalls is cold and cruel and without principles.

HASTINGS: Is he?

SERGE: But is it not clear? Mr. Ingalls he seduced the wife of Mr. Breckenridge. Mr. Breckenridge discovered it this afternoon.

HASTINGS: Now there, Mr. Sookin, you have an interesting point. Very interesting. There's never been any trouble between Mr. Ingalls and Mr. Breckenridge—until this afternoon. This evening, Mr. Breckenridge is found murdered. Convenient. A bit too convenient, don't you think? If Mr. Ingalls murdered Mr. Breckenridge—wouldn't it be dangerous for him to do it tonight? On the other hand, if someone else murdered Mr. Breckenridge—wouldn't he choose precisely tonight, when suspicion could be thrown so easily on Mr. Ingalls?

SERGE: But that is not all! Mr. Breckenridge he wanted to give this great invention to all the poor humanity. But Mr. Ingalls wanted to make the money for himself. Is it not to his advantage to kill Mr. Breckenridge?

HASTINGS: Sure. Except that Steve never cared for money.

SERGE: No? When he said so himself? When he shouted so? When I heard him?

HASTINGS: Sure. I heard him, too. Many times. Except that Steve never shouts.

SERGE: But then, if you heard it, too—

HASTINGS: Come on, Mr. Sookin, you can't be as stupid

as you're trying to appear. Who doesn't care for money? You name one. But here's the difference: the man who admits that he cares for money is all right. He's usually worth the money he makes. He won't kill for it. He doesn't have to. But watch out for the man who yells too loudly how much he scorns money. Watch out particularly for the one who yells that others must scorn it. He's after something much worse than money.

INGALLS: Thanks, Greg.

HASTINGS: Don't thank me too soon. [*Picks up the fingerprint cards*] You see, the fingerprints on that gun are yours. [*The others gasp*]

ADRIENNE: [*Jumping up*] That's horrible! It's horrible! It's unfair! Of course they're Steve's. Steve handled that gun today! Everybody saw him do it!

HASTINGS: Oh? . . . Tell me about that, Miss Knowland.

ADRIENNE: It was . . . it was this afternoon. We were talking about Walter being afraid of guns. Walter said he wasn't, said he had a gun and he told Steve to look in that drawer. Steve took the gun out, and looked at it, and then put it back. And we all saw it. And someone . . . someone got the horrible idea . . .

HASTINGS: Yes, Miss Knowland, I think so, too. [*Walks to cabinet, opens the drawer, looks in, then closes it*] Yes, it's gone. . . . Sit down, Miss Knowland. There's no need to be upset about this. Nobody who's ever seen a movie would commit murder holding a gun with his bare hand. Now, if Steve did it, he would certainly think of wiping off the fingerprints that he'd left on that gun earlier. But if somebody else did it, he'd certainly be damn glad to leave Steve's fingerprints where they were. Convenient, isn't it? . . . Now, who saw Steve handling that gun today? All of you here?

ADRIENNE: All—except Billy and Flash and Curtiss.

HASTINGS: [*Nods*] Interesting. . . . You see, Steve, that was one of the reasons why I said I thought certain things let you out. I saw that there were prints on that gun and I didn't think you'd be stupid enough to leave them there. I didn't think you'd drop the gun like that, either. Not with a deep lake close by. . . . The other reason was that I don't think you'd shoot a man in the back.

TONY: [*Gasps at a sudden thought*] Mr. Hastings! . . . I just thought of something!

HASTINGS: Yes?

TONY: What if Serge is a Communist spy? [SERGE *gasps and leaps to his feet*]

HASTINGS: [*Shakes his head at* TONY *reproachfully*] Why, Tony. You didn't really think that I hadn't thought of that already?

SERGE: [*To* TONY] You swine! *I*—a Communist? I who go to church? I who have suffered—

HASTINGS: Look, Mr. Sookin, be sensible about it. If you're not a Communist spy—you'd be angry. But if you *are* a Communist spy—you'd be much angrier, so where does it get you?

SERGE: But it is the insult! I, who have faith in the Holy Mother Russia—

HASTINGS: All right. Drop it. [*To* TONY] You see, Mr. Goddard, it's possible, but it doesn't jell. If Mr. Sookin were a Soviet agent, he'd be after the invention, of course. But nobody touched that machine. Besides, I understand that Mr. Sookin heartily supported Mr. Breckenridge in his decision to give this invention away to the world.

SERGE: I did! I am a humanitarian.

HASTINGS: What? Another one?

INGALLS: He did more than that. It was he who gave Walter the idea of the gift in the first place.

SERGE: That is true! But how did you know it?

INGALLS: I guessed it.

HASTINGS: Tell me, what is that invention actually good for? I mean, in practical application.

INGALLS: Oh, for a source of cheap power. For lighting the slums, for instance, or running factory motors.

HASTINGS: Is that all?

INGALLS: That's all.

HASTINGS: Well, you see? If it's a purely commercial invention, why should the Soviets be anxious to get exclusive control of it? They would try to steal it, of course. But once Mr. Breckenridge had decided to save them the trouble and give it away, they would

cheer him as their best friend. They spend billions
trying to prompt giveaways of that kind. They would
guard his life—at least until tomorrow noon. They
wouldn't send any spies around to kill him.

SERGE: But Mr. Hastings!

HASTINGS: Yes?

SERGE: I am *not* a Soviet spy!

HASTINGS: Okay. I haven't said you were. [*To the others*]
Well, here's how we stand. On one side, we have
Steve, who had not one, but two possible motives. He
has no alibi at all and his fingerprints are on the gun.
On the other side, we have Mr. Sookin, who has a
perfect alibi and no possible motive.

SERGE: But then why do you not act? What more do
you want? When you have the so good case against
Mr. Ingalls?

HASTINGS: That's why, Serge—because it *is* so good. It's
too good.

SERGE: Why do you not let the jury decide that?

HASTINGS: Because I am afraid that the average jury
would agree with you.

[DIXON *enters from the garden. He carries on his palm
a tiny object wrapped in cellophane. He hands it to*
HASTINGS]

DIXON: Found in the grass near the machine.

HASTINGS: [*Unwraps the cellophane. Looks, sighs with
disgust*] Oh Lord! . . . A cigarette butt. . . . I didn't
think murderers went around doing that anymore.
[*Waves to* DIXON, *who exits into the garden.* HASTINGS
picks up the cigarette butt, examines it] A Camel . . .
burned just to the brand. . . . How convenient. . . .
[*Puts the butt down. Says wearily:*] All right, who
smokes Camels around here? [INGALLS *takes out his
cigarette case, opens it, and extends it to* HASTINGS. HAS-
TINGS *looks and nods*]

INGALLS: It doesn't surprise you?

HASTINGS: No. [*To the others*] Does anyone else here
smoke Camels? [*They shake their heads*]

ADRIENNE: *I* do.

INGALLS: You don't smoke, Adrienne.

ADRIENNE: I do—on the stage. . . . I'm very good at staging things.

HASTINGS: I'm not too sure of that.

INGALLS: [*In a warning tone*] Adrienne . . .

ADRIENNE: [*To* HASTINGS] Keep him out of this. Are you running this investigation or is he? You've been reviewing things a lot around here. How about my doing that for a change?

HASTINGS: Go right ahead.

ADRIENNE: Well, for instance, look at me. I had two motives. I wanted to break my contract. If you wish to know how badly I wanted it—well, I tried to kill myself a year ago. If I'd try that, wouldn't I try something else, as desperate—or worse? Today I asked Walter, for the last time, to release me. He refused. That alone would be enough, wouldn't it? But that's not all. I love Steve Ingalls. I've been in love with him for years. Oh, it's all right for me to say that—because he doesn't give a damn about me. Today—I learned that he loves Helen. [*Looks at* HASTINGS] Well? Am I going to finish? Or will *you*?

INGALLS: [*To* ADRIENNE] You're going to shut up.

HASTINGS: No, Steve, I'd rather let Miss Knowland finish.

ADRIENNE: All right. Wouldn't I be smart enough to kill Walter and frame Steve for it? Wouldn't I figure that even if he's not convicted, Helen will never be able to get him—because if he married her, it would be like signing a confession? How's that? Pretty good case?

HASTINGS: Very good.

INGALLS: [*Stepping forward*] Adrienne . . .

ADRIENNE: [*Snaps angrily*] It's your turn to shut up! [*To* HASTINGS] And besides, that business about the murderer interrupting the fireworks—that's nothing but your own guess. What is there to prove it? Drop that—and my alilbi is as bad as Steve's. Worse. Because I went out looking for Walter. Nothing wrong with *this* case, is there?

HASTINGS: Yes. There is. That's why it's good.

INGALLS: Greg, I won't allow this.

HASTINGS: Come on, Steve, that's the first foolish thing I've heard you say. What's the matter with you? How can you stop me? [*To* ADRIENNE] Miss Knowland, have you noticed that you're the only one here who's been contradicting herself?

ADRIENNE: How?

HASTINGS: That's why I like your case. Because it's not perfect. I don't like perfect cases. . . . How? Well, if Steve was framed, I see only two people who had a motive for framing him. Mr. Sookin and you. Mr. Sookin hates Steve. You love him—which is much more damning. Now look at Mr. Sookin. If he framed Steve, he's been acting like a fool here, laying it on too thick. Now what would he do if he weren't a fool?

SERGE: [*With a new kind of dangerous, mocking note in his voice*] He'd pretend to be one.

HASTINGS: [*Looks at him with new interest, says slowly:*] Quite so. [*Then lightly again:*] Congratulations, Mr. Sookin. You're beginning to understand my ways of thinking. You may be right. But there's another possible method of being clever. The person who framed Steve might do his best to act afterward as if he were *protecting* him.

INGALLS: Greg!

HASTINGS: [*His voice driving on intensely*] Keep still, all of you! Do you see, Miss Knowland? You've put on a beautiful show of protecting Steve. And yet, it was you who gave away the story of that interrupted love scene. Why? To show us that you were jealous? Or to damn Steve?

INGALLS: [*In a tone of such authority that* HASTINGS *has to remain silent*] All right, Greg. That's enough. [*His tone makes everyone look at him*] You wanted to know how I could stop you? Very simply. [*Takes a notebook out of his pocket and throws it down on the table. Takes out a pencil and stands holding it in his hand, over the paper*] Unless you leave Adrienne out of this, I'm going to write a confession that *I* did it.

[ADRIENNE *stands stock-still, like a person hit over the head*]

HASTINGS: But, Steve, you didn't do it!

INGALLS: That's your concern. Mine is only that *she* didn't do it. I'm not going to put on a show of protecting her—as she's been trying to protect me, very crudely. I'm not going to hint and throw suspicion on myself. That's been done for me—quite adequately. I'm simply going to blackmail you. You understand? If I sign a confession—with the evidence you have on me, you'll be forced to put me on trial. You'll have no choice. You might know that I didn't do it, but the jury won't be so subtle. The jury will be glad to pounce upon the obvious. Have I made myself clear? Leave Adrienne out of this, unless you want an unsolved murder on your record—and on your conscience.

ADRIENNE: [*It is a scream of terror, of triumph, of release all at once—and the happiest sound in the world*] Steve! [*He turns to look at her. They stand holding the glance. It is more revealing than any love scene. They look at each other as if they were alone in the room and in the world. . . . Then she whispers, choking:*] Steve . . . you, who've never believed in self-sacrifice . . . you, who've preached selfishness and egoism and . . . you wouldn't do this, unless . . . unless it's—

INGALLS: [*In a low, tense voice, more passionate than the tone of a love confession*]—unless it's for the most selfish reason in the world. [*She closes her eyes. He turns away from her slowly.* HELEN, *who has been watching them, lets her head drop, hopelessly*]

HASTINGS: [*Breaking the silence*] God help us when people begin protecting each other! When they start that—I'm through. [*Throws the notebook to* INGALLS] All right, Steve. Put it away. You win—for the moment. I'll have a few questions to ask you about this— but not right now. [*To* ADRIENNE] Miss Knowland, if you were actually protecting him, you have no respect for my intelligence at all. You should have known I wouldn't believe that Steve is guilty. I know a frame-up when I see one. [*To the others*] And for the information of the scoundrel who did this, I'd like to say that he's an incredible fool. Did he really expect me to believe that Steve Ingalls—with his brilliant, methodical, scientific mind—would commit a sloppy crime like this? I could readily accept Steve as capable of murder. But if he ever committed one, it would be the finest job in the world. There wouldn't be a hair's weight of a clue. He'd have an alibi—as perfect as a precision instrument. But to think of Steve leaving fingerprints and cigarette butts behind! . . . I'd like to get the bastard who planned this and punch him in the nose. It's not a case, it's a personal insult to me!

TONY: And to Steve.

HASTINGS: [*Rising*] I've had enough of this for tonight. Let's get some sleep and some sense. I shall ask everybody not to leave this house, of course. I'll have my men remain here—in this room and in the garden. I'll be back early in the morning. I won't ask you who killed Walter Breckenridge. I'll know that when I find the answer to another question: *who framed Steve Ingalls?* . . . Good night. [*Exits into the garden, calling:*] Dixon! [*As the others move to rise slowly or look at one another,* INGALLS *turns and walks to the stairs.* ADRIENNE—*who has looked at no one but him—makes a step to follow him. He stops on the stairs, turns to her, says calmly:*]

INGALLS: I told you to wait. Sound vibrations travel very slowly, Adrienne. Not yet. [*Turns and exits up the stairs, as she stands looking after him*]

CURTAIN

SCENE 2

Early next morning. The room seems to be glowing. There is a clear blue sky outside and the house is flooded with sunlight.

    HELEN *and* FLEMING *are sitting at a table, deep in conversation. It is a serious conversation, but their voices are simple, light, natural.*

FLEMING: Would we go by boat or by train?

HELEN: A plane would be best, don't you think? Easier for Billy and he'll enjoy it.

FLEMING: Do we have to make arrangements with Dr. Harlan in advance?

HELEN: I think so. I'll telephone him today.

FLEMING: Long-distance?

HELEN: Yes, of course. Why not?

FLEMING: Helen . . . is it going to be very expensive— the operation and all?

HELEN: We don't have to worry about that.

FLEMING: Yes, Helen. We do.

HELEN: [*Looks at him. Then:*] Of course. Forgive me. Bad habits are very hard to lose.

FLEMING: I thought—

[ARIENNE *comes down the stairs. She walks as if her feet do not need to touch the ground. She wears a gay, simple summer dress. She looks like a person whose presence in a room would compete with the sunlight. But her manner is very simple; it is the manner of so profound a happiness that it cannot be anything but simple*]

ADRIENNE: Good morning.

FLEMING: [*Brightly*] Good morning, Adrienne.

HELEN: [*With a little effort*] Good morning.

ADRIENNE: Mr. Hastings arrived?

FLEMING: Not yet.

ADRIENNE: [*Looking through cigarette boxes*] Any Camels around here? I think I'll take up smoking. Camels are wonderful things. God bless every Camel butt in the world! [*Finds a cigarette and lights it*]

FLEMING: Never saw you look like that, Adrienne. Slept well?

ADRIENNE: [*Walking to French doors*] Haven't slept at all. I don't see why people insist on sleeping. You feel so much better if you don't. And how can anybody want to lose a minute—a single minute of being alive?

FLEMING: What's the matter, Adrienne?

ADRIENNE: Nothing. [*Points to the garden*] It's the Fourth of July. [*Exits into the garden*]

HELEN: [*Looks after her, then forces herself to return to the conversation*] When we go to Montreal—

FLEMING: Look, Helen, here's what I thought: I'll have to take the money from you for Billy's operation. That's one time when it's proper for a man to accept help. But don't *give* me the money. Lend it. And charge me a fair interest on it. That, you see, would really be an act of humanity.

HELEN: Yes, Harvey. That's what we'll do.

FLEMING: [*In a low voice*] Thank you.

HELEN: And, of course, we'll take legal steps to make him "Billy Fleming" again. . . . But you won't forbid me to visit him, will you?

FLEMING: [*Smiles happily, shaking his head. Then, at a sudden grim thought:*] Helen. There's one more thing. It's still possible that they'll decide that one of us . . . that . . .

HELEN: Yes. That one of us is the murderer.

FLEMING: Well . . . shall we agree that . . . if it's one of us . . . the other will take Billy to Montreal?

HELEN: Yes, Harvey. And if it's not one of us, then we'll go together.

[INGALLS *enters, coming down the stairs*]

INGALLS: Good morning.

HELEN: Good morning, Steve.

FLEMING: [*Looks at the two of them, then:*] Is Billy up yet?

INGALLS: Don't know. I haven't been downstairs.

FLEMING: Guess I'll go to see if he's up. [*Exits Right*]

INGALLS: [*Turning to* HELEN] Helen.

HELEN: [*Quietly*] I know.

INGALLS: Helen, will you marry me?

HELEN: [*Looks at him, startled, then shakes her head slowly*] No, Steve.

INGALLS: Do you think that I am afraid?

HELEN: No. But if I told you what I think of this, you'd be very angry. You're never angry, except when people say nice things about you. [*As he is about to speak*] No, Steve. You don't love me. Perhaps you thought you did. Perhaps you didn't know who it was that you really loved. I think you know it now. I do. You can't hurt me, Steve, except if you refuse to admit this. Because, then, I'll know that you have no respect for me at all.

INGALLS: [*In a low voice*] I'm sorry, Helen.

HELEN: [*Nods her head slowly. Then forces herself to say lightly:*] Besides, you should have noticed that I never said I loved you.

INGALLS: I noticed something else.

HELEN: Oh, that? Well, you must be generous, Steve. You mustn't hold a moment's weakness against me. After all, you're very attractive, and . . . and Adrienne was right about your manner of making love.

INGALLS: Helen, I'm making it harder for you.

HELEN: [*Calmly, her head high, looking straight at him*]

No, Steve, no. I wanted to say it. And now I want you to forget it. No, I don't love you. I've never loved you. I've known you all these years—I've seen you so often—I've looked at you—I've heard your voice. . . . But I never loved you.

INGALLS: Helen . . .

HELEN: And that, Steve, is all you have a right to remember.

[*She turns, walks to stairs. The doorbell rings. She stops on the stairs.* INGALLS *opens the door.* HASTINGS *enters*]

HASTINGS: Good morning.

HELEN: Good morning, Mr. Hastings.

INGALLS: Hello, Greg.

HASTINGS: [*To* INGALLS] It would be your face that I'd have to see first. All right, I suppose I'd better take you first. [*To* HELEN] Will you excuse me, Mrs. Breckenridge? This case has upset all my theories. I'll have to revert to the conventional and question some of the people in private.

HELEN: Yes, of course. I shall be upstairs if you want me. [*Exits up the stairs*]

HASTINGS: [*Sitting down*] Goddamn this case. Couldn't eat a bite of breakfast this morning.

INGALLS: Oh, I did. I had scrambled eggs and bacon and fresh strawberries and coffee and—

HASTINGS: All right, all right. It doesn't prove anything. You'd eat as well whether you'd done it or not. Did you do it?

INGALLS: What do you think?

HASTINGS: You know what I think. But damn it, Steve, if I don't solve this, it's you that they'll throw to the lions. The jury lions.

INGALLS: I don't think I'm a good type for a martyr.

HASTINGS: No. But a swell type for a murderer.

INGALLS: Oh yes.

[DIXON *enters Right, carrying a stack of newspapers and a phonograph record*]

DIXON: Good morning, Chief. Here it is. [*Deposits his load on a table*]

HASTINGS: What about the shrubbery outside and the balcony?

DIXON: In perfect order. No broken branches. No footprints. Nothing. [*Picking up the record*] Rachmaninoff's Prelude in G Minor all right. And the newspapers.

HASTINGS: [*Looks through the newspapers, stops at one*] *Who* reads the *Red Worker*?

DIXON: Mrs. Pudget.

HASTINGS: [*Having gone to the bottom of the pile*] No *Courier*?

DIXON: No *Courier*.

HASTINGS: Damn it, Dixon, we've got to find it—or prove that it wasn't here at all!

INGALLS: But it was here. I saw it.

HASTINGS: That's the hell of it! Too many of you saw it. I don't think that little Holy Russian rat would've had the guts to fake it with an earlier edition. And yet I know there's something phony about that alibi. Dixon, look through the garbage cans, the incinerators, everything!

DIXON: We did.

HASTINGS: Look again.

DIXON: Okay, Chief. [*Exits Right*]

HASTINGS: Steve, don't be too damn noble and tell me who'd really have a reason to frame you around here!

INGALLS: If you'll take my word for it—and I wish you would—no one.

HASTINGS: No one?

INGALLS: I wouldn't vouch for Serge. But I know of no reason why he'd kill Walter.

HASTINGS: You know, I'm sure he's done it. Look at how it was done. So crude, so obvious. I don't see anyone else staging a frame-up quite so blatantly and hoping to get away with it. It just smells "Serge" all over. A dull, presumptuous, Communist mind that counts on its insolence to overcome the intelligence of anyone else.

INGALLS: But you've got to prove it.

HASTINGS: Yes. And I can't. Well, let's see about the others. Tony Goddard? No reason for him to frame you. Fleming? Possible. Out of fear. Drunkards are not very strong people.

INGALLS: I'll vouch for Fleming.

HASTINGS: Mrs. Breckenridge? No reason. Miss Knowland? . . . Now don't pull out any notebooks. Steve, don't refuse to answer this. I've got to ask it. You're in love with Adrienne Knowland, aren't you?

INGALLS: Desperately. Miserably. Completely. For many years.

HASTINGS: Why "miserably" for many years—when she loves you?

INGALLS: Because neither of us thought it possible of the other. . . . Why did you have to ask this?

HASTINGS: Because—what, then, was that love scene with Mrs. Breckenridge?

INGALLS: [*Shrugging*] A moment's weakness. Despair, perhaps. Because I didn't think that I could ever have the woman I wanted.

HASTINGS: You chose a nice day to be weak on.

INGALLS: Yes, didn't I?

HASTINGS: [*Rising*] Well, I think I'll have a little talk with Fleming now.

INGALLS: Will you be long?

HASTINGS: I don't think so. [SERGE *enters Right.* HASTINGS *turns at the stairs*] Ah, good morning, Commissar.

SERGE: [*Stiffly*] That is not funny.

HASTINGS: No. But it could be. [*Exits up the stairs*]

SERGE: [*Sees the papers, hurries to look through them*] Ah, the newspapers. Have they the *Courier* found?

INGALLS: No.

SERGE: But that is unbelievable! I cannot understand it!

INGALLS: Don't worry. They'll find it—when the time comes. . . . You have nothing to worry about. Look at *me*.

SERGE: [*Interested*] You are worried?

INGALLS: Well, wouldn't you be? It's all right for Greg to amuse himself with fancy deductions and to believe the most improbable. A jury won't do that. A jury will love a case like mine. It's easy on their conscience.

SERGE: [*As persuasively as he can make it*] That is true. I think the jury it would convict you. I think you have no chance.

INGALLS: Oh, I might have a chance. But it will take money.

SERGE: [*Attentively*] Money?

INGALLS: Lots of money. I'll need a good lawyer.

SERGE: Yes. You will need a very good lawyer. And that is expensive.

INGALLS: Very expensive.

SERGE: Your case it is bad.

INGALLS: Very bad.

SERGE: You feel certain that you will be put on trial?

INGALLS: Looks like it.

SERGE: And . . . you do not have the money?

INGALLS: Oh, I suppose I can scrape some together, but you see, I've never made very much. Not like Walter. And what I made I put back into the laboratory. Oh, I guess I could raise some cash on that, but what's the use? Even if I'm acquitted, I'll be broke when I get out of it.

SERGE: You are not the type of man who will like it—being broke.

INGALLS: I won't like it at all.

SERGE: And besides, you believe that your own interest—it comes first?

INGALLS: That's what I believe.

SERGE: [*Throws a quick glance around, then leans over the table, close to* INGALLS, *and speaks rapidly, in a low, hard, tense voice—a new* SERGE *entirely. Even his English is better, but his accent remains*] Listen. No jokes and no clowning about what you knew or what you guessed. We haven't the time. And it's your neck to be saved. Five hundred thousand dollars—now—in your hands—for that invention.

INGALLS: [*Whistles*] Why, Serge, at the rate of fifteen dollars a week, it will take you—

SERGE: Cut it out. You know. You knew all the time. I knew that you knew. And it didn't do you any good, did it? There's no time for showing how smart you are. Now it's either you want it or you don't. And it must be quick.

INGALLS: Well, looks like you've got me, doesn't it?

SERGE: Yes. So don't start talking about your conscience or your patriotism or things like that. You and I, we understand each other.

INGALLS: I think we've understood each other from the first. [*Chuckles*] A gift to mankind, eh, Serge? Just to light the slums and put the greedy utility companies out of business?

SERGE: We have not time for laughing. Yes or no?

INGALLS: Do you carry five hundred thousand bucks, like that, in your pocket?

SERGE: I will write you a check.

INGALLS: How will I know it's any good?

SERGE: You'll know it when you see on whose account it's drawn. Beyond that, you'll have to take the chance. Because I want that graph right now.

INGALLS: Now?

SERGE: I can't come for it when you're in jail, can I? [*Pulls a sheet of paper and a pencil out of a drawer and throws them down on the table*] Now. On this sheet of paper. Before you touch the check.

INGALLS: Aren't you afraid of giving me a check? It could be used as evidence against you.

SERGE: You had evidence against me yesterday. You didn't use it. You saved me. Why?

INGALLS: I think you know that.

SERGE: Yes. There was one thing which you said yesterday—and when you said it, I knew I could have you.

INGALLS: I know what that was. But Greg Hastings didn't notice it.

SERGE: There were many things he didn't notice. Of course, you and I we know who killed Breckenridge.

INGALLS: I'm sure one of us does.

SERGE: It was Adrienne Knowland.

INGALLS: Was it?

SERGE: Good God, it's obvious, isn't it? But we don't care who did it, you and I. It was very convenient, that's all.

INGALLS: Yes.

SERGE: Well, do I get the graph?

INGALLS: I have no choice, have I? I suppose I'll get used to it in time, but it's rather uncomfortable— becoming a scoundrel.

SERGE: That won't bother you for long.

INGALLS: No, not for long. . . . Write that check.

[SERGE *takes a checkbook and a pen out of his pocket, sits down at the table, across from* INGALLS, *writes the check, then extends it, showing it to* INGALLS, *but not letting him touch it.* INGALLS *looks at the check, reads:*]

"The Soviet Culture and Friendship Society." Fancy that! What a coincidence.

SERGE: [*Contemptuously*] If I were doing what you are doing, at least I would not laugh about it.

INGALLS: That's the trouble with you, Serge. You have no sense of humor.

SERGE: You are a very contemptible person.

INGALLS: But I thought you knew that. [*Extends his hand for the check*]

SERGE: [*Pulls the check back, puts it down on the table in front of himself, and pushes the sheet of paper toward* INGALLS] Now get to work. Quick.

INGALLS: Why quite so much hurry? Can't you let me degrade myself gracefully?

SERGE: Shut up! The graph now!

INGALLS: [*Picking up the pencil*] Oh yes, the graph. [*Taps his chin with the pencil thoughfully*] Have you ever thought, Serge, what a strange thing life is? There's so much about it that we don't understand.

SERGE: Hurry up, you fool!

INGALLS: Oh yes. [*Leans over the paper, the pencil ready, then looks up*] And when we don't understand things, we make mistakes.

SERGE: Shut up! Write!

INGALLS: What? Oh, the graph. Well you see cosmic rays are tiny particles which bombard the earth from outer space, carrying an electric charge of—[*Looks up*] For instance, we never understood that incident when someone shot at Walter a month ago. Or did we? [SERGE *looks at him.* INGALLS *holds the glance. Then:*] Shall I write?

SERGE: What about that incident?

INGALLS: Doesn't anything strike you as funny, Serge?

SERGE: What about that incident?

INGALLS: Oh, I thought you knew that I knew everything. Well, I know, for instance, that what you planned then—has succeeded now. Brilliantly, completely, and as you wanted it. Only much better planned than the first time. And a little late. One month too late.

[SERGE *jumps up*] I'm sorry. You want the graph. Cosmic rays, when drawn into a single stream by means of . . . Incidentally, you're not a good shot, Serge. You're much better at housebreaking—or at breaking locks on bags, to be exact. You should have searched that bag, though. It would have looked less obvious.

SERGE: You understood—

INGALLS: Of course, Serge. If that murder had succeeded, the gun would have been found in my bag. And you wouldn't have had time to break the lock *after* the shot. You were very foresighted. But obvious.

SERGE: You can't prove that.

INGALLS: No. I can't prove it. And the gun in my bag wouldn't have proved much, either. Not much. Just enough to put me on trial. And you would have had one man who knew that graph dead, and the other in desperate need of money. But you're a bad shot. You're a much better psychologist. The gift to mankind idea worked smoother and safer.

SERGE: You can't prove—

INGALLS: No. I can't prove anything. And you know, Serge, I don't really think that you did it, this time. But doesn't it strike you as funny that someone has done it for you?

SERGE: I don't care what you think or know. It worked.

INGALLS: Yes. It worked.

SERGE: Then write, Goddamn you!

INGALLS: If you wish.

[*There is the sound of a door opening upstairs.* SERGE *whirls around.* INGALLS *slams his right hand, palm down, over the check on the table, as* HASTINGS *comes down the stairs*]

HASTINGS: [*Notices* INGALLS' *hand at once, says lightly:*] I'm not interrupting anything, am I?

[SERGE *stands by the table, doing a very bad job of disguising his anxiety.* INGALLS *is perfectly calm*]

INGALLS: No. No.

HASTINGS: Imagine finding the two of you in a friendly tête-à-tête.

INGALLS: Oh, we were discussing going into vaudeville together. In a mind-reading act. We're very good at reading each other's mind. Though I think I'm better at it than Serge.

HASTINGS: [*Looks at* INGALLS' *right hand on the table, imitating his tone*] You have an interesting hand, Steve. Ever had your palm read?

INGALLS: No. I don't believe in palmistry.

HASTINGS: [*Takes out a cigarette*] Give me a light, Steve. [INGALLS *reaches into his pocket, takes out his lighter, snaps it on, and offers it to* HASTINGS—*all with his left hand*] Didn't know you were left-handed.

INGALLS: I'm not. I'm just versatile.

HASTINGS: Come on, Steve, how long are you going to play the fool? Lift that hand.

INGALLS: Well, *Serge* enjoyed it. [*Lifts his hand as* SERGE *leaps toward it, but* HASTINGS *pushes* SERGE *aside and seizes the check*]

HASTINGS: [*Reading the check*] "Pay to the order of Steven Ingalls . . ." Well, well, well. Had I come down a minute later, you'd have been half-a-millionaire, Steve.

INGALLS: Yes. Why did you have to hurry?

SERGE: [*Screams at the top of his voice, whirling upon* INGALLS] You swine! You did it on purpose!

HASTINGS: [*In mock astonishment*] *No?*

SERGE: [*To* INGALLS] You lied! You betrayed me! You never intended to sell yourself! You're unprincipled and dishonest!

INGALLS: You shouldn't have trusted me like that.

[HELEN *and* TONY *enter hurriedly at the top of the stairs*]

HELEN: [*Anxiously*] What's going on here?

HASTINGS: Nothing much. Just Serge throwing five-hundred-thousand-dollar checks around.

[HELEN *gasps.* TONY *follows her down the stairs*]

SERGE: [*Screaming defiantly to* INGALLS *and* HASTINGS]

Well? What are you going to do about it? You can't prove anything!

[FLEMING *hurries in Right and stops short at the door*]

HASTINGS: [*Reproachfully*] Now, Serge. We can prove that you're defrauding the Refugees' Committee out of fifteen bucks a week, for instance. And we can prove that I'm right about people who have no motive.

TONY: [*Almost regretfully*] Gee, I hoped it wouldn't be Serge. I hate having to be grateful to Serge for the rest of my life.

[ADRIENNE *comes in from the garden, followed a little later by* DIXON]

SERGE: What motive? What can you prove? That I tried to buy an invention from a murderer who needed the money—nothing else. It's just a simple commercial invention. *Isn't* it, Mr. Ingalls?

INGALLS: Yes.

HASTINGS: Goddamn it, we've got to find that newspaper!

SERGE: Now you understand, Mr. Hastings? Prove that I wasn't in Stamford! Prove it! I don't care whether you find that paper or not! Your own dear friends will have to swear they saw it!

HASTINGS: They don't know what edition it was.

SERGE: That's right! They don't know! Then how do they know it wasn't the last one? Prove that!

FLEMING: [*Looking around the room uselessly, frantically*] We ought to tear this house down and find the lousy sheet! [TONY *joins him in searching*]

SERGE: Prove that I lied to you! Find a jury, even a dumb American jury, that will want to look at me, when they hear of this very heroic genius—[*Points at* INGALLS]—alone in the garden, leaving his fingerprints on the gun!

[*During the last few speeches,* INGALLS *takes out his cigarette case, takes a cigarette, takes a match folder from the table, strikes a match, lights the cigarette and*] *tosses the lighted match into the fireplace.* ADRIENNE, *who has been looking at him, follows it with her eyes, screams suddenly, and dives for the fireplace to put out the fire set to the charred, rolled remnant of a newspaper*]

ADRIENNE: Steve! Look! [*Rises from her knees, with the rolled newspaper in her hand.* HASTINGS *seizes it from her. He unrolls it frantically, looks for the upper front page. Stands perfectly still and silent for a moment. Then raises his head to look at the others, and says quietly, almost wearily:*]
HASTINGS: The early edition of yesterday's *Courier*.

[*Silence. Then* SERGE *lunges for the paper*]

SERGE: You're lying!
HASTINGS: [*Pushing him aside*] Oh no, you don't!

[DIXON *steps to* SERGE's *side.* HASTINGS *extends the newspaper headline toward* SERGE, *but at a safe distance*]

See for yourself. But don't touch it.
SERGE: It's not the paper! It's not the same paper! It was the last edition! I know it was! I looked for the mark when I got it! It was the last edition that I specially wanted!
HASTINGS: [*Shaking his head*] And that, Serge, proves I'm right about people who have good alibis.
SERGE: Who put it in that fireplace? Who burned it like this? I didn't do that! [*Whirls on* INGALLS] He did it! Of course! I gave it to him! When I arrived I gave the paper to him! He changed it for this one! He put it there in the fireplace and—
HASTINGS:—and almost burned the evidence, just now, that's going to save his life? Come on, Serge, how much do you expect me to believe?
SERGE: But I didn't—
HASTINGS: You did. But very badly. Like all the rest of it. You were in a hurry when you started burning that paper. You were interrupted. So you stuck it there, hoping to get it later. But you couldn't—not with my man here all night. . . . Well, I'm almost as big a fool

as you are. Do you know why I took that alibi of yours seriously? Because I didn't think you'd have the guts to pull what you pulled. You could shoot a man in the back all right. But to risk showing a paper to all those people—when your life depended on whether they'd notice the edition or not—*that* took the kind of courage you haven't got. Or so I thought. I owe you an apology there.

SERGE: But you can't prove I did it! You can't prove this is the paper I brought!

HASTINGS: All right, produce the other one.

SERGE: You can't convict me on that!

HASTINGS: I can have a pretty good try at it.

SERGE: [*Real terror showing in his face for the first time*] You're going to—

HASTINGS: I'm going to let you explain it all to a jury.

SERGE: [*Screaming*] But you can't! You can't! Listen! I'm innocent! But if you put me on trial, they'll kill me, don't you understand? Not your jury! My own chiefs! All right! I *am* a Soviet agent! And they don't forgive an agent who gets put on trial! They'll kill me—my own chiefs at home! Don't you understand? Even if I'm acquitted, it will be a death sentence for me just the same! [*Pulls a gun out*] Stand still, all of you!

[SERGE *whirls around and rushes out through the French doors.* DIXON *flies after him, pulling out his gun. They disappear in the garden, as* HASTINGS *starts to follow them. There are two shots. After a moment,* HASTINGS *comes back slowly*]

HASTINGS: That's that.

HELEN: Is he dead?

HASTINGS: Yes. [*Then adds:*] Perhaps it's best this way. It saves us from a long and painful trial. The case is closed. I'm glad—for all of you. [*To* HELEN] I hope, Mrs. Breckenridge, that when you've been a neighbor of ours longer, you will forgive us for giving you on your first day here—

HELEN: I shall be a neighbor of yours, Mr. Hastings— perhaps—later. Not this summer. I'm going to sell this house. Harvey and I are going to Montreal.

TONY: And I'm going to Gimbel's.

[HASTINGS *bows as* HELEN *exits up the stairs with* TONY. FLEMING *exits Right*]

HASTINGS: [*Walks to door Left, turns to* INGALLS] It's as I've always said, Steve. There *is* no perfect crime.

INGALLS: [*Who has not moved from near the fireplace*] No, Greg. There isn't.

[HASTINGS *exits Left.* INGALLS *turns to look at Adrienne*]

ADRIENNE: What are you going to do now, Steve?

INGALLS: I'm going to ask you to marry me. [*As she makes a movement forward*] But before you answer, there's something I'm going to tell you. Yesterday, when you looked at those fireworks and suddenly thought of something—it was not of me or of Helen, was it?

ADRIENNE: No.

INGALLS: I know what you thought. You see, I know who killed Walter Breckenridge. I want you to know it. Listen and don't say anything until I finish.

[*The lights black out completely. Then a single spotlight hits the center of the stage. We can see nothing beyond, only the figures of the two men in the spotlight:* WALTER BRECKENRIDGE *and* STEVE INGALLS. BRECKENRIDGE *is operating the levers of a portable electric switchboard.* INGALLS *stands beside him.* INGALLS *speaks slowly, evenly, quietly, in the expressionless tone of an irrevocable decision*]

INGALLS: If, tomorrow at noon, Walter, you give this invention to the world—then, the day after tomorrow, Soviet Russia, Communist China, and every other dictatorship, every other scum on the face of the earth, will have the secret of the greatest military weapon ever invented.

BRECKENRIDGE: Are you going to start on that again? I thought we had settled it this afternoon.

INGALLS: This afternoon, Walter, I begged you. I had never begged a man before. I am not doing that now.

BRECKENRIDGE: You're interfering with the fireworks. Drop it, Steve. I'm not interested.

INGALLS: No, you're not interested in the consequences. Humanitarians never are. All you see ahead is lighted slums and free electric power on the farms. But you don't want to know that the same invention and the same grand gesture of yours will also send death through the air, and blow up ammunition depots, and turn cities into rubble.

BRECKENRIDGE: I am not concerned with war. I am taking a much farther perspective. I am looking down the centuries. What if one or two generations have to suffer?

INGALLS: And so, at a desperate time, when your country needs the exclusive secret and control of a weapon such as this, you will give it away to anyone and everyone.

BRECKENRIDGE: My country will have an equal chance with the rest of the world.

INGALLS: An equal chance to be destroyed? Is that what you're after? But you will never understand. You have no concern for your country, for your friends, for your property, or for yourself. You don't have the courage to hold that which is yours, to hold it proudly, wisely, openly, and to use it for your own honest good. You don't even know that that takes courage.

BRECKENRIDGE: I do not wish to discuss it.

INGALLS: You are not concerned with mankind, Walter. If you were, you'd know that when you give things to mankind, you give them also to mankind's enemies.

BRECKENRIDGE: You have always lacked faith in your fellow men. Your narrow patriotism is old-fashioned, Steve. And if you think that my decision is so dangerous, why don't you report me to the government?

INGALLS: There are too many friends of Serge Sookin's in the government—at present. It's I who must stop you.

BRECKENRIDGE: You? There's nothing you can do about it. You're only a junior partner.

INGALLS: Yes, Walter, that's all I am. Sixteen years ago,

when we formed our partnership and started the Breckenridge Laboratories, I was very young. I did not care for mankind and I did not care for fame. I was willing to give you most of the profits, and all the glory, and your name on my inventions—they were *my* inventions, Walter, mine alone, all of them, and nobody knew it outside the laboratory. I cared for nothing but my work. You knew how to handle people. I didn't. And I agreed to everything you wanted— just to have a chance at the work I loved. You told me that I was selfish, while you—you loved people and wanted to help them. Well, I've seen your kind of help. And I've seen also that it was I, I the selfish individualist, who helped mankind by producing the Vitamin X separator and the cheap violet ray and the electric saw—[*Points to machine*]—and this. While you accepted gratitude for it—and ruined all those you touched. I've seen what you've done to men. It was *I* who gave you the means to do it. It was I who made it possible for you. It is my responsibility now. I created you—I'm going to destroy you. [BRECKENRIDGE *glances up at him swiftly, understands, jerks his hand away from the machine and to his coat pocket*] What are you looking for? This? [*Takes the gun out of his pocket and shows it to* BRECKENRIDGE. *Then slips it back into his pocket*] Don't move, Walter.

BRECKENRIDGE: [*His voice a little hoarse, but still assured*] Have you lost your mind? Do you expect me to believe that you're going to kill me, here, now, with a house full of people a few steps away?

INGALLS: Yes, Walter.

BRECKENRIDGE: Are you prepared to hang for it?

INGALLS: No.

BRECKENRIDGE: How do you expect to get away with it? [INGALLS *does not answer, but takes out a cigarette and lights it*] Stop playing for effects! Answer me!

INGALLS: I am answering you. [*Indicating the cigarette*] Watch this cigarette, Walter. You have as long a time left to live as it will take this cigarette to burn. When it burns down to the brand, I'm going to throw it here in the grass. It will be found near your body. The gun will be found here—with my fingerprints on it. My handkerchief will be found here on a branch. Your watch will be smashed to set the time. I will have no alibi of any kind. It will be the sloppiest and most obvious murder ever committed. And that is why it will be the perfect crime.

BRECKENRIDGE: [*Fear coming a little closer to him*] You . . . you wouldn't . . .

INGALLS: But that's not all. I'm going to let your friend Serge Sookin hang for your murder. He's tried once to do just what I'm going to do for him. Let him take his punishment now. I'm going to frame myself. And I'm also going to frame him to look as if he'd framed *me.* I'll give him an alibi—and then I'll blow it up. Right now, he is in Stamford, buying a newspaper. But it won't do him any good, because, at this moment, up in my room, I have an early edition of today's *Courier.* Do you understand, Walter?

BRECKENRIDGE: [*His voice hoarse, barely audible*] You . . . Goddamn fiend . . .!

INGALLS: You wanted to know why I let you see me kissing Helen today. To give myself a plausible motive of sorts. Just the kind that would tempt a Serge to frame me. You see, I can't let Greg Hastings guess my real motive. I didn't know that Helen would play her part so well. I never dreamed that possible or I wouldn't have done it. It's the only thing that I regret.

BRECKENRIDGE: You . . . won't . . . get away with it. . . .

INGALLS: The greatest chance I'm taking is that I must not let Greg Hastings guess the real nature of my invention. If he guesses that—he'll know I did it. But I have to take that chance. [*Looks at his cigarette*] Your time is up. [*Puts the butt out and tosses it aside*]

BRECKENRIDGE: [*In utter panic*] No! You won't! You won't! You can't! [*Makes a movement to run*]

INGALLS: [*Whipping the gun out*] I told you not to move. [BRECKENRIDGE *stops*] Don't run, Walter. Take it straight for once. If you run—you'll only help me. I'm a good shot—and nobody would believe that I'd shoot a man in the back. [*And now* this *is the real* STEVE INGALLS—*hard, alive, taut with energy, his voice ringing—the inventor, the chance-taker, the genius—as he stands pointing the gun at* BRECKENRIDGE] Walter!

I won't let you do to the world what you've done to all your friends. We can protect ourselves against men who would do us evil. But God save us from the men who would do us good! This is the only humanitarian act I've ever committed—the only one any man can ever commit. I'm setting men free. Free to suffer. Free to struggle. Free to take chances. But free, Walter, *free*! Don't forget, tomorrow is Independence Day!

[BRECKENRIDGE *whirls around and disappears in the dark.* INGALLS *does not move from the spot, only turns without hurry, lifts the gun, and fires into the darkness*]

[*The spotlight vanishes. Blackout*]

[*When the full lights come back,* INGALLS *is sitting calmly in a chair, finishing his story.* ADRIENNE *stands tensely, silently before him*]

INGALLS: I've told you this because I wanted you to know that I don't regret it. Had circumstances forced me to take a valuable life—I wouldn't hesitate to offer my own life in return. But I don't think that of Walter. Nor of Serge. . . . Now you know what I am. [*Rises, stands looking at her*] Now, Adrienne, repeat it—if you still want me to hear it.

ADRIENNE: [*Looking at him, her head high*] No, Steve. I can't repeat it now. I said that I was inexcusably, contemptibly in love with you and had been for years. I can't say that any longer. I will say that I'm in love with you—so terribly *proudly* in love with you—and will be for years . . . and years . . . and forever. . . .
[*He does not move, only bows his head slowly, accepting his vindication*]

CURTAIN

"Do you think," Ayn Rand said to me when I finished reading, "that I would ever give the central action in a story of mine to anyone but the hero?"

The Fountainhead
(unpublished excerpts)

1938

Editor's Preface

In 1938, after devoting about three years to architectural research, Ayn Rand started writing *The Fountainhead*. She finished in late 1942, and the novel was published the next year. In less than a decade, the book became world-famous; by now, it has sold more than six million copies. Ayn Rand's own view of *The Fountainhead* can be found in her introduction to the 25th Anniversary Edition.

For this anthology, I have selected two sets of excerpts cut by Miss Rand from the original manuscript; these are the only unpublished passages of substantial length. Both are from the early part of the novel, written in 1938. As is true of the passages from *We the Living*, neither has received Ayn Rand's customary final editing, and the titles are my own invention.

"Vesta Dunning" is the story of Howard Roark's first love affair, with a young actress, before he found Dominique. In the manuscript, the story is interwoven with other plot developments; it is offered here as a continuous, uninterrupted narrative.

Vesta Dunning is an eloquent example of a person of "mixed premises," to use a term of Ayn Rand's. In part, Vesta shares Howard Roark's view of life; in part, she is a secondhander, willing to prostitute her talent in order to win the approval of others, a policy she tries to defend as a means to a noble end. Miss Rand cut Vesta from the novel, she told me, when she realized that there was too great a similarity between Vesta and Gail Wynand, the newspaper publisher (who also pursued a secondhander's course in the name of achieving noble ends). In some respects, there is a marked similarity between Vesta and Peter Keating, too; in fact, as the material makes plain, some of Keating's dialogue was written originally for Vesta.

"Roark and Cameron" comprises two distinct scenes involving both men. The first takes place when Roark is working in New York City for Henry Cameron, the once-famous architect who is now forgotten by the world; the second occurs some time later, at the site of the Heller house, Roark's first commission after starting in private architectural practice on his own. Evidently, Miss Rand cut the scenes because she decided that so detailed a treatment of Roark's relationship to Cameron was inessential to the purpose of the novel at this point—that is, the establishing of Roark's character and the development of the plot.

Despite the intrinsic interest of this manuscript material, I have serious misgivings about publishing it. In certain respects, the scenes are inconsistent with the final novel (which may very well have contributed to their being cut). It is doubtful to me whether Roark, as presented in the novel, would have had an affair with Vesta. It is doubtful whether, in the Cameron scene, Roark would have lost his temper to the extent of punching a man. Furthermore, Roark's statements are not always as exact philosophically as Miss Rand's final editing would have made them. The Roark in the novel, for instance, would not have said that he is too selfish to love anyone (in the novel he says that selfishness is a precondition of love); nor would he have said, without a clearer context, that he hates the world. Aside from these specifics, the general tone of Roark's characterization does not always seem right; without the context of the rest of the novel, he comes across, I think, as overly severe at times to Vesta, and also as overly abstracted and antisocial. Undoubtedly, this is also partly an issue of exact nuance and wording, which Miss Rand would have adjusted had she decided to retain the material.

The admirers of *The Fountainhead* see the novel, and Roark, as finished realities. The author obviously shared this view. I must therefore stress that the following is *not* to be taken as part of *The Fountainhead*. These scenes do not contribute to the novel's theme or meaning, and they do not cast further light on Roark's character or motivation. They are offered as individual, self-contained pieces, to be read as such. If I may state the point paradoxically, for emphasis: these events did not happen to Roark—they are pure fiction!

Despite my misgivings, I could not convince myself to keep the material hidden, for a single reason: it is too well written. Miss Rand told me once that she regretted having to cut the Vesta Dunning affair because it contained "some of my best writing." This is true, and it is from this perspective that the passages are best approached. Even in this unedited material, one can see some characteristic features of Ayn Rand's mature literary style. More than any other single attribute of her writing, her style reveals the extent of her growth in the space of a decade.

The feature of Ayn Rand's style most apparent in these scenes is one that perfectly reflects her basic philosophy. I mean her ability to integrate *concretes* and *abstractions*.

Philosophically, Ayn Rand is Aristotelian. She does not believe in any Platonic world of abstractions; nor does she accept the view that concepts are merely arbitrary social conventions, with its implication that reality consists of unintelligible concretes. Following Aristotle, she holds that the world of physical entities is reality, *and* that it can be understood by man through the use of his conceptual faculty. Concepts, she holds, are not supernatural or conventional; they are objective forms of cognition based on, and ultimately making comprehensible, the facts of reality perceived by our senses. (Ayn Rand's distinctive theory of concepts is presented in her *Introduction to Objectivist Epistemology*.) For man, therefore, the proper method of knowledge is not perception alone or conception alone, but the integration of the two—which means, in effect, the union of concretes and abstractions.

One literary expression of this epistemology is Ayn Rand's commitment to integrating theme and plot. The plot of an Ayn Rand novel is a purposeful progression of events, not a series of random occurrences. The events add up to a general thematic idea, which is thus implicit in and conveyed by the story, not arbitrarily superimposed on it. The plot, in short, is a progression of concretes integrated by and conveying an abstraction.

The same epistemology is essential to Ayn Rand's style of writing, whether she is describing physical nature, human action, or the most delicate, hidden emotion. The style consists in integrating the *facts* being described and their *meaning*.

Consider, for example, the following paragraph, which describes Vesta on the screen:

> . . . She had not learned the proper camera angles, she had not learned the correct screen makeup; her mouth was too large, her cheeks too gaunt, her hair uncombed, her movements too jerky and angular. She was like nothing ever seen in a film before, she was a contradiction to all standards, she was awkward, crude, shocking, she was like a breath of fresh air. The studio had expected her to be hated; she was suddenly worshiped by the public. She was not pretty, nor gracious, nor gentle, nor sweet; she played the part of a young girl not as a tubercular flower, but as a steel knife. A reviewer said that she was a cross between a medieval pageboy and a gun moll. She achieved the incredible: she was the first woman who ever allowed herself to make strength attractive on the screen.

The paragraph begins with a description of Vesta's mouth, her hair, her movements, etc. This description re-creates the concrete reality, sets the physical essentials of a young Katharine Hepburn type before us, so that we can, in effect, perceive the event (Vesta onscreen) through our own eyes. On this basis, we are offered some preliminary abstractions, giving a first layer of meaning to these facts; Vesta comes across, we learn, not as pretty, gentle, sweet, but as crude, shocking, fresh—and we accept this account, we see its inner logic, because we know the supporting facts. Then we are given some vivid images comparing Vesta to utterly different entities of a similar meaning (a steel knife, a gun moll, etc.); this helps both to keep the reality real (i.e., to keep it concrete) and to develop the meaning further. The images seem to flow naturally out of the earlier material; they do not strike us as forced or as superfluous, "literary" embellishments. Finally, after this buildup, we are given a single abstraction which unites all of it— the facts, the preliminary abstractions, the images. We are given an integrating concept, which names a definitive meaning, to carry forward with us: ". . . she was the first woman who ever allowed herself to make strength attractive on the screen." By this time, we do not have to guess at the meaning of "strength," even though it is a very broad abstraction; we know what is meant by it in this context, because we have seen the data that give rise to the concept here. And we believe the term; we do not feel that it is empty or arbitrary, or that we have to take the author's word for it. We do not even feel that it is the conclusion of an extended argument (though in effect it is). We take it here virtually as a statement of the self-evident, as a statement of what we ourselves by now are ready to conclude.

This method is not, of course, repeated in every paragraph. It is applied only where the material requires it. Nor is the order of development always the same; nor are the specific steps—there may be more or fewer of them. But this kind of approach, in some form and on some level, *is* always present. It is one of the elements that make Ayn Rand's writing so powerful. Concretes by themselves are meaningless, and cannot even be retained for long; abstractions by themselves are vague or empty. But concretes illuminated by an abstraction acquire meaning, and thereby permanence in our minds; and abstractions illustrated by concretes acquire specificity, reality, the power to convince. The result is that *both* aspects of the writing become important to the reader, who experiences at once the vividness of sensory perception and the clarity of a rational thought process.

Essential to Ayn Rand's method is that the concretes really be concrete, i.e., *perceptual*. The entity or attribute must be described as the reader would actually see it if he were present. Yet, at the same time, the description must pave the way for the abstraction. The description, therefore, must be highly selective; it must dispense with all premature commentary and all irrelevant data, however naturalistic. It must present those facts, and those only, that are essential if the reader is to apprehend the scene from the angle the author requires. This demands of the writing an extreme ingenuity and purposefulness. The author must continuously invent the telling detail, the fresh perspective, the eloquent juxtaposition, that will create in the reader the awareness of a perceptual reality—which contains an implicit meaning, the specific meaning intended by the author.

As a small instance: at one point, Miss Rand wishes to convey Vesta's feeling of helplessness in Roark's bed, her desperate need to confess her love to him and yet at the same time to hide it because of his aloofness. Miss Rand does not describe this conflict in any such terms, which are mere generalities. She makes the conflict real by a *perceptual* description, at once strikingly original and yet nothing more than a selective account of an ordinary physical fact: "He listened silently to her breathless voice whispering to him, when she could not stop it: 'I love you, Howard . . . I love you . . . I love you . . .' her lips pressed to his arm, to his shoulder, as if her mouth were telling it to his skin, and it was not from her nor for him." One can *see* the mouth on the skin as a kind of movie close-up; and implicit in the sight, in this context, is the meaning, the attempt at concealment ("and it was not from her nor for him").

A further requirement of Ayn Rand's method is that she use language *exactly*.

Miss Rand must name the precise data which lead to the abstraction, and the precise abstraction to which they lead. On either level, a mere approximation, or any touch of vagueness, will not do; such defaults would weaken or destroy the inner logic of the writing, and thereby its power and integrity. Miss Rand, therefore, is sensitive to the slightest shade of wording or connotation that might possibly be overgeneralized, unclear, or misleading; she is sensitive to any wording that might blur what she is seeking to capture. She wishes both the facts and the meaning to confront the reader cleanly, starkly, unmistakably. (Thus her scorn for those writers who equate artistry with ambiguity.)

When Roark first meets Vesta, for instance, he likes her—that is the fact—but "liking" by itself is not enough here. What is his exact feeling? "He liked that face, coldly, impersonally, almost indifferently; but sharply and quite personally, he liked the thing in her voice which he had heard before he entered." Or, on the level of meaning: when Vesta feels Roark's aloofness in bed, "it was as if the nights they shared gave her no rights." The last two words are followed immediately by: ". . . not the right to the confidence of a friend, not the right to the consideration of an acquaintance, not even the right to the courtesy of a stranger passing her on the street." Now we *know* what it means for her to have "no rights."

The same use of language governs Ayn Rand's dialogue. An admirer of her work once observed that her characters do not talk naturalistically—that is, the way people talk. They state the essence of what people *mean*. And they state it exactly. (This is true even of villains in her novels, who seek not to communicate, but to evade.) When Vesta feels ambivalence for Roark, as an example, there is a kind of surgical conscientiousness involved as she struggles to name it, to name the exact shade of her feeling, in all its complexity and contradiction.

Howard, I love you. I don't know what it is. I don't know why it should be like this. I love you and I can't stand you. And also, I wouldn't love you if I could stand you, if you were any different. But what you are—that frightens me, Howard. I don't know why. It frightens me because it's something in me which I don't want. No.

Because it's something in me which I do want, but I'd rather not want it. . . .

Such painstaking, virtually scientific precision could by itself constitute an admirable literary style. But in Ayn Rand's work it is integrated with what may seem to some to be an opposite, even contradictory feature: extravagant drama, vivid imagery, passionate evaluations (by the characters *and* the author)—in short, a pervasive *emotional* quality animating the writing. The emotional quality is not a contradiction; it is an essential attribute of the style, a consequence of the element of abstractions. A writer who identifies the conceptual meaning of the facts he conveys is able to judge and communicate their *value* significance. The mind that stops to ask about something, "*What* is it?" goes on to ask, "So what?" and to let us know the answer. A style describing concretes without reference to their abstract meaning would tend to emerge as dry or repressed (for example, the style of Sinclair Lewis or John O'Hara). A style featuring abstractions without reference to concretes would, if it tried to be evaluative, emerge as bombastic or feverish (for example, the style of Thomas Wolfe). In contrast to both types, Ayn Rand offers us a rare combination: the most scrupulous, subtly analyzed factuality, giving rise to the most violent, freewheeling emotionality. The first makes the second believable and worthy of respect; the second makes the first exciting.

Serious Romantic writers in the nineteenth century (there are none left now) stressed values in their work, and often achieved color, drama, passion. But they did it, usually, by retreating to a realm of remote history or of fantasy—that is, by abandoning actual, contemporary reality. Serious Naturalists of one or two generations ago stressed facts, and often achieved an impressively accurate reproduction of contemporary reality—but, usually, at the price of abandoning broad abstractions, universal meanings, value judgments. (Today's writers generally abandon everything and achieve nothing.) By uniting the two essentials of human cognition, perception and conception, Ayn Rand's writing (like her philosophy) is able to unite facts *and* values.

Ayn Rand described her literary orientation as Romantic Realism (see *The Romantic Manifesto*). The term is applicable on every level of her writing. For her, "romanticism" does not mean escape from life; nor does "realism" mean escape from values. The universe she creates in her novels is not a realm of impossible fantasy, but the world as it might be (the principle of Realism)—*and* as it ought to be (the principle of Romanticism). Her characters are not knights in armor or Martians in spaceships, but architects, businessmen, scientists, politicians—men of our era dealing with real, contemporary problems (Realism)—and she presents these characters not as helpless victims of society, but as heroes (or villains) shaped by their own choices and values (Romanticism).

"Romantic Realism" applies equally to her style. The re-creation of concretes, the commitment to perceptual fact, the painstaking precision and clarity of the descriptions—this is Realism in a sense deeper than fidelity to the man on the street. It is fidelity to physical reality as such. The commitment to abstractions, to broader significance, to evaluation, drama, passion—this is the Romanticist element.

Ayn Rand's writing (like everyone else's) is made only of abstractions (words). Because of her method, however, she can make words convey at the same time the reality of a given event, its meaning, and its feeling. The reader experiences the material as a surge of power that reaches him on all levels: it reaches his senses and his mind, his mind and his emotions.

Although Ayn Rand's writing is thoroughly conscious, it is not self-conscious; it is natural, economical, flowing. It does not strike one as literary pyrotechnics (although it is that). Like all great literature, it strikes one as a simple statement of the inevitable.

The above indicates my reasons for wanting to publish these scenes. Taken by themselves as pieces of writing, "Vesta Dunning" and "Roark and Cameron" are a fitting conclusion to this survey of Ayn Rand's early work and development.

The following is what the author of "The Husband I Bought" was capable of twelve years later.

—L. P.

Vesta Dunning

The snow fell in a thick curtain, as if a pillow were being shaken from the top windows of the tenement, and through the flakes sticking to his eyelashes, Roark could barely see the entrance of his home. He shook the iced drops from the upturned collar of his coat, a threadbare coat that served meagerly through the February storms of New York. He found the entrance and stopped in the dark hall, where a single yellow light bulb made a mosaic of glistening snakes in the melting slush on the floor, and he shook his cap out, gathering a tiny pool of cold, biting water in the palm of his hand. He swung into the black hole of the stairway, for the climb to the sixth floor.

It was long past the dinner hour, and only a faint odor of grease and onions remained in the stairshaft, floating from behind the closed, grimy doors on the landings. He had worked late. Three new commissions had come unexpectedly into the office, and Cameron had exhausted his stock of blasphemy, a bracing, joyous blasphemy ringing through the drafting room as a tonic. "Just like in the old days," Simpson had said, and in the early dusk of the office, in the unhealthy light, in the freezing drafts from the snow piled on the window ledges there had reigned for days an air of morning and spring. Roark was tired tonight, and he went up the stairs closing his eyes often, pressing his lids down to let them rest from the strain of microscopically thin black lines that had had to be drawn unerringly all day long, lines that stood now as a white cobweb on dark red whenever he closed his eyes. But he went up swiftly, his body alive in a bright, exhilarating exhaustion, a weariness demanding action, not rest, to relieve it.

He had reached the fourth floor, and he stopped. High on the dark wall facing the smeared window, the red glow of a soda-biscuit sign across the river lighted the landing, and black dots of snowflakes' shadows rolled, whirling, over the red patch. Two flights up, behind the closed door of his room, he heard a voice speaking.

He rose a few steps, and stood pressed to the wall, and listened. It was a woman's voice, young, clear, resonant, and it was raised in full force, as if addressing a huge crowd. He heard, incredibly, this:

. . . but do not question me. I do not answer questions.
You have a choice to make: accept me now
or go your own silent, starless way
to an unsung defeat in uncontested battle.
I stand before you here, I am unarmed;
I offer you tonight my only weapon—
the weapon of that certainty I carry,
unchangeable, untouched and unshared.
Tomorrow's battle I have won tonight
if you but follow me. We'll lift together
the siege of Orleans and win the freedom
I am alone to see and to believe. . . .

The voice was exultant, breaking under an emotion it could not control. It seemed to fail suddenly in the wrong places, speaking the words not as they should have been spoken on a stage, but as a person would fling them out in delirium, unable to hold them, choking upon them. It was the voice of a somnambulist, unconscious of its own sounds, knowing only the violence and the ecstasy of the dream from which it came.

Then it stopped and there was no sound in the room above. Roark went up swiftly and threw the door open.

A girl stood in the middle of the room, with her back to him. She whirled about, when she heard the door knock against the wall. His eyes could not catch the speed of her movement. He had not seen her turn. But there she was suddenly, facing him, as if she had sprung up from the floor and frozen for a second. Her short brown hair stood up wildly with the wind of the motion. Her thin body stood as it had stopped, twisted in loose, incredible angles, awkward, except for her long, slim legs that could not be awkward, even when planted firmly, stubbornly wide apart, as they were now.

"What do you want here?" she snapped ferociously.

"Well," said Roark, "don't you think that I should ask you that?"

She looked at him, at the room.

"Oh," she said, something extinguishing itself in her voice, "I suppose it's your room. I'm sorry."

She made a brusque movement to go. But he stepped in front of the door.

"What were you doing here?" he asked.

"It's your own fault. You should lock your room when you go out. Then you won't have to be angry at people for coming in."

"I'm not angry. And there's nothing here to lock up."

"Well, *I* am angry! You heard me here, didn't you? Why didn't you knock?"

But she was looking at him closely, her eyes widening, clearing slowly with the perception of his face; he could almost see each line of his face being imprinted, reflected upon hers; and suddenly she smiled, a wide, swift, irresistible smile that seemed to click like a windshield wiper and sweep everything else, the anger, the doubt, the wonder, off her face. He could not decide whether she was attractive or not; somehow, one couldn't be aware of her face, but only of its expressions: changing, snapping, jerking expressions, like projections of a jolting film that unrolled somewhere beyond the muscles of her face. He noticed a wide mouth, a short, impertinent nose turned up, dark, greenish eyes. There was a certain quality for which he looked unconsciously upon every face that passed him; a quality of awareness, of will, of purpose, a quality hard and precise; lacking it, the faces passed him unnoticed; with its presence—and he found it rarely—they stopped his eyes for a brief, curious moment of wonder. He saw it now, undefinable and unmistakable, upon her face; he liked that face, coldly, impersonally, almost indifferently; but sharply and quite personally, he liked the thing in her voice which he had heard before he entered.

"I'm sorry you heard me," she said, smiling, still with a hard little tone of reproach in her voice. "I don't want anyone to hear that. . . . But then, it's you," she added. "So I guess it's all right."

"Why?" he asked.

"I don't know. Do you?"

"Yes, I think so. It is all right. What were you reciting?"

"Joan d'Arc. It's from an old German play I found. It's of no interest to you or anyone."

"Where are you going to do it?"

"I'm not doing it anywhere—yet. It's never been produced here. What I'm doing is the part of Polly Mae—five sides—in *You're Telling Me* at the Majestic. Opens February the nineteenth. Don't come. I won't give you any passes and I don't want you to see it."

"I don't want to see it. But I want to know how you got here."

"Oh. . . ." She laughed, suddenly at ease. "Well, sit down. . . . Oh, it's really you who should invite me to sit down." With which she was sitting on the edge of his table, her shoulders hunched, her legs flung out, sloppily contorted, one foot twisted, pointing in, and grotesquely graceful. "Don't worry," she said, "I haven't touched anything here. It's on account of Helen. She's my roommate. I have nothing against her, except the eight-hour working day."

"What?"

"I mean she's got to be home at five. I wish someone'd exploit her good and hard for a change, but no, she gets off every single evening. She's secretary to a warehouse around here. You have a marvelous room. Sloppy, but look at the space! You can't appreciate what it means to live in a clothes closet—or have you seen the other rooms in this house? Anyway, mine's on the fifth floor, just below you. And when I want to rehearse in the evenings, with Helen down there, I have to do it on the stairs. You see?"

"No."

"Well, go out and see how cold it is on the stairs

today. And I saw your door half open. So I couldn't resist it. And then, it was too grand a chance up here to waste it on Polly Mae. Did you ever notice what space will do to your voice? I guess I forgot that someone would come here eventually. . . . My name's Vesta Dunning. Yours is Howard Roark—it's plastered here all over the place—you have a funny handwriting—and you're an architect."

"So you haven't touched anything here?"

"Oh, I just looked at the drawings. There's one—it's crazy, but it's marvelous!" She was up and across the room in a streak, and she stopped, as if she had applied brakes at full speed, at the shelf he had built for his drawings. She always stopped in jerks, as if the momentum of her every movement would carry her on forever and it took a conscious effort to end it. She had the inertia of motion; only stillness seemed to require the impulse of energy.

"This one," she said, picking out a sketch. "What on earth ever gave you an idea like that? When I'm a famous actress, I'll hire you to build this for me."

He was standing beside her; she felt his sleeve against her arm as he took the sketch from her, looked at it, put it back on the shelf.

"When you're a famous actress," he said, "you won't want a house like that."

"Why?" she asked. "Oh, you mean because of Polly Mae, don't you?" Her voice was hard. "You're a strange person. I didn't think anyone would understand it like that, like I do. . . . But you've heard the other also."

"Yes," he said, looking at her.

"You've heard it. You know. You know what it will mean when I'm a famous actress."

"Do you think your public will like it?"

"What?"

"Joan d'Arc."

"I don't care if they don't. I'll make them like it. I don't want to give them what they ask for. I want to make them ask for what I want to give. What are you laughing at?"

"Nothing. I'm not laughing. Go on."

"I know, you think it's cheap and shabby, acting and all that. I do too. But not what I'm going to make of it. I don't want to be a star with a permanent wave. I'm not good-looking anyway. That's not what I'm after. I hate her—Polly Mae. But I'm not afraid of her. I've got to use her to go where I'm going. And where I'm going—it's to the murder of Polly Mae. The end of her in all the minds that have been told to like her. Just to show them what else is possible, what can exist, but doesn't, but will exist through me, to make it real when God failed to . . . Look, I've never spoken of it to anyone, why am I telling it to you? . . . Well, I don't care if you hear this also, whether you understand it or not, and I think you understand, but what I want is . . ."

". . . the weapon of that certainty I carry, unchangeable, untouched and unshared."

"Don't!" she screamed furiously. "Oh," she said softly, "how did you remember it? You liked it, didn't you?" She stood close to him, her face hard. "Didn't you?"

"Yes," he said. She was smiling. "Don't be pleased," he added. "It probably means that no one else will."

She shrugged. "To hell with that."

"How old are you?"

"Eighteen. Why?"

"Don't people always ask you that when you speak of something that's important to you? They always ask me."

"Have you noticed that? What is it that happens to them when they grow older?"

"I don't know."

"Maybe we'll never know, you and I."

"Maybe."

She saw a package of cigarettes in his coat pocket, extended her hand for it, took it out, calmly offered it to him, and took one for herself. She stood smoking, looking at him through the smoke.

"Do you know," she said, "you're terribly good-looking."

"What?" He laughed. "It's the first time I've ever heard that."

"Well, you really aren't. Only I like to look at your face. It's so . . . untouchable. It makes me want to see you break down."

"Well, you're honest."

"So are you. And terribly conceited."

"Probably. Call it that. Why?"

"Because you didn't seem to notice that I paid you a compliment."

She was smiling at him openly, unconcerned and impersonal. There was no invitation, no coquetry in her face, only a cool, wondering interest. But, somehow, it was not the same face that had spoken of Joan d'Arc, and he frowned, remembering that he was tired.

"Don't pay me any compliments," he said, "if you want to come here again."

"May I come here again?" she asked eagerly.

"Look, here's what we'll do. I'll leave you my key in the mornings—I'd better lock the room from now on, I don't want anyone else studying my handwriting around here—I'll slip the key under your door. You can rehearse here all day long, but try to get out by seven. I don't want visitors when I get home. Drop the key in my mailbox."

She looked at him, her eyes radiant.

"It's the nastiest way I've ever heard anyone offering the nicest thing," she said. "All right, I won't bother you again. But leave the key. It's the third door down the hall, to the right."

"You'll have it tomorrow. Now run along. I have work to do."

"Can't I," she asked, "be a little late some evenings and overstep the seven-o'clock deadline by ten minutes?"

"I don't know. Maybe."

"Goodnight, Howard." She smiled at him from the threshold. "Thank you."

"Goodnight, Vesta."

In the spring, the windows of Roark's room stood open, and through the long, bright evenings Vesta Dunning sat on a windowsill, strands of lights twinkling through the dark silhouettes of the city behind her, the luminous spire of a building far away at the tip of her nose. Roark lay stretched on his stomach on the floor, his elbows propped before him, his chin in his hands, and looked up at her and at the glowing sky. Usually, he saw neither. But she had noticed that in him long ago and had come to take it for granted, without resentment or wonder. She breathed the cool air of the city and smiled secretly to herself, to the thought that he allowed her sitting there and that he did notice it sometimes.

She had broken her deadline often, remaining in his room to see him come home; at first, because she forgot the time in her work; then, because she forgot the work and watched the clock anxiously for the hour of his return. On some evenings, he ordered her out because he was busy; on others he let her stay for an hour or two; it did not seem to matter much, in either case, and this made her hate him, at first, then hate herself—for the joy of the pain of his indifference.

They talked lazily, aimlessly, of many things, alone over the city in the evenings. She talked, usually; sometimes, he listened. She had few friends; he had none. It was impossible to predict what subject she would fling out suddenly in her eager, jerking voice; everything seemed to interest her; nothing interested him. She would speak of plays, of men, of books, of holdups, of perfumes, of buildings; she would say suddenly: "What do you think of that gas-station murder?" "What gas-station murder?" "Don't you read the news? You should see what the Wynand papers are making of it. It's beautiful, what an orgy they're having with it." "Nobody reads the Wynand papers but housewives and whores." "Oh, but they have such nice grisly pictures!" . . . Then: "Howard, do you think that there is such a thing as infinity? Because if you try to think of it one way or the other, it doesn't make sense—and I thought that . . ." Then: "Howard, Howard, do you still think that I'll be a great actress someday? You said so once." Then her voice would be low, and even, and hard, and reluctant somehow.

He noticed that this was the one thing which made her hesitant and still and drawn. When she spoke of her future, she was like an arrow, stripped to a thin shaft, poised, ready, aimed at a single point far away, an arrow resting on so taut a string that one wished it to start upon its flight before the string would break. She hated to speak of it; but she had to speak of it, and something in him forced her to speak, and then she would talk for hours, her voice flat, unfriendly, without expression, but her lips trembling. Then she would not notice him listening; and then he would be listening, and his eyes would be open, as if a shutter had clicked off, and his eyes would be aware of her, of her thin, slouched shoulders, of the line of her throat against the sky, of her twisted [pose],* always wrong, always graceful.

She did not know that she had courage or purpose. She struggled as she was struggling because she had been born that way and she had no choice in the matter, nor the time to wonder about an alternative. She did not notice her own dismal poverty, nor her fear of the landlord, nor the days when she went without dinner. *You're Telling Me,* the show which she would not allow Roark to see, had closed within two weeks. She had made the rounds of theatrical producers, after that, grimly, stubbornly, without plaints or questions. She had found no work, and it gave her no anger and no doubts.

She was eighteen, without parents, censors, or morals, and she was, indifferently and incongruously, a virgin.

She was desperately in love with Roark.

She knew that he knew it, even though she had never spoken of it. He seemed neither flattered nor annoyed. She wondered sometimes why he allowed her to see him so often and why they were friends when she meant nothing to him. Then she thought that she did mean something, but what or how she could never decide. He liked her presence, but he liked it in that strange way which seemed to tell her that he would not turn his head were she to drop suddenly beyond the window ledge. Her body grew rigid sometimes with the sudden desire to touch his arm, to run her fingers on the soft edge of the collarbone in his open shirt; yet she knew that were she to sink her fingers into his freckled skin, were she

*The manuscript is illegible at this point.

to hold that head by its orange hair, she could never hold it close enough, nor reach it, nor own it. There were days when she hated him and felt relieved at the knowledge that she could exist without needing him. She always came back, for that look of indifferent curiosity in his eyes; it was indifferent, but it was curiosity and it was directed at her. She had learned it was more than others ever drew from him.

Sometimes, in the warm spring evenings, they would go together for a ride on the Staten Island Ferry. It was a trip he liked, and she loved and dreaded. She loved to be alone with him, late at night, on a half-empty deck, with the sky black and low, pressing down to her forehead, so that she felt lost in a vast darkness, in spite of the raw lights on deck, as if she could see in the dark, and see the hard, straight, slanting line of his nose, his chin against the black water beyond them, and the night gathered in little pools on his hollow cheeks. Then he would lean against the railing and stand looking at the city, at the high pillars of twinkling dots pierced through an empty sky where no buildings could be seen or seemed to have existed. Then she knew how it would feel to die, because she did not exist then, save in the knowledge of her nonbeing, because the boat did not exist, nor the water, nothing but the man at the railing and what he saw beyond those strings of light. Sometimes, she would lean close to him and let her hand on the railing press against his; he would not move his hand away; he would do worse; he would not notice it.

In the summer, she went away for three months with the road tour of a stock company. She did not write to him and he had not asked her to write. When she returned, in the fall, he was glad to see her, glad enough to show her that he was glad; but it did not make her happy, because he showed also that he knew she would return and return exactly as she did: hard, unsmiling, hungrier for him than ever, angry and tingling under the pleasure of the contempt in his slow, understanding smile.

She managed—by losing her patience and calling a producer the names she had always wanted to call him— to get a part in a new play, that fall. It was not a big part, but she had one good scene. She let Roark come to the opening. What he saw, for six minutes on that stage, was a wild, incredible little creature whom he barely recognized as Vesta Dunning, a thing so free and natural and simple that she seemed fantastic. She was unconscious of the room, of the eyes watching her, and of all rules: her postures absurd, reversed, her limbs swinging loosely, aimlessly—and ending in the precision of a sudden gesture, unexpected and thrillingly right, her voice stopping on the wrong words, hard in tenderness, smiling in sorrow, everything wrong and everything exactly as it had to be, inevitable in a crazy perfection of her own. And for six minutes, there was no theater and no stage, only a young, radiant voice too full of its own power and its own promise. One review, on the following day, mentioned the brilliant scene of a girl named Vesta Dunning, a beginner, it stated, worth watching. Vesta cut the review out of the paper and carried it about with her for weeks; she would take it out of her bag, in Roark's room, and spread it on the floor and sit before it, her chin in her hands, her eyes glowing; until, one night, he kicked it with his foot from under her face and across the room.

"You're disgusting," he said. "Why such concern over something someone said about you?"

"But, Howard, he liked me. I want them all to like me."

He shrugged. She picked up her review and folded it carefully, but never brought it to his room again.

The play settled down for a run of many months. And as the months advanced into winter, she found herself cursing the first hit in which she had ever appeared, watching the audience anxiously each night, looking hopefully for the holes of empty seats, waiting for signs of the evening when the show would close; the evening when she would be free to sit again in Roark's room and wait for his return from work and hear his steps up the stairs. Now she could only drop in on him, late at night, and she rushed home after the performance, without stopping to remove her makeup, ignoring the people in the subway, who stared at the bright-tan greasepaint on her face. She flew up the stairs, she burst into his room without knocking, she stood breathless, not knowing why she had had to hurry, not knowing what to do now that she was here; she stood, mascara smeared on her cheeks, her dress buttoned hastily on the wrong buttons. Sometimes he allowed her to remain there for a while. Sometimes he said: "You look like hell. Go take the filth off your face." She resolved fiercely not to see him too often; every night, she came up, promising herself to miss the next time.

On the evenings when he was willing to stop and rest and talk to her, it was she who often broke off the conversation and left him as soon as she could. She had accepted the feeling of her disappearance, which she had known so often with him; but she could not bear the feeling of his own destruction. On those evenings, between long stretches of work, he sat there before her, he spoke, he listened, he answered her and it seemed normal and reasonable, but she felt cold with panic suddenly, without tangible cause. It was as if something had wiped them out of existence; it was as if he did not know in what position his limbs had fallen as he lay stretched on his old cot, or whether he had any limbs; he did not know his words beyond the minute. He was vague, quiet, tired. She could have faced active hatred toward her, toward the room, toward the world. But the utter void of a complete indifference made her shudder and think of things she had learned vaguely in physics, things supposed to be impossible on earth: the absolute zero, the total vacuum. Sometimes, he would stop in the middle of a sentence and not know that he had stopped. He would sit still, looking at something so definite that she would turn and follow the direction of his glance but find nothing there. Then she would guess, not see, the hint of a shadow of a smile in the hard corners of his lips. She would see the long fingers of his hand grow tense and move strangely, stretching, spreading slowly. Then it would stop abruptly, and he would raise his head and ask: "Was I saying something?"

Long in advance, she had asked him to let her celebrate the New Year with him, the two of them together, she planned, alone in his room. He had promised. Then, one night, he told her quietly: "Look, Vesta, stay away from here, will you? I'm busy. Leave me alone for a couple of weeks."

"But, Howard," she whispered, her heart sinking, "the New Year . . ."

"That's ten days off. That will be fine. Come back New Year's Eve. I'll be waiting for you then."

She stayed away. And through the fury of her desire for him there grew slowly a burning resentment. She found that his absence was a relief. It was a gray relief, but it was comfortable. She felt as if she were returning to a green cow pasture after the white crystal of the north pole. She went to parties with her friends from the theater, she danced, she laughed, she felt insignificant and safe. The relief was not in his absence, but in the disappearance of that feeling of her own importance which his mere presence, even his contempt gave her. Without him, she did not have to look up to herself.

She decided that she would never see him again. She made the violence of her longing for him into the violence of her rebellion. She resolved to make of the one night, which she had awaited breathlessly for so many weeks, the symbol of her defiance: she would not spend New Year's Eve with him. She accepted an invitation to a party for that night. And at eleven o'clock, her head high, her lips set, enjoying the torture of her new hatred, she climbed firmly the stairs to his room, to tell him that she was not coming.

She knew, when she entered, that he had forgotten the day and the date. He was sitting on a low box by the window, one shoulder raised, contorted behind him, his elbow resting on the windowsill, his head thrown back, his eyes closed. She saw the fingers of his hand hanging at his shoulder, the long line of his thigh thrust forward, his knee bent, his leg stretched limply, slanting down to the floor. She had never seen him in such exhaustion. He raised his head slowly and looked at her. His eyes were not tired. She stood still under his glance. She had never loved him as in that moment.

"Hello, Vesta," he said. He seemed a little astonished

to see her. She knew, in the bright clarity of one swift instant, that she was afraid of him; not of her love for him, but of something deeper, more important, more permanent in the substance of his being. She wanted to escape it. She wanted to be free of him. She felt her muscles become rigid with the spasm of all the hatred she had felt for him in the days of his absence and felt more sharply now. She said, her voice precise, measured, husky:

"I came to tell you that I'm not staying here tonight."

"Tonight?" he asked, astonished. "Why come to tell me that?"

"Because it's New Year's Eve, as of course you've forgotten."

"Oh, yes. So it is."

"And you can celebrate it alone, if at all. I'm not staying."

"No?" he said. "Why?"

"Because I'm going to a party." She knew, without his mocking glance, that it had sounded silly. She said through her teeth: "Or, if you want to know, because I don't want to see you."

He looked at her, his lower lids raised across his eyes.

"I don't want to see you," she said. "Not tonight or ever. I wanted you to know that. You see, here, I'm saying it to you. I don't want to see you. I don't need you. I want you to know that."

He did not seem surprised by the irrelevance of her words. He understood what had never been said between them, what should have been said to make her words coherent. He sat watching her silently.

"You think you know what I think of you, don't you?" she said, her voice rising. "Well, you don't. It isn't that. I can't stand you. You're not a human being. You're a monster of some kind. I would like to hurt you. You're abnormal. You're a perverted egotist. You're a monster of egotism. You shouldn't exist."

It was not the despair of her love. It was hatred and it was real. Her voice, clear and breaking, was free of him. But she could not move. His presence held her there, rooted to one spot. She threw her shoulders back, her arms taut behind her, bent slightly at the elbows, her hands closed, her wrists heavy, beating. She said, her voice choked:

"I'm saying this because I've always wanted to say it and now I can. I just want to say it, like this, to your face. It's wonderful. Just to say that you don't own me and you never will. Not you. Anyone but you. To say that you're nothing, you, nothing, and I can laugh at you. And I can loathe you. Do you hear me? You . . ."

And then she saw that he was looking at her as he had never looked before. He was leaning forward, his arm across his knee, and his hand, hanging in the air, seemed to support the whole weight of his body, a still, heavy, gathered weight. In his eyes, she saw for the first time a new, open, eager interest, an attention so avid that her breath stopped. What she saw in his face terrified her: it was cold, bare, raw cruelty. She was conscious suddenly, overwhelmingly of what she had never felt in that room before: that a man was looking at her.

She could not move from that spot. She whispered, her eyes closed:

"I don't want you . . . I don't want you . . ."

He was beside her. She was in his arms, her body jerked tight against his, his mouth on hers.

She knew that it was not love and that she was to expect no love. She knew that she did not want that which would happen to her, because she was afraid, because she had never thought of that as real. She knew also that none of this mattered, nothing mattered except his desire and that she could grant him his desire. When he threw her down on the bed, she thought that the sole thing existing, the substance of all reality for her and for everyone, was only to do what he wanted.

[One] evening, Keating climbed, unannounced, to Roark's room and knocked, a little nervously, and entered cheerfully, brisk, smiling, casual. He found Roark sitting on the windowsill, smoking, swinging one leg absentmindedly, and Vesta Dunning on the floor, by a lamp, sewing buttons on his old shirt.

"Just passing by," said Keating brightly, having acknowledged an introduction to Vesta, "just passing by with an evening to kill and happened to think that that's where you live, Howard, and thought I'd drop in to say hello, haven't seen you for such a long time."

"I know what you want," said Roark. "All right. How much?"

"How . . . What do you mean, Howard?"

"You know what I mean. How much do you offer?"

"I . . . Fifty a week," Keating blurted out involuntarily. This was not at all the elaborate approach he had prepared, but he had not expected to find that no approach would be necessary. "Fifty to start with. Of course, if you think it's not enough, I could maybe . . ."

"Fifty will do."

"You . . . you'll come with us, Howard?"

"When do you want me to start?"

"Why . . . God! as soon as you can. Monday?"

"All right."

Gee, Howard, thanks!" said Keating and wondered while pronouncing it why he was saying this, when Roark should have been the one to thank him, and wondered what it was that Roark always did to him to throw him off the track completely.

"Now listen to me," said Roark. "I'm not going to do any designing. No, not any. No details. No Louis XV skyscrapers. Just keep me off aesthetics if you want to keep me at all. I have nothing to learn about design at Francon & Heyer's. Put me in the engineering department. Send me on inspections. I want to get out in the field. That's all I can learn at your place. Now, do you still want me?"

"Oh, sure, Howard, sure, anything you say. You'll like the place, just wait and see. You'll like Francon. He's one of Cameron's men himself."

"He shouldn't boast about it."

"Well . . . that is . . ."

"No. Don't worry. I won't say it to his face. I won't say anything to anyone. I won't embarrass you. I won't preach any modernism. I won't say what I think of the work I'll see there. I'll behave. Is that what you wanted to know?"

"Oh, no, Howard, I know I can trust your good judgment, really, I wasn't worried, I wasn't even thinking of it."

"Well, it's all settled then? Goodnight. See you Monday."

"Well, yes . . . that is . . . I . . . I'm in no special hurry to go, really I came to see you and . . ."

"What's the matter, Peter? Something bothering you?"

"Why, no . . . I . . ."

"You want to know why I'm doing it?" Roark looked at him and smiled, without resentment or interest. "Is that it? I'll tell you, if you want to know. I don't give a damn where I work next. There's no architect in town that I'd cross the street to work for. And since I have to work somewhere, it might as well be your Francon— if I can get what I want from you. Don't worry. I'm selling myself, and I'll play the game that way—for the time being."

"Really, Howard, you don't have to look at it like that. There's no limit to how far you can go with us, once you get used to it. You'll see, for a change, what a real office looks like. After Cameron's, you'll find such a scope for your talent that . . ."

"We'll shut up about that, won't we, Peter?"

"Oh . . . I . . . I didn't mean to . . . I didn't mean anything." And he kept still. He did not quite know what to say nor what he should feel. It was a victory, but it was hollow somehow. Still, it was a victory and he felt that he wanted to feel affection for Roark.

Keating smiled warmly, cheerily, and he saw Vesta smiling in answer, in approval and understanding; but Roark would not smile; Roark looked at him steadily, his gray eyes at their most exasperating, without expression, without hint of thought or feeling.

"Gee, Howard," Keating tried with resolute brightness, "it will be wonderful to have you with us. Just like in the old days. Just like . . ." It petered out; he had nothing to say.

"It's wonderful of you to be doing this, Mr. Keating," said Vesta. She was not looking at Roark.

"Oh, not at all, Miss Dunning, not at all." It was like a shot in the arm to Keating, and the sudden, supple lift of his head was his own again, his usual own, in the manner with which he moved everywhere else. He loved Roark in that moment. "Say, Howard, how about our going out for a little drink somewhere, Miss Dunning and you and I, just sort of to celebrate the occasion?"

"Swell," said Vesta. "I'd love to."

"Sorry, Peter," said Roark. "That isn't part of the job."

"Well, as you wish," said Keating, rising. "See you Monday, Howard." He looked at Roark, and his eyes narrowed, and he smiled, too pleasantly. "Nine o'clock, Howard. Do be on time. That's one thing we insist upon. We've had a time clock installed for the draftsmen—my idea—you won't mind, of course?" He swung his overcoat closed, with a swift, sweeping gesture he had learned from Francon, a gesture that seemed to display the luster of the cloth and the cost of it and everything that the cost implied. He stood buttoning it casually, with straight fingertips, not looking down at his hands. "I shall be responsible for you, Howard. You'll be under me personally, by the way. Goodnight, Howard."

He left. Roark lit a cigarette and sat down, one foot on the windowsill, his knee bent, his head thrown back. Vesta looked at the curve of his neck, at the smoke rising in a straight, even streak with his even breathing. She knew that he had forgotten her presence.

"Why did you have to act like that?" she snapped.

"Huh?" he asked, his eyes closed.

"Why did you have to insult Mr. Keating?"

"Oh? Did I?"

"It was darn decent of him. And he tried so hard to be friendly. I thought he's such a nice person. Why did you have to go out of your way to be nasty? Can't you ever be human? After all, he was doing you a favor. And you accepted it. You took it and you treated him like dirt under your feet. You . . . Are you listening to me, Howard?"

"No."

She stood looking at him, her hands tight, grasping the cloth of her blouse at her shoulders, pulling it savagely so that she felt the collar cutting the back of her neck. She tried to think of something that would bring him to the humiliation of anger. She couldn't. She felt the anger growing within her instead, and she forced herself to say nothing until she could keep her voice from shaking.

It was not the scene she had witnessed that made her hate him for the moment. It was something she had felt present in that scene, something in him which she could not name, the thing she dreaded, the thing she had fought—and loved—for a year.

That year of her life had given her no happiness; only bewilderment and doubts and fear; a fear underscored by rare moments of a joy which was too much to bear. . . . She never felt the distance between them as she felt it lying in his arms, in his bed. It was as if the nights they shared gave her no rights, not the right to the confidence of a friend, not the right of the consideration of an acquaintance, not even the right to the courtesy of a stranger passing her on the street. He listened silently to her breathless voice whispering to him, when she could not stop it: "I love you, Howard . . . I love you . . . I love you . . ." her lips pressed to his arm, to his shoulder, as if her mouth were telling it to his skin, and it was not from her nor for him. She could be grateful only that he heard. He never answered.

She spoke to him of his meaning to her, of her life, of every thought, every spring of her life. He said nothing. He shared nothing. He never came to her for consolation, for encouragement, not even as to a mirror to reflect him and to listen. He had never known the need of someone listening. He had never known need. He did not need her. It was this—hidden, unconfessed, unacknowledged, but present, there, there within her—which made her afraid. She would have given anything, she would have lost him happily afterwards, if only she could see once one sign, one hint of his need for her, for anything of her. She could never see it.

She asked sometimes, her arms about him: "Howard, do you love me?" He answered: "No." She expected no other answer; somehow, the simple honesty in his voice, as he answered, the gentleness, the quiet unconsciousness of any cruelty made her accept it without hurt.

"Howard, do you think you'll ever love anyone?"

"No."

"You're too selfish!"

"Oh, yes."

"And conceited."

"No. I'm too selfish to be conceited."

Yet he was not indifferent to her. There were moments when she felt his attention, to her voice, to her every movement in the room, and behind his silence a question mark that was almost admiration. In such moments, she was not afraid of him and she felt closer to him than to any being in the world. Those were the moments when she did not laugh and did not feel comfortable, but felt happy instead and spoke of her work. She had had several parts after her first small success; they were not good parts and the shows had not lasted, and on some she had received no notice at all. But she was moving forward, and the more she hated the empty words she had to speak each evening in some half-empty theater, the more eagerly she could think of things she would do some day, when she reached the freedom to do them, of the women she would play, of Joan d'Arc. She found that she could speak of it to Roark, that it was easier, speaking of it to him than dreaming it secretly. His mere presence, his silence, his eyes, still and listening to her, gave it a reality she could not create alone. She was so aware of him, when she spoke of it, that she could forget his presence and yet feel it in all of her body, in the sharp, quickened, exhilarated tension of her muscles, and she could read the words of Joan d'Arc aloud, turned away from him, not seeing him, not knowing him, but reading it to him for him, with every vibration of her ecstatic voice. "Howard," she said sometimes, breaking off her lincs, her back turned to him, not feeling the necessity to face him, because he was everywhere around her, and his name was only a mechanical convention for the thing she was addressing, "there are things that are normal and comfortable and easy, and that's most of life for all of us. And then there are also things above it, things so much more than human, and not many can bear it and then not often, but that's the only reason for living at all. Things that make you very quiet and still and it's difficult to breathe. Can I explain that to the people who've never seen it? Can I show it to them? Can I? That's what I'll do some-day with her, with Joan d'Arc, to make them look up, up, Howard. . . . You see it, don't you?" And when she looked at him, his eyes were wide and open to her, and in that instant there were no secrets in him hidden from her, and she knew him, knowing also that she would lose him again in a moment, and she felt that her legs could not hold her, and she was sitting on the floor, her head buried against his knees, and she was whispering: "How-ard, I'm afraid of you . . . I'm afraid of myself because of you . . . Howard . . . Howard . . ." She felt his lips on the back of her neck and she felt a thing incredible from him, incredible and right, right only in that mo-ment: tenderness.

Then she knew, not that he loved her, but that he granted her a strange value, not for him, but in herself alone, apart from him, not needing her, but admiring her. And she felt at once that this was right and what she wanted and what she loved in him, and also that it was inhuman, bewildering, cold, and not the love others called love. She felt both things, confused, inextricable, and she knew only, with a certainty beyond explanation, that she was happy in that moment and would hate him for it when the moment passed and life became nor-mal again.

That norm, the hours succeeding one another, the days and the months, were becoming easier and pleas-anter for her; the pleasanter they became the heavier was the burden of a mere thought about him. She had never had many friends, but she was acquiring them now, because people in her profession, in the producers' offices, in the drugstores where actors gathered, were beginning to know her, to notice her and to like her. She was asked to parties, to luncheons, she was given passes to shows. He would never accompany her. He refused to meet her friends. The few whom she intro-duced to him told her afterwards that they had never encountered a man more unpleasant than that friend of hers . . . what was his name? Roark? who does he think he is?—even though Roark had said very little to them and had been very polite. He would go with her to the theater sometimes and would seldom enjoy the play. He would never go to a movie nor to a speakeasy, nor dance, nor accept invitations.

"What for, Vesta? I have nothing to talk about."

"Don't you want to meet people, to know them, to exchange ideas?"

"I know them. I haven't any ideas to exchange."

"Don't you ever get bored?"

"Always. Terribly. Except when I'm alone."

"You're not normal, Howard!"

"No."

"Why don't you do something about it? It bothers everyone who meets you."

"It doesn't bother me."

There had been—in all their life together—no gay memories, no tender moments to relive, no companionship, very little laughter; there had been "no fun," she said to herself sometimes, and felt dimly guilty of the word, then angry. When she was away from him, among people, the thought of him was like a weight in her mind, spoiling the comfortable gaiety of the moment. It was like a silent reproach somewhere—and she defied it by drinking a little too much and laughing too loudly. After all, she said to herself, looking at the couples dancing around her, one could not be a Joan d'Arc all the time.

And tonight, alone with him after Keating had left, she felt the resentment rising even here, in his room, in his presence. She looked at him, angry, trying to think of how she could make him understand, angry because she knew that he understood it already, and it was useless, and no word could reach him.

"Howard, listen to me please. Why did you have to do that? Why couldn't you be nice to Mr. Keating?"

"What have I done?"

"It isn't what you did. It's what you didn't do."

"What?"

"Oh, nothing . . . everything! Why do you hate him?"

"But I don't hate him."

"Well, that's it! Why don't you hate him at least?"

"For what?"

"Just to give him something. You can't like anyone, so you can at least be courteous enough to show it. And kind enough."

"I'm not kind, Vesta."

"How do you expect to get along in the world? You have to live with people, you know. Look, I . . . I want to understand. There are two ways. You can join people or you can fight them. But you don't seem to be doing either."

"What is it? What are you after specifically right now?"

"Well, for instance, why couldn't you go out with Keating for a drink? When he asked you so nicely. And I wanted to go."

"But I didn't."

"Why not?"

"What for?"

"Do you always have to have a purpose for everything? Do you always have to be so serious? Can't you ever do things, just do them, without reason, just like everybody? Can't you . . . oh, for God's sake, can't you be simple and silly, just once?"

"No."

"What's the matter with you, Howard? Can't you be natural?"

"But I am."

"Can't you relax, just once in your life?"

He looked at her and smiled, because he was sitting on the windowsill, leaning sloppily against the wall, his legs sprawled, his limbs loose, in perfect relaxation.

"That's not what I mean," she said angrily. "That's just sheer laziness. I don't know whether you're the tensest or the laziest man on earth."

"Well, make up your mind."

"It won't make any difference, if I do."

"No."

"Howard, do you ever think of how hard this is for me?"

"No."

"I always think of how you'll react to everything I do."

"Don't. I don't like it."

"But it is hard for me, Howard."

"Leave me then."

"You want me to?"

"No. Not yet."

"But you'd let me go, rather than do anything for me?"

"Yes."

"Howard!"

"But you haven't asked me to do anything for you."

"Well . . . oh, God damn you, Howard, it's so difficult to speak to you! I know what I want to say and I don't know how to say it!"

"That's because you don't want to know what you're really trying to say. Not yet. But I know it and I'm not going to help you say it. Because when you do say it, I'll throw you out of here. Only it won't be necessary. You won't want to be here then. . . . Is that of any help?"

He had said it evenly, quietly, without emphasis or concern. She felt cold with panic. It had suddenly been too near, that possibility of losing him, and she was not prepared to face it. She stood, her hands clutching the shirt at her sides, moving convulsively through the cloth, hanging on, because she wanted to reach for him, to grasp him, to hold him. But she could not trust herself to touch him, not then, because she would betray too much. After a while, she walked to him, and then she could slip her arms gently about him and put her chin on his shoulder, her head against his.

"All right, Howard," she whispered, "I won't say anything. . . . Can I . . . can I congratulate you on the job, at least? I'm really terribly glad you got it."

"Thanks."

"Look, Howard, are you going to move out of here? I'd hate to see you go, but you can get a better place somewhere close by or maybe right in the building."

"No. I'm staying here."

"But on fifty a week you can afford not to live in

this horrible dump. And we'll see each other just as often."

"I'll need every cent of that money."

"But why?"

"Because I won't last there."

She looked at him in consternation.

"Howard, why do you start in with an attitude like that? Are you planning to quit already?"

"No. They'll fire me."

"When?"

"Sooner or later."

"Why will they fire you?"

"That would take much too long to explain."

"You're not awfully glad of the job, are you?"

"I expected it."

"It's pretty grand, though, isn't it? I've heard of them vaguely—Francon & Heyer. They're really awfully big and famous, aren't they?"

"They are."

"You could really get somewhere with them."

"I doubt it."

"But isn't it going to be better than that hopeless place where you worked? Won't you be happier in a real, important office, successful and respected and . . ."

"We'll keep still about that, Vesta, and we'll do it damn fast."

"Oh, Howard!" she cried, losing all control. "I can't talk to you at all! What's the matter with you tonight?"

"Why tonight?"

"No, that's true! It's not tonight! It's always! I can't stand it, Howard!"

He looked at her without moving. He asked:

"What do you want?"

"Listen, Howard . . ." she whispered gently. Her fingers were rolled together in a little ball at her throat, her eyes were wide and pleading and defenseless; she had never looked lovelier. "Listen, my darling, my dearest one, I love you. I'm not reproaching you. I'm only begging you. I want you. I've never really had you, Howard. I want to know you. I want to understand. I'm . . . lonely."

"I'm not a crutch, Vesta."

"But I want you to help me! I want to know that you want to help me!"

"I wouldn't, if I were you. If I come to wanting to help a person, I'll not want that person nor to help any longer."

"Howard!" she screamed. "Howard, how can you say a thing like that!"

And then she was sobbing suddenly, before she could stop it, sobbing openly, convulsively, not trying to hide the single, shameful fact of pain, sobbing with her head against the crook of his elbow. He said nothing and did not move. Her head slipped down to his hand, she pressed her face against it, she could feel her tears on the skin of his hand. The hand did not move; it did not seem alive. When she raised her head, at last, empty of tears, of sounds, even of pain, the pain swallowed under a numb stupor, only her throat still jerking silently, when she looked at him, she saw a face that had not changed, had not been reached, had no answer to give her. He asked:

"Can you go now?"

She nodded, humbly, almost indifferently, indifferent to her own pain and to the lack of answer which was such an eloquent answer. She backed slowly to the door, she went out silently, her eyes fastened to the last moment, incredulous and bewildered, upon his face, upon the vast, incomprehensible cruelty of his face.

At the end of March, a new play opened in New York and on the following morning the dramatic reviews dedicated most of their space to Vesta Dunning.

Her part was described officially as the second feminine lead, but for those who saw the opening performance there had been no leads and no other actors in the cast and hardly any play: there had been only a miracle, the impossible made real, a woman no one had ever met, yet everyone knew and recognized and believed boundlessly for two and a half hours. It was the part of a wild, stubborn, sparkling, dreadful girl who drove to despair her family and all those approaching her. Vesta Dunning streaked across the stage with her swift, broken, contorted gait; or she stood still, her body an arc, her arms flung out, her voice a whisper; or she destroyed a profound speech with one convulsed shrug of her thin shoulders; or she laughed and all the words on that stage were wiped off by her laughter. She did not hear the applause afterwards. She bowed to it, not knowing that anyone applauded her, not knowing that she bowed.

She did not hear what was said to her in the dressing room that night. She did not wait for the reviews. She ran away to find Roark, who was waiting for her at the stage door, and she seized his arm to help her stand up, but she said nothing, and they rode home in a cab, silently, not touching each other. Then, in his room, she stood before him, she looked at him, she was speaking, not knowing that she spoke aloud, words like fragments of the thing that was bursting within her:

"Howard . . . that was it . . . there it was . . . you see, I liked her . . . she's the first one I ever liked doing . . . it was right . . . oh, Howard, Howard! It was right . . . I don't care what they'll say . . . I don't care about the reviews . . . whether it runs or not, I've done it once . . . I've done it . . . and that's the way now, Howard . . . it's open . . . to Joan d'Arc . . . they'll let me do it . . . they'll let me do it someday. . . ."

He drew her close to him, and she stood while he sat, his arms tight about her, his face buried against her stomach, holding her, holding something that was not to be lost. In that moment, she forgot the fear that had been following her for days, the fear of the slow, open, inevitable growth of his indifference.

He did not tell Vesta about it for several days. He had seen her seldom in the last few months; her success was working a change in her, which he did not want to see. When he told her at last that he had lost his job, she looked at him coldly and shrugged: "It may teach you a few things for the future."

"It did," said Roark.

"Don't expect me to sympathize. Whatever it was that you did, I'm sure you jolly well deserved it."

"I did."

"For God's sake, Howard, when are you going to

come down to earth? You can't think that you're the only one who's always right and everybody else wrong!"

"I'm too tired to quarrel with you tonight, Vesta."

"You've got to learn to curb yourself and cooperate with other people. That's it, cooperate. People aren't as stupid as you think. They appreciate real worth when there's any to appreciate."

"I don't doubt it."

"Stop talking as if you're throwing sentences in the wastebasket! Stop being so damn smug! Don't you realize what's happened to you? You had a chance at a real career with a real, first-class firm and you didn't have sense enough to keep it! You had a chance to get out of the gutter and you threw it away! You had to be Joan d'Arc'ish all over the place and . . ."

"Shut up, Vesta," he said quietly.

When he came home in the evenings, Vesta was there sometimes, waiting for him. She asked: "Found anything?" When he answered, "No," she put her arms around him and said she felt sure he would find it. But secretly, involuntarily, hating herself for it, she felt glad of his failure: it was a vindication of her own unspoken thoughts, of the new appearance the world was presenting to her, of her new security, of her reconciliation with the world, a security which he threatened, a reconciliation against which he stood as a reproach, even though he said nothing and, perhaps, saw nothing. She did not want to acknowledge these thoughts; she needed him, she would not be torn away from him. She could not tell whether he guessed. She knew only that his eyes were watching her, and he said nothing.

Vesta entered the room in a streak, without knocking, and stopped abruptly, her skirt flying in a wide triangle and flapping back tightly against her knees. She stood, her mouth half open, her hair thrown back, as she always stood—as if in a gust of wind, her thin body braced, her eyes wide, impatient, full of a flame that seemed to flicker in the wind.

"Howard! I have something to tell you! Where on earth have you been? I've come up three times this evening. You weren't looking for work at this hour, were you?—you couldn't."

"I . . ." he began, but she went on:

"Something wonderful's happened to me! I'm signing the contract tomorrow. I'm going to Hollywood."

He sat silently, his arms on the table before him, and looked at her.

"I'm going as soon as the play closes," she said, and threw her hands up, and whirled on one toe, her skirt flaring like a dancer's. "I didn't tell you, but they took a test of me—weeks ago—and I saw it, I don't really look very pretty, but they said they could fix that and that I had personality and they'll give me a chance, and I'm signing a contract!"

"For how long?" he asked.

"Oh, that? That's nothing. It's for five years, but it's only options, you know, I don't have to stay there that long."

He snapped his finger against the edge of a sheet of newspaper and the click of his nail sent it across the table with a thin, whining crackle, like a string plucked, and he said nothing.

"Oh, no," she said, too emphatically, "I'm not giving up the stage. It's just to make some quick money."

"You don't need it. You said you could have any part you chose next year."

"Sure. I can always have that—after those notices."

"Next year, you could do what you've wanted to do."

"I'm doing that."

"So I see."

"Well, why not? It's such a chance."

"For what?"

"Oh, for . . . for . . . Hell, I don't see why you have to disapprove!"

"I haven't said that."

"Oh, no! You never say anything. Well, what's wrong with it?"

"Nothing. Only that you're lying."

"How?"

"You're not going for the money."

"Well . . . well, for what then? And isn't it better—

whatever you mean than to go for money? I thought you wouldn't approve of my going after money."

"No, Vesta. You thought I might approve. That's why you said it."

"Well, is it all right if it's for the money?"

"It might be. But that's not what you're after."

"What am I after?"

"People."

"What people?"

"Millions of them. Carloads. Tons. Swarms of them. To look at you. To admire you. No matter what they're admiring you for."

"You're being silly. I don't know what you're driving at. And besides, if I make good, I don't have to play in stupid movies. I can select my parts. I can do as much as on the stage. More. Because it will reach so many more people and . . ." He was laughing. "Oh, all right, don't be so smart! You'll see. I can do what I want on the screen, too. Just give me time. I'll do everything I want."

"Joan d'Arc?"

"Why not? Besides, it'll help. I'll make a name for myself, then watch me come back to the stage and do Joan d'Arc! And furthermore . . ."

"Look, Vesta, I'm not arguing. You're going. That's fine. Don't explain too much."

"You don't have to look like a judge dishing out a life sentence! And I don't care whether you approve or not!"

"I haven't said I didn't."

"I thought you'd be glad for me. Everybody else was. But you have to spoil it."

"How?"

"Oh, how! How do you always manage to spoil everything? And here I was so anxious to tell you! I couldn't wait. Where on earth have you been all evening, by the way?"

"Working."

"What? Where?"

"In the office."

"What office? Have you found a job?"

"Two weeks ago."

"Oh! . . . Well, how nice. . . . Doing what?"

"Well, what do you suppose?"

"Oh, you got a real job? With an architect? So you found one to take you after all?"

"Yes."

"Well . . . it's wonderful . . . I'm awfully glad. . . . Oh, I'm awfully glad. . . ." She heard her own voice, flat and empty and with a thin, strange, distant note in it, a note that was anger without reason; she wondered whether it sounded like that to him also. She said quickly: "I hope you're set this time. I hope you'll be successful someday—like everybody else."

He leaned back and looked at her. She stood defiantly, holding his eyes, saying nothing, flaunting her consciousness of the meaning of his silence.

"You're not glad that I got it," he said. "You hope I won't last. That's the next best to the thing you really hope—that I'll be successful someday *like everybody else.*"

"You're talking nonsense. I don't know what you're saying."

He sat, looking at her, without moving. She shrugged and turned away; she picked up the newspaper and flipped its pages violently, as if the loud crackling could shut out the feeling of his eyes on her.

"All right," he said slowly. "Now say it."

"What?" she snapped, whirling around.

"What you've wanted to say for a long time."

She flung the newspaper aside. She said: "I don't know what you're talking about."

"Say it, Vesta."

"Oh, you're impossible! You're . . ." And then her voice dropped suddenly, and she spoke softly, simply, pleading: "Howard, I love you. I don't know what it is. I don't know why it should be like this. I love you and I can't stand you. And also, I wouldn't love you if I could stand you, if you were any different. But what you are—that frightens me, Howard. I don't know why. It frightens me because it's something in me which I don't want. No. Because it's something in me which I do want, but I'd rather not want it, and . . . Oh, you can't understand any of it!"

"Go on."

"Yes, damn you, you do understand! . . . Oh, don't look at me like that! . . . Howard, Howard, please listen. It's this: you want the impossible. You are the impossible yourself—and you expect the impossible. I can't feel human around you. I can't feel simple, natural, comfortable. And one's got to be comfortable sometime! It's like . . . like as if you had no weekdays at all in your life, nothing but Sundays, and you expect me always to be on my Sunday behavior. Everything is important to you, everything is great, significant in some way, every minute, even when you keep still. God, Howard, one can't stand that! It becomes unbearable . . . if . . . if I could only put it into words!"

"You have. Very nicely."

"Oh, please, Howard, don't look like that! I'm not . . . I'm not criticizing you. I understand. I know what you want of life. I want it too. That's why I love you. But, Howard! You can't be that all the time! God, not all the time! One's got to be human also."

"What?"

"Human! One has to relax. One gets tired of the heroic."

"What's heroic about me?"

"Nothing. Everything! . . . No, you don't do anything. You don't say anything. I don't know. It's only what you make people feel in your presence."

"What?"

"The abnormal. The overnormal. The strain. When I'm with you—it's always like a choice. A choice between you—and the rest of the world. I don't want such a choice. I'm afraid because I want you too much—but I don't want to give up everybody, everything. I want to be a part of the world. They like me, they recognize me now, I don't want to be an outsider. There's so much that's beautiful in the world, and gay and simple and pleasant. It's not all a fight and a renunciation. It doesn't have to be. It is—with you."

"What have I ever renounced?"

"Oh, you'll never renounce anything. You'll walk over corpses for what you want. But it's what you've renounced by never wanting it. What you've closed your eyes to—what you were born with your eyes closed to."

"Don't you think that perhaps one can't have one's eyes open to both?"

"Everybody else can! Everybody but you. You're so old, Howard. So old, so serious. . . . And there's something else. What you said about my going after people. Look, Howard, don't other people mean anything to you at all? I know, you like some of them and you hate others, but neither really makes much difference to you. That's what's horrifying. Everyone's a blank around you. They're there, but they don't touch you in any way, not in any single way. You're so closed, so finished. It's unbearable. All of us react upon one another in some way, I don't mean that we have to be slaves of others, or be influenced, or changed, no, not that, but we react. You don't. We're aware of others. You're not. You don't hate people—that's the ghastliness of it. If you did—it would be simple to face. But you're worse. You're a fiend. You're the real enemy of all mankind—because one can't do anything against your kind of weapon—your utter, horrible, inhuman indifference!"

She stood waiting. She stood, as if she had slapped his face and triumphantly expected the answer. He looked at her. She saw that his lips were opening wide, his mouth loose, young, easy; she could not believe for a moment that he was laughing. She did not believe what he said either. He said:

"I'm sorry, Vesta."

Then she felt frightened. He said very gently:

"I didn't want it to come to this. I think I knew also that it would, from the first. I'm sorry. There are chances I shouldn't take. You see—I'm weak, like everybody else. I'm not closed enough nor certain enough. I see hope sometimes where I shouldn't. Now forget me. It will be easier than it seems to you right now."

"You . . . you don't mean for me . . . to leave you?"

"Yes."

"Oh, no, Howard! Not like that! Not now!"

"Like that, Vesta. Now."

"Why?"

"You know that."

"Howard . . ."

"I think you know also that you'll be glad of it later. Maybe tomorrow. Just forget me. If you want to see me affected by someone else—well, I'll tell you that I'm sorry."

"No, you aren't. Not to lose me."

"No. Not any more. But to see what will happen to you . . . no. Not that either. But this: to see what will never happen to you."

"What?"

"*That* is what you don't want to know. So forget it."

"Oh, Howard! Howard . . ."

Her voice broke, as the consciousness of what had happened, like a blow delayed, reached her at last. She stood, her shoulders drooping forward, her hands hanging uselessly, awkwardly, suddenly conscious of her hands and not knowing where to put them, her body huddled and loose, looking at him, her eyes clear and too brilliant, her mouth twisted. She swallowed slowly, with a hard effort, as if her whole energy had gone into the movement of her throat, into the purpose of knowing that her throat could be made to move. It was a bewilderment of pain, helpless and astonished, as an animal wondering what had happened, knowing only that it was hurt, but not how or why, puzzled that it should be hurt and that this was the shape of pain.

"Howard . . ." she whispered softly, as simply as if she were addressing herself and no stress, no emotion, no clarity of words were necessary. "It's funny . . . what is it? . . . It couldn't happen like this . . . and it did . . . I think I'm hurt, Howard . . . terribly . . . I want to cry or do something . . . and I can't. . . . What is it? . . . I can't do anything before you . . . I want to say something . . . I should . . . it doesn't happen like this . . . and I can't . . . It's funny . . . isn't it? . . . You understand?"

"Yes," he said softly.

"Are you hurt too?" she asked, suddenly eager, as if she had caught at the thread of a purpose. "Are you? Are you? You must be!"

"Yes, Vesta."

"No, you aren't! You don't say it as it would sound if you . . . You can't be hurt. You can never be hurt!"

"I suppose not."

"Howard, why? Why do this? When I need you so much!"

"To end it before we start hating each other. You've started already."

"Oh, no, Howard! No! I don't! Not now! Can't you believe me?"

"I believe you. Not now. But the moment you leave this room. And at every other time."

"Howard, I'll try . . ."

"No, Vesta. Those things can't be tried. You'd better go now."

"Howard, can't you feel . . . sorry for me? I know, it's a terrible thing to say. I wouldn't want it from anyone else. But that . . . that's all I can have from you. . . . Howard? Can't you?"

"No, Vesta."

She spread her hands out helplessly, still wondering, a bewildered question remaining in her eyes, and moved her lips to speak, but didn't, and turned, small, awkward, uncertain, and left.

She walked down the stairs and knew that she would cry in her room, cry for many hours. But one sentence he had spoken came back to her, one sentence clear and alone in the desolate emptiness of her mind: "You'll be glad of it later. Maybe tomorrow." She knew that she was glad already. It terrified her, it made the pain sharper. But she was glad.

He had not seen Vesta again before she left for California. She did not write to him and he had long since forgotten her, except for wondering occasionally, when passing by a movie theater, why he'd heard of no film in which she was to appear. Hollywood seemed to have forgotten her also; she was given no parts.

Then, in the spring, he saw her picture in the paper; she stood, dressed in a polka-dot bathing suit, holding coyly, unnaturally a huge beach ball over her head; except for the pose, it was still Vesta, the odd, impatient face, the wild hair, the ease and freedom in the lines of the body; but one had to look twice to notice it; the photograph was focused upon her long, bare legs, as all the photographs appearing in that corner of that section had always been. The caption read: "This cute little number is Sally Ann Blainey, Lux Studio's starlet. Before she was discovered by Lux scouts, Miss Blainey achieved some measure of distinction on the Broadway stage, where she was known as Vesta Dunning. The studio bosses, however, have given her a less ungainly name." It was not mentioned when she would be put to work.

"Child of Divorce" was released in January 1927, and it made film history. It was not an unusual picture and it starred an actor who was quite definitely on his downgrade, but it had Sally Ann Blainey in a smaller part. Lux Studios had not expected much of Sally Ann Blainey; she had not been advertised, and a week after the picture's completion her contract had been dropped. But on the day after the film's release, she was signed again, on quite different terms, and her name appeared in electric lights upon the marquees of theaters throughout the country, over that of the forgotten star.

Roark went to see the picture. It was still Vesta, as he had seen her last. She had lost nothing and learned nothing. She had not learned the proper camera angles, she had not learned the correct screen makeup; her mouth was too large, her cheeks too gaunt, her hair uncombed, her movements too jerky and angular. She was like nothing ever seen in a film before, she was a contradiction to all standards, she was awkward, crude, shocking, she was like a breath of fresh air. The studio had expected her to be hated; she was suddenly worshiped by the public. She was not pretty, nor gracious, nor gentle, nor sweet; she played the part of a young girl not as a tubercular flower, but as a steel knife. A reviewer said that she was a cross between a medieval pageboy and a gun moll. She achieved the incredible: she was the first woman who ever allowed herself to make strength attractive on the screen.

For a few moments after he left the theater, Roark

almost wished to have her back. But he forgot it by the time he got home. Afterwards, he remembered, sometimes, that magnificent performance; he wondered whether he had been wrong and she would win her battle, after all; but he could no longer feel it as a thing too close to him.

Roark and Cameron

In the daytime, Cameron's feelings were not expressed in any way, save, perhaps, in the fact that he seldom called Roark by name. "Here, pokerface," he would say, "get this done and step on it." "Look, carrot-top, what in hell did you mean by this? Lost your senses, have you?" "That's great. That's splendid. Excellent. Now throw it in the wastebasket and do it over again, you damned icicle." Loomis was baffled and Simpson scratched his head, wondering: a casual familiarity toward an employee was not a thing that Simpson had ever observed in his forty years of service with Cameron.

At night, when the work was done and the others had gone, Cameron asked Roark, sometimes, to remain. Then they sat together for hours in his dim office, and Cameron talked. The radiators of the building were usually out of order and Cameron had an old Franklin heater burning in the middle of the room. He would pull his chair to the heater, and Roark would sit on the floor, the bluish glow of the flame upon the knuckles of his hands clasping his knees. When he spoke, Cameron was no longer an old man starving slowly in an office near the Battery; nor was he a great architect scorning his vain competitors; he was the only builder in the world and he was reshaping the face of America. His words pressed down like the plunger of a fuse box setting off the explosion; and the explosion swept out the miles, the thousands of miles of houses upon which every sin of their owners stood written as a scar, as a sore running in crumbling plaster; the houses like mirrors, flaunting to the streets the naked soul of those within and the ugliness of it; the vanity, gathering soot upon twisted, flowered ledges, the ostentation, swelling like a goiter in bloated porches, the fear, the fear of the herd, cringing under columns stuck there because all the neighbors had them, the stupidity, choking in fetid air under the gables of garrets. After the explosion, his voice, his hands moving slowly as he spoke, like planes smoothing unseen walls, raised broad, clean streets and houses in the likeness of what those within should be and would be made to become by these houses: straight and simple and honest, wise and clear in their purpose, copying nothing, following nothing but the needs of those living within— and let the needs of no [one] living be those of his neighbor! To give them, Cameron was saying, what they want, but first to teach them to want—to want with their own eyes, their own brains, their own hearts. To teach them to dream—then give the dream to them in steel and mortar, and let them follow it with dreams in muscle and blood. To make them true, Howard, to make them true to themselves and give them the selves, to kill the slave in them, Howard, Howard, don't you see?—the slaves of slaves served by slaves for the sake of slaves!

He was the only builder in the world, as he spoke, but even he was not there, in that room, nor the boy who sat, taut and silent, at his feet; only that thing, that truth trembling in his hard voice, was present; he spoke of that alone and, speaking of it, he made real, tangible in the dark room, his own being and that of the boy. The heater hissed softly, with little puffing, choked explosions. The two lines on Cameron's face stood out like black gashes on the lighted patches of his cheeks, two patches floating upon the blackness that swallowed his forehead, his eyes, his beard. There was, turned up to him from the dark, a wedge of soft, living gold cut by the fringe of long lashes, then darkness again like a soft black stone and, rising upon it, a luminous vein in the stone cut as a cameo, a chin with a long mouth, a speck of fire trembling on the lower lip.

He never spoke again of his past nor of Roark's future. He never said why he talked to him thus through the long winter evenings, admitting no questions and no wonder upon it, not saying what necessity drove him to speak nor what granted Roark the right to listen. He never said whether he cared for Roark's presence there or in the world, whether it mattered to him that Roark heard or existed. Only once did he say suddenly, at the end of a long speech: ". . . and, yes, it may seem strange to give a life for the sake of steel skeletons and windows, your life also—my dearest one—because it's necessary. . . ." He had gone on to speak about windows, and he had never said it again.

But in the mornings, as Cameron entered his office sharply on the dot of nine, he would stop first at the door of the drafting room, throw a long, sharp glance at the men, then slam the door behind him. Loomis had said once, not suspecting the accuracy of what he thought to be a good joke, that Cameron had the look of a man who'd seen a miracle and wanted to make sure it hadn't gone.

Then came the morning when Cameron was late. The clock on the wall of the drafting room was moving past the mark of ten, and Roark noticed that Loomis and Simpson were exchanging glances, silent, significant glances heavy with a secret he did not share. Loomis clucked his tongue once, looking at the clock, with a wet, bitter, mocking sound. Simpson sighed heavily and bent over his table, his old head bobbing softly up and down several times, in hopeless resignation.

At half past ten, Trager shuffled into the drafting room and stood on the threshold, seeing nobody.

"Mr. Darrow calling," he said to no one at all, the sounds of his voice like a string of precision dancers, all stiff and all alike, "says something awful's happened at the Huston Street job and he's going down there and for Mr. Cameron to meet him there at once. I guess one of you guys will have to go."

Darrow was the consulting structural engineer on the Huston Street job, and such a message from him went like a cold gust through the room. But it was the "I guess" that seemed to leap out of Trager's words, weighted with the secret meaning of why he guessed so and of why he expected them to know it. Loomis and Simpson looked helplessly at one another, and Loomis chuckled. Roark said brusquely, not knowing what had put anger into his voice: "Mr. Cameron said yesterday that he was going to inspect the Huston Street job. That's probably why he's late. Tell Darrow that he's on his way there now."

Loomis whistled through his teeth, and it seemed to Roark that the sound was laughing, bursting like steam from under tons of pressure of contempt. Trager would not move, would not look at Roark, but glanced slowly at the others. The others had nothing to say.

"Okay," said Trager, at last, to Roark, a flat, short sound concentrating within it a long sentence, saying that Trager would obey, because he didn't give a damn, even though he hadn't believed a single word of Roark's, because Roark knew better, or should. Trager turned and shuffled back to his telephone.

Half an hour later, he returned.

"Mr. Darrow calling from Huston Street," he said, his voice dull and even and sleepy, as if he were reporting on the amount of new pencils to be ordered, "he says to please send someone over and pour Mr. Cameron out of there, also to see what's to be done."

In the silence, Roark's T-square clattered loudly to the floor. The three men looked at him, and Loomis grinned viciously, triumphantly. But there was nothing to be seen on Roark's face. Roark turned to Trager slowly.

"I'm going there," said Roark.

"No, I guess you can't," mumbled Simpson. "I guess I gotta go."

"What can you do there?" Loomis snapped at Roark, more insolently than he had ever dared before. "What in hell do *you* know about construction? Let Simpson go."

"*I'm* going," said Roark.

He had his coat and cap on, he was out, before the others knew what to say; they knew also that they had better keep quiet.

Roark jumped into a cab, ordering: "Step on it! Fly, go through the lights!" He had in his pocket five dollars and forty-six cents, saved painstakingly from seven months of work. He hoped it would be enough to pay for the cab.

The Huston Street job was a twenty-story office building in a squalid block of lofts. It was the most important commission that Cameron had had for a long time. He had said nothing about it, but Roark knew that it was precious to the old master as a newborn child, as a first son. Once again, Cameron thought, he had a chance to show the indifferent city what he could do, how cheaply, how efficiently he could do it. Cameron, the bitter, the cynical, the hater of all men, had never lost the expectation of a miracle. He kept waiting, saying to himself always, "Next time," next time someone would see, next time the men who spent fortunes on grocery displays of marble vegetables and cursed the twisted, botched space within would realize the simplicity, the economy, the wisdom of his work, would come to him if he gave them but one more example. The example was granted to him again. And Cameron, who cursed all builders and owners, who laughed in their faces, prayed now that nothing would go wrong with the Huston Street job. Everything had gone wrong with it from the beginning.

The structure was owned by two brothers. It was the younger one who had insisted upon choosing Cameron as the architect, because he had seen Cameron's old buildings and a glimmer of sense had settled itself stubbornly within his brain; it was the older who had resented it, while giving in, had doubted the choice, and had selected as contractor for the building an old friend of his, who had little reputation but much contempt for architects. It had been a silent, vicious war from the beginning, with the contractor disregarding Cameron's orders, botching instructions, ignoring specifications, then running to the owners with complaints against ignorant architects whom he intended to teach a thing or two about building. The owners always took the side of the contractor, who was, they felt certain, protecting their interests against malignant strangers. There had been delays. There had been strikes among the building workers, due to unfair, planless, purposeless management. The delays cost money. It was not Cameron's fault, but there was no court before which he could prove it. The court that passed judgment upon him would be the spreading whispers: "Oh, yeah, Cameron. He starts with a budget of four hundred thousand and it's six hundred before the steel's up. Have you heard what that building of his down in Huston Street has cost?"

Roark thought of that as the cab whirled into Huston Street. Then he forgot it for a moment, forgot Cameron, forgot everything else. He was looking at a cage of steel rising in a gash between streaked, sooted brick walls. There it was, steel columns pointing at the sky, gray arches of floors mounting like even shelves, tangled in wires, in ropes and cables and grimy planks, with scaffoldings clinging to its empty flanks, gray overalls burrowing through its bowels, derricks like fountains of iron flung up from its veins. It was only a raw chaos of beams to those passing it in the street, but Roark thought that those on the street had the narrow, dissecting eyes of the X-ray marking nothing save bones, while he saw the whole body completed, the shape of living flesh, the walls, the angles, the windows. He could never look at the structure of a building, which he had seen born in lines and dots and squares upon a piece of paper, without feeling his throat tighten, his breath plunge to his stomach, and the silly desire, dim and real in his hand, to take his hat off. His fingers tightened on the edge of the cab window. When the car stopped, he got out supply, he walked to the building swiftly, confidently, his head high and light as if he were coming home, as if the steel hulk were gathering assurance from him and he— from its naked beams. Then, he stopped.

Cameron stood leaning against the boards of the superintendent's shanty. Cameron was erect, with an air of self-possessed, utter, terrifying dignity. Only his eyes, dun, swimming, unfocused, were blinking at Roark with a heavy, offensive persistence.

"Who are you?" asked Cameron.

The voice, thick, blurred, spongy, was not one that Roark had ever heard.

Cameron lunged towards him, swayed, stretched an arm to hold on to the wall, stood uncertainly, the weight of his short, thick body sagging suspended to his arm, with five stubby fingers spread on the planks, like leeches sucking into wood.

"Hey, you," he said to Roark softly, waving a limp finger in his face, "I'll tell you something. I've got something to tell you. It's on account of the drill. You know the drill? It drills a little hole, so softly, it purrs like a bee in springtime, it drills right down through your throat, through your stomach, through the earth below, there's no bottom to that hole, no end, no stopping. There's a hole in the earth and it widens all the time and things whirl in it, spirals, widening. It hurts so very terribly . . . I know a fellow who's hurt so much that I hear him screaming all the time. But I don't know him very well. . . . That's why I've got something to tell you. If you're looking at this thing here behind us, go and get a good laugh. It's wonderful what they've done to it. But walk carefully, there's spirals in the ground, widening . . . you see? . . ."

"Mr. Cameron," said Roark softly, "sit down." His strong hands closed over the old man's forearms, forcing him gently down upon a pile of planks. Cameron did not resist; he sat, looking up, muttering feebly: "That's funny . . . very funny . . . I know someone who looks just like you. . . ."

Then Roark noticed the men who stood watching him curiously. Among them, he saw Darrow, a lanky, stooped, elderly giant with an impassive face; and the contractor's chief estimator, a muscular individual with his hands in his pockets, a pale, puffed face, a dab of mustache in the too wide space between his nose and mouth. He knew the contractor's estimator; Cameron had thrown him out of his office two weeks ago, concluding the last of his too frequent visits.

"What's happened here?" Roark asked.

"Oh, what the hell!" said the estimator. "Darrow's been calling your place all morning and then *this* shows up all of a sudden!" He jerked his thumb at Cameron.

"What were you calling about? Where's the trouble?"

"Well, Roark, I don't know if you can do anything about it . . ." Darrow began, but the estimator interrupted him.

"Aw, what the hell! We got no time to waste explaining to punk kids!"

Roark was looking at Darrow.

"Well?" Roark asked, and the question was a command.

"It's the concrete," said Darrow impassively. "The penthouse, the elevator machinery-room floor arches. It's running under test. It won't stand the load. I told the bastards not to pour it in this weather. But they went right ahead. Now it's set. And it's no good. What are you going to do about it?"

Roark stood, his head thrown back, looking at the gray shadow of the penthouse among the gray clouds far away. Then he turned to the estimator.

"Well?" Roark asked.

"Well, what?" the estimator snapped, and added, his voice whining: "Aw, we couldn't help it!"

"Talk fast," said Roark.

"Aw, what the hell! We were behind schedule and the boss was stepping on us and the old man's sniveling about all the dough this thing's costing him as it is, and so we figured we'd save time, what the hell, nothing's ever happened before, and anyway you know how concrete is, it's a killer, you never can tell how the damn stuff will set, it's not our fault, it can happen to anybody, we couldn't help it. . . . And anyway, if your damn drawings weren't so damn fancy, we could've . . . A good architect'd know how to fix it up, even if . . ." His voice just petered out before the eyes that faced him.

"Well, what's the use of bellyaching now?" the estimator snapped as Roark said nothing. "I say, let it go. It'll stand all right. If Darrow here wasn't so damn finicky . . . And anyway, it's a fine time to be getting soused on us! What can you expect with the kind of fine architect we got around here?"

"Look, Roark," Darrow said quietly, "the work's held up. Someone's got to decide."

Behind them, Cameron burst into laughter suddenly, a high, monotonous, senseless, agonized laughter. He was still sitting there, on the planks, and he looked up, and his face seemed contorted, even though not a muscle of it moved.

"What are you doing here?" he asked, staring at Roark, his eyes stubbornly insistent and disturbed. "That's what I want to know, what you're doing here. You look funny. You look damn funny. I like your face, do you know that? Yes, I like it. Look, get out of here. You should be home. You should be home and in bed. You don't feel well. Look, don't worry about what you see here, about this . . ." He waved his arm vaguely at the building. "It's no use. It's absolutely no use. It doesn't matter. Also they have a drill in there. You don't see it, but that's because they're clever, they've hidden it. What do you want to get hurt for? It doesn't matter anyway."

"There!" said the estimator triumphantly. "See?"

Cameron sat, breathing heavily, wisps of steam trembling from his open mouth up into the frozen air, his stiff, cold fingers convulsed on the edge of a plank, and he looked up at the men.

"You think I'm drunk, don't you?" he asked, his eyes narrow and sly. "You damn fools! All of you, the red-headed one in particular! You think I'm drunk. That's where you're wrong. This is the time when I'm sober. The only time. And then I can have peace. Otherwise, I'm drunk always. Drunk all the time. Seeing things that don't exist. Me, I drink to stop the DT's. I drink to see clearly for once. To know that it doesn't matter . . . Nothing. . . . Not at all. . . . It's so easy. Drink to learn to hate things. I've never felt better in my life."

"Pretty, ain't it?" said the estimator.

"Shut up," said Darrow.

"God damn you all!" the estimator screamed suddenly. "We wouldn't have had any trouble if they'd hired a real architect! That's what happens when people get charitable and pick out a worthless bum who's never been any good, an old drunk who . . ."

Roark turned to him. Roark's arm went back and down, and then forward slowly, as if gathering the weight of air upon the crook of his elbow; it was only a flash, but it seemed to last for minutes, the movement stopped, the taut arm motionless in speed, and then his knuckles shot up, to the man's jaw, and the estimator was on the ground, his knees bent, upturned, his hand on his cheek. Roark stood, his legs spread apart, his arms hanging indifferently by his sides.

"Let's go up," said Roark, turning to Darrow. "Get the superintendent. I'll tell you what's to be done."

They went inside the structure, behind them Cameron staring stupidly ahead and the estimator scrambling slowly to his feet, dusting himself, muttering to no one: "Aw, what the hell, I didn' mean no harm, what the hell, you can't do that to me, you son of a bitch, I'll get you canned for this, I didn' mean no harm . . ."

The construction superintendent followed Roark and Darrow to the elevator, silently, reluctantly, glancing dubiously at Roark. The elevator—a few planks with a precarious railing—shot upward along the side of the building, swaying, shuddering, its cables creaking. The pavements dropped below them, the tops of automobiles descending softly down into an abyss till only flat little squares remained, flowing evenly through the thin channels of streets; the windows of houses streamed down, past them, and roofs flashed by, as flat breaks in the stream, as pedals pressing the houses down, out of the way of their flight. The superintendent picked his teeth thoughtfully; Darrow held on to the wooden railing; Roark stood, his hand closed about a cable, his legs apart, and looked at the structure, at the layers of floor arches flying past.

Twenty floors above the pavement, they stepped out onto a gray mat of concrete in the open cages that were to be the penthouse. "You can see," Darrow was saying, "it's worse than the tests showed."

Roark saw it at once, the odd gray color of the concrete, not the healthy, normal gray of the floors below; he could hear it with his eyes, the cry of warning, the alarm bell rising from the cold, hard, flat stretch of gray under his feet. It was as a disease written upon the skin of this thing he loved, this thing delivered suddenly to his care, and he stood over it as a doctor too sure of the symptoms when he had not wanted to be sure. He ran his fingers over the cold edge of a column encased in that treacherous gray; softly, absently, as if caressing the hand of a precious patient in sympathy, in understanding, in reassurance, to give comfort and to gain it in return.

"Well, Mr. Roark?" the superintendent asked. "What's going to happen?"

"Just this," said Roark. "When you get your elevator machinery up here, it will go straight through this, straight down to the basement."

"But, Jesus! What're we going to do now?"

Roark walked away from the two men, who stood watching him; he walked slowly, his eyes taking in every column, every beam, every foot of space, his steps ringing hard and hollow against the naked concrete. Then he stopped; he stood, his hands in his pockets, his collar raised, a tall figure against the empty gray sky beyond, one strand of red hair fluttering under his old cap. It was up to him, he thought, and each hour counted, each hour adding to that cost that stood as a monster somewhere, leering at them all; to do it over, to remove that concrete—it would mean two weeks of blasting to destroy one day's work, of blasting that might shake the building to its roots, if it could stand the strain at all. He would have to let the concrete remain, he thought, and then he would have to devise supports for these floors—when so little space was available, when every foot of it had been assigned to a purpose in the strict, meticulous economy of Cameron's plan. To devise it somehow, he thought, and to change nothing, not to alter one foot, one line of the building's silhouette, of its crown, of its proud profile, that had to be as Cameron had wished it to be, as each clear, powerful, delicate line rising from the ground demanded it to be. To decide, he thought, to take that into his hands, Cameron's work, to save it, to put his own thoughts irrevocably into steel and mortar— and he was not ready for that, he could not be ready. But it was only one part of him that thought this, dimly, not in words and logic, only as a twisted little ball of emotion in the pit of his stomach, a ball that would have broken into these words had he stopped to unravel it. He did not stop. The ball was only driving on the rest of him, and the rest of him was cold, clear, precise.

He stood without moving for a long time. Then he seized a piece of board from the ground and a pencil from his pocket. He stood, one foot resting on a pile of planks, the board on his knee, his hand flashing in swift, straight jerks, the outlines of steel supports rising on the wood. He sketched for a long time. The two men walked to him, stood watching his hand silently from behind his shoulder. Then, as the scheme became clear, it was the superintendent who spoke first, to gasp incredulously: "Jesus! It'll work! So that's what you're driving at!" Roark nodded and went on.

When he had finished, he handed the board to the superintendent, saying briefly, unnecessarily, because the crude, hurried lines on the board said everything: "Take the columns you have stored down below . . . put supports here . . . see? . . . and here . . . you clear the elevator shafts like this, see? . . . and here . . . clear the conduits . . . there's the general scheme."

"Jesus!" said the superintendent, frightened and delighted. "It's never been done that way before."

"You're going to do it."

"It'll hold," said Darrow, studying the sketch. "We may have to check some of these beams of yours . . . this business here, for instance . . . but it'll hold."

"The owners won't like it," said the superintendent, as a regretful afterthought.

"They'll take it and keep their damn mouths shut," said Roark. "Give me another board. Now look. Here's what you do on the two floors below." He went on drawing for a long time, throwing words over his shoulder once in a while.

"Yes," whispered the superintendent. "But . . . but what'll I say if someone asks if . . ."

"Say I gave the orders. Now keep these and get started." He turned to Darrow. "I'll draw up the plans and you'll have them this afternoon to check, and let him have them as soon as possible." He turned to the superintendent. "Now go ahead."

"Yes, sir," said the superintendent. He said it respectfully.

They went down silently in the elevator. The superintendent was studying the drawings, Darrow was studying Roark, Roark was looking at the building.

They reached the ground below and Roark went back

to Cameron. He took Cameron's elbows and helped him slowly to his feet. The estimator had disappeared.

"I'll take you home, Mr. Cameron," Roark said gently.

"Huh?" muttered Cameron. "Yes . . . oh, yes. . . ." He nodded vaguely, in assent to nothing comprehensible.

Roark led him away. Then Cameron shook off the hands holding him, tottered and turned around. He stood, looking up at the steel skeleton, his head thrown back. He flung his arms out wide, and stood still, only his fingers moving weakly, uselessly, as if reaching for something. His lips moved; he wanted to speak; he said nothing.

"Look . . ." he whispered at last. "Look . . ." His voice was soft, choked, pleading, pleading desperately for the words he could not find. "Look . . ." He had so much to say. "Look . . ." he muttered hopelessly.

When Roark took his arm again, he did not resist. Roark led him to a cab and they drove to Cameron's home. Roark knew Cameron's address, but had never been inside his one stuffy, unkempt furnished room that bore on its walls, as its single distinction, framed photographs of his buildings. The bed stood untouched, unused the night before. Cameron had followed docilely up the stairs. But the sight of his room seemed to awaken something in his brain. He jerked loose suddenly; he whirled upon Roark, and his face was white with rage.

"What are you doing here?" he screamed, choking, his voice gulping in his throat. "What are you following me for? I hate you, whoever you are. I know what's the matter with me. It's because I can't bear the sight of you. There you stand reproaching me!"

"I don't," whispered Roark.

"God damn you! That's what's been following me. You're the one who's making me miserable. Everything else's all right, but you're the one who's putting me through hell. You're out to kill me, you . . ." And then there followed a torrent of such blasphemy as Roark had never heard on any waterfront, in any construction gang. Roark stood silently, waiting.

"Get out!" roared Cameron, lurching toward him. "Get out of here! Get out of my sight! Get out!"

Roark did not move. Cameron raised his hand and struck him across the mouth.

Roark fell back against a bedstand, but caught his balance, his feet steady, his body huddled against the stand, his hands behind him, pressed to its sides. He looked at Cameron. The sound of the blow had knocked Cameron into a sudden, lucid, sober pause of consciousness. He stared at Roark, his mouth half-open, his eyes dull, blank, frightened, but focused.

"Howard . . ." he muttered. "Howard, what are you doing here?"

His hand went across his wet forehead, trying vainly to remember.

"Howard, what was it? What happened?"

"Nothing, Mr. Cameron," Roark whispered, his handkerchief hidden in his hand, pressed to his mouth, swiftly wiping off the blood. "Nothing."

"Something's happened. Are you all right, Howard?"

"I'm all right, Mr. Cameron. But you'd better go to bed. I'll help you."

The old man did not resist, his legs giving way under him, his eyes empty, while Roark undressed him and pulled the blanket over him.

"Howard," he whispered, his face white on the pillow, his eyes closed, "I never wanted you to see it. But now you've seen it. Now you know."

"Try to sleep, Mr. Cameron."

"An honor . . ." Cameron whispered, without opening his eyes, "an honor that I could not have deserved. . . . Who said that?"

"Go to sleep, Mr. Cameron. You'll be all right tomorrow."

"You hate me now," said Cameron, raising his head, looking at Roark, a soft, lost, unexpecting smile in his eyes, "don't you?"

"No," said Roark. "But I hate everyone else in the world."

Cameron's head fell back on the pillow. He lay still, his hands small, drawn, and yellow on the white bedcloth. Then he was asleep.

There was no one to call. Roark asked the sleepy,

indifferent landlady to look after Cameron, and returned to the office.

He went straight to his table, noticing no one. He pulled a sheet of paper forward and went to work silently.

"Well?" asked Loomis. "What happened down there?" asked Simpson.

"Penthouse floor arches," Roark answered without raising his head.

"Jesus!" gasped Simpson. "Now what?"

"It will be all right," said Roark. "You'll take these down to Huston Street when I finish, Loomis."

"Yes," said Loomis, his mouth hanging open.

That afternoon, Trager came into the drafting room, his glance directed, fixed upon a definite object.

"There's a Mr. Mead outside," he said. "He had an appointment with Mr. Cameron about that hotel down in Connecticut. What shall I tell him, Mr. Roark?"

Roark jerked his thumb at the door of Cameron's office.

"Send him in," said Roark. "I'll see him."

On a day when the [Heller] house was nearing completion, Roark noticed, driving towards it one morning, an old, hunched figure standing at the foot of the hill, alone on the rocky shore, ignored by the cars flying past and by the noisy activity of the workers above. He knew the broad, bent back of that figure, but what it appeared to be was incredible. He stopped his car with a violent screech of brakes, and leaped out, and ran forward, frightened. He saw the heavy cane and the two hands leaning agonizingly upon its handle, the old body braced in supreme effort against one steady shaft, grinding its tip into the earth.

Roark stood before him and opened his mouth and said nothing.

"Well?" asked Cameron. "What are you staring at?"

Roark couldn't answer.

"Now you're not going to say anything," Cameron snapped. "Why the hell did you have to come here today? I didn't want you to know."

"How . . . how could Miss Cameron let you . . ."

"She didn't let me," said Cameron triumphantly. "I escaped." His eyes twinkled slyly, with the boasting of a boy playing hookey. "I just sneaked out of the house when she went to church. I can hire taxis and get on trains just like anybody else. I'll slap your face if you go on standing there with that stupid look proclaiming to the world that it's so unusual for me to crawl out of the grave. Really, you know, you're more of a fool than I thought you were. You should have expected me here someday." The cane staggered and he caught at Roark's arm for support. He added softly: "Do you know what Victor Hugo said? Victor Hugo said that there may be indifferent fathers, but there can't be indifferent grandfathers. Help me up the hill."

"No!" said Roark. "You can't!"

"I said help me up the hill," Cameron pronounced slowly, icily, with the tone of addressing an insolent draftsman.

Roark had to obey. His hands closed about Cameron's elbows, and he pulled the old body gently, tightly against his own, and they went forward slowly. Cameron's feet stepped with long, deliberate precision, each step—a purpose begun and carried on and completed consciously, his mind concentrated upon each step. The cane left a long, zigzagging string of dots stamped on the earth behind them. Cameron barely felt the pressure of Roark's hands on his elbows, but the hands led him, held him in tight safety, as if some fluid energy of motion flowed from these hands through his body, as if Cameron were carried forward not by his feet, but by Roark's hands. They stopped frequently, upon each ledge they reached, and stood silently, Cameron trying to hide the gasps of his breath, and looked up. Then they went on.

When they reached the top, they sat down on the steps of the entrance and rested for a long time. Then they walked slowly through all the rooms of the house. The workers looked with indifferent curiosity upon the old cripple whom it pleased the architect to drag through the building. No one knew Cameron. Cameron made no comments, beyond snapping briefly, once in a while: "That's a bum job of plastering here. Don't let them get away with it. Have it done over. . . . Watch out for air currents in this hall. Adjust the ventilation. . . . You'll want another electric outlet on these stairs. . . ." Then they came out again and Cameron stood, without help, leaning on his cane, his back to the house, looking over the vast spread of the countryside for a long time. When he turned his head to Roark, he said nothing, but nodded slowly in a great, silent affirmation.

After a while, Roark said: "I'll drive you back now."

"No," said Cameron. "I'll stay here till evening— while I'm here. You go ahead with whatever you have to do. I'll just sit here. Don't make such a fuss about me."

Roark brought the leather seats from his car, and spread them on the ground in the shade of a tree, and helped Cameron to settle down comfortably upon them. Then he went back to his work in the house. Cameron sat looking at the sea and at the walls before him. His cane, stretched limply forward between his hands, tapped softly against a stone, once in a while, two brief little thumps, then two more a long time later, as if punctuating the course of his thoughts.

At noon, they shared the box lunch Roark had brought with him; they ate, Roark sitting on the ground beside him, and they spoke of the various qualities of Connecticut granite as compared with the stone from other quarries. And later, when Roark had nothing further to do for the day, he stretched down beside Cameron, and they sat through many hours, unconscious of their long silences and of the few sentences they spoke, vague, unfinished, half-answered sentences, unconscious of the time that passed and of the necessity for any aim in sitting there.

Long after the workers had left, when the sea became a soft purple and the windows of the empty, silent house flared up in unmoving yellow fire, Roark said: "We're going now," and Cameron nodded silently.

When they had reached the car below, Cameron leaned suddenly against its door, his face white from an exhaustion he could not hide. He pushed Roark's hands away. "In a moment . . ." he whispered humbly. "All right in a moment. . . ." Then he raised his head and said: "Okay." Roark helped him into the car.

They had driven for half a mile, before Roark asked: "Are you sure you're all right?"

"I'm not," said Cameron. "To hell with that. I'll have to go back to the wheelchair for a month, I suppose. . . . Keep still. You know better than to regret it."

The Simplest Thing in the World

1940

Editor's Preface

This 1940 story, with Ayn Rand's prefatory note, is reprinted from *The Romantic Manifesto*.

She wrote it about a creative writer, while she was deep in the writing of *The Fountainhead*. By that time, *The Fountainhead* had been rejected by some twelve publishers.

—R.E.R.

The Simplest Thing in the World

*(This story was written in 1940. It did not ap-
pear in print until the November 1967 issue
of* THE OBJECTIVIST, *where it was published in
its original form, as written.*

*The story illustrates the nature of the cre-
ative process—the way in which an artist's
sense of life directs the integrating functions
of his subconscious and controls his creative
imagination.—A. R.)*

Henry Dorn sat at his desk and looked at a sheet of
blank paper. Through a feeling of numb panic, he said
to himself: this is going to be the easiest thing you've
ever done.

Just be stupid, he said to himself. That's all. Just relax
and be as stupid as you can be. Easy, isn't it? What are
you scared of, you damn fool? You don't think you can
be stupid, is that it? You're conceited, he said to himself
angrily. That's the whole trouble with you. You're conceited as hell. So you can't be stupid, can you? You're
being stupid right now. You've been stupid about this
thing all your life. Why can't you be stupid on order?

I'll start in a minute, he said. Just one minute more
and then I'll start. I will, this time. I'll just rest for a
minute, that's all right, isn't it? I'm very tired. You've
done nothing today, he said. You've done nothing for
months. What are you tired of? That's why I'm tired—
because I've done nothing. I wish I could . . . I'd give

anything if I could again . . . Stop that. Stop it quick.
That's the one thing you mustn't think about. You're to
start in a minute and you were almost ready. You won't
be ready if you think of that.

Don't look at it. Don't look at it. Don't look at . . .
He had turned. He was looking at a thick book in a
ragged blue jacket, lying on a shelf, under old magazines.
He could see, on its spine, the white letters merging with
the faded blue: *Triumph* by Henry Dorn.

He got up and pushed the magazines down to hide
the book. It's better if you don't see it while you're
doing it, he said. No. It's better if it doesn't see you
doing it. You're a sentimental fool, he said.

It was not a good book. How do you know it was a
good book? No, that won't work. All right, it *was* a good
book. It's a great book. There's nothing you can do
about that. It would be much easier if you could. It
would be much easier if you could make yourself believe
that it was a lousy book and that it had deserved what
had happened to it. Then you could look people straight
in the face and write a better one. But you didn't believe
it. And you had tried very hard to believe that. But
you didn't.

All right, he said. Drop that. You've gone over that,
over and over again, for two years. So drop it. Not
now . . . It wasn't the bad reviews that I minded. It was
the good ones. Particularly the one by Fleurette Lumm
who said it was the best book she'd ever read—because
it had such a touching love story.

He had not even known that there was a love story
in his book, and he had not known that what there was
of it was touching. And the things that were there, in
his book, the things he had spent five years thinking
of and writing, writing as carefully, as scrupulously, as
delicately as he knew how—these things Fleurette
Lumm had not mentioned at all. At first, after he had
read the reviews, he had thought that these things were
not in his book at all; he had only imagined they were;
or else the printer had left them out—only the book
seemed very thick, and if the printer had left them out,
what filled all those pages? And it wasn't possible that
he had not written the book in English, and it wasn't

ossible that so many bright people couldn't read English, and it wasn't possible that he was insane. So he read his book over again, very carefully, and he was happy when he found a bad sentence in it, or a muddled paragraph, or a thought that did not seem clear; he said, they're right, it isn't there, it isn't clear at all, it was perfectly fair of them to miss it and the world is a human place to live in. But after he had read all of his book, to the end, he knew that it *was* there, that it was clear and beautiful and very important, that he could not have done it any better—and that he'll never understand the answer. That he had better not try to understand it, if he wished to remain alive.

All right, he said. That's about enough now, isn't it? You've been at it longer than a minute. And you said you would start.

The door was open and he looked into the bedroom. Kitty sat there at a table, playing solitaire. Her face looked as if she were very successful at making it look as if everything were all right. She had a lovely mouth. You could always tell things about people by their mouth. Hers looked as if she wanted to smile at the world, and if she didn't it was her own fault, and she really would in a moment, because she was all right and so was the world. In the lamplight her neck looked white and very thin, bent attentively over the cards. It didn't cost any money to play solitaire. He heard the cards thumping down gently, and the steam crackling in the pipe in the corner.

The doorbell rang, and Kitty came in quickly to open the door, not looking at him, her body tight and purposeful under the childish, wide-skirted, print dress, a very lovely dress, only it had been bought two years ago and for summer wear. He could have opened the door, but he knew why she wanted to open it.

He stood, his feet planted wide apart, his stomach drawn, not looking at the door, listening. He heard a voice and then he heard Kitty saying: "No, I'm sorry, but we really don't need an Electrolux." Kitty's voice was almost a song of release; as if she were making an effort not to sound too foolish; as if she loved the Electrolux man and wished she could ask him in to visit. He knew why Kitty's voice sounded like that. She had thought it was the landlord.

Kitty closed the door, and looked at him, crossing the room, and smiled as if she were apologizing—humbly and happily—for her existence, and said: "I don't want to interrupt you, dear," and went back to her solitaire.

All you have to do, he said to himself, is think of Fleurette Lumm and try to imagine what she likes. Just imagine that and then write it down. That's all there is to it. And you'll have a good commercial story that will sell immediately and make you a lot of money. It's the simplest thing in the world.

You can't be the only one who's right and everybody else wrong, he said. Everybody's told you that that's what you must do. You've asked for a job and nobody would give you one. Nobody would help you find one. Nobody had even seemed interested or serious about it. They said, a brilliant young man like you! Look at Paul Pattison, they said. Eighty thousand a year and not half your brain. But Paul knows what the public likes to read and gives it to them. If you'd just stop being so stubborn, they said. You don't have to be intellectual all the time. Why not be practical for a while, and then, after you've made your first fifty thousand dollars, you can sit back and indulge yourself in some more high literature which will never sell. They said, why waste your time on a job? What can you do? You'll be lucky if you get twenty-five a week. It's foolish, when you've got a great talent for words, you know you have, if you'd only be sensible about it. It ought to be easy for you. If you can write fancy, difficult stuff like that, it ought to be a cinch to toss off a popular serial or two. Any fool can do it. They said, stop dramatizing yourself. Do you enjoy being a martyr? They said, look at your wife. They said, if Paul Pattison can do it, why can't you?

Think of Fleurette Lumm, he said to himself, sitting down at his desk. You imagine that you can't understand her, but you can, if you want to. Don't try to be so complicated. Be simple. She's simple to understand. That's it. Be simple about everything. Just write a simple story. The simplest, most unimportant story you can imagine. For God's sake, can't you think of anything nat's not important, not important at all, not of the slightest possible importance? Can't you? Are you as good as that, you conceited fool? Do you really think you're as good as that? That you can't do anything unless it's great, profound, important? Do you *have* to be a world-saver all the time? Do you *have* to be a damn Joan d'Arc?

Stop kidding yourself, he said. You can. You're no better than anyone else. He chuckled. *That's* the kind of rotter you are. People tell themselves they're no worse than anyone else when they need courage. You tell yourself you're no better. I wish you'd tell me where you got that infernal conceit of yours. That's all it is. Not any great talent, not any brilliant mind—just conceit. You're not a noble martyr to your art. You're an inflated egotist—and you're getting just what you deserve.

Good, are you? What makes you think you're good? What right have you to hate what you're going to do? You haven't written anything for months. You couldn't. You can't write any more. You never will again. And if you can't write what you want to write—what business have you to despise the things people want you to write? That's all you're good for anyway, not for any great epics with immortal messages, and you ought to be damn glad to try and do it, not sit here like a convict in a death cell waiting for his picture to be taken for the front pages.

Now that's better. I think you have the right spirit now. Now you can start.

How does one start those things? . . . Well, let's see . . . It must be a simple, human story. Try to think of something human . . . How does one make one's mind work? How does one invent a story? How can people ever be writers? Come on, you've written before. How did you start then? No, you can't think of that. Not of that. If you do—you'll go completely blank again, or worse. Think that you've never written before. It's a new start. You're turning over a new leaf. There! That was good. If you can think in lousy bromides like that, you'll do it. You're beginning to get it . . .

Think of something human . . . Oh, come on, think hard . . . Well, try it this way: think of the word "human," think of what it means—you'll get an idea somewhere . . . Human . . . What's the most human thing there is? What's the quality that all the people you know have got, the outstanding quality in all of them? Their motive power? Fear. Not fear of anyone in particular, just fear. Just a great, blind force without object. Malicious fear. The kind that makes them want to see you suffer. Because they know that they, too, will have to suffer and it makes it easier, to know that you do also. The kind that makes them want to see you being small and funny and smutty. Small people are safe. It's not really fear, it's more than that. Like Mr. Crawford, for instance, who's a lawyer and who's glad when a client of his loses a suit. He's glad, even though he loses money on it; even though it hurts his reputation. He's glad, and he doesn't even know that he's glad. God, what a story there is in Mr. Crawford! If you could put him down on paper as he is, and explain just why he is like that, and . . .

Yeah, he said to himself. In three volumes which no one would ever publish, because they'd say it was not true and call me a hater of humanity. Stop it. Stop it fast. That's not at all what they mean when they say a story is human. But it's human. But it's not what they mean. What do they mean? You'll never know. Oh yes, you do. You know it. You know it very well—without knowing. Oh, stop this! . . .

Why must you always know the meaning of everything? There's your first mistake—right there. Do it without thinking. It mustn't have any meaning. It must be written as if you'd never tried to find any meaning in anything, not ever in your life. It must sound as if that's the kind of person you are. Why do people resent people who look for a meaning? What's the real reason that . . .

STOP IT! . . .

All right. Let's try to go at it in a different way entirely. Don't start with an abstraction. Start with something definite. Anything. Think of something simple, obvious and bad. So bad that you won't care, one way or the other. Say the first thing you can think of.

For instance, a story about a middle-aged millionaire who tries to seduce a poor young working girl. *That's*

ood. That's very good. Now go on with it. Quick. Don't
think. Go on with it.

Well, he's a man of about fifty. He's made a fortune,
unscrupulously, because he's ruthless. She's only twenty-
two, and very beautiful, and very sweet, and she works
in the five-and-ten. Yes, in the five-and-ten. And he
owns it. That's what he is—a big tycoon who owns a
whole slew of five-and-ten's. This is good.

One day he comes to this particular store, and he sees
this girl and he falls in love with her. Why would he fall
in love with her? Well, he's lonely. He's very terribly
lonely. He hasn't got a friend in the world. People don't
like him. People never like a man who's made a success
of himself. Also, he's ruthless. You can't make a success
of yourself unless you hold onto your one goal and drop
everything else. When you have a great devotion to a
goal—people call you ruthless. And when you work
harder than anyone else, when you work like a freight
engine while others take it easy, and so you beat them
at it—people call you unscrupulous. That's human also.

You don't work like that just to make money. It's
something else. It's a great, driving energy—a creative
energy?—no, it's the principle of creation itself. It's what
makes everything in the world. Dams and skyscrapers
and transatlantic cables. Everything we've got. It comes
from men like that. When he started the shipyards—oh,
he's a five-and-ten tycoon—no, he isn't, to hell with the
five-and-ten!—when he started the shipyards that he
made his fortune from, there was nothing there but a
few shacks and a lot of clam shells. He made the town,
he made the harbor, he gave jobs to hundreds of people,
they'd still be digging for clams if he hadn't come along.
And now they hate him. And he's not bitter about it.
He's accepted that long ago. He just doesn't understand.
Now he's fifty years old, and circumstances have forced
him to retire. He's got millions—and he's the most miserable man in the world. Because he wants to work—
not to make money, just to work, just to fight and take
chances—because that great energy cannot be kept still.

Now when he meets the girl—what girl?—oh, the one
in the five-and-ten . . . Oh, to hell with her! What do
you need her for? He's married long ago—and that's not

the story at all. What he meets is a poor, struggling young man. And he envies this boy—because the boy's great struggle is still ahead of him. But this boy—now *that's* the point—this boy doesn't want to struggle at all. He's a nice, able, likeable kid, but he has no real, driving desire for anything. He's been adequate at several different jobs and he's dropped them all. There's no passion to him, no goal. What he wants above all is security. He doesn't care what he does or how or who tells him to do it. He's never created anything. He's given nothing to the world and he never will. But he wants security from the world. And he's liked by everybody. And he has everybody's sympathy. And there they are—the two men. Which one is right? Which one is good? Which one's got the truth? What happens when life brings them face to face?

Oh, what a story! Don't you see? It's not just the two of them. It's more, much more. It's the whole tragedy of the world today. It's our greatest problem. It's the most important . . .

Oh, God!

Do you think you can? Do you think you'll get away with it maybe, if you're very clever, if you disguise it, so they'll think it's just a story about an old man, nothing very serious, I don't mind if they miss it, I hope they miss it, let them think they're reading trash, if they'll only let me write it. I don't have to stress it, I don't have to have much of it, of what's good, I can hide it, I can apologize for it with a lot of human stuff about boats and women and swimming pools. They won't know. They'll let me.

No, he said, they won't. Don't fool yourself. They're as good at it as you are. They know their kind of story just like you do yours. They might not even be able to explain it, what it is or where, but they'll know. They always know what's theirs and what isn't. Besides, it's a controversial issue. The leftists won't like it. It will antagonize a lot of people. What do you want a controversial issue for—in a popular magazine story?

No, go back to the beginning, where he's a five-and-ten tycoon . . . No. I can't. I can't waste it. I've got to use that story. I'll write it. But not now. I'll write it after 've written this one commercial piece. That will be the first thing I'll write after I have money. That's worth waiting for.

Now start all over again. On something else. Come on, it isn't so bad now, is it? You see, it wasn't difficult at all, thinking. It came by itself. Just start on something else.

Get an interesting beginning, something good and startling, even if you don't know what it's all about and where to go from there. Suppose you open with a young girl who lives on a rooftop, in one of those storerooms above a loft-building, and she's sitting there on the roof, all alone, it's a beautiful summer evening, and suddenly there's a shot and a window in the next building cracks open, glass flying all over the place, and a man jumps out of the window onto her roof.

There! You can't possibly go wrong on that. It's so bad that it's sure to be right.

Well . . . Why would a girl live in a loft-building? Because it's cheap. No, the Y.W.C.A. would be cheaper. Or sharing a furnished room with a girlfriend. That's what a girl would do. No, not this girl. She can't get along with people. She doesn't know why. But she can't. So she'd rather be alone. She's been very much alone all her life. She works in a huge, busy, noisy, stupid office. She likes her rooftop because when she's there alone at night, she has the whole city to herself, and she sees it, not as it is, but as it could have been. As it should have been. That's her trouble—always wanting things to be what they should be, and never are. She looks at the city and she thinks of what's going on in the penthouses, little islands of light in the sky, and she thinks of great, mysterious, breath-stopping things, not of cocktail parties, and drunks in bathrooms, and kept women with dogs.

And the building next door—it's a smart hotel, and there's this one large window right over her roof, and the window is of frosted glass, because the view is so ugly. She can't see anything in that window—only the silhouettes of people against the light. Only the shadows. And she sees this one man there—he's tall and slender and he holds his shoulders as if he were giving orders to the whole world. And he moves as if that were a light and easy job for him to do. And she falls in love with him. With his shadow. She's never seen him and she doesn't want to. She doesn't know anything about him and she never tries to learn. She doesn't care. It's not what he is. It's what she thinks of him as being. It's a love without future, without hope or the need of hope, a love great enough to find happiness in nothing but its own greatness, unreal, inexpressible, undemanding—and more real than anything around her. And . . .

Henry Dorn sat at his desk, seeing what men cannot see except when they do not know they are seeing it, seeing his own thoughts in a way of sight brighter than any perception of the things around him, seeing them, not pushing them forward, but seeing them as a detached observer without control of their shape, each thought a corner, and a bright astonishment meeting him behind each corner, not creating anything, but being carried along, not helping and not resisting, through minutes of a feeling like a payment for all the agony he would ever bear, a feeling continuing only while you do not know that you feel it . . .

And then, that evening, she is sitting alone on the roof, and there's a shot, and that window is shattered, and that man leaps out onto her roof. She sees him for the first time—and this is the miracle: for once in her life, he *is* what she had wanted him to be, he looks as she had wanted him to look. But he has just committed a murder. I suppose it will have to be some kind of justifiable murder . . . No! No! No! It's not a justifiable murder at all. We don't even know what it is—and she doesn't know. But here is the dream, the impossible, the ideal—against the laws of the whole world. Her own truth—against all mankind. She has to . . .

Oh, stop it! Stop it! Stop it!

Well . . . ?

Pull yourself together, man. Pull yourself together . . .

Well? For whom is it you're writing that story? For the *Women's Kitchen Friend*?

No, you're not tired. You're all right. It's all right.

You'll write this story later. You'll write it after you have money. It's all right. It won't be taken away from you. Now sit quiet. Count ten.

No! I tell you, you *can*. You can. You haven't tried hard enough. You let it get away with you. You begin to think. Can't you think without thinking?

Listen, can't you understand a different way of doing it? Don't think of the fantastic, don't think of the unusual, don't think of the opposite of what anyone else'd want to think, but go after the obvious, the easy. Easy—for whom? Come on now. It's this: it's because you ask yourself "what if . . . ?" That starts the whole trouble. "What if it's not what it seems to be at all . . . Wouldn't it be interesting if . . ." That's what you do, and you mustn't. You mustn't think of what would be interesting. But how can I do anything if I know it isn't interesting? But it will be—to them. That's just why it will be to them—because it isn't to you. That's the whole secret. But then how do I know what, or where, or why?

Listen, can't you stop it for a little while? Can't you turn it off—that brain of yours? Can't you make it work without letting it work? Can't you be stupid? Can't you be consciously, deliberately, cold-bloodedly stupid? Can't that be done in some way? Everybody is stupid about some things, the best of us and the brightest. Everybody has blind spots, they say. Can't you make it be this?

Dear God, let me be stupid! Let me be dishonest! Let me be contemptible! Just once. Because I must.

Don't you see? It's a matter of one reversal. Just make one single reversal: instead of believing that one must try to be intelligent, different, honest, challenging, that one must do the best possible to the best of one's ability and then stretch it some more to do still better—believe that one must be dull, stale, sweet, dishonest and safe. That's all. Is that the way other people do it? No, I don't think so. They'd end up in an insane asylum in six months. Then what is it? I don't know. It isn't that—but it works out like that. Maybe if we were told from the beginning to reverse it . . . But we aren't. But some of us get wise to it early—and then they're all right. But why should it be like that? Why should we . . .

Drop it. You're not settling world problems. You're writing a commercial story.

All right. Quick and cold now. Hold yourself tight and don't let yourself like the story. Above all, don't let yourself like it.

Let's make it a detective story. A murder mystery. You can't possibly have a murder mystery with any serious meaning. Come on. Quick, cold and simple.

There must be two villains in a mystery story: the victim and the murderer—so nobody would feel too sorry for either of them. That's the way it's always done. Well, you can have some leeway on the victim, but the murderer's *got* to be a villain . . . Now the murderer must have a motive. It must be a contemptible motive . . . Let's see . . . I've got it: the murderer is a professional blackmailer who's holding a lot of people in his clutches, and the victim is the man who's about to expose him, so the blackmailer kills this man. That's as low a motive as you could imagine. There's no excuse for that . . . Or is there? What if . . . Wouldn't it be interesting if you could prove that the murderer was justified?

What if all those people he blackmails are utter lice? The kind that do horrible things, but just manage to remain within the law, so there's no way of defending yourself against them. And this man chooses deliberately to become a crusading blackmailer. He gets things on all those people and he forces them to do justice. A lot of men make careers for themselves by knowing where some body or other is buried. Well, this man goes out after such "bodies," only he doesn't use them for personal advancement, he uses them to undo the harm these people are doing. He's a Robin Hood of blackmail. He gets them in the only way they can be gotten. For instance, one of them is a corrupt politician, and the hero—no, the murderer—no, the *hero* gets the dope on him and forces him to vote right on a certain measure. Another one is a big Hollywood producer who's ruined a lot of lives—and the hero makes him give a talented actress a break without forcing her to become his mistress. Another one is a crooked businessman—and the hero forces him to play straight. And when the worst ne of the lot—what's the worst one of the lot? a hypo-critical reformer, I think—no, that's dangerous to touch, too controversial—oh, what the hell!—when this reformer traps the hero and is about to expose him, the hero kills him. Why shouldn't he? And the interesting thing about the story is that all those people will be presented just as they appear in real life. Nice people, pillars of society, liked, admired and respected. And the hero is just a hard, lonely kind of outcast.

Oh, what a story! Prove that! Prove what some of our popular people are really like! Blow the lid off society! Show it for what it's worth! Prove that the lone wolf is not always a wolf! Prove honesty and courage and strength and dedication! Prove it through a blackmailer and a murderer! Have a story with a murderer for a hero and let him get away with it! A great story! An important story which . . .

Henry Dorn sat very still, his hands folded in his lap, hunched, seeing nothing, thinking of nothing.

Then he pushed the sheet of blank paper aside and reached for the *Times'* "Help Wanted" ads.

The Genius of Ayn Rand

THE VIRTUE OF SELFISHNESS:
A New Concept of Egoism

Ayn Rand explains what "selfishness" is, and why the pursuit of his or her own rational self-interest is every individual's highest moral obligation.

RETURN OF THE PRIMITIVE:
The Anti-Industrial Revolution

Edited with an introduction and additional essays by Peter Schwartz. Ayn Rand identifies the intellectual roots of "political correctness," urging people to repudiate its mindless nihilism and to uphold a philosophy of reason, individualism, capitalism, and technological progress.

S464/Rand

Inside the Mind of Ayn Rand

The Ayn Rand Reader
Edited by Gary Hull. Introduction by Leonard Peikoff. Containing excerpts from various works of Ayn Rand, both fiction and nonfiction, this reader provides an illuminating glimpse for beginners into the art and philosophy of the legendary writer.

Journals of Ayn Rand
Edited by David Harriman. Foreword by Leonard Peikoff. Providing access to Ayn Rand's intimate thoughts and feelings, this book reveals the evolution of Ayn Rand as an artist and as a philosopher. Includes all her notes on her novels in progress.

Letters of Ayn Rand
Edited by Michael S. Berliner. Introduction by Leonard Peikoff. Containing letters from Ayn Rand ranging in tone from warm affection to icy fury. Here is a chronicle across fifty years that captures the inspiring drama of a towering literary genius and her amazing life.

The Romantic Manifesto:
A Philosophy of Literature
Ayn Rand's declaration of her reasons for rejecting both Naturalism and Modernism in art, while upholding Romanticism.

Available wherever books are sold or at penguin.com

A fascinating and illuminating guide to
Ayn Rand's Objectivist philosophy

THE AYN RAND LEXICON
Objectivism from A to Z

Edited by **Harry Binswanger**
With an Introduction by **Leonard Peikoff**

A comprehensive, alphabetical encyclopedia of
Objectivist thought, this is the definitive guide
to the works of one of the most important
writers of our century. A highly accessible
compilation of key statements on over 400
topics in philosophy and related fields, selected
from Ayn Rand's articles, essays, lectures and
books. This unique volume brings together for
the fist time all the key ideas of Objectivism, as
brilliantly dramatized in Miss Rand's novels
We the Living, The Fountainhead,
and *Atlas Shrugged.*

Available wherever books are sold or at
penguin.com

S468/Rand